Chronicles of The Black Company

TOR BOOKS BY GLEN COOK

An Ill Fate Marshalling
Reap the East Wind
The Swordbearer
The Tower of Fear

THE BLACK COMPANY

The Black Company (The First Chronicle)
Shadows Linger (The Second Chronicle)
The White Rose (The Third Chronicle)
Shadow Games (The First Book of the South)
Dreams of Steel (The Second Book of the South)
The Silver Spike
Bleak Seasons (Book One of Glittering Stone)
She Is the Darkness (Book Two of Glittering Stone)
Water Sleeps (Book Three of Glittering Stone)
Soldiers Live (Book Four of Glittering Stone)

Chronicles of the Black Company
(comprising *The Black Company,*
Shadows Linger, and *The White Rose*)

THE INSTRUMENTALITIES OF THE NIGHT

The Tyranny of the Night
Lord of the Silent Kingdom

CHRONICLES of THE BLACK COMPANY

GLEN COOK

TOR®

A TOM DOHERTY ASSOCIATES BOOK / NEW YORK

This is a work of fiction. All of the characters, organizations, and events portrayed in these novels are either products of the author's imagination or are used fictitiously.

CHRONICLES OF THE BLACK COMPANY

A Tor Book
Published by Tom Doherty Associates, LLC
175 Fifth Avenue
New York, NY 10010

www.tor.com

Library of Congress Cataloging-in-Publication Data

Cook, Glen.
Chronicles of the Black Company / Glen Cook.—1st ed.
p. cm.
Contents: The Black Company—Shadows Linger—The White Rose.
"A Tom Doherty Associates book."
ISBN-13: 978-0-7653-1923-4
ISBN-10: 0-7653-1923-3
I. Title.

PS3553.O5536 C48 2007
813'.54—dc22

2007024922

Printed in the United States of America

0 9 8

Contents

The Black Company

This one is for the people of the
St. Louis Science Fiction Society.
Love you all.

1

Legate

There were prodigies and portents enough, One-Eye says. We must blame ourselves for misinterpreting them. One-Eye's handicap in no way impairs his marvelous hindsight.

Lightning from a clear sky smote the Necropolitan Hill. One bolt struck the bronze plaque sealing the tomb of the forvalaka, obliterating half the spell of confinement. It rained stones. Statues bled. Priests at several temples reported sacrificial victims without hearts or livers. One victim escaped after its bowels were opened and was not recaptured. At the Fork Barracks, where the Urban Cohorts were billeted, the image of Teux turned completely around. For nine evenings running, ten black vultures circled the Bastion. Then one evicted the eagle which lived atop the Paper Tower.

Astrologers refused readings, fearing for their lives. A mad soothsayer wandered the streets proclaiming the imminent end of the world. At the Bastion, the eagle not only departed, the ivy on the outer ramparts withered and gave way to a creeper which appeared black in all but the most intense sunlight.

But that happens every year. Fools can make an omen of anything in retrospect.

We *should* have been better prepared. We did have four modestly accomplished wizards to stand sentinel against predatory tomorrows—though never by any means as sophisticated as divining through sheeps' entrails.

Still, the best augurs are those who divine from the portents of the past. They compile phenomenal records.

Beryl totters perpetually, ready to stumble over a precipice into chaos. The

Queen of the Jewel Cities was old and decadent and mad, filled with the stench of degeneracy and moral dryrot. Only a fool would be surprised by anything found creeping its night streets.

I had every shutter thrown wide, praying for a breath off the harbor, rotting fish and all. There wasn't enough breeze to stir a cobweb. I mopped my face and grimaced at my first patient. "Crabs again, Curly?"

He grinned feebly. His face was pale. "It's my stomach, Croaker." His pate looks like a polished ostrich egg. Thus the name. I checked the watch schedule and duty roster. Nothing there he would want to avoid. "It's bad, Croaker. Really."

"Uhm." I assumed my professional demeanor, sure what it was. His skin was clammy, despite the heat. "Eaten outside the commissary lately, Curly?" A fly landed on his head, strutted like a conqueror. He didn't notice.

"Yeah. Three, four times."

"Uhm." I mixed a nasty, milky concoction. "Drink this. All of it."

His whole face puckered at the first taste. "Look, Croaker, I. . . ."

The *smell* of the stuff revolted me. "Drink, friend. Two men died before I came up with that. Then Pokey took it and lived." Word was out about that.

He drank.

"You mean it's poison? The damned Blues slipped me something?"

"Take it easy. You'll be okay. Yeah. It looks that way." I'd had to open up Walleye and Wild Bruce to learn the truth. It was a subtle poison. "Get over there on the cot where the breeze will hit you—if the son of a bitch ever comes up. And lie still. Let the stuff work." I settled him down.

"Tell me what you ate outside." I collected a pen and a chart tacked onto a board. I had done the same with Pokey, and with Wild Bruce before he died, and had had Walleye's platoon sergeant backtrack his movements. I was sure the poison had come from one of several nearby dives frequented by the Bastion garrison.

Curly produced one across-the-board match. "Bingo! We've got the bastards now."

"Who?" He was ready to go settle up himself.

"You rest. I'll see the Captain." I patted his shoulder, checked the next room. Curly was it for morning sick call.

I took the long route, along Trejan's Wall, which overlooks Beryl's harbor. Halfway over I paused, stared north, past the mole and lighthouse and Fortress Island, at the Sea of Torments. Particolored sails speckled the dingy grey-brown water as coastal dhows scooted out along the spiderweb of routes linking the Jewel Cities. The upper air was still and heavy and hazy. The horizon could not be discerned. But down on the water the air was in motion. There was always a breeze out around the Island, though it avoided the shore as if fearing leprosy. Closer at hand, the wheeling gulls were as surly and lackadaisical as the day promised to make most men.

Another summer in service to the Syndic of Beryl, sweating and grimy, thanklessly shielding him from political rivals and his undisciplined native troops. Another summer busting our butts for Curly's reward. The pay was good, but not in coin of the soul. Our forebrethren would be embarrassed to see us so diminished.

Beryl is misery curdled, but also ancient and intriguing. Its history is a bottomless well filled with murky water. I amuse myself plumbing its shadowy depths, trying to isolate fact from fiction, legend, and myth. No easy task, for the city's earlier historians wrote with an eye to pleasing the powers of their day.

The most interesting period, for me, is the ancient kingdom, which is the least satisfactorily chronicled. It was then, in the reign of Niam, that the forvalaka came, were overcome after a decade of terror, and were confined in their dark tomb atop the Necropolitan Hill. Echoes of that terror persist in folklore and matronly admonitions to unruly children. No one recalls what the forvalaka were, now.

I resumed walking, despairing of beating the heat. The sentries, in their shaded kiosks, wore towels draped around their necks.

A breeze startled me. I faced the harbor. A ship was rounding the Island, a great lumbering beast that dwarfed the dhows and feluccas. A silver skull bulged in the center of its full-bellied black sail. That skull's red eyes glowed. Fires flickered behind its broken teeth. A glittering silver band encircled the skull.

"What the hell is that?" a sentry asked.

"I don't know, Whitey." The ship's size impressed me more than did its flashy sail. The four minor wizards we had with the Company could match that showmanship. But I'd never seen a galley sporting five banks of oars.

I recalled my mission.

I knocked on the Captain's door. He did not respond. I invited myself inside, found him snoring in his big wooden chair. "Yo!" I hollered. "Fire! Riots in the Groan! Dancing at the Gate of Dawn!" Dancing was an old time general who nearly destroyed Beryl. People still shudder at his name.

The Captain was cool. He didn't crack an eyelid or smile. "You're presumptuous, Croaker. When are you going to learn to go through channels?" Channels meant bug the Lieutenant first. Don't interrupt his nap unless the Blues were storming the Bastion.

I explained about Curly and my chart.

He swung his feet off the desk. "Sounds like work for Mercy." His voice had a hard edge. The Black Company does not suffer malicious attacks upon its men.

Mercy was our nastiest platoon leader. He thought a dozen men would suffice, but let Silent and me tag along. I could patch the wounded. Silent would be useful if the Blues played rough. Silent held us up half a day while he made a quick trip to the woods.

"What the hell you up to?" I asked when he got back, lugging a ratty-looking sack.

He just grinned. Silent he is and silent he stays.

The place was called Mole Tavern. It was a comfortable hangout. I had passed many an evening there. Mercy assigned three men to the back door, and a pair each to the two windows. He sent another two to the roof. Every building in Beryl has a roof hatch. People sleep up top during the summer.

He led the rest of us through the Mole's front door.

Mercy was a smallish, cocky fellow, fond of the dramatic gesture. His entry should have been preceded by fanfares.

The crowd froze, stared at our shields and bared blades, at snatches of grim faces barely visible through gaps in our face guards. "Verus!" Mercy shouted. "Get your butt out here!"

The grandfather of the managing family appeared. He sidled toward us like a mutt expecting a kick. The customers began buzzing. "Silence!" Mercy thundered. He could get a big roar out of his small body.

"How may we help you, honored sirs?" the old man asked.

"You can get your sons and grandsons out here, Blue."

Chairs squeaked. A soldier slammed his blade into a tabletop.

"Sit still," Mercy said. "You're just having lunch, fine. You'll be loose in an hour."

The old man began shaking. "I don't understand, sir. What have we done?"

Mercy grinned evilly. "He plays the innocent well. It's murder, Verus. Two charges of murder by poisoning. Two of attempted murder by poisoning. The magistrates decreed the punishment of slaves." He was having fun.

Mercy wasn't one of my favorite people. He never stopped being the boy who pulled wings off flies.

The punishment of slaves meant being left up for scavenger birds after public crucifixion. In Beryl only criminals are buried uncremated, or not buried at all.

An uproar rose in the kitchen. Somebody was trying to get out the back door. Our men were objecting.

The public room exploded. A wave of dagger-brandishing humanity hit us. They forced us back to the door. Those who were not guilty obviously feared they would be condemned with those who were. Beryl's justice is fast, crude, and harsh, and seldom gives a defendant opportunity to clear himself.

A dagger slipped past a shield. One of our men went down. I am not much as a fighter, but I stepped into his place. Mercy said something snide that I did not catch. "That's your chance at heaven wasted," I countered. "You're out of the Annals forever."

"Crap. You don't leave out anything."

A dozen citizens went down. Blood pooled in low places on the floor. Spectators gathered outside. Soon some adventurer would hit us from behind.

A dagger nicked Mercy. He lost patience. "Silent!"

Silent was on the job already, but he was Silent. That meant no sound, and very little flash or fury.

Mole patrons began slapping their faces and pawing the air, forsaking us. They hopped and danced, grabbed their backs and behinds, squealed and howled piteously. Several collapsed.

"What the hell did you do?" I asked.

Silent grinned, exposing sharp teeth. He passed a dusky paw across my eyes. I saw the Mole from a slightly altered perspective.

The bag he had lugged in from out of town proved to be one of those hornets' nests you can, if you're unlucky, run into in the woods south of Beryl. Its tenants were the bumblebee-looking monsters peasants call bald-faced hornets. They have a foul temper unrivalled anywhere in Nature. They cowed the Mole crowd fast, without bothering our lads.

"Fine work, Silent," Mercy said, after having vented his fury on several hapless patrons. He herded the survivors into the street.

I examined our injured brother while the unharmed soldiers finished the wounded. Saving the Syndic the cost of a trial and a hangman, Mercy called that. Silent looked on, still grinning. He's not nice either, though he seldom participates directly.

We took more prisoners than expected. "Was a bunch of them." Mercy's eyes twinkled. "Thanks, Silent." The line stretched a block.

Fate is a fickle bitch. She'd led us to Mole Tavern at a critical moment. Poking around, our witch man had unearthed a prize, a crowd concealed in a hideout beneath the wine cellar. Among them were some of the best known Blues.

Mercy chattered, wondering aloud how large a reward our informant deserved. No such informant existed. The yammer was meant to save our tame wizards from becoming prime targets. Our enemies would scurry around looking for phantom spies.

"Move them out," Mercy ordered. Still grinning, he eyed the sullen crowd.

"Think they'll try something?" They did not. His supreme confidence cowed anyone who had ideas.

We wound through mazelike streets half as old as the world, our prisoners shuffling listlessly. I gawked. My comrades are indifferent to the past, but I cannot help being awed—and occasionally intimidated—by how time-deep Beryl's history runs.

Mercy called an unexpected halt. We had come to the Avenue of the Syndics, which winds from the Customs House uptown to the Bastion's main gate. There was a procession on the Avenue. Though we reached the intersection first, Mercy yielded the right-of-way.

The procession consisted of a hundred armed men. They looked tougher than anyone in Beryl but us. At their head rode a dark figure on the biggest black stallion I've ever seen. The rider was small, effeminately slim, and clad in worn black leather. He wore a black morion which concealed his head entirely. Black gloves concealed his hands. He seemed to be unarmed.

"Damn me," Mercy whispered.

I was disturbed. That rider chilled me. Something primitive deep inside me wanted to run. But curiosity plagued me more. Who was he? Had he come off that strange ship in the harbor? Why was he here?

The eyeless gaze of the rider swept across us indifferently, as though passing over a flock of sheep. Then it jerked back, fixing on Silent.

Silent met stare for stare, and showed no fear. And still he seemed somehow diminished.

The column passed on, hardened, disciplined. Shaken, Mercy got our mob moving again. We entered the Bastion only yards behind the strangers.

We had arrested most of the more conservative Blue leadership. When word of the raid spread, the volatile types decided to flex their muscles. They sparked something monstrous.

The perpetually abrasive weather does things to men's reason. The Beryl mob is savage. Riots occur almost without provocation. When things go bad the dead number in the thousands. This was one of the worst times.

The army is half the problem. A parade of weak, short-term Syndics let discipline lapse. The troops are beyond control now. Generally, though, they will act against rioters. They see riot suppression as license to loot.

The worst happened. Several cohorts from the Fork Barracks demanded a special donative before they would respond to a directive to restore order. The Syndic refused to pay.

The cohorts mutinied.

Mercy's platoon hastily established a strongpoint near the Rubbish Gate and held off all three cohorts. Most of our men were killed, but none ran. Mercy himself lost an eye, a finger, was wounded in shoulder and hip, and had more than a hundred holes in his shield when help arrived. He came to me more dead than alive.

In the end, the mutineers scattered rather than face the rest of the Black Company.

The riots were the worst in memory. We lost almost a hundred brethren trying to suppress them. We could ill afford the loss of one. In the Groan the streets were carpeted with corpses. The rats grew fat. Clouds of vultures and ravens migrated from the countryside.

The Captain ordered the Company into the Bastion. "Let it run its course," he said. "We've done enough." His disposition had gone beyond sour, disgusted. "Our commission doesn't require us to commit suicide."

Somebody made a crack about us falling on our swords.

"Seems to be what the Syndic expects."

Beryl had ground our spirits down, but had left none so disillusioned as the Captain. He blamed himself for our losses. He did, in fact, try to resign.

The mob had fallen into a sullen, grudging, desultory effort to sustain chaos, interfering with any attempt to fight fires or prevent looting, but otherwise just roamed. The mutinous cohorts, fattened by deserters from other units, were systematizing the murder and plunder.

The third night I stood a watch on Trejan's Wall, beneath the carping stars, a fool of a volunteer sentinel. The city was strangely quiet. I might have been more anxious had I not been so tired. It was all I could do to stay awake.

Tom-Tom came by. "What are you doing out here, Croaker?"

"Filling in."

"You look like death on a stick. Get some rest."

"You don't look good yourself, runt."

He shrugged. "How's Mercy?"

"Not out of the woods yet." I had little hope for him really. I pointed. "You know anything about that out there?" An isolated scream echoed in the distance. It had a quality which set it aside from other recent screams. Those had been filled with pain, rage, and fear. This one was redolent of something darker.

He hemmed and hawed in that way he and his brother One-Eye have. If you don't know, they figure it's a secret worth keeping. Wizards! "There's a rumor that the mutineers broke the seals on the tomb of the forvalaka while they were plundering the Necropolitan Hill."

"Uh? Those things are loose?"

"The Syndic thinks so. The Captain don't take it seriously."

I didn't either, though Tom-Tom looked concerned. "They looked tough. The ones who were here the other day."

"Ought to have recruited them," he said, with an undertone of sadness. He and One-Eye have been with the Company a long time. They have seen much of its decline.

"Why were they here?"

He shrugged. "Get some rest, Croaker. Don't kill yourself. Won't make a bit of difference in the end." He ambled away, lost in the wilderness of his thoughts.

I lifted an eyebrow. He was *way* down. I turned back to the fires and lights and disturbing absence of racket. My eyes kept crossing, my vision clouding. Tom-Tom was right. I needed sleep.

From the darkness came another of those strange, hopeless cries. This one was closer.

Up, Croaker." The Lieutenant was not gentle. "Captain wants you in the officers' mess."

I groaned. I cursed. I threatened mayhem in the first degree. He grinned, pinched the nerve in my elbow, rolled me onto the floor. "I'm up already," I grumbled, feeling around for my boots. "What's it about?"

He was gone.

"Will Mercy pull through, Croaker?" the Captain asked.

"I don't think so, but I've seen bigger miracles."

The officers and sergeants were all there. "You want to know what's happening," the Captain said. "The visitor the other day was an envoy from overseas. He offered an alliance. The north's military resources in exchange for the support of Beryl's fleets. Sounded reasonable to me. But the Syndic is being stubborn. He's still upset about the conquest of Opal. I suggested he be more flexible. If these northerners are villains then the alliance option could be the least of several evils. Better an ally than a tributary. Our problem is, where do we stand if the legate presses?"

Candy said, "We should refuse if he tells us to fight these northerners?"

"Maybe. Fighting a sorcerer could mean our destruction."

Wham! The mess door slammed open. A small, dusky, wiry man, preceded by a great humped beak of a nose, blew inside. The Captain bounced up and clicked his heels. "Syndic."

Our visitor slammed both fists down on the tabletop. "You ordered your men withdrawn into the Bastion. I'm not paying you to hide like whipped dogs."

"You're not paying us to become martyrs, either," the Captain replied in his reasoning-with-fools voice. "We're a bodyguard, not police. Maintaining order is the task of the Urban Cohorts."

The Syndic was tired, distraught, frightened, on his last emotional legs. Like everyone else.

"Be reasonable," the Captain suggested. "Beryl has passed a point of no return. Chaos rules the streets. Any attempt to restore order is doomed. The cure now is the disease."

I liked that. I had begun to hate Beryl.

The Syndic shrank into himself. "There's still the forvalaka. And that vulture from the north, waiting off the Island."

Tom-Tom started out of a half-sleep. "Off the Island, you say?"

"Waiting for me to beg."

"Interesting." The little wizard lapsed into semi-slumber.

The Captain and the Syndic bickered about the terms of our commission. I produced our copy of the agreement. The Syndic tried to stretch clauses with, "Yeah, but." Clearly, he wanted to fight if the legate started throwing his weight around.

Elmo started snoring. The Captain dismissed us, resumed arguing with our employer.

I suppose seven hours passes as a night's sleep. I didn't strangle Tom-Tom when he wakened me. But I did grouse and crab till he threatened to turn me into a jackass braying at the Gate of Dawn. Only then, after I had dressed and we had joined a dozen others, did I realize that I didn't have a notion what was happening.

"We're going to look at a tomb," Tom-Tom said.

"Huh?" I am none too bright some mornings.

"We're going to the Necropolitan Hill to eyeball that forvalaka tomb."

"Now wait a minute. . . ."

"Chicken? I always thought you were, Croaker."

"What're you talking about?"

"Don't worry. You'll have three top wizards along, with nothing to do but babysit your ass. One-Eye would go too, but the Captain wants him to hang around."

"Why is what I want to know."

"To find out if vampires are real. They could be a put-up from yon spook ship."

"Neat trick. Maybe we should have thought of it." The forvalaka threat had done what no force of arms could: stilled the riots.

Tom-Tom nodded. He dragged fingers across the little drum that gave him his name. I filed the thought. He's worse than his brother when it comes to admitting shortcomings.

The city was as still as an old battlefield. Like a battlefield, it was filled with stench, flies, scavengers, and the dead. The only sound was the tread of our boots and, once, the mournful cry of a sad dog standing sentinel over its fallen master. "The price of order," I muttered. I tried to run the dog off. It wouldn't budge.

"The cost of chaos," Tom-Tom countered. *Thump* on his drum. "Not quite the same thing, Croaker."

The Necropolitan Hill is taller than the heights on which the Bastion stands. From the Upper Enclosure, where the mausoleums of the wealthy stand, I could see the northern ship.

"Just lying out there waiting," Tom-Tom said. "Like the Syndic said."

"Why don't they just move in? Who could stop them?"

Tom-Tom shrugged. Nobody else offered an opinion.

We reached the storied tomb. It looked the part it played in rumor and legend. It was very, very old, definitely lightning-blasted, and scarred with tool marks. One thick oak door had burst asunder. Toothpicks and fragments lay scattered for a dozen yards around.

Goblin, Tom-Tom, and Silent put their heads together. Somebody made a crack about that way they might have a brain between them. Goblin and Silent then took stations flanking the door, a few steps back. Tom-Tom faced it head on. He shuffled around like a bull about to charge, found his spot, dropped into a crouch with his arms flung up oddly, like a parody of a martial arts master.

"How about you fools open the door?" he growled. "Idiots. I had to bring idiots." *Wham-wham* on the drum. "Stand around with their fingers in their noses."

A couple of us grabbed the ruined door and heaved. It was too warped to give much. Tom-Tom rapped his drum, let out a villainous scream, and jumped inside. Goblin bounced to the portal behind him. Silent moved up in a fast glide.

Inside, Tom-Tom let out a rat squeak and started sneezing. He stumbled out, eyes watering, grinding his nose with the heels of his hands. He sounded like he had a bad cold when he said, "Wasn't a trick." His ebony skin had gone grey.

"What do you mean?" I demanded.

He jerked a thumb toward the tomb. Goblin and Silent were inside now. They started sneezing.

I sidled to the doorway, peeked. I couldn't see squat. Just dust thick in the sunlight close to me. Then I stepped inside. My eyes adjusted.

There were bones everywhere. Bones in heaps, bones in stacks, bones sorted neatly by something insane. Strange bones they were, similar to those of men, but of weird proportion to my physician's eye. There must have been fifty bodies originally. They'd really packed them in, back when. Forvalaka for sure, then, because Beryl buries its villains uncremated.

There were fresh corpses too. I counted seven dead soldiers before the sneezing started. They wore the colors of a mutinous cohort.

I dragged a body outside, let go, stumbled a few steps, was noisily sick. When I regained control, I turned back to examine my booty.

The others stood around looking green. "No phantom did that," Goblin said. Tom-Tom bobbed his head. He was more shaken than anyone. More shaken than the sight demanded, I thought.

Silent got on with business, somehow conjuring a brisk, small maid of a breeze that scurried in through the mausoleum door and bustled out again, skirts laden with dust and the smell of death.

"You all right?" I asked Tom-Tom.

He eyed my medical kit and waved me off. "I'll be okay. I was just remembering."

I gave him a minute, then prodded, "Remembering?"

"We were boys, One-Eye and me. They'd just sold us to N'Gamo, to become his apprentices. A messenger came from a village back in the hills." He knelt beside the dead soldier. "The wounds are identical."

I was rattled. Nothing human killed that way, yet the damage seemed deliberate, calculated, the work of a malign intelligence. That made it more horrible.

I swallowed, knelt, began my examination. Silent and Goblin eased into the tomb. Goblin had a little amber ball of light rolling around his cupped hands. "No bleeding," I observed.

"It takes the blood," Tom-Tom said. Silent dragged another corpse out. "And the organs when it has time." The second body had been split from groin to gullet. Heart and liver were missing.

Silent went back inside. Goblin came out. He settled on a broken grave marker and shook his head. "Well?" Tom-Tom demanded.

"Definitely the real thing. No prank by our friend." He pointed. The northerner continued its patrol amidst a swarm of fishermen and coasters. "There were fifty-four of them sealed up here. They ate each other. This was the last one left."

Tom-Tom jumped as if slapped.

"What's the matter?" I asked.

"That means the thing was the nastiest, cunningest, cruelest, and craziest of the lot."

"Vampires," I muttered. "In this day."

Tom-Tom said, "Not strictly a vampire. This is the wereleopard, the man-leopard who walks on two legs by day and on four by night."

I'd heard of werewolves and werebears. The peasants around my home city tell such tales. I'd never heard of a wereleopard. I told Tom-Tom as much.

"The man-leopard is from the far south. The jungle." He stared out to sea. "They have to be buried alive."

Silent deposited another corpse.

Blood-drinking, liver-eating wereleopards. Ancient, darkness-wise, filled with a millennium of hatred and hunger. The stuff of nightmare all right. "Can you handle it?"

"N'Gamo couldn't. I'll never be his match, and he lost an arm and a foot trying to destroy a young male. What we have here is an old female. Bitter, cruel, and clever. The four of us might hold her off. Conquer her, no."

"But if you and One-Eye know this thing. . . ."

"No." He had the shakes. He gripped his drum so tight it creaked. "We can't."

Chaos died. Beryl's streets remained as starkly silent as those of a city overthrown. Even the mutineers concealed themselves till hunger drove them to the city granaries.

The Syndic tried to tighten the screws on the Captain. The Captain ignored him. Silent, Goblin, and One-Eye tracked the monster. The thing functioned on a purely animal level, feeding the hunger of an age. The factions besieged the Syndic with demands for protection.

The Lieutenant again summoned us to the officers' mess. The Captain wasted no time. "Men, our situation is grim." He paced. "Beryl is demanding a new Syndic. Every faction has asked the Black Company to stand aside."

The moral dilemma escalated with the stakes.

"We aren't heroes," the Captain continued. "We're tough. We're stubborn. We try to honor our commitments. But we don't die for lost causes."

I protested, the voice of tradition questioning his unspoken proposition.

"The question on the table is the survival of the Company, Croaker."

"We have taken the gold, Captain. Honor is the question on the table. For four centuries the Black Company has met the letter of its commissions. Consider the Book of Set, recorded by Annalist Coral while the Company was in service to the Archon of Bone, during the Revolt of the Chiliarchs."

"You consider it, Croaker."

I was irritated. "I stand on my right as a free soldier."

"He has the right to speak," the Lieutenant agreed. He is more a traditionalist than I.

"Okay. Let him talk. We don't have to listen."

I reiterated that darkest hour in the Company's history . . . till I realized I was arguing with myself. Half of me wanted to sell out.

"Croaker? Are you finished?"

I swallowed. "Find a legitimate loophole and I'll go along."

Tom-Tom gave me a mocking drumroll. One-Eye chuckled. "That's a job for Goblin, Croaker. He was a lawyer before he worked his way up to pimping."

Goblin took the bait. "*I* was a lawyer? Your mother was a lawyer's. . . ."

"Enough!" The Captain slapped the tabletop. "We've got Croaker's okay. Go with it. Find an out."

The others looked relieved. Even the Lieutenant. My opinion, as Annalist, carried more weight than I liked.

"The obvious out is the termination of the man holding our bond," I observed. That hung in the air like an old, foul smell. Like the stench in the tomb of the forvalaka. "In our battered state, who could blame us if an assassin slipped past?"

"You have a disgusting turn of mind, Croaker," Tom-Tom said. He gave me another drumroll.

"Pots calling kettles? We'd retain the appearance of honor. We *do* fail. As often as not."

"I like it," the Captain said. "Let's break this up before the Syndic comes asking what's up. You stay, Tom-Tom. I've got a job for you."

It was a night for screamers. A broiling, sticky night of the sort that abrades that last thin barrier between the civilized man and the monster crouched in his soul. The screams came from homes where fear, heat, and overcrowding had put too much strain on the monster's chains.

A cool wind roared in off the gulf, pursued by massive storm clouds with lightning prancing in their hair. The wind swept away the stench of Beryl. The downpour scoured its streets. By morning's light Beryl seemed a different city, still and cool and clean.

The streets were speckled with puddles as we walked to the waterfront. Runoff still chuckled in the gutters. By noon the air would be leaden again, and more humid than ever.

Tom-Tom awaited us on a boat he had hired. I said, "How much did you pocket on this deal? This scow looks like it'd sink before it cleared the Island."

"Not a copper, Croaker." He sounded disappointed. He and his brother are great pilferers and black-marketeers. "Not a copper. This here is a slicker job than it looks. Her master is a smuggler."

"I'll take your word. You'd probably know." Nevertheless, I stepped gingerly as I boarded. He scowled. We were supposed to pretend that the avarice of Tom-Tom and One-Eye did not exist.

We were off to sea to make an arrangement. Tom-Tom had the Captain's carte blanche. The Lieutenant and I were along to give him a swift kick if he got carried away. Silent and a half dozen soldiers accompanied us for show.

A customs launch hailed us off the Island. We were gone before she could get underway. I squatted, peered under the boom. The black ship loomed bigger and bigger "That damned thing is a floating island."

"Too big," the Lieutenant growled. "Ship that size couldn't hold together in a heavy sea."

"Why not? How do you know?" Even boggled I remained curious about my brethren.

"Sailed as a cabin boy when I was young. I learned ships." His tone discouraged further interrogation. Most of the men want their antecedents kept private. As you might expect in a company of villains held together by its now and its us-against-the-world gone befores.

"Not too big if you have the thaumaturgic craft to bind it," Tom-Tom countered. He was shaky, tapping his drum in random, nervous rhythms. He and One-Eye both hate water.

So. A mysterious northern enchanter. A ship as black as the floors of hell. My nerves began to fray.

Her crew dropped an accommodation ladder. The Lieutenant scampered up. He seemed impressed.

I'm no sailor, but the ship did look squared away and disciplined.

A junior officer sorted out Tom-Tom, Silent, and myself and asked us to accompany him. He led us down stairs and through passageways, aft, without speaking.

The northern emissary sat crosslegs amidst rich cushions backed by the ship's open sternlights, in a cabin worthy of an eastern potentate. I gaped. Tom-Tom smouldered with avarice. The emissary laughed.

The laughter was a shock. A high-pitched near giggle more appropriate to some fifteen-year-old madonna of the tavern night than to a man more powerful than any king. "Excuse me," he said, placing a hand daintily where his mouth would have been had he not been wearing that black morion. Then, "Be seated."

My eyes widened against my will. Each remark came in a distinctly different voice. Was there a committee inside that helmet?

Tom-Tom gulped air. Silent, being Silent, simply sat. I followed his example, and tried not to become too offensive with my frightened, curious stare.

Tom-Tom wasn't the best diplomat that day. He blurted, "The Syndic won't last much longer. We want to make an arrangement. . . ."

Silent dug a toe into his thigh.

I muttered, "This is our daring prince of thieves? Our man of iron nerve?"

The legate chuckled. "You're the physician? Croaker? Pardon him. He knows me."

A cold, cold fear enfolded me in its dark wings. Sweat moistened my temples. It had nothing to do with heat. A cool sea breeze flowed through the sternlights, a breeze for which men in Beryl would kill.

"There is no cause to fear me. I was sent to offer an alliance meant to benefit Beryl as much as my people. I remain convinced that agreement can be forged—though not with the current autocrat. You face a problem requiring the same solution as mine, but your commission puts you in a narrow place."

"He knows it all. No point talking," Tom-Tom croaked. He thumped his drum, but his fetish did him no good. He was choking up.

The legate observed, "The Syndic is not invulnerable. Even guarded by you." A great big cat had Tom-Tom's tongue. The envoy looked at me. I shrugged. "Suppose the Syndic expired while your company was defending the Bastion against the mob?"

"Ideal," I said. "But it ignores the question of our subsequent safety."

"You drive the mob off, then discover the death. You're no longer employed, so you leave Beryl."

"And go where? And outrun our enemies how? The Urban Cohorts would pursue us."

"Tell your Captain that, on discovery of the Syndic's demise, if I receive a written request to mediate the succession, my forces will relieve you at the Bastion. You should leave Beryl and camp on the Pillar of Anguish."

The Pillar of Anguish is an arrowhead of a chalk headland wormholed with countless little caverns. It thrusts out to sea a day's march east of Beryl. A lighthouse/watchtower stands there. The name comes from the moaning the wind makes passing through the caverns.

"That's a goddamned deathtrap. Those bugger-masters would just besiege us and giggle till we ate each other."

"A simple matter to slip boats in and take you off."

Ding-ding. An alarm bell banged away four inches behind my eyes. This sumbitch was running a game on us. "Why the hell would you do that?"

"Your company would be unemployed. I would be willing to assume the commission. There is a need for good soldiers in the north."

Ding-ding. That old bell kept singing. He wanted to take us on? What for?

Something told me that was not the moment to ask. I shifted my ground. "What about the forvalaka?" Zig where they expect you to zag.

"The thing out of the crypt?" The envoy's voice was that of the woman of your dreams, purring "come on." "I may have work for it too."

"You'll get it under control?"

"Once it serves its purpose."

I thought of the lightning bolt that had obliterated a spell of confinement on a plaque that had resisted tampering for a millennium. I kept my suspicions off my face, I'm sure. But the emissary chuckled. "Maybe, physician. Maybe not. An interesting puzzle, no? Go back to your captain. Make up your minds. Quickly. Your enemies are ready to move." He made a gesture that dismissed us.

* * *

Just deliver the case!" the Captain snarled at Candy. "Then get your butt back here."

Candy took the courier case and went.

"Anybody else want to argue? You bastards had your chance to get rid of me. You blew it."

Tempers were hot. The Captain had made the legate a counter-proposal, been offered his patronage should the Syndic perish. Candy was running the Captain's reply to the envoy.

Tom-Tom muttered, "You don't know what you're doing. You don't know who you're signing with."

"Illuminate me. No? Croaker. What's it like out there?" I had been sent to scout the city.

"It's plague all right. Not like any I've seen before, though. The forvalaka must be the vector."

The Captain gave me the squinty eye.

"Doctor talk. A vector is a carrier. The plague comes in pockets around its kills."

The Captain growled, "Tom-Tom? You know this beast."

"Never heard of one spreading disease. And all of us who went into the tomb are still healthy."

I chimed in, "The carrier doesn't matter. The plague does. It'll get worse if people don't start burning bodies."

"It hasn't penetrated the Bastion," the Captain observed. "And it's had a positive effect. The regular garrison have stopped deserting."

"I encountered a lot of antagonism in the Groan. They're on the edge of another explosion."

"How soon?"

"Two days? Three at the outside."

The Captain chewed his lip. The tight place was getting tighter. "We've got to. . . ."

A tribune of the garrison shoved through the door. "There's a mob at the gate. They have a ram."

"Let's go," the Captain said.

It took only minutes to disperse them. A few missiles and a few pots of hot water. They fled, pelting us with curses and insults.

Night fell. I stayed on the wall, watching distant torches roam the city. The mob was evolving, developing a nervous system. If it developed a brain we would find ourselves caught in a revolution.

The movement of torches eventually diminished. The explosion would not come tonight. Maybe tomorrow, if the heat and humidity became too oppressive.

Later I heard scratching to my right. Then clackings. Scrapings. Softly, softly, but there. Approaching. Terror filled me. I became as motionless as the gargoyles perched over the gate. The breeze became an arctic wind.

Something came over the battlements. Red eyes. Four legs. Dark as the night. Black leopard. It moved as fluidly as water running downhill. It padded down the stair into the courtyard, vanished.

The monkey in my backbrain wanted to scamper up a tall tree, screeching, to hurl excrement and rotted fruit. I fled toward the nearest door, took a protected route to the Captain's quarters, let myself in without knocking.

I found him on his cot, hands behind his head, staring at the ceiling. His room was illuminated by a single feeble candle. "The forvalaka is in the Bastion. I saw it come over the wall." My voice squeaked like Goblin's.

He grunted.

"You hear me?"

"I heard, Croaker. Go away. Leave me alone."

"Yes sir." So. It was eating him up. I backed toward the door. . . .

The scream was loud and long and hopeless, and ended abruptly. It came from the Syndic's quarters. I drew my sword, charged through the door—smack into Candy. Candy went down. I stood over him, numbly wondering why he was back so soon.

"Get in here, Croaker," the Captain ordered. "Want to get yourself killed?" There were more cries from the Syndic's quarters. Death was not being selective.

I yanked Candy inside. We bolted and barred the door. I stood with my back against it, eyes closed, panting. Chances are it was imagination, but I thought I heard something growl as it padded past.

"Now what?" Candy asked. His face was colorless. His hands were shaking.

The Captain finished scribbling a letter. He handed it over. "Now you go back."

Someone hammered on the door. "What?" the Captain snapped.

A voice muted by thick wood responded. I said, "It's One-Eye."

"Open up."

I opened. One-Eye, Tom-Tom, Goblin, Silent, and a dozen others pushed inside. The room got hot and tight. Tom-Tom said, "The man-leopard is in the Bastion, Captain." He forgot to punctuate with his drum. It seemed to droop at his hip.

Another scream from the Syndic's quarters. My imagination *had* tricked me.

"What're we going to do?" One-Eye asked. He was a wrinkled little black man no bigger than his brother, usually possessed by a bizarre sense of humor. He was a year older than Tom-Tom, but at their age no one was counting. Both were over a hundred, if the Annals could be believed. He was terrified. Tom-Tom was on the edge of hysteria. Goblin and Silent, too, were rocky. "It can take us off one by one."

"Can it be killed?"

"They're almost invincible, Captain."

"Can they be killed?" The Captain put a hard edge on his voice. He was frightened too.

"Yes," One-Eye confessed. He seemed a whisker less scared than Tom-Tom. "Nothing is invulnerable. Not even that thing on the black ship. But this is strong, fast, and smart. Weapons are of little avail. Sorcery is better, but even that isn't much use." Never before had I heard him admit limitations.

"We've talked enough," the Captain growled. "Now we act." He was difficult to know, our commander, but was transparent now. Rage and frustration at an impossible situation had fixed on the forvalaka.

Tom-Tom and One-Eye protested vehemently.

"You've been thinking about this since you found out that thing was loose," the Captain said. "You decided what you'd do if you had to. Let's do it."

Another scream. "The Paper Tower must be an abattoir," I muttered. "The thing is hunting down everybody up there."

For a moment I thought even Silent would protest.

The Captain strapped on his weapons. "Match, assemble the men. Seal all the entrances to the Paper Tower. Elmo, pick some good halberdiers and crossbowmen. Quarrels to be poisoned."

Twenty minutes fled. I lost count of the cries. I lost track of everything but a growing trepidation and the question, *why* had the forvalaka invaded the Bastion? Why did it persist in its hunt? More than hunger drove it.

That legate had hinted at having a use for it. What? This? What were we doing working with someone who could do that?

All four wizards collaborated on the spell that preceded us, crackling. The air itself threw blue sparks. Halberdiers followed. Crossbowmen backed them. Behind them another dozen of us entered the Syndic's quarters.

Anticlimax. The antechamber to the Paper Tower looked perfectly normal. "It's upstairs," One-Eye told us.

The Captain faced the passageway behind us. "Match, bring your men inside." He planned to advance room by room, sealing all exits but one for retreat. One-Eye and Tom-Tom did not approve. They said the thing would be more dangerous cornered. Ominous silence surrounded us. There had been no cries for several minutes.

We found the first victim at the base of the stair leading into the Tower proper. "One of ours," I grumbled. The Syndic always surrounded himself with a squad from the Company. "Sleeping quarters upstairs?" I'd never been inside the Paper Tower.

The Captain nodded. "Kitchen level, stores level, servants' quarters on two levels, then family, then the Syndic himself. Library and offices at the top. Wants to make it hard to get to him."

I examined the body. "Not quite like the ones at the tomb. Tom-Tom. It didn't take the blood or organs. How come?"

He had no answer. Neither did One-Eye.

The Captain peered into the shadows above. "Now it gets tricky. Halberdiers, one step at a time. Keep your points low. Crossbows, stay four or five steps behind. Shoot anything that moves. Swords out, everybody. One-Eye, run your spell ahead."

Crackle. Step, step, quietly. Stench of fear. *Quang!* A man discharged his crossbow accidentally. The Captain spit and grumbled like a volcano in bad temper.

There wasn't a damned thing to see.

Servants' quarters. Blood splashed the walls. Bodies and pieces of bodies lay everywhere amidst furniture invariably shredded and wrecked. There are hard men in the Company, but even the hardest was moved. Even I, who as physician see the worst the battlefield offers.

The Lieutenant said, "Captain, I'm getting the rest of the Company. This thing isn't getting away." His tone brooked no contradiction. The Captain merely nodded.

The carnage had that effect. Fear faded somewhat. Most of us decided the thing had to be destroyed.

A scream sounded above. It was like a taunt hurled our way, daring us to come on. Hard-eyed men started up the stair. The air crackled as the spell preceded them. Tom-Tom and One-Eye bore down on their terror. The death hunt began in earnest.

A vulture had evicted the eagle nesting atop the Paper Tower, a fell omen indeed. I had no hope for our employer.

We climbed past five levels. It was gorily obvious the forvalaka had visited each. . . .

Tom-Tom whipped up a hand, pointed. The forvalaka was nearby. The halberdiers knelt behind their weapons. The crossbowmen aimed at shadows. Tom-Tom waited half a minute. He, One-Eye, Silent, and Goblin posed intently, listening to something the rest of the world could only imagine. Then, "It's waiting. Be careful. Don't give it an opening."

I asked a dumb question, altogether too late for its answer to have bearing. "Shouldn't we use silver weapons? Quarrel heads and blades?"

Tom-Tom looked baffled.

"Where I come from the peasants say you have to kill werewolves with silver."

"Crap. You kill them same as you kill anything else. Only you move faster and hit harder 'cause you only get one shot."

The more he revealed the less terrible the creature seemed. This was like hunting a rogue lion. Why all the fuss?

I recalled the servants' quarters.

"Everybody just stand still," Tom-Tom said. "And be quiet. We'll try a sending." He and his cohorts put their heads together. After a while he indicated we should resume our advance.

We eased onto a landing, packed tightly, a human hedgehog with quills of steel. The wizards sped their enchantment. An angry roar came from the shadows ahead, followed by the scrape of claws. Something moved. Crossbows twanged. Another roar, almost mocking. The wizards put their heads together again. Downstairs the Lieutenant was ordering men into positions the forvalaka would have to pass to escape.

We eased into the darkness, tension mounting. Bodies and blood made the footing treacherous. Men hastened to seal doors. Slowly, we penetrated a suite of offices. Twice movement drew fire from the crossbows.

The forvalaka yowled not twenty feet away. Tom-Tom released a sigh that was half groan. "Caught it," he said, meaning they had reached it with their spell.

Twenty feet away. Right there with us. I could see nothing. . . . Something moved. Quarrels flew. A man cried out. . . . "Damn!" the Captain swore. "Somebody was still alive up here."

Something as black as the heart of night, as quick as unexpected death, arced over the halberds. I had one thought, *Fast!*, before it was among us. Men flew around, yelled, got into one another's way. The monster roared and growled, threw claws and fangs too fast for the eye to follow. Once I thought I slashed a flank of darkness, before a blow hurled me a dozen feet.

I scrambled up, got my back to a pillar. I was sure I was going to die, sure the thing would kill us all. Pure hubris, us thinking we could handle it. Only seconds had passed. Half a dozen men were dead. More were injured. The forvalaka didn't seem slowed, let alone harmed. Neither weapons nor spells hampered it.

Our wizards stood in a little knot, trying to produce another enchantment. The Captain cored a second clump. The rest of the men were scattered. The monster flashed around, picking them off.

Grey fire ripped through the room, for an instant exposing its entirety, branding the carnage on the backs of my eyeballs. The forvalaka screamed, this time with genuine pain. Point for the wizards.

It streaked toward me. I hacked in panic as it whipped past. I missed. It whirled, took a running start, leapt at the wizards. They met it with another flashy spell. The forvalaka howled. A man shrieked. The beast thrashed on the floor like a dying snake. Men stabbed it with pikes and swords. It regained its feet and streaked out the exit we had kept open for ourselves.

"It's coming!" the Captain bellowed to the Lieutenant.

I sagged, knowing nothing but relief. It was gone. . . . Before my butt hit the floor One-Eye was dragging me up. "Come on, Croaker. It hit Tom-Tom. You got to help."

I staggered over, suddenly aware of a shallow gash down one leg. "Better clean it good," I muttered. "Those claws are bound to be filthy."

Tom-Tom was a twist of human wreckage. His throat had been torn out, his belly opened. His arms and chest had been ripped to the bone. Amazingly, he was still alive, but there was nothing I could do. Nothing any physician could have done. Not even a master sorcerer, specializing in healing, could have salvaged the little black man. But One-Eye insisted I try, and try I did till the Captain dragged me off to attend men less certain of dying. One-Eye was bellowing at him as I left.

"Get some lights in here!" I ordered. At the same time the Captain began assembling the uninjured at the open doorway, telling them to hold it.

As the light grew stronger the extent of the debacle became more evident. We had been decimated. Moreover, a dozen brothers who had not been with us lay scattered around the chamber. They had been on duty. Among them were as many more of the Syndic's secretaries and advisers.

"Anybody see the Syndic?" the Captain demanded. "He must have been here." He and Match and Elmo started searching. I did not have much chance to follow that. I patched and sewed like a madman, comandeering all the help I could. The forvalaka left deep claw wounds which required careful and skillful suturing.

Somehow, Goblin and Silent managed to calm One-Eye enough so he could help. Maybe they did something to him. He worked in a daze barely this side of unconsciousness.

I took another look at Tom-Tom when I got a chance. He was *still* alive, clutching his little drum. Damn! That much stubbornness deserved reward. But how? My expertise simply was not adequate.

"Yo!" Match shouted. "Captain!" I glanced over. He was tapping a chest with his sword.

The chest was of stone. It was a strongbox of a type favored by Beryl's wealthy. I guess this one weighed five hundred pounds. Its exterior had been fancifully carved. Most of the decoration had been demolished. By the tearing of claws?

Elmo smashed the lock and pried the lid open. I glimpsed a man lying atop gold and jewels, arms around his head, shaking. Elmo and the Captain exchanged grim looks.

I was distracted by the Lieutenant's arrival. He had held on downstairs till he got worried about nothing having happened. The forvalaka had not gone down.

"Search the tower," the Captain told him. "Maybe it went up." There were a couple levels above us.

When next I glanced at the chest it was closed again. Our employer was nowhere in evidence. Match was seated atop it, cleaning his nails with a dagger. I eyed the Captain and Elmo. There was something the slightest bit odd about them.

They would not have finished the forvalaka's task for her, would they? No. The Captain couldn't betray Company ideals that way. Could he?

I did not ask.

The search of the tower revealed nothing but a trail of blood leading to the tower top, where the forvalaka had lain gathering strength. It had been badly hurt, but it had escaped by descending the outer face of the tower.

Someone suggested we track it. To that the Captain replied, "We're leaving Beryl. We're no longer employed. We have to get out before the city turns on us." He sent Match and Elmo to keep an eye on the native garrison. The rest evacuated the wounded from the Paper Tower.

For several minutes I remained unchaperoned. I eyed the big stone chest. Temptation arose, but I resisted. I did not want to know.

Candy got back after all the excitement. He told us the legate was at the pier offloading his troops.

The men were packing and loading, some muttering about events in the Paper Tower, others bitching about having to leave. You stop moving and immediately put down roots. You accumulate things. You find a woman. Then the inevitable happens and you have to leave it all. There was a lot of pain floating around our barracks.

I was at the gate when the northerners came. I helped turn the capstan that raised the portcullus. I felt none too proud. Without my approval the Syndic might never have been betrayed.

The legate occupied the Bastion. The Company began its evacuation. It was then about the third hour after midnight and the streets were deserted.

Two-thirds of the way to the Gate of Dawn the Captain ordered a halt. The sergeants assembled everyone able to fight. The rest continued with the wagons.

The Captain took us north on the Avenue of the Older Empire, where

Beryl's emperors had memorialized themselves and their triumphs. Many of the monuments are bizarre, and celebrate such minutia as favorite horses, gladiators, or lovers of either sex.

I had a bad feeling even before we reached the Rubbish Gate. Uneasiness grew into suspicion, and suspicion blossomed into grim certainty as we entered the martial fields. There is nothing near the Rubbish Gate but the Fork Barracks.

The Captain made no specific declaration. When we reached the Fork compound every man knew what was afoot.

The Urban Cohorts were as sloppy as ever. The compound gate was open and the lone watchman was asleep. We trooped inside unresisted. The Captain began assigning tasks.

Between five and six thousand men remained there. Their officers had restored some discipline, having enticed them into restoring their weapons to the armories. Traditionally, Beryl's captains trust their men with weapons only on the eve of battle.

Three platoons moved directly into the barracks, killing men in their beds. The remaining platoon established a blocking position at the far end of the compound.

The sun was up before the Captain was satisfied. We withdrew and hurried after our baggage train. There wasn't a man among us who hadn't had his fill.

We were not pursued, of course. No one came besieging the camp we established on the Pillar of Anguish. Which was what it was all about. That and the release of several years of pent-up anger.

Elmo and I stood at the tip of the headland, watching the afternoon sun play around the edges of a storm far out to sea. It had danced in and swamped our encampment with its cool deluge, then had rolled off across the water again. It was beautiful, though not especially colorful.

Elmo had not had much to say recently. "Something eating you, Elmo?" The storm moved in front of the light, giving the sea the look of rusted iron. I wondered if the cool had reached Beryl.

"Reckon you can guess, Croaker."

"Reckon I can." The Paper Tower. The Fork Barracks. Our ignoble treatment of our commission. "What do you think it will be like, north of the sea?"

"Think the black witch will come, eh?"

"He'll come, Elmo. He's just having trouble getting his puppets to jig to his tune." As who did not, trying to tame that insane city?

"Uhm." And, "Look there."

A pod of whales plunged past rocks lying off the headland. I tried to appear unimpressed, and failed. The beasts were magnificent, dancing in the iron sea.

We sat down with our backs toward the lighthouse. It seemed we looked at a world never defiled by Man. Sometimes I suspect it would be better for our absence.

"Ship out there," Elmo said.

I didn't see it till its sail caught the fire of the afternoon sun, becoming an orange triangle edged with gold, rocking and bobbing with the rise and fall of the sea. "Coaster. Maybe a twenty tonner."

"That big?"

"For a coaster. Deep water ships sometimes run eighty tons."

Time pranced along, fickle and faggoty. We watched ship and whales. I began to daydream. For the hundredth time I tried to imagine the new land, building upon traders' tales heard secondhand. We would likely cross to Opal. Opal was a reflection of Beryl, they said, though a younger city. . . .

"That fool is going to pile onto the rocks."

I woke up. The coaster was perilously near said danger. She shifted course a point and eluded disaster by a hundred yards, resumed her original course.

"That put some excitement into our day," I observed.

"One of these days you're going to say something without getting sarcastic and I'll curl up and die, Croaker."

"Keeps me sane, friend."

"That's debatable, Croaker. Debatable."

I went back to staring tomorrow in the face. Better than looking backward. But tomorrow refused to shed its mask.

"She's coming around," Elmo said.

"What? Oh." The coaster wallowed in the swell, barely making way, while her bows swung toward the strand below our camp.

"Want to tell the Captain?"

"I expect he knows. The men in the lighthouse."

"Yeah."

"Keep an eye out in case anything else turns up."

The storm was sliding to the west now, obscuring that horizon and blanketing the sea with its shadow. The cold grey sea. Suddenly, I was terrified of the crossing.

That coaster brought news from smuggler friends of Tom-Tom and One-Eye. One-Eye became even more dour and surly after he received them, and he had reached all time lows already. He even eschewed squabbling with Goblin, which he made a second career. Tom-Tom's death had hit him hard, and would not turn loose. He would not tell us what his friends had to say.

The Captain was little better. His temper was an abomination. I think he both longed for and dreaded the new land. The commission meant potential rebirth for the Company, with our sins left behind, yet he had an intimation of the service we were entering. He suspected the Syndic had been right about the northern empire.

The day following the smuggler's visit brought cool northern breezes. Fog nuzzled the skirts of the headland early in the evening. Shortly after nightfall, coming out of that fog, a boat grounded on the beach. The legate had come.

We gathered our things and began taking leave of camp followers who had trickled out from the city. Our animals and equipment would be their reward for faith and friendship. I spent a sad, gentle hour with a woman to whom I meant more than I suspected. We shed no tears and told one another no lies. I left her with memories and most of my pathetic fortune. She left me with a lump in my throat and a sense of loss not wholly fathomable.

"Come on, Croaker," I muttered as I clambered down to the beach. "You've been through this before. You'll forget her before you get to Opal."

A half dozen boats were drawn up on the strand. As each filled northern sailors shoved it into the surf. Oarsmen drove it into the waves, and in seconds it vanished into the fog. Empty boats came bobbing in. Every other boat carried equipment and possessions.

A sailor who spoke the language of Beryl told me there was plenty of room aboard the black ship. The legate had left his troops in Beryl as guards for the new puppet Syndic, who was another Red distantly related to the man we had served.

"Hope they have less trouble than we did," I said, and went away to brood.

The legate was trading his men for us. I suspected we were going to be used, that we were headed into something grimmer than we could imagine.

Several times during the wait I heard a distant howl. At first I thought it the song of the Pillar. But the air was not moving. When it came again I lost all doubt. My skin crawled.

The quartermaster, the Captain, the Lieutenant, Silent, Goblin, One-Eye, and I waited till the last boat. "I'm not going," One-Eye announced as a boatswain beckoned us to board.

"Get in," the Captain told him. His voice was gentle. That is when he is dangerous.

"I'm resigning. Going to head south. Been gone long enough, they should've forgotten me."

The Captain jabbed a finger at the Lieutenant, Silent, Goblin, and me, jerked his thumb at the boat. One-Eye bellowed. "I'll turn the lot of you into ostriches. . . ." Silent's hand sealed his mouth. We ran him to the boat. He wriggled like a snake in a firepit.

"You stay with the family," the Captain said softly.

"On three," Goblin squealed merrily, then quick-counted. The little black man arced into the boat, twisting in flight. He bobbed over the gunwale cursing, spraying us with saliva. We laughed to see him showing some spirit. Goblin led the charge that nailed him to a thwart.

Sailors pushed us off. The moment the oars bit water One-Eye subsided. He had the look of a man headed for the gallows.

The galley took form, a looming, indeterminate shape slightly darker than the surrounding darkness. I heard the fog-hollowed voices of seamen, timbers creaking, tackle working, long before I was sure of my eyes. Our boat nosed in to the foot of an accommodation ladder. The howl came again.

One-Eye tried to dive overboard. We restrained him. The Captain applied a bootheel to his butt. "You had your chance to talk us out of this. You wouldn't. Live with it."

One-Eye slouched as he followed the Lieutenant up the ladder, a man without hope. A man who had left a brother dead and now was being forced to approach that brother's killer, upon which he was powerless to take revenge.

We found the Company on the maindeck, snuggled amongst mounds of gear. The sergeants threaded the mess toward us.

The legate appeared. I stared. This was the first I had seen him afoot, standing. He was *short.* For a moment I wondered if he were male at all. His voices were often otherwise.

He surveyed us with an intensity that suggested he was reading our souls. One of his officers asked the Captain to fall the men in the best he could on the crowded deck. The ship's crew were taking up the center flats decking over the open well that ran from the bow almost to the stern, and from deck level down to the lower oar bank. Below, there was muttering, clanking, rattling, as the oarsmen wakened.

The legate reviewed us. He paused before each soldier, pinned a reproduction of the device on his sail over each heart. It was slow going. We were under way before he finished.

The nearer the envoy approached, the more One-Eye shook. He almost fainted when the legate pinned him. I was baffled. Why so much emotion?

I was nervous when my turn came, but not frightened. I glanced at the badge as delicate gloved fingers attached it to my jerkin. Skull and circle in silver, on jet, elegantly crafted. A valuable if grim piece of jewelry. Had he not been so rattled, I would have thought One-Eye to be considering how best to pawn it.

The device now seemed vaguely familiar. Outside the context of the sail, which I had taken as showmanship and ignored. Hadn't I read or heard about a similar seal somewhere?

The legate said, "Welcome to the service of the Lady, physician." His voice was distracting. It did not fit expectations, ever. This time it was musical, lilting, the voice of a young woman putting something over on wiser heads.

The Lady? Where had I encountered that word used that way, emphasized as though it was the title of a goddess? A dark legend out of olden times. . . .

A howl of outrage, pain, and despair filled the ship. Startled, I broke ranks and went to the lip of the air well.

The forvalaka was in a big iron cage at the foot of the mast. In the shadows it seemed to change subtly as it prowled, testing every bar. One moment it was an athletic woman of about thirty, but seconds later it had assumed the aspect of a black leopard on its hind legs, clawing the imprisoning iron. I recalled the legate saying he might have a use for the monster.

I faced him. And the memory came. A devil's hammer drove spikes of ice into the belly of my soul. I knew why One-Eye did not want to cross the sea. The ancient evil of the north. . . . "I thought you people died three hundred years ago."

The legate laughed. "You don't know your history well enough. We weren't destroyed. Just chained and buried alive." His laughter had an hysterical edge. "Chained, buried, and eventually liberated by a fool named Bomanz, Croaker."

I dropped to my haunches beside One-Eye, who buried his face in his hands.

The legate, the terror called Soulcatcher in old tales, a devil worse than any dozen forvalaka, laughed madly. His crewmen cringed. A great joke, enlisting the Black Company in the service of evil. A great city taken and little villains suborned. A truly cosmic jest.

The Captain settled beside me. "Tell me, Croaker."

So I told him about the Domination, and the Dominator and his Lady. Their rule had spanned an empire of evil unrivalled in Hell. I told him about the Ten Who Were Taken (of whom Soulcatcher was one), ten great wizards, near-demigods in their power, who had been overcome by the Dominator and compelled into his service. I told him about the White Rose, the lady general who had brought the Domination down, but whose power had been insufficient to destroy the Dominator, his Lady, and the Ten. She had interred the lot in a charm-bound barrow somewhere north of the sea.

"And now they're restored to life, it seems," I said. "They rule the northern empire. Tom-Tom and One-Eye must have suspected. . . . We've enlisted in their service."

"Taken," he murmured. "Rather like the forvalaka."

The beast screamed and hurled itself against the bars of its cage. Soulcatcher's laughter drifted across the foggy deck. "Taken by the Taken," I agreed. "The parallel is uncomfortable." I had begun to shake as more and more old tales surfaced in my mind.

The Captain sighed and stared into the fog, toward the new land.

One-Eye stared at the thing in the cage, hating. I tried to ease him away. He shook me off. "Not yet, Croaker. I have to figure this."

"What?"

"This isn't the one that killed Tom-Tom. It doesn't have the scars we put on it."

I turned slowly, studied the legate. He laughed again, looking our way.

One-Eye never figured it out. And I never told him. We have troubles enough.

2 Raven

The crossing from Beryl proves my point," One-Eye growled over a pewter tankard. "The Black Company doesn't belong on water. Wench! More ale!" He waved his tankard. The girl could not understand him otherwise. He refused to learn the languages of the north.

"You're drunk," I observed.

"How perceptive. Will you take note, gentlemen? The Croaker, our esteemed master of the arts cleric and medical, has had the perspicacity to discover that I am drunk." He punctuated his speech with belches and mispronunciations. He surveyed his audience with that look of sublime solemnity only a drunk can muster.

The girl brought another pitcher, and a bottle for Silent. He, too, was ready for more of his particular poison. He was drinking a sour Beryl wine perfectly suited to his personality. Money changed hands.

There were seven of us altogether. We were keeping our heads down. The place was full of sailors. We were outsiders, outlanders, the sort picked for pounding when the brawling started. With the exception of One-Eye, we prefer saving our fight for when we are getting paid.

Pawnbroker stuck his ugly face in through the street doorway. His beady little eyes tightened into a squint. He spotted us.

Pawnbroker. He got that name because he loansharks the Company. He doesn't like it, but says anything is better than the monniker hung on him by his peasant parents: Sugar Beet.

"Hey! It's the Sweet Beet!" One-Eye roared. "Come on over, Sugar Baby. Drinks on One-Eye. He's too drunk to know any better." He was. Sober, One-Eye is tighter than a collar of day-old rawhide.

Pawnbroker winced, looked around furtively. He has that manner. "The Captain wants you guys."

We exchanged glances. One-Eye settled down. We had not seen much of the Captain lately. He was all the time hanging around with bigwigs from the Imperial Army.

Elmo and the Lieutenant got up. I did too, and started toward Pawnbroker.

The barkeeper bellowed. A serving wench darted to the doorway, blocked it. A huge, dull bull of a man lumbered out of a back room. He carried a prodigious gnarly club in each hogshead hand. He looked confused.

One-Eye snarled. The rest of our crowd rose, ready for anything.

The sailors, smelling a riot, started choosing sides. Mostly against us.

"What the hell is going on?" I shouted.

"Please, sir," said the girl at the door. "Your friends haven't paid for their last round." She sped the barkeeper a vicious look.

"The hell they didn't." House policy was payment on delivery. I looked at the Lieutenant. He agreed. I glanced at the barkeep, sensed his greed. He thought we were drunk enough to pay twice.

Elmo said, "One-Eye, you picked this thieves' den. You straighten them out."

No sooner said than done. One-Eye squealed like a hog meeting the butcher. . . .

A chimp-sized, four-armed bundle of ugly exploded from beneath our table. It charged the girl at the door, left fang-marks on her thigh. Then it climbed all over the club-wielding mountain of muscle. The man was bleeding in a dozen places before he knew what was happening.

A fruit bowl on a table at the room's center vanished in a black fog. It reappeared a second later—with venomous snakes boiling over its rim.

The barkeep's jaw dropped. And scarab beetles poured out of his mouth.

We made our exit during the excitement. One-Eye howled and giggled for blocks.

The Captain stared at us. We leaned on one another before his table. One-Eye still suffered the occasional spate of giggles. Even the Lieutenant could not keep a straight face. "They're drunk," the Captain told him.

"We're drunk," One-Eye agreed. "We're palpably, plausibly, pukingly drunk."

The Lieutenant jabbed him in the kidney.

"Sit down, men. Try to behave while you're here."

Here was a posh garden establishment socially miles above our last port of call. Here even the whores had titles. Plantings and tricks of landscaping broke the gardens into areas of semi-seclusion. There were ponds, gazebos, stone walkways, and an overwhelming perfume of flowers in the air.

"A little rich for us," I remarked.

"What's the occasion?" the Lieutenant asked. The rest of us jockied for seats.

The Captain had staked out a huge stone table. Twenty people could have sat around it. "We're guests. Act like it." He toyed with the badge over his heart, identifying him as receiving the protection of Soulcatcher. We each possessed one but seldom wore them. The Captain's gesture suggested we correct that deficiency.

"We're guests of the Taken?" I asked. I fought the effects of the ale. This should go into the Annals.

"No. The badges are for the benefit of the house." He gestured. Everyone visible wore a badge declaring an alignment with one or another of the Taken. I recognized a few. The Howler. Nightcrawler. Stormbringer. The Limper.

"Our host wants to enlist in the Company."

"He wants to join the Black Company?" One-Eye asked. "What's wrong with the fool?" It had been years since we had taken a new recruit.

The Captain shrugged, smiled. "Once upon a time a witchdoctor did."

One-Eye grumbled, "He's been sorry ever since."

"Why is he still here?" I asked.

One-Eye did not answer. Nobody leaves the Company, except feet first. The outfit is home.

"What's he like?" the Lieutenant asked.

The Captain closed his eyes. "Unusual. He could be an asset. I like him. But judge for yourselves. He's here." He flicked a finger at a man surveying the gardens.

His clothing was grey, tattered, and patched. He was of modest height, lean, dusky. Darkly handsome. I guessed him to be in his late twenties. Unprepossessing. . . .

Not really. On second glance you noted something striking. An intensity, a lack of expression, something in his stance. He was not intimidated by the gardens.

People looked and wrinkled their noses. They did not see the man, they saw rags. You could feel their revulsion. Bad enough that we had been allowed inside. Now it was ragpickers.

A grandly accoutred attendant went to show him an entrance he'd obviously entered in error.

The man came toward us, passing the attendant as if he did not exist. There was a jerkiness, a stiffness, to his movements which suggested he was recovering from recent wounds. "Captain?"

"Good afternoon. Have a seat."

A ponderous staff general detached himself from a clutch of senior officers and svelte young women. He took a few steps our way, paused. He was tempted to make his prejudices known.

I recognized him. Lord Jalena. As high as you could get without being one of the Ten Who Were Taken. His face was puffed and red. If the Captain noticed him, he pretended otherwise.

"Gentlemen, this is . . . Raven. He wants to join us. Raven isn't his birthname. Doesn't matter. The rest of you lied too. Introduce yourselves and ask questions."

There was something odd about this Raven. We were his guests, apparently. His manner was not that of a street beggar, yet he looked like a lot of bad road.

Lord Jalena arrived. His breath came in wheezes. Pigs like him I would love to put through half what they inflict on their troops.

He scowled at the Captain. "Sir," he said between puffs, "your connections are such that we can't deny *you*, but. . . . The Gardens are for persons of refinement. They have been for two hundred years. We don't admit. . . ."

The Captain donned a quizzical smile. Mildly, he replied, "I'm a guest, Milord. If you don't like my company, complain to my host." He indicated Raven.

Jalena made a half-right turn. "Sir. . . ." His eyes and mouth went round. "You!"

Raven stared at Jalena. Not one muscle twitched. Not an eyelash flickered. The color fled the fat man's cheeks. He glanced at his own party almost in supplication, looked at Raven again, turned to the Captain. His mouth worked but no words came out.

The Captain reached toward Raven. Raven accepted Soulcatcher's badge. He pinned it over his heart.

Jalena went paler still. He backed away.

"Seems to know you," the Captain observed.

"He thought I was dead."

Jalena rejoined his party. He gabbled and pointed. Pale-faced men looked our way. They argued briefly, then the whole lot fled the garden.

Raven did not explain. Instead, he said, "Shall we get to business?"

"Care to illuminate what just happened?" The Captain's voice had a dangerous softness.

"No."

"Better reconsider. Your presence could endanger the whole Company."

"It won't. It's a personal matter. I won't bring it with me."

The Captain thought about it. He is not one to intrude on a man's past. Not without cause. He decided he had cause. "How can you avoid bringing it? Obviously, you mean something to Lord Jalena."

"Not to Jalena. To friends of his. It's old history. I'll settle it before I join you. Five people have to die to close the book."

This sounded interesting. Ah, the smell of mystery and dark doings, of skulduggery and revenge. The meat of a good tale. "I'm Croaker. Any special reason for not sharing the story?"

Raven faced me, obviously under rigid self-control. "It's private, it's old, and it's shameful. I don't want to talk about it."

One-Eye said, "In that case I can't vote for acceptance."

Two men and a woman came down a flagstone pathway, paused overlooking the place where Lord Jalena's party had been. Latecomers? They were surprised. I watched them talk it over.

Elmo voted with One-Eye. So did the Lieutenant.

"Croaker?" the Captain asked.

I voted aye. I smelled a mystery and did not want it to get away.

The Captain told Raven, "I know part of it. That's why I'm voting with One-Eye. For the Company's sake. I'd like to have you. But. . . . Settle it before we leave."

The latecomers headed our way, noses in the air but determined to learn what had become of their party.

"When are you leaving?" Raven asked. "How long do I have?"

"Tomorrow. Sunrise."

"What?" I demanded.

"Hold on," One-Eye said. "How come already?"

Even the Lieutenant, who never questions anything, said, "We were supposed to get a couple weeks." He had found a lady friend, his first since I had known him.

The Captain shrugged. "They need us up north. The Limper lost the fortress at Deal to a Rebel named Raker."

The latecomers arrived. One of the men demanded, "What became of the party in the Camellia Grotto?" His voice had a whiny, nasal quality. My hackles rose. It reeked of arrogance and contempt. I hadn't heard its like since I joined the Black Company. People in Beryl hadn't used that tone.

They don't know the Black Company in Opal, I told myself. Not yet, they don't.

The voice hit Raven like a sledge whack on the back of the head. He stiffened.

For a moment his eyes were pure ice. Then a smile crinkled their corners—as evil a smile as I have ever seen.

The Captain whispered, "I know why Jalena suffered his attack of indigestion."

We sat motionless, frozen by deadly imminence. Raven turned slowly, rising. Those three saw his face.

Whiny-voice choked. His male companion began shaking. The woman opened her mouth. Nothing came out.

Where Raven got the knife I do not know. It went almost too fast to follow. Whiny-voice bled from a cut throat. His friend had steel in his heart. And Raven had the woman's throat in his left hand.

"No. Please," she whispered without force. She expected no mercy.

Raven squeezed, forced her to her knees. Her face purpled, bloated. Her tongue rolled out. She seized his wrist, shuddered. He lifted her, stared into her eyes till they rolled up and she sagged. She shuddered again, died.

Raven jerked his hand away. He stared at that rigid, shaking claw. His face was ghastly. He surrendered to the all-over shakes.

"Croaker!" the Captain snapped. "Don't you claim to be a physician?"

"Yeah." People were reacting. The whole garden was watching. I checked Whiny-voice. Dead as a stone. So was his sidekick. I turned to the woman.

Raven knelt. He held her left hand. There were tears in his eyes. He removed a gold wedding band, pocketed it. That was all he took, though she sported a fortune in jewelry.

I met his gaze over the body. The ice was in his eyes again. It dared me to voice my guess.

"I don't want to sound hysterical," One-Eye growled, "but why don't we get the hell out of here?"

"Good thinking," Elmo said, and started heeling and toeing it.

"Get moving!" the Captain snapped at me. He took Raven's arm. I trailed.

Raven said, "I'll have my affairs settled by dawn."

The Captain glanced back. "Yeah," was all he said.

I thought so too.

But we would leave Opal without him.

The Captain received several nasty messages that night. His only comment was, "Those three must have been part of the in-crowd."

"They wore the Limper's badges," I said. "What's the story on Raven, anyway? Who is he?"

"Somebody who didn't get along with the Limper. Who was done dirty and left for dead."

"Was the woman something he didn't tell you?"

The Captain shrugged. I took that as an affirmative.

"Bet she was his wife. Maybe she betrayed him." That kind of thing is common here. Conspiracies and assassinations and naked power-grabs. All the fun of decadence. The Lady does not discourage anything. Maybe the games amuse her.

As we travelled north we moved ever nearer the heart of the empire. Each day took us into emotionally bleaker country. The locals became ever more dour, grim, and sullen. These were not happy lands, despite the season.

The day came when we had to skirt the very soul of the empire, the Tower at Charm, built by the Lady after her resurrection. Hard-eyed cavalrymen escorted us. We got no closer than three miles. Even so, the Tower's silhouette loomed over the horizon. It is a massive cube of dark stone. It stands at least five hundred feet high.

I studied it all day. What was our mistress like? Would I ever meet her? She intrigued me. That night I wrote an exercise in which I tried to characterize her. It degenerated into a romantic fantasy.

Next afternoon we encountered a pale-faced rider galloping south in search of our Company. His badges proclaimed him a follower of the Limper. Our outriders brought him to the Lieutenant.

"You people are taking your damned sweet time, aren't you? You're wanted in Forsberg. Quit shitting around."

The Lieutenant is a quiet man accustomed to the respect due his rank. He was so startled he said nothing. The courier became more offensive. Then the Lieutenant demanded, "What's your rank?"

"Corporal Courier to the Limper. Buddy, you'd better get hauling. He don't put up with no shit."

The Lieutenant is the Company disciplinarian. It is a load he takes off the Captain. He is a reasonable, just sort of guy.

"Sergeant!" he snapped at Elmo. "I want you." He was angry. Usually only the Captain calls Elmo Sergeant.

Elmo was riding with the Captain at the time. He trotted up the column. The Captain tagged along. "Sir?" Elmo asked.

The Lieutenant halted the Company. "Flog some respect into this peasant."

"Yes sir. Otto. Crispin. Turn a hand here."

"Twenty strokes should do it."

"Twenty strokes it is, sir."

"What the hell do you think you're pulling? No stinking hiresword is going to. . . ."

The Captain said, "Lieutenant, I think that calls for another ten lashes."

"Yes sir. Elmo?"

"Thirty it is, sir." He struck out. The courier flopped out of his saddle. Otto and Crispin picked him up and ran him to a rail fence, draped him over it. Crispin slit the back of his shirt.

Elmo plied the strokes with the Lieutenant's riding crop. He did not lean into it. There was no rancor in this, just a message to those who thought the Black Company second-class.

I was there with my kit when Elmo finished. "Try to relax, lad. I'm a physician. I'll clean your back and bandage you." I patted his cheek. "You took it pretty good for a northerner."

Elmo gave him a new shirt when I finished. I offered some unsolicited advice on treatment, then suggested, "Report to the Captain as if this hadn't happened." I pointed toward the Captain. . . . "Well."

Friend Raven had rejoined us. He watched from the back of a sweaty, dusty roan.

The messenger took my advice. The Captain said, "Tell the Limper I'm travelling as fast as I can. I won't push so hard I'll be in no shape to fight when I get there."

"Yes sir. I'll tell him, sir." Gingerly, the courier mounted his horse. He concealed his feelings well.

Raven observed, "The Limper will cut your heart out for that."

"The Limper's displeasure doesn't concern me. I thought you were going to join us before we left Opal."

"I was slow closing accounts. One wasn't in the city at all. Lord Jalena warned the other. It took me three days to find him."

"The one out of town?"

"I decided to join you instead."

That was not a satisfactory answer, but the Captain slid around it. "I can't let you join us while you have outside interests."

"I let it go. I repaid the most important debt." He meant the woman. I could taste it.

The Captain eyed him sourly. "All right. Ride with Elmo's platoon."

"Thank you. Sir." That sounded strange. He was not a man accustomed to sirring anyone.

Our northward journey continued, past Elm, into the Salient, past Roses, and northward still, into Forsberg. That one-time kingdom had become a bloody killing-ground.

The city of Oar lies in northernmost Forsberg, and in the forests above lies the Barrowland, where the Lady and her lover, the Dominator, were interred four centuries ago. The stubborn necromantic investigations of wizards from Oar had resurrected the Lady and Ten Who Were Taken from their dark, abiding dreams. Now their guilt-ridden descendants battled the Lady.

Southern Forsberg remained deceptively peaceful. The peasantry greeted us without enthusiasm, but willingly took our money.

"That's because seeing the Lady's soldiers pay is such a novelty," Raven claimed. "The Taken just grab whatever strikes their fancy."

The Captain grunted. We would have done so ourselves had we not had instructions to the contrary. Soulcatcher had directed us to be gentlemen. He had given the Captain a plump war chest. The Captain was willing. No point making enemies needlessly.

We had been travelling two months. A thousand miles lay behind us. We were exhausted. The Captain decided to rest us at the edge of the war zone. Maybe he was having second thoughts about serving the Lady.

Anyway, there is no point hunting trouble. Not when not fighting pays the same.

The Captain directed us into a forest. While we pitched camp, he talked with Raven. I watched.

Curious. There was a bond developing there. I could not understand it because I did not know enough about either man. Raven was a new enigma, the Captain an old one.

In all the years I have known the Captain I have learned almost nothing about him. Just a hint here and there, fleshed out by speculation.

He was born in one of the Jewel Cities. He was a professional soldier. Something overturned his personal life. Possibly a woman. He abandoned commission and titles and became a wanderer. Eventually he hooked up with our band of spiritual exiles.

We all have our pasts. I suspect we keep them nebulous not because we are hiding from our yesterdays but because we think we will cut more romantic figures if we roll our eyes and dispense delicate hints about beautiful women forever beyond our reaches. Those men whose stories I have uprooted are running from the law, not a tragic love affair.

The Captain and Raven, though, obviously found one another kindred souls.

The camp was set. The pickets were out. We settled in to rest. Though that was busy country, neither contending force noticed us immediately.

Silent was using his skills to augment the watchfulness of our sentries. He detected spies hidden inside our outer picket line and warned One-Eye. One-Eye reported to the Captain.

The Captain spread a map atop a stump we had turned into a card table, after evicting me, One-Eye, Goblin, and several others. "Where are they?"

"Two here. Two more over there. One here."

"Somebody go tell the pickets to disappear. We'll sneak out. Goblin. Where's Goblin? Tell Goblin to get with the illusions." The Captain had decided not to start anything. A laudable decision, I thought.

A few minutes later, he asked, "Where's Raven?"

I said, "I think he went after the spies."

"What? Is he an idiot?" His face darkened. "What the hell do you want?"

Goblin squeaked like a stomped rat. He squeaks at the best of times. The Captain's outburst had him sounding like a baby bird. "You called for me."

The Captain stamped in a circle, growling and scowling. Had he the talent of a Goblin or a One-Eye, smoke would have poured from his ears.

I winked at Goblin, who grinned like a big toad. This shambling little war dance was just a warning not to trifle with him. He shuffled maps. He cast dark looks. He wheeled on me. "I don't like it. Did you put him up to it?"

"Hell no." I do not try to create Company history. I just record it.

Then Raven showed up. He dumped a body at the Captain's feet, proffered a string of grisly trophies.

"What the hell?"

"Thumbs. They count coup in these parts."

The Captain turned green around the gills. "What's the body for?"

"Stick his feet in the fire. Leave him. They won't waste time wondering how we knew they were out there."

One-Eye, Goblin, and Silent cast a glamour over the Company. We slipped away, slick as a fish through the fingers of a clumsy fisherman. An enemy battalion, which had been sneaking up, never caught a whiff of us. We headed straight north. The Captain planned to find the Limper.

Late that afternoon One-Eye broke into a marching song. Goblin squawked in protest. One-Eye grinned and sang all the louder.

"He's changing the words!" Goblin squealed.

Men grinned, anticipating. One-Eye and Goblin have been feuding for ages. One-Eye always starts the scraps. Goblin can be as touchy as a fresh burn. Their spats are entertaining.

This time Goblin did not reciprocate. He ignored One-Eye. The little black man got his feelings hurt. He got louder. We expected fireworks. What we got is bored. One-Eye could not get a rise. He started sulking.

A bit later, Goblin told me, "Keep your eyes peeled, Croaker. We're in strange country. Anything could happen." He giggled.

A horsefly landed on the haunch of One-Eye's mount. The animal screamed, reared. Sleepy One-Eye tumbled over its tail. Everybody guffawed. The wizened little wizard came up out of the dust cursing and swatting with his battered old hat. He punched his horse with his free hand, connecting with the beast's forehead. Then he danced around moaning and blowing on his knuckles.

His reward was a shower of catcalls. Goblin smirked.

Soon One-Eye was dozing again. It's a trick you learn after enough weary miles on horseback. A bird settled on his shoulder. He snorted, swatted. . . . The bird left a huge, fetid purple deposit. One-Eye howled. He threw things. He shredded his jerkin getting it off.

Again we laughed. And Goblin looked as innocent as a virgin. One-Eye scowled and growled but did not catch on.

He got a glimmer when we crested a hill and beheld a band of monkey-sized pygmies busily kissing an idol reminiscent of a horse's behind. Every pygmy was a miniature One-Eye.

The little wizard turned a hideous look on Goblin. Goblin responded with an innocent, don't look at me shrug.

"Point to Goblin," I judged.

"Better watch yourself, Croaker," One-Eye growled. "Or you'll be doing the kissing right here." He patted his fanny.

"When pigs fly." He is a more skilled wizard than Goblin or Silent, but not half what he would have us believe. If he could execute half his threats, he would be a peril to the Taken. Silent is more consistent, Goblin more inventive.

One-Eye would lie awake nights thinkings of ways to get even for Goblin's having gotten even. A strange pair. I do not know why they have not killed one another.

Finding the Limper was easier said than done. We trailed him into a forest, where we found abandoned earthworks and a lot of Rebel bodies. Our path tilted downward into a valley of broad meadows parted by a sparkling stream.

"What the hell?" I asked Goblin. "That's strange." Wide, low, black humps pimpled the meadows. There were bodies everywhere.

"That's one reason the Taken are feared. Killing spells. Their heat sucked the ground up."

I stopped to study a hump.

The blackness could have been drawn with a compass. The boundary was as sharp as a penstroke. Charred skeletons lay within the black. Swordblades and spearheads looked like wax imitations left too long in the sun. I caught One-Eye staring. "When you can do this trick you'll scare me."

"If I could do that I'd scare myself."

I checked another circle. It was a twin of the first. Raven reined in beside me. "The Limper's work. I've seen it before."

I sniffed the wind. Maybe I had him in the right mood. "When was that?"

He ignored me.

He would not come out of his shell. Would not say hello half the time, let alone talk about who or what he was.

He is a cold one. The horrors of that valley did not touch him.

"The Limper lost this one," the Captain decided. "He's on the run."

"Do we keep after him?" the Lieutenant asked.

"This is strange country. We're in more danger operating alone."

We followed a spoor of violence, a swath of destruction. Ruined fields fell behind us. Burned villages. Slaughtered people and butchered livestock. Poisoned wells. The Limper left nothing but death and desolation.

Our brief was to help hold Forsberg. Joining the Limper was not mandatory. I wanted no part of him. I did not want to be in the same province.

As the devastation grew more recent, Raven showed elation, dismay, introspection easing into determination, and ever more of that rigid self-control he so often hid behind.

When I reflect on my companions' inner natures I usually wish I controlled one small talent. I wish I could look inside them and unmask the darks and brights that move them. Then I take a quick look into the jungle of my own soul and thank heaven that I cannot. Any man who barely sustains an armistice with himself has no business poking around in an alien soul.

I decided to keep closer watch on our newest brother.

We did not need Doughbelly coming in from the point to tell us we were close. All the forward horizon sprouted tall, leaning trees of smoke. This part of Forsberg was flat and open and marvelously green, and against the turquoise sky those oily pillars were an abomination.

There was not much breeze. The afternoon promised to be scorching.

Doughbelly swung in beside the Lieutenant. Elmo and I stopped swapping tired old lies and listened. Doughbelly indicated a smoke spire. "Still some of the Limper's men in that village, sir."

"Talk to them?"

"No sir. Longhead didn't think you'd want us to. He's waiting outside town."

"How many of them?"

"Twenty, twenty-five. Drunk and mean. The officer was worse than the men."

The Lieutenant glanced over his shoulder. "Ah. Elmo. It's your lucky day. Take ten men and go with Doughbelly. Scout around."

"Shit," Elmo muttered. He is a good man, but muggy spring days make him lazy. "Okay. Otto. Silent. Peewee. Whitey. Billygoat. Raven. . . ."

I coughed discreetly.

"You're out of your head, Croaker. All right." He did a quick count on his fingers, called three more names. We formed outside the column. Elmo gave us the once-over to make sure we hadn't forgotten our heads. "Let's go."

We hurried forward. Doughbelly directed us into a woodlot overlooking the stricken town. Longhead and a man called Jolly waited there. Elmo asked, "Any developments?"

Jolly, who is professionally sarcastic, replied, "The fires are burning down."

We looked at the village. I saw nothing that did not turn my stomach. Slaughtered livestock. Slaughtered cats and dogs. The small, broken forms of dead children.

"Not the kids too," I said, without realizing I was speaking. "Not the babies again."

Elmo looked at me oddly, not because he was unmoved himself but because I was uncharacteristically sympathetic. I have seen a lot of dead men. I did not enlighten him. For me there is a big difference between adults and kids. "Elmo, I have to go in there."

"Don't be stupid, Croaker. What can you do?"

"If I can save one kid. . . ."

Raven said, "I'll go with him." A knife appeared in his hand. He must have learned that trick from a conjurer. He does it when he is nervous or angry.

"Think you can bluff twenty-five men?"

Raven shrugged. "Croaker is right, Elmo. It's got to be done. Some things you don't tolerate."

Elmo surrendered. "We'll all go. Pray they aren't so drunk they can't tell friend from foe."

Raven started riding.

The village was good-sized. There had been more than two hundred homes before the Limper's advent. Half were burned or burning. Bodies littered the streets. Flies clustered around their sightless eyes. "Nobody of military age," I noted.

I dismounted and knelt beside a boy of four or five. His skull had been smashed, but he was breathing. Raven dropped beside me. "Nothing I can do," I said.

"You can end his ordeal." There were tears in Raven's eyes. Tears and anger. "There's no excuse for this." He moved to a corpse lying in shadow.

This one was about seventeen. He wore the jacket of a Rebel Mainforcer. He had died fighting. Raven said, "He must have been on leave. One boy to protect them." He pried a bow from lifeless fingers, bent it. "Good wood. A few thousand of these could rout the Limper." He slung the bow and appropriated the boy's arrows.

I examined another two children. They were beyond help. Inside a burned hut I found a grandmother who had died trying to shield an infant. In vain.

Raven exuded disgust. "Creatures like the Limper create two enemies for every one they destroy."

I became aware of muted weeping, and of cursing and laughter somewhere ahead. "Let's see what that is."

Beside the hut we found four dead soldiers. The lad had left his mark. "Good shooting," Raven observed. "Poor fool."

"Fool?"

"He should've had the sense to run. Might've gone easier on everyone." His intensity startled me. What did he care about a boy from the other side? "Dead heroes don't get a second chance."

Aha! He was drawing a parallel with an event in his own mysterious past.

The cursing and weeping resolved into a scene fit to disgust anyone tainted with humanity.

There were a dozen soldiers in the circle, laughing at their own crude jokes. I remembered a bitch dog surrounded by males who, contrary to custom, were not fighting for mounting rights but were taking turns. They might have killed her had I not intervened.

Raven and I mounted up, the better to see.

The victim was a child of nine. Welts covered her. She was terrified, yet making no sound. In a moment I understood. She was a mute.

War is a cruel business prosecuted by cruel men. The gods know the Black Company are no cherubim. But there *are* limits.

They were making an old man watch. He was the source of both curses and weeping.

Raven put an arrow into a man about to assault the girl.

"Dammit!" Elmo yelled. "Raven! . . ."

The soldiers turned on us. Weapons appeared. Raven loosed another arrow. It dropped the trooper holding the old man. The Limper's men lost any inclination to fight. Elmo whispered, "Whitey, go tell the old man to haul ass over here."

One of the Limper's men took a like notion. He scampered off. Raven let him run.

The Captain would have his behind on a platter.

He did not seem concerned. "Old timer. Come here. Bring the child. And get some clothes on her."

Part of me could not help but applaud, but another part called Raven a fool.

Elmo did not have to tell us to watch our backs. We were painfully aware that we were in big trouble. Hurry, Whitey, I thought.

Their messenger reached their commander first. He came tottering up the street. Doughbelly was right. He was worse than his men.

The old timer and girl clung to Raven's stirrup. The old man scowled at our badges. Elmo nudged his mount forward, pointed at Raven. I nodded.

The drunken officer stopped in front of Elmo. Dull eyes assayed us. He seemed impressed. We have grown hard in a rough trade, and look it.

"You!" he squealed suddenly, exactly the way Whiny-voice had done in Opal. He stared at Raven. Then he spun, ran.

Raven thundered, "Stand still, Lane! Take it like a man, you gutless thief!" He snatched an arrow from his quiver.

Elmo cut his bowstring.

Lane stopped. His response was not gratitude. He cursed. He enumerated the horrors we could expect at the hand of his patron.

I watched Raven.

He stared at Elmo in cold fury. Elmo faced it without flinching. He was a hard guy himself.

Raven did his knife trick. I tapped his blade with my swordtip. He mouthed one soft curse, glared, relaxed. Elmo said, "You left your old life behind, remember?"

Raven nodded once, sharply. "It's harder than I thought." His shoulders sagged. "Run away, Lane. You're not important enough to kill."

A clatter rose behind us. The Captain was coming.

That little wart of the Limper's puffed up and wriggled like a cat about to pounce. Elmo glared at him down the length of his sword. He got the hint.

Raven muttered, "I should know better anyway. He's only a butt boy."

I asked a leading question. It drew a blank stare.

The Captain rattled up. "What the hell is going on?"

Elmo began one of his terse reports. Raven interrupted. "Yon sot is one of Zouad's jackals. I wanted to kill him. Elmo and Croaker stopped me."

Zouad? Where had I heard that name? Connected with the Limper. Colonel Zouad. The Limper's number one villain. Political liaison, among other euphemisms. His name had occurred in a few overheard conversations between Raven and the Captain. Zouad was Raven's intended fifth victim? Then the Limper himself must have been behind Raven's misfortunes.

Curiouser and curiouser. Also scarier and scarier. The Limper is not anybody to mess with.

The Limper's man shouted, "I want this man arrested." The Captain gave him a look. "He murdered two of my men."

The bodies were there in plain sight. Raven said nothing. Elmo stepped out of character and volunteered, "They were raping the child. Their idea of pacification."

The Captain stared at his opposite number. The man reddened. Even the blackest villain will feel shame if caught unable to justify himself. The Captain snapped, "Croaker?"

"We found one dead Rebel, Captain. Indications were this sort of thing started before he became a factor."

He asked the sot, "These people are subjects of the Lady? Under her protection?" The point might be arguable in other courts, but at the moment it told. By his lack of a defense the man confessed a moral guilt.

"You disgust me." The Captain used his soft, dangerous voice. "Get out of here. Don't cross my path again. I'll leave you to my friend's mercy if you do." The man stumbled away.

The Captain turned to Raven. "You mother-lorn fool. Do you have any idea what you've done?"

Wearily, Raven replied, "Probably better than you do, Captain. But I'd do it again."

"And you wonder why we dragged our feet taking you on?" He shifted subject. "What are you going to do with these people, noble rescuer?"

That question had not occurred to Raven. Whatever the upheaval in his life, it had left him living entirely in the present. He was compelled by the past and oblivious to the future. "They're my responsibility, aren't they?"

The Captain gave up trying to catch the Limper. Operating independently now seemed the lesser evil.

The repercussions began four days later.

We had just fought our first significant battle, having crushed a Rebel force twice our size. It had not been difficult. They were green, and our wizards helped. Not many escaped.

The battlefield was ours. The men were looting the dead. Elmo, myself, the Captain, and a few others were standing around feeling smug. One-Eye and Goblin were celebrating in their unique fashion, taunting one another through the mouths of corpses.

Goblin suddenly stiffened. His eyes rolled up. A whine slipped past his lips, rose in pitch. He crumpled.

One-Eye reached him a step ahead of me, began slapping his cheeks. His habitual hostility had vanished.

"Give me some room!" I growled.

Goblin wakened before I could do more than check his pulse. "Soulcatcher," he murmured. "Making contact."

At that moment I was glad I did not own Goblin's talents. Having one of the Taken inside my mind seemed a worse violation than rape. "Captain," I called. "Soulcatcher." I stayed close.

The Captain ran over. He never runs unless we are in action. "What is it?"

Goblin sighed. His eyes opened. "He's gone now." His skin and hair were soaked with sweat. He was pale. He started shaking.

"Gone?" the Captain demanded. "What the hell?"

We helped Goblin get comfortable. "The Limper went to the Lady instead of coming at us head on. There's bad blood between him and Soulcatcher. He thinks we came out here to undermine him. He tried to turn the tables. But Soulcatcher is in high favor since Beryl, and the Limper isn't because of his failures. The Lady told him to leave us alone. Soulcatcher didn't get the Limper replaced, but he figures he won the round."

Goblin paused. One-Eye handed him a long drink. He drained it in an instant. "He says stay out of the Limper's way. He might try to discredit us somehow, or even steer the Rebel toward us. He says we should recapture the fortress at Deal. That would embarrass the Rebel and the Limper both."

Elmo muttered, "He wants flashy, why don't he have us round up the Circle of Eighteen?" The Circle is the Rebel High Command, eighteen wizards who think that between them they have what it takes to challenge the Lady and the Taken. Raker, the Limper's nemesis in Forsberg, belonged to the Circle.

The Captain looked thoughtful. He asked Raven, "You get the feeling there's politics involved?"

"The Company is Soulcatcher's tool. That's common knowledge. The puzzle is what he plans to do with it."

"I got that feeling in Opal."

Politics. The Lady's empire purports to be monolithic. The Ten Who Were Taken expend terrible energies keeping it that way. And spend as much more squabbling among themselves like toddlers fighting over toys, or competing for Mother's affection.

"Is that it?" the Captain grumbled.

"That's it. He says he'll keep in touch."

So we went and did it. We captured the fortress at Deal, in the dead of night, within howling distance of Oar. They say both Raker and the Limper flew into insane rages. I figure Soulcatcher ate that up.

One-Eye flipped a card into the discard pile. He muttered, "Somebody's sandbagging."

Goblin snapped the card up, spread four knaves and discarded a queen. He grinned. You knew he was going down next time, holding nothing heavier than a deuce. One-Eye smacked the tabletop, hissed. He hadn't won a hand since sitting down.

"Go low, guys," Elmo warned, ignoring Goblin's discard. He drew, scrunched his cards around just inches from his face, spread three fours and discarded a deuce. He tapped his remaining pair, grinned at Goblin, said, "That better be an ace, Chubby."

Pickles snagged Elmo's deuce, spread four of a kind, discarded a trey. He plied Goblin with an owl-like stare that dared him to go down. It said an ace would not keep him from getting burned.

I wished Raven were there. His presence made One-Eye too nervous to cheat. But Raven was on turnip patrol, which is what we called the weekly mission to Oar to purchase supplies. Pickles had his chair.

Pickles is Company quartermaster. He usually went on turnip patrol. He begged off this one because of stomach troubles.

"Looks like everybody was sandbagging," I said, and glared at a hopeless hand. Pair of sevens, pair of eights, and a nine to go with one of the eights, but no run. Almost everything I could use was in the discard pile. I drew. Sumbitch. Another nine, and it gave me a run. I spread it, dumped the off seven, and prayed. Prayer was all that could help.

One-Eye ignored my seven. He drew. "Damn!" He dumped a six on the bottom of my straight and discarded a six. "The moment of truth, Porkchop," he told Goblin. "You going to try Pickles?" And, "These Forsbergers are crazy. I've never seen anything like them."

We had been in the fortress a month. It was a little big for us, but I liked it. "I could get to like them," I said. "If they could just learn to like me." We had beaten off four counterattacks already. "Shit or get off the pot, Goblin. You know you got me and Elmo licked."

Pickles ticked the corner of his card with his thumbnail, stared at Goblin. He said, "They've got a whole Rebel mythos up here. Prophets and false prophets. Prophetic dreams. Sendings from the gods. Even a prophecy that a child somewhere around here is a reincarnation of the White Rose."

"If the kid's already here, how come he's not pounding on us?" Elmo asked.

"They haven't found him yet. Or her. They have a whole tribe of people out looking."

Goblin chickened. He drew, sputtered, discarded a king. Elmo drew and discarded another king. Pickles looked at Goblin. He smiled a small smile, took a card, did not bother looking at it. He tossed a five onto the six One-Eye had dumped on my run and flipped his draw into the discard pile.

"A five?" Goblin squeaked. "You were holding a five? I don't believe it. He had a five." He slapped his ace onto the tabletop. "He had a damned five."

"Temper, temper," Elmo admonished. "You're the guy who's always telling One-Eye to simmer down, remember?"

"He bluffed me with a damned five?"

Pickles wore that little smile as he stacked his winnings. He was pleased with himself. He had pulled a good bluff. I would have bet he was holding an ace myself.

One-Eye shoved the cards to Goblin. "Deal."

"Oh, come on. He was holding a five, and I got to deal too?"

"It's your turn. Shut up and shuffle."

I asked Pickles, "Where'd you hear that reincarnation stuff?"

"Flick." Flick was the old man Raven had saved. Pickles had overcome the old man's defenses. They were getting thick.

The girl went by the name Darling. She had taken a big shine to Raven. She followed him around, and drove the rest of us crazy sometimes. I was glad Raven had gone to town. We would not see much of Darling till he got back.

Goblin dealt. I checked my cards. The proverbial hand so bad it could not make a foot. Damned near one of Elmo's fabled Pismo straights, or no two cards of the same suit.

Goblin looked his over. His eyes got big. He slapped them down face upward. "Tonk! Goddammed tonk. Fifty!" He had dealt himself five royal cards, an automatic win demanding a double payoff.

"The only way he can win is deal them to himself," One-Eye grumped.

Goblin chortled, "You ain't winning even when you deal, Maggot Lips."

Elmo started shuffling.

The next hand went the distance. Pickles fed us snippets of the reincarnation story between plays.

Darling wandered by, her round, freckled face blank, her eyes empty. I tried imagining her in the White Rose role. I could not. She did not fit.

Pickles dealt. Elmo tried to go down with eighteen. One-Eye burned him. He held seventeen after his draw. I raked the cards in, started shuffling.

"Come on, Croaker," One-Eye taunted. "Let's don't fool around. I'm on a streak. One in a row. Deal me them aces and deuces." Fifteen and under is an automatic win, same as forty-nine and fifty.

"Oh. Sorry. I caught myself taking this Rebel superstition seriously."

Pickles observed, "It's a persuasive sort of nonsense. It hangs together in a certain elegant illusion of hope." I frowned his way. His smile was almost shy. "It's hard to lose when you *know* fate is on your side. The Rebel knows. Anyway, that's what Raven says." Our grand old man was getting close to Raven.

"Then we'll have to change their thinking."

"Can't. Whip them a hundred times and they'll keep on coming. And because of that they'll fulfill their own prophecy."

Elmo grunted, "Then we have to do more than whip them. We have to humiliate them." *We* meant everybody on the Lady's side.

I flipped an eight into another of the countless discard piles which have become the milemarks of my life. "This is getting old." I was restless. I felt an undirected urge to be doing something. Anything.

Elmo shrugged. "Playing passes the time."

"This is the life, all right," Goblin said. "Sit around and wait. How much of that have we done over the years?"

"I haven't kept track," I grumbled. "More of that than anything else."

"Hark!" Elmo said. "I hear a little voice. It says my flock are bored. Pickles. Break out the archery butts and. . . ." His suggestion died under an avalanche of groans.

Rigorous physical training is Elmo's prescription for ennui. A dash through his diabolical obstacle course kills or cures.

Pickles extended his protest beyond the obligatory groan. "I'm gonna have wagons to unload, Elmo. Those guys should be back any time. You want these clowns to exercise, give them to me."

Elmo and I exchanged glances. Goblin and One-Eye looked alert. Not back yet? They should have been in before noon. I figured they were sleeping it off. Turnip patrol always came back wasted.

"I figured they were in," Elmo said.

Goblin flipped his hand at the discard pile. His cards danced for a moment, suspended by his trickery. He wanted us to know he was letting us off. "I better check this out."

One-Eye's cards slithered across the table, humping like inchworms. "I'll look into it, Chubby."

"I called it first, Toad Breath."

"I got seniority."

"Both of you do it," Elmo suggested. He turned to me. "I'll put a patrol together. You tell the Lieutenant." He tossed his cards in, started calling names. He headed for the stables.

Hooves pounded the dust beneath a continuous, grumbling drumbeat. We rode swiftly but warily. One-Eye watched for trouble, but performing sorceries on horseback is difficult.

Still, he caught a whiff in time. Elmo fluttered hand signals. We split into two groups, ploughed into the tall roadside weeds. The Rebel popped up and found us at his throat. He never had a chance. We were travelling again in minutes.

One-Eye told me, "I hope nobody over there starts wondering why we always know what they're going to try."

"Let them think they're up to their asses in spies."

"How did a spy get the word to Deal so fast? Our luck looks too good to be true. The Captain should get Soulcatcher to pull us out while we still have some value."

He had a point. Once our secret got out, the Rebel would neutralize our wizards with his own. Our luck would take a header.

The walls of Oar hove into view. I started getting the queasy regrets. The Lieutenant hadn't really approved this adventure. The Captain himself would ream me royal. His cussing would scorch the hair off my chin. I would be old before the restrictions ran out. So long madonnas of the streetside!

I was supposed to know better. I was halfway an officer.

The prospect of careers cleaning the Company stables and heads did not intimidate Elmo or his corporals. Forward! they seemed to be thinking. Onward, for the glory of the band. Yech!

They were not stupid, just willing to pay the price of disobedience.

That idiot One-Eye actually started singing as we entered Oar. The song was his own wild, nonsensical composition sung in a voice utterly incapable of carrying a tune.

"Can it, One-Eye," Elmo snarled. "You're attracting attention."

His order was pointless. We were too obviously who we were, and just as obviously were in vile temper. This was no turnip patrol. We were looking for trouble.

One-Eye whooped his way into a new song. "Can the racket!" Elmo thundered. "Get on your goddamned job."

We turned a corner. A black fog formed around our horses' fetlocks as we did. Moist black noses poked up and out and sniffed the fetid evening air. They wrinkled. Maybe they had become as countrified as I. Out came almond eyes glowing like the lamps of Hell. A susurrus of fear swept the pedestrians watching from the streetsides.

Up they sprang, a dozen, a score, five score phantoms born in that snakepit One-Eye calls a mind. They streaked ahead, weasely, toothy, sinuous black things that darted at the people of Oar. Terror outpaced them. In minutes we shared the streets with no one but ghosts.

This was my first visit to Oar. I looked it over like I had just come in on the pumpkin wagon.

"Well, look here," Elmo said as we turned into the street where the turnip patrol usually quartered. "Here's old Cornie." I knew the name, though not the man. Cornie kept the stable where the patrol always stayed.

An old man rose from his seat beside a watering trough. "Heared you was coming," he said. "Done all what I could, Elmo. Couldn't get them no doctor, though."

"We brought our own." Though Cornie was old and had to hustle to keep pace, Elmo did not slow down.

I sniffed the air. It held a taint of old smoke.

Cornie dashed ahead, around an angle in the street. Weasel things flashed around his legs like surf foaming around a boulder on the shore. We followed, and found the source of the smoke smell.

Someone had fired Cornie's stable, then jumped our guys as they ran out. The villains. Wisps of smoke still rose. The street in front of the stable was filled with casualties. The least injured were standing guard, rerouting traffic.

Candy, who commanded the patrol, limped toward us. "Where do I start?" I asked.

He pointed. "Those are the worst. Better begin with Raven, if he's still alive."

My heart jumped. Raven? He seemed so invulnerable.

One-Eye scattered his pets. No Rebel would sneak up on us now. I followed Candy to where Raven lay. The man was unconscious. His face was paper-white. "He the worst?"

"The only one I thought wouldn't make it."

"You did all right. Did the tourniquets the way I taught you, didn't you?" I looked Candy over. "You should be lying down yourself." Back to Raven. He had close to thirty cuts on his face side, some of them deep. I threaded my needle.

Elmo joined us after a quick look around the perimeter. "Bad?" he asked.

"Can't tell for sure. He's full of holes. Lost a lot of blood. Better have One-Eye make up some of his broth." One-Eye makes an herb and chicken soup that will bring new hope to the dead. He is my only assistant.

Elmo asked, "How did it happen, Candy?"

"They fired the stable and jumped us when we ran out."

"I can see that."

Cornie muttered, "The filthy murderers." I got the feeling he was mourning his stable more than the patrol, though.

Elmo made a face like a man chewing on a green persimmon. "And no dead? Raven is the worst? That's hard to believe."

"One dead," Candy corrected. "The old guy. Raven's sidekick. From that village."

"Flick," Elmo growled. Flick was not supposed to have left the fortress at Deal. The Captain did not trust him. But Elmo overlooked that breach of regulations. "We're going to make somebody sorry they started this," he said. There wasn't a bit of emotion in his voice. He might have been quoting the wholesale price of yams.

I wondered how Pickles would take the news. He was fond of Flick. Darling would be shattered. Flick was her grandfather.

"They were only after Raven," Cornie said. "That's why he got cut so bad."

And Candy, "Flick threw himself in their way." He gestured. "All the rest of this is because we wouldn't stand back."

Elmo asked the question puzzling me. "Why would the Rebel be that hot to get Raven?"

Doughbelly was hanging around waiting for me to get to the gash in his left forearm. He said, "It wasn't Rebels, Elmo. It was that dumbshit captain from where we picked up Flick and Darling."

I swore.

"You stick to your needlepoint, Croaker," Elmo said. "You sure, Doughbelly?"

"Sure I'm sure. Ask Jolly. He seen him too. The rest was just street thugs. We whipped them good once we got going." He pointed. Near the unburned side of the stable were a dozen bodies stacked like cordwood. Flick was the only one I recognized. The others wore ragged local costume.

Candy said, "I saw him too, Elmo. And he wasn't top dog. There was another guy hanging around back in the shadows. He cleared out when we started winning."

Cornie had been hanging around, looking watchful and staying quiet. He volunteered, "I know where they went. Place over to Bleek Street."

I exchanged glances with One-Eye, who was putting his broth together using this and that from a black bag of his own. "Looks like Cornie knows our crowd," I said.

"Know you well enough to know you don't want nobody getting away with nothing like this."

I looked at Elmo. Elmo stared at Cornie. There always was some doubt about the stablekeeper. Cornie got nervous. Elmo, like any veteran sergeant, has a baleful stare. Finally, "One-Eye, take this fellow for a walk. Get his story."

One-Eye had Cornie under hypnosis in seconds. The two of them roamed around chatting like old buddies.

I shifted my attention to Candy. "That man in the shadows. Did he limp?"

"Wasn't the Limper. Too tall."

"Even so, the attack would have had the spook's blessing. Right, Elmo?"

Elmo nodded. "Soulcatcher would get severely pissed if he figured it out. The okay to risk that had to come from the top."

Something like a sigh came out of Raven. I looked down. His eyes were open a crack. He repeated the sound. I put my ear next to his lips. "Zouad . . ." he murmured.

Zouad. The infamous Colonel Zouad. The enemy he had renounced. The Limper's special villain. Raven's knight-errantry had generated vicious repercussions.

I told Elmo. He did not seem surprised. Maybe the Captain had passed Raven's history on to his platoon leaders.

One-Eye came back. He said, "Friend Cornie works for the other team." He grinned a malific grin, the one he practices so he can scare kids and dogs. "Thought you might want to take that into consideration, Elmo."

"Oh, yes." Elmo seemed delighted.

I went to work on the man next worse off. More sewing to do. I wondered if I would have enough suture. The patrol was in bad shape. "How long till we get some of that broth, One-Eye?"

"Still got to come up with a chicken."

Elmo grumbled, "So have somebody go steal one."

One-Eye said, "The people we want are holed up in a Bleek Street dive. They've got some rough friends."

"What are you going to do, Elmo?" I asked. I was sure he would do something. Raven had put us under obligation by naming Zouad. He thought he was dying. He would not have named the name otherwise. I knew him that well, if I didn't know anything about his past.

"We've got to arrange something for the Colonel."

"You go looking for trouble, you're going to find it. Remember who he works for."

"Bad business, letting somebody get away with hitting the Company, Croaker. Even the Limper."

"That's taking pretty high policy on your own shoulders, isn't it?" I could not disagree, though. A defeat on the battlefield is acceptable. This was not the same. This was empire politics. People should be warned that it could get hairy if they dragged us in. The Limper *and* Soulcatcher had to be shown. I asked Elmo, "What kind of repercussions do you figure on?"

"One hell of a lot of pissing and moaning. But I don't reckon there's much they can *do.* Hell, Croaker, it ain't your no nevermind anyway. You get paid to patch guys up." He stared at Cornie thoughtfully. "I reckon the fewer witnesses left over, the better. The Limper can't scream if he can't prove nothing. One-Eye. You go on talking to your pet Rebel there. I got a nasty little idea shaping up in the back of my head. Maybe he has the key."

One-Eye finished dishing out his soup. The earliest partakers had more color in their cheeks already. Elmo stopped paring his nails. He skewered the stablekeeper with a hard stare. "Cornie, you ever hear of Colonel Zouad?"

Cornie stiffened. He hesitated just a second too long. "Can't say as I have."

"That's odd. Figured you would have. He's the one they call the Limper's left hand. Anyway, I figure the Circle would do most anything to lay hands on him. What do you think?"

"I don't know nothing about the Circle, Elmo." He gazed out over the rooftops. "You telling me this fellow over to Bleek is this Zouad?"

Elmo chuckled. "Didn't say that at all, Cornie. Did I give that impression, Croaker?"

"Hell no. What would Zouad be doing hanging around a crummy whorehouse in Oar? The Limper is up to his butt in trouble over east. He'd want all the help he could get."

"See, Cornie? But look here. Maybe I do know where the Circle could find the Colonel. Now, him and the Company ain't no friends. On the other hand, we ain't friends with the Circle, neither. But that's business. No hard feelings. So I was thinking. Maybe we could trade a favor for a favor. Maybe some big-time Rebel could drop by that place in Bleek Street and tell the owners he don't think they ought to be looking out for those guys. You see what I mean? If it was to go that way, Colonel Zouad just might drop into the Circle's lap."

Cornie got the look of a man who knows he is trapped.

He had been a good spy when we had had no reason to worry about him. He had been just plain old Cornie, friendly stablekeeper, whom we had tipped a little extra and talked around no more nor less than anyone else outside the Company. He had been under no pressure. He hadn't had to be anything but himself.

"You got me all wrong, Elmo. Honest. I don't never get involved in politics. The Lady or the Whites, it's all the same to me. Horses need feeding and stabling no matter who rides them."

"Reckon you're right there, Cornie. Excuse me for being suspicious." Elmo winked at One-Eye.

"That's the Amador where those fellows are staying, Elmo. You better go over there before somebody tells them you're in town. Me, I'd better start getting this place cleaned up."

"We're in no hurry, Cornie. But you go ahead with whatever you've got to do."

Cornie eyed us. He went a few steps toward what was left of his stable. He looked us over. Elmo considered him blandly. One-Eye lifted his horse's left foreleg to check its hoof. Cornie ducked into the ruin. "One-Eye?" Elmo asked.

"Right on out the back. Heeling and toeing."

Elmo grinned. "Keep your eye on him. Croaker, take notes. I want to know who he tells. And who they tell. We gave him something that ought to spread like the clap."

Zouad was a dead man from the minute Raven named his name," I told One-Eye. "Maybe from the minute he did whatever it was back when."

One-Eye grunted, discarded. Candy picked up and spread. One-Eye cursed. "I can't play with these guys, Croaker. They don't play right."

Elmo galloped up the street, dismounted. "They're moving in on that whorehouse. Got something for me, One-Eye?"

The list was disappointing. I gave it to Elmo. He cursed, spat, cursed again. He kicked the planks we were using as a card table. "Pay attention to your damned jobs."

One-Eye controlled his temper. "They're not making mistakes, Elmo. They're covering their asses. Cornie has been around us too long to trust."

Elmo stomped around and breathed fire. "All right. Backup plan number one. We watch Zouad. See where they take him after they grab him. We'll rescue him when he's about ready to croak, wipe out any Rebels around the place, then hunt down anybody who checked in there."

I observed, "You're determined to show a profit, aren't you?"

"Damned straight. How's Raven?"

"Looks like he'll pull through. The infection is under control, and One-Eye says he's started to heal."

"Uhn. One-Eye, I want Rebel names. Lots of names."

"Yes sir, boss, sir." One-Eye produced an exaggerated salute. It became an obscene gesture when Elmo turned away.

"Push those planks together, Doughbelly," I suggested. "Your deal, One-Eye."

He did not respond. He did not bitch or gripe or threaten to turn me into a newt. He just stood there, numb as death, eye barely cracked.

"Elmo!"

Elmo got in front of him and stared from six inches away. He snapped his fingers under One-Eye's nose. One-Eye did not respond. "What do you think, Croaker?"

"Something is happening at that whorehouse."

One-Eye did not move a muscle for ten minutes. Then the eye opened, unglazed, and he relaxed like a wet rag. Elmo demanded, "What the hell happened?"

"Give him a minute, will you?" I snapped.

One-Eye collected himself. "The Rebel got Zouad, but not before he contacted the Limper."

"Uhm?"

"The spook is coming to help him."

Elmo turned a pale shade of grey. "Here? To Oar?"

"Yep."

"Oh, shit."

Indeed. The Limper was the nastiest of the Taken. "Think fast, Elmo. He'll trace our part in it. . . . Cornie is the cutout link."

"One-Eye, you find that old shit. Whitey. Still. Pokey. Got a job for you." He gave instructions. Pokey grinned and stroked his dagger. Bloodthirsty bastard.

I cannot adequately portray the unease One-Eye's news generated. We knew the Limper only through stories, but those stories were always grim. We were scared. Soulcatcher's patronage was no real protection against another of the Taken.

Elmo punched me. "He's doing it again."

Sure enough. One-Eye was stiff. But this time he went beyond rigidity. He toppled, began thrashing and foaming at the mouth.

"Hold him!" I ordered. "Elmo, give me that baton of yours." A half dozen men piled on One-Eye. Small though he was, he gave them a ride.

"What for?" Elmo asked.

"I'll put it in his mouth so he doesn't chew his tongue." One-Eye made the weirdest sounds I've ever heard, and I have heard plenty on battlefields. Wounded men make noises you would swear could not come from a human throat.

The seizure lasted only seconds. After one final, violent surge, One-Eye lapsed into a peaceful slumber.

"Okay, Croaker. What the hell happened?"

"I don't know. The falling sickness?"

"Give him some of his own soup," somebody suggested. "Serve him right." A tin cup appeared. We forced its contents down his throat.

His eye clicked open. "What are you trying to do? Poison me? Feh! What was that? Boiled sewage?"

"Your soup," I told him.

Elmo jumped in. "What happened?"

One-Eye spat. He grabbed a nearby wineskin, sucked a mouthful, gargled, spat again. "Soulcatcher happened, that's what. Whew! I feel for Goblin now."

My heart started skipping every third beat. A nest of hornets swarmed in my gut. First the Limper, now Soulcatcher.

"So what did the spook want?" Elmo demanded. He was nervous too. He is not usually impatient.

"He wanted to know what the hell is going on. He heard the Limper was all excited. He checked with Goblin. All Goblin knew was that we headed here. So he climbed into my head."

"And was amazed at all the wide open space. Now he knows everything you know, eh?"

"Yes." Obviously, One-Eye did not like the idea.

Elmo waited several seconds. "Well?"

"Well what?" One-Eye covered his grin by pulling on the wineskin.

"Dammit, what did he say?"

One-Eye chuckled. "He approves of what we're doing. But he thinks we're showing all the finesse of a bull in rut. So we're getting a little help."

"What kind of help?" Elmo sounded like he knew things were out of control, but could not see where.

"He's sending somebody."

Elmo relaxed. So did I. As long as the spook himself stayed away. "How soon?" I wondered aloud.

"Maybe sooner than we'd like," Elmo muttered. "Lay off the wine, One-Eye. You still got to watch Zouad."

One-Eye grumbled. He went into that semi-trance that means he is looking around somewhere else. He was gone a long time.

"So!" Elmo growled when One-Eye came out of it. He kept looking around like he expected Soulcatcher to pop out of thin air.

"So take it easy. They've got him tucked away in a secret sub-basement about a mile south of here."

Elmo was as restless as a little boy with a desperate need to pee. "What's the matter with you?" I asked.

"A bad feeling. Just a bad, bad feeling, Croaker." His roving gaze came to rest. His eyes got big. "I was right. Oh, damn, I was right."

It looked as tall as a house and half as wide. It wore scarlet bleached by time, moth-eaten, and tattered. It came up the street in a sort of shamble, now fast, now slow. Wild, stringy grey hair tangled around its head. Its bramble patch of a beard was so thick and matted with filth that its face was all but invisible. One pallid, liver-spotted hand clutched a pole of a staff that was a thing of beauty defiled by its bearer's touch. It was an immensely elongated female body, perfect in every detail.

Someone whispered, "They say that was a real woman back during the Domination. They say she cheated on him."

You could not blame the woman. Not if you gave Shifter a good look.

Shapeshifter is Soulcatcher's closest ally among the Ten Who Were Taken. His enmity for the Limper is more virulent than our patron's. The Limper was the third corner in the triangle explaining Shifter's staff.

He stopped a few feet away. His eyes burned with an insane fire that made them impossible to meet. I cannot recall what color they were. Chronologically, he was the first great wizard-king seduced, suborned, and enslaved by the Dominator and his Lady.

Shaking, One-Eye stepped out front. "I'm the wizard," he said.

"Catcher told me." Shifter's voice was resonant and deep and big for even a man of his size. "Developments?"

"I've traced Zouad. Nothing else."

Shifter scanned us again. Some folks were doing a fade. He smiled behind his facial brush.

Down at the bend in the street civilians were gathering to gape. Oar had not yet seen any of the Lady's champions. This was the city's lucky day. Two of the maddest were in town.

Shifter's gaze touched me. For an instant I felt his cold contempt. I was a sour stench in his nostrils.

He found what he was looking for. Raven. He moved forward. We dodged the way small males duck the dominant baboon at the zoo. He stared at Raven for several minutes, then his vast shoulders hunched in a shrug. He placed the toes of his staff on Raven's chest.

I gasped. Raven's color improved dramatically. He stopped sweating. His features relaxed as the pain faded. His wounds formed angry red scar tissue which faded to the white of old scars in minutes. We gathered in a tighter and tighter circle, awed by the show.

Pokey came trotting up the street. "Hey, Elmo. We did it. What's going on?" He got a look at Shifter, squeaked like a caught mouse.

Elmo had himself together again. "Where's Whitey and Still?"

"Getting rid of the body."

"Body?" Shifter asked. Elmo explained. Shifter grunted. "This Cornie will become the basis of our plan. You." He speared One-Eye with a sausage-sized finger. "Where are those men?"

Predictably, One-Eye located them in a tavern. "You." Shifter indicated Pokey. "Tell them to bring the body back here."

Pokey got grey around the edges. You could see the protests piling up inside him. But he nodded, gulped some air, and trotted off. Nobody argues with the Taken.

I checked Raven's pulse. It was strong. He looked perfectly healthy. As diffidently as I could, I asked, "Could you do that for the others? While we're waiting?"

He gave me a look I thought would curdle my blood. But he did it.

"What happened? What are you doing here?" Raven frowned up at me. Then it came back to him. He sat up. "Zouad. . . ." He looked around.

"You've been out for two days. They carved you up like a goose. We didn't think you'd make it."

He felt his wounds. "What's going on, Croaker? I ought to be dead."

"Soulcatcher sent a friend. Shifter. He fixed you up." He had fixed everybody. It was hard to stay terrified of a guy who would do that for your outfit.

Raven surged to his feet, wobbled dizzily. "That damned Cornie. He set it up." A knife appeared in his hand. "Damn. I'm weak as a kitten."

I had wondered how Cornie could know so much about the attackers. "That isn't Cornie there, Raven. Cornie is dead. That's Shifter practicing to be Cornie." He did not need practice. He was Cornie enough to fool Cornie's mother.

Raven settled back beside me. "What's going on?"

I brought him up to date. "Shifter wants to go in using Cornie as credentials. They probably trust him now."

"I'll be right behind him."

"He might not like that."

"I don't care what he likes. Zouad isn't getting out of it this time. The debt is too big." His face softened and saddened. "How's Darling? She hear about Flick yet?"

"I don't think so. Nobody's been back to Deal. Elmo figures he can do whatever he wants here as long as he don't have to face the Captain till it's over."

"Good. I won't have to argue it with him."

"Shifter isn't the only Taken in town," I reminded him. Shifter had said he sensed the Limper. Raven shrugged. The Limper did not matter to him.

The Cornie simulacrum came toward us. We rose. I was shaky, but did note that Raven grew a shade paler. Good. He wasn't a cold stone all the time.

"You will accompany me," he told Raven. He eyed me. "And you. And the sergeant."

"They know Elmo," I protested. And he grinned.

"You will appear to be Rebels. Only one of the Circle would detect the deception. None of them are in Oar. The Rebel here is independently minded. We will take advantage of his failure to summon support." The Rebel is as plagued by personality politics as is our side.

Shifter beckoned One-Eye. "Status of Colonel Zouad?"

"He hasn't cracked."

"He's tough," Raven said, begrudging the compliment.

"You getting any names?" Elmo asked me.

I had a nice list. Elmo was pleased.

"We'd better go," Shifter said. "Before Limper strikes."

One-Eye gave us the passwords. Scared, convinced I was not ready for this, more convinced that I did not dare contest Shifter's selections, I trudged along in the Taken's wake.

I don't know when it happened. I just glanced up and found myself walking with strangers. I gobbled at Shifter's back.

Raven laughed. I understood then. Shifter had cast his glamour over us. We now appeared to be captains of the Rebel persuasion. "Who are we?" I asked.

Shifter indicated Raven. "Harden, of the Circle. Raker's brother-in-law. They hate one another the way Catcher and Limper hate one another." Next, Elmo. "Field Major Reef, Harden's chief of staff. You, Harden's nephew, Motrin Hanin, as vicious an assassin as ever lived."

We had heard of none of them, but Shifter assured us their presence would not be questioned. Harden was in and out of Forsberg all the time, making life tough for his wife's brother.

Right, I thought. Fine and dandy. And what about the Limper? What do we do if he shows up?

The people at the place where they were holding Zouad were more embarrassed than curious when Cornie announced Harden. They had not deferred to the Circle. They did not ask questions. Apparently the real Harden possessed a vile, volatile, unpredictable temper.

"Show them the prisoner," Shifter said.

One Rebel gave Shifter a look that said, "Just you wait, Cornie."

The place was packed with Rebels. I could almost hear Elmo thinking out his plan of attack.

They took us down into a basement, through a cleverly concealed doorway, and down deeper still, into a room with earthen walls and ceiling supported by beams and timbers. The decor came straight out of a fiend's imagination.

Torture chambers exist, of course, but the mass of men never see them, so they never really believe in them. I'd never seen one before.

I surveyed the instruments, looked at Zouad there strapped into a huge, bizarre chair, and wondered why the Lady was considered such a villain. These people said they were the good guys, fighting for the right, liberty, and the dignity of the human spirit, but in method they were no better than the Limper.

Shifter whispered to Raven. Raven nodded. I wondered how we would get our cues. Shifter had not rehearsed us much. These people would expect us to act like Harden and his cutthroats.

We seated ourselves and observed the interrogation. Our presence inspired the questioners. I closed my eyes. Raven and Elmo were less disturbed.

After a few minutes "Harden" ordered "Major Reef" to go handle some piece of business. I do not recall the excuse. I was distracted. Its purpose was to put Elmo back on the street so he could start the roundup.

Shifter was winging it. We were supposed to sit tight till he cued us. I gathered we would make our move when Elmo closed in and panic started seeping down from above. Meantime, we would watch Colonel Zouad's demolition.

The Colonel was not that impressive, but then the torturers had had him a while. I expect anyone would look hollow and shrunken after enduring their mercies.

We sat like three idols. I sent mental hurryups to Elmo. I had been trained to take pleasure in the healing, not the breaking, of human flesh.

Even Raven seemed unhappy. Doubtless he had fantasized torments for Zouad, but when it came to the actuality his basic decency triumphed. His style was to stick a knife in a man and have done.

The earth lurched as if stomped by a huge boot. Soil fell from the walls and overhead. The air filled with dust. "Earthquake!" somebody yelled, and the Rebels all scrambled for the stair. Shifter sat still and smiled.

The earth shuddered again. I fought the instinct of the herd and remained seated. Shifter was not worried. Why should I be?

He pointed at Zouad. Raven nodded, rose, went over. The Colonel was conscious and lucid and frightened by the quaking. He looked grateful when Raven started unbuckling him.

The great foot stamped again. Earth fell. In one corner a supporting upright toppled. A trickle of loose soil began running into the basement. The other beams groaned and shifted. I barely controlled myself.

Sometime during the tremor Raven stopped being Harden. Shifter stopped being Cornie. Zouad looked them over and caught on. His face hardened, went pale. As if he had more to fear from Raven and Shapeshifter than from the Rebel.

"Yeah," Raven said. "It's payoff time."

The earth bucked. Overhead there was a remote rumble of falling masonry. Lamps toppled and went out. The dust made the air almost unbreathable. And Rebels came tumbling back down the stair, looking over their shoulders.

"Limper is here," Shifter said. He did not seem displeased. He rose and faced the stair. He was Cornie again, and Raven was Harden once more.

Rebels piled into the room. I lost track of Raven in the press and poor light. Somebody sealed the door up top. The Rebels got quiet as mice. You could almost hear hearts hammering as they watched the stair and wondered if the secret entrance were well enough hidden.

Despite several yards of intervening earth, I heard something moving through the basement above. Drag-thump. Drag-thump. The rhythm of a crippled man walking. My gaze, too, locked on the secret door.

The earth shook its most violent yet. The doorway exploded inward. The far end of the sub-basement caved in. Men screamed as the earth swallowed them. The human herd shoved this way and that in search of an escape that did not exist. Only Shifter and I were not caught up in it. We watched from an island of calm.

All the lamps had died. The only light came from the gap at the head of the stair, sliding around a silhouette which, at that moment, seemed vile just in its stance. I had cold, clammy skin and violent shakes. It was not just because I had heard so much about the Limper. He exuded something that made me feel the way an arachnophobe might if you dropped a big hairy spider into his lap.

I glanced at Shifter. He was Cornie, just another of the Rebel crew. Did he have some special reason for not wanting to be recognized by the Limper?

He did something with his hands.

A blinding light filled the pit. I could not see. I heard beams creaking and giving way. This time I did not hesitate. I joined the rush to the stair.

I suppose the Limper was more startled than anyone else. He had not expected any serious opposition. Shifter's trick caught him off guard. The rush swept over him before he could protect himself.

Shifter and I were the last up the stair. I skipped over the Limper, a small man in brown who did not look terrible at all as he writhed on the floor. I looked for the stair to the street level. Shifter grabbed my arm. His grip was undeniable. "Help me." He planted a boot against the Limper's ribs, started rolling him through the entrance to the sub-basement.

Down below, men groaned and cried out for help. Sections of floor on our level were sagging, collapsing. More in fear that I would be trapped if we did not hurry than out of any desire to inconvenience the Limper, I helped Shifter dump the Taken into the pit.

Shifter grinned, gave me a thumbs up. He did something with his fingers. The collapse accelerated. He seized my arm and headed for the stair. We piled into the street amidst the grandest uproar in Oar's recent history.

The foxes were in the henhouse. Men were running hither and yon yelling incoherently. Elmo and the Company were all around them, driving them inward, cutting them down. The Rebels were too confused to defend themselves.

Had it not been for Shifter, I suppose, I would not have survived that. He did something that turned the points of arrows and swords. Cunning beast that I am, I stayed in his shadow till we were safely behind Company lines.

It was a great victory for the Lady. It exceeded Elmo's wildest hopes. Before the dust settled the purge had taken virtually every committed Rebel in Oar. Shifter stayed in the thick of it. He gave us invaluable assistance and had a grand time smashing things up. He was as happy as a child starting fires.

Then he disappeared as utterly as if he had never existed. And we, so exhausted we were crawling around like lizards, assembled outside Cornie's stable. Elmo took the roll.

All accounted for but one. "Where's Raven?" Elmo asked.

I told him, "I think he got buried when that house fell in. Him and Zouad both."

One-Eye observed, "Kind of fitting. Ironic but fitting. Hate to see him go, though. He played a mean game of Tonk."

"The Limper is down there too?" Elmo asked.

I grinned. "I helped bury him."

"And Shifter is gone."

I had begun to sense a disturbing pattern. I wanted to know if it was just my imagination. I brought it up while the men were getting ready to return to Deal. "You know, the only people who saw Shifter were on our side. The Rebel and the Limper saw a lot of us. Especially of you, Elmo. And me and Raven. Cornie will turn up dead. I have a feeling Shifter's finesse didn't have much to do with getting Zouad or wiping out the local Rebel hierarchy. I think we were put on the spot where the Limper is concerned. Very craftily."

Elmo likes to come across as a big, dumb country boy turned soldier, but he is sharp. He not only saw what I meant, he immediately connected it with the broader picture of politicking among the Taken. "We've got to get the hell away from here before the Limper digs his way out. And I don't mean just away from Oar. I mean Forsberg. Soulcatcher has put us on the board as his frontline pawns. We're liable to get caught between a rock and a hard place." He chewed his lip for a second, then started acting like a sergeant, bellowing at anybody not moving fast enough to suit him.

He was in a near panic, but was a soldier to the bone. Our departure was no rout. We went out escorting the provision wagons Candy's patrol had come to collect. He told me, "I'll go crazy after we get back. I'll go out and chew down a tree, or something." And after a few miles, thoughtfully, "Been trying to decide who ought to break the news to Darling. Croaker, you just volunteered. You've got the right touch."

So I had me something to keep my mind occupied during the ride. Damn that Elmo!

The great brouhaha in Oar was not the end of it. Ripples spread. Consequences piled up. Fate shoved its badfinger in.

Raker launched a major offensive while the Limper was digging his way out of the rubble. He did so unaware that his enemy was absent from the field, but the effect was the same. The Limper's army collapsed. Our victory went for naught. Rebel bands whooped through Oar, hunting the Lady's agents.

We, thanks to Soulcatcher's foresight, were moving south when the collapse came, so we avoided becoming involved. We went into garrison at Elm credited with several dramatic victories, and the Limper fled into the Salient with the remnants of his force, branded as an incompetent. He knew who had done him in, but there wasn't anything he could do. His relationship with the Lady was too precarious. He dared do nothing but remain her faithful lapdog. He would have to come up with some outstanding victories before he thought about settling with us or Soulcatcher.

I did not feel that comforted. The worm has a way of turning, given time.

Raker was so enthusiastic over his success that he did not slow down after he conquered Forsberg. He turned southward. Soulcatcher ordered us out of Elm only a week after we had settled in.

Did the Captain get upset about what had happened? Was he displeased because so many of his men had gone off on their own, exceeding or stretching his instructions? Let's just say the extra duty assignments were enough to break the back of an ox. Let's say the madonnas of the night in Elm were severely disappointed in the Black Company. I do not want to think about it. The man is a diabolic genius.

The platoons were on review. The wagons were loaded and ready to roll.

The Captain and Lieutenant were conferring with their sergeants. One-Eye and Goblin were playing some sort of game with little shadow creatures making war in the corners of the compound. Most of us were watching and betting this way or that depending on shifts of fortune. The gateman shouted, "Rider coming in."

Nobody paid any attention. Messengers came and went all day.

The gate swung inward. And Darling began clapping her hands. She ran toward the gateway.

Through it, looking as rough as the day we had met him, rode our Raven. He scooped up Darling and gave her a big hug, perched her astride his mount before him, and reported to the Captain. I heard him say that all his debts were paid, and that he no longer had any interests outside the Company.

The Captain stared at him a long time, then nodded and told him to take his place in ranks.

He had used us, and while doing so had found himself a new home. He was welcome to the family.

We rode out, bound for a new garrison in the Salient.

Raker

The wind tumbled and bumbled and howled around Meystrikt. Arctic imps giggled and blew their frigid breath through chinks in the walls of my quarters. My lamplight flickered and danced, barely surviving. When my fingers stiffened, I folded them round the flame and let them toast.

The wind was a hard blow out of the north, gritty with powdered snow. A foot had fallen during the night. More was coming. It would bring more misery with it. I pitied Elmo and his gang. They were out Rebel hunting.

Meystrikt Fortress. Pearl of the Salient defenses. Frozen in winter. Swampy in spring. An oven in summer. White Rose prophets and Rebel mainforcers were the least of our troubles.

The Salient is a long arrowhead of flatland pointing south, between mountain ranges. Meystrikt lies at its point. It funnels weather and enemies down onto the stronghold. Our assignment is to hold this anchor of the Lady's northern defenses.

Why the Black Company?

We are the best. The Rebel infection began seeping through the Salient soon after the fall of Forsberg. The Limper tried to stop it and failed. The Lady set us to clean up the Limper's mess. Her only other option was to abandon another province.

The gate watch sounded a trumpet. Elmo was coming in.

There was no rush to greet him. The rules call for casualness, for a pretense that your guts are not churning with dread. Instead, men peeped from hidden places, wondering about brothers who had gone a-hunting. Anybody lost? Anyone bad hurt? You know them better than kin. You had fought side by side for years. Not all of them were friends, but they were family. The only family you had.

The gateman hammered ice off the windlass. Shrieking its protests, the portcullis rose. As Company historian I could go greet Elmo without violating the unwritten rules. Fool that I am, I went out into the wind and chill.

A sorry lot of shadows loomed through the blowing snow. The ponies were dragging. Their riders slumped over icy manes. Animals and men hunched into themselves, trying to escape the wind's scratching talons. Clouds of breath smoked from mounts and men, and were ripped away. This, in painting form, would have made a snowman shiver.

Of the whole Company only Raven ever saw snow before this winter. Some welcome to service with the Lady.

The riders came closer. They looked more like refugees than brothers of the Black Company. Ice-diamonds twinkled in Elmo's mustache. Rags concealed the rest of his face. The others were so bundled I could not tell who was who. Only Silent rode resolutely tall. He peered straight ahead, disdaining that pitiless wind.

Elmo nodded as he came through the gate. "We'd started to wonder," I said. Wonder means worry. The rules demand a show of indifference.

"Hard travelling."

"How'd it go?"

"Black Company twenty-three, Rebel zip. No work for you, Croaker, except Jo-Jo has a little frostbite."

"You get Raker?"

Raker's dire prophecies, skilled witchcraft, and battlefield cunning had made a fool of the Limper. The Salient had been ready to collapse before the Lady ordered us to take over. The move had sent shock waves throughout the empire. A mercenary captain had been assigned forces and powers usually reserved for one of the Ten!

Salient winter being what it was, only a shot at Raker himself made the Captain field this patrol.

Elmo bared his face and grinned. He was not talking. He would just have to tell it again for the Captain.

I considered Silent. No smile on his long, dreary face. He responded with a slight jerk of his head. So. Another victory that amounted to failure. Raker had escaped again. Maybe he would send us scampering after the Limper, squeaking mice who had grown too bold and challenged the cat.

Still, chopping twenty-three men out of the regional Rebel hierarchy counted for something. Not a bad day's work, in fact. Better than any the Limper turned in.

Men came for the patrol's ponies. Others set out mulled wine and warm food in the main hall. I stuck with Elmo and Silent. Their tale would get told soon enough.

Meystrikt's main hall is only slightly less draughty than its quarters. I treated Jo-Jo. The others attacked their meals. Feast complete, Elmo, Silent, One-Eye, and Knuckles convened around a small table. Cards materialized. One-Eye scowled my way. "Going to stand there with your thumb in your butt, Croaker? We need a mark."

One-Eye is at least a hundred years old. The Annals mention the wizened little black man's volcanic tempers throughout the last century. There is no telling when he joined. Seventy years' worth of Annals were lost when the Company's positions were overrun at the Battle of Urban. One-Eye refuses to illuminate the missing years. He says he does not believe in history.

Elmo dealt. Five cards to each player and a hand to an empty chair. "Croaker!" One-Eye snapped. "You going to squat?"

"Nope. Sooner or later Elmo is going to talk." I tapped my pen against my teeth.

One-Eye was in rare form. Smoke poured out of his ears. A screaming bat popped out of his mouth.

"He seems annoyed," I observed. The others grinned. Baiting One-Eye is a favorite pastime.

One-Eye hates field work. And hates missing out even more. Elmo's grins and Silent's benevolent glances convinced him he had missed something good.

Elmo redistributed his cards, peered at them from inches away. Silent's eyes glittered. No doubt about it. They had a special surprise.

Raven took the seat they had offered me. No one objected. Even One-Eye never objects to anything Raven decides to do.

Raven. Colder than our weather since Oar. A dead soul now, maybe. He can make a man shudder with a glance. He exudes a stench of the grave. And yet, Darling loves him. Pale, frail, ethereal, she kept one hand on his shoulder while he ordered his cards. She smiled for him.

Raven is an asset in any game including One-Eye. One-Eye cheats. But never when Raven is playing.

She stands in the Tower, gazing northward. Her delicate hands are clasped before Her. A breeze steals softly through Her window. It stirs the midnight silk of Her hair. Tear diamonds sparkle on the gentle curve of Her cheek."

"Hoo-wee!"

"Oh, wow!"

"Author! Author!"

"May a sow litter in your bedroll, Willie." Those characters got a howl out of my fantasies about the Lady.

The sketches are a game I play with myself. Hell, for all they know, my inventions might be on the mark. Only the Ten Who Were Taken ever see the Lady. Who knows if she is ugly, beautiful, or what?

"Tear diamonds sparkling, eh?" One-Eye said. "I like that. Figure she's pining for you, Croaker?"

"Knock it off. I don't make fun of your games."

The Lieutenant entered, seated himself, regarded us with a black scowl. Lately his mission in life has been to disapprove.

His advent meant the Captain was on his way. Elmo folded his hand, composed himself.

The place fell silent. Men appeared as if by magic. "Bar the damned door!" One-Eye muttered. "They keep stumbling in like this, I'll freeze my ass off. Play the hand out, Elmo."

The Captain came in, took his usual seat. "Let's hear it, Sergeant."

The Captain is not one of our more colorful characters. Too quiet. Too serious.

Elmo laid his cards down, tapped their edges into alignment, ordered his thoughts. He can become obsessed with brevity and precision.

"Sergeant?"

"Silent spotted a picket line south of the farm, Captain. We circled north. Attacked after sunset. They tried to scatter. Silent distracted Raker while we handled the others. Thirty men. We got twenty-three. We yelled a lot about not letting our spy get hurt. We missed Raker."

Sneaky makes this outfit work. We want the Rebel to believe his ranks are shot with informers. That hamstrings his communications and decision-making, and makes life less chancy for Silent, One-Eye, and Goblin.

The planted rumor. The small frame. The touch of bribery or blackmail. Those are the best weapons. We opt battle only when we have our opponents mousetrapped. At least ideally.

"You returned directly to the fortress?"

"Yes sir. After burning the farmhouse and outbuildings. Raker concealed his trail well."

The Captain considered the smoke-darkened beams overhead. Only One-Eye's snapping of his cards broke the silence. The Captain dropped his gaze. "Then, pray, why are you and Silent grinning like a pair of prize fools?"

One-Eye muttered, "Proud they came home empty-handed."

Elmo grinned some more. "But we didn't."

Silent dug inside his filthy shirt, produced the small leather bag that always hangs on a thong around his neck. His trick bag. It is filled with noxious oddments like putrified bat's ears or elixir of nightmare. This time he produced a folded piece of paper. He cast dramatic glances at One-Eye and Goblin, opened the packet fold by fold. Even the Captain left his seat, crowded the table.

"Behold!" said Elmo.

Tain't nothing but hair." Heads shook. Throats grumbled. Somebody questioned Elmo's grasp on reality. But One-Eye and Goblin had three big coweyes between them. One-Eye chirruped inarticulately. Goblin squeaked a few times, but, then, Goblin always squeaks. "Is it really his?" he managed at last. "Really his?"

Elmo and Silent radiated the smugness of eminently successful conquistadors. "Absodamnlutely," Elmo said. "Right off the top of his bean. We had that old man by the balls and he knew it. He was heeling and toeing it out of there so fast he smacked his noggin on a doorframe. Saw it myself, and so did Silent. Left these on the beam. Whoo, that gaffer can step."

And Goblin, an octave above his usual rusty hinge squall, dancing in his excitement, said, "Gents, we've got him. He's as good as hanging on a meathook right now. The big one." He meowed at One-Eye. "What do you think of that, you sorry little spook?"

A herd of minuscule lightning bugs poured out of One-Eye's nostrils. Good soldiers all, they fell into formation, spelling out the words *Goblin is a Poof.* Their little wings hummed the words for the benefit of the illiterate.

There is no truth to that canard. Goblin is thoroughly heterosexual. One-Eye was trying to start something.

Goblin made a gesture. A great shadow-figure, like Soulcatcher but tall enough to brush the ceiling beams, bent and skewered One-Eye with an accusing finger. A sourceless voice whispered, "It was you that corrupted the lad, sodder."

One-Eye snorted, shook his head, shook his head and snorted. His eye glazed. Goblin giggled, stifled himself, giggled again. He spun away, danced a wild victory jig in front of the fireplace.

Our less intuitive brethren grumbled. A couple of hairs. With those and two bits silver you could get rolled by the village whores.

"Gentlemen!" The Captain understood.

The shadow-show ceased. The Captain considered his wizards. He thought. He paced. He nodded to himself. Finally, he asked, "One-Eye. Are they enough?"

One-Eye chuckled, an astonishingly deep sound for so small a man. "One hair, sir, or one nail paring, is enough. Sir, we have him."

Goblin continued his weird dance. Silent kept grinning. Raving lunatics, the lot of them.

The Captain thought some more. "We can't handle this ourselves." He circled the hall, his pacing portentous. "We'll have to bring in one of the Taken."

One of the Taken. Naturally. Our three sorcerers are our most precious resource. They must be protected. But. . . . Cold stole in and froze us into statues. One of the Lady's shadow disciples. . . . One of those dark lords here? No. . . .

"Not the Limper. He's got a hard-on for us."

"Shifter gives me the creeps."

"Nightcrawler is worse."

"How the hell do you know? You never seen him."

One-Eye said, "We can handle it, Captain."

"And Raker's cousins would be on you like flies on a horseapple."

"Soulcatcher," the Lieutenant suggested. "He *is* our patron, more or less."

The suggestion carried. The Captain said, "Contact him, One-Eye. Be ready to move when he gets here."

One-Eye nodded, grinned. He was in love. Already, tricky, nasty plots were afoot in his twisted mind.

It should have been Silent's game, really. The Captain gave it to One-Eye because he cannot come to grips with Silent's refusal to talk. That scares him for some reason.

Silent did not protest.

Some of our native servants are spies. We know who they are, thanks to One-Eye and Goblin. One, who knew nothing about the hair, was allowed to flee with the news that we were setting up an espionage headquarters in the free city Roses.

When you have the smaller battalions you learn guile.

* * *

Every ruler makes enemies. The Lady is no exception. The Sons of the White Rose are everywhere. . . . If one chooses sides on emotion, then the Rebel is the guy to go with. He is fighting for everything men claim to honor: freedom, independence, truth, the right. . . . All the subjective illusions, all the eternal trigger-words. We are minions of the villain of the piece. We confess the illusion and deny the substance.

There are no self-proclaimed villains, only regiments of self-proclaimed saints. Victorious historians rule where good or evil lies.

We abjure labels. We fight for money and an indefinable pride. The politics, the ethics, the moralities, are irrelevant.

One-Eye had contacted Soulcatcher. He was coming. Goblin said the old spook howled with glee. He smelled a chance to raise his stock and scuttle that of the Limper. The Ten squabble and backbite worse than spoiled children.

Winter relaxed its siege briefly. The men and native staff began clearing Meystrikt's courtyards. One of the natives disappeared. In the main hall, One-Eye and Silent looked smug over their cards. The Rebel was being told exactly what they wanted.

"What's happening on the wall?" I asked. Elmo had rigged block and tackle and was working a crennel stone loose. "What're you going to do with that block?"

"A little sculpture, Croaker. I've taken up a new hobby."

"So don't tell me. See if I care."

"Take that attitude if you want. I was going to ask if you could go after Raker with us. So you could put it in the Annals right."

"With a word about One-Eye's genius?"

"Credit where credit is due, Croaker."

"Then Silent is due a chapter, isn't he?"

He sputtered. He grumbled. He cursed. "You want to play a hand?" They had only three players, one of whom was Raven. Tonk is more interesting with four or five.

I won three hands straight.

"Don't you have anything to do? A wart to cut off, or something?"

"You asked him to play," a kibbitzing soldier observed.

"You like flies, Otto?"

"Flies?"

"Going to turn you into a frog if you don't shut your mouth."

Otto was not impressed. "You couldn't turn a tadpole into a frog."

I snickered. "You asked for it, One-Eye. When is Soulcatcher going to show?"

"When he gets here."

I nodded. There is no apparent rhyme or reason to the way the Taken do things. "Regular Cheerful Charlies today, aren't we? How much has he lost, Otto?"

Otto just smirked.

Raven won the next two hands.

One-Eye swore off talking. So much for discovering the nature of his project. Probably for the best. An explanation never made could not be overheard by the Rebel's spies.

Six hairs and a block of limestone. What the hell?

For days Silent, Goblin, and One-Eye took turns working that stone. I visited the stable occasionally. They let me watch, and growl when they would not answer questions.

The Captain, too, sometimes poked his head in, shrugged, and went back to his quarters. He was juggling strategies for a spring campaign which would throw all available Imperial might against the Rebel. His rooms were impenetrable, so thick were the maps and reports.

We meant to hurt the Rebel some once the weather turned.

Cruel it may be, but most of us enjoy what we do—and the Captain more than anyone. This is a favorite game, matching wits with a Raker. He is blind to the dead, to the burning villages, to the starving children. As is the Rebel. Two blind armies, able to see nothing but one another.

Soulcatcher came in the deep hours, amidst a blizzard which beggared the one Elmo endured. The wind wailed and howled. Snow drifted against the northeast corner of the fortress, battlement-high, and spilled over. Wood and hay stores were becoming a concern. Locals said it was the worst blizzard in history.

At its height, Soulcatcher came. The boom-boom-boom of his knock awakened all Meystrikt. Horns sounded. Drums rolled. The gatehouse watch screeched against the wind. They could not open the gate.

Soulcatcher came over the wall via the drift. He fell, nearly vanished in the loose snow in the forecourt. Hardly a dignified arrival for one of the Ten.

I hurried to the main hall. One-Eye, Silent, and Goblin were there already, with the fire blazing merrily. The Lieutenant appeared, followed by the Captain. Elmo and Raven came with the Captain. "Send the rest back to bed," the Lieutenant snapped.

Soulcatcher came in, removed a heavy black greatcloak, squatted before the fire. A calculatedly human gesture? I wondered.

Soulcatcher's slight body is always sheathed in black leather. He wears that head-hiding black morion, and the black gloves and black boots. Only a couple of silver badges break the monotony. The only color about him is the uncut ruby forming the pommel of his dagger. A five-taloned claw clutches the gem to the handle of the weapon.

Small, soft curves interrupt the flatness of Soulcatcher's chest. There is a feminine flair to his hips and legs. Three of the Taken are female, but which are which only the Lady knows. We call them all he. Their sex won't ever mean a thing to us.

Soulcatcher claims to be our friend, our champion. Even so, his presence brought a different chill to the hall. The cold of him has nothing to do with climate. Even One-Eye shivers when he is around.

And Raven? I do not know. Raven seems incapable of feeling anymore, except where Darling is concerned. Someday that great stone face is going to break. I hope I am there to see it.

Soulcatcher turned his back to the fire. "So." High-pitched. "Fine weather for an adventure." Baritone. Strange sounds followed. Laughter. The Taken had made a joke.

Nobody laughed.

We were not supposed to laugh. Soulcatcher turned to One-Eye. "Tell me." This in tenor, slow and soft, with a muffled quality, as if it were coming through a thin wall. Or, as Elmo says, from beyond the grave.

There was no bluster or showman in One-Eye now. "We'll start from the beginning. Captain?"

The Captain said, "One of our informants caught wind of a meeting of the Rebel captains. One-Eye, Goblin, and Silent followed the movements of known Rebels. . . ."

"You let them run around loose?"

"They lead us to their friends."

"Of course. One of the Limper's shortcomings. No imagination. He kills them where he finds them—along with everyone else in sight." Again that weird laughter. "Less effective, yes?" There was another sentence, but in no language I know.

The Captain nodded. "Elmo?"

Elmo told his part as he had before, word for word. He passed the tale to One-Eye, who sketched a scheme for taking Raker. I did not understand, but Soulcatcher caught it instantly. He laughed a third time.

I gathered we were going to unleash the dark side of human nature.

One-Eye took Soulcatcher to see his mystery stone. We moved closer to the fire. Silent produced a deck. There were no takers.

Sometimes I wonder how the regulars stay sane. They are around the Taken all the time. Soulcatcher is a sweetheart compared to the others.

One-Eye and Soulcatcher returned, laughing. "Two of a kind," Elmo muttered, in a rare statement of opinion.

Soulcatcher recaptured the fire. "Well done, gentlemen. Very well done. Imaginative. This could break them in the Salient. We start for Roses when the weather breaks. A party of eight, Captain, including two of your witch men." Each sentence was followed by a break. Each was in a different voice. Weird.

I have heard those are the voices of all the people whose souls Soulcatcher has caught.

Bolder than my wont, I volunteered for the expedition. I wanted to see how Raker could be taken with hair and a block of limestone. The Limper had failed with all his furious power.

The Captain thought about it. "Okay, Croaker. One-Eye and Goblin. You, Elmo. And pick two more."

"That's only seven, Captain."

"Raven makes eight."

"Oh. Raven. Of course."

Of course. Quiet, deadly Raven would be the Captain's alter ego. The bond between those men surpasses understanding. Guess it bothers me because Raven scares the hell out of me lately.

Raven caught the Captain's eye. His right eyebrow rose. The Captain replied with a ghost of a nod. Raven twitched a shoulder. What was the message? I could not guess.

Something unusual was in the wind. Those in the know found it delicious. Though I could not guess what it was, I knew it would be slick and nasty.

The storm broke. Soon the Roses road was open. Soulcatcher fretted. Raker had two weeks start. It would take us a week to reach Roses. One-Eye's planted tales might lose their efficacy before we arrived.

We left before dawn, the limestone block aboard a wagon. The wizards had done little but carve out a modest declivity the size of a large melon. I could not fathom its value. One-Eye and Goblin fussed over it like grooms over new brides. One-Eye answered my questions with a big grin. Bastard.

The weather held fair. Warm winds blew out of the south. We encountered long stretches of muddy road. And I witnessed an outrageous phenomenon. Soulcatcher got down in the mud and dragged that wagon with the rest of us. That great lord of the empire.

Roses is the queen city of the Salient, a teeming sprawl, a free city, a republic. The Lady has not seen fit to revoke its traditional autonomy. The world needs places where men of all stripes and stations can step outside the usual strictures.

So. Roses. Owning no master. Filled with agents and spies and those who live on the dark side of the law. In that environment, One-Eye claimed, his scheme had to prosper.

Roses' red walls loomed over us, dark as old blood in the light of the setting sun, when we arrived.

Goblin ambled into the room we had taken. "I found the place," he squeaked at One-Eye.

"Good."

Curious. They had not exchanged a cross word in weeks. Usually an hour without a squabble was a miracle.

Soulcatcher shifted in the shadowed corner where he remained planted like a lean black bush, a crowd softly debating with itself. "Go on."

"It's an old public square. A dozen alleys and streets going in and out. Poorly lighted at night. No reason for any traffic after dark."

"Sounds perfect," One-Eye said.

"It is. I rented a room overlooking it."

"Let's take a look," Elmo said. We all suffered from cabin fever. An exodus started. Only Soulcatcher stayed put. Perhaps he understood our need to get away.

Goblin was right about the square, apparently. "So what?" I asked. One-Eye grinned. I snapped, "Clam-lips! Play games."

"Tonight?" Goblin asked.

One-Eye nodded. "If the old spook says go."

"I'm getting frustrated," I announced. "What's going on? All you clowns do is play cards and watch Raven sharpen his knives." That went on for hours at a time, the movement of whetstone across steel sending chills down my spine. It was an omen. Raven does not do that unless he expects the situation to get nasty.

One-Eye made a sound like a cawing crow.

We rolled the wagon at midnight. The stablekeeper called us madmen. One-Eye gave him one of his famous grins. He drove. The rest of us walked, surrounding the wagon.

There had been changes. Something had been added. Someone had incised the stone with a message. One-Eye, probably, during one of his unexplained forays out of headquarters.

Bulky leather sacks and a stout plank table had joined the stone. The table looked capable of bearing the block. Its legs were of a dark, polished wood. Inlaid in them were symbols in silver and ivory, very complex, hieroglyphical, mystical.

"Where did you get the table?" I asked. Goblin squeaked, laughed. I growled, "Why the hell can't you tell me now?"

"Okay," One-Eye said, chuckling nastily. "We made it."

"What for?"

"To sit our rock on."

"You're not telling me anything."

"Patience, Croaker. All in due time." Bastard.

There was a strangeness about our square. It was foggy. There had been no fog anywhere else.

One-Eye stopped the wagon in the square's center. "Out with that table, boys."

"Out with you," Goblin squawked. "Think you can malinger your way through this?" He wheeled on Elmo. "Damned old cripple's always got an excuse."

"He's got a point, One-Eye." One-Eye protested. Elmo snapped, "Get your butt down off there."

One-Eye glared at Goblin. "Going to get you someday, Chubbo. Curse of impotence. How does that sound?"

Goblin was not impressed. "I'd put a curse of stupidity on you if I could improve on Nature."

"Get the damned table down," Elmo snapped.

"You nervous?" I asked. He never gets riled at their fussing. Treats it as part of the entertainment.

"Yeah. You and Raven get up there and push."

That table was heavier than it looked. It took all of us to get it off the wagon. One-Eye's faked grunts and curses did not help. I asked him how he got it on.

"Built it there, dummy," he said, then fussed at us, wanting it moved a half inch this way, then a half inch that.

"Let it be," Soulcatcher said. "We don't have time for this." His displeasure had a salutary effect. Neither Goblin nor One-Eye said another word.

We slid the stone onto the table. I stepped back, wiped sweat from my face. I was soaked. In the middle of winter. That rock radiated heat.

"The bags," Soulcatcher said. That voice sounded like a woman I would not mind meeting.

I grabbed one, grunted. It was heavy. "Hey. This is money."

One-Eye snickered. I heaved the sack into the pile under the table. A damned fortune there. I had never seen so much in one place, in fact.

"Cut the bags," Soulcatcher ordered. "Hurry it up!"

Raven slashed the sacks. Treasure dribbled onto the cobblestones. We stared, lusting in our hearts.

Soulcatcher caught One-Eye's shoulder, took Goblin's arm. Both wizards seemed to shrink. They faced table and stone. Soulcatcher said, "Move the wagon."

I still had not read the immortal message they had carved on the rock. I darted in for a look.

LET HE WHO WOULD CLAIM THIS WEALTH
SEAT THE HEAD OF THE CREATURE
RAKER
WITHIN THIS THRONE OF STONE

Ah. Aha. Plainspoken. Straightforward. Simple. Just our style. Ha.

I stepped back, tried to guess the magnitude of Soulcatcher's investment. I spied gold amidst the hill of silver. One bag leaked uncut gems.

"The hair," Soulcatcher demanded. One-Eye produced the strands. Soulcatcher thumbed them into the walls of the head-sized cavity. He stepped back, joined hands with One-Eye and Goblin.

They made magic.

Treasure, table, and stone began to shed a golden glow.

Our archfoe was a dead man. Half the world would try to collect this bounty. It was too big to resist. His own people would turn on him.

I saw one slim chance for him. He could steal the treasure himself. Tough job, though. No Rebel Prophet could out-magic one of the Taken.

They completed their spell-casting. "Somebody test it," One-Eye said.

There was a vicious crackle when Raven's daggertip pricked the plane of the tablelegs. He cursed, scowled at his weapon. Elmo thrust with his sword. *Crackle!* The tip of his blade glowed white.

"Excellent," Soulcatcher said. "Take the wagon away."

Elmo detailed a man. The rest of us fled to the room Goblin had rented.

At first we crowded the window, willing something to happen. That palled fast. Roses did not discover the doom we had set for Raker till sunrise.

Cautious entrepreneurs found a hundred ways to go after that money. Crowds came just to see. One enterprising band started tearing up the street to dig under. Police ran them off.

Soulcatcher took a seat beside the window and never moved. Once he told me, "Have to modify the spells. I didn't anticipate this much ingenuity."

Surprised at my own audacity, I asked, "What's the Lady like?" I had just finished one of my fantasy sketches.

He turned slowly, stared briefly. "Something that will bite steel." His voice was female and catty. An odd answer. Then, "Have to keep them from using tools."

So much for getting an eyewitness report. I should have known better. We mortals are mere objects to the Taken. Our curiosities are of supreme indifference. I retreated to my secret kingdom and its spectrum of imaginary Ladies.

Soulcatcher modified the ward sorceries that night. Next morning there were corpses in the square.

One-Eye wakened me the third night. "Got a customer."

"Hunh?"

"A guy with a head." He was pleased.

I stumbled to the window. Goblin and Raven were there already. We crowded one side. Nobody wanted to get too close to Soulcatcher.

A man stole across the square below. A head dangled from his left hand. He carried it by its hair. I said, "I wondered how long it would be before this started."

"Silence," Soulcatcher hissed. "He's out there."

"Who?"

He was patient. Remarkably patient. Another of the Taken would have struck me down. "Raker. Don't give us away."

I do not know how he knew. Maybe I would not want to find out. Those things scare me.

"A sneak visit was in the scenario," Goblin whispered, squeaking. How can he squeak when he whispers? "Raker *has* to find out what he's up against. He can't do that from anywhere else." The fat little man seemed proud.

The Captain calls human nature our sharpest blade. Curiosity and a will to survive drew Raker into our cauldron. Maybe he would turn it on us. We have a lot of handles sticking out ourselves.

Weeks passed. Raker came again and again, apparently content to observe. Soulcatcher told us to let him be, no matter how easy a target he made of himself.

Our mentor might be considerate of us, but he has his cruel streak. It seemed he wanted to torment Raker with the uncertainty of his fate.

"This berg is going bounty-crazy," Goblin squealed. He danced one of his jigs. "You ought to get out more, Croaker. They're turning Raker into an industry." He beckoned me into the corner farthest from Soulcatcher, opened a wallet. "Look here," he whispered.

He had a double fistful of coins. Some were gold. I observed, "You're going to be walking tilted to one side."

He grinned. Goblin grinning is a sight to behold. "Made this selling tips on where to find Raker," he whispered. With a glance toward Soulcatcher, "Bogus tips." He put a hand on my shoulder. He had to stretch up to do it. "You can get rich out there."

"I didn't know we were in this to get rich."

He scowled, his round, pale face becoming all wrinkles. "What are you? Some kind of . . .?"

Soulcatcher turned. Goblin croaked, "Just an argument about a bet, sir. Just a bet."

I laughed aloud. "Really convincing, Chubbo. Why not just hang yourself?"

He pouted, but not for long. Goblin is irrepressible. His humor breaks through in the most depressing situations. He whispered, "Shit, Croaker, you should see what One-Eye is doing. Selling amulets. Guaranteed to tell if there's a Rebel close by." A glance toward Soulcatcher. "They really work, too. Sort of."

I shook my head. "At least he'll be able to pay his card debts." That was One-Eye all over. He had had it rough at Meystrikt, where there was no room for his usual forays into the black market.

"You guys are supposed to be planting rumors. Keeping the pot boiling, not. . . ."

"Sshh!" He glanced at Soulcatcher again. "We are. Every dive in town. Hell, the rumor mill is berserk out there. Come on. I'll show you."

"No." Soulcatcher was talking more and more. I had hopes of inveigling a real conversation.

"Your loss. I know a bookmaker taking bets on when Raker will lose his head. You got inside dope, you know."

"Scoot out of here before you lose yours."

I went to the window. A minute later Goblin scampered across the square below. He passed our trap without glancing its way.

"Let them play their games," Soulcatcher said.

"Sir?" My new approach. Brown-nosing.

"My ears are sharper than your friend realizes."

I searched the face of that black morion, trying to capture some hint of the thoughts behind the metal.

"It's of no consequence." He shifted slightly, stared past me. "The underground is paralyzed by dismay."

"Sir?"

"The mortar in that house is rotting. It'll crumble soon. That would not have happened had we taken Raker immediately. They would have made a martyr of him. The loss would have saddened them, but they would have gone on. The Circle would have replaced Raker in time for the spring campaigns."

I stared into the plaza. Why was Soulcatcher telling me this? And all in one voice. Was it the voice of the real Soulcatcher?

"Because you thought I was being cruel for cruelty's sake."

I jumped. "How did you . . .?"

Soulcatcher made a sound which passed as laughter. "No. I didn't read your mind. I know how minds work. I am the Catcher of Souls, remember?"

Do the Taken get lonely? Do they yearn for simple companionship? Friendship?

"Sometimes." This in one of the female voices. A seductive one.

I half-turned, then faced the square quickly, frightened.

Soulcatcher read that, too. He went back to Raker. "Simple elimination was never my plan. I want the hero of Forsberg to discredit himself."

Soulcatcher knew our enemy better than we suspected. Raker was playing his game. Already he had made two spectacular, vain attempts on our trap. Those failures had ruined his stock with fellow-travellers. To hear tell, Roses seethed with pro-Empire sentiment.

"He'll make a fool of himself, then we'll squash him. Like a noxious beetle."

"Don't underestimate him." What audacity. Giving advice to one of the Taken. "The Limper. . . ."

"That I won't do. I'm not the Limper. He and Raker are two of a kind. In the old times. . . . The Dominator would have made him one of us."

"What was he like?" Get him talking, Croaker. From the Dominator it is only one step to the Lady.

Soulcatcher's right hand rolled palm upward, opened, slowly made a claw. The gesture rattled me. I imagined that claw ripping at my soul. End of conversation.

Later on I told Elmo, "You know, that thing out there didn't have to be real. Anything would have done the job if the mob couldn't get to it."

Soulcatcher said, "Wrong. Raker had to know it was real."

Next morning we heard from the Captain. News, mostly. A few Rebel partisans were surrendering their weapons in response to an amnesty offer. Some mainforcers who had come south with Raker were pulling out. The confusion had reached the Circle. Raker's failure in Roses worried them.

"Why's that?" I asked. "Nothing has really happened."

Soulcatcher replied, "It's happening on the other side. In people's minds." Was there a hint of smugness there? "Raker, and by extension the Circle, looks impotent. He should have yielded the Salient to another commander."

"If I was a bigtime general, I probably wouldn't admit to a screwup either," I said.

"Croaker," Elmo gasped, amazed. I do not speak my mind, usually.

"It's true, Elmo. Can you picture any general—ours or theirs—asking somebody to take over for him?"

That black morion faced me. "Their faith is dying. An army without faith in itself is beaten more surely than an army defeated in battle." When Soulcatcher gets on a subject nothing deflects him.

I had a funny feeling he might be the type to yield command to someone better able to exercise it.

"We tighten the screws now. All of you. Tell it in the taverns. Whisper it in the streets. Burn him. Drive him. Push him so hard he doesn't have time to think. I want him so desperate he tries something stupid."

I thought Soulcatcher had the right idea. This fragment of the Lady's war would not be won on any battlefield. Spring was at hand, yet fighting had not yet begun. The eyes of the Salient were locked on the free city, awaiting the outcome of this duel between Raker and the Lady's champion.

Soulcatcher observed, "It's no longer necessary to kill Raker. His credibility is dead. Now we're destroying the confidence of his movement." He resumed his vigil at the window.

Elmo said, "Captain says the Circle ordered Raker out. He wouldn't go."

"He revolted against his own revolution?"

"He wants to beat this trap."

Another facet of human nature working for our side. Overweening pride.

"Get some cards out. Goblin and One-Eye have been robbing widows and orphans again. Time to clean them out."

Raker was on his own, hunted, haunted, a whipped dog running the alleys of the night. He could trust no one. I felt sorry for him. Almost.

He was a fool. Only a fool keeps betting against the odds. The odds against Raker were getting longer by the hour.

I jerked a thumb at the darkness near the window. "Sounds like a convening of the Brotherhood of Whispers."

Raven glanced over my shoulder, said nothing. We were playing head to head Tonk, a dull time-killer of a game.

A dozen voices murmured over there. "I smell it." "You're wrong." "It's in from the south." "End it now." "Not yet." "It's time." "Needs a while longer." "Pushing our luck. The game could turn." " 'Ware pride." "It's here. The stench of it runs before it like the breath of a jackal."

"Wonder if he ever loses an argument with himself?"

Still Raven said nothing. In my more daring moods I have been trying to draw him out. Without luck. I was doing better with Soulcatcher.

Soulcatcher rose suddenly, an angry noise rising from deep inside him.

"What is it?" I asked. I was tired of Roses. I was disgusted with Roses. Roses bored and frightened me. It was worth a man's life to go into those streets alone.

One of those spook voices was right. We were approaching a point of diminishing returns. I was developing a grudging admiration for Raker myself. The man refused to surrender or run.

"What is it?" I asked again

"The Limper. He's in Roses."

"Here? Why?"

"He smells a big kill. He wants to steal the credit."

"You mean muscle in on our action?"

"That's his style."

"Wouldn't the Lady . . .?"

"This is Roses. She's a long way off. And she doesn't care who gets him."

Politics among the Lady's viceroys. It is a strange world. I do not understand people outside the Company.

We lead a simple life. No thinking required. The Captain takes care of that. We just follow orders. For most of us the Black Company is a hiding place, a refuge from yesterday, a place to become a new man.

"What do we do?" I asked.

"I'll handle the Limper." He began seeing to his apparel.

Goblin and One-Eye staggered in. They were so drunk they had to prop each other up. "Shit," Goblin squeaked. "Snowing again. Goddamned snow. I thought winter was over."

One-Eye burst into song. Something about the beauties of winter. I could not follow him. His speech was slurred and he had forgotten half the words.

Goblin fell into a chair, forgetting One-Eye. One-Eye collapsed at his feet. He vomited on Goblin's boots, tried to continue his song. Goblin muttered, "Where the hell is everybody?"

"Out carousing around." I exchanged looks with Raven. "Do you believe this? Those two getting drunk together?"

"Where you going, old spook?" Goblin squeaked at Soulcatcher. Soulcatcher went out without answering. "Bastard. Hey. One-Eye, old buddy. That right? Old spook a bastard?"

One-Eye levered himself off the floor, looked around. I don't think he was seeing with the eye he had. "S'right." He scowled at me. "Bassard. All bassard." Something struck him funny. He giggled.

Goblin joined him. When Raven and I did not get the joke, he put on a very dignified face and said, "Not our kind in here, old buddy. Warmer out in the snow." He helped One-Eye stand. They staggered out the door.

"Hope they don't do anything stupid. More stupid. Like show off. They'll kill themselves."

"Tonk," Raven said. He spread his cards. Those two might not have come in for all the response he showed.

Ten or fifty hands later one of the soldiers we had brought burst in. "You seen Elmo?" he demanded.

I glanced at him. Snow was melting in his hair. He was pale, scared. "No. What happened, Hagop?"

"Somebody stabbed Otto. I think it was Raker. I run him off."

"Stabbed? He dead?" I started looking for my kit. Otto would need me more than he would need Elmo.

"No. He's cut bad. Lot of blood."

"Why didn't you bring him?"

"Couldn't carry him."

He was drunk too. The attack on his friend had sobered him some, but that would not last. "You sure it was Raker?" Was the old fool trying to hit back?

"Sure. Hey, Croaker. Come on. He's gonna die."

"I'm coming. I'm coming."

"Wait." Raven was pawing through his gear. "I'm going." He balanced a pair of finely-honed knives, debating a choice. He shrugged, stuck both inside his belt. "Get yourself a cloak, Croaker. It's cold out there."

While I found one he grilled Hagop about Otto's whereabouts, told him to stay put till Elmo showed. Then, "Let's go, Croaker."

Down the stairs. Into the streets. Raven's walk is deceptive. He never seems hurried, but you have to hustle to stay up.

Snowing was not the half of it. Even where the streets were lighted you could not see twenty feet. It was six inches deep already. Heavy, wet stuff. But the temperature was falling, and a wind was coming up. Another blizzard? Damn! Hadn't we had enough?

We found Otto a quarter block from where he was supposed to be. He had dragged himself under some steps. Raven went right to him. How he knew where to look I will never know. We carried Otto to the nearest light. He could not help himself. He was out.

I snorted. "Dead drunk. Only danger was freezing to death." He had blood all over him but his wound was not bad. Needed some stitches, that is all. We lugged him back to the room. I stripped him and got sewing while he was in no shape to bitch.

Otto's sidekick was asleep. Raven kicked him till he woke up. "I want the truth," Raven said. "How did it happen?"

Hagop told it, insisting, "It was Raker, man. It was Raker."

I doubted that. So did Raven. But when I finished my needlepoint, Raven said, "Get your sword, Croaker." He had the hunter look. I did not want to go out again, but even less did I want to argue with Raven when he was in that mood. I got my swordbelt.

The air was colder. The wind was stronger. The snowflakes were smaller and more biting when they hit my cheek. I stalked along behind Raven, wondering what the hell we were doing.

He found the place where Otto was knifed. New snow had not yet obliterated the marks on the old. Raven squatted, stared. I wondered what he saw. There was not enough light to tell anything, so far as I could see.

"Maybe he wasn't lying," he said at last. He stared into the darkness of the alley whence the attacker had come.

"How do you know?"

He did not tell me. "Come on." He stalked into the alley.

I do not like alleys. I especially do not like them in cities like Roses, where they harbor every evil known to man, and probably a few still undiscovered. But Raven was going in. . . . Raven wanted my help. . . . Raven was my brother in the Black Company. . . . But, damn, a hot fire and warm wine would have been nicer.

I do not think I spent more than three or four hours exploring the city. Raven had gone out less than I had. Yet he seemed to know where he was going. He led me up side streets and down alleys, across thoroughfares and over bridges. Roses is pierced by three rivers, and a web of canals connect them. The bridges are one of Roses' claims to fame.

Bridges did not intrigue me at the moment. I was preoccupied with keeping up and trying to stay warm. My feet were hunks of ice. Snow kept getting into my boots, and Raven was in no mood to stop every time that happened.

On and on. Miles and hours. I never saw so many slums and stews. . . .

"Stop!" Raven flung an arm across my path.

"What?"

"Quiet." He listened. I listened. I did not hear a thing. I had not seen much during our headlong rush, either. How could Raven be tracking Otto's assailant? I did not doubt that he was, I just could not figure it.

Truth told, nothing Raven did surprised me. Nothing had since the day I watched him strangle his wife.

"We're almost up with him." He peered into the blowing snow. "Go straight ahead, the pace we've been going. You'll catch him in a couple blocks."

"What? Where're you going?" I was carping at a fading shadow. "Damn you." I took a deep breath, cursed again, drew my sword, and started forward. All I could think was, How am I going to explain if we've got the wrong man?

Then I saw him in the light from a tavern door. A tall, lean man shuffling dispiritedly, oblivious to his surroundings. Raker? How would I know? Elmo and Otto were the only ones who had been along on the farm raid. . . .

Came the dawn. Only they could identify Raker for the rest of us. Otto was wounded and Elmo had not been heard from. . . . Where was he? Under a blanket of snow in some alley, cold as this hideous night?

My fright retreated before anger.

I sheathed my sword and drew a dagger. I kept it hidden inside my cloak. The figure ahead did not glance back as I overtook it, drew even.

"Rough night, eh, old-timer?"

He grunted noncommittally. Then he looked at me, eyes narrowing, when I fell into step beside him. He eased away, watched me closely. There was no fear in his eyes. He was sure of himself. Not the sort of old man you found wandering the streets of the slums. They are scared of their own shadows.

"What do you want?" It was a calm, straightforward question.

He did not have to be frightened. I was scared enough for both of us. "You knifed a friend of mine, Raker."

He halted. A glint of something strange showed in his eye. "The Black Company?"

I nodded.

He stared, eyes narrowing thoughtfully. "The physician. You're the physician. The one they call Croaker."

"Glad to meet you." I am sure my voice sounded stronger than I felt.

I thought, what the hell do I do now?

Raker flung his cloak open. A short stabbing sword thrust my way. I slid aside, opened my own cloak, dodged again and tried to draw my sword.

Raker froze. He caught my eye. His eyes seemed to grow larger, larger. . . . I was falling into twin grey pools. . . . A smile tugged at the corners of his mouth. He stepped toward me, blade rising. . . .

And grunted suddenly. A look of total amazement came over his face. I shook his spell, stepped back, came to guard.

Raker turned slowly, faced the darkness. Raven's knife protruded from his back. Raker reached back and withdrew it. A mewl of pain passed his lips. He glared at the knife, then, ever so slowly, began to sing.

"Move, Croaker!"

A spell! Fool! I had forgotten what Raker was. I charged.

Raven arrived at the same instant.

I looked at the body. "Now what?"

Raven knelt, produced another knife. It had a serrated edge. "Somebody claims Soulcatcher's bounty."

"He'd have a fit."

"You going to tell him?"

"No. But what will we do with it?" There had been times when the Black Company was prosperous, but never when it was rich. Accumulation of wealth is not our purpose.

"I can use some of it. Old debts. The rest. . . . Divide it up. Send it back to Beryl. Whatever. It's there. Why let the Taken keep it?"

I shrugged. "Up to you. I just hope Soulcatcher won't think we crossed him."

"Only you and me know. I won't tell him." He brushed the snow off the old man's face. Raker was cooling fast.

Raven used his knife.

I am a physician. I have removed limbs. I am a soldier. I have seen some bloody battlefields. Nevertheless, I was queasy. Decapitating a dead man did not seem right.

Raven secured our grisly trophy inside his cloak. It did not bother him. Once, on the way to our part of town, I asked, "Why did we go after him, anyway?"

He did not answer immediately. Then, "The Captain's last letter said to get it over with if I had the chance."

As we neared the square, Raven said, "Go upstairs. See if the spook is there. If he's not, send the soberest man after our wagon. You come back here."

"Right." I sighed, hurried to our quarters. Anything for a little warmth.

The snow was a foot deep now. I was afraid my feet were permanently damaged.

"Where the hell have you been?" Elmo demanded when I stumbled through the doorway. "Where's Raven?"

I looked around. No Soulcatcher. Goblin and One-Eye were back, dead to the world. Otto and Hagop were snoring like giants. "How's Otto?"

"Doing all right. What've you been up to?"

I settled myself beside our fire, prized my boots off. My feet were blue and numb but not frozen. Soon they tingled painfully. My legs ached from all that walking through the snow, too. I told Elmo the whole story.

"You killed him?"

"Raven said the Captain wants done with the project."

"Yeah. I didn't figure Raven would go cut his throat."

"Where's Soulcatcher?"

"Hasn't been back." He grinned. "I'll get the wagon. Don't tell anybody else. Too many big mouths." He flung his cloak about his shoulders, stamped out.

My hands and feet felt halfway human. I scooted over and nabbed Otto's boots. He was about my size, and he did not need them.

Out into the night again. Morning, almost. Dawn was due soon.

If I expected any remonstrance from Raven I was disappointed. He just looked at me. I think he actually shivered. I remember thinking, maybe he is human after all. "Had to change my boots. Elmo is getting the wagon. The rest of them are passed out."

"Soulcatcher?"

"Not back yet."

"Let's plant this seed." He strode into the swirling flakes. I hurried after him.

The snow had not collected on our trap. It sat there glowing gold. Water puddled beneath it and trickled away to become ice.

"You think Soulcatcher will know when this thing gets discharged?" I asked.

"It's a good bet. Goblin and One-Eye, too."

"The place could burn down around those two and they wouldn't turn over."

"Nevertheless. . . . Sshh! Somebody out there. Go that way." He moved the other direction, circling.

What am I doing this for? I wondered as I skulked through the snow, weapon in hand. I ran into Raven. "See anything?"

He glared into the darkness. "Somebody was here." He sniffed the air, turned his head slowly right and left. He took a dozen quick steps, pointed down.

He was right. The trail was fresh. The departing half looked hurried. I stared at those marks. "I don't like it, Raven." Our visitor's spoor indicated that he dragged his right foot. "The Limper."

"We don't know for sure."

"Who else? Where's Elmo?"

We returned to the Raker trap, waited impatiently. Raven paced. He muttered. I could not recall ever having seen him this unsettled. Once, he said, "The Limper isn't Soulcatcher."

Really. Soulcatcher is almost human. Limper is the sort that enjoys tormenting babies.

A jangle of traces and squeak of poorly greased wheels entered the plaza. Elmo and the wagon appeared. Elmo pulled up and jumped down.

"Where the hell you been?" Fear and weariness made me cross.

"Takes time to dig out a stableboy and get a team ready. What's the matter? What happened?"

"The Limper was here."

"Oh, shit. What did he do?"

"Nothing. He just. . . ."

"Let's move," Raven snapped. "Before he comes back." He took the head to the stone. The wardspells might not have existed. He fitted our trophy into the waiting declivity. The golden glow winked out. Snowflakes began accumulating on head and stone.

"Let's go," Elmo gasped. "We don't have much time."

I grabbed a sack and heaved it into the wagon. Thoughtful Elmo had laid out a tarp to keep loose coins from dribbling between the floorboards.

Raven told me to rake up the loose stuff under the table. "Elmo, dump some of those sacks out and give them to Croaker."

They heaved bags. I scrambled after loose coins.

"One minute gone," Raven said. Half the bags were in the wagon.

"Too much loose stuff," I complained.

"We'll leave it if we have to."

"What're we going to do with it? How will we hide it?"

"In the hay in the stable," Raven said. "For now. Later we put a false bed in the wagon. Two minutes gone."

"What about wagon tracks?" Elmo asked. "He could follow them to the stable."

"Why should he care in the first place?" I wondered aloud.

Raven ignored me. He asked Elmo, "You didn't conceal them coming here?"

"Didn't think of it."

"Damn!"

All the sacks were aboard. Elmo and Raven helped with the loose stuff.

"Three minutes," Raven said, then, "Quiet!" He listened. "Soulcatcher couldn't be here already, could he? No. The Limper again. Come on. You drive, Elmo. Head for a thoroughfare. Lose us in traffic. I'll follow you. Croaker, go try to cover Elmo's backtrail."

"Where is he?" Elmo asked, staring into the falling snow.

Raven pointed. "We'll have to lose him. Or he'll take it away. Go on, Croaker. Get moving. Elmo."

"Get up!" Elmo snapped his traces. The wagon creaked away.

I ducked under the table and stuffed my pockets, then ran away from where Raven said the Limper was.

I do not know that I had much luck obscuring Elmo's backtrail. I think we were helped more by morning traffic than by anything I did. I did get rid of the stableboy. I gave him a sock full of gold and silver, more than he could make in years of stable work, and asked him if he could lose himself. Away from Roses, preferably. He told me, "I won't even stop to get my things." He dropped his pitchfork and headed out, never to be seen again.

I hied myself back to our room.

Everyone was sleeping but Otto. "Oh, Croaker," he said. " 'Bout time."

"Pain?"

"Yeah."

"Hangover?"

"That too."

"Let's see what we can do. How long you been awake?"

"An hour, I guess."

"Soulcatcher been here?"

"No. What happened to him, anyway?"

"I don't know."

"Hey. Those are my boots. What the hell do you think you're doing, wearing my boots?"

"Take it easy. Drink this."

He drank. "Come on. What're you doing wearing my boots?"

I removed the boots and set them near the fire, which had burned quite low. Otto kept after me while I added coal. "If you don't calm down you're going to rip your stitches."

I will say this for our people. They pay attention when my advice is medical. Angry as he was, he lay back, forced himself to lie still. He did not stop cussing me.

I shed my wet things and donned a nightshirt I found lying around. I do not know where it came from. It was too short. I put on a pot of tea, then turned to Otto. "Let's take a closer look." I dragged my kit over.

I was cleaning around the wound and Otto was cursing softly when I heard the sound. *Scrape-clump, scrape-clump.* It stopped outside the door.

Otto sensed my fear. "What's the matter?"

"It's. . . ." The door opened behind me. I glanced back. I had guessed right.

The Limper went to the table, dropped into a chair, surveyed the room. His gaze skewered me. I wondered if he recalled what I had done to him in Oar.

Inanely, I said, "I just started tea."

He stared at the wet boots and cloak, then at each man in the room. Then at me again.

The Limper is not big. Meeting him in the street, not knowing what he is, you would not be impressed. Like Soulcatcher, he wears a single color, a dingy brown. He was ragged. His face was concealed by a battered leather mask which drooped. Tangled threads of hair protruded from under his hood and around his mask. It was grey peppered with black.

He did not say a word. Just sat there and stared. Not knowing what else to do, I finished tending Otto, then made the tea. I poured three tin cups, gave one to Otto, set one before the Limper, took the third myself.

What now? No excuse to be busy. Nowhere to sit but at that table. . . . Oh, shit!

The Limper removed his mask. He raised the tin cup. . . .

I could not tear my gaze away.

His was the face of a dead man, of a mummy improperly preserved. His eyes were alive and baleful, yet directly beneath one was a patch of flesh which had rotted. Beneath his nose, at the right corner of his mouth, a square inch of lip was missing, revealing gum and yellowed teeth.

The Limper sipped tea, met my eye, and smiled.

I nearly dribbled down my leg.

I went to the window. There was some light out there now, and the snowfall was weakening, but I could not see the stone.

The stamp of boots sounded on the stair. Elmo and Raven shoved into the room. Elmo growled, "Hey, Croaker, how the hell did you get rid of that . . .?" His words grew smaller as he recognized the Limper.

Raven gave me a questioning look. The Limper turned. I shrugged when his back was to me. Raven moved to one side, began removing his wet things.

Elmo got the idea. He went the other way, stripped beside the fire. "Damn, it's good to get out of those. How's the boy, Otto?"

"There's fresh tea," I said.

Otto replied, "I hurt all over, Elmo."

The Limper peered at each of us, and at One-Eye and Goblin, who had yet to stir. "So. Soulcatcher brings the Black Company's best." His voice was a whisper, yet it filled the room. "Where is he?"

Raven ignored him. He donned dry breeches, sat beside Otto, double-checked my handiwork. "Good job of stitching, Croaker."

"I get plenty of practice with this outfit."

Elmo shrugged in response to the Limper. He drained his cup, poured tea all around, then filled the pot from one of the pitchers. He planted a boot in One-Eye's ribs while the Limper glared at Raven.

"You!" the Limper snapped. "I haven't forgotten what you did in Opal. Nor during the campaign in Forsberg."

Raven settled with his back against the wall. He produced one of his more wicked knives and began cleaning his fingernails. He smiled. At the Limper, he smiled, and there was mockery in his eyes.

Didn't anything scare that man?

"What did you do with the money? That wasn't Soulcatcher's. The Lady gave it to me."

I took courage from Raven's defiance. "Aren't you supposed to be in Elm? The Lady ordered you out of the Salient."

Anger distorted that wretched face. A scar ran down his forehead and left cheek. It stood out. Supposedly it continued down his left breast. The blow had been struck by the White Rose herself.

The Limper rose. And that damned Raven said, "Got the cards, Elmo? The table is free."

The Limper scowled. The tension level was rising fast. He snapped, "I want that money. It's mine. Your choice is to cooperate or not. I don't think you'll enjoy it if you don't."

"You want it, you go get it," Raven said. "Catch Raker. Chop off his head. Take it to the stone. That ought to be easy for the Limper. Raker is only a bandit. What chance would he stand against the Limper?"

I thought the Taken would explode. He did not. For an instant he was baffled.

He was not off balance long. "All right. If you want it the hard way." His smile was wide and cruel.

The tension was near the snapping point.

* * *

A shadow moved in the open doorway. A lean, dark figure appeared, stared at the Limper's back. I sighed in relief.

The Limper spun. For a moment the air seemed to crackle between the Taken.

From the corner of one eye I noted that Goblin was sitting up. His fingers were dancing in complex rhythms. One-Eye, facing the wall, was whispering into his bedroll. Raven reversed his knife for a throw. Elmo got a grip on the tea pot, ready to fling hot water.

There was no missile within grabbing distance of me. What the hell could I contribute? A chronicle of the blowup afterward, if I survived?

Soulcatcher made a tiny gesture, stepped around the Limper, deposited himself in his usual chair. He flung a toe out, hooked one of the chairs away from the table, put his feet up. He stared at the Limper, his fingers steepled before his mouth. "The Lady sent a message. In case I ran into you. She wants to see you." Soulcatcher used only one voice throughout. A hard female voice. "She wants to ask you about the uprising in Elm."

The Limper jerked. One hand, extended over the table, twitched nervously. "Uprising? In Elm?"

"Rebels attacked the palace and barracks."

The Limper's leathery face lost color. The twitching of his hand became more pronounced.

Soulcatcher said, "She wants to know why you weren't there to head them off."

The Limper stayed about three seconds more. In that time his face became grotesque. Seldom have I seen such naked fear. Then he spun and fled.

Raven flipped his knife. It stuck in the doorframe. The Limper did not notice.

Soulcatcher laughed. This was not the laugh of earlier days, but a deep, harsh, solid, vindictive laughter. He rose, turned to the window. "Ah. Someone has claimed our prize? When did that happen?"

Elmo masked his response by going to close the door. Raven said, "Toss me my knife, Elmo." I eased up beside Soulcatcher, looked out. The snowfall had ceased. The stone was visible. Cold, unglowing, with an inch of white on top.

"I don't know." I hoped I sounded sincere. "The snow was heavy all night. Last time I looked—before *he* showed up—I couldn't see a thing. Maybe I'd better go down there."

"Don't bother." He adjusted his chair so he could watch the square. Later, after he had accepted tea from Elmo and finished it—concealing his face by turning away—he mused, "Raker eliminated. His vermin in panic. And, sweeter still, the Limper embarrassed again. Not a bad job."

"Was that true?" I asked. "About Elm?"

"Every word," in a fey, merry voice. "One does wonder how the Rebel knew the Limper was out of town. And how Shapeshifter caught wind of the trouble quickly enough to show up and quash the uprising before it amounted to anything." Another pause. "No doubt the Limper will ponder that while he is recuperating." He laughed again, more softly, more darkly.

Elmo and I busied ourselves preparing breakfast. Otto usually handled the cooking, so we had an excuse for breaking routine. After a time, Soulcatcher observed, "There's no point to you people staying here. Your Captain's prayers have been answered."

"We can go?" Elmo asked.

"No reason to stay, is there?"

One-Eye had reasons. We ignored them.

"Start packing after breakfast," Elmo told us.

"You're going to travel in this weather?" One-Eye demanded.

"Captain wants us back."

I took Soulcatcher a platter of scrambled eggs. I do not know why. He did not eat often, and breakfast almost never. But he accepted it, turned his back.

I looked out the window. The mob had discovered the change. Someone had brushed the snow off Raker's face. His eyes were open, seemed to be watching. Weird.

Men were scrambling around under the table, fighting over the coins we had left behind. The pileup seethed like maggots in a putrid corpse. "Somebody ought to do him honor," I murmured. "He was a hell of an opponent."

"You have your Annals," Soulcatcher told me. And, "Only a conquerer bothers to honor a fallen foe."

I was headed for my own plate by then. I wondered what he meant, but a hot meal was more important at the moment.

They were all down at the stable except me and Otto. They were going to bring the wagon around for the wounded soldier. I had given him something to get him through the rough handling to come.

They were taking their time. Elmo wanted to rig a canopy to shield Otto from the weather. I played solitaire while I waited.

Out of nowhere, Soulcatcher said, "She's *very* beautiful, Croaker. Young-looking. Fresh. Dazzling. With a heart of flint. The Limper is a warm puppy by comparison. Pray you never catch her eye."

Soulcatcher stared out the window. I wanted to ask questions, but none would come at that moment. Damn. I really wasted a chance then.

What color was her hair? Her eyes? How did she smile? It all meant a lot to me when I could not know.

Soulcatcher rose, donned his cloak. "If only for the Limper, it's been worth it," he said. He paused at the door, pierced me with his stare. "You and Elmo and Raven. Drink a toast to me. Hear?"

Then he was gone.

Elmo came in a minute later. We lifted Otto and started back to Meystrikt. My nerves were not worth a damn for a long time.

Whisper

The engagement gave us the most gain for least effort of any I can remember. It was pure serendipity that went one hundred percent our way. It was a disaster for the Rebel.

We were in flight from the Salient, where the Lady's defenses had collapsed almost overnight. Running with us were five or six hundred regulars who had lost their units. For speed's sake, the Captain had chosen to cut straight through the Forest of Cloud to Lords, instead of following the longer southern road around.

A Rebel mainforce battalion was a day or two behind us. We could have turned and whipped them, but the Captain wanted to give them the slip instead. I liked his thinking. The fighting around Roses had been grim. Thousands had fallen. With so many extra bodies attaching themselves to the Company, I had been losing men for lack of time to treat them.

Our orders were to report to Nightcrawler at Lords. Soulcatcher thought Lords would be the target of the next Rebel thrust. Tired as we were, we expected to see more bitter fighting before winter slowed the war's pace.

"Croaker! Lookee here!" Whitey came charging toward where I sat with the Captain and Silent and one or two others. He had a naked woman draped over his shoulder. She might have been attractive had she not been so thoroughly abused.

"Not bad, Whitey. Not bad," I said, and went back to my journal. Behind Whitey the whooping and screaming continued. The men were harvesting the fruits of victory.

"They're barbarians," the Captain observed without rancor.

"Got to let them cut loose sometimes," I reminded him. "Better here than with the people of Lords."

The Captain agreed reluctantly. He just does not have much stomach for plunder and rape, much as they are part of our business. I think he is a secret romantic, at least when females are involved.

I tried to soften his mood. "They asked for it, taking up arms."

Bleakly, he asked me, "How long has this been going on, Croaker? Seems like forever, doesn't it? Can you even remember a time when you weren't a soldier? What's the point? Why are we even here? We keep winning battles, but the Lady is losing the war. Why don't they just call the whole thing off and go home?"

He was partially right. Since Forsberg it has been one retreat after another, though we have done well. The Salient had been secure till Shapeshifter and the Limper got into the act.

Our latest retreat had brought us stumbling into this Rebel base camp. We presumed it was the main training and staging center for the campaign against Nightcrawler. Luckily, we spotted the Rebel before he spotted us. We surrounded the place and roared in before dawn. We were badly outnumbered, but the Rebel did not put up much of a fight. Most were green volunteers. The startling aspect was the presence of an amazon regiment.

We had heard of them, of course. There were several in the east, around Rust, where the fighting is more bitter and sustained than here. This was our first encounter. It left the men disdainful of women warriors, despite their having fought better than their male compatriots.

Smoke began drifting our way. The men were firing the barracks and headquarters buildings. The Captain muttered, "Croaker, go make sure those fools don't fire the forest."

I rose, picked up my bag, ambled down into the din.

There were bodies everywhere. The fools must have felt completely safe. They hadn't put up a stockade or trenched around the encampment. Stupid. That is the first thing you do, even when you *know* there is no enemy within a hundred miles. You put a roof over your head later. Wet is better than dead.

I should be used to this. I have been with the Company a long time. And it does bother me less than it used to. I have hung armor plate over my moral soft spots. But I still try to avoid looking at the worst.

You who come after me, scribbling these Annals, by now realize that I shy off portraying the whole truth about our band of blackguards. You know they are vicious, violent, and ignorant. They are complete barbarians, living out their cruelest fantasies, their behavior tempered only by the presence of a few decent men. I do not often show that side because these men are my brethren, my family, and I was taught young not to speak ill of kin. The old lessons die hardest.

Raven laughs when he reads my accounts. "Sugar and spice," he calls them, and threatens to take the Annals away and write the stories the way he sees them happen.

Hardass Raven. Mocking me. And who was that out there roaming around the camp, breaking it up wherever the men were amusing themselves with a little torture? Who had a ten-year-old girl trailing him on an old jack mule? Not Croaker, brothers. Not Croaker. Croaker isn't no romantic. That is a passion reserved for the Captain and Raven.

Naturally, Raven has become the Captain's best friend. They sit around together like a couple of rocks, talking about the same things boulders do. They are content just to share one another's company.

Elmo was leading the arsonists. They were older Company men who had sated their less intense hungers for flesh. Those still mauling the ladies were mostly our young regular hangers-on.

They had given the Rebel a good fight at Salient, but he had been too strong. Half the Circle of Eighteen had ranged themselves against us there. We had had only the Limper and Shapeshifter on our side. Those two spent more time trying to sabotage one another than trying to repel the Circle. Result, a debacle. The Lady's most humiliating defeat in a decade.

The Circle pulls together most of the time. They do not spend more energy abusing one another than they spend on their enemies.

"Hey! Croaker!" One-Eye called. "Join the fun." He tossed a burning brand through a barracks doorway. The building promptly exploded. Heavy oaken shutters blew off the windows. A gout of flame enveloped One-Eye. He came charging out, kinky hair smouldering below the band of his weird, floppy hat. I wrestled him down, used that hat to slap his hair. "All right. All right," he growled. "You don't have to enjoy yourself so damned much."

Unable to stifle a grin, I helped him up. "You all right?"

"Singed," he said, assuming that air of phony dignity cats adopt after some particularly inept performance. Something like, "That's what I meant to do all along."

The fire roared. Pieces of thatch soared and bobbed over the building. I observed, "The Captain sent me to make sure you clowns didn't start a forest fire."

Just then Goblin ambled around the side of the flaming building. His broad mouth stretched in a smirk.

One-Eye took one look and shrieked. "You maggot brain! You set me up for that." He let out a spine-tingling howl and started dancing. The roar of the flames deepened, became rhythmic. Soon it seemed I could see something prancing among the flames behind the windows.

Goblin saw it too. His smirk vanished. He gulped, went white, began a little dance of his own. He and One-Eye howled and squawked and virtually ignored one another.

A watering trough disgorged its contents, which arced through the air and splashed the flames. The contents of a water barrel followed. The roar of the fire dwindled.

One-Eye pranced over and took a poke at Goblin, trying to break his concentration. Goblin weaved and bobbed and squeaked and kept on dancing. More water hit the fire.

"What a pair."

I turned. Elmo had come over to watch. "A pair indeed," I replied. Fussing, feuding, whining, they could be an allegory of their bigger brethren in the trade. Except their conflict does not run half to the bone, like that between Shifter and the Limper. When you slice through the fog, you find that these two are friends. There are no friends among the Taken.

"Got something to show you," Elmo said. He would not say anything more. I nodded and followed him.

Goblin and One-Eye kept at it. Goblin appeared to be ahead. I stopped worrying about the fire.

You figured how to read these northern chicken tracks?" Elmo asked. He had led me into what must have been the headquarters for the whole camp. He indicated a mountain of papers his men had piled on the floor, evidently as tinder for another fire.

"I think I can puzzle it out."

"Thought you might find something in this stuff."

I selected a paper at random. It was a copy of an order directing a specific Rebel mainforce battalion to filter into Lords and disappear into the homes of local sympathizers till called to strike at Lords' defenders from within. It was signed *Whisper*. A list of contacts was appended.

"I'll say," I said, suddenly short of breath. That one order betrayed a half-dozen Rebel secrets, and implied several more. "I'll say." I grabbed another. Like the first, it was a directive to a specific unit. Like the first, it was a window into the heart of current Rebel strategy. "Get the Captain," I told Elmo.

"Get Goblin and One-Eye and the Lieutenant and anybody else who maybe ought to be. . . ."

I must have looked weird. Elmo wore a strange, nervous expression when he interrupted. "What the hell is it, Croaker?"

"All the orders and plans for the campaign against Lords. The complete order of battle." But that was not the bottom line. That I was going to save for the Captain himself. "And hurry. Minutes might be critical. And stop them from burning anything like this. For Hell's sake, stop them. We've hit paydirt. Don't send it up in smoke."

Elmo slammed through the door. I heard his bellows fade into the distance. A good sergeant, Elmo. He does not waste time asking questions. Grunting, I settled myself on the floor and began scanning documents.

The door creaked. I did not look up. I was in a fever, glancing at documents as fast as I could yank them off the pile, sorting them into smaller stacks. Muddy boots appeared at the edge of my vision. "Can you read these, Raven?" I had recognized his step.

"Can I? Yes."

"Help me see what we've got here."

Raven settled himself opposite me. The pile lay between us, nearly blocking our view of one another. Darling positioned herself behind him, out of his way but well within the shadow of his protection. Her quiet, dull eyes still reflected the horror of that far village.

In some ways Raven is a paradigm for the Company. The difference between him and the rest of us is that he is a little more of everything, a little bigger than life. Maybe, by being the newcomer, the only brother from the north, he is symbolic of our life in the Lady's service. His moral agonies have become our moral agonies. His silent refusal to howl and beat his breast in adversity is ours as well. We prefer to speak with the metallic voice of our arms.

Enough. Why venture into the meaning of it all? Elmo had struck paydirt. Raven and I went sifting for nuggets.

Goblin and One-Eye drifted in. Neither could read the northern script. They started to amuse themselves by sending sourceless shadows chasing one another around the walls. Raven gave them a nasty look. Their ceaseless clowning and bickering can be tiresome when you have something on your mind.

They looked at him, dropped the game, sat down quietly, almost like children admonished. Raven has that knack, that energy, that impact of personality, to make men, more dangerous than he, shudder in his cold dark wind.

The Captain arrived, accompanied by Elmo and Silent. Through the doorway I glimpsed several men hanging around. Funny the way they smell things shaping up.

"What have you got, Croaker?" the Captain asked.

I figured he had milked Elmo dry, so I got straight to the kicker. "These orders." I tapped one of my stacks. "All these reports." I tapped another. "They're all signed by Whisper. We're kicking up the veggies in Whisper's private garden." My voice was up in the high squeak range.

For a while nobody said anything. Goblin made a few squeaky noises when Candy and the other sergeants rushed in. Finally, the Captain asked Raven, "That right?"

Raven nodded. "Judging by the documents, she's been in and out since early spring."

The Captain folded his hands, began pacing. He looked like a tired old monk on his way to evening prayer.

Whisper is the best known of the Rebel generals. Her stubborn genius has held the eastern front together despite the best efforts of the Ten. She is also the most dangerous of the Circle of Eighteen. She is known for the thoroughness with which she plans campaigns. In a war which, too often, resembles armed chaos on both sides, her forces stand out for their tight organization, discipline, and clarity of purpose.

The Captain mused, "She's supposed to be commanding the Rebel army at Rust. Right?" The struggle for Rust was three years old. Rumor had hundreds of square miles laid waste. During the winter past both sides had been reduced to eating their own dead to survive.

I nodded. The question was rhetorical. He was thinking out loud.

"And Rust has been a killing ground for years. Whisper won't break. The Lady won't back off. But if Whisper is coming here, then the Circle has decided to let Rust fall."

I added, "It means they're shifting from an eastern to a northern strategy." The north remains the Lady's weak flank. The west is prostrate. The Lady's allies rule the sea to the south. The north has been ignored since the Empire's frontiers reached the great forests above Forsberg. It is in the north that the Rebel has managed his most spectacular successes.

The Lieutenant observed, "They have the momentum, with Forsberg taken, the Salient overrun, Roses gone, and Rye besieged. There are Rebel mainforcers headed for Wist and Jane. They'll be stopped, but the Circle must know that. So they're dancing on the other foot and coming at Lords. If Lords goes, they're almost to the edge of the Windy Country. Cross the Windy Country, climb the Stair of Tear, and they're looking down at Charm from a hundred miles away."

I continued scanning and sorting. "Elmo, you might look around and see if you can come up with anything else. She might have something tucked away."

"Use One-Eye, Goblin, and Silent," Raven suggested. "Better chance of finding something."

The Captain okayed the proposal. He told the Lieutenant, "Get that business out there wrapped up. Carp, you and Candy get the men ready to move out. Match, double your perimeter guard."

"Sir?" Candy asked.

"You don't want to be here when Whisper gets back, do you? Goblin, come back here. Get ahold of Soulcatcher. This goes to the top. Now."

Goblin made an awful face, then went into a corner and began murmuring to himself. It was a quiet little sorcery—to start.

The Captain rolled on. "Croaker, you and Raven pack these documents when you're done. We'll want them along."

"I maybe better save the best out for Catcher," I said. "Some will need immediate attention if we're to get any use out of them. I mean, something will have to be done before Whisper can put the word out."

He cut me off. "Right. I'll send you a wagon. Don't dilly-dally." He looked grey around the edges as he stalked outside.

A new strain of terror entered the screaming and shouting outside. I untangled my aching legs and went to the door. They were herding the Rebels together on their drill field. The prisoners sensed the Company's sudden eagerness to cut and run. They thought they were about to die just minutes before salvation arrived.

Shaking my head, I returned to my reading. Raven gave me a look that might have meant he shared my pain. On the other hand, it might have contained contempt for my weakness. With Raven it is hard to tell.

One-Eye shoved through the door, stomped over, dumped an armload of bundles wrapped in oilskin. Moist clods clung to them. "You were right. We dug these up behind her sleeping quarters."

Goblin let out a long, shrill screech as chilling as an owl's when you are alone in the woods at midnight. One-Eye charged the sound.

Such moments make me doubt the sincerity of their animosity.

Goblin moaned, "He's in the Tower. He's with the Lady. I see Her through his eyes . . . his eyes . . . his eyes. . . . The darkness! Oh, God, the darkness! No! Oh, God, no! No!" His words twisted into a shriek of pure terror. That faded to, "The Eye. I see the Eye. It's looking right through me."

Raven and I exchanged frowns and shrugs. We did not know what he was talking about.

Goblin sounded like he was regressing toward childhood. "Make it stop looking at me. Make it stop. I've been good. Make it go away."

One-Eye was on his knees beside Goblin. "It's all right. It's all right. It's not real. It's going to be all right."

I exchanged glances with Raven. He turned, began gesturing at Darling. "I'm sending her to fetch the Captain."

Darling left reluctantly. Raven took another sheet from the pile and resumed reading. Cool as a stone, that Raven.

Goblin screamed for a while, then got quiet as death. I jerked around. One-Eye lifted a hand to tell me I was not needed. Goblin had finished delivering his message.

Goblin relaxed slowly. The terror left his face. His color improved. I knelt, touched his carotid. His heart was hammering, but its beat was slowing. "Surprised it didn't kill him this time," I said. "It ever been this bad before?"

"No." One-Eye dropped Goblin's hand. "We'd better not put it on him next time."

"Is it progressive?" My trade borders theirs along the shadowed edges, but only in small ways. I did not know.

"No. His confidence will need support for a while. Sounded like he caught Soulcatcher right at the heart of the Tower. I think that would leave anybody rocky."

"While in the presence of the Lady," I breathed. I could not contain my excitement. Goblin had seen the inside of the Tower! He might have seen the Lady! Only the Ten Who Were Taken ever came out of the Tower. Popular imagination invests its interior with a thousand gruesome possibilities. And I had me a live witness!

"You just let him be, Croaker. He'll tell you when he's ready." There was a hard edge to One-Eye's voice.

They laugh at my little fantasies, tell me I have fallen in love with a spook. Maybe they are right. Sometimes my interest scares me. It gets close to becoming an obsession.

For a time I forgot my duty to Goblin. For a moment he stopped being a man, a brother, an old friend. He became a source of information. Then, shamed, I retreated to my papers.

The Captain arrived, puzzled, dragged by a determined Darling. "Ah. I see. He made contact." He studied Goblin. "Said anything yet? No? Wake him up, One-Eye."

One-Eye started to protest, thought better of it, shook Goblin gently. Goblin took his time awakening. His sleep was almost as deep as a trance.

"Was it rough?" the Captain asked me.

I explained. He grunted, said, "That wagon is on its way. One of you start packing."

I started straightening my piles.

"One of you means Raven, Croaker. You stand by here. Goblin doesn't look too good."

He did not. He had gone pale again. His breath was coming shallower and quicker, getting ragged. "Give him a slap, One-Eye," I said. "He might think he's still out there."

The slap did the job. Goblin opened eyes filled with panic. He recognized One-Eye, shuddered, took a deep breath, and squeaked, "I have to come back to this? After that?" But his voice gave the lie to his protest. The relief there was thick enough to cut.

"He's all right," I said. "He can bitch."

The Captain squatted. He did not say anything. Goblin would talk when he was ready.

He took several minutes to get himself together, then said, "Soulcatcher says to get the hell out of here. Fast. He'll meet us on the way to Lords."

"That's it?"

That is all there ever is, but the Captain keeps hoping for more. The game does not seem worth the candle when you see what Goblin goes through.

I looked at him hard. It was one hell of a temptation. He looked back. "Later, Croaker. Give me time to get it straightened out in my head."

I nodded, said, "A little herb tea will perk you up."

"Oh, no. You're not giving me any of that rat piss of One-Eye's."

"Not his. My own." I measured enough for a strong quart, gave it to One-Eye, closed my kit, returned to the papers as the wagon creaked up outside.

As I carried my first load out, I noticed that the men were at the coup de grace stage on the drill field. The Captain was not fooling around. He wanted to put a lot of distance between himself and the camp before Whisper returned.

Can't say I blame him. Her reputation is thoroughly vile.

I did not get to the oilskin packets till we were travelling again. I sat up beside the driver and started the first, vainly trying to ignore the savage jouncing of the springless vehicle.

I went through the packets twice, growing ever more distressed.

A real dilemma. Should I tell the Captain what I had learned? Should I tell One-Eye or Raven? Each would be interested. Should I save everything for Soulcatcher? No doubt he would prefer that. My question was, did this information fall inside or outside my obligation to the Company? I needed an adviser.

I jumped down from the wagon, let the column drift past till Silent caught up. He had middle guard. One-Eye was on the point and Goblin back in the rear. Each was worth a platoon of outriders.

Silent looked down from the back of the big black he rides when he is in a villainous mood. He scowled. Of our wizards he is the nearest to what you could call evil, though, like so many of us, he is more image than substance.

"I've got a problem," I told him. "A big one. You're the best sounding board." I looked around. "I don't want anyone else to hear this."

Silent nodded. He made complicated, fluid gestures too quick to follow. Suddenly, I could not hear anything from more than five feet away. You would be amazed how many sounds you do not notice till they are gone. I told Silent what I had found.

Silent is hard to shock. He has seen and heard it all. But he looked properly astonished this time.

For a moment I thought he was going to say something.

"Should I tell Soulcatcher?"

Vigorous affirmative nod. All right. I hadn't doubted that. The news was too big for the Company. It would eat us up if we kept it to ourselves.

"How about the Captain? One-Eye? Some of the others?"

He was less quick to respond, and less decisive. His advice was negative. With a few questions and the intuition one develops on long exposure, I understood Silent to feel that Soulcatcher would want to spread the word on a need-to-know basis.

"Right, then," I said, and, "Thanks," and started trotting up the column. When I was out of sight of Silent, I asked one of the men, "You seen Raven?"

"Up with the Captain."

That figured. I resumed trotting.

After a moment of reflection I had decided to buy a little insurance. Raven was the finest policy I could imagine.

"You read any of the old languages?" I asked him. It was hard talking to him. He and the Captain were mounted and Darling was right behind them. Her mule kept trying to tromp my heels.

"Some. All part of a classical education. Why?"

I scrambled a few steps ahead. "We're going to be having mule stew if you don't watch it, animal." I swear, that beast sneered. I told Raven, "Some of those papers aren't modern. The ones One-Eye dug up."

"Not important then, are they?"

I shrugged and ambled along beside him, picking my words carefully. "You never know. The Lady and the Ten, they go way back." I let out a yelp, spun, ran backward gripping my shoulder where the mule had nipped me. The animal looked innocent, but Darling was grinning impishly.

It was almost worth the pain, just to see her smile. She did so so seldom.

I cut across the column and drifted back till I was walking beside Elmo. He asked, "Is something wrong, Croaker?"

"Uhm? No. Not really."

"You look scared."

I *was* scared. I had tipped the lid off a little box, just to see what was inside, and had found it filled with nastiness. The things I had read could not be unlearned.

When next I saw Raven his face was as grey as mine. Maybe more so. We walked together while he sketched what he had learned from the documents I had not been able to read.

"Some of them belonged to the wizard Bomanz," he told me. "Others date from the Domination. Some are TelleKurre. Only the Ten use that language anymore."

"Bomanz?" I asked.

"Right. The one who wakened the Lady. Whisper got ahold of his secret papers somehow."

"Oh."

"Indeed. Yes. Oh."

We parted, each to be alone with his fears.

Soulcatcher came sneakily. He wore clothing not unlike ours outside his customary leathers. He slipped into the column unremarked. How long he was there I do not know. I became aware of him as we were leaving the forest, after three eighteen-hour days of heavy marching. I was putting one foot ahead of the other, aching, and mumbling about getting too old when a soft feminine voice inquired, "How are you today, physician?" It lilted with amusement.

Had I been less exhausted I might have jumped ten feet, screaming. As it was, I just took my next step, cranked my head around, and muttered, "Finally showed up, eh?" Profound apathy was the order of the moment.

A wave of relief would arrive later, but just then my brain was running as sluggishly as my body. After so long on the run it was hard to get the adrenaline pumping. The world held no sudden excitements or terrors.

Soulcatcher marched beside me, matching stride for stride, occasionally glancing my way. I could not see his face, but I sensed his amusement.

The relief came, and was followed by a wave of awe at my own temerity. I had talked back like Catcher was one of the guys. It was thunderbolt time.

"So why don't we look at those documents?" he asked. He seemed positively cheerful. I showed him to the wagon. We scrambled aboard. The driver gave us one wide-eyed look, then stared determinedly forward, shivering and trying to become deaf.

I went straight to the packets that had been buried, started to slip out. "Stay," he said. "They don't need to know yet." He sensed my fear, giggled like a young girl. "You're safe, Croaker. In fact, the Lady sends her personal thanks." He laughed again. "She wanted to know all about you, Croaker. All about you. You've caught her imagination too."

Another hammer blow of fear. Nobody wants to catch the Lady's eye.

Soulcatcher enjoyed my discomfiture. "She might grant you an interview, Croaker. Oh, my. You're so pale. Well, it isn't mandatory. To work, then."

Never have I seen anyone read so fast. He went through the old documents and the new, zip.

Catcher said, "You weren't able to read all of this." He used his businesslike female voice.

"No."

"Neither can I. Some only the Lady will be able to decipher."

Odd, I thought. I expected more enthusiasm. The seizure of the documents represented a coup for him because he had had the foresight to enlist the Black Company.

"How much did you get?"

I talked about the Rebel plan for a thrust through Lords, and about what Whisper's presence implied.

He chuckled. "The old documents, Croaker. Tell me about the old documents."

I was sweating. The softer, the more gentle he became, the more I felt I had to fear. "The old wizard. The one who wakened you all. Some of them were his papers." Damn. I knew I had stuck my foot in my mouth before I finished. Raven was the only man in the Company who could have identified Bomanz's papers as his.

Soulcatcher chuckled, gave me a comradely shoulder slap. "I thought so, Croaker. I wasn't sure, but I thought so. I didn't think you could resist telling Raven."

I did not respond. I wanted to lie, but he *knew*.

"You couldn't have known any other way. You told him about the references to the Limper's true name, so he just had to read everything he could. Right?"

Still I kept my peace. It was true, though my motives had not been wholly brotherly. Raven has his scores to settle, but Limper wants *all* of *us*.

The most jealously guarded secret of any wizard, of course, is his true name. An enemy armed with that can stab through any magic or illusion straight to the heart of the soul.

"You only guessed at the magnitude of what you found, Croaker. Even I can only guess. But what will come of it is predictable. The biggest disaster ever for Rebel arms, and a lot of rattling and shaking among the Ten." He slapped my shoulder again. "You've made me the second most powerful person in the Empire. The Lady knows all our true names. Now I know three of the others, and I've gotten my own back."

No wonder he was effusive. He had ducked an arrow he had not known was coming, and had lucked onto a stranglehold on the Limper at the same time. He had stumbled over a rainbow pot of power.

"But Whisper. . . ."

"Whisper will have to go." The voice he used was deep and chill. It was the voice of an assassin, a voice accustomed to pronouncing death sentences. "Whisper has to die fast. Otherwise nothing is gained."

"Suppose she told someone else?"

"She didn't. Oh, no. I know Whisper. I fought her at Rust before the Lady sent me to Beryl. I fought her at Were. I chased her through the talking menhirs upon the Plain of Fear. I know Whisper. She's a genius, but she's a loner. Had she lived during the first era, the Dominator would have made her one of his own. She serves the White Rose, but her heart is as black as the night of Hell."

"That sounds like the whole Circle to me."

Catcher laughed. "Yes. Every one a hypocrite. But there isn't a one like Whisper. This is incredible, Croaker. How did she unearth so many secrets? How did she get *my* name? I had it hidden perfectly. I admire her. Truly. Such genius. Such audacity. A strike through Lords, across the Windy Country, and up the Stair of Tear. Incredible. Impossible. And it would have worked but for the accident of the Black Company, and you. You'll be rewarded. I guarantee it. But enough of this. I've got work to do. Nightcrawler needs this information. The Lady has to see these papers."

"I hope you're right," I grumbled. "Kick ass, then take a break. I'm worn out. We've been humping and fighting for a year."

Dumb remark, Croaker. I felt the chill of the frown inside the black morion. How long had Soulcatcher been humping and fighting? An age. "You go on now," he told me. "I'll talk to you and Raven later." Cold, cold voice. I got the hell out of there.

It was all over in Lords when we got there. Nightcrawler had moved fast and had hit hard. You could not go anywhere without finding Rebels hanging from the trees and lampposts. The Company went into barracks expecting a quiet, boring winter, and a spring spent chasing Rebel leftovers back to the great northern forests.

Ah, it was a sweet illusion while it lasted.

Tonk!" I said, slapping down five face cards given me on the deal. "Ha! Double, you guys. Double. Pay up."

One-Eye grumbled and growled and shoved coins across the table. Raven chuckled. Even Goblin perked up enough to smile. One-Eye had not won a hand all morning, even when he cheated.

"Thank you, gentlemen. Thank you. Deal, One-Eye."

"What're you doing, Croaker? Eh? How are you doing it?"

"The hand is quicker than the eye," Elmo suggested.

"Just clean living, One-Eye. Clean living."

The Lieutenant shoved through the door, face drawn into a fierce scowl. "Raven. Croaker. The Captain wants you. Chop-chop." He surveyed the various card games. "You degenerates."

One-Eye sniffed, then worked up a wan smile. The Lieutenant was a worse player than he.

I looked at Raven. The Captain was his buddy. But he shrugged, tossed his cards in. I filled my pockets with my winnings and followed him to the Captain's office.

Soulcatcher was there. We had not seen him since that day at the edge of the forest. I had hoped he had gotten too busy to get back to us. I looked at the Captain, trying to divine the future from his face. I saw that he was not happy.

If the Captain was not happy, I wasn't.

"Sit," he said. Two chairs were waiting. He prowled around, fidgeting. Finally, he said, "We have movement orders. Straight from Charm. Us and Nightcrawler's whole brigade." He gestured toward Soulcatcher, passing the explaining to him.

Catcher seemed lost in thought. Barely audibly, he finally asked, "How are you with a bow, Raven?"

"Fair. No champion."

"Better than fair," the Captain countered. "Damned good."

"You, Croaker?"

"I used to be good. I haven't drawn one for years."

"Get some practice." Catcher started pacing too. The office was small. I expected a collision momentarily. After a minute, Soulcatcher said, "There have been developments. We tried to catch Whisper at her camp. We just missed her. She smelled the trap. She's still out there somewhere, hiding. The Lady is sending in troops from all sides."

That explained the Captain's remark. It did not tell me why I was supposed to hone my archery skills.

"Near as we can tell," Soulcatcher continued, "the Rebel doesn't know what happened out there. Yet. Whisper hasn't found the nerve to pass the word about her failure. She's a proud woman. Looks like she wants to try recouping first."

"With what?" Raven asked. "She couldn't put together a platoon."

"With memories. Memories of the material you found buried. We don't think she knows we got it. She didn't get close to her headquarters before Limper tipped our hand and she fled into the forest. And just we four, and the Lady, know of the documents."

Raven and I nodded. Now we understood Catcher's restlessness. Whisper knew his true name. He was on the bull's-eye.

"What do you want with us?" Raven asked suspiciously. He was afraid

Catcher thought we had deciphered that name ourselves. He'd even suggested we kill the Taken before he killed us. The Ten are neither immortal nor invulnerable, but they are damned hard to reach. I did not, ever, want to have a try at one.

"We have a special mission, we three."

Raven and I exchanged glances. Was he setting us up?

Catcher said, "Captain, would you mind stepping outside for a minute?"

The Captain shambled through the doorway. His bear act is all for show. I don't suppose he realizes that we have had it figured for years. He keeps on with it, trying for effect.

"I'm not going to take you off where I can kill you quietly," Soulcatcher told us. "No, Raven, I don't think you figured out my true name."

Spooky. I scrunched my head down against my shoulders. Raven flicked a hand. A knife appeared. He began cleaning already immaculate nails.

"The critical development is this: Whisper suborned the Limper after we made a fool of him in the Raker affair."

I burst out, "That explains what happened in the Salient. We had it sewed up. It fell apart overnight. And he was a pure shit during the battle at Roses."

Raven agreed. "Roses was his fault. But nobody thought it was treason. After all, he's one of the Ten."

"Yes," Catcher said. "It explains many things. But the Salient and Roses are yesterday. Our interest now is tomorrow. It's getting rid of Whisper before she gifts us with another disaster."

Raven eyed Catcher, eyed me, pursued his needless manicure. I was not taking the Taken at face value either. We lesser mortals are but toys and tools to them. They are the kind of people who dig up the bones of their grandmothers to win points with the Lady.

"This is our edge on Whisper," Soulcatcher said. "We know she has agreed to meet the Limper tomorrow. . . ."

"How?" Raven demanded.

"*I* don't know. The Lady told *me*. Limper doesn't know we know about him, but he does know he can't last much longer. He'll probably try to make a deal so the Circle will protect him. He knows if he doesn't, he's dead. What the Lady wants is them to die together so the Circle will suspect she was selling out to the Limper instead of the other way around."

"It won't wash," Raven grumbled.

"They'll believe it."

"So we're going to knock him off," I said. "Me and Raven. With bows. And how are we supposed to find them?" Catcher would not be there himself, no matter how he talked. Both the Limper and Whisper would sense his presence long before he came within bowshot.

"Limper will be with the forces moving into the forest. Not knowing that he's suspected, he won't hide from the Lady's Eye. He'll expect his movements to be taken as part of the search. The Lady will report his whereabouts to me. I'll put you on his trail. When they meet, you take them out."

"Sure," Raven sneered. "Sure. It'll be a turkey shoot." He threw his knife. It bit deep into a windowsill. He stomped out of the room.

The deal sounded no better to me. I stared at Soulcatcher and debated with myself for about two seconds before I let fear push me in Raven's wake.

My last glimpse of Catcher was of a weary person slumped in unhappiness. I guess it is hard for them to live with their reputations. We all want people to like us.

I was doing one of my little fantasies about the Lady while Raven systematically plunked arrows into a red rag pinned to a straw butt. I had had trouble hitting the butt itself my first round, let alone the rag. It seemed Raven could not miss.

This time I was playing around with her childhood. That is something I like to look at with any villain. What twists and knots went into the thread tying the creature at Charm to the little girl who was? Consider little children. There are not many of them not cute and lovable and precious, sweet as whipped honey and butter. So where do all the wicked people come from? I walk through our barracks and wonder how a giggling, inquisitive toddler could have become a Three Fingers, a Jolly, or a Silent.

Little girls are twice as precious and innocent as little boys. I do not know a culture that does not make them that way.

So where does a Lady come from? Or, for that matter, a Whisper? I was speculating in this latest tale.

Goblin sat down beside me. He read what I had written. "I don't think so," he said. "I think she made a conscious decision in the beginning."

I turned toward him slowly, acutely conscious of Soulcatcher standing only a few yards behind me, watching the arrows fly. "I didn't really think it was this way, Goblin. It's a. . . . Well, you know. You want to understand, so you put it together some way you can handle."

"We all do that. In everyday life it's called making excuses." True, raw motives are too rough to swallow. By the time most people reach my age, they have glossed their motives so often and so well they fall completely out of touch with them.

I became conscious of a shadow across my lap. I glanced up. Soulcatcher extended a hand, inviting me to take my turn with the bow. Raven had recovered his arrows, and was standing by, waiting for me to step to the mark.

My first three shafts plunked into the rag. "How about that?" I said, and turned to take a bow.

Soulcatcher was reading my little fantasy. He raised his gaze to mine. "Really, Croaker! It wasn't like that at all. Didn't you know that she murdered her twin sister when she was fourteen?"

Rats with icy claws scrambled around on my spine. I turned, let a shaft fly. It ripped wide right of the butt. I sprayed a few more around, and did nothing but irritate the pigeons in the background.

Catcher took the bow. "Your nerves are going, Croaker." In a blur, he snapped three arrows into a circle less than an inch across. "Keep at it. You'll be under more pressure out there." He handed the bow back. "The secret is concentration. Pretend you're doing surgery."

Pretend I'm doing surgery. Right. I have managed some fancy emergency work in the middle of battlefields. Right. But this was different.

The grand old excuse. Yes, but. . . . This is different.

I calmed down enough to hit the butt with the rest of my shafts. After recovering them, I stood aside for Raven.

Goblin handed me my writing materials. Irritably, I crumpled my little fable.

"Need something for your nerves?" Goblin asked.

"Yeah. The iron filings or whatever it is Raven eats." My self-esteem was pretty shaky.

"Try this." Goblin offered me a little six-pointed silver star hanging on a neck chain. At its center was a Medusa head in jet.

"An amulet?"

"Yes. We thought you might need it tomorrow."

"Tomorrow?" Nobody was supposed to know what was happening.

"We have eyes, Croaker. This is the Company. Maybe we don't know what, but we can tell when something is going on."

"Yeah. I suppose so. Thanks, Goblin."

"Me and One-Eye and Silent, we all worked on it."

"Thanks. What about Raven?" When somebody makes a gesture like that, I feel more comfortable shifting the subject.

"Raven doesn't need one. Raven is his own amulet. Sit down. Let's talk."

"I can't tell you about it."

"I know. I thought you wanted to know about the Tower." He had not talked about his visit yet. I had given up on him.

"All right. Tell me." I stared at Raven. Arrow after arrow skewered the rag.

"Aren't you going to write it down?"

"Oh. Yeah." I readied pen and paper. The men are tremendously impressed by the fact that I keep these Annals. Their only immortality will be here. "Glad I didn't bet him."

"Bet who?"

"Raven wanted to make a wager on our marksmanship."

Goblin snorted. "You're getting too smart to get hooked by a sucker bet? Get your pen ready." He launched his story.

He did not add much to rumors I had picked up here and there. He described the place he had gone as a big, drafty box of a room, gloomy and dusty. About what I expected of the Tower. Or of any castle.

"What did she look like?" That was the most intriguing part of the puzzle. I had a mental picture of a dark-haired, ageless beauty with a sexual presence that hit mere mortals with the impact of a mace. Soulcatcher said she was beautiful, but I had no independent corroboration.

"I don't know. I don't remember."

"What do you mean, you don't remember? How can you not remember?"

"Don't get all excited, Croaker. I can't remember. She was there in front of me, then. . . . Then all I could see was that giant yellow eye that kept getting bigger and bigger and stared right through me, looking at every secret I ever had. That's all I remember. I still have nightmares about that eye."

I sighed, exasperated. "I guess I should've expected that. You know, she could come walking by right now and nobody would know it was her."

"I expect that's the way she wants it, Croaker. If it does all fall apart, the way it looked before you found those papers, she can just walk away. Only the Ten could identify her, and she would make sure of them somehow."

I doubt it would be that simple. People like the Lady have trouble assuming a lesser role. Deposed princes keep acting like princes.

"Thanks for taking the trouble to tell me about it, Goblin."

"No trouble. I didn't have anything to tell. Only reason I put it off was it upset me so much."

Raven finished retrieving his arrows. He came over and told Goblin, "Why don't you go put a bug in One-Eye's bedroll, or something? We've got work to do." He was nervous about my erratic marksmanship.

We had to depend on one another. If either missed, chances were we would die before a second shaft could be sped. I did not want to think about that.

But thinking about it improved my concentration. I got most of my arrows into the rag this time.

It was a pain in the ass damned thing to have to do, night before whatever faced Raven and me, but the Captain refused to part with a tradition three centuries old. He also refused to entertain protests about our having been drafted by Soulcatcher, or demands for the additional knowledge he obviously commanded. I mean, I understood what Catcher wanted done and why, I just could not make sense of why he wanted Raven and me to do it. Having the Captain back him only made it more confusing.

"Why, Croaker?" he finally demanded. "Because I gave you an order, that's why. Now get out there and do your reading."

Once each month, in the evening, the entire Company assembles so the Annalist can read from his predecessors. The readings are supposed to put the men in touch with the outfit's history and traditions, which stretch back centuries and thousands of miles.

I placed my selection on a crude lectern and went with the usual formula. "Good evening, brothers. A reading from the Annals of the Black Company, last of the Free Companies of Khatovar. Tonight I'm reading from the Book of Kette, set down early in the Company's second century by Annalists Lees, Agrip, Holm, and Straw. The Company was in service to the Paingod of Cho'n Delor at that time. That was when the Company really was black.

"The reading is from Annalist Straw. It concerns the Company's role in events surrounding the fall of Cho'n Delor." I began to read, reflecting privately that the Company has served many losing causes.

The Cho'n Delor era bore many resemblances to our own, though then, standing more than six thousand strong, the Company was in a better position to shape its own destiny.

I lost track entirely. Old Straw was hell with a pen. I read for three hours, raving like a mad prophet, and held them spellbound. They gave me an ovation when I finished. I retreated from the lectern feeling as though my life had been fulfilled.

The physical and mental price of my histrionics caught up as I entered my barracks. Being a semi-officer, I rated a small cubicle of my own. I staggered right to it.

Raven was waiting. He sat on my bunk doing something artistic with an arrow. Its shaft had a band of silver around it. He seemed to be engraving something. Had I not been exhausted, I might have been curious.

"You were superb," Raven told me. "Even I felt it."

"Eh?"

"You made me understand what it meant to be a brother of the Black Company back then."

"What it still means to some."

"Yes. And more. You reached them where they lived."

"Yeah. Sure. What're you doing?"

"Fixing an arrow for the Limper. With his true name on it. Catcher gave it to me."

"Oh." Exhaustion kept me from pursuing the matter. "What did you want?"

"You made me feel something for the first time since my wife and her lovers tried to murder me and steal my rights and titles." He rose, closed one eye, looked down the length of his arrow. "Thanks, Croaker. For a while I felt human again." He stalked out.

I collapsed on the bunk and closed my eyes, recalling Raven strangling his wife, taking her wedding ring, and saying not a word. He had revealed more in that one rapid-fire sentence than since the day we had met. Strange.

I fell asleep reflecting that he had evened scores with everyone but the ultimate source of his despair. The Limper had been untouchable because he was one of the Lady's own. But no more.

Raven would be looking forward to tomorrow. I wondered what he would dream tonight. And if he would have much purpose left if the Limper died. A man cannot survive on hatred alone. Would he bother trying to survive what was coming?

Maybe that was what he wanted to say.

I was scared. A man thinking that way could get a little flashy, a little dangerous to those around him.

A hand closed on my shoulder. "Time, Croaker." The Captain himself was doing the wakeup calls.

"Yeah. I'm awake." I had not slept well.

"Catcher is ready to go."

It was still dark out. "Time?"

"Almost four. He wants to be gone before first light."

"Oh."

"Croaker? Be careful out there. I want you back."

"Sure, Captain. You know I don't take chances. Captain? Why me and Raven, anyway?" Maybe he would tell me now.

"He says the Lady calls it a reward."

"No shit? Some reward." I felt around for my boots as he moved to the door. "Captain? Thanks."

"Sure." He knew I meant thanks for caring.

Raven stuck his head in as I was lacing my jerkin. "Ready?"

"One minute. Cold out there?"

"Nippy."

"Take a coat?"

"Wouldn't hurt. Mail shirt?" He touched my chest.

"Yeah." I pulled my coat on, picked up the bow I was taking, bounced it on my palm. For an instant Goblin's amulet lay cool on my breastbone. I hoped it would work.

Raven cracked a smile. "Me too."

I grinned back. "Let's go get them."

Soulcatcher was waiting on the court where we had practiced our archery. He was limned by light from the company mess. The bakers were hard at work already. Catcher stood at a stiff parade rest, a bundle under his left arm. He stared toward the Forest of Cloud. He wore only leathers and morion. Unlike some of the Taken, he seldom carries weapons. He prefers relying on his thaumaturgic skills.

He was talking to himself. Weird stuff. "Want to see him go down. Been waiting four hundred years." "We can't get that close. He'll smell us coming." "Put aside all Power." "Oh! That's too risky!" A whole chorus of voices got into the act. It got really spooky when two of them talked at once.

Raven and I exchanged glances. He shrugged. Catcher did not faze him. But, then, he grew up in the Lady's dominions. He has seen all the Taken. Soulcatcher is supposedly one of the least bizarre.

We listened for a few minutes. It did not get any saner out. Finally, Raven growled, "Lord? We're ready." He sounded a little shaky.

I was beyond speech myself. All I could think of was a bow, an arrow, and a job I was expected to do. I rehearsed the draw, release, and flight of my shaft over and over again. Unconsciously, I rubbed Goblin's gift. I would catch myself doing that often.

Soulcatcher shuddered like a wet dog, drew himself together. Without looking at us, he gestured, said, "Come," and started walking.

Raven turned. He yelled, "Darling, you get back in there like I told you. Go on now."

"How is she supposed to hear you?" I asked, looking back at the child watching from a shadowed doorway.

"She won't. But the Captain will. Go on now." He gestured violently. The Captain appeared momentarily. Darling vanished. We followed Soulcatcher. Raven muttered to himself. He worried about the child.

Soulcatcher set a brisk pace, out of the compound, out of Lords itself, across fields, never looking back. He led us to a large woodlot several bowshots from the wall, to a glade at the lot's heart. There, on the bank of a creek, lay a ragged carpet stretched on a crude wooden frame about a foot high and six feet by eight. Soulcatcher said something. The carpet twitched, wriggled a little, stretched itself taut.

"Raven, you sit here." Catcher indicated the right hand corner nearest us. "Croaker, over here." He indicated the left corner.

Raven placed a foot on the carpet gingerly, seemed surprised that the works did not collapse.

"Sit down." Soulcatcher placed him just so, with his legs crossed and his weapons lying beside him near the carpet's edge. He did the same with me. I was suprised to find the carpet rigid. It was like sitting on a tabletop. "It's imperative that you don't move around," Catcher said, wriggling himself into position ahead of us, centered a foot forward of the carpet's midline. "If we don't stay balanced, we fall off. Understand?"

I did not, but I agreed with Raven when he said yes.

"Ready?"

Raven said yes again. I guess he knew what was happening. I was taken by surprise.

Soulcatcher laid his hands out palms upward beside him, said a few strange words, raised his hands slowly. I gasped, leaned. The ground was receding.

"Sit still!" Raven snarled. "You trying to kill us?"

The ground was only six feet down. Then. I straightened up and went rigid. But I did turn my head enough to check a movement in the brush.

Yes. Darling. With her mouth an O of amazement. I faced forward, gripped my bow so tightly I thought I would crush handprints into it. I wished I dared finger my amulet. "Raven, did you make arrangements for Darling? In case, you know. . . ."

"The Captain will look out for her."

"I forgot to fix it with somebody for the Annals."

"Don't be so optimistic," he said sarcastically. I shivered uncontrollably.

Soulcatcher did something. We started gliding over the treetops. Chill air whispered past us. I glanced over the side. We were a good five stories high and climbing.

The stars twisted overhead as Catcher changed course. The wind rose till we seemed to be flying into the face of a gale. I leaned farther and farther forward, afraid it would push me off. There was nothing behind me but several hundred feet and an abrupt stop. My fingers ached from gripping my bow.

I have learned one thing, I told myself. How Catcher manages to show up so fast when he is always so far from the action when we get in touch.

It was a silent journey. Catcher stayed busy doing whatever it was he did to make his steed fly. Raven closed in on himself. So did I. I was scared silly. My stomach was in revolt. I do not know about Raven.

The stars began to fade. The eastern horizon lightened. The earth materialized below us. I chanced a look. We were over the Forest of Cloud. A little more light. Catcher grunted, considered the east, then the distances ahead. He seemed to listen for a moment, then nodded.

The carpet raised its nose. We climbed. The earth rocked and dwindled till it looked like a map. The air became ever more chill. My stomach remained rebellious.

Way off to our left I glimpsed a black scar on the forest. It was the encampment we had overrun. Then we entered a cloud and Catcher slowed our rush.

"We'll drift a while," he said. "We're thirty miles south of the Limper. He's riding away from us. We're overtaking him fast. When we're almost up to where he might detect me, we'll go down." He used the businesslike female voice.

I started to say something. He snapped, "Be quiet, Croaker. Don't distract me."

We stayed in that cloud, unseen and unable to see, for two hours. Then Catcher said, "Time to go down. Grip the frame members and don't let go. It may be a little unsettling."

The bottom fell out. We went down like a stone dropped from a cliff. The carpet began to rotate slowly, so the forest seemed to turn below us. Then it began to slide back and forth like a feather falling. Each time it tilted my way I thought I would tumble over the side.

A good scream might have helped, but you could not do that in front of characters like Raven and Soulcatcher.

The forest kept getting closer. Soon I could distinguish individual trees . . . when I dared to look. We were going to die. I knew we were going to smash right down through the forest canopy fifty feet into the earth.

Catcher said something. I did not catch it. He was talking to his carpet anyway. The rocking and spinning gradually stopped. Our descent slowed. The carpet nosed down slightly and began to glide forward. Eventually Catcher took us below treetop level, into the aisle over a river. We scooted along a dozen feet above the water, with Soulcatcher laughing as birds scattered in panic.

He brought us to earth in a glen beside the river. "Off and stretch," he told us. After we had loosened up, he said, "The Limper is four miles north of us. He's reached the meeting place. You'll go on from here without me. He'll detect me if I get any closer. I want your badges. He can detect those too."

Raven nodded, surrendered his badge, strung his bow, nocked an arrow, pulled back, relaxed. I did the same. It settled my nerves.

I was so grateful to be on the ground I could have kissed it.

"The bole on the big oak." Raven pointed across the river. He let fly. His shaft struck a few inches off center. I took a deep, relaxing breath, followed suit. My shaft struck an inch nearer center. "Should have bet me that time," he remarked. To Catcher, "We're ready."

I added, "We'll need more specific directions."

"Follow the river bank. There are plenty of game trails. The going shouldn't be hard. No need to hurry anyway. Whisper shouldn't be there for hours yet."

"The river heads west," I observed.

"It loops back. Follow it for three miles, then turn a point west of north and go straight through the woods." Catcher crouched and cleared the leaves and twigs off some bare earth, used a stick to sketch a map. "If you reach this bend, you've gone too far."

Then Catcher froze. For a long minute he listened to something only he could hear. Then he resumed, "The Lady says you'll know you're close when you reach a grove of huge evergreens. It was the holy place of a people who died out before the Domination. The Limper is waiting at the center of the grove."

"Good enough," Raven said.

I asked, "You'll wait here?"

"Have no fear, Croaker."

I took another of my relaxing breaths. "Let's go, Raven."

"One second, Croaker," Soulcatcher said. He retrieved something from his bundle. It proved to be an arrow. "Use this."

I eyed it uncertainly, then placed it in my quiver.

Raven insisted on leading. I did not argue. I was a city boy before I joined the Company. I cannot become comfortable with forests. Especially not woods the size of the Forest of Cloud. Too much quiet. Too much solitude. Too easy to get lost. For the first two miles I worried more about finding my way back than I did about the coming encounter. I spent a lot of time memorizing landmarks.

Raven did not speak for an hour. I was busy thinking myself. I did not mind.

He raised a hand. I stopped. "Far enough, I think," he said. "We go that way now."

"Uhm."

"Let's rest." He settled on a huge tree root, his back against a trunk. "Awful quiet today, Croaker."

"Things on my mind."

"Yeah." He smiled. "Like what kind of reward we're set up for?"

"Among other things." I drew out the arrow Catcher had given me. "You see this?"

"A blunt head?" He felt it. "Soft, almost. What the hell?"

"Exactly. Means I'm not supposed to kill her."

There was no question of who would let fly at whom. The Limper was Raven's all the way.

"Maybe. But I'm not going to get killed trying to take her alive."

"Me either. That's what's bothering me. Along with about ten other things, like why the Lady *really* picked you and me, and why she wants Whisper alive. . . . Oh, the hell with it. It'll give me ulcers."

"Ready?"

"I guess."

We left the riverbank. The going became more difficult, but soon we crossed a low ridgeline and reached the edge of the evergreens. Not much grew beneath them. Very little sunlight leaked through their boughs. Raven paused to urinate. "Won't be any chance later," he explained.

He was right. You do not want that sort of problem when you are in ambush a stone's throw from an unfriendly Taken.

I was getting shaky. Raven laid a hand on my shoulder. "We'll be okay," he promised. But he did not believe it himself. His hand was shaky too.

I reached inside my jerkin and touched Goblin's amulet. It helped.

Raven raised an eyebrow. I nodded. We resumed walking. I chewed a strip of jerky, which burned off nervous energy. We did not speak again.

There were ruins among the trees. Raven examined the glyphs incised in the stones. He shrugged. They meant nothing to him.

Then we came to the big trees, the grandfathers of those through which we had been passing. They towered hundreds of feet high and had trunks as thick as the spans of two men's arms. Here and there, the sun thrust swords of light down through the boughs. The air was thick with resin smells. The silence was overwhelming. We moved one step at a time, making sure our footfalls sent no warnings ahead.

My nervousness peaked out, began to fade. It was too late to run, too late to change my mind. My brain cancelled all emotion. Usually that only happened when I was forced to treat casualties while people were killing one another all around me.

Raven signalled a halt. I nodded. I had heard it too. A horse snorting. Raven gestured for me to stay put. He eased to our left, keeping low, and disappeared behind a tree about fifty feet away.

He reappeared in a minute, beckoned. I joined him. He led me to a spot from which I could look into an open area. The Limper and his horse were there.

The clearing was maybe seventy feet long by fifty wide. A tumble of crumbling stone stood at its center. The Limper sat on one fallen rock and leaned against another. He seemed to be sleeping. One corner of the clearing was occupied by the trunk of a fallen giant that had not been down long. It showed very little weathering.

Raven tapped the back of my hand, pointed. He wanted to move on.

I did not like moving now that we had the Limper in sight. Each step meant another chance to alert the Taken to his peril. But Raven was right. The sun was dropping in front of us. The longer we stayed put, the worse the light would become. Eventually, it would be in our eyes.

We moved with exaggerated care. Of course. One mistake and we were dead. When Raven glanced back I saw sweat on his temples.

He stopped, pointed, smiled. I crept up beside him. He pointed again.

Another fallen tree lay ahead. This one was about four feet in diameter. It looked perfect for our purpose. It was big enough to hide us, low enough to let fly over. We found a spot providing a clean aisle of fire to the heart of the clearing.

The light was good, too. Several spears broke through the canopy and illuminated most of the clearing. There was a little haze in the air, pollen perhaps, which made the beams stand out. I studied the clearing for several minutes, imprinting it on my mind. Then I sat behind the log and pretended I was a rock. Raven took the watch.

It seemed weeks passed before anything happened.

Raven tapped my shoulder. I looked up. He made a walking motion with two fingers. The Limper was up and prowling. I rose carefully, watched.

The Limper circled the pile of stones a few times, bad leg dragging, then sat down again. He picked up a twig and broke it into small pieces, tossing each at some target only he could see. When the twig was gone, he scooped up a handful of small cones and threw them lazily. Portrait of a man killing time.

I wondered why he had come on horseback. He could get places fast when he wanted. I supposed because he had been close by. Then I worried that some of his troops might show up.

He got up and walked around again, collecting cones and chucking them at the fallen behemoth across the clearing. Damned, but I wished we could take him then, and have done.

The Limper's mount's head jerked up. The animal whickered. Raven and I sank down, crushed ourselves into the shadows and needles beneath our trunk. A crackling tension radiated from the clearing.

A moment later I heard hooves crunching needles. I held my breath. From the corner of my eye I caught flickers of a white horse moving among the trees. Whisper? Would she see us?

Yes and no. Thank whatever gods there are, yes and no. She passed within fifty feet without noticing us.

The Limper called something. Whisper replied in a melodious voice that did not at all fit the wide, hard, homely woman I had seen pass. She sounded seventeen and gorgeous, looked forty-five and like she had been around the world three times.

Raven prodded me gently.

I rose about as fast as a flower blooms, scared they would hear my sinews crackle. We peeped over the fallen tree. Whisper dismounted and took one of the Limper's hands in both of hers.

The situation could not have been more perfect. We were in shadow, they were fixed in a shaft of sunlight. Golden dust sparkled around them. And they were restricting one another by holding hands.

It had to be now. We both knew it, both bent our bows. We both had additional arrows gripped against our weapons, ready to be snapped to our strings. "Now," Raven said.

My nerves did not bother me till my arrow was in the air. Then I went cold and shaky.

Raven's shaft went in under the Limper's left arm. The Taken made a sound like a rat getting stomped. He arched away from Whisper.

My shaft smashed against Whisper's temple. She was wearing a leather helmet, but I was confident the impact would down her. She spun away from the Limper.

Raven sped a second arrow, I fumbled mine. I dropped my bow and vaulted over the log. Raven's third arrow whistled past me.

Whisper was on her knees when I arrived. I kicked her in the head, whirled to face the Limper. Raven's arrows had struck home, but even his special shaft had not ended the Taken's story. He was trying to growl out a spell through a throat filled with blood. I kicked him too.

Then Raven was there with me. I spun back to Whisper.

That bitch was as tough as her reputation. Woozy as she was, she was trying to get up, trying to draw her sword, trying to mouth a spell. I scrambled her brains again, got rid of her blade. "I didn't bring any cord," I gasped. "You bring any cord, Raven?"

"No." He just stood there staring at the Limper. The Taken's battered leather mask had slipped sideways. He was trying to straighten it so he could see who we were.

"How the hell am I going to tie her up?"

"Better worry about gagging her first." Raven helped the Limper with his mask, smiling that incredibly cruel smile he gets when he is about to cut a special throat.

I yanked out my knife and hacked at Whisper's clothing. She fought me. I had to keep knocking her down. Finally, I had strips of rag to bind her and to stuff into her mouth. I dragged her over to the pile of stones, propped her up, turned to see what Raven was doing.

He had ripped the Limper's mask away, exposing the desolation of the Taken's face.

"What are you doing?" I asked. He was binding the Limper. I wondered why he was bothering.

"Got to thinking maybe I don't have the talent to handle this." He dropped into a squat and patted the Limper's cheek. The Limper radiated hatred. "You know me, Croaker. I'm an old softy. I'd just kill him and be satisfied. But he deserves a harder death. Catcher has more experience in these things." He chuckled wickedly.

The Limper strained against his bonds. Despite the three arrows, he seemed normally strong. Even vigorous. The shafts certainly did not inconvenience him.

Raven patted his cheek again. "Hey, old buddy. Word of warning, one friend to another. . . . Wasn't that what you told me about an hour before Morningstar and her friends ambushed me in that place you sent me? Word of warning? Yeah. Look out for Soulcatcher. He got ahold of your true name. Character like that, there's no telling what he might do."

I said, "Take it easy on the gloating, Raven. Watch him. He's doing something with his fingers." He was wriggling them rhythmically.

"Aye!" Raven shouted, laughing. He grabbed the sword I had taken from Whisper and chopped fingers off each of the Limper's hands.

Raven rides me for not telling the whole truth in these Annals. Someday maybe he will look at this and be sorry. But, honestly, he was not nice people that day.

I had a similar problem with Whisper. I chose a different solution. I cut off her hair and used it to tangle her fingers together.

Raven tormented the Limper till I could stand no more. "Raven, that's really enough. Why don't you back off and keep them covered?" He had been given no specific instructions about what to do after we captured Whisper, but I figured the Lady would tell Catcher and he would drop in. We just had to keep things under control till he arrived.

Soulcatcher's magic carpet dropped from the sky half an hour after I chased Raven away from the Limper. It settled a few feet from our captives. Catcher stepped off, stretched, looked down at Whisper. He sighed, observed, "Not a pretty sight, Whisper," in that businesslike female voice. "But then you never were. Yes. My friend Croaker found the buried packets."

Whisper's hard, cold eyes sought me. They were informed with a savage impact. Rather than face that, I moved. I did not correct Soulcatcher.

He turned to the Limper, shook his head sadly. "No. It's not personal. You used up your credit. *She* ordered this."

The Limper went rigid.

Soulcatcher asked Raven, "Why didn't you kill him?"

Raven sat on the trunk of the larger fallen tree, bow across his lap, staring at the earth. He did not reply. I said, "He figured you could think of something better."

Catcher laughed. "I thought about it coming over here. Nothing seemed adequate. I'm taking Raven's way out. I told Shifter. He's on his way." He looked down at the Limper. "You're in trouble, aren't you?" To me, "You'd think a man this old would have garnered some wisdom along the way." He turned to Raven. "Raven, he was the Lady's reward to you."

Raven grunted. "I appreciate it."

I had figured that out already. But I was supposed to get something out of this too, and I had not seen anything remotely fulfilling any dream of mine.

Soulcatcher did his mindreading trick. "Yours has changed, I think. It hasn't been delivered yet. Make yourself comfortable, Croaker. We'll be here a long time."

I went and sat beside Raven. We did not talk. There was nothing I wanted to say, and he was lost somewhere inside himself. Like I said, a man cannot live on hatred alone.

Soulcatcher double-checked our captives' bonds, dragged his carpet rack into the shadows, then perched himself on the stone pile.

Shapeshifter arrived twenty minutes later, as huge, ugly, dirty, and stinking as ever. He looked the Limper over, conferred with Catcher, growled at the Limper for half a minute, then remounted his flying carpet and soared away. Catcher explained, "He's passing it on too. Nobody wants the final responsibility."

"Who could he pass it to?" I wondered. The Limper had no heavy enemies left.

Catcher shrugged and returned to the stone pile. He muttered in a dozen voices, drawing into himself, almost shrinking. I think he was as happy to be there as was I.

Time trudged on. The slant of the bars of sunlight grew ever steeper. One after another winked out. I began to wonder if Raven's suspicions had not been correct. We would be easy pickings after dark. The Taken do not need the sun to see.

I looked at Raven. What was happening inside his head? His face was a morose blank. It was the face he wore while playing cards.

I dropped off the log and prowled, following the pattern set by the Limper. There was nothing else to do. I whipped a pine cone at a burl on the log Raven and I had used for cover . . . and it ducked! I started a headlong charge toward Whisper's bloody sword before I fully realized what I had seen.

"What's wrong?" Soulcatcher asked as I pulled up.

I improvised. "Pulled muscle, I think. I was going to loosen up with some sprints, but something happened in my leg." I massaged my right calf. He seemed satisfied. I glanced toward the log, saw nothing.

But I knew Silent was there. Would be there if he was needed.

Silent. How the hell had he gotten here? Same way as the rest of us? Did he have tricks that nobody suspected?

After the appropriate theatrics, I limped over and joined Raven. By gesturing I tried to make him understand that we would have help if push came to shove, but the message did not penetrate. He was too withdrawn.

* * *

It was dark. There was a half moon overhead, poking a few mild silvery bars into the clearing. Catcher remained on the stone pile. Raven and I remained on the log. My behind was aching. My nerves were raw. I was tired and hungry and scared. I had had enough, but did not have the courage to say so.

Raven shed his funk suddenly. He assayed the situation, asked, "What the hell are we doing?"

Soulcatcher woke up. "Waiting. Shouldn't be much longer."

"Waiting for what?" I demanded. I can be brave with Raven backing me. Soulcatcher stared my way. I became aware of an unnatural stir in the grove behind me, of Raven coiling himself for action. "Waiting for what?" I repeated weakly.

"For me, physician." I felt the speaker's breath on the back of my neck.

I jumped halfway to Catcher, and did not stop till I reached Whisper's blade. Catcher laughed. I wondered if he had noticed that my leg had gotten better. I glanced at the smaller log. Nothing.

A glorious light poured over the log I had quitted. I did not see Raven. He had vanished. I gripped Whisper's sword and resolved to lay a good one on Soulcatcher.

The light floated over the fallen giant, settled in front of Catcher. It was too brilliant to look at long. It illuminated the whole clearing.

Soulcatcher dropped to one knee. And then I understood.

The Lady! This fiery glory was the Lady. We had been waiting for the Lady! I stared till my eyes ached. And dropped to one knee myself. I offered Whisper's sword on my palms, like a knight doing homage to his king. The Lady!

Was this my reward? To actually meet Her? That something that called to me from Charm twisted, filled me, and for one foolish instant I was totally in love. But I could not see Her. I wanted to see what She looked like.

She had that capacity I found so disconcerting in Soulcatcher. "Not this time, Croaker," she said. "But soon, I think." She touched my hand. Her fingers burned me like the first sexual touch of my first lover. Remember that racing, stunning, raging instant of excitement?

"The reward comes later. This time you'll be permitted to witness a rite unseen for five hundred years." She moved. "That has to be uncomfortable. Get up."

I rose, backed away. Soulcatcher stood in his parade rest stance, watching the light. Its intensity was falling. I could watch without pain. It drifted around the stone pile to our prisoners, waning till I could discern a feminine shape inside.

The Lady looked at the Limper a long time. The Limper looked back. His face was empty. He was beyond hope or despair.

The Lady said, "You served me well for a while. And your treachery helped more than it hurt. I am not without mercy." She flared on one side. A shadow diminished. There stood Raven, arrow across bow. "He's yours, Raven."

I looked at the Limper. He betrayed excitement and a strange hope. Not that he would survive, of course, but that he would die quickly, simply, painlessly.

Raven said, "No." Nothing else. Just a flat refusal.

The Lady mused, "Too bad, Limper." She arched back and screamed something at the sky.

Limper flopped violently. The gag flew out of his mouth. His ankle bonds parted. He gained his feet, tried to run, tried to mouth some spell that would protect him. He had gone thirty feet when a thousand fiery snakes streaked out of the night and swarmed him.

They covered his body. They slithered into his mouth and nose, into his eyes and ears. They went in the easy way and came gnawing out through his back and chest and belly. And he screamed. And screamed. And screamed. And the same terrible vitality which had fought off the lethality of Raven's arrows kept him alive throughout this punishment.

I heaved up the jerky that had been my only meal all day.

The Limper was a long time screaming, and never did die. Eventually, the Lady tired and sent the serpents away. She spun a whispery cocoon around the Limper, shouted another series of syllables. A gigantic luminescent dragonfly dropped from the night, snapped him up, and hummed away toward Charm. The Lady said, "He'll provide years of entertainment." She glanced at Soulcatcher, making sure the lesson had not gone over his head.

Catcher had not moved a muscle. He did not do so now.

The Lady said, "Croaker, what you are about to witness exists only in a few memories. Even most of my champions have forgotten."

What the hell was she talking about?

She looked down. Whisper cringed. The Lady said, "No, not all that. You've been such an outstanding enemy, I'm going to reward you." Strange laughter. "There is a vacancy among the Taken."

So. The blunted arrow, the weird circumstances leading to that moment, came clear. The Lady had decided that Whisper should replace the Limper.

When? Just when had she made that decision? The Limper had been in bad trouble for a year, suffering one humiliation after another. Had she orchestrated those? I think she had. A clue here, a clue there, a strand of gossip and a stray memory. . . . Catcher had been in on part of it, using us. Maybe he had been in on it as far back as when he had enlisted us. Surely our crossing paths with Raven had been no accident. . . . Ah, she was a cruel, wicked, deceitful, calculating bitch.

But everyone knew that. That was her story. She had dispossessed her own husband. She had murdered her sister, if Soulcatcher could be believed. So why was I disappointed and surprised?

I glanced at Catcher. He had not moved, but there was a subtle change in his stance. He was dazed by surprise. "Yes," the Lady told him. "You thought only the Dominator could Take." Soft laughter. "You were wrong. Pass that along to anyone still thinking about resurrecting my husband."

Catcher moved slightly. I could not read the movement's significance, but the Lady seemed satisfied. She faced Whisper again.

The Rebel general was more terrified than the Limper had been. She was about to become the thing she hated most—and she could do nothing.

The Lady knelt and began whispering to her.

I watched, and still I do not know what went on. Nor can I describe the Lady, any more than Goblin could, despite having been near her all night. Or maybe for several nights. Time had a surreal quality. We lost some days somewhere. But see her I did, *and* I witnessed the rite that converted our most dangerous enemy into one of our own.

I recall one thing with a razor-edged clarity. A huge yellow eye. The same eye that so croggled Goblin. It came and looked into me and Raven and Whisper.

It did not shatter me the way it had Goblin. Maybe I am less sensitive. Or just more ignorant. But it was bad. Like I said, some days disappeared.

That eye is not infallible. It does not do well with short term memories. The Lady remained unaware of Silent's proximity.

Of the rest of it there are only flickers of recollection, most filled with Whisper's screams. There was a moment when the clearing filled with dancing devils all glowing with their inner wickedness. They fought for the privilege of mounting Whisper. There was a time when Whisper faced the eye. A time when, I think, Whisper died and was resurrected, died and was resurrected, till she became intimate with death. There were times when she was tortured. And another time with the eye.

The fragments I retain suggest that she was shattered, slain, revived, and reassembled as a devoted slave. I recall her pledge of fealty to the Lady. Her voice dripped a craven eagerness to please.

Long after it was over I wakened confused and lost, and terrified. It took a while to reason out. The confusion was part of the Lady's protective coloration. What I could not remember could not be used against her.

Some reward.

She was gone. Likewise Whisper. But Soulcatcher remained, pacing the clearing, muttering in a dozen frantic voices. He fell silent the instant I tried to sit up. He stared, head thrust forward suspiciously.

I groaned, tried to rise, fell back. I crawled over and propped myself on one of the stones. Catcher brought me a canteen. I drank clumsily. He said, "You can eat after you pull yourself together."

Which remark alerted me to ravenous hunger. How long had it been? "What happened?"

"What do you remember?"

"Not much. Whisper was Taken?"

"She's replacing Limper. The Lady took her to the eastern front. Her knowledge of the other side should shake things loose out there."

I tried to shake the cobwebs. "I thought they were shifting to a northern strategy."

"They are. And as soon as your friend recovers, we have to return to Lords." In a soft, female voice, he admitted, "I didn't know Whisper as well as I thought. She did pass the word when she learned what happened at her camp. For once the Circle responded quickly. They avoided the usual infighting. They smell blood. They accepted their losses, and let us divert ourselves while they started their maneuvers. Kept them damned well hidden. Now Harden's army is headed toward Lords. Our forces are still scattered throughout the forest. She turned the trap around on us."

I did not want to hear it. A year of bad news is enough. Why couldn't one of our coups remain solid? "She sacrificed herself intentionally?"

"No. She wanted to run us around the woods to buy time for the Circle. She didn't know the Lady knew about the Limper. I thought I knew her, but I was wrong. We'll benefit eventually, but there are going to be hard times till Whisper straightens out the east."

I tried to rise, could not.

"Take it easy," he suggested. "First time with the Eye is always rough. Think you could eat something now?"

"Drag one of those horses over here."

"Better go easy at first."

"How bad is it?" I was not quite sure what I was asking. He assumed I meant the strategic situation.

"Harden's army is bigger than any we've yet faced up here. And it's only one of the groups that are on the move. If Nightcrawler doesn't reach Lords first, we'll lose the city and kingdom. Which might give them the momentum to drive us out of the north entirely. Our forces at Wist, Jane, Wine, and so forth, aren't up to a major campaign. The north has been a sideshow till now."

"But. . . . After all we've been through? We're worse off than when we lost Roses? Damn! That isn't fair." I was tired of retreating.

"Not to worry, Croaker. If Lords goes, we'll stop them at the Stair of Tear. We'll hold them there while Whisper runs wild. They can't ignore her forever. If the east collapses, the rebellion will die. The east is their strength." He sounded like a man trying to convince himself. He had been through these oscillations before, during the last days of the Domination.

I buried my head in my hands, muttered, "I thought we had them whipped." Why the hell had we left Beryl?

Soulcatcher prodded Raven with a toe. Raven did not stir. "Come on!" Catcher grumbled. "They need me at Lords. Nightcrawler and I may end up trying to hold the city by ourselves."

"Why didn't you just leave us if the situation is so critical?"

He hemmed and hawed and slid around it, and before he finished I suspected that this one Taken had a sense of honor, a sense of duty toward those who had accepted his protection. He would not admit it, though. Never. That would not fit the image of the Taken.

I thought about another journey through the sky. I thought hard. I am as lazy as the next guy, but I could not take that. Not now. Not feeling the way I did. "I'd fall off for sure. There's no point you hanging around. We won't be ready for days. Hell, we can walk out." I thought about the forest. Walking did not appeal to me either. "Give us our badges back. So you can locate us again. Then you can pick us up if you get time."

He grumbled. We batted it back and forth. I kept on about how shaky I was, about how shaky Raven would be.

He was anxious to get moving. He let me convince him. He unloaded his carpet—he had gone somewhere while I was unconscious—and climbed aboard. "I'll see you in a few days." His carpet rose far faster than it had done with Raven and me aboard. And then it was gone. I dragged myself to the things he had left behind.

"You bastard." I chuckled. His protest had been a shuck. He had left food, our own weapons that we had left in Lords, and odds and ends we might need to survive. Not a bad boss, for one of the Taken. "Hey! Silent! Where the hell are you?"

Silent drifted into the clearing. He looked at me, at Raven, at the supplies, and did not say anything. Of course not. He is Silent.

He looked ragged around the edges. "Not enough sleep?" I asked. He nodded. "You see what happened here?" He nodded again. "I hope you remember it better than I do." He shook his head. Damn. So it will go into the Annals unclear.

It is a weird way to hold a conversation, one man talking and the other head-shaking. Getting information across can be incredibly difficult. I should study the communicative gestures Raven has learned from Darling. Silent is her second best friend. It would be interesting just to eavesdrop on their conversations.

"Let's see what we can do for Raven," I suggested.

Raven was sleeping the sleep of the exhausted. He did not come out of it for hours. I used the interim to interrogate Silent.

The Captain had sent him. He had come on horseback. He was, in fact, on his way before Raven and I were summoned for our interview with Soulcatcher. He had ridden hard, day and night. He had reached the clearing only a short while before I spotted him.

I asked how he had known where to go, granting that the Captain would have nursed enough information from Catcher to get him started—a move which fit the Captain's style. Silent admitted he had not known where he was headed, except generally, till we had reached the area. Then he had tracked us through the amulet Goblin had given me.

Crafty little Goblin. He had not betrayed a hint. Good thing, too. The eye would have found the knowledge. "You think you could have done something if we'd really needed help?" I asked.

Silent smiled, shrugged, stalked over to the stone pile and seated himself. He was done with the question game. Of all the Company he is the least concerned about the image he will present in the Annals. He does not care whether people like or hate him, does not care where he has been or where he is going. Sometimes I wonder if he cares whether he lives or dies, wonder what makes him stay. He must have some attachment to the Company.

Raven finally came around. We nursed him and fed him and, finally, bedraggled, we rounded up Whisper's and the Limper's horses and headed for Lords. We travelled without enthusiasm, knowing we were headed for another battlefield, another land of standing dead men.

We could not get close. Harden's Rebels had the city besieged, circumvallated and bottled in a double fosse. A grim black cloud concealed the city itself. Cruel lightning rambled its edges, dueling the might of the Eighteen. Harden had not come alone.

The Circle seemed determined to avenge Whisper.

"Catcher and Nightcrawler are playing rough," Raven observed, after one particularly violent exchange. "I suggest we drift south and wait. If they abandon Lords, we'll join back up when they run toward the Windy Country." His face twisted horribly. He did not relish that prospect. He knew the Windy Country.

So south we scooted, and joined up with other stragglers. We spent twelve days in hiding, waiting. Raven organized the stragglers into the semblance of a military unit. I passed the time writing and thinking about Whisper, wondering how much she would influence the eastern situation. The rare glimpses I got of Lords convinced me that she was our side's last real hope.

Rumor had the Rebel applying just as much pressure elsewhere. The Lady supposedly had to transfer the Hanged Man and Bonegnasher from the east to stiffen resistance. One rumor had Shapeshifter slain in the fighting at Rye.

I worried about the Company. Our brethren had gotten into Lords before Harden's arrival.

Not a man falls without my telling his tale. How can I do that from twenty miles away? How many details will be lost in the oral histories I will have to collect after the fact? How many men will fall without their deaths being observed at all?

But mostly I spend my time thinking about the Limper and the Lady. And agonizing.

I do not think that I will be writing any more cute, romantic fantasies about our employer. I have been too close to her. I am not in love now.

I am a haunted man. I am haunted by the Limper's screams. I am haunted by the Lady's laughter. I am haunted by my suspicion that we are furthering the cause of something that deserves to be scrubbed from the face of the earth. I am haunted by the conviction that those bent upon the Lady's eradication are little better than she.

I am haunted by the clear knowledge that, in the end, evil always triumphs.

Oh, my. Trouble. There is a nasty black cloud crawling over the hills to the northeast. Everybody is running around, grabbing weapons and saddling horses. Raven is yelling at me to get my butt moving. . . .

5

Harden

The wind howled and flung blasts of dust and sand against our backs. We retreated into it, walking backward, the gritty storm finding every gap in armor and clothing, combining with sweat in a stinking, salty mud. The air was hot and dry. It sucked the moisture away quickly, leaving the mud dried in clots. We all had lips cracked and swollen, tongues like moldy pillows choking on the grit crusting the insides of our mouths.

Stormbringer had gotten carried away. We were suffering almost as much as was the Rebel. Visibility was a scant dozen yards. I could barely see the men to my right and left, and only two guys in the rearguard line, walking backward before me. Knowing our enemies had to come after us facing into the wind did not cheer me much.

The men in the other line suddenly scuttled around, plying their bows. Tall somethings loomed out of the swirling dust, cloakshadows swirling around them, flapping like vast wings. I drew my bow and let fly, sure my shaft would drift astray.

It did not. A horseman threw up his hands. His animal whirled and ran before the wind, pursuing riderless companions.

They were pushing hard, keeping close, trying to pick us off before we escaped the Windy Country to the more defensible Stair of Tear. They wanted every man of us stretched dead and plundered beneath the unforgiving desert sun.

Step back. Step back. So damned slow. But there was no choice. If we turned our backs they would swarm over us. We had to make them pay for every approach, to intimidate their exuberance thoroughly.

Stormbringer's sending was our best armor. The Windy Country is wild and brisk at the best of times, flat, barren, and dry, uninhabited, a place where sandstorms are common. But never had it seen a storm like this, that went on hour after hour and day after day, relenting only in the hours of darkness. It made the Windy Country no fit place for any living thing. And only that kept the Company alive.

There were three thousand of us now, falling back before the inexorable tide that had swamped Lords. Our little brotherhood, by refusing to break, had become the nucleus to which the fugitives from the disaster had attached themselves once the Captain had fought his way through the siege lines. We had become the brains and nerves of this fleeing shadow of an army. The Lady herself had sent orders for all Imperial officers to defer to the Captain. Only the Company had produced any signal successes during the northern campaign.

Someone came out of the dust and howl behind me, tapped my shoulder. I whirled. It was not yet time to leave the line.

Raven faced me. The Captain had figured out where I was.

Raven's whole head was wrapped in rags. I squinted, one hand raised to block the biting sand. He screamed something like, "Ta kata wa ya." I shook my head. He pointed rearward, grabbed me, yelled into my ear. "The Captain wants you."

Of course he did. I nodded, handed over bow and arrows, leaned into the wind and grit. Weapons were in short supply. The arrows I had given him were spent Rebel shafts gleaned after they had come wobbling out of the brownish haze.

Trudge trudge trudge. Sand pattering against the top of my head as I walked with chin against chest, hunched, eyes slitted. I did not want to go back. The Captain was not going to say anything I wanted to hear.

A big bush came spinning and bounding toward me. It nearly bowled me over. I laughed. We had Shapeshifter with us. The Rebel would waste a lot of arrows when that hit their lines. They outnumbered us ten or fifteen to one, but numbers could not soften their fear of the Taken.

I stamped into the fangs of the wind till I was sure I had gone too far, or had lost my bearings. It was always the same. After I decided to give up, there it was, the miraculous isle of peace. I entered it, staggering in the sudden absence of wind. My ears roared, refusing to believe the quiet.

Thirty wagons rolled along in tight formation inside the quiet, wheel to wheel. Most were filled with casualties. A thousand men surrounded the wagons, tramping doggedly southward. They stared at the earth and dreaded the coming of their turns out on the line. There was no conversation, no exchange of witticisms. They had seen too many retreats. They followed the Captain only because he promised a chance to survive.

"Croaker! Over here!" The Lieutenant beckoned me from the formation's extreme right flank.

The Captain looked like a naturally surly bear wakened from hibernation prematurely. The grey at his temples wriggled as he chewed his words before spitting them out. His face sagged. His eyes were dark hollows. His voice was infinitely tired. "Thought I told you to stick around."

"It was my turn. . . ."

"You don't take a turn, Croaker. Let me see if I can put it into words simple enough for you. We have three thousand men. We're in continuous contact with the Rebel. We've got one half-assed witchdoctor and one real doctor to take care of those boys. One-Eye has to spend half his energy helping maintain this dome of peace. Which leaves you to carry the medical load. Which means you don't risk yourself out on the line. Not for any reason."

I stared into the emptiness above his left shoulder, scowling at the sand swirling around the sheltered area.

"Am I getting through, Croaker? Am I making myself clear? I appreciate your devotion to the Annals, your determination to get the feel of the action, but. . . ."

I bobbed my head, glanced at the wagons and their sad burdens. So many wounded, and so little I could do for them. He did not see the helpless feeling that caused. All I could do was sew them up and pray, and make the dying comfortable till they went—whereupon we dumped them to make room for newcomers.

Too many were lost who need not have been, had I had time, trained help, and a decent surgery. Why did I go out to the battle line? Because I could accomplish something there. I could strike back at our tormentors.

"Croaker," the Captain growled. "I get the feeling you're not listening."

"Yes sir. Understood, sir. I'll stay here and tend to my sewing."

"Don't look so bleak." He touched my shoulder. "Catcher says we'll reach the Stair of Tear tomorrow. Then we can do what we all want. Bloody Harden's nose."

Harden had become the senior Rebel general. "Did he say how we're going to manage that, outnumbered a skillion to one?"

The Captain scowled. He did his shuffling little bear dance while he phrased a reassuring answer.

Three thousand exhausted, beaten men turn back Harden's victory-hopped horde? Not bloody likely. Not even with three of the Ten Who Were Taken helping.

"I thought not," I sneered.

"That's not your department, though, is it? Catcher doesn't second-guess your surgical procedures, does he? Then why question the grand strategy?"

I grinned. "The unwritten law of all armies, Captain. The lower ranks have the privilege of questioning the sanity and competence of their commanders. It's the mortar holding an army together."

The Captain eyed me from his shorter stature, wider displacement, and from beneath shaggy brows. "That holds them together, eh? And you know what keeps them moving?"

"What's that?"

"Guys like me ass-kicking guys like you when they start philosophizing. If you get my drift."

"I believe I do, sir." I moved out, recovered my kit from the wagon where I had stashed it, went to work. There were few new casualties.

Rebel ambition was wearing down under Stormbringer's ceaseless assault.

I was loafing along, waiting for a call, when I spotted Elmo loping out of the weather. I hadn't seen him for days. He fell in beside the Captain. I ambled over.

". . . sweep around our right," he was saying. "Maybe trying to reach the Stair first." He glanced at me, lifted a hand in greeting. It shook. He was pallid with weariness. Like the Captain, he had had little rest since we had entered the Windy Country.

"Pull a company out of reserve. Take them in flank," the Captain replied. "Hit them hard, and stand fast. They won't expect that. It'll shake them. Make them wonder what we're up to."

"Yes sir." Elmo turned to go.

"Elmo?"

"Sir?"

"Be careful out there. Save your energy. We're going to keep moving tonight."

Elmo's eyes spoke tortured volumes. But he did not question his orders. He is a good soldier. And, as did I, he knew they came from above the Captain's head. Perhaps from the Tower itself.

Hitherto, night had brought a tacit truce. The rigors of the days had left both armies unwilling to take one needless step after dark. There had been no nighttime contact.

Even those hours of respite, when the storm slept, were not enough to keep the armies from marching with their butts drooping against their heels. Now our high lords wanted an extra effort, hoping to gain some tactical advantage. Get to the Stair by night, get dug in, make the Rebel come at us out of perpetual storm. It made sense. But it was the sort of move ordered by an armchair general three hundred miles behind the fighting.

"You hear that?" the Captain asked me.

"Yeah. Sounds dumb."

"I agree with the Taken, Croaker. The travelling will be easier for us and more difficult for the Rebel. Are you caught up?"

"Yes."

"Then try to stay out of the way. Go hitch a ride. Take a nap."

I wandered away, cursing the ill fortune that had stripped us of most of our mounts. Gods, walking was getting old.

I did not take the Captain's advice, though it was sound. I was too keyed up to rest. The prospect of a night march had shaken me.

I roamed around seeking old friends. The Company had scattered throughout the larger mob, as cadre for the Captain's will. Some men I hadn't seen since Lords. I did not know if they were still alive.

I could find no one but Goblin, One-Eye, and Silent. Today Goblin and One-Eye were no more communicative than Silent. Which said a lot about morale.

They trudged doggedly onward, eyes on the dry earth, only rarely making some gesture or muttering some word to maintain the integrity of our bubble of peace. I trudged with them. Finally, I tried breaking the ice with a "Hi."

Goblin grunted. One-Eye gave me a few seconds of evil stare. Silent did not acknowledge my existence.

"Captain says we're going to march through the night," I told them. I had to make someone else as miserable as I was.

Goblin's look asked me why I wanted to tell that kind of lie. One-Eye muttered something about turning the bastard into a toad.

"The bastard you're going to have to turn is Soulcatcher," I said smugly.

He gave me another evil look. "Maybe I'll practice on you, Croaker."

One-Eye did not like the night march, so Goblin immediately approved the genius of the man who had initiated the idea. But his enthusiasm was so slight One-Eye did not bother taking the bait.

I thought I would give it another try. "You guys look as sour as I feel."

No rise. Not even a turn of the head. "Be that way." I drooped too, put one foot ahead of the other, blanked my mind.

They came and got me to take care of Elmo's wounded. There were a dozen of them, and that was it for the day. The Rebel had run out of do or die.

Darkness came early under the storm. We went about business as usual. We got a little away from the Rebel, waited for the storm to abate, pitched a camp with fires built of whatever brush could be scrounged. Only this time it was just a brief rest, till the stars came out. They stared down with mockery in their twinkles, saying all our sweat and blood really had no meaning in the long eye of time. Nothing we did would be recalled a thousand years from now.

Such thoughts infected us all. No one had any ideals or glory-lust left. We just wanted to get somewhere, lie down, and forget the war.

The war would not forget us. As soon as he believed the Rebel to be satisfied that we were encamped, the Captain resumed the march, now in a ragged column snaking slowly across moonlighted barrens.

Hours passed and we seemed to get nowhere. The land never changed. I glanced back occasionally, checking the renewed storm Stormbringer was hurling against the Rebel camp. Lightning rippled and flickered in this one. It was more furious than anything they had faced so far.

The shadowed Stair of Tear materialized so slowly that it was there for an hour before I realized it was not a bank of cloud low on the horizon. The stars began to fade and the east to lighten before the land started rising.

The Stair of Tear is a rugged, wild range virtually impassable except for the one steep pass from which the cordillera takes its name. The land rises gradually till it reaches sudden, towering red sandstone bluffs and mesas which stretch either way for hundreds of miles. In the morning sun they looked like the weathered battlements of a giant's fortress.

The column wound into a canyon choked with talus, halted while a path was cleared for the wagons. I dragged myself to a bluff top and watched the storm. It was moving our way.

Would we get through before Harden arrived?

The blockage was a fresh fall which covered only a quarter mile of road. Beyond it lay the route travelled by caravans before the war interrupted trade.

I faced the storm again. Harden was making good time. I suppose anger drove him. He was not about to turn loose. We had killed his brother-in-law, and had engineered the Taking of his cousin. . . .

Movement to the west caught my eye. A whole range of ferocious thunderheads was moving toward Harden, rumbling and brawling among themselves. A funnel cloud spun off and streaked toward the sandstorm. The Taken play rough.

Harden was stubborn. He kept coming through everything.

"Yo! Croaker!" someone shouted. "Come on."

I looked down. The wagons were through the worst. Time to go.

Out on the flats the thunderheads spun off another funnel cloud. I almost felt sorry for Harden's men.

Soon after I rejoined the column the ground shuddered. The bluff I had climbed quivered, groaned, toppled, sprawled across the road. Another little gift for Harden.

We reached our stopping place shortly before nightfall. Decent country at last! Real trees. A gurgling creek. Those who had any strength left began digging in or cooking. The rest fell in their tracks. The Captain did not press. The best medicine at the moment was the simple freedom to rest.

I slept like the proverbial log.

One-Eye wakened me at rooster time. "Let's get to work," he said. "The Captain wants a hospital set up." He made a face. His looks like a prune at the best of times. "We're supposed to have some help coming up from Charm."

I groaned and moaned and cursed and got up. Every muscle was stiff. Every bone ached. "Next time we're someplace civilized enough to have taverns remind me to drink a toast to eternal peace," I grumbled. "One-Eye, I'm ready to retire."

"So who isn't? But you're the Annalist, Croaker. You're always rubbing our noses in tradition. You know you only got two ways out while we've got this commission. Dead or feet first. Shove some chow in your ugly face and let's get cracking. I got more important things to do than play nursemaid."

"Cheerful this morning, aren't we?"

"Positively rosy." He grumped around while I got myself into an approximation of order.

The camp was coming to life. Men were eating and washing the desert off their bodies. They were cussing and fussing and bitching. Some were even talking to one another. The recovery had begun.

Sergeants and officers were out surveying the lie of the slope, seeking the most defensible strongpoints. This, then, was the place where the Taken wanted to make a stand.

It was a good spot. It was that part of the pass which gave the Stair its name, a twelve hundred foot rise overlooking a maze of canyons. The old road wound back and forth across the mountainside in countless switchbacks, so that from a distance it looked like a giant's lopsided stairway.

One-Eye and I drafted a dozen men and began moving the wounded to a quiet grove well above the prospective battleground. We spent an hour making them comfortable and getting set for future business.

"What's that?" One-Eye suddenly demanded.

I listened. The din of preparation had died. "Something up," I said.

"Genius," he countered. "Probably the people from Charm."

"Let's take a look." I tramped out of the grove and down toward the Captain's headquarters. The newcomers were obvious the moment I left the trees.

I would guess there were a thousand of them, half soldiers from the Lady's personal Guard in brilliant uniforms, the rest apparently teamsters. The train of wagons and livestock were more exciting than the reinforcements. "Feast time tonight," I called to One-Eye, who was following me. He looked the wagons over and smiled. Pure pleasure smiles from him are only slightly more common than the fabled hen's teeth. They are certainly worth recording in these Annals.

With the Guards battalion was the Taken called the Hanged Man. He was improbably tall and lean. His head was twisted way over to one side. His neck was swollen and purpled from the bite of a noose. His face was frozen into the bloated expression of one who has been strangled. I expect he had considerable difficulty speaking.

He was the fifth of the Taken I had seen, following Soulcatcher, the Limper, Shapeshifter, and Whisper. I missed Nightcrawler in Lords, and had not yet seen Stormbringer, despite proximity. The Hanged Man was different. The others usually wore something to conceal head and face. Excepting Whisper, they had spent ages in the ground. The grave had not treated them kindly.

Soulcatcher and Shapeshifter were there to greet the Hanged Man. The Captain was nearby, back to them, listening to the commander of the Lady's guardsmen. I eased closer, hoping to eavesdrop.

The guardsman was being surly because he had to place himself at the Captain's disposal. None of the regulars liked taking orders from a come-lately mercenary from overseas.

I sidled nearer the Taken. And found I could not understand a word of their conversation. They were speaking TelleKurre, which had died with the fall of the Domination.

A hand touched mine, lightly. Startled, I looked down into the wide brown eyes of Darling, whom I had not seen for days. She made rapid gestures with her fingers. I have been learning her signs. She wanted to show me something.

She led me to Raven's tent, which was not far from the Captain's. She scrambled inside, returned with a wooden doll. Loving craftsmanship had gone into its creation. I could not imagine the hours Raven must have put into it. I could not imagine where he had found them.

Darling slowed her finger talk so I could follow more easily. I was not yet very facile. She told me Raven made the doll, as I had guessed, and that now he was sewing up a wardrobe. She thought she had a great treasure. Recalling the village where we had found her, I could not doubt that it was the finest toy she had ever possessed.

Revealing object, when you think about Raven, who comes across so bitter, cold, and silent, whose only use for a knife seems so sinister.

Darling and I conversed for several minutes. Her thoughts are delightfully straightforward, a refreshing contrast in a world filled with devious, prevaricating, unpredictable, scheming people.

A hand squeezed my shoulder, halfway between angry and companionable. "The Captain is looking for you, Croaker." Raven's dark eyes glinted like obsidian under a quarter moon. He pretended the doll was invisible. He *likes* to come across hard, I realized.

"Right," I said, making manual good-byes. I enjoyed learning from Darling. She enjoyed teaching me. I think it gave her a feeling of worth. The Captain was considering having everyone learn her sign language. It would make a valuable supplement to our traditional but inadequate battle signals.

The Captain gave me a black look when I arrived, but spared me a lecture. "Your new help and supplies are over yonder. Show them where to go."

"Yes sir."

The responsibility was getting to him. He hadn't ever commanded so many men, nor faced conditions so adverse, with orders so impossible, staring at a future so uncertain. From where he stood it looked like we would be sacrificed to buy time.

We of the Company are not enthusiastic fighters. But the Stair of Tear could not be held by trickery.

It looked like the end had come.

No one will sing songs in our memory. We are the last of the Free Companies of Khatovar. Our traditions and memories live only in these Annals. We are our only mourners.

It is the Company against the world. Thus it has been and ever will be.

My aid from the Lady consisted of two qualified battlefield surgeons and a dozen trainees of various degrees of skill, along with a brace of wagons brimming with medical supplies. I was grateful. Now I stood a chance of saving a few men.

I took the newcomers to my grove, explained how I worked, turned them loose on my patients. After making sure they were not complete incompetents, I turned the hospital over and left.

I was restless. I did not like what was happening to the Company. It had acquired too many new followers and responsibilities. The old intimacy was gone. Time was, I saw every one of the men every day. Now there were some I had not seen since before the debacle at Lords. I did not know if they were dead, alive, or captive. I was almost neurotically anxious that some men had been lost and would be forgotten.

The Company is our family. The brotherhood makes it go. These days, with all these new northern faces, the prime force holding the Company together is a desperate effort by the brethren to reachieve the old intimacy. The strain of trying marks every face.

I went out to one of the forward watchpoints, which overlooked the fall of the brook into the canyons. Way, way down there, below the mist, lay a small, glimmering pool. A thin trickle left it, running toward the Windy Country. It would not complete its journey. I searched the chaotic ranks of sandstone towers and buttes. Thunderheads with lightning swords aflash on their brows grumbled and pounded the badlands, reminding me that trouble was not far away.

Harden was coming despite Stormbringer's wrath. He would make contact tomorrow, I guessed. I wondered how much the storms had hurt him. Surely not enough.

I spied a brown hulk shambling down the switchback road. Shapeshifter, going out to practice his special terrors. He could enter the Rebel camp as one of them, practice poison magics upon their cookpots or fill their drinking water with disease. He could become the shadow in the darkness that all men fear, taking them one at a time, leaving only mangled remains to fill the living with terror. I envied him even while I loathed him.

The stars twinkled above the campfire. It had burned low while some of us old hands played Tonk. I was a slight winner. I said, "I'm quitting while I'm ahead. Anybody want my place?" I unwound my aching legs and moved away, settled against a log, stared at the sky. The stars seemed merry and friendly.

The air was cool and fresh and still. The camp was quiet. Crickets and nightbirds sang their soothing songs. The world was at peace. It was hard to believe that this place was soon to become a battlefield. I wriggled till I was comfortable, watched for shooting stars. I was determined to enjoy the moment. It might be the last such I would know.

The fire spit and crackled. Somebody found ambition enough to add a little wood. It blazed up, sent piney smoke drifting my way, launched shadows which danced over the intent faces of the card players. One-Eye's lips were taut because he was losing. Goblin's frog mouth was stretched in an unconscious grin.

Silent was a blank, being Silent. Elmo was thinking hard, scowling as he calculated odds. Jolly was more sour than customary. It was good to see Jolly again. I had feared him lost at Lords.

Only one puny meteor rolled across the sky. I gave it up, closed my eyes, listened to my heartbeat. *Harden is coming. Harden is coming,* it said. It pounded out a drumbeat, mimicking the tread of advancing legions.

Raven settled down beside me. "Quiet tonight," he observed.

"Calm before the storm," I replied. "What's cooking with the high and the mighty?"

"Lot of argument. The Captain, Catcher, and the new one are letting them yap. Letting them get it out of their systems. Who's ahead?"

"Goblin."

"One-Eye isn't dealing from the bottom of the deck?"

"We never caught him."

"I heard that," One-Eye growled. "One of these days, Raven. . . ."

"I know. Zap. I'm a frog prince. Croaker, you been up the hill since it got dark?"

"No. Why?"

"Something unusual over in the east. Looks like a comet."

My heart did a small flip. I calculated quickly. "You're probably right. It's due back." I rose. He did too. We walked uphill.

Every major event in the saga of the Lady and her husband has been presaged by a comet. Countless Rebel prophets have predicted that she will fall while a comet is in the sky. But their most dangerous prophecy concerns the child who will be a reincarnation of the White Rose. The Circle is spending a lot of energy trying to locate the kid.

Raven led me to a height from which we could see the stars lying low in the east. Sure enough, something like a faraway silver spearhead rode the sky there. I stared a long time before observing, "It seems to be pointed at Charm."

"I thought so too." He was silent for a while. "I'm not much on prophecies, Croaker. They sound too much like superstition. But this makes me nervous."

"You've heard those prophecies all your life. I'd be surprised if they *hadn't* touched you."

He grunted, not satisfied. "The Hanged Man brought news of the east. Whisper has taken Rust."

"Good news, good news," I said, with considerable sarcasm.

"She's taken Rust *and* surrounded Trinket's army. We can have the whole east by next summer."

We faced the canyon. A few of Harden's advance units had reached the foot of the switchbacks. Stormbringer had broken off his long assault in order to prepare for Harden's attempt to break through here.

"So it comes down to us," I whispered. "We have to stop them here or the whole thing goes because of a sneak attack through the back way."

"Maybe. But don't count the Lady out even if we fail. The Rebel hasn't yet faced Her. And they know it to a man. Each mile they move toward the Tower will fill them with greater dread. Terror itself will defeat them unless they find their prophesied child."

"Maybe." We watched the comet. It was far, far away yet, just barely detectable. It would be up there a long time. Great battles would be fought before it departed.

I made a face. "Maybe you shouldn't have shown me. Now I'll dream about the damned thing."

Raven flashed a rare grin. "Dream us a victory," he suggested.

I did some dreaming aloud. "We've got the high ground. Harden has to bring his men up twelve hundred feet of switchback. They'll be easy meat when they get here."

"Whistling in the dark, Croaker. I'm going to turn in. Good luck tomorrow."

"Same to you," I replied. He would be in the thick of it. The Captain had chosen him to command a battalion of veteran regulars. They would be holding one flank, sweeping the road with arrow flights.

I dreamed, but my dreams were not what I expected. A wavering golden thing came, hovered above me, glowing like shoals of faraway stars. I was not sure whether I was asleep or awake, and still have not satisfied myself either way. I will call it dream because it sits more comfortably that way. I do not like to think the Lady had taken that much interest in me.

It was my own fault. All those romances I wrote about her had gone to seed on the fertile stable floor of my imagination. Such presumption, my dreams. The Lady Herself send Her spirit to comfort one silly, war-weary, quietly frightened soldier? In the name of heaven, why?

That glow came and hovered above me, and sent reassurances overtoned by harmonics of amusement. *Fear not, my faithful. The Stair of Tear is not the Lock of the Empire. It can be broken without harm. Whatever happens, my faithful will remain safe. The Stair is but a milemark along the Rebel's road to destruction.*

There was more, all of a puzzlingly personal nature. My wildest fantasies were being reflected back upon me. At the end, for just an instant, a face peeked from the golden glow. It was the most beautiful female face I have ever seen, though I cannot now recall it.

Next morning I told One-Eye about the dream as I hounded my hospital into life. He looked at me and shrugged. "Too much imagination, Croaker." He was preoccupied, anxious to complete his medical chores and get gone. He hated the work.

My work caught up, I meandered toward the main encampment. My head was stuffy and my mood sour. The cool, dry mountain air was not as invigorating as it should have been.

I found the temper of the men as sour as my own. Below, Harden's forces were moving.

Part of winning is a downdeep certainty that, no matter how bad things look, a road to victory will open. The Company carried that conviction through the debacle at Lords. We'd always found a way to bloody the Rebel's nose, even while the Lady's armies were in retreat. Now, though. . . . The conviction has begun to waver.

Forsberg, Roses, Lords, and a dozen lesser defeats. Part of losing is the converse of winning. We were haunted by a secret fear that, despite the obvious advantages of terrain and backing by the Taken, something would go wrong.

Maybe they cooked it up themselves. Maybe the Captain was behind it, or even Soulcatcher. Possibly it came about naturally, as these things once did. . . .

One-Eye had trooped downhill behind me, sour, surly, grumbling to himself, and spoiling for a row. His path crossed Goblin's.

Slugabed Goblin had just dragged out of his bedroll. He had a bowl of water and was washing up. He is a fastidious little wart. One-Eye spotted him and saw a chance to punish somebody with his foul mood. He muttered a string of strange words and went into a curious little fling that looked half ballet and half primitive war dance.

Goblin's water changed.

I smelled it from twenty feet away. It had turned a malignant brown. Sickening green gobs floated on its surface. It even *felt* foul.

Goblin rose with magnificent dignity, turned. He looked an evilly grinning One-Eye in the eye for several seconds. Then he bowed. When his head came up he wore a huge frog smile. He opened his mouth and let fly the most godawful, earthshaking howl I have ever heard.

They were off, and damned be the fool who got in their way. Shadows scattered around One-Eye, wriggling across the earth like a thousand hasty serpents. Ghosts danced, crawling from under rocks, jumping down from trees, hopping out of bushes. The latter squealed and howled and giggled and chased One-Eye's shadow snakes.

The ghosts stood two feet tall and very much resembled half-pint One-Eyes with double-ugly faces and behinds like those of female baboons in season. What they did with captured shadow snakes, taste forbids me tell.

One-Eye, foiled, leapt into the air. He cursed, shrieked, foamed at the mouth. To us old hands, who had witnessed these hatter-mad battles before, it was obvious that Goblin had been laying in the weeds, waiting for One-Eye to start something.

This was one time when One-Eye had more than a lone bolt to shoot.

He banished the snakes. The rocks, bushes, and trees that had belched Goblin's critters now disgorged gigantic, glossy-green dung beetles. The big bugs jumped Goblin's elves, rolled them right up, and began tumble-bugging them toward the edge of the cliff.

Needless to say, all the whoop and holler drew an audience. Laughter ripped out of us old hands, long familiar with this endless duel. It spread to the others once they realized this was not sorcery run amok.

Goblin's red-bottomed ghosts sprouted roots and refused to be tumbled. They grew into huge, drooling-mawed carnivorous plants fit to inhabit the cruelest jungle of nightmare. Clickety-clackety-crunch, all across the slope, carapaces broke between closing vegetable jaws. That spine-shaking, tooth-grinding feeling you get when you crunch a big cockroach slithered across the slopes, magnified a thousand times, birthing a plague of shudders. For a moment even One-Eye remained motionless.

I glanced around. The Captain had come to watch. He betrayed a satisfied smile. It was a precious gem, that smile, rarer than roc's eggs. His companions, regular officers and Guards captains, appeared baffled.

Someone took up position beside me, at an intimate, comradely distance. I glanced sideways, found myself shoulder to shoulder with Soulcatcher. Or elbow to shoulder. The Taken does not stand very tall.

"Amusing, yes?" he said in one of his thousand voices.

I nodded nervously.

One-Eye shuddered all over, jumped high in the air again, wailed and howled, then went down kicking and flopping like a man with the falling sickness.

The surviving beetles rushed together, zip-zap, clickety-clack, into two seething piles, clacking their mandibles angrily, scraping against one another chitinously. Brown smog wriggled from the piles in thick ropes, twisted and joined, became a curtain concealing the frenzied bugs. The smoke contracted into globules which bounced, bounding higher after each contact with the earth. Then they did not come down, but rather drifted on the breeze, sprouting what grew into gnarly digits.

What we had here were replicas of One-Eye's horny paws a hundred times life size. Those hands went weed-plucking through Goblin's monster garden, ripping his plants up by the roots, knotting their stems together in elegant, complicated sailor's knots, forming an ever-elongating braid.

"They do have more talent than one would suspect," Soulcatcher observed. "But so wasted on frivolity."

"I don't know." I gestured. The show was having an invigorating effect on morale. Feeling a breath of that boldness which animates me at odd moments,

I suggested, "This is a sorcery they can appreciate, unlike the oppressive, bitter wizardries of the Taken."

Catcher's black morion faced me for a few seconds. I imagined fires burning behind the narrow eyeslits. Then a girlish giggle slipped forth. "You're right. We're so filled with doom and gloom and brooding and terror we infect whole armies. One soon forgets the emotional panorama of life."

How odd, I thought. This was a Taken with a chink in its armor, a Soulcatcher drawing aside one of the veils concealing its secret being. The Annalist in me caught the scent of a tale and began to bay.

Catcher sidestepped me as though reading my thoughts. "You had a visitation last night?"

The Annalist-hound's voice died in midcry. "I had a strange dream. About the Lady."

Catcher chuckled, a deep, bass rumble. That constant changing of voices can rattle the most stolid of men. It put me on the defensive. His very comradeliness, too, disturbed me.

"I think she favors you, Croaker. Some little thing about you has captured her imagination, just as she has caught yours. What did she have to say?"

Something way back told me to be careful. Catcher's query was warm and offhand, yet there was a hidden intensity there which said that the question was not at all casual.

"Just reassurances," I replied. "Something about the Stair of Tear not being all that critical in her scheme. But it was only a dream."

"Of course." He seemed satisfied. "Only a dream." But the voice was the female one he used when he was most serious.

The men were oohing and ahing. I turned to check the progress of the contest.

Goblin's skein of pitcher-plants had transmogrified into a huge airborne man-of-war jellyfish. The brown hands were entangled in its tentacles, trying to tear themselves free. And over the cliff face, observing, floated a giant pink face, bearded, surrounded by tangled orange hair. One eye was half closed, sleepily, by a livid scar. I frowned, baffled. "What's that?" I knew it was not any doing of Goblin's or One-Eye's, and wondered if Silent had joined the game, just to show them up.

Soulcatcher made a sound that was a creditable imitation of a bird's dying squawk. "Harden," he said, and whirled to face the Captain, bellowing, "To arms. They come."

In seconds men were flying toward their positions. The last hints of the struggle between Goblin and One-Eye became misty tatters floating on the wind, drifting toward the leering Harden face, giving it a loathsome case of acne where they touched. A cute fillip, I thought, but don't try to take him heads up, boys. He won't play games.

The answer to our scramble was a lot of horn-blowing from below, and a grumble of drums which echoed in the canyons like distant thunder.

The Rebel poked at us all day, but it was obvious that he was not serious, that he was just prodding the hornets' nest to see what would happen. He was well aware of the difficulty of storming the Stair.

All of which portended Harden having something nasty up his sleeve.

Overall, though, the skirmishes boosted morale. The men began to believe there was a chance they could hold.

Though the comet swam among the stars, and a galaxy of campfires speckled the Stair below, the night gave the lie to my feeling that the Stair was the heart of war. I sat on an outcrop overlooking the enemy, knees up under my chin, musing on the latest news from the east. Whisper was besieging Frost now, after having finished Trinket's army and having defeated Moth and Sidle among the talking menhirs of the Plain of Fear. The east looked a worse disaster for the Rebel than was the north for us.

It could get worse here. Moth and Sidle and Linger had joined Harden. Others of the Eighteen were down there, as yet unidentified. Our enemies did smell blood.

I have never seen the northern auroras, though I am told we would have gotten glimpses had we held Oar and Deal long enough to have wintered there. The tales I have heard about those gentle, gaudy lights make me think they are the only thing to compare with what took shape over the canyons, as the Rebel campfires dwindled. Long, long, thin banners of tenuous light twisted up toward the stars, shimmering, undulating like seaweed in a gentle current. Soft pinks and greens, yellows and blues, beautiful hues. A phrase leapt into my mind. An ancient name. The Pastel Wars.

The Company fought in the Pastel Wars, long, long ago. I tried to recall what the Annals said about those conflicts. It would not all come to the fore, but I remembered enough to become frightened. I hurried toward the officers' compound, seeking Soulcatcher.

I found him, and told him what I remembered, and he thanked me for my concern, but said he was familiar with both the Pastel Wars and the Rebel cabal sending up these lights. We had no worries. This attack had been anticipated and the Hanged Man was here to abort it.

"Take yourself a seat somewhere, Croaker. Goblin and One-Eye put on their show. Now it's the turn of the Ten." He oozed a confidence both strong and malignant, so that I supposed the Rebel had fallen into some Taken trap.

I did as he suggested, venturing back out to my lonely watchpost. Along the way I passed through a camp aroused by the growing spectacle. A murmur of fear ran hither and yon, rising and falling like the mutter of distant surf.

The colored streamers were stronger now, and there was a frenetic jerkiness to their movements which suggested a thwarted will. Maybe Catcher was right. Maybe this would come to nothing but a flashy show for the troops.

I resumed my perch. The canyon bottom no longer twinkled. It was a sea of ink down there, not at all softened by the glow of the writhing streamers. But if nothing could be seen, plenty could be heard. The acoustics of the land were remarkable.

Harden was on the move. Only the advance of his entire army could generate so much metallic rattle and tinkle.

Harden and his henchmen were confident too.

A soft green light banner floated up into the night, fluttering lazily, like a streamer of tissue in an updraft. It faded as it rose, and disintegrated into dying sparks high overhead.

What snipped it loose? I wondered. Harden or the Hanged Man? Did this bode good or ill?

It was a subtle contest, almost impossible to follow. It was like watching superior fencers duel. You could not follow everything unless you were an expert yourself. Goblin and One-Eye had gone at it like a couple of barbarians with broadswords, comparatively speaking.

Little by little, the colorful aurora died. That had to be the doing of the Hanged Man. The unanchored light banners did us no harm.

The racket below got closer.

Where was Stormbringer? We had not heard from him for a while. This seemed an ideal time to gift the Rebel with miserable weather.

Catcher, too, seemed to be lying down on the job. In all the time we have been in service to the Lady we have not seen him do anything really dramatic. Was he less mighty than his reputation, or, perhaps, saving himself for some extremity only he foresaw?

Something new was happening below. The canyon walls had begun to glow in stripes and spots, a deep, deep red that was barely noticeable at first. The red became brighter. Only after patches began to drip and ooze did I notice the hot draft riding up the cliff face.

"Great gods," I murmured, stricken. Here was a deed worthy of my expectations of the Taken.

Stone began to grumble and roar as molten rock ran away and left mountainsides undermined. There were cries from below, the cries of the hopeless who see doom coming and can do nothing to stay or evade it. Harden's men were being cooked and crushed.

They were in the witch's cauldron for sure, but something made me uneasy anyway. There seemed to be too little yelling for a force the size of Harden's.

In spots the rock became so hot it caught fire. The canyon expelled a furious updraft. The wind howled over the hammering of falling rocks. The light grew bright enough to betray Rebel units climbing the switchbacks.

Too few, I thought. . . . A lonely figure on another outcrop caught my eye. One of the Taken, though in the shifting, uncertain light I could not be certain which. It was nodding to itself as it observed the enemy's travails.

The redness, the melting, the collapsing and burning spread till the whole panorama was veined with red and poked with bubbling pools.

A drop of moisture hit my cheek. I looked up, startled, and a second fat drop smacked the bridge of my nose.

The stars had vanished. The spongy bellies of fat grey clouds raced overhead, almost low enough to touch, garishly tinted by the hellscape below.

The bellies of the clouds opened over the canyon. Caught on the edge of the downpour, I was nearly beaten to my knees. Out there it was more savage.

Rain hit molten rock. The roar of steam was deafening. Particolored, it stormed toward the sky. The fringe I caught, as I turned to run, was hot enough to redden patches of skin.

Those poor Rebel fools, I thought. Steamed like lobsters. . . .

I had been dissatisfied because I had seen little spectacular from the Taken? Not anymore. I had trouble keeping my supper down as I reflected on the cold, cruel calculation that had gone into the planning of this.

I suffered one of those crises of conscience familiar to every mercenary, and which few outside the profession understand. My job is to defeat my employer's enemies. Usually any way I can. And heaven knows the Company has served some blackhearted villains. But there was something *wrong* about what was happening below. In retrospect, I think we all felt it. Perhaps it sprang from a misguided sense of solidarity with fellow soldiers dying without an opportunity to defend themselves.

We *do* have a sense of honor in the Company.

The roar of downpour and steam faded. I ventured back to my vantage point. Except for small patches, the canyon was dark. I looked for the Taken I had seen earlier. He was gone.

Above, the comet came out from behind the last clouds, marring the night like a tiny, mocking smile. It had a distinct bend in its tail. Over on the sawtoothed horizon, a moon took a cautious peek at the tortured land.

Horns blared in that direction, their tinny voices distinctly edged with panic. They gave way to a distant muddled sound of fighting, an uproar which swelled rapidly. The fighting sounded heavy and confused. I started toward my makeshift hospital, confident there would be work for me soon. For some reason I was not particularly startled or upset.

Messengers dashed past me, zipping around purposefully. The Captain had done that much with those stragglers. He had restored their senses of order and discipline.

Something whooshed overhead. A seated man riding a dark rectangle swooped through the moonlight, banking toward the uproar. Soulcatcher on his flying carpet.

A bright violet shell flared around him. His carpet rocked violently, slid sideways for a dozen yards. The light faded, shrank in upon him and vanished, leaving me with spots before my eyes. I shrugged, tramped on up the hill.

The early casualties beat me to the hospital. In a way, I was pleased. That indicated efficiency and retention of cool heads under fire. The Captain had worked wonders.

The clatter of companies moving through the darkness confirmed my suspicion that this was more than a nuisance attack by men who seldom dared the dark. (The night belongs to the Lady.) Somehow, we had been flanked.

"About damned time you showed your ugly face," One-Eye growled. "Over there. Surgery. I had them start setting up lights."

I washed and got to it. The Lady's people joined me, and pitched in heroically, and for the first time since we had taken the commission I felt I was doing the wounded some good.

But they just kept pouring in. The clangor continued to rise. Soon it was evident that the Rebel's canyon thrust had been but a feint. All that showy drama had been to little purpose.

Dawn was coloring the sky when I glanced up and found a tattered Soulcatcher facing me. He looked like he had been roasted over a slow fire, and basted in something bluish, greenish, and nasty. He exuded a smoky aroma.

"Start loading your wagons, Croaker," he said in his businesslike female voice. "The Captain is sending you a dozen helpers."

All the transport, including that come up from the south, was parked above my open-air hospital. I glanced that way. A tall, lean, crooked-necked individual was harrassing the teamsters into hitching up. "The battle going sour?" I asked. "Caught you by surprise, didn't they?"

Catcher ignored the latter remark. "We have achieved most of our goals. Only one task remains unfulfilled." The voice he chose was deep, sonorous, slow, a speechmaker's voice. "The fighting may go either way. It's too soon to tell. Your Captain has given this rabble backbone. But lest defeat catch you up, get your charges moving."

A few wagons were creaking down toward us already. I shrugged, passed the word, found the next man who needed my attention. While I worked, I asked Catcher, "If the thing is in the balance, shouldn't you be over there pounding on the Rebel?"

"I'm doing the Lady's bidding, Croaker. Our goals are almost met. Linger and Moth are no more. Sidle is grievously injured. Shifter has accomplished his deceit. There is naught left but to deprive the Rebel of their general."

I was confused. Divergent thoughts found their ways to my tongue and betrayed themselves. "But shouldn't we try to break them here?" And, "This northern campaign has been hard on the Circle. First Raker, then Whisper. Now Linger and Moth."

"With Sidle and Harden to go. Yes. They beat us again and again, and each time it costs them the heart of their strength." He gazed downhill, toward a small company coming our way. Raven was in the lead. Catcher faced the wagon park. The Hanged Man stopped gesturing and struck a pose: man listening.

Suddenly, Soulcatcher resumed talking. "Whisper has breached the walls of Frost. Nightcrawler has negotiated the treacherous menhirs on the Plain of Fear, and approaches the suburbs of Thud. The Faceless is on the Plain now, moving toward Barns. They say Parcel committed suicide last night at Ade, to avoid capture by Bonegnasher. Things aren't the disaster they seem, Croaker."

The hell they aren't, I thought. That's the east. This is here. I could not get excited about victories a quarter of the world away. Here we were getting stomped, and if the Rebel broke through to Charm, nothing that happened in the east would matter.

Raven halted his group and approached me alone. "What do you want them to do?"

I assumed the Captain had sent him, so was sure the Captain had ordered the withdrawal. He would not play games for Catcher. "Put the ones we've treated into the wagons." The teamsters were arraying themselves in a nice line. "Send a dozen or so walking wounded with each wagon. Me and One-Eye and the rest will keep cutting and sewing. What?"

He had a look in his eye. I did not like it. He glanced at Soulcatcher. So did I.

"I haven't told him yet," Catcher said.

"Told me what?" I knew I would not like it when I heard it. They had that nervous smell about them. It screamed bad news.

Raven smiled. Not a happy smile, but a sort of gruesome rictus. "You and me, we've been drafted again, Croaker."

"What? Come on! Not again!" I still got the shakes thinking about helping do in the Limper and Whisper

"You have the practical experience," Catcher said.

I kept shaking my head.

Raven growled, "I have to go, so do you, Croaker. Besides, you'll want to get it in the Annals, how you took out more of the Eighteen than any of the Taken."

"Crap. What am I? A bounty hunter? No. I'm a physician. The Annals and fighting are incidental."

Raven told Catcher, "This is the man the Captain had to drag off the line when we were crossing the Windy Country." His eyes were narrow, his cheeks taut. He did not want to go either. He was displacing his resentment by chiding me.

"There is no option, Croaker," Soulcatcher said in a child's voice. "The Lady chose you." He tried to soften my disappointment by adding, "She rewards well those who please her. And you have caught her fancy."

I damned myself for my earlier romanticism. That Croaker who had come north, so thoroughly bemused by the mysterious Lady, was another man. A stripling, filled with the foolish ignorances of youth. Yeah. Sometimes you lie to yourself just to keep going.

Catcher told me, "We're not going it alone this time, Croaker. We'll have help from Crooked Neck, Shifter, and Stormbringer."

Sourly, I remarked, "Takes the whole gang to scrub one bandit, eh?"

Catcher did not take the bait. He never does. "The carpet is over there. Collect your weapons and join me." He stalked away.

I took my ire out on my helpers, completely unfairly. Finally, when One-Eye was ready to blow, Raven remarked, "Don't be an asshole, Croaker. We've got to do it, let's do it."

So I apologized to everyone and marched down to join Soulcatcher.

Soulcatcher said, "Get aboard," indicating places. Raven and I assumed the positions we had used before. Catcher handed us lengths of cord. "Tie yourselves securely. This could get rough. I don't want you falling off. And keep a knife handy so you can cut loose when we go in."

My heart fluttered. To tell the truth, I was excited about flying again. Moments from my previous flight haunted me with their joy and beauty. There is a glorious feeling of freedom up there with the cool wind and the eagles.

Catcher even tied himself. Bad sign. "Ready?" Not awaiting an answer, he started muttering. The carpet rocked gently, floated upward light as down on a breeze.

We cleared the treetops. Framewood smacked me in the behind. My guts sank. Air whipped around me. My hat blew off. I grabbed and missed. The carpet tilted precariously. I found myself gaping down at an earth receding rapidly. Raven grabbed me. Had we not been tied we both would have gone over the side.

We drifted out over the canyons, which looked like a crazy maze from above. The Rebel mass looked like army ants on the march.

I glanced around the sky, which itself is a marvel from that perspective. There were no eagles on the wing. Just vultures. Catcher made a dash through one flight, scattered them.

Another carpet floated up, passed nearby, drifted away till it became but a distant speck. It carried the Hanged Man and two heavily armed Imperials.

"Where's Stormbringer?" I asked.

Catcher extended an arm. Squinting, I discerned a dot on the blue over the desert.

We drifted till I began to wonder if anything was going to happen. Studying the Rebel's progress palled fast. He was making too much headway.

"Get ready," Catcher called over his shoulder.

I gripped my ropes, anticipating something nervewracking.

"Now."

The bottom fell out. And stayed out. Down, down, and down we plunged. The air screamed. The earth rolled and twisted and hurtled upward. The distant specks that were Stormbringer and the Hanged Man also plummeted. They grew more distinct as we slanted in from three directions.

We whipped past the level where our brethren were striving to stem the Rebel flood. Down we continued, into a less steep glide, rolling, twisting, fishtailing to avoid colliding with wildly eroded sandstone towers. Some I could have touched as we hurtled past.

A small meadow appeared ahead. Our velocity dropped dramatically, till we hovered. "He's there," Catcher whispered. We slid forward a few yards, floated just peeping round a pillar of sandstone.

The once green meadow had been churned by the passage of horses and men. A dozen wagons and their teamsters remained there. Catcher cursed under his breath.

A shadow flew from between rock spires to our left. *Flash!* Thunder shook the canyon. Sod hurtled into the air. Men cried out, staggered around, scrambled for their weapons.

Another shadow whipped through from another direction. I do not know what the Hanged Man did, but the Rebels began clawing their throats, gasping.

One big man shook the magic and staggered toward a huge black horse tethered to a picket post at the nether end of the meadow. Catcher took our carpet in fast. The earth slammed against its frame. "Off!" he growled as we bounced. He snatched a sword himself.

Raven and I clambered off and followed Catcher on unsteady legs. The Taken swooped down on the choking teamsters and raged among them, blade throwing gore. Raven and I contributed to the massacre, I hope with less enthusiasm.

"What the hell are you doing here?" Catcher raved at his victims. "He was supposed to be alone."

The other carpets returned and settled nearer the fleeing man. The Taken and their henchmen pursued him on wobbly legs. He vaulted onto the horse's back and parted the picket rope with a vicious swordstroke. I stared. I had not expected Harden to be so intimidating. He was every bit as ugly as the apparition that had appeared during Goblin's bout with One-Eye.

Catcher cut down the last Rebel teamster. "Come!" he snapped. We dogged him as he loped toward Harden. I wondered why I did not have sense enough to hang back.

The Rebel general stopped fleeing. He felled one of the Imperials, who had outdistanced everybody, let out a great bellow of laughter, then howled something unintelligible. The air crackled with the imminence of sorcery.

Violet light flared around all three Taken, more intense than when it had hit Catcher during the night. It stopped them in their tracks. It was a most puissant sorcery. It occupied them totally. Harden turned his attention to the rest of us.

The second Imperial reached him. His great sword hammered down, pounding through the soldier's guard. The horse ambled forward at Harden's urging, gingerly stepping over the fallen. Harden looked at the Taken and cursed the animal, flailed around with his blade.

The horse moved no faster. Harden smote its neck savagely, then howled. His hand would not come free of its mane. His cry of rage became one of despair. He turned his blade on the beast, could not harm it, instantly hurled the weapon at the Taken. The violet surrounding them had begun to weaken.

Raven was two steps from Harden, I three behind him. Stormbringer's men were as close, approaching from the other side.

Raven slashed, a strong, upward cutting stroke. His swordtip thumped Harden's belly—and rebounded. Chain mail? Harden's big fist lashed out and connected with Raven's temple. He wobbled a step and sagged.

Without thought I shifted aim and slashed at Harden's hand. We both yelled when iron bit bone and scarlet flowed.

I leapt over Raven, stopped, spun. Stormbringer's soldiers were hacking at Harden. His mouth was open. His scarred face was contorted as he concentrated on ignoring pain while he used his powers to save himself. The Taken remained out of it for the moment. He faced three ordinary men. But all that did not register till later.

I could see nothing but Harden's steed. The animal was melting. . . . No. Not melting. Changing.

I giggled. The great Rebel general was astride Shapeshifter's back.

My giggles became crazy laughter.

My little fit cost me my opportunity to participate in the death of a champion. Stormbringer's two soldiers cut Harden to pieces while Shifter held and stifled him. He was dead meat before I regained my self-control.

The Hanged Man, too, missed the denouement. He was busy dying, Harden's great thrown blade buried in his skull. Soulcatcher and Stormbringer moved toward him.

Shifter completed his change into a great, greasy, stinking, fat, naked creature which, despite standing on its hind legs, seemed no more human than the beast he had portrayed. He kicked Harden's remains and quaked with mirth, as though his deadly trick had been the finest jest of the century.

Then he saw the Hanged Man. Shudders ran through his flab. He hastened toward the other Taken, incoherencies frothing his lips.

Crooked Neck worked the sword loose from his skull. He tried to say something, had no luck. Stormbringer and Soulcatcher made no move to help.

I stared at Stormbringer. Such a tiny thing she was. I knelt to test Raven's pulse. She was no bigger than a child. How could such a small package chain such terrible wrath?

Shifter shambled toward the tableau, anger knotting the muscles under the fat across his shaggy shoulders. He halted, faced Catcher and Stormbringer from a tense stance. Nothing was said, but it seemed the Hanged Man's fate was being decided. Shifter wanted to help. The others did not.

Puzzling. Shifter is Catcher's ally. Why this sudden conflict?

Why this daring of the Lady's wrath? She would not be pleased if the Hanged Man died.

Raven's pulse was fluttery when first I touched his throat, but it firmed up. I breathed a little easier.

Stormbringer's soldiers eased up toward the Taken, eying Shifter's gross back.

Catcher exchanged glances with Stormbringer. The woman nodded. Soulcatcher whirled. The slits in his mask blazed a lava red.

Suddenly, there was no Catcher. There was a cloud of darkness ten feet high and a dozen across, black as the inside of a coal sack, thicker than the densest fog. The cloud jumped quicker than an adder's strike. There was one mouselike squeak of surprise, then a sinister, enduring silence. After all the roar and clangor, the quiet was deadly ominous.

I shook Raven violently. He did not respond.

Shifter and Stormbringer stood over the Hanged Man, staring at me. I wanted to scream, to run, to crawl into the ground to hide. I was a magic man, able to read their thoughts. I knew too much.

Terror froze me.

The coal dust cloud vanished as quickly as it had appeared. Soulcatcher stood between the soldiers. Both toppled slowly, with the majesty of stately old pines.

I gouged Raven. He groaned. His eyes flickered open and I caught a glimpse of pupil, Dilated. Concussion. Damn it! . . .

Catcher looked at his partners in crime. Then, slowly, he turned on me.

The three Taken closed in. In the background, the Hanged Man went on dying. He was very noisy about it. I did not hear him, though. I rose, knees watery, and faced my doom.

It's not supposed to end this way, I thought. This isn't right. . . .

All three stood there and stared.

I stared back. Nothing else I could do.

Brave Croaker. Guts enough, at least, to stare Death in the eye.

You didn't see a thing, did you?" Catcher asked softly. Cold lizards slithered down my spine. That voice was one that one of the dead soldiers had used while hacking away at Harden.

I shook my head.

"You were too busy fighting Harden, then you were occupied with Raven."

I nodded weakly. My knee joints were jelly. I would have bolted otherwise. Foolish as that would have been. Catcher said, "Get Raven onto Bringer's carpet." He pointed.

Nudging, whispering, cajoling, I helped Raven walk. He hadn't the least idea where he was or what he was doing. But he let me steer him.

I was worried. I could find no obvious damage, yet he was not acting right. "Take him straight to my hospital," I said. I could not look Stormbringer in the eye, nor did I achieve the inflection I wanted. My words came out sounding like a plea.

Catcher summoned me to his carpet. I went with all the enthusiasm of a hog to the slaughter chute. He could be playing a game. A fall from his carpet would be a permanent cure for any doubts he harbored about my ability to keep quiet.

He followed me, tossed his bloody sword aboard, settled himself. The carpet floated upward, crawled toward the great scrap of the Stair.

I glanced back at the still forms on the meadow, nagged by undirected feelings of shame. That had not been right. . . . And yet, what could I have done?

Something golden, something like a pale nebula in the farthest circle of the midnight sky, moved in the shade cast by one of the sandstone towers.

My heart nearly stopped.

The Captain sucked the headless and increasingly demoralized Rebel army into a trap. A great slaughter ensued. Lack of numbers and sheer exhaustion kept the Company from hurling the Rebel off the mountain. Nor did the complacency of the Taken help. One fresh battalion, one sorcerous assault, might have given us the day.

I treated Raven on the run, after placing him aboard the last wagon to head south. He would remain odd and remote for days. Care of Darling fell my way by default. The child was a fine distraction from the depression of yet another retreat.

Maybe that was the way she had rewarded Raven for his generosity.

"This is our last withdrawal," the Captain promised. *He* would not call it a retreat, but hadn't the gall to call it an advance to the rear, retrograde action, or any of that gobbledegook. He did not mention the fact that any further withdrawal would come after the end. Charm's fall would mark the death-date of the Lady's Empire. In all probability it will terminate these Annals, and scriven the end of Company history.

Rest in peace, you last of the warrior brotherhoods. You were home and family to me. . . .

News came which had not been allowed to reach us at the Stair of Tear. Tidings of other Rebel armies advancing from the north along routes more westerly than our line of retreat. The list of cities lost was long and disheartening, even granting exaggeration by the reporters. Soldiers defeated always overestimate the strength of their foe. That soothes egos suspecting their own inferiority.

Walking with Elmo, down the long, gentle south slope, toward the fertile farmlands north of Charm, I suggested, "Sometime when there aren't any Taken around, how about you hint to the Captain that it might be wise if he started disassociating the Company from Soulcatcher."

He looked at me oddly. My old comrades had been doing that lately. Since Harden's fall I had been moody, dour, and uncommunicative. Not that I was a bonfire at the best of times, mind. The pressure was crushing my spirit. I denied myself my usual outlet, the Annals, for fear Soulcatcher would somehow detect what I had written.

"It might be better if we weren't too closely identified with him," I added.

"What happened out there?" By then everyone knew the basic tale. Harden slain. The Hanged Man fallen. Raven and I the only soldiers who got out alive. Everybody had an insatiable thirst for details.

"I can't tell you. But you tell him. When none of the Taken are around."

Elmo did his sums and came to the conclusion not far off the mark. "All right, Croaker. Will do. Take care."

Take care I would. If Fate let me.

That was the day we received word of new victories in the east. The Rebel redoubts were collapsing as fast as the Lady's armies could march.

It was also the day we heard that all four northern and western Rebel armies had halted to rest, recruit, and refit for an assault on Charm. Nothing stood between them and the Tower. Nothing, that is, but the Black Company and its accumulation of beaten men.

The great comet is in the sky, that evil harbinger of all great shifts of fortune.

The end is near.

We are retreating still, toward our final appointment with Destiny.

I must record one final incident in the tale of the encounter with Harden. It took place three days north of the Tower, and consisted of another dream like the one I suffered at the head of the Stair. The same golden dream, which might have been no dream at all, promised me, "My faithful need have no fear." Once again it allowed me a glimpse of that heart-stopping face. And then it was gone, and the fear returned, not lessened in the least.

The days passed. The miles wore away. The great ugly block of the Tower hove over the horizon. And the comet grew ever more brilliant in the nighttime sky.

6

Lady

The land slowly became silvery green. Dawn scattered feathers of crimson upon the walled town. Golden flashes freckled its battlements where the sun touched dew. The mists began to slide into the hollows. Trumpets sounded the morning watch.

The Lieutenant shaded his eyes, squinted. He grunted disgustedly, glanced at One-Eye. The little black man nodded. "Time, Goblin," the Lieutenant said over his shoulder.

Men stirred back in the woods. Goblin knelt beside me, peered out at the farmland. He and four other men were clad as poor townswomen, with their heads wrapped in shawls. They carried pottery jars swinging from wooden yokes, had their weapons hidden inside their clothing.

"Go. The gate is open," the Lieutenant said. They moved out, following the edge of the wood downhill.

"Damn, it's good to be doing this kind of thing again," I said.

The Lieutenant grinned. He had smiled seldom since we had left Beryl.

Below, the five fake women slipped through shadow toward the spring beside the road to town. Already a few townswomen were headed down to draw water.

We expected little trouble getting to the gatekeepers. The town was filled with strangers, refugees and Rebel campfollowers. The garrison was small and lax. The Rebel had no cause to suppose the Lady would strike this far from Charm. The town had no significance in the grand struggle.

Except that two of the Eighteen, privy to Rebel strategies, were quartered there.

We had lurked in those woods three days, watching. Feather and Journey, recently promoted to the Circle, were honeymooning there before moving south to join the assault on Charm.

Three days. Three days of no fires during the chill nights, of dried food at every meal. Three days of misery. And our spirits were their highest in years. "I think we'll pull it off," I opined.

The Lieutenant gestured. Several men stole after the disguised.

One-Eye remarked, "Whoever thought this up knew what he was doing." He was excited.

We all were. It was a chance to do that at which we are best. For fifty days we had done plain physical labor, preparing Charm for the Rebel onslaught, and for fifty nights we had agonized about the coming battle.

Another five men slipped downhill.

"Bunch of women coming out now," One-Eye said. Tension mounted.

Women paraded toward the spring. There would be a flow all day, unless we interrupted. They had no water source inside the wall.

My stomach sank. Our infiltrators had started uphill. "Stand ready," the Lieutenant said.

"Loosen up," I suggested. Exercise helps dissipate nervous energy.

No matter how long you soldier, fear always swells as combat nears. There is always the dread that the numbers will catch up. One-Eye enters every action sure the fates have checked his name off their list.

The infiltrators exchanged falsetto greetings with the townswomen. They arrived at the gate undiscovered. It was guarded by a single militiaman, a cobbler busy hammering brass nails into the heel of a boot. His halberd was ten feet away.

Goblin scampered back outside. He clapped his hands overhead. A *crack* reverberated across the countryside. His arms fell level with his shoulders, palms up. A rainbow arced between his hands.

"Always has to ham it up," One-Eye grumbled. Goblin did a jig.

The patrol swept forward. The women at the spring screamed and scattered. Wolves jumping into a sheepfold, I thought. We ran hard. My pack hammered my kidneys. After two hundred yards I was stumbling over my bow. Younger men began passing me.

I reached the gate unable to whip a grandmother. Lucky for me, the grandmas were goofing off. The men swept through the town. There was no resistance.

We who were to tackle Feather and Journey hastened to the tiny citadel. That was no better defended. The Lieutenant and I followed One-Eye, Silent, and Goblin inside.

We encountered no resistance below the top level. There, incredibly, the newlyweds were still entangled in sleep. One-Eye brushed their guards aside with a terrifying illusion. Goblin and Silent shattered the door to the lovenest.

We stormed inside. Even sleepy, baffled, and frightened, they were feisty. They bruised several of us good before we got gags into their mouths and bonds onto their wrists.

The Lieutenant told them, "We're supposed to bring you back alive. That don't mean we can't hurt you some. Come quiet, do what you're told, and you'll be all right." I halfway expected him to sneer, twirl the end of his mustache, and punctuate with evil laughter. He was clowning, assuming the villain's role the Rebel insists we play.

Feather and Journey would give us all the trouble they could. They knew the Lady hadn't sent us to bring them round for tea.

Halfway back to friendly territory. On our bellies on a hilltop, studying an enemy encampment. "Big," I said. "Twenty-five, thirty thousand men." It was one of six such camps on an arc bending north and west of Charm.

"They sit on their hands much longer, they're in trouble," the Lieutenant said.

They should have attacked immediately after the Stair of Tear. But the loss of Harden, Sidle, Moth, and Linger had set lesser captains to squabbling over supreme command. The Rebel offensive had stalled. The Lady had regained her balance.

Her patrols-in-force now harassed Rebel foragers, exterminated collaborators, scouted, destroyed everything the enemy might find useful. Despite vastly superior numbers, the Rebel's stance was becoming defensive. Every day in camp sapped his psychological momentum.

Two months ago our morale was lower than a snake's butt. Now it was on the rebound. If we made it back it would soar. Our coup would stun the Rebel movement.

If we made it back.

We lay motionless upon steep lichened limestone and dead leaves. The creek below chuckled at our predicament. Shadows of naked trees stippled us. Low-grade spells by One-Eye and his cohorts further camouflaged us.

The smell of fear and of sweaty horses taunted my nostrils. From the road above came the voices of Rebel cavalrymen. I could not understand their tongue. They were arguing, though.

Scattered with undisturbed leaves and twigs, the road had looked unpatrolled. Weariness had overcome our caution. We had decided to follow it. Then we had rounded a turn and found ourselves facing a Rebel patrol across the meadowed valley into which the creek below flowed.

They were cursing our disappearance. Several dismounted and urinated down the bank. . . .

Feather started thrashing.

Damn! I screamed inside. Damn! Damn! I knew it!

The Rebels yammered and lined the edge of the road.

I smacked the woman's temple. Goblin clipped her from the other side. Quick-thinking Silent wove nets of spell with tentacle-limber fingers dancing close to his chest.

A ragged bush shivered. A fat old badger waddle-ran down the bank and crossed the creek, vanishing into a dense stand of poplars.

Cursing, the Rebels threw rocks. They clattered like dropped stoneware as they skipped off boulders in the streambed. The soldiers stamped around telling one another we had to be nearby. We could not have gotten much farther on foot. Logic might undo the best efforts of our wizards.

I was scared with a knee-knocking, hand-shaking, gut-emptying kind of fear. It had built steadily, through too many narrow escapes. Superstition told me my odds were getting too long.

So much for that earlier gust of refreshed morale. The unreasoning fear betrayed it for the illusion it was. Beneath its patina I retained the defeatist attitude brought down from the Stair of Tear. My war was over and lost. All I wanted to do was run.

Journey showed signs of getting frisky too. My glare was fierce. He subsided.

A breeze stirred the dead leaves. The sweat on my body chilled. My fear cooled somewhat.

The patrol remounted. Still fussing, they rode on up the road. I watched them come into sight where the way curled eastward with the canyon. They wore scarlet tabards over good link mail. Their helmets and arms were of excellent quality. The Rebel was getting prosperous. They had started out as a rabble armed with tools.

"We could have taken them," someone said.

"Stupid!" the Lieutenant snapped. "Right now they aren't sure who they saw. If we fought, they would know."

We did not need the Rebel getting a line on us this close to home. There was no room for maneuvering.

The man who had spoken was one of the stragglers we had accumulated during the long retreat. "Brother, you better learn one thing if you want to stick with us. You fight when there ain't no other choice. Some of us would have gotten hurt too, you know."

He grunted.

"They're out of sight," the Lieutenant said. "Let's move." He took the point, headed for the rugged hills beyond the meadow. I groaned. More crosscountry.

My every muscle ached already. Exhaustion threatened to betray me. Man was not meant for endless dawn to dusk marching with sixty pounds on his back.

"Damned fast thinking back there," I told Silent.

He accepted praise with a shrug, saying nothing. As always.

A cry from the rear. "They're coming back."

We sprawled on the flank of a grassy hill. The Tower rose above the horizon due south. That basaltic cube was intimidating even from ten miles away and implausible in its setting. Emotion demanded a surround of fiery waste, or at best a land perpetually locked in winter. Instead, this country was a vast green pasture, gentle hills with small farms dotting their southern hips. Trees lined the deep, slow brooks snaking between.

Nearer the Tower the land became less pastoral, but never reflected the gloom Rebel propagandists placed around the Lady's stronghold. No brimstone and barren, broken plains. No bizarre, evil creatures strutting over scattered human bones. No dark clouds ever rolling and grumbling in the sky.

The Lieutenant said, "No patrols in sight. Croaker, One-Eye, do your stuff."

I strung my bow. Goblin brought three prepared arrows. Each had a maleable blue ball at its head. One-Eye sprinkled one with grey dust, passed it to me. I aimed at the sun, let fly.

Blue fire too bright to view flared and sank into the valley below. Then a second, and a third. The fireballs dropped in a neat column, appearing to drift down more than fall.

"Now we wait," Goblin squeaked, and threw himself down in the tall grass.

"And hope our friends arrive first." Any nearby Rebel surely would investigate the signal. Yet we had to call for help. We could not penetrate the Rebel cordon unnoticed.

"Get down!" the Lieutenant snapped. The grass was tall enough to conceal a supine figure. "Third squad, take the watch."

Men grumbled and claimed it was another squad's turn. But they took sentinel positions with that minimal, obligatory complaint. Their mood was bright. Hadn't we lost those fools back in the hills? What could stop us now?

I made a pillow of my pack and watched cumulus mountains drift over in stately legions. It was a gorgeous, crisp, springlike day.

My gaze dropped to the Tower. My mood darkened. The pace would pick up. The capture of Feather and Journey would spur the Rebel into action. Surrender secrets those two would. There was no way to hide or lie when the Lady asked a question.

I heard a rustle, turned my head, found myself eye to eye with a snake. It wore a human face. I started to yell—then recognized that silly grin.

One-Eye. His ugly mug in miniature, but with both eyes and no floppy hat on top. The snake snickered, winked, slithered across my chest.

"Here they go again," I murmured, and sat up to watch.

There was a sudden, violent thrashing in the grass. Farther on, Goblin popped up wearing a shit-eating grin. The grass rustled. Animals the size of rabbits trooped past me, carrying chunks of snake in bloody needle teeth. Homemade mongooses, I guessed.

Goblin had anticipated One-Eye again.

One-Eye let out a howl and jumped up cursing. His hat spun around. Smoke poured out of his nostrils. When he yelled, fire roared in his mouth.

Goblin capered like a cannibal just before they dish up the long pig. He described circles with his forefingers. Rings of pale orange glimmered in the air. He flipped them at One-Eye. They settled around the little black man. Goblin barked like a seal. The hoops tightened.

One-Eye made weird noises and negated the rings. He made throwing motions with both hands. Brown balls streaked toward Goblin. They exploded, yielding clouds of butterflies that went for Goblin's eyes. Goblin did a backflip, scampered through the grass like a mouse fleeing an owl, popped up with a counterspell.

The air sprouted flowers. Each bloom had a mouth. Each mouth boasted walruslike tusks. The flowers skewered butterfly wings with their tusks, then complacently munched butterfly bodies. Goblin fell over giggling.

One-Eye cussed a literal blue streak, a cerulean banner trailing from his lips. Argent lettering proclaimed his opinion of Goblin.

"Knock it off!" the Lieutenant thundered belatedly. "We don't need you attracting attention."

"Too late, Lieutenant," somebody said. "Look down there."

Soldiers were headed our way. Soldiers wearing red, with the White Rose emblazoned on their tabards. We dropped into the grass like ground squirrels into their holes.

Chatter ran across the hillside. Most threatened One-Eye with dire dooms. A minority included Goblin for having shared in the betraying fireworks.

Trumpets sounded. The Rebel dispersed for an assault on our hill.

* * *

The air whined in torment. A shadow flashed over the hilltop, rippling across windblown grass. "Taken," I murmured, and popped up for the instant needed to spot a flying carpet banking into the valley. "Soulcatcher?" I couldn't be sure. At that distance it could have been any of several Taken.

The carpet dove into massed arrow fire. Lime fog enveloped it, trailed behind it, for a moment recalled the comet which overhung the world. The lime haze scattered resolved into threadlike snippets. A few filaments caught the breeze and drifted our way.

I glanced up. The comet hung on the horizon like a ghost of a god's scimitar. It had been in the sky so long we scarcely noticed it now. I wondered if the Rebel had become equally indifferent. For him it was one of the great portents of impending victory.

Men screamed. The carpet had passed along the Rebel line and now drifted like down on the wind just beyond bowshot. The lime-colored thread was so scattered it was barely visible. The screams came from men who had suffered its touch. Grisly green wounds opened wherever there was contact.

Some thread seemed determined to come our way.

The Lieutenant saw it. "Let's move out, men. Just in case." He pointed across the wind. The thread would have to drift sideways to catch us.

We hustled maybe three hundred yards. Writhing, the thread crawled on air, coming our way. It *was* after us. The Taken watched intently, ignoring the Rebel.

"That bastard wants to kill us!" I exploded. Terror turned my legs to gelatin. Why would one of the Taken want us to become victims of an accident?

If that *was* Catcher. . . . But Catcher was our mentor. Our boss. We wore his badges. He wouldn't. . . .

The carpet snapped into motion so violently its rider almost tumbled off. It hurtled toward the nearest wood, vanished. The thread lost volition and drifted down, disappearing in the grass.

"What the devil?"

"Holy Hell!"

I whirled. A vast shadow moved toward us, expanding, as a gigantic carpet descended. Faces peeped over its edges. We froze, bristling with ready weapons.

"The Howler," I said, and had my guess confirmed by a cry like that of a wolf challenging the moon.

The carpet grounded. "Get aboard, you idiots. Come on. Move it."

I laughed, tension draining away. That was the Captain. He danced like a nervous bear along the near edge of the carpet. Others of our brethren accompanied him. I threw my pack aboard, accepted a hand up. "Raven. You showed up in the nick this time."

"You'll wish we'd let you take your chances."

"Eh?"

"Captain will tell you."

The last man scrambled aboard. The Captain gave Feather and Journey the hard eye, then marched around getting the men evenly distributed. At the rear of the carpet, unmoving, shunned, sat a child-sized figure concealed in layers of indigo gauze. It howled at random intervals.

I shuddered. "What are you talking about?"

"Captain will tell you," he repeated.

"Sure. How's Darling?"

"Doing all right." Lots of words in our Raven.

The Captain settled beside me. "Bad news, Croaker," he said.

"Yeah?" I reached for my vaunted sarcasm. "Give it to me straight. I can take it."

"Tough guy," Raven observed.

"That's me. Eat nails for breakfast. Whip wildcats with my bare hands."

The Captain shook his head. "Hang on to that sense of humor. The Lady wants to see you. Personally."

My stomach dropped to the ground, which was a couple hundred feet down. "Oh, shit," I whispered. "Oh, damn."

"Yeah."

"What did I do?"

"You'd know better than I do."

My mind hurtled around like a herd of mice fleeing a cat. In seconds I was soaked with sweat.

Raven observed, "Can't be as bad as it sounds. She was almost polite."

The Captain nodded. "It was a request."

"Sure it was."

Raven said, "If she had a grudge you'd just disappear."

I did not feel reassured.

"One too many romances," the Captain chided. "Now she's in love with you too."

They never forget, never let up. It had been months since I had written one of those romances. "What's it about?"

"She didn't say."

Silence reigned the rest of the way. They sat beside me and tried to reassure me with traditional Company solidarity. As we came in on our encampment, though, the Captain did say, "She told us to bring our strength up to the thousand mark. We can enlist volunteers from the lot we brought out of the north."

"Good news, good news." That *was* cause for jubilation. For the first time in two centuries we were going to grow. Plenty of stragglers would be eager to exchange their oaths to the Taken for oaths to the Company. We were in high favor. We had mana. And, being mercenaries, we got more leeway than anyone else in the Lady's service.

I could not get excited, though. Not with the Lady waiting.

The carpet grounded. Brethren crowded around, anxious to see how we had done. Lies and jocular threats flew.

The Captain said, "You stay aboard, Croaker. Goblin, Silent, One-Eye, you too." He indicated the prisoners. "Deliver the merchandise."

As the men slid over the side, Darling came bouncing out of the mob. Raven hollered at her, but of course she could not hear. She scrambled aboard, carrying the doll Raven had carved. It was dressed neatly in clothing of superb miniature detail. She handed it to me and started flashing finger language.

Raven hollered again. I tried to interrupt, but Darling was intent on telling me about the doll's wardrobe. Some might have thought her retarded, to be so excited about such things at her age. She was not. She had a mind like a razor. She knew what she was doing when she boarded the carpet. She was stealing a chance to fly.

"Honey," I said, both aloud and with signs, "You've got to get off. We're going. . . ."

Raven yelled in outrage as the Howler lifted off. One-Eye, Goblin, and Silent all glared at him. He howled. The carpet continued to rise.

"Sit down," I told Darling. She did so, not far from Feather. She forgot the doll, wanted to know about our adventure. I told her. It kept me occupied. She spent more time looking over the side than paying attention to me, yet she missed nothing. When I finished she looked at Feather and Journey with adult pity. She was unconcerned about my appointment with the Lady, though she did give me a reassuring hug good-bye.

The Howler's carpet drifted away from the Tower top. I waved a feeble farewell. Darling blew me a kiss. Goblin patted his breast. I touched the amulet he had given me in Lords. Small comfort, that.

Imperial Guards strapped Journey and Feather onto litters. "What about me?" I asked shakily.

A captain told me, "You're supposed to wait here." He stayed when the others left. He tried to make small talk, but I wasn't in the mood.

I wandered to the Tower's edge, looked out on the vast engineering project being undertaken by the Lady's armies.

At the time of the Tower's construction huge basalt billets had been imported. Shaped on site, they had been stacked and fused into this gigantic cube of stone. The waste, chips, blocks broken during shaping, billets found unsuitable and overage, had been left scattered around the Tower in a vast wild jumble more effective than any moat. It extended a mile.

In the north, though, a depressed piece-of-pie section remained unlittered. This constituted the only approach to the Tower on the ground. In that arc the Lady's forces prepared for the Rebel onslaught.

No one down there believed his labor would shape the battle's outcome. The comet was in the sky. But every man worked because labor provided surcease from fear.

The pie-slice rose to either side, meeting the rock jumble. A log palisade spanned the slice's wide end. Our camps lay behind that. Behind the camps was a trench thirty feet deep and thirty wide. A hundred yards nearer the Tower there was another trench, and a hundred yards nearer still, a third, still being dug.

The excavated earth had been transported nearer the Tower and dumped behind a twelve foot log retaining wall spanning the slice. From this elevation men would hurl missiles on an enemy attacking our infantry on ground level.

A hundred yards back stood a second retaining wall, providing another two fathom elevation. The Lady meant to array her forces in three distinct armies, one on each level, and force the Rebel to fight three battles in series.

An earthen pyramid was abuilding a dozen rods behind the final retaining wall. It was seventy feet high already, its sides sloping about thirty-five degrees.

Obsessive neatness characterized everything. The plain, in places scraped down several feet, was as level as a tabletop. It had been planted with grass. Our animals kept that cropped like a well-kempt lawn. Stone roadways ran here and there, and woe betide the man who strayed off without orders.

Below, on the middle level, bowmen were ranging fire on the ground between the nearer trenches. While they loosed, their officers adjusted the positions of racks from which they drew their arrows.

On the upper terrace Guards bustled around ballistae, calculating fire lanes and survivability, ranging their engines on targets farther away. Carts laden with ammunition sat near each weapon.

Like the grass and mannered roadways, these preparations betrayed an obsession with order.

On the bottom level workmen had begun demolishing short sections of retaining wall. Baffling.

I spotted a carpet coming in, turned to watch. It settled to the roof. Four stiff, shaky, wind-burned soldiers stepped off. A corporal led them away.

The armies of the east were headed our way, hoping to arrive before the Rebel assault, with little hope of actually making it. The Taken were flying day and night bringing in what manpower they could.

Men shouted below. I turned to look. . . . Threw up an arm. Slam! Impact threw me a dozen feet, spinning. My Guard guide yelled. The Tower roof came up to meet me. Men shouted and ran my way.

I rolled, tried to get up, slipped in a slick of blood. Blood! My blood! It spurted from the inside of my left upper arm. I stared at the wound with dull, amazed eyes. What the hell?

"Lie down," the Guard captain ordered. "Come on." He slapped me a good one. "Quick. Tell me what to do."

"Tourniquet," I croaked. "Tie something around it. Stop the bleeding."

He yanked his belt off. Good, quick thinking. One of the best tourniquets there is. I tried to sit up, to advise while he worked.

"Hold him down," he told several bystanders. "Foster. What happened?"

"One of the weapons fell off the upper tier. It went off when it fell. They're running around like chickens."

"Wasn't no accident," I gasped. "Somebody wanted to kill me." Getting hazy, I could think of nothing but lime thread crawling against the wind. "Why?"

"Tell me and we'll both know, friend. You men. Get a litter." He snugged the belt tighter. "Going to be all right, fellow. We'll have you to a healer in a minute."

"Severed artery," I said. "That's tricky." My ears hummed. The world began to turn slowly, getting cold. Shock. How much blood did I lose? The captain had moved fast enough. Plenty of time. If the healer was not some butcher. . . .

The captain grabbed a corporal. "Go find out what happened down there. Don't take any bullshit answers."

The litter came. They lifted me in, hoisted me, and I passed out. I wakened in a small surgery, tended by a man who was as much sorcerer as surgeon. "Better job than I could have done," I told him when he finished.

"Any pain?"

"Nope."

"Going to ache like hell in a while."

"I know." How many times had I said the same?

The Guard captain came. "Going all right?"

"Done," the surgeon replied. To me, "No work. No activity. No sex. You know the drill."

"I do. Sling?"

He nodded. "We'll bind your arm to your side, too, for a few days."

The captain was antsy. "Find out what happened?" I asked.

"Not really. The ballista crew couldn't explain. It just got away from them somehow. Maybe you got lucky." He recalled me saying somebody was trying to kill me.

I touched the amulet Goblin had given me. "Maybe."

"Hate to do it," he said. "But I've got to take you for your interview."

Fear. "What about?"

"You'd know better than I."

"But I don't." I had a remote suspicion, but had forced that out of mind.

There seemed to be two Towers, one sheathing the other. The outer was the seat of Empire, manned by the Lady's functionaries. The inner, as intimidating to them as was the whole to us outside, took up a third of the volume and could be entered at only one point. Few ever did so.

The entrance was open when we reached it. There were no guards. I suppose none were needed. I should have been more scared, but was too dopey. The captain said, "I'll wait here." He had placed me in a wheeled chair, which he rolled through the doorway. I went in with my eyes sealed and heart hammering.

The door chunked shut. The chair rolled a long way, making several turns. I don't know what impelled it. I refused to look. Then it stopped moving. I waited. Nothing happened. Curiosity got the best of me. I blinked.

She stands in the Tower, gazing northward. Her delicate hands are clasped before Her. A breeze steals softly through Her window. It stirs the midnight silk of Her hair. Tear diamonds sparkle on the gentle curve of Her cheek.

My own words, written more than a year before, came back. It was that scene, from that romance, to the least detail. To detail I had imagined but never written. As if that fantasy instant had been ripped from my brain whole and given the breath of life.

I did not believe it for a second, of course. I was in the bowels of the Tower. There were no windows in that grim structure.

She turned. And I saw what every man sees in dreams. Perfection. She did not have to speak for me to know her voice, her speech rhythms, the breathiness between phrases. She did not have to move for me to know her mannerisms, the way she walked, the odd way she would lift her hand to her throat when she laughed. I had known her since adolescence.

In seconds I understood what the old stories meant about her overwhelming presence. The Dominator himself must have swayed in her hot wind.

She rocked me, but did not sweep me away. Though half of me hungered, the remainder recalled my years around Goblin and One-Eye. Where there is sorcery nothing is what it seems. Nice, yes, but sugar candy.

She studied me as intently as I studied her. Finally, "We meet again." The voice was everything I expected and more. It had humor, too.

"Indeed," I croaked.

"You're frightened."

"Of course I am." Maybe a fool would have denied it. Maybe.

"You were injured." She drifted closer. I nodded, my heartbeat increasing. "I wouldn't subject you to this if it wasn't important."

I nodded again, too shaky to speak, totally baffled. This was the Lady, the villain of the ages, the Shadow animate. This was the black widow at the heart of darkness's web, a demi-goddess of evil. What could be important enough for her to take note of the likes of me?

Again, I did have suspicions I would not admit to myself. My moments of critical congress with anyone important were not numerous.

"Someone tried to kill you. Who?"

"I don't know." Taken on the wind. Lime thread.

"Why?"

"I don't know."

"You know. Even if you think you don't." Flint razored through that perfect voice.

I had come expecting the worst, had been taken in by the dream, had let my defenses fall.

The air hummed. A lemon glow formed above her. She moved closer, becoming hazy—except for that face and that yellow. That face expanded, vast, intense, swooping closer. Yellow filled the universe. I saw nothing but the eye. . . .

The Eye! I remembered the Eye in the Forest of Cloud. I tried to throw my arm across my face. I could not move. I think I screamed. Hell. I know I screamed.

There were questions I did not hear. Answers spooled across my mind, in rainbows of thought, like oil droplets spreading on still, crystal water. I had no more secrets.

No secrets. No thought I'd ever had was hidden.

Terror writhed in me like snakes afraid. I had written those silly romances, true, but I also had my doubts and disgusts. A villain as black as she would destroy me for having seditious thoughts. . . .

Wrong. She was secure in the strength of her wickedness. She did not need to quash the questions and doubts and fears of her minions. She could laugh at our consciences and moralities.

This was no repeat of our encounter in the forest. I did not lose my memories. I just did not hear her questions. Those could be inferred from my answers about my contacts with the Taken.

She was hunting the something I began to suspect at the Stair of Tear. I had stumbled into as deadly a trap as ever snapped shut; Taken as the one jaw, the Lady as the other.

Darkness. And awakening.

She stands in the Tower, gazing northward. . . . Tear diamonds sparkle on Her cheek.

A spark of Croaker remained unintimidated. "This is where I came in."

She faced me, smiled. She stepped over and touched me with the sweetest fingers ever woman possessed.

All fear went away.

All darkness closed in again.

Passageway walls were rolling by when I recovered. The Guard captain was pushing me. "How are you doing?" he asked.

I took stock. "Good enough. Where you taking me now?"

"The front door. She said cut you loose."

Just like that? Hmm. I touched my wound. Healed. I shook my head. Things like this did not happen to me.

I paused at the place where the ballista had had its mishap. There was nothing to see and no one to question. I descended to the middle level and visited one of the crews excavating there. They had orders to install a cubicle twelve feet wide and eighteen deep. They had no idea why.

I scanned the length of the retaining wall. A dozen such sites were under construction.

The men eyed me intently when I limped into camp. They choked on questions they could not ask, on concern they could not express. Only Darling refused to play the traditional game. She squeezed my hand, gave me a big smile. Her little fingers danced.

She asked the questions machismo forbid the men. "Slow down," I told her. I was not yet proficient enough to catch everything she signed. Yet her joy communicated itself. I had a big grin on when I became aware that someone was in my way. I looked up. Raven.

"Captain wants you," he said. He seemed cool.

"Figures." I signed good-bye, strolled toward headquarters. I felt no urgency. No mere mortal could intimidate me now.

I glanced back. Raven had his arm across Darling's shoulder, proprietary, looking puzzled.

The Captain was off his style. He dispensed with the customary growling. One-Eye was the only third party present, and he, too, was interested in nothing but business.

"We got trouble?" the Captain asked.

"What do you mean?"

"What happened in the hills. No accident, eh? The Lady summons you, and half an hour later one of the Taken goes zuzu. Then there's your accident at the Tower. You're bad hurt and nobody can explain."

One-Eye observed, "Logic insists a connection."

The Captain added, "Yesterday we heard you were dying. Today you're fine. Sorcery?"

"Yesterday?" Time had gotten away again. I pushed the tent flap aside, stared at the Tower. "Another night in elf hill."

"*Was* it an accident?" One-Eye asked.

"It wasn't accidental." The Lady hadn't thought so.

"Captain, that jibes."

The Captain said, "Somebody tried to knife Raven last night. Darling ran him off."

"Raven? Darling?"

"Something woke her up. She whacked the guy in the head with her doll. Whoever it was got away."

"Weird."

"Decidedly," One-Eye said. "Why would Raven sleep through and a deaf kid wake up? Raven can hear the footfall of a gnat. Smells of sorcery. Cockeyed sorcery. The kid shouldn't have awakened."

The Captain jumped in. "Raven. You. Taken. The Lady. Murder attempts. An interview in the Tower. You have the answer. Spill it."

My reluctance showed.

"You told Elmo we should disassociate ourselves from Catcher. How come? Catcher treats us good. What happened when you took out Harden? Spread it around and there wouldn't be any point to killing you."

Good argument. Only I like to be sure before I shoot my mouth off. "I think there's a plot against the Lady. Soulcatcher and Stormbringer might be involved." I related details of Harden's fall and Whisper's taking. "Shifter was really upset because they let the Hanged Man die. I don't think the Limper was part of anything. He was set up, and manipulated craftily. The Lady was too. Maybe the Limper and the Hanged Man were her supporters."

One-Eye looked thoughtful. "You sure Catcher is in on it?"

"I'm not sure of anything. I wouldn't be surprised by anything, either. Ever since Beryl I've thought he was using us."

The Captain nodded. "Definitely. I told One-Eye to cook up an amulet that'll warn you if one of the Taken gets too close. For what good it'll do. I don't think you'll be bothered again, though. The Rebel is on the move. That'll be everybody's first order of business."

A chain of logic lightninged to a conclusion. The data was there all the time. It just needed a nudge to drop into place. "I think I know what it's about. The Lady being an usurper."

One-Eye asked, "One of the boys in the masks wants to do her the way she done her old man?"

"No. They want to bring back the Dominator."

"Eh?"

"He's still up north, in the ground. The Lady just kept him from returning when the wizard Bomanz opened the way for her. He could be in touch with Taken who are faithful to him. Bomanz proved communication with those buried in the Barrowland was possible. He could even be guiding some of the Circle. Harden was as big a villain as any of the Taken."

One-Eye pondered, then prophesied. "The battle will be lost. The Lady will be overthrown. Her loyal Taken will be laid low and her loyal troops wiped out. But they will take the most idealistic elements among the Rebel with them, meaning, essentially, a defeat for the White Rose."

I nodded. "The comet is in the sky, but the Rebel hasn't found his mystic child."

"Yeah. You're probably right on the mark when you say maybe the Dominator is influencing the Circle. Yeah."

"And in the chaos afterward, while they're squabbling over the spoils, up jumps the devil," I said.

"So where do we fit?" the Captain asked.

"The question," I replied, "is how do we get out from under."

Flying carpets buzzed around the Tower like flies around a corpse. The armies of Whisper, the Howler, the Nameless, Bonegnasher, and Moonbiter were eight to twelve days away, converging. Eastern troops were pouring in by air.

The gate in the palisade was busy with the comings and goings of parties harassing the Rebel. The Rebel had moved his camps to within five miles of the Tower. Some company troops made the occasional night raid, abetted by Goblin, One-Eye, and Silent, but the effort seemed pointless. The numbers were too overwhelming for hit and run to have any substantial effect. I wondered why the Lady wanted the Rebel kept stirred up.

Construction was complete. The obstacles were prepared. Boobytraps were in place. There was little to do but wait.

Six days had passed since our return with Feather and Journey. I'd expected their capture to electrify the Rebel into striking, but still they were stalling. One-Eye believed they had hopes of a last-minute finding of their White Rose.

Only the drawing of lots remained undone. Three of the Taken, with armies assigned them, would defend each level. It was rumored that the Lady herself would command forces stationed on the pyramid.

Nobody wanted to be on the front line. No matter how things went, those troops would be badly hurt. Thus the lottery.

There had been no more attempts on Raven or myself. Our antagonist was covering his tracks some other way. Too late to do unto us, anyway. I'd seen the Lady.

The tenor changed. Returning skirmishers began to look more battered, more desperate. The enemy was moving his camps again.

A messenger reached the Captain. He assembled the officers. "It's begun. The Lady has called the Taken to the lottery." He wore an odd expression. The main ingredient was astonishment. "We have special orders. From the Lady herself."

Whisper-murmur-rustle-grumble, everyone shaken. She was giving us all the rough jobs. I envisioned having to anchor the first line against Rebel elite troops.

"We're to strike camp and assemble on the pyramid." A hundred questions buzzed like hornets. He said, "She wants us for bodyguards."

"The Guard won't like that," I said. They did not like us anyway, having had to submit to the Captain's orders at the Stair of Tear.

"Think they'll give her a hard way to go, Croaker? Gents, the boss says go. So we go. You want to talk about it, do it while you're breaking camp. Without the men hearing."

For the troops this was great news. Not only would we be behind the worst fighting, we would be in a position to fall back into the Tower.

Was I that sure we were doomed? Did my negativism mirror a general attitude? Was this an army defeated before the first blow?

The comet was in the sky.

Considering that phenomenon while we moved, amidst animals being driven into the Tower, I understood why the Rebel had stalled. They had hoped to find their White Rose at the last minute, of course. And they had been waiting for the comet to attain a more auspicious aspect, its closest approach.

I grumbled to myself.

Raven, trudging beside me burdened with his own gear and a bundle belonging to Darling, grunted, "Huh?"

"They haven't found their magic kid. They won't have everything going their way."

He looked at me oddly, almost suspiciously. Then, "Yet," he said. "Yet."

There was a big clamor as Rebel cavalry hurled javelins at sentinels on the palisade. Raven did not look back. It was just a probe.

We had a hell of a view from the pyramid, though it was crowded up there. "Hope we're not stuck here long, I said. And, "Going to be hell treating casualties."

The Rebel had moved his camps to within a half mile of the stockade. They blended into one. There was constant skirmishing at the palisade. Most of our troops had taken their places on the tiers.

The first level forces consisted of those who had served in the north, fleshed out by garrison troops from cities abandoned to the Rebel. There were nine thousand of them, divided into three divisions. The center had been assigned to Stormbringer. Had I been running things, she would have been on the pyramid hurling cyclones.

The wings were commanded by Moonbiter and Bonegnasher, two Taken I'd never encountered.

Six thousand men occupied the second level, also divided into three divisions. Most were archers from the eastern armies. They were tough, and far less uncertain than the men below them. Their commanders, from left to right, were: the Faceless or Nameless Man, the Howler, and Nightcrawler. Countless racks of arrows had been provided them. I wondered how they would manage if the enemy broke the first line.

The third tier was manned by the Guard at the ballistae, Whisper on the left with fifteen hundred veterans from her own eastern army, and Shifter on the right with a thousand westerners and southerners. In the middle, below the pyramid, Soulcatcher commanded the Guard and allies from the Jewel Cities. His troops numbered twenty-five hundred.

And on the pyramid was the Black Company, one thousand strong, with banners bright and standards bold and weapons ready to hand.

So. Roughly twenty-one thousand men, against more than ten times that number. Numbers aren't always critical. The Annals recall many moments when the Company beat the odds. But not like this. This was too static. There was no room for retreat, for maneuver, and an advance was out of the question.

The Rebel got serious. The palisade's defenders withdrew quickly, dismantling the spans across the three trenches. The Rebel did not pursue. Instead, he began demolishing the stockade.

"They look as methodical as the Lady," I told Elmo.

"Yep. They'll use the timber to bridge the trenches."

He was wrong, but we would not learn that immediately.

"Seven days till the eastern armies get here," I muttered at sunset, glancing back at the huge, dark bulk of the Tower. The Lady had not come forth for the initial scrimmage.

"More like nine or ten," Elmo countered. "They'll want to get here all together."

"Yeah. Should've thought of that."

We ate dried food and slept on the earth. And in the morning we rose to the bray of Rebel trumpets.

The enemy formations stretched as far as the eye could see. A line of mantlets started forward. They had been built from timber scavenged from our palisade. They formed a moving wall stretched across the pie-slice. The heavy ballistae thumped away. Large trebuchets hurled stones and fireballs. The damage they did was inconsequential.

Rebel pioneers began bridging the first trench, using timber brought from their camps. The foundations for these were huge beams, fifty feet long, impervious to missile fire. They had to use cranes to position them. They exposed themselves while assembling and operating the devices. Well-ranged Guard engines made that expensive.

Where the palisade had stood Rebel engineers were assembling wheeled towers from which bowmen could shoot, and wheeled ramps to roll up to the first tier. Carpenters were making ladders. I saw no artillery. I guess they planned to swamp us once they crossed the trenches.

The Lieutenant knew siegework well. I went to him. "How they going to bring up those ramps and towers?"

"They'll fill the ditches."

He was right. As soon as they had bridges across the first, and started moving mantlets over, carts and wagons appeared, carrying earth and stone. Teamsters and animals took a beating. Many a corpse went into the fill.

The pioneers moved up to the second trench, assembled their cranes. The Circle gave them no armed support. Stormbringer sent archers to the lip of the final trench. The Guard laid down heavy fire with the ballistae. The pioneers suffered heavy casualties. The enemy command simply sent more men.

The Rebel began moving mantlets across the second trench an hour before noon. Wagons and carts crossed the first, carrying fill.

The pioneers encountered withering fire moving up to bridge the final ditch. The archers on the second tier sped their shafts high. They fell nearly straight down. The trebuchets shifted their aim, blasting mantlets into toothpicks and timbers. But the Rebel kept coming. On Moonbiter's flank they got a set of supporting beams across.

Moonbiter attacked, crossing with a picked force. His assault was so ferocious he drove the pioneers back over the second trench. He destroyed their equipment, attacked again. Then the Rebel command brought up a strong heavy infantry column. Moonbiter withdrew, leaving the second trench bridges ruined.

Inexorably, the Rebel bridged again, moved to the final trench with soldiers to protect his workmen. Stormbringer's snipers retreated.

The arrows from the second tier fell like flakes in a heavy winter snow, steadily and evenly. The carnage was spectacular. Rebel troops rolled into the witch's cauldron in a flood. A river of wounded flowed out. At the last trench the pioneers began keeping to the shelter of their mantlets, praying those would not be shattered by the Guard.

Thus it stood as the sun settled, casting long shadows across the field of blood. I'd guess the Rebel lost ten thousand men without bringing us to battle.

Through that day neither the Taken nor the Circle unleashed their powers. The Lady did not venture out of the Tower.

One less day to await the armies of the east.

Hostilities ended at sunset. We ate. The Rebel brought another shift to work the trenches. The newcomers went at it with the gusto their predecessors had lost. The strategy was obvious. They would rotate fresh troops in and wear us down.

The dark was the time of the Taken. Their passivity ended.

I could see little initially, so cannot for certain say who did what. Shifter, I suspect, changed shape and crossed into enemy territory.

The stars began to fade behind onrushing storm clouds. Cold air rushed across the earth. The wind rose, howled. Riding it came a horde of things with leathery wings, flying serpents the length of a man's arm. Their hissing overshadowed the tumult of the storm. Thunder crashed and lightning stalked, jabbing enemy works with its spears. The flashes revealed the ponderous advance of giants from the rock wastes. They hurled boulders the way children throw balls. One snatched up a bridge beam and used it as a two-handed club, smashing siege towers and ramps. The look of them, in the treacherous light, was of creatures of stone, basaltic rubble cobbled together in grotesque, gargantuan parody of the human form.

The earth shivered. Patches of plain glowed a bilious green. Radiant ten-foot, blood-streaked orange worms slithered amongst the foe. The heavens opened and dumped rain and burning brimstone.

The night coughed up more horrors. Killing fogs. Murderous insects. A beginning glow of magma such as we had seen at the Stair of Tear. And all this in just minutes. Once the Circle responded, the terrors faded, though some it took hours to neutralize. They never took the offensive. The Taken were too strong.

By midnight all was quiet. The Rebel had given up everything but fill work at the far trench. The storm had become a steady rain. It made the Rebel miserable but did him no harm. I wriggled down amongst my companions and fell asleep thinking how nice it was that our part of the world was dry.

Dawn. First view of the Taken's handiwork. Death everywhere. Horribly mutilated corpses. The Rebel labored till noon cleaning up. Then he resumed his assault on the trenches.

The Captain received a message from the Tower. He assembled us. "Word is, we lost Shifter last night." He gave me a look meant to be significant. "The circumstances were questionable. We've been told to stay alert. That means you,

One-Eye. And you, Goblin and Silent. You send a yell to the Tower if you see anything suspicious. Understand?" They nodded.

Shapeshifter gone. That must have taken some doing.

"The Rebel lose anybody important?" I asked.

"Whiskers. Roper. Tamarask. But they can be replaced. Shifter can't."

Rumors floated around. The deaths of members of the Circle had been caused by some catlike beast so strong and quick even the powers of its victims were of no consequence. Several score senior Rebel functionaries had fallen victim as well.

The men recalled a similar beast from Beryl. There were whispers. Catcher had brought the forvalaka over on the ship. Was he using it against the Rebel?

I thought not. The attack fit Shifter's style. Shifter loved sneaking into the enemy camp. . . .

One-Eye went around wearing a thoughtful look, so self-engrossed he bumped into things. Once he stopped and smashed a fist into a ham hanging near the newly erected cook tents.

He had it figured out. How Catcher could send the forvalaka into the Bastion to slaughter the Syndic's entire household, and end up controlling the city through a puppet, through no cost to the Lady's overextended resources. Catcher and Shifter were thick then, weren't they?

He had figured out who killed his brother—too late to exact revenge.

He went around and beat on that ham several times during the course of the day.

I joined Raven and Darling later. They were watching the action. I checked Shapeshifter's force. His standard had been replaced. "Raven. Isn't that Jalena's banner?"

"Yes." He spat.

"Shifter wasn't a bad guy. For one of the Taken."

"None of them are. For Taken. As long as you don't get in their way." He spat again, eyed the Tower. "What's going on here, Croaker?"

"Eh?" He was as civil as he had been since our return from the field.

"What's this show all about? Why is she doing it this way?"

I was not sure what he was asking. "I don't know. She doesn't confide in me."

He scowled. "No?" As though he did not believe me! Then he shrugged. "Be interesting to find out."

"No doubt." I watched Darling. She was inordinately intrigued by the attack. She asked Raven a stream of questions. They were not simple. You might expect their like from an apprentice general, a prince, someone expected to assume eventual command.

"Shouldn't she be somewhere safer?" I asked. "I mean. . . ."

"Where?" Raven demanded. "Where would she be safer than with me?" His voice was hard, his eyes narrow with suspicion. Startled, I dropped the subject.

Was he jealous because I had become Darling's friend? I don't know. Everything about Raven is strange.

Stretches of the farther trench had vanished. In places the middle trench had been filled and tamped. The Rebel had moved his surviving towers and ramps up to the extreme limit of our artillery. New towers were abuilding. New mantlets were everywhere. Men huddled behind every one.

Braving merciless fire, Rebel pioneers bridged the final trench. Counterattacks stalled them again and again, yet they kept coming. They completed their eighth bridge about the third hour after noon.

Vast infantry formations moved forward. They swarmed across the bridges, into the teeth of the arrowstorm. They hit our first line randomly, pelting in like sleet, dying against a wall of spears and shields and swords. Bodies piled up. Our bowmen threatened to fill the ditches around the bridges. And still they came.

I recognized a few banners seen at Roses and Lords. The elite units were coming up.

They crossed the bridges and formed up, advanced in fair order, exerted heavy pressure on our center. Behind them a second line formed, stronger, deeper, and broader. When it was solid its officers moved it forward a few yards, had their men crouch behind their shields.

Pioneers moved mantlets across, joined them in a sort of palisade. Our heaviest artillery concentrated on these. Behind the ditch, hordes ran fill to selected points.

Though the men on the bottom level were our least reliable—I suspect the lottery was rigged—they repelled the Rebel elite. Success gave them only a brief respite. The next mass attacked.

Our line creaked. It might have broken had the men had anywhere to run. They had the habit of fleeing. But here they were trapped, with no chance of getting up the retaining wall.

That wave receded. On his end Moonbiter counterattacked and routed the enemy before him. He destroyed most of their mantlets and briefly threatened their bridges. I was impressed by his aggressiveness.

It was late. The Lady had not come forth. I suppose she had not doubted we would hold. The enemy launched a last assault, a human wave attack, that came within a whisper of swamping our men. In places the Rebel reached the retaining wall and tried to scale or dismantle it. But our men did not collapse. The incessant rain of arrows broke the Rebel determination.

They withdrew. Fresh units filled in behind the mantlets. A temporary peace settled in. The field belonged to their pioneers.

"Six days," I said to no one in particular. "I don't think we can hang on."

The first line shouldn't survive tomorrow. The horde would storm the second level. Our archers were deadly as archers, but I doubted they would do well hand-to-hand. Moreover, once forced into close combat they could no longer punish the enemy coming up. Then the Rebel towers would do them as they had been done.

We had cut a narrow trench near the rear of the pyramid top. It served as our latrine. The Captain caught me at my most inelegant. "They need you down on the bottom level, Croaker. Take One-Eye and your crew."

"What?"

"You're a physician, aren't you?"

"Oh." Silly of me. Should have known I could not remain an observer.

The rest of the Company went down too, to perform other tasks.

Getting down was no trouble, though traffic was heavy on the temporary ramps. Men from the upper level and pyramid top hauled munitions down to the bowmen (the Lady must have squirreled arrows for a generation), brought corpses and casualties up.

"Be a good time to jump us," I told One-Eye. "Just scamper up the ramps."

"They're too busy doing the same things we are." We passed within ten feet of Soulcatcher. I lifted a hand in tentative greeting. He did the same after a pause. I got the feeling he was startled.

Down we went, and down again, into Stormbringer's territory.

It was hell down there. Every battlefield is, after, but never had I seen anything like this. Men were down everywhere. Many were Rebels our men hadn't the energy to finish. Even the troops from up top just booted them aside so they could collect our people. Forty feet away, ignored, Rebel soldiers were gathering their own people and ignoring ours. "It's like something out of the old Annals," I told One-Eye. "Maybe the battle at Torn."

"Torn wasn't this bloody."

"Uhm." He was there. He went back a long way.

I found an officer and asked where we should set up shop. He suggested we'd be the most use to Bonegnasher.

Going, we passed uncomfortably near Stormbringer. One-Eye's amulet burned my wrist.

"Friend of yours?" One-Eye asked sarcastically.

"What?"

"Such a look you got from the old spook."

I shuddered. Lime thread. Taken on the wind. That could have been Stormbringer.

Bonegnasher was a big one, bigger than Shifter, eight feet tall and six hundred pounds of iron mean muscle. He was so strong it was grotesque. He had a mouth like a crocodile, and supposedly had eaten his enemies in the old days. A few of the old stories also call him Bonecrusher, because of his strength.

While I stared, one of his lieutenants told us to go out to the far right flank, where fighting had been so light no medical team had yet been assigned.

We located the appropriate battalion commander. "Set up right here," he told us. "I'll have the men brought to you." He looked sour.

One of his staff volunteered, "He was a company commander this morning. It was hard on officers today." When you have heavy casualties among your officers, they are leading from the front to keep the men from breaking.

One-Eye and I started patching. "Thought you had it easy over here."

"Easy is relative." He looked at us hard, talking about easy when we had spent the day loafing on the pyramid.

Torchlight medicine is a bunch of fun. Between us we treated several hundred men. Whenever I paused to work the pain and stiffness out of my hands and shoulders, I glanced at the sky, perplexed. I had expected the Taken to go crazy again tonight.

Bonegnasher ambled into our makeshift surgery, naked to the waist, maskless, looking like an oversized wrestler. He said nothing. We tried to ignore him. His piggy little eyes remained tight as he watched.

One-Eye and I were working on the same man, from opposite ends. He stopped suddenly, head coming up like that of a startled horse. His eye got big. He looked around wildly. "What is it?" I asked.

"I don't. . . . Odd. It's gone. For a second. . . . Never mind."

I kept an eye on him. He was frightened. More frightened than the presence of the Taken justified. As if some personal danger threatened him. I glanced at Bonegnasher. He was watching One-Eye too.

One-Eye did it again later, while we were working separate patients. I looked up. Beyond him, down at waist level, I caught the glow of eyes. A chill scrambled down my spine.

One-Eye watched the darkness, nervousness increasing. When he finished with his patient he cleansed his hands and drifted toward Bonegnasher.

An animal screamed. A dark shape hurtled into the circle of light, toward me. "Forvalaka!" I gasped, and threw myself aside. The beast passed over me, one claw ripping my jerkin.

Bonegnasher reached the man-leopard's point of impact the moment it did so. One-Eye unleashed a spell that blinded me, the forvalaka, and everyone watching. I heard the beast roar. Anger became agony. My vision returned. Bonegnasher had the monster in a deadly hug, right arm crushing its windpipe, left its ribs. It clawed air futilely. It was supposed to have the strength of a dozen natural leopards. In Bonegnasher's arms it was helpless. The Taken laughed, took a bite from its left shoulder.

One-Eye staggered over to me. "Should have had that guy with us in Beryl," I said. My voice quavered.

One-Eye was so frightened he was gagging. He did not laugh. I did not have much humor in me, either, frankly. Just a reflex sarcasm. Gallows humor.

Trumpets filled the night with their cries. Men ran to their stations. The rattle of arms overrode the strangling of the forvalaka.

One-Eye grabbed my arm. "Got to get out of here," he said. "Come on."

I was mesmerized by the struggle. The leopard was trying to change. It looked vaguely womanish.

"Come on!" One-Eye swore sulphurously. "That thing was after you, you know. Sent. Let's move before it gets away."

It had no end of energy, despite Bonegnasher's immense strength and savagery. The Taken had destroyed its left shoulder with his teeth.

One-Eye was right. Across the way the Rebel was getting excited. Fighting could break out. Time to make tracks, for both reasons. I grabbed my kit and scooted.

We passed both Stormbringer and Soulcatcher getting back. I gave each a mocking salute, driven by I don't know what tomfool bravado. One, I was sure, initiated the attack. Neither responded.

Reaction did not set in till I was safe atop the pyramid, with the Company, with nothing to do but think about what could have happened. Then I started shaking so bad One-Eye gave me one of my own knockout draughts.

Something visited my dreams. Old friend now. Golden glow and beautiful face. As before, "My Faithful need not fear."

There was a hint of light in the east when the drug wore off. I wakened less frightened, but hardly confident. Three times they had tried. Anyone that set on killing me would find a way. No matter what the Lady said.

One-Eye appeared almost immediately. "You all right?"

"Yeah. Fine."

"You missed a hell of a show."

I raised an eyebrow.

"The Circle and the Taken went at it after your lights went out. Only stopped a little while ago. A little hairy around the edges this time. Bonegnasher and Stormbringer got skragged. Looks like they did it to each other. Come here. I want to show you something."

Grumbling, I followed him. "How bad did the Rebel get hurt?"

"You hear different stories. But plenty. At least four of them bought it." He halted at the front edge of the pyramid top, gestured dramatically.

"What?"

"You blind? I got only one eye and I can see better than you?"

"Give me a hint."

"Look for a crucifixion."

"Oh." That told, I had no trouble finding the cross planted near Stormbringer's command post. "Okay. So what?"

"That's your friend. The forvalaka."

"Mine?"

"Ours?" A delightfully wicked expression crossed his face. "End of a long story, Croaker. And a satisfying one. Either way it was, whoever killed Tom-Tom, I lived to see them reach an evil end."

"Yeah." To our left Raven and Darling watched the Rebel move up. Their fingers blurred. They were too far for me to catch much. It was like overhearing a conversation in a language with which you have only a formal acquaintance. Goobledegook. "What's eating Raven lately?"

"What do you mean?"

"He don't have anything to do with anybody but Darling. Don't even hang around the Captain anymore. Hasn't gotten into a card game since we brought in Feather and Journey. Gets all sour whenever you try to be nice to Darling. Something happen while we were away?"

One-Eye shrugged. "I was with you, Croaker. Remember? Nobody ain't said nothing. But now you mention it, yeah, he is acting strange." He chuckled. "For Raven, strange."

I surveyed the Rebel's preparations. They seemed halfhearted and disorganized. Even so, despite the fury of the night, he had finished filling the farther two trenches. His efforts at the nearest had provided a half dozen crossing places.

Our second and third level forces looked thin. I asked why.

"The Lady ordered a bunch down to the first level. Especially off the top."

Mostly from Soulcatcher's division, I realized. His outfit looked puny. "Think they'll break through today?"

One-Eye shrugged. "If they stay as stubborn as they were. But look. They ain't eager no more. They found out we weren't going to be easy. We made them start to wonder. To remember the old spook in the Tower. She hasn't come out yet. Maybe they're getting worried."

I suspected it was more because of casualties among the Circle than because of growing trepidation among the soldiers. The Rebel command structure must be chaotic. Any army falters when nobody knows who is in charge.

Nevertheless, four hours after dawn they began dying for their cause. Our front line braced itself. The Howler and the Faceless Man had replaced Stormbringer and Bonegnasher, leaving the second level to Nightcrawler.

The fighting had become formularized. The horde swept forward, into the teeth of the arrowstorm, crossed the bridges, hid behind the mantlets, streamed around those to hit our first line. They kept coming, a never-ending stream. Thousands fell before reaching their foes. Many who did make it battled only a short while, then wandered off, sometimes helping injured comrades, more often just getting out of harm's way. Their officers had no control.

The reinforced line consequently held together longer and more resolutely than I anticipated. Nevertheless, the weight of numbers and accumulated fatigue eventually told. Gaps appeared. Enemy troops reached the retaining wall. The Taken organized counterattacks, most of which did not attain the momentum to carry through. Here, there, weaker willed troopers tried to flee to the higher level. Nightcrawler distributed squads along the edge. They threw the fugitives back. Resistance stiffened.

Still, the Rebel now scented victory. He became more enthusiastic.

The distant ramps and towers started forward. Their advance was ponderous, a few yards a minute. One tower toppled when it hit fill inadequately tamped in the far trench. It crushed a ramp and several dozen men. The remaining engines came on. The Guard redirected its heaviest weapons, throwing fireballs.

A tower caught. Then another. A ramp came to a halt, in flames. But the other engines rolled steadily forward, reaching the second trench.

The lighter ballistae shifted aim as well, savaging the thousands hauling the engines forward.

At the nearest trench pioneers kept filling and tamping. And falling to our bowmen. I had to admire them. They were the bravest of the foe.

The Rebel star was rising. He overcame his weak start and became as ferocious as before. Our first level units fractured into ever smaller knots, whirling, swirling. The men Nightcrawler had scattered to keep ours from fleeing now battled overbold Rebels who clambered up the retaining wall. In one spot Rebel troops pulled some of the logs free and tried to excavate a pathway up.

It was the middle of the afternoon. The Rebel still had hours of daylight. I began to get the shakes.

One-Eye, whom I hadn't seen since it started, joined me again. "Word from the Tower," he said. "They lost six of the Circle last night. Means there are only maybe eight left out there. Probably none who were in the Circle when we first came north."

"No wonder they started slow."

He eyed the fighting. "Don't look good, does it?"

"Hardly."

"Guess that's why she's coming out." I turned. "Yeah. She's on her way. In person."

Cold. Cold-cold-cold. I do not know why. Then I heard the Captain yelling, the Lieutenant and Candy and Elmo and Raven and who knows all else, all yelling for us to get into formation. Grab-ass time was over. I withdrew to my surgery, which was a clump of tents at the rear, unfortunately on the downwind side of the latrine. "Quick inspection," I told One-Eye. "See that everything is squared away."

The Lady came on horseback, up the ramp climbing from near the Tower entrance. She rode an animal bred for the part. It was huge and spirited, a glossy roan that looked like an artist's conception of equine perfection. She was very stylish, in red and gold brocade, white scarves, gold and silver jewelry, a few black accents. Like a rich lady one might see in the streets of Opal. Her hair was darker than midnight, and hung long from beneath an elegant white and lace tricorne hat trailing white ostrich plumes. A net of pearls kept it constrained. She looked twenty at the oldest. Quiet islanded her as she passed. Men gaped. Nowhere did I see a hint of fear.

The Lady's companions were more in keeping with her image. Of medium height, all swathed in black, faces concealed behind black gauze, mounted upon black horses harnessed and saddled in black leather, they resembled the popular picture of the Taken. One bore a long black spear tipped with blackened steel, the other a big silver horn. One rode to either flank, trailing by a rigid yard.

She honored me with one sweet smile as she passed. Her eyes sparkled with humor and invitation. . . .

"She still loves you," One-Eye quipped.

I shuddered. "That's what I'm afraid of."

She rode through the Company, straight to the Captain, spoke to him for half a minute. He showed no emotion, coming face to face with this old evil. Nothing shakes him when he assumes his iron commander mask.

Elmo came hustling up. "How you doing, buddy?" I asked. I had not seen him in days.

"She wants you."

I said something like "Glug." Real intelligent.

"I know what you mean. Enough is enough. But what can you do? Get yourself a horse."

"A horse? Why? Where?"

"Just carrying a message, Croaker. Don't ask me. . . . Speak of the devil."

A young trooper, wearing the Howler's colors, appeared over the edge of the rear of the pyramid. He led a string of horses. Elmo trotted over. After a brief exchange, he beckoned me. Reluctantly, I joined him. "Take your pick, Croaker."

I selected a chestnut mare with good lines and apparent docility, swung aboard. It felt good to be in the saddle. It had been a while. "Wish me luck, Elmo." I wanted to sound flip. It came out squeaky.

"You got it." And as I started away, "Teach you to write those silly stories."

"Let up, eh?" As I went forward I did wonder, for a moment, how much art does affect life. *Could* I have brought this on myself?

The Lady did not look back as I approached. She did make a small gesture. The horseman on her right edged away, leaving me room. I took the hint, halted, concentrated on the panorama instead of looking at her. I sensed her amusement.

The situation had worsened in the minutes I had been away. Rebel soldiers had attained several footholds on the second tier. On the first our formations had been shattered. The Howler had relented and was letting his men help those below scramble up the retaining wall. Whisper's troops, on the third level, were using bows for the first time.

The assault ramps were almost up to the nearest ditch. The great towers had halted. Over half were out of action. The remainder had been manned, but were so far away the bowmen there were doing no damage. Thank heaven for small favors.

The Taken on the first level were using their powers, but were in so much danger they had little chance to wield them effectively.

The Lady said, "I wanted you to see this, Annalist."

"Eh?" Another sparkling gem from the Company wit.

"What is about to transpire. So that it is properly recorded in at least one place."

I snuck a glance at her. She wore a teasing little smile. I shifted my attention to the fighting. What she did to me, just sitting there, amidst the fury of the end of the world, was more frightening than the prospect of a death in battle. I am too old to boil like a horny fifteen-year-old.

The Lady snapped her fingers.

The rider on her left raised the silver horn, cleared the gauze from her face so she could bring the instrument to her lips. Feather! My gaze flicked to the Lady. She winked.

Taken. Feather and Journey had been Taken, like Whisper before them. What power and might they possessed was now at the Lady's disposal. . . . My mind scampered around that. Implications, implications. Old Taken fallen, new Taken stepping in to replace them. . . .

The horn called out, a sweet note, like that of an angel summoning the hosts of heaven. It was not loud, yet it rang out everywhere, as if coming from the very firmament. The fighting stopped cold. All eyes turned to the pyramid.

The Lady snapped her fingers. The other rider (Journey, I presumed) lifted his spear high, let its head fall.

The forward retaining wall exploded in a dozen places. Bestial trumpeting filled the silence. Even before I saw them burst forth I knew, and laughed.

"Elephants!" I hadn't seen war elephants since my first year with the Company. "Where did you get elephants?"

The Lady's eyes sparkled. She did not respond.

The answer was obvious. From overseas. From her allies among the Jewel cities. How she had gotten them here unnoted, and kept them concealed, ah, that was the mystery.

It was a delectable surprise to spring on the Rebel at the moment of his apparent triumph. Nobody in these parts had ever seen war elephants, let alone had any notion how to fight them.

The great grey pachyderms smashed into the Rebel horde. The mahouts had great fun, charging their beasts back and forth, trampling Rebels by the hundred, totally shattering their morale. They pulled the mantlets down. They lumbered across the bridges and went after the siege towers, toppling them one by one.

There were twenty-four of the beasts, two for each place of hiding. They had been provided with armor, and their drivers were encased in metal, yet here and there the random spear or arrow found a chink, either felling a mahout or pricking a beast enough to enrage it. Elephants that lost riders lost interest in the fray. The wounded animals went crazy. They did more damage than those still under control.

The Lady gestured again. Again Journey signalled. Troops below lowered the ramps we had used for hauling materiel down and casualties up. The troops of the third level, saving the Guard, marched down, formed up, launched an attack upon chaos. Considering the respective numbers, that seemed mad. But considering the wild swing in fortunes, morale was more important.

Whisper on the left wing, Catcher in the center, fat old Lord Jalena on the right. Drums pounding. They rolled forward, slowed only by the problem of slaughtering the panicked thousands. The Rebel was afraid not to run, yet afraid to flee toward the rampaging elephants between him and his camp. He did little to defend himself.

Clear to the first ditch. Biter, the Howler, and the Faceless whipped their survivors into line, cursed and frightened them into moving forward, to fire all the enemy works.

Attackers to the second ditch, swirling over and around the abandoned towers and ramps, passing on, following the bloody trail of the elephants. Now fires among the engines as the men from the first level arrived. The attackers advancing toward the nether ditch. The whole field carpeted with enemy dead. Dead in numbers unlike anything I had seen anywhere before.

The Circle, what remained of it, finally recovered enough to try its powers against the beasts. They scored a few successes before being neutralized by the Taken. Then it depended on the men in the field.

As always, the Rebel had the numbers. One by one, the elephants fell. The enemy piled up before the attacking line. We had no reserves. Fresh troops streamed from the Rebel camps, without enthusiasm but sufficiently strong to turn our advance. A withdrawal became necessary.

The Lady signalled it through Journey.

"Very good," I muttered. "Very good indeed," as our men returned to their positions, sank down in weariness. Darkness was not far away. We had made it through another day. "But now what? Those fools won't quit while the comet is in the sky. And we've shot our last bolt."

The Lady smiled. "Record it as you saw it, Annalist." She and her companions rode away.

"What am I going to do with this horse?" I grumbled.

There was a battle of powers that night, but I missed it. I do not know for whom it was the greater disaster. We lost Moonbiter, the Faceless Man, and Nightcrawler. Only Nightcrawler fell to enemy action. The others were consumed by the feud among the Taken.

A messenger came not an hour after sundown. I was readying my team to go below, after having fed them. Elmo ran the relay again. "Tower, Croaker. Your girlfriend wants you. Take your bow along."

There is only so much you can fear someone, even someone like the Lady. Resigned, I asked, "Why a bow?"

He shrugged.

"Arrows too?"

"No word on that. Doesn't sound smart."

"You're probably right. One-Eye, it's all yours."

Silver lining time. At least I would not spend my night amputating limbs, sewing cuts, and reassuring youngsters whom I knew would not survive the week. Serving with the Taken gives a soldier a better chance of surviving wounds, but still gangrene and peritonitis take their tolls.

Down the long ramp, to the dark gate. The Tower loomed like something out of myth, awash in the silver light of the comet. Had the Circle blundered? Waited too long? Was the comet no longer a favorable omen once it began to wane?

How close were the eastern armies? Not close enough. But our strategy did not seem predicated on stalling. If that were the plan, we would have marched into the Tower and sealed the door. Wouldn't we?

I dithered. Natural reluctance. I touched the amulet Goblin had given me back when, the amulet One-Eye had presented more recently. Not much assurance there. I glanced at the pyramid, thought I saw a stocky silhouette up top. The Captain? I raised a hand. The silhouette responded. Cheered, I turned.

The gate looked like the mouth of the night, but a step forward took me into a wide, lighted passageway. It reeked of the horses and cattle which had been driven in an age ago.

A soldier awaited me. "Are you Croaker?" I nodded. "Follow me." He was not a Guard, but a young infantryman from the Howler's army. He seemed bewildered. Here, there, I saw more of his ilk. It hit me. The Howler had spent his nights ferrying troops while the rest of the Taken battled the Circle and one another. None of those men had come to the battlefield.

How many were there? What surprises did the Tower conceal?

I entered the inner Tower through the portal I had used before. The soldier halted where the Guard captain had. He wished me luck in a pale, shaky voice. I thanked him squeakily.

She played no games. At least, nothing flashy. And I did not slip into my role as sex-brained boy. This was business all the way.

She seated me at a dark wood table with my bow lying before me, said, "I have a problem."

I just looked at her.

"Rumors are running wild out there, aren't they? About what's happened among the Taken?"

I nodded. "This isn't like the Limper going bad. They're murdering each other. The men don't want to get caught in the crossfire."

"My husband isn't dead. You know that. He's behind it all. He's been awakening. Very slowly, but enough to have reached some of the Circle. Enough to have touched the females among the Taken. They'll do anything for him. The bitches. I watch them as closely as I can, but I'm not infallible. They get away with things. This battle. . . . It isn't what it seems. The Rebel army was brought here by members of the Circle under my husband's influence. The fools. They thought they could use *him*, to defeat me and grab power for themselves. They're all gone now, slain, but the thing they set in motion goes on. I'm not fighting the White Rose, Annalist—though a victory over that silliness could come from this as well. I'm fighting the old slaver, the Dominator. And if I lose I lose the world."

Cunning woman. She did not assume the role of maiden in distress. She played it as one equal to another, and that won my sympathy more surely. She knew I knew the Dominator as well as did any mundane now alive. Knew I must fear him far more than her, for who fears a woman more than a man?

"I know you, Annalist. I have opened your soul and peered inside. You fight for me because your Company has undertaken a commission it will pursue to the bitter end—because its principal personalities feel its honor was stained in Beryl. And that though most of you think you're serving Evil.

"Evil is relative, Annalist. You can't hang a sign on it. You can't touch it or taste it or cut it with a sword. Evil depends on where you are standing, pointing your indicting finger. Where you stand now, because of your oath, is opposite the Dominator. For you he is where your Evil lies."

She paced a moment, perhaps anticipating a response. I made none. She had encapsulated my own philosophy.

"That evil tried to kill you three times, physician. Twice for fear of your knowledge, once for fear of your future."

That woke me up. "My future?"

"The Taken sometimes glimpse the future. Perhaps this conversation was foreseen."

She had me baffled. I sat there looking stupid.

She left the room momentarily, returned carrying a quiver of arrows, spilled them on the table. They were black and heavy, silver-headed, inscribed with almost invisible lettering. While I examined them she took my bow, exchanged it for another of identical weight and pull. It was a gorgeous match for the arrows. Too gorgeous to be used as a weapon.

She told me, "Carry these. Always."

"I'll have to use them?"

"It's possible. Tomorrow will see the end of the matter, one way or the other. The Rebel has been mauled, yet he retains vast manpower reserves. My strategy may not succeed. If I fail, my husband wins. Not the Rebel, not the White Rose, but the Dominator, that hideous beast lying restless in his grave. . . ."

I avoided her gaze, eyed the weapons, wondered what I was supposed to say, to not hear, what I was supposed to do with those death tools, and if I could do it when the time came.

She knew my mind. "You'll know the moment. And you'll do what you think is right."

I looked up now, frowning, wishing. . . . Even knowing what she was, wishing. Maybe my idiot brothers were right.

She smiled, reached with one of those too-perfect hands, clasped my fingers. . . .

I lost track. I think. I do not recall anything happening. Yet my mind did fuzz for a second, and when it unfuzzed, she was holding my hand still, smiling, saying, "Time to go, soldier. Rest well."

I rose zombielike and shambled toward the door. I had a distinct feeling that I had missed something. I did not look back. I couldn't.

I stepped into the night outside the Tower and immediately knew I had lost time again. The stars had moved across the sky. The comet was low. Rest well? The hours for rest were nearly gone.

It was peaceful out, cool, with crickets chirping. Crickets. Who would believe it? I looked down at the weapon she had given me. When had I strung it? Why was I carrying an arrow across it? I could not recall taking them off the table. . . . For one frightened instant I thought my mind was going. Cricket song brought me back.

I looked up the pyramid. Someone was up top, watching. I raised a hand. He responded. Elmo, by the way he moved. Good old Elmo.

Couple hours till dawn. I could get a little shuteye if I didn't dawdle.

A quarter way up the ramp I got a funny feeling. Halfway there I realized what it was. One-Eye's amulet! My wrist was burning. . . . Taken! Danger!

A cloud of darkness reared out of the night, from some imperfection in the side of the pyramid. It spread like the sail of a ship, flat, and moved toward me. I responded the only way I could. With an arrow.

My shaft ripped through that sheet of darkness. And a long wail surrounded me, filled with more surprise than rage, more despair than agony. The sheet of darkness shredded. Something manshaped scuttled across the slope. I watched it go, never thinking of spending another arrow, though I laid another across the bow. Boggled, I resumed my climb.

"What happened?" Elmo asked when I got to the top.

"I don't know," I said. "I honestly don't have the foggiest what the hell happened tonight."

He gave me the once-over. "You look pretty rocky. Get some rest."

"I need it," I admitted. "Pass it to the Captain. She says tomorrow is the day. Win or lose." Much good the news would do him. But I thought he would like to know.

"Yeah. They do something to you in there?"

"I don't know. I don't think so."

He wanted to talk more, despite his admonition about resting. I pushed him away gently, went into one of my hospital tents and curled up in a tight corner like a wounded animal denning up. I had been touched somehow, even if I could not name it. I needed time to recover. Probably more time than I would be given.

They sent Goblin to wake me. I was my usual charming morning self, threatening blood feud with anyone fool enough to disturb my dreams. Not that they didn't deserve disturbing. They were foul. I was doing unspeakable things with a couple of girls who could not have been more than twelve, and making them love it. It's disgusting, the shadows that lurk in the mind.

Revolting as my dreams were, I did not want to get up. My bedroll was toasty warm.

Goblin said, "You want I should play rough? Listen, Croaker. Your girlfriend is coming out. Captain wants you up to meet her."

"Yeah. Sure." I grabbed my boots with one hand, parted the tent flap with the other. I growled, "What the hell time is it? Looks like the sun's been up for hours."

"It has. Elmo figured you needed the rest. Said you had it rough last night."

I grunted, hastily put myself together. I considered washing up, but Goblin headed me off. "Get your war gear on. The Rebel is headed this way."

I heard distant drums. The Rebel had not used drums before. I asked about it.

Goblin shrugged. He was looking pale. I suppose he had heard my message to the Captain. Win or lose. Today. "They've elected themselves a new council." He began to natter, as men will do when frightened, telling me the night's history of the feud among the Taken, and of how the Rebel had suffered. I heard nothing cheering. He helped me don what armor I possessed. I hadn't worn anything but a mail shirt since the fighting around Roses. I collected the weapons the Lady had given me and stepped out into one of the most glorious mornings I'd ever seen.

"Hell of a day for dying," I said.

"Yeah."

"How soon is she going to be here?" The Captain would want us on station when she arrived. He liked to present a portrait of order and efficiency.

"When she gets here. We just had a message saying she would be out."

"Uhm." I surveyed the pyramid top. The men were about their business, preparing for a fight. Nobody seemed in any hurry. "I'm going to wander around."

Goblin did not say anything. He just followed, pallid face pulled into a concerned frown. His eyes moved constantly, watching everything. From the set of his shoulders and careful way he moved, I realized he had a spell ready for instant use. It was not till he had dogged me a while that I realized he was bodyguarding.

I was both pleased and distressed. Pleased because people cared enough to look out for me, distressed because my situation had become so bad. I glanced at my hands. Unconsciously, I had strung the bow and laid an arrow across. Part of me was on maximum alert too.

Everyone eyed the weapons, but no one asked. I suspect stories were making the rounds. Strange that my comrades did not corner me to double-check.

The Rebel arrayed his forces carefully, methodically, beyond the reach of our weapons. Whoever had taken charge had restored discipline. And had constructed a whole armada of new engines during the night.

Our forces had abandoned the lower level. All that remained down there was a crucifix with a figure writhing upon it. . . . Writhing. After all it had suffered, including having been nailed up on that cross, the forvalaka remained alive!

The troops had been shuffled. The archers were upon the third level now, Whisper having taken command of that whole tier. The allies, the survivors from the first level, Catcher's forces, and what not, were on the second level. Catcher had the center, Lord Jalena the right, and the Howler the left. An effort had been made to restore the retaining wall, but it remained in terrible shape. It would be a poor obstacle.

One-Eye joined us. "You guys hear the latest?"

I lifted an inquiring eyebrow.

"They claim they've found their White Rose child."

After reflection I responded, "Dubious."

"For sure. Word from the Tower is, she's a fake. Just something to get the troops fired up."

"I figured. Surprised they didn't think of it before."

"Speak of the devil," Goblin squeaked. He pointed.

I had to search a moment before spotting the soft glow advancing along the aisles between enemy divisions. It surrounded a child on a big white horse, bearing a standard of red emblazoned with a white rose.

"Not even good showmanship," One-Eye complained. "That guy on the bay is making the light."

My insides had knotted in fear that this was the real thing after all. I looked down at my hands, wondering if this child was the target the Lady had in mind. But no. I had no impulse to speed a shaft in that direction. Not that I could have gotten one halfway there.

I glimpsed Raven and Darling on the far side of the pyramid, hands going zip-zip. I headed that way.

Raven spotted us when we were twenty feet away. He glanced at my weapons. His face tightened. A knife appeared in his hand. He started cleaning his nails.

I stumbled, so startled was I. The knife business was a tick. He did it only under stress. Why with me? I was no enemy.

I tucked my bow and arrow under my left arm, greeted Darling. She gave me a big grin, quick hug. *She* didn't have anything against me. She asked if she could see the bow. I let her look but did not turn loose. I couldn't.

Raven was as restless as a man seated on a griddle.

"What the hell is the matter with you?" I demanded. "You been acting like the rest of us have the plague." His behavior hurt. We had been through some shit together, Raven and I. He had no call to turn on me.

His mouth tightened to a tiny point. He dug under his nails till it seemed he had to be hurting himself.

"Well?"

"Don't push me, Croaker."

With my right hand I scratched Darling's back as she leaned against me. My left tightened on my bow. My knuckles turned the color of old ice. I was ready to thump the man. Take that dagger away and I stood a chance. He is a tough bastard, but I've had a few years to get tough myself.

Darling seemed oblivious to the tension between us.

Goblin stepped in. He faced Raven, his stance as belligerent as mine. "You've got a problem, Raven. I think maybe we better have a sitdown with the Captain."

Raven was startled. He realized, if only for a moment, that he was making enemies. It's damned hard to make Goblin mad. Really mad, not mad like he gets with One-Eye.

Something died behind Raven's eyes. He indicated my bow. "Lady's leman," he accused.

I was more baffled than angry. "Not true," I said. "But so what if it was?"

He moved restlessly. His gaze kept flicking to Darling, leaning against me. He wanted her away, but could not put the demand into acceptable words.

"First sucking up to Soulcatcher all the time. Now to the Lady. What are you doing, Croaker? Who are you selling?"

"What?" Only Darling's presence kept me from going after him.

"That's enough," Goblin said. His voice was hard, without a hint of squeak. "I'm pulling rank. On everybody. Right now. Right here. We're going to the Captain and get this talked out. Or we're unvoting your membership in the Company, Raven. Croaker is right. You've been a pure ass lately. We don't need it. We've got enough trouble out there." He stabbed a finger at the Rebel.

The Rebel answered with trumpets.

There was no confab with the Captain.

It was obvious somebody new was in charge. The enemy divisions came forward in lockstep, slowly, their shields arrayed in proper turtle fashion, turning most of our arrows. Whisper adjusted quickly, concentrating the guard's fire on one formation at a time, having the archers wait till the heavy weapons broke the turtle. Effective, but not effective enough.

The siege towers and ramps rumbled forward as fast as men could drag them. The Guard did their best, but could destroy only a few. Whisper was in a dilemma. She had to choose between targets. She elected to concentrate on breaking turtles.

The towers came closer this time. The Rebel archers were able to reach our men. That meant our archers could reach them, and ours were better marksmen.

The enemy crossed the nearest ditch, encountering massed missile fire from both levels. Only when they reached the retaining wall did they break their formations, streaming to the weak points, where they had little success.

They then attacked everywhere at once. Their ramps were slow arriving. Men with ladders rushed forward.

The Taken did not hold back. They threw everything they could. Rebel wizards fought them all the way, and, despite the harm they had suffered, for the most part kept them neutralized. Whisper did not participate. She was too busy.

The Lady and her companions arrived. Again I was summoned. I clambered aboard my horse and joined her, bow across my lap.

They came on and on. Occasionally I glanced at the Lady. She remained an ice queen, utterly without expression.

The Rebel gained foothold after foothold. He tore whole sections of retaining wall away. Men with shovels hurled earth around, building natural ramps. The wooden ramps continued their advance, but would not arrive soon.

There was one island of peace out there, around the crucified forvalaka. The attackers gave it a wide berth.

Lord Jalena's troops began to waver. You could see a collapse threatening even before men turned to eye the retaining wall behind them.

The Lady gestured. Journey spurred his horse forward, down the face of the pyramid. He passed behind Whisper's men, through them, stationed himself at the edge of the level, behind Jalena's division. He raised his spear. It blazed. Why I don't know, but Jalena's troops took heart, solidified, began to push the Rebel back.

The Lady gestured to her left. Feather went down the slope like a daredevil, winding her horn. Its silver call drowned the blare of Rebel trumpets. She passed through the third level troops and leapt her horse off the wall. The drop would have killed any horse I'd ever seen. This one landed heavily, gained its balance, reared, neighed in triumph as Feather winded her horn. As on the right, the troops took heart and began driving the Rebel back.

A small indigo shape clambered up the wall and scuttled to the rear, skirting the base of the pyramid. It ran all the way to the Tower. The Howler. I frowned, puzzled. Had he been relieved?

Our center became the focus of battle, Catcher struggling valiantly to keep his line.

I heard sounds, glanced over, saw that the Captain had come up on the Lady's far side. He was mounted. I looked back. A number of horses had been brought up. I stared down that long steep slope at the narrowness of the third level, and my heart sank. She was not planning a cavalry charge, was she?

Feather and Journey were big medicine, but not medicine big enough. They stiffened resistance only till the Rebel ramps arrived.

The level went. Slower than I expected, but it went. No more than a thousand men escaped. I looked at the Lady. Her face remained ice, yet I felt she was not displeased.

Whisper poured arrows into the mass below. Guards fired ballistae point blank.

A shadow crept over the pyramid. I looked up. The Howler's carpet drifted out over the foe. Men crouched along its edges, dropping balls the size of heads. Those plummeted into the Rebel mass without visible effect. The carpet crawled toward the enemy camp, raining those pointless objects.

It took the Rebel an hour to establish solid bridgeheads upon the third level, and another hour to bring up enough men to press the attack. Whisper, Feather, Journey, and Catcher mauled them mercilessly. Oncoming troops clambered over drifts of their comrades to reach the top.

The Howler carried his ball-dropping to the Rebel camp. I doubted there was anyone out there. They were all in the pie-slice, awaiting their turns at us.

The false White Rose sat her horse out about the second trench, glowing, surrounded by the new Rebel council. They remained frozen, acting only when one of the Taken used their powers. They had done nothing about the Howler, though. Apparently there was nothing they could do.

I checked the Captain, who had been up to something. . . . He was lining horsemen up across the front of the pyramid. We *were* going to attack down that slope! What idiocy!

A voice inside told me, *My faithful need not fear*. I faced the Lady. She looked at me coolly, regally. I turned back to the battle.

It would not be long. Our troops had put aside their bows and abandoned the heavy weapons. They were bracing themselves. On the plain the whole horde was in motion. But a vaguely slowed, indecisive motion, it seemed. This was the moment when they should have run headlong, swamping us, roaring into the Tower before the gate could be closed. . . .

The Howler came roaring back from the enemy camp, moving a dozen times faster than any horse could run. I watched the big carpet pass over, even now unable to restrain my awe. For an instant it masked the comet, then passed on, toward the Tower. A strange howl wafted down, unlike any Howler cry I had heard before. The carpet dipped slightly, tried to slow, ploughed into the Tower a few feet below its top.

"My god," I murmured, watching the thing crumple, watching men tumble down the five hundred foot fall. "My god." Then the Howler died or lost consciousness. The carpet itself began to fall.

I shifted my gaze to the Lady, who had been watching too. Her expression did not change in the slightest. Softly, in a voice only I heard, she said, "You *will* use the bow."

I shuddered. And for a second images flashed through my mind, a hundred of them too quickly for any to be caught. I seemed to be drawing the bow. . . .

She was angry. Angry with a rage so great I shook just contemplating it, even knowing it was not directed at me. Its object was not hard to determine. The Howler's demise was not caused by enemy action. There was but one Taken likely to be responsible. Soulcatcher. Our former mentor. The one who had used us in so many schemes.

The Lady murmured something. I am not sure I heard it right. Sounded like, "I gave her every chance."

I whispered, "We weren't part of it."

"Come." She kneed her animal. It went over the edge. I threw one despairing look at the Captain and followed.

She went down that slope with the speed that Feather had shown. My mount seemed determined to keep pace.

We plunged toward an island of screaming men. It centered on a fountain of lime thread which boiled up and spread on the wind, taking Rebel and friend alike. The Lady did not swerve.

Soulcatcher was in flight already. Friend and enemy were eager to get out of his way. Death surrounded him. He ran at Journey, leapt, knocked him off his horse, bestrode the animal himself, leapt it down to the second level, ploughed through the enemy there, descended to the plain, and roared away.

The Lady followed the path he blazed, dark hair streaming. I stayed in her wake, utterly baffled yet unable to change what I was doing. We reached the plain three hundred yards behind Soulcatcher. The Lady spurred her mount. Mine kept pace. I was sure one or both animals would stumble over abandoned equipment or bodies. Yet they, and Catcher's beast too, were as sure-footed as horses on a track.

Catcher sped directly to the enemy encampment, and through. We followed. In the open country beyond we began to gain. Those beasts, all three, were as tireless as machines. Miles rolled away. We gained fifty yards with every one. I clutched my bow and clung to the nightmare. I've never been religious, but that was a time when I was tempted to pray.

She was as implacable as death, my Lady. I pitied Soulcatcher when she caught him.

Soulcatcher raced along a road winding through one of the valleys west of Charm. We were near the place where we had rested on a hilltop, and encountered lime thread. I recalled what we had ridden through, back at Charm. A fountain of the stuff, and it hadn't touched us.

What was happening back there? Was this some scheme to leave our people at the Rebel's mercy? It had become clear, toward the end, that the Lady's strategy involved maximum destruction. That she wanted only a small minority of either side to survive. She was cleaning house. She had but one enemy left among the Taken. Soulcatcher. Catcher, who had been almost good to me. Who had saved my life at least once, at the Stair of Tear, when Stormbringer would have slain Raven and me. Catcher, who was the only Taken to speak to me as a man, to tell me a bit about the old days, to respond to my insatiable curiosities. . . .

What the devil was I doing here, in a hellride with the Lady, hunting a thing that could gobble me up without blinking?

Catcher turned the flank of a hill and when, seconds later, we rounded the same impediment, had disappeared. The Lady slowed for a moment, head turning slowly, then yanked her reins, swung toward woods that swept down to the edge of the road. She halted when she reached the first trees. My beast stopped beside hers.

The Lady threw herself off her mount. I did the same without thinking. By the time I gained my feet her animal was collapsing and mine was dead, standing on stiff legs. Both had fist-sized black burns upon their throats.

The Lady pointed, started forward. Crouching, arrow across bow, I joined her. I went carefully, soundlessly, sliding through the brush like a fox.

She stopped, crouched, pointed. I looked along her arm. Flicker, flicker, two seconds of rapid images. They stopped. I saw a figure perhaps fifty feet distant, back to us, kneeling, doing something swiftly. No time for the moral questions I had debated riding out. That creature had made several attempts on my life. My arrow was in the air before I realized what I was doing.

It smacked into the head of the figure. The figure pitched forward. I gaped a second, then released a long breath. So easy. . . .

The Lady took three quick steps forward, frowning. There was a rapid rustle to our right. Something rattled brush. She whirled and ran for open country, slapping my arm as she passed.

In seconds we were on the road. Another arrow lay across my bow. Her arm rose, pointing. . . . A squarish shape slid out of the woods fifty yards away. A figure aboard made a throwing motion our way. I staggered under the impact of the blow from no visible source. Spiderwebs seemed drawn across my eyes, blurring my vision. Vaguely, I sensed the Lady making a gesture. The webs disappeared. I felt whole. She pointed as the carpet began to rise and move away.

I drew and loosed, with no hope my arrow would strike a moving target at that range.

It did not, but only because the carpet jerked violently downward and to one side while the arrow was in the air. My shaft ripped past inches behind the carpet rider's head.

The Lady did something. The air hummed. From nowhere came a giant dragonfly like the one I had seen in the Forest of Cloud. It streaked toward the carpet, hit. The carpet spun, flipped, jerked around. Its rider fell free, plummeted with a despairing cry. I loosed another shaft the instant the man hit earth. He twitched a moment, lay still. And we were upon him.

The Lady ripped the black morion off our victim. And cursed. Softly, steadily, she cursed like a senior sergeant.

"What?" I finally asked. The man was dead enough to satisfy me.

"It's not her." She whirled, faced the wood. Her face blanked for several seconds. Then she faced the drifting carpet. She jerked her head at the wood. "Go see if that's a woman. See if the horse is there." She began making come-hither gestures at Catcher's carpet.

I went, mind aboil. Catcher was a woman, eh? Crafty, too. All prepared to be chased here, by the Lady herself.

Fear grew as I slipped through the wood, slow, silent. Catcher had played a game on everyone, and far more shrewdly than even the Lady had anticipated. What next, then? There had been so many attempts on my life. . . . Might this not be the moment to end whatever threat I represented?

Nothing happened, though. Except that I crept up to the corpse in the wood, ripped off a black morion, and found a handsome youth inside. Fear, anger, and frustration overwhelmed me. I kicked him. Some good, abusing dead meat.

The fit did not last. I began looking around the camp where the substitutes had waited. They had been there a while, and been prepared to stay a while longer. They had supplies for a month.

A large bundle caught my eye. I cut the cords binding it, peeped inside. Papers. A bale that must have weighed eighty pounds. Curiosity grabbed me.

I looked around hastily, saw nothing threatening, probed a little deeper. And immediately realized what I had. These were part of the hoard we had unearthed in the Forest of Cloud.

What were they doing here? I'd thought Catcher had turned them over to the Lady. Eh! Plot and counterplot. Maybe he *had* delivered some. And maybe he kept back others he thought would be useful later. Maybe we had been so close on his heels he had not had time to collect them. . . .

Maybe he would be back. I looked around again, frightened once more.

Nothing stirred.

Where was he?

She, I reminded myself. Catcher was one of the shes.

I looked around, hunting evidence of the Taken's departure, soon discovered hoofprints leading deeper into the wood. A few paces beyond the camp they reached a narrow trail. I crouched, looking down an aisle of forest, through golden motes floating in shafts of sunlight. I tried to work myself up to go on.

Come, a voice said in my mind. *Come.*

The Lady. Relieved not to have to follow that trail, I turned back. "It was a man," I said as I approached the Lady.

"I thought so." She had the carpet under one hand, floating two feet off the earth. "Get aboard."

I swallowed, did as I was told. It was like climbing aboard a boat from deep water. I almost fell off twice. As she followed me aboard, I told her, "He—*she*—stayed on the horse and went on down the trail through the woods."

"What direction?"

"South."

The carpet rose swiftly. The dead horses dwindled beneath us. We began to drift over the wood. My stomach felt like I had drunk several gallons of wine the night before.

The Lady cursed softly under her breath. Finally, in a louder voice, she said, "The bitch. She ran a game on us all. My husband included."

I said nothing. I was debating whether or not to mention the papers. She would be interested. But so was I, and if I mentioned them now I'd never get a chance to poke through them.

"I'll bet that was what she was doing. Getting rid of the other Taken by pretending to be part of their plot. Then it would have been me. Then she would just leave the Dominator in the ground. She would have it all, and be able to keep him restrained. He can't break out without help." She was thinking aloud more than speaking to me. "And I missed the evidence. Or ignored it. It was right there all the time. Cunning bitch. She'll burn for that."

We began to fall. I nearly lost what little my stomach contained. We fell into a valley deeper than most in the area, though the hills to either hand stood no more than two hundred feet high. We slowed.

"Arrow," she said. I had forgotten to ready another.

We drifted down the valley a mile or so, then upslope till we floated beside an outcrop of sedimentary rock. There we hovered, nudging the stone. There was a brisk cold wind. My hands grew numb. We were far from the Tower, into country where winter held full sway. I shivered continuously.

The only warning was a soft, "Hang on."

The carpet shot forward. A quarter mile distant was a figure lying low on the neck of a racing horse. The Lady dropped till we hurtled along just two feet off the ground.

Catcher saw us. She threw up a hand in a warding gesture. We were upon her. I released my shaft.

The carpet slammed up against me as the Lady pulled it upward, trying to clear horse and rider. She did not pull up enough. Impact made the carpet lurch. Frame members cracked, broke. We spun. I hung on desperately while sky and earth wheeled about me. There was another shock as we hit ground, more spinning as we went over and over. I threw myself clear.

I was on my feet in an instant, wobbling, slapping another arrow across my bow. Catcher's horse was down with a broken leg. Catcher was beside her, on hands and knees, stunned. A silver arrowhead protruded from her waist, indicting me.

I loosed my shaft. And another, and another, recalling the terrible vitality the Limper had shown in the Forest of Cloud, after Raven had felled him with an arrow bearing the power of his true name. Still in fear, I drew my sword once my final arrow was gone. I charged. I do not know how I retained the weapon through everything that had happened. I reached Catcher, raised the blade high, swung with a vicious two-handed stroke. It was the most fearful, violent blow I have ever struck. Soulcatcher's head rolled away. The morion's face guard popped open. A woman's face stared at me with accusing eyes. A woman almost identical in appearance to the one with whom I had come.

Catcher's eyes focused upon me. Her lips tried to form words. I stood there frozen, wondering what the hell it all meant. And life faded from Catcher before I caught the message she tried to impart.

I would return to that moment ten thousand times, trying to read those dying lips.

The Lady crept up beside me, dragging one leg. Habit forced me to turn, kneel. . . . "It's broken," she said. "Never mind. It can wait." Her breathing was shallow, rapid. For a moment I thought it was the pain. Then I saw she was looking at the head. She began to giggle.

I looked at that face so like her own, then at her. She rested a hand on my shoulder, allowing me to take some of her weight. I rose carefully, slid an arm around her. "Never did like that bitch," she said. "Even when we were children. . . ." She glanced at me warily, shut up. The life left her face. She became the ice lady once more.

If ever there was some weird love spark within me, as my brothers accused, it flickered its last. I saw plainly what the Rebel wanted to destroy—that part of the movement which was true White Rose, not puppet to the monster who had created this woman and now wanted her destroyed so it could bring its own breed of terror back to the world. At that moment I'd gladly have deposited her head beside her sister's.

Second time, if Catcher could be believed. Second sister. This deserved no allegiance.

There are limits to one's luck, one's power, to how much one dares resist. I hadn't the nerve to follow through on my impulse. Later, maybe. The Captain had made a mistake, taking service with Soulcatcher. Was my unique position adequate to argue him out of that service on grounds that our commission ended with Catcher's death?

I doubted it. It would take a battle, to say the least. Especially if, as I suspected, he had helped the Syndic along in Beryl. The Company's existence did not appear to be in absolute jeopardy, assuming we survived the battle. He would not countenance another betrayal. In the conflict of moralities he would find that the greater evil.

Was there a Company now? The battle of Charm had not ended because the Lady and I had absented ourselves. Who knew what had happened while we were haring after a renegade Taken?

I glanced at the sun, was astonished to discover that only a little over an hour had passed.

The Lady recalled Charm too. "The carpet, physician," she said. "We'd better get back."

I helped her hobble to the remnant of Catcher's carpet. It was half a ruin, but she believed it would function. I deposited her, collected the bow she had given me, sat in front of her. She whispered. Creaking, the carpet rose. It provided a very unstable seat.

I sat with eyes closed, debating myself, as she circled the site of Catcher's fall. I could not get my feelings straight. I did not believe in evil as an active force, only as a matter of viewpoint, yet I had seen enough to make me question my philosophy. If the Lady were not evil incarnate, then she was as close as made no difference.

We began limping toward the Tower. When I opened my eyes I could see that great dark block tilting on the horizon, gradually swelling. I did not want to go back.

We passed over the rocky ground west of Charm, a hundred feet up, barely creeping along. The Lady had to concentrate totally to keep the carpet aloft. I was terrified the thing would go down there, or gasp its last over the Rebel army. I leaned forward, studying the jumble, trying to pick a place to crash.

That was how I saw the girl.

We were three quarters of the way across. I saw something move. "Eh?" Darling looked up at us, shading her eyes. A hand whipped out of shadow, dragged her into hiding.

I glanced at the Lady. She had noticed nothing. She was too busy staying aloft.

What was going on? Had the Rebel driven the Company into the rocks? Why wasn't I seeing anyone else?

Straining, the Lady gradually gained altitude. The slice-of-pie expanded before me.

Land of nightmare. Tens of thousands of dead Rebels carpeted it. Most had fallen in formation. The tiers were inundated in dead of both persuasions. A White Rose banner on a leaning pole fluttered atop the pyramid. Nowhere did I see anyone moving. Silence gripped the land, except for the murmur of a chill northern wind.

The Lady lost it for an instant. We plunged. She caught us a dozen feet short of crashing.

Nothing stirred but wind-rippled banners. The battlefield looked like something from the imagination of a mad artist. The top layer of Rebel dead lay as though they had died in terrible pain. Their numbers were incalculable.

We rose above the pyramid. Death had swept around it, toward the Tower. The gate remained open. Rebel bodies lay in its shadow.

They had gotten inside.

There were but a handful of bodies atop the pyramid, all Rebel. My comrades must have made it inside.

They had to be fighting still, inside those twisted corridors. The place was too vast to overrun quickly. I listened, but heard nothing.

The Tower top was three hundred feet above us. We couldn't get any higher. . . . A figure appeared there, beckoning. It was short and clad in brown. I gaped. I recalled only one Taken who wore brown. It moved to a slightly better vantage, limping, still beckoning. The carpet rose. Two hundred feet to go. One hundred. I looked back on the panorama of death. Quarter of a million men? Mind-boggling. Too vast to have real meaning. Even in the Dominator's heyday battles never approached that scale. . . .

I glanced at the Lady, She had engineered it. She would be total mistress of the world now—if the Tower survived the battle underway inside. Who could oppose her? The manhood of a continent lay dead. . . .

A half dozen Rebels came out the gate. They launched arrows at us. Only a few wobbled as high as the carpet. The soldiers stopped loosing, waited. They knew we were in trouble.

Fifty feet. Twenty-five. The Lady struggled, even with Limper's help. I shivered in the wind, which threatened to bounce us off the Tower. I recalled the Howler's long plunge. We were as high as he had been.

A glance at the plain showed me the forvalaka. It hung limp upon its cross, but I knew it was alive.

Men joined the Limper. Some carried ropes, some lances or long poles. We rose ever more slowly. It became a ridiculously tense game, safety almost within reaching distance, yet never quite at hand.

A rope dropped into my lap. A Guard sergeant shouted, "Harness her up."

"What about me, asshole?" I moved about as fast as a rock grows, afraid I'd upset the carpet's stability. I was tempted to tie some false knot that would give way under strain. I did not like the Lady much anymore. The world would be better for her absence. Catcher was a murdering schemer whose ambitions sent hundreds to their deaths. She deserved her fate. How much more so this sister who had hurried thousands down the shadowed road?

A second line came down. I tied myself. We were five feet from the top, unable to get higher. The men on the lines took in the slack. The carpet slid in against the Tower. Poles reached down. I grabbed one.

The carpet dropped away.

For a second I thought I was gone. Then they hauled me in.

There was heavy fighting downstairs, they said. The Limper ignored me completely, hurried away to get in on the action. I just sprawled atop the Tower, glad to be safe. I even napped. I wakened alone with the north wind, and an enfeebled comet on the horizon. I went down to audit the endgame of the Lady's grand design.

She won. Not one in a hundred Rebels survived, and most of those deserted early.

The Howler spread disease with the globes he dropped. It reached its critical stage soon after the Lady and I departed, chasing Soulcatcher. The Rebel wizards could not stem it on any significant scale. Thus the windrows of dead.

Even so, many of the enemy proved partially or wholly immune, and not all of ours escaped infection. The Rebel took the top tier.

The plan, at that point, called for the Black Company to counterattack. The Limper, rehabilitated, was to assist them with men from inside the Tower. But the Lady was not there to order the charge. In her absence Whisper ordered a withdrawal into the Tower.

The interior of the Tower was a series of death traps manned not only by the Howler's easterners but by wounded taken inside previous nights and healed by the Lady's powers.

It ended long before I could thread the maze to my comrades. When I did cross their trail, I learned I was hours behind. They had departed the Tower under orders to establish a picket line where the stockade had stood.

I reached ground level well after nightfall. I was tired. I just wanted peace, quiet, maybe a garrison post in a small town. . . . My mind wasn't working well. I had things to do, arguments to argue, a battle to fight with the Captain. He would not want to betray another commission. There are the physically dead and the morally dead. My comrades were among the latter. They would not understand me. Elmo, Raven, Candy, One-Eye, Goblin, they would act like I was talking a foreign language. And yet, could I condemn them? They were my brothers, my friends, my family, and acted moral within that context. The weight of it fell on me. I had to convince them there was a larger obligation.

I crunched through dried blood, stepping over corpses, leading horses I had liberated from the Lady's stables. Why I took several is a mystery, except for a vague notion that they might come in handy. The one that Feather had ridden I took because I did not feel like walking.

I paused to stare at the comet. It seemed drained. "Not this time, eh?" I asked it. "Can't say I'm totally dismayed." Fake chuckle. How could I be? Had this been the Rebel's hour, as he had believed, I would be dead.

I stopped twice more before reaching camp. The first time I heard soft cursing as I descended the remnants of the lower retaining wall. I approached the sound, found One-Eye seated beneath the crucified forvalaka. He talked steadily in a soft voice, in a language I did not understand. So intent was he that he did not hear me come. Neither did he hear me go a minute later, thoroughly disgusted.

One-Eye was collecting for the death of his brother Tom-Tom. Knowing him, he would stretch it out for days.

I paused again where the false White Rose had watched the battle. She was there still, very dead at a very young age. Her wizard friends had made her death harder by trying to save her from the Howler's disease.

"So much for that." I looked back at the Tower, at the comet. She had won. . . .

Or had she? What had she accomplished, really? The destruction of the Rebel? But he had become the instrument of her husband, an even greater evil. It had been he defeated here, if only he, she, and I knew that. The greater wickedness had been forestalled. Moreover, the Rebel ideal had passed through a cleansing, tempering flame. A generation hence. . . .

I am not religious. I cannot conceive of gods who would give a damn about humanity's frothy carryings-on. I mean, logically, beings of that order just wouldn't. But maybe there is a force for greater good, created by our unconscious minds conjoined, that becomes an independent power greater than the sum of its parts. Maybe, being a mindthing, it is not time-bound. Maybe it can see everywhere and everywhen and move pawns so that what seems to be today's victory becomes the cornerstone of tomorrow's defeat.

Maybe weariness did things to my mind. For a few seconds I believed I saw the landscape of tomorrow, saw the Lady's triumph turning like a serpent and generating her destruction during the next passage of the comet. I saw a true White Rose carrying her standard to the Tower, saw her and her champions as clearly as if I were there that day myself. . . .

I swayed atop that beast of Feather's, stricken and terrified. For if it were a true vision, I *would* be there. If it were a true vision, I knew the White Rose. Had known her for a year. She was my friend. And I had discounted her because of a handicap. . . .

I urged the horses toward camp. By the time a sentinel challenged me I had regained enough cynicism to have discounted the vision. I'd just been through too much in one day. Characters like me don't become prophets. Especially not from the wrong side.

Elmo's was the first familiar face I saw. "God, you look awful," he said. "You hurt?"

I could do nothing but shake my head. He dragged me off the horse and put me away somewhere and that was the last I knew for hours. Except that my dreams were as disjointed and time-loose as the vision, and I did not like them at all. And I could not escape them.

The mind is resilient, though. I managed to forget the dreams within moments of awakening.

7

Rose

The argument with the Captain raged for two hours. He was unyielding. He did not accept my arguments, legal or moral. Time brought others into the fray, as they came to the Captain on business. By the time I really lost my temper most of the principals of the Company were present: the Lieutenant, Goblin, Silent, Elmo, Candy, and several new officers recruited here at Charm. What little support I received came from surprising quarters. Silent backed me. So did two of the new officers.

I stamped out. Silent and Goblin followed. I was in a towering rage, though unsurprised by their response. With the Rebel beaten there was little to encourage the Company's defection. They would be hogs knee-deep in slops now. Questions of right and wrong sounded stupid. Basically, who cared?

It was still early, the day after the battle. I had not slept well, and was full of nervous energy. I paced vigorously, trying to walk it off.

Goblin timed me, stepped into my path after I settled down. Silent observed from nearby. Goblin asked, "Can we talk?"

"I've been talking. Nobody listens."

"You're too argumentative. Come over here and sit down." Over here proved to be a pile of gear near a campfire where some men were cooking, others were playing Tonk. The usual crowd. They looked at me from the corners of their eyes and shrugged. They all seemed worried. Like they were concerned for my sanity.

I guess if any of them had done what I had, a year ago, I would have felt the same. It was honest confusion and concern based in care for a comrade.

Their thickheadedness irritated me, yet I could not sustain that irritation because by sending Goblin around, they had proven they wanted to understand.

The game went along, quiet and sullen initially, growing animated as they exchanged gossip about the course of the battle.

Goblin asked, "What happened yesterday, Croaker?"

"I told you."

Gently, he suggested, "How about we go over it again? Get more of the detail." I knew what he was doing. A little mental therapy based on an assumption that prolonged proximity to the Lady had unsettled my mind. He was right. It had. It had opened my eyes, too, and I tried to make that clear as I reiterated my day, calling on such skills as I have developed scribbling these Annals, hoping to convince him that my stance was rational and moral and everyone else's was not.

"You see what he did when those Oar boys tried to get behind the Captain?" one of the cardplayers asked. They were gossiping about Raven. I had forgotten him till then. I pricked up my ears and listened to several stories of his savage heroics. To hear them talk, Raven had saved everybody in the Company at least once.

Somebody asked, "Where is he?"

Lots of headshaking. Someone suggested, "Must have gotten killed. The Captain sent a detail after our dead. Guess we'll see him go in the ground this afternoon."

"What happened to the kid?"

Elmo snorted. "Find him and you'll find her."

"Talking about the kid, you see what happened when they tried to clobber second platoon with some kind of knockout spell? It was weird. The kid acted like nothing ever happened. Everybody else went down like a rock. She just looked kind of puzzled and shook Raven. Up he came, bam, hacking away.

She shook them all back awake. Like the magic couldn't touch her, or something."

Somebody else said, "Maybe that's cause she's deaf. Like maybe the magic was sound."

"Ah, who knows? Pity she didn't make it, though. Kind of got used to her hanging around."

"Raven, too. Need him to keep old One-Eye from cheating." Everybody laughed.

I looked at Silent, who was eavesdropping on my conversation with Goblin. I shook my head. He raised an eyebrow. I used Darling's signs to tell him, *They aren't dead.* He liked Darling too.

He rose, walked behind Goblin, jerked his head. He wanted to see me alone. I extricated myself and followed him.

I explained that I had seen Darling while returning from my venture with the Lady, that I suspected Raven was deserting by the one route he thought would not be watched. Silent frowned and wanted to know why.

"You got me. You know how he's been lately." I did not mention my vision or dreams, all of which seemed fantastic now. "Maybe he got fed up with us."

Silent smiled a smile that said he did not believe a word of that. He sighed, *I want to know why. What do you know?* He assumed I knew more about Raven and Darling than anyone else because I was always probing for personal details to put into the Annals.

"I don't know anything you don't. He hung around with the Captain and Pickles more than anybody else."

He thought for about ten seconds, then signed, *You saddle two horses. No, four horses, with some food. We may be a few days. I will go ask questions.* His manner did not brook argument.

That was fine with me. A ride had occurred to me while I was talking to Goblin. I had given up the notion because I could think of no way to pick up Raven's trail.

I went to the picket where Elmo had taken the horses last night. Four of them. For an instant I reflected on the chance a greater force existed, moving us. I conned a couple men into saddling the beasts for me while I went and finagled some food out of Pickles. He was not easy to get around. He wanted the Captain's personal authorization. We worked out a deal where he would get a special mention in the Annals.

Silent joined me at the tail of the negotiations. Once we had strapped the supplies aboard the horses, I asked, "You learn anything?"

He signed, *Only that the Captain has some special knowledge he will not share. I think it had more to do with Darling than with Raven.*

I grunted. Here it was again. . . . The Captain had come up with a notion like mine? And had had it this morning, while we were arguing? Hmm. He had a tricky mind. . . .

I think Raven left without the Captain's permission, but has his blessing. Did you interrogate Pickles?

"Thought you were going to do that."

He shook his head. He hadn't had time.

"Go ahead now. Still a few things I want to get together." I hustled to the hospital tent, accoutred myself with my weapons and dug out a present I had been saving for Darling's birthday. Then I hunted Elmo up and told him I could use some of my share of the money we had kyped in Roses.

"How much?"

"Much as I can get."

He looked at me long and hard, decided to ask no questions. We went to his tent and counted it out quietly. The men knew nothing about that money. The secret remained with those of us who had gone to Roses after Raker. There were those, though, who wondered how One-Eye managed to keep paying his gambling debts when he never won and had no time for his usual black marketeering.

Elmo followed me when I left his tent. We found Silent already mounted up, the horses ready to go. "Going for a ride, eh?" he asked.

"Yeah." I secured the bow the Lady had given me to my saddle, mounted up.

Elmo searched our faces with narrowed eyes, then said, "Good luck." He turned and walked away. I looked at Silent.

He signed, *Pickles claims ignorance too. I did trick him into admitting he had given Raven extra rations before the fighting started yesterday. He knows something too.*

Well, hell. Everybody seemed to be in on the guesswork. As Silent led off, I turned my thoughts to the morning's confrontation, seeking hints of things askew. And I found a few. Goblin and Elmo had their suspicions too.

There was no avoiding a passage through the Rebel camp. Pity. I would have preferred to avoid it. The flies and stench were thick. When the Lady and I rode through, it looked empty. Wrong. We'd simply not seen anyone. The enemy wounded and camp followers were there. The Howler had dropped his globes on them too.

I'd selected animals well. In addition to having taken Feather's mount, I had acquired others of the same tireless breed. Silent set a brisk pace, eschewing communication till, as we hastened down the outer border of the rocky country, he reined in and signed for me to study my surroundings. He wanted to know the line of flight the Lady had followed approaching the Tower.

I told him I thought we had come in about a mile south of where we were then. He gave me the extra horses and edged near the rocks, proceeded slowly, studying the ground carefully. I paid little attention. He could find sign better than I.

I could have found this trail, though. Silent threw up a hand, then indicated the ground. They had departed the badlands about where the Lady and I had crossed the boundary going the other way. "Trying to make time, not cover his trail," I guessed.

Silent nodded, stared westward. He signed questions about roads.

The main north-south high road passes three miles west of the Tower. It was the road we followed to Forsberg. We guessed he would head there first. Even in these times there would be traffic enough to conceal the passage of a man and child. From ordinary eyes. Silent believed he could follow.

"Remember, this is his country," I said. "He knows it better than we do."

Silent nodded absently, unconcerned. I glanced at the sun. Maybe two hours of daylight left. I wondered how big a lead they had.

We reached the high road. Silent studied it a moment, rode south a few yards, nodded to himself. He beckoned me, spurred his mount.

And so we rode those tireless beasts, hard, hour after hour, after the sun went down, all the night long, into the next day, heading toward the sea, till we were far ahead of our quarry. The breaks were few and far between. I ached everywhere. It was too soon after my venture with the Lady for this.

We halted where the road hugged the foot of a wooded hill. Silent indicated a bald spot that made a good watchpoint. I nodded. We turned off and climbed.

I took care of the horses, then collapsed. "Getting too old for this," I said, and fell asleep immediately.

Silent wakened me at dusk. "They coming?" I asked.

He shook his head, signed that he did not expect them before tomorrow. But I should keep an eye out anyway, in case Raven was travelling by night.

So I sat under the pallid light of the comet, wrapped in a blanket, shivering in the winter wind, for hour upon hour, alone with thoughts I did not want to think. I saw nothing but a brace of roebuck crossing from woods to farmland in hopes of finding better forage.

Silent relieved me a couple hours before dawn. Oh joy, oh joy. Now I could lie down and shiver and think thoughts I did not want to think. But I did fall asleep sometime, because it was light when Silent squeezed my shoulder. . . .

"They coming?"

He nodded.

I rose, rubbed my eyes with the backs of my hands, stared up the road. Sure enough, two figures were coming south, one taller than the other. But at that distance they could have been any adult and child. We packed and readied the horses hurriedly, descended the hill. Silent wanted to wait down the road, around the bend. He told me to get on the road behind them, just in case. You never knew about Raven.

He left. I waited, shivering still, feeling very lonely. The travellers breasted a rise. Yes. Raven and Darling. They walked briskly, but Raven seemed unafraid, certain no one was after him. They passed me. I waited a minute, eased out of the woods, followed them around the toe of the hill.

Silent sat his mount in the middle of the road, leaning forward slightly, looking lean and mean and dark. Raven had stopped fifty feet away, exposed his steel. He held Darling behind him.

She noticed me coming, grinned and waved. I grinned back, despite the tension of the moment.

Raven whirled. A snarl stretched his lips. Anger, possibly even hatred, smouldered in his eyes. I stopped beyond the reach of his knives. He did not look willing to talk.

We all remained motionless for several minutes. Nobody wanted to speak first. I looked at Silent. He shrugged. He had come to the end of his plan.

Curiosity had brought me here. I had satisfied part of it. They were alive, and were running. Only the why remained shadowy.

To my amazement Raven yielded first. "What're you doing here, Croaker?" I'd thought him able to outstubborn a stone.

"Looking for you."

"Why?"

"Curiosity. Me and Silent, we got an interest in Darling. We were worried."

He frowned. He was not hearing what he had expected.

"You can see she's all right."

"Yeah. Looks like. How about you?"

"I look like I'm not?"

I glanced at Silent. He had nothing to contribute. "One wonders, Raven. One wonders."

He was on the defensive. "What the hell does that mean?"

"Fellow freezes out his buddies. Treats them like shit. Then he deserts. Makes people wonder enough to go find out what's happening."

"The Captain know you're here?"

I glanced at Silent again. He nodded. "Yeah. Want to let us in on it, old buddy? Me, Silent, the Captain, Pickles, Elmo, Goblin, we all maybe got an idea. . . ."

"Don't try to stop me, Croaker."

"Why are you always looking for a fight? Who said anything about stopping you? They wanted you stopped, you wouldn't be out here now. You'd never have gotten away from the Tower."

He was startled.

"They saw it coming, Pickles and the Old Man. They let you go. Some of the rest of us, we'd like to know why. I mean, like, we think we know, and if it's what we think, then at least you have *my* blessing. And Silent's. And I guess everybody's who didn't hold you back."

Raven frowned. He knew what I was hinting, but couldn't make sense of it. His not being old line Company left a communications gap.

"Put it this way," I said. "Me and Silent figure you're going down as killed in action. Both of you. Nobody needs to know any different. But, you know, it's like you're running away from home. Even if we wish you well, we maybe feel a little hurt on account of the way you do it. You were voted into the Company. You went through hell with us. You. . . . Look what you and me went through together. And you treat us like shit. That don't go down too well."

It sank in. He said, "Sometimes something comes up that's so important you can't tell your best friends. Could get you all killed."

"Figured that was it. Hey! Take it easy."

Silent had dismounted and begun an exchange with Darling. She seemed oblivious to the strain between her friends. She was telling Silent what they had done and where they were headed.

"Think that's smart?" I asked. "Opal? Couple things you should know, then. One, the Lady won. Guess you figured that. Saw it coming, or you wouldn't have pulled out. Okay. More important. The Limper is back. She didn't do him in. She shaped him up and he's her number one boy now."

Raven turned pale. It was the first I could recall seeing him truly frightened. But his fear was not for himself. He considered himself a walking dead man, a man with nothing to lose. But now he had Darling, and a cause. He had to stay alive.

"Yeah. The Limper. Me and Silent went over this a lot." Actually, this had occurred to me only a moment earlier. I felt it would go better if he thought some considered deliberation had gone into it. "We figure the Lady will catch on sooner or later. She'll want to make a move. If she connects you, you'll have the Limper on your trail. He knows you. He'd start looking in your old stomping grounds, figuring you'd get in touch with old friends. You got any friends who could hide you from the Limper?"

Raven sighed, seemed to lose stature. He put his steel away. "That was my plan. Thought we'd cross to Beryl and hide out there."

"Beryl is technically only the Lady's ally, but her word is law there. You've got to go somewhere where they've never heard of her."

"Where?"

"This isn't my part of the world." He seemed calm enough now, so I dismounted. He eyed me warily, then relaxed. I said, "I pretty much know what I came to find out. Silent?"

Silent nodded, continued his conversation with Darling.

I took the money bag from my bedroll, tossed it to Raven. "You left your share of the Roses take." I brought the spare horses up. "You could travel faster if you were riding."

Raven struggled with himself, trying to say thank you, unable to get through the barriers he had built around the man inside. "Guess we could head toward. . . ."

"I don't want to know. I've met the Eye twice already. She's got a thing about getting her side set down for posterity. Not that she wants to look good, just that she wants it down true. She knows how history rewrites itself. She doesn't want that to happen to her. And I'm the boy she's picked to do the writing."

"Get out, Croaker. Come with us. You and Silent. Come with us."

It had been a long, lonely night. I had thought about it a lot. "Can't, Raven. The Captain has to stay where he's at, even if he don't like it. The Company has to stay. I'm Company. I'm too old to run away from home. We'll fight the same fight, you and me, but I'll do my share staying with the family."

"Come on, Croaker. A bunch of mercenary cutthroats. . . ."

"Whoa! Hold it." My voice hardened more than I wanted. He stopped. I said, "Remember that night in Lords, before we went after Whisper? When I read from the Annals? What you said?"

He did not respond for several seconds. "Yes. That you'd made me feel what it meant to be a member of the Black Company. All right. Maybe I don't understand it, but I did feel it."

"Thanks." I took another package from my bedroll. This one was for Darling. "You talk to Silent a while, eh? I got a birthday present here."

He looked at me a moment, then nodded. I turned so my tears would not be so obvious. And after I said my goodbyes to the girl, and cherished her delight in my feeble present, I went to the roadside and had myself a brief, quiet cry. Silent and Raven pretended blindness.

I would miss Darling. And I would spend the rest of my days frightened for her. She was precious, perfect, always happy. The thing in that village was behind her. But ahead lay the most terrible enemy imaginable. None of us wanted that for her.

I rose, erased the evidence of tears, took Raven aside. "I don't know your plans. I don't want to know. But just in case. When the Lady and I caught up with Soulcatcher the other day, he had a whole bale of those papers we dug up in Whisper's camp. He never turned them over to her. She doesn't know they exist." I told him where they could be found. "I'll ride out that way in a couple weeks. If they're still there, I'll see what I can find in them myself."

He looked at me with a cool, expressionless face. He was thinking my death warrant was signed if I came under the Eye again. But he did not say it. "Thanks, Croaker. If I'm ever up that way, I'll check into it."

"Yeah. You ready to go, Silent?"

Silent nodded.

"Darling, come here." I squeezed her in a long, tight hug. "You be good for Raven." I unfastened the amulet One-Eye had given me, fixed it on her wrist, told Raven, "That'll let her know if any unfriendly Taken comes around. Don't ask me how, but it works. Luck."

"Yeah." He stood there looking at us as we mounted, still baffled. He raised a hand tentatively, dropped it.

I told Silent, "Let's go home." And we rode away.

Neither of us looked back.

It was an incident that never happened. After all, hadn't Raven and his orphan died at the gates of Charm?

Back to the Company. Back to business. Back to the parade of years. Back to these Annals. Back to fear.

Thirty-seven years before the comet returns. The vision has to be false. I'll never survive that long. Will I?

Shadows Linger

For David G. Hartwell,
without whom there would be neither Sword
nor Dread Empire nor Starfishers

I

Juniper

All men are born condemned, so the wise say. All suckle the breast of Death.

All bow before that Silent Monarch. That Lord in Shadow lifts a finger. A feather flutters to the earth. There is no reason in His song. The good go young. The wicked prosper. He is king of the Chaos Lords. His breath stills all souls.

We found a city dedicated to His worship, long ago, but so old now it has lost that dedication. The dark majesty of his godhead has frayed, been forgotten by all but those who stand in his shadow. But Juniper faced a more immediate fear, a specter from yesteryear leaking into the present upon a height overlooking the city. And because of that the Black Company went there, to that strange city far beyond the bounds of the Lady's empire. . . . But this is not the beginning. In the beginning we were far away. Only two old friends and a handful of men we would meet later stood nose-to-nose with the shadow.

2

Tally Roadside

The children's heads popped from the weeds like groundhog heads. They watched the approaching soldiers. The boy whispered, "Must be a thousand of them." The column stretched back and back. The dust it raised drifted up the face of a far hill. The creak and jangle of harness grew ever louder.

The day was hot. The children were sweating. Their thoughts lingered on a nearby brook and a dip in a pool they had found there. But they had been set to watch the road. Rumor said the Lady meant to break the renascent Rebel movement in Tally province.

And here her soldiers came. Closer now. Grim, hard-looking men. Veterans. Easily old enough to have helped create the disaster which had befallen the Rebel six years ago, claiming, among a quarter million men, their father.

"It's them!" the boy gasped. Fear and awe filled his voice. Grudging admiration edged it. "That's the Black Company."

The girl was no student of the enemy. "How do you know?"

The boy indicated a bear of a man on a big roan. He had silvery hair. His bearing said he was accustomed to command. "That's the one they call the Captain. The little black one beside him would be the wizard called One-Eye. See his hat? That's how you tell. The ones behind them must be Elmo and the Lieutenant."

"Are any of the Taken with them?" The girl rose higher, for a better look. "Where are the other famous ones?" She was the younger. The boy, at ten, already considered himself a soldier of the White Rose.

He yanked his sister down. "Stupid! Want them to see you?"

"So what if they do?"

The boy sneered. She had believed their uncle Neat when he had said that the enemy would not harm children. The boy hated his uncle. The man had no guts.

Nobody pledged to the White Rose had any guts. They just played at fighting the Lady. The most daring thing they did was ambush the occasional courier. At least the enemy had courage.

They had seen what they had been sent to see. He touched the girl's wrist. "Let's go." They scurried through the weeds, toward the wooded creek bank.

A shadow lay upon their path. They looked up and went pale. Three horsemen stared down at them. The boy gaped. Nobody could have slipped up unheard. "Goblin!"

The small, frog-faced man in the middle grinned. "At your service, laddy-boy."

The boy was terrified, but his mind remained functional. He shouted, "Run!" If one of them could escape. . . .

Goblin made a circular gesture. Pale pink fire tangled his fingers. He made a throwing motion. The boy fell, fighting invisible bonds like a fly caught in a spider's web. His sister whimpered a dozen feet away.

"Pick them up," Goblin told his companions. "They should tell an interesting tale."

Juniper: The Iron Lily

The Lily stands on Floral Lane in the heart of the Buskin, Juniper's worst slum, where the taste of death floats on every tongue and men value life less than they do an hour of warmth or a decent meal. Its front sags against its neighbor to the right, clinging for support like one of its own drunken patrons. Its rear cants in the opposite direction. Its bare wood siding sports leprous patches of grey rot. Its windows are boarded with scraps and chinked with rags. Its roof boasts gaps through which the wind howls and bites when it blows off the Wolander Mountains. There, even on a summer's day, the glaciers twinkle like distant veins of silver.

Sea winds are little better. They bring a chill damp which gnaws the bones and sends ice floes scampering across the harbor.

The shaggy arms of the Wolanders reach seaward, flanking the River Port, forming cupped hands which hold the city and harbor. The city straddles the river, creeping up the heights on both sides.

Wealth rises in Juniper, scrambling up and away from the river. The people of the Buskin, when they lift their eyes from their misery, see the homes of the wealthy above, noses in the air, watching one another across the valley.

Higher still, crowning the ridges, are two castles. On the southern height stands Duretile, hereditary bastion of the Dukes of Juniper. Duretile is in scandalous disrepair. Most every structure in Juniper is.

Below Duretile lies the devotional heart of Juniper, the Enclosure, beneath which lie the Catacombs. There half a hundred generations rest, awaiting the Day of Passage, guarded by the Custodians of the Dead.

On the north ridge stands an incomplete fortress called, simply, the black castle. Its architecture is alien. Grotesque monsters leer from its battlements. Serpents writhe in frozen agonies upon its walls. There are no joints in the obsidian-like material. And the place is growing.

The people of Juniper ignore the castle's existence, its growth. They do not want to know what is happening up there. Seldom do they have time to pause in their struggle for survival to lift their eyes that high.

4

Tally Ambush

I drew a seven, spread, discarded a trey, and stared at a lone ace. To my left, Pawnbroker muttered, "That did it. He's down to a rock."

I eyed him curiously. "What makes you say that?"

He drew, cursed, discarded. "You get a face like a corpse when you've got it cold, Croaker. Even your eyes."

Candy drew, cursed, discarded a five. "He's right, Croaker. You get so unreadable you're readable. Come on, Otto."

Otto stared at his hand, then at the pile, as though he could conjure victory from the jaws of defeat. He drew. "Shit." He discarded his draw, a royal card. I showed them my ace and raked in my winnings.

Candy stared over my shoulder while Otto gathered the cards. His eyes were hard and cold. "What?" I asked.

"Our host is working up his courage. Looking for a way to get out and warn them."

I turned. So did the others. One by one the tavern-keeper and his customers dropped their gazes and shrank into themselves. All but the tall, dark man seated alone in shadows near the fireplace. He winked and lifted a mug, as if in salute. I scowled. His response was a smile.

Otto dealt.

"One hundred ninety-three," I said.

Candy frowned. "Damn you, Croaker," he said, without emotion. I had been counting hands. They were perfect ticks of the clocks of our lives as brothers of the Black Company. I had played over ten thousand hands since the battle at Charm. Only the gods themselves know how many I played before I started keeping track.

"Think they got wind of us?" Pawnbroker asked. He was edgy. Waiting does that.

"I don't see how." Candy arrayed his hand with exaggerated care. A dead giveaway. He had something hot. I reexamined mine. Twenty-one. Probably get burned, but the best way to stop him. . . . I went down. "Twenty-one."

Otto sputtered. "You son-of-a-bitch." He laid down a hand strong for going low. But it added to twenty-two because of one royal card. Candy had three nines, an ace and a trey. Grinning, I raked it in again.

"You win this one, we're going to check your sleeves," Pawnbroker grumbled. I collected the cards and started shuffling.

The back door hinges squealed. Everyone froze, stared at the kitchen door. Men stirred beyond it.

"Madle! Where the hell are you?"

The tavern-keeper looked at Candy, agonized. Candy cued him. The taverner called, "Out here, Neat."

Candy whispered, "Keep playing." I started dealing.

A man of forty came from the kitchen. Several others followed. All wore dappled green. They had bows across their backs. Neat said, "They must've got the kids. I don't know how, but. . . ." He saw something in Madle's eyes. "What's the matter?"

We had Madle sufficiently intimidated. He did not give us away.

Staring at my cards, I drew my spring tube. My companions did likewise. Pawnbroker discarded the card he had drawn, a deuce. He usually tries to go low. His play betrayed his nervousness.

Candy snagged the discard and spread an ace-deuce-trey run. He discarded an eight.

One of Neat's companions whined, "I told you we shouldn't send kids." It sounded like breathing life into an old argument.

"I don't need any I-told-you-so," Neat growled. "Madle, I spread the word for a meeting. We'll have to scatter the outfit."

"We don't know nothing for sure, Neat," another green man said. "You know kids."

"You're fooling yourself. The Lady's hounds are on our trail."

The whiner said, "I told you we shouldn't hit those. . . ." He fell silent, realizing, a moment too late, that strangers were present, that the regulars all looked ghastly.

Neat went for his sword.

There were nine of them, if you counted Madle and some customers who got involved. Candy overturned the card table. We tripped the catches on our spring tubes. Four poisoned darts snapped across the common room. We drew swords.

It lasted only seconds.

"Everybody all right?" Candy asked.

"Got a scratch," Otto said. I checked it. Nothing to worry about.

"Back behind the bar, friend," Candy told Madle, whom he had spared. "The rest of you, get this place straightened up. Pawnbroker, watch them. They even think about getting out of line, kill them."

"What do I do with the bodies?"

"Throw them down the well."

I righted the table again, sat down, unfolded a sheet of paper. Sketched upon it was the chain of command of the insurgents in Tally. I blacked out NEAT. It stood at mid-level. "Madle," I said. "Come here."

The barkeep approached with the eagerness of a dog to a whipping.

"Take it easy. You'll get through this all right. If you cooperate. Tell me who those men were."

He hemmed and hawed. Predictably.

"Just names," I said. He looked at the paper, frowning. He could not read. "Madle? Be a tight place to swim, down a well with a bunch of bodies."

He gulped, surveyed the room. I glanced at the man near the fireplace. He hadn't moved during the encounter. Even now he watched with apparent indifference.

Madle named names.

Some were on my list and some were not. Those that were not I assumed to be spear carriers. Tally had been well and reliably scouted.

The last corpse went out. I gave Madle a small gold piece. He goggled. His customers regarded him with unfriendly eyes. I grinned. "For services rendered."

Madle blanched, stared at the coin. It was a kiss of death. His patrons would think he had helped set the ambush. “Gotcha,” I whispered. “Want to get out of this alive?”

He looked at me in fear and hatred. “Who the hell are you guys?” he demanded in a harsh whisper.

“The Black Company, Madle. The Black Company.”

I don’t know how he managed, but he went even whiter.

Juniper: Marron Shed

The day was cold and grey and damp, still, misty, and sullen. Conversation in the Iron Lily consisted of surly monosyllables uttered before a puny fire.

Then the drizzle came, drawing the curtains of the world in tight. Brown and grey shapes hunched dispiritedly along the grubby, muddy street. It was a day ripped full-grown from the womb of despair. Inside the Lily, Marron Shed looked up from his mug-wiping. Keeping the dust off, he called it. Nobody was using his shoddy stoneware because nobody was buying his cheap, sour wine. Nobody could afford it.

The Lily stood on the south side of Floral Lane. Shed’s counter faced the doorway, twenty feet deep into the shadows of the common room. A herd of tiny tables, each with its brood of rickety stools, presented a perilous maze for the customer coming out of sunlight. A half-dozen roughly cut support pillars formed additional obstacles. The ceiling beams were too low for a tall man. The boards of the floor were cracked and warped and creaky, and anything spilled ran downhill.

The walls were decorated with old-time odds and ends and curios left by customers which had no meaning for anyone entering today. Marron Shed was too lazy to dust them or take them down.

The common room L-ed around the end of his counter, past the fireplace, near which the best tables stood. Beyond the fireplace, in the deepest shadows, a yard from the kitchen door, lay the base of the stair to the rooming floors.

Into that darksome labyrinth came a small, weasely man. He carried a bundle of wood scraps. "Shed? Can I?"

"Hell. Why not, Asa? We'll all benefit." The fire had dwindled to a bank of grey ash.

Asa scuttled to the fireplace. The group there parted surlily. Asa settled beside Shed's mother. Old June was blind. She could not tell who he was. He placed his bundle before him and started stirring the coals.

"Nothing down to the docks today?" Shed asked.

Asa shook his head. "Nothing came in. Nothing going out. They only had five jobs. Unloading wagons. People were fighting over them."

Shed nodded. Asa was no fighter. Asa was not fond of honest labor, either. "Darling, one draft for Asa." Shed gestured as he spoke. His serving girl picked up the battered mug and took it to the fire.

Shed did not like the little man. He was a sneak, a thief, a liar, a mooch, the sort who would sell his sister for a couple of copper gersh. He was a whiner and complainer and coward. But he had become a project for Shed, who could have used a little charity himself. Asa was one of the homeless Shed let sleep on the common room floor whenever they brought wood for the fire. Letting the homeless have the floor did not put money into the coin box, but it did assure some warmth for June's arthritic bones.

Finding free wood in Juniper in winter was harder than finding work. Shed was amused by Asa's determination to avoid honest employment.

The fire's crackle killed the stillness. Shed put his grimy rag aside. He stood behind his mother, hands to the heat. His fingernails began aching. He hadn't realized how cold he was.

It was going to be a long, cold winter. "Asa, do you have a regular wood source?" Shed could not afford fuel. Nowadays firewood was barged down the Port from far upstream. It was expensive. In his youth. . . .

"No." Asa stared into the flames. Piney smells spread through the Lily. Shed worried about his chimney. Another pine scrap winter, and he hadn't had the chimney swept. A chimney fire could destroy him.

Things had to turn around soon. He was over the edge, in debt to his ears. He was desperate.

"Shed."

He looked to his tables, to his only real paying customer. "Raven?"

"Refill, if you please."

Shed looked for Darling. She had disappeared. He cursed softly. No point yelling. The girl was deaf, needed signs to communicate. An asset, he had thought when Raven had suggested he hire her. Countless secrets were whispered in the

Lily. He had thought more whisperers might come if they could speak without fear of being overheard.

Shed bobbed his head, captured Raven's mug. He disliked Raven, partially because Raven was successful at Asa's game. Raven had no visible means of support, yet always had money. Another reason was because Raven was younger, tougher and healthier than the run of the Lily's customers. He was an anomaly. The Lily was on the downhill end of the Buskin, close to the waterfront. It drew all the drunkards, the worn-out whores, the dopers, the derelicts and human flotsam who eddied into that last backwater before the darkness overhauled them. Shed sometimes agonized, fearing his precious Lily was but a final way station.

Raven did not belong. He could afford better. Shed wished he dared throw the man out. Raven made his skin crawl, sitting at his corner table, dead eyes hammering iron spikes of suspicion into anyone who entered the tavern, cleaning his nails endlessly with a knife honed razor-sharp, speaking a few cold, toneless words whenever anyone took a notion to drag Darling upstairs. . . . That baffled Shed. Though there was no obvious connection, Raven protected the girl as though she were his virgin daughter. What the hell was a tavern slut for, anyway?

Shed shuddered, pushed it out of mind. He needed Raven. Needed every paying guest he could get. He was surviving on prayers.

He delivered the wine. Raven dropped three coins into his palm. One was a silver leva. "Sir?"

"Get some decent firewood in here, Shed. If I wanted to freeze, I'd stay outside."

"Yes, sir!" Shed went to the door, peeked into the street. Latham's wood yard was just a block away.

The drizzle had become an icy rain. The mucky lane was crusting. "Going to snow before dark," he informed no one in particular.

"In or out," Raven growled. "Don't waste what warmth there is."

Shed slid outside. He hoped he could reach Latham's before the cold began to ache.

Shapes loomed out of the icefall. One was a giant. Both hunched forward, rags around their necks to prevent ice from sliding down their backs.

Shed charged back into the Lily. "I'll go out the back way." He signed, "Darling, I'm going out. You haven't seen me since this morning."

"Krage?" the girl signed.

"Krage," Shed admitted. He dashed into the kitchen, snagged his ragged coat off its hook, wriggled into it. He fumbled the door latch twice before he got it loose.

An evil grin with three teeth absent greeted him as he leaned into the cold.

Foul breath assaulted his nostrils. A filthy finger gouged his chest. "Going somewhere, Shed?"

"Hi, Red. Just going to see Latham about firewood."

"No, you're not." The finger pushed. Shed fell back till he was in the common room.

Sweating, he asked, "Cup of wine?"

"That's neighborly of you, Shed. Make it three."

"Three?" Shed's voice squeaked.

"Don't tell me you didn't know Krage is on his way."

"I didn't," Shed lied.

Red's snaggle-toothed smirk said he knew Shed was lying.

6

Tally Mix-Up

You try your damnedest, but something always goes wrong. That's life. If you're smart, you plan for it.

Somehow, somebody got away from Madle's, along about the twenty-fifth Rebel who stumbled into our web, when it really looked like Neat had done us a big favor, summoning the local hierarchy to a conference. Looking backward, it is hard to fix blame. We all did our jobs. But there are limits to how alert you stay under extended stress. The man who disappeared probably spent hours plotting his break. We did not notice his absence for a long time.

Candy figured it out. He threw his cards in at the tail of a hand, said, "We're minus a body, troops. One of those pig farmers. The little guy who *looked* like a pig."

I could see the table from the corner of my eye. I grunted. "You're right. Damn. Should have taken a head count after each trip to the well."

The table was behind Pawnbroker. He did not turn around. He waited a hand, then ambled to Madle's counter and bought a crock of beer. While his rambling distracted the locals, I made rapid signs with my fingers, in deaf-speech. "Better be ready for a raid. They know who we are. I shot my mouth off."

The Rebel would want us bad. The Black Company has earned a widespread reputation as a successful eradicator of the Rebel pestilence, wherever it appears. Though we are not as vicious as reputed, news of our coming strikes terror wherever we go. The Rebel often goes to ground, abandoning his operations, where we appear.

Yet here were four of us, separated from our companions, evidently unaware that we were at risk. They would try. The question at hand was how hard.

We did have cards up our sleeves. We never play fair if we can avoid it. The Company philosophy is to maximize effectiveness while minimizing risk.

The tall, dark man rose, left his shadow, stalked toward the stair to the sleeping rooms. Candy snapped, "Watch him, Otto." Otto hurried after him, looking feeble in the man's wake. The locals watched, wondering.

Pawnbroker used signs to ask, "What now?"

"We wait," Candy said aloud, and with signs added, "Do what we were sent to do."

"Not much fun, being live bait," Pawnbroker signed back. He studied the stair nervously. "Set Otto up with a hand," he suggested.

I looked at Candy. He nodded. "Why not? Give him about seventeen." Otto would go down first time around every time if he had less than twenty. It was a good percentage bet.

I quick figured the cards in my head, and grinned. I could give him seventeen and have enough low cards left to give each of us a hand that would burn him. "Give me those cards."

I hurried through the deck, building hands. "There." Nobody had higher than a five. But Otto's hand had higher cards than the others.

Candy grinned. "Yeah."

Otto did not come back. Pawnbroker said, "I'm going up to check."

"All right," Candy replied. He went and got himself a beer. I eyed the locals. They were getting ideas. I stared at one and shook my head.

Pawnbroker and Otto returned a minute later, preceded by the dark man, who returned to his shadow. Pawnbroker and Otto looked relieved. They settled down to play.

Otto asked, "Who dealt?"

"Candy did," I said. "Your go."

He went down. "Seventeen."

"Heh-heh-heh," I replied. "Burned you. Fifteen."

And Pawnbroker said, "Got you both. Fourteen."

And Candy, "Fourteen. You're hurting, Otto."

He just sat there, numbed, for several seconds. Then he caught on. "You bastards! You stacked it! You don't think I'm going to pay off. . . ."

"Settle down. Joke, son," Candy said. "Joke. It was your deal anyhow." The cards went around and the darkness came. No more insurgents appeared. The locals grew ever more restless. Some worried about their families, about being late. As everywhere else, most Tallylanders are concerned only with their own lives. They don't care whether the White Rose or the Lady is ascendant.

The minority of Rebel sympathizers worried about when the blow might fall. They were afraid of getting caught in the crossfire.

We pretended ignorance of the situation.

Candy signed, "Which ones are dangerous?"

We conferred, selected three men who might become trouble. Candy had Otto bind them to their chairs.

It dawned on the locals that we knew what to expect, that we were prepared. Not looking forward, but prepared.

The raiders waited till midnight. They were more cautious than the Rebel we encountered ordinarily. Maybe our reputation was *too* strong. . . .

They burst in in a rush. We discharged our spring tubes and began swinging swords, retreating to a corner away from the fireplace. The tall man watched indifferently.

There were a lot of Rebels. Far more than we had expected. They kept storming inside, crowding up, getting into one another's ways, climbing over the corpses of their comrades. "Some trap," I gasped. "Must be a hundred of them."

"Yeah," Candy said. "It don't look good." He kicked at a man's groin, cut him when he covered up.

The place was wall-to-wall insurgents, and from the noise there were a hell of a lot more outside. Somebody didn't want us getting away.

Well, that was the plan.

My nostrils flared. There was an odor in the air, just the faintest off-key touch, subtle under the stink of fear and sweat. "Cover up!" I yelled, and whipped a wad of damp wool from my belt pouch. It stunk worse than a squashed skunk. My companions followed suit.

Somewhere a man screamed. Then another. Voices rose in a hellish chorus. Our enemies surged around, baffled, panicky. Faces twisted in agony. Men fell down in writhing heaps, clawing their noses and throats. I was careful to keep my face in the wool.

The tall, thin man came out of his shadows. Calmly, he began despatching guerrillas with a fourteen-inch, silvery blade. He spared those customers we had not bound to their chairs.

He signed, "It's safe to breathe now."

"Watch the door," Candy told me. He knew I had an aversion to this kind of slaughter. "Otto, you take the kitchen. Me and Pawnbroker will help Silent."

The Rebel outside tried to get us by speeding arrows through the doorway. He had no luck. Then he tried firing the place. Madle suffered paroxysms of rage. Silent, one of the three wizards of the Company, who had been sent into Tally weeks earlier, used his powers to squelch the fire. Angrily, the Rebel prepared for a siege.

"Must have brought every man in the province," I said.

Candy shrugged. He and Pawnbroker were piling corpses into defensive barricades. "They must have set up a base camp near here." Our intelligence about the Tally guerrillas was extensive. The Lady prepares well before she sends us in. But we hadn't been told to expect such strength available at short notice.

Despite our successes, I was scared. There was a big mob outside, and it sounded like more were arriving regularly. Silent, as an ace in the hole, hadn't much more value.

"You send your bird?" I demanded, assuming that had been the reason for his trip upstairs. He nodded. That provided some relief. But not much.

The tenor changed. They were quieter outside. More arrows zipped through the doorway. It had been ripped off its hinges in the first rush. The bodies heaped in it would not slow the Rebel long. "They're going to come," I told Candy.

"All right." He joined Otto in the kitchen. Pawnbroker joined me. Silent, looking mean and deadly, stationed himself in the center of the common room.

A roar went up outside.

"Here they come!"

We held the main rush, with Silent's help, but others began to batter the window shutters. Then Candy and Otto had to concede the kitchen. Candy killed an overzealous attacker and spun away long enough to bellow, "Where the hell are they, Silent?"

Silent shrugged. He seemed almost indifferent to the proximity of death. He hurled a spell at a man being boosted through a window.

Trumpets brayed in the night. "Ha!" I shouted. "They're coming!" The last gate of the trap had closed.

One question remained. Would the Company close in before our attackers finished us?

More windows gave. Silent could not be everywhere. "To the stair!" Candy shouted. "Fall back to the stair."

We raced for it. Silent called up a noxious fog. It was not the deadly thing he had used before. He could not do that again, now. He hadn't time to prepare.

The stair was easily held. Two men, with Silent behind them, could hold it forever.

The Rebel saw that. He began setting fires. This time Silent could not extinguish all the flames.

7

Juniper: Krage

The front door opened. Two men shoved into the Lily, stamped their feet and beat the ice off themselves. Shed scuttled over to help. The bigger man pushed him away. The smaller crossed the room, kicked Asa away from the fire, squatted with his hands extended. Shed's guests stared into the flames, seeing and hearing nothing.

Except Raven, Shed noted. Raven looked interested, and not particularly disturbed.

Shed sweated. Krage finally turned around. "You didn't stop by yesterday, Shed. I missed you."

"I couldn't, Krage. I didn't have anything to bring you. Look in my coin box. You know I'll pay you. I always do. I just need a little time."

"You were late last week, Shed. I was patient. I know you're having problems. But you were late the week before that, too. And the week before that. You're making me look bad. I know you mean it when you say you'll pay me. But what will people think? Eh? Maybe they start thinking it's all right for them to be late, too. Maybe they start thinking they don't have to pay at all."

"Krage, I can't. Look in my box. As soon as business picks up. . . ."

Krage gestured. Red reached behind the counter. "Business is bad everywhere, Shed. I got problems, too. I got expenses. I can't meet mine if you don't meet yours." He ambled around the common room, examining the furnishings.

Shed could read his mind. He wanted the Lily. Wanted Shed in a hole so deep he would have to give the place up.

Red handed Shed's box to Krage. Krage made a face. "Business really is bad." He gestured. The big man, Count, seized Shed's elbows from behind. Shed nearly fainted. Krage grinned wickedly. "Pat him down, Red. See if he's holding out." He emptied the coin box. "On account, Shed."

Red found the silver leva Raven had given Shed.

Krage shook his head. "Shed, Shed, you lied to me." Count pressed his elbows together painfully.

"That isn't mine," Shed protested. "That belongs to Raven. He wanted me to buy wood. That's why I was headed for Latham's."

Krage eyed him. Shed knew Krage knew he was telling the truth. He didn't have the guts to lie.

Shed was scared. Krage might bust him up just so he would give up the Lily to buy his life.

What then? He would be without a gersh, and in the street with an old woman to look after.

Shed's mother cursed Krage. Everyone ignored her, including Shed. She was harmless. Darling stood in the kitchen doorway, frozen, one hand fisted before her mouth, eyes full of appeal. She watched Raven more than Krage and Shed.

"What do you want me to break, Krage?" Red asked. Shed cringed. Red enjoyed his work. "You shouldn't hold out on us, Shed. You shouldn't lie to Krage." He unleashed a vicious punch. Shed gagged, tried to fall forward. Count held him upright. Red hit him again.

A soft, cold voice said, "He told the truth. I sent him for wood."

Krage and Red shifted formation. Count did not relax his grip. "Who are you?" Krage demanded.

"Raven. Let him be."

Krage exchanged glances with Red. Red said, "I think maybe you'd better not talk that way to Mister Krage."

Raven's gaze rose. Red's shoulders tightened defensively. Then, aware of his audience, he stepped over and threw an open-palmed punch.

Raven plucked his hand out of the air, twisted. Red went to his knees, grinding his teeth on a whimper. Raven said, "That was stupid."

Astonished, Krage replied, "Smart is as smart does, mister. Let him go while you're healthy."

Raven smiled for the first time in Shed's recollection. "*That* wasn't smart." There was an audible *pop*. Red screamed.

"Count!" Krage snapped.

Count hurled Shed aside. He was twice Red's size, quick, strong as a mountain, and barely as smart. Nobody survived Count.

A wicked nine-inch dagger appeared in Raven's hand. Count stopped so violently his feet tangled. He fell forward, rolling off the edge of Raven's table.

"Oh, shit," Shed groaned. Somebody was going to get killed. Krage wouldn't put up with this. It would be bad for business.

But as Count rose, Krage said, "Count, help Red." His tone was conversational.

Count obediently turned to Red, who had dragged himself away to nurse his wrist.

"Maybe we had a little misunderstanding here," Krage said. "I'll put it plain, Shed. You've got one week to pay me. The big and the nut both."

"But. . . ."

"No buts, Shed. That's according to terms. Kill somebody. Rob somebody. Sell this dump. But get the money." The or-elses did not have to be explained.

I'll be all right, Shed promised himself. He won't hurt me. I'm too good a customer.

How the hell would he come up with it? He couldn't sell out. Not with winter closing in. The old woman couldn't survive in the street.

Cold air gusted into the Lily as Krage paused at the door. He glared at Raven. Raven did not bother looking back.

"Some wine here, Shed," Raven said. "I seem to have spilled mine."

Shed hustled despite his pain. He could not help fawning. "I thank you, Raven, but you shouldn't have interfered. He'll kill you for that."

Raven shrugged. "Go to the wood-seller before somebody else tries to take my money."

Shed looked at the door. He did not want to go outside. They might be waiting. But then he looked at Raven again. The man was cleaning his nails with that wicked knife. "Right away."

It was snowing now. The street was treacherous. Only a thin white mask covered the mud.

Shed could not help wondering why Raven had intervened. To protect his money? Reasonable. . . . Only, reasonable men stayed quiet around Krage. He would cut your throat if you looked at him wrong.

Raven was new around here. Maybe he did not know about Krage.

He would learn the hard way. His life wasn't worth two gersh anymore.

Raven seemed well-heeled. He wouldn't carry his whole fortune around with him, would he? Maybe he kept part hidden in his room. Maybe enough to pay off Krage. Maybe he could set Raven up. Krage would appreciate that.

"Let's see your money," Latham said when he asked for wood. Shed produced Raven's silver leva. "Ha! Who died this time?"

Shed reddened. An old prostitute had died at the Lily last winter. Shed had rifled her belongings before summoning the Custodians. His mother had lived warm for the rest of the winter. The whole Buskin knew because he had made the mistake of telling Asa.

By custom, the Custodians took the personal possessions of the newly dead. Those and donations supported them and the Catacombs.

"Nobody died. A guest sent me."

"Ha! The day you have a guest who can afford generosity. . . ." Latham shrugged. "But what do I care? The coin is good. I don't need its provenance. Grab some wood. You're headed that way."

Shed staggered back to the Lily, face burning, ribs aching. Latham hadn't bothered to hide his contempt.

Back home, with the fire taking hold of the good oak, Shed drew two mugs of wine and sat down opposite Raven. "On the house."

Raven stared momentarily, took a sip, maneuvered the mug to an exact spot upon the tabletop. "What do you want?"

"To thank you again."

"There's nothing to thank me for."

"To warn you, then. You didn't take Krage serious enough."

Latham tramped in with an armload of firewood, grumbling because he couldn't get his wagon out. He would be back and forth for a long time.

"Go away, Shed." And, as Shed rose, face hot, Raven snapped, "Wait. You think you owe me? Then someday I'll ask a favor. You do it. Right?"

"Sure, Raven. Anything. Just name it."

"Go sit by the fire, Shed."

Shed squeezed in between Asa and his mother, joining their surly silence. That Raven really was creepy.

The man in question was engaged in a lively exchange of signs with the deaf serving girl.

8

Tally: Close-Up

I let the tip of my blade drop to the inn floor. I slumped in exhaustion, coughing weakly in the smoke. I swayed, feebly reached for the support of an overturned table. Reaction was setting in. I had been sure this time was the end. If they hadn't been forced to extinguish the fires themselves. . . .

Elmo crossed the room and threw an arm around me. "You hurt, Croaker? Want me to find One-Eye?"

"Not hurt. Just burned out. Been a long time since I been so scared, Elmo. Thought I was a goner."

He righted a chair with a foot and sat me down. He was my closest friend, a wiry, old hardcase seldom given to moodiness. Wet blood reddened his left sleeve. I tried to stand. "Sit," he ordered. "Pockets can take care of it."

Pockets was my understudy, a kid of twenty-three. The Company is getting older—at least at its core, my contemporaries. Elmo is past fifty. The Captain and Lieutenant straddle that five-zero. I wouldn't see forty again. "Get them all?"

"Enough." Elmo settled on another chair. "One-Eye and Goblin and Silent went after the ones who took off." His voice was vacant. "Half the Rebels in the province, first shot."

"We're getting too old for this." The men began bringing prisoners inside, sifting them for characters who might know something useful. "Ought to leave this stuff to the kids."

"They couldn't handle it." He stared into nothing, at long ago and far away.

"Something wrong?"

He shook his head, then contradicted himself. "What are we doing, Croaker? Isn't there any end to it?"

I waited. He did not go on. He doesn't talk much. Especially not about his feelings. I nudged. "What do you mean?"

"Just goes on and on. Hunting Rebels. No end to the supply. Even back when we worked for the Syndic in Beryl. We hunted dissidents. And before

Beryl. . . . Thirty-six years of same old same old. And me never sure I was doing right. Especially now."

It was like Elmo to keep his reservations in abeyance eight years before airing them. "We're in no position to change anything. The Lady won't take kindly to us if we suddenly say we're only going to do thus and so, and none of that."

The Lady's service has not been bad. Though we get the toughest missions, we never have to do the dirty stuff. The regulars get those jobs. Preemptive strikes sometimes, sure. The occasional massacre. But all in the line of business. Militarily necessary. We'd never gotten involved in atrocities. The Captain wouldn't permit that.

"It's not the morality, Croaker. What's moral in war? Superior strength. No. I'm just tired."

"Not an adventure anymore, eh?"

"Stopped being that a long time ago. Turned into a job. Something I do because I don't know anything else."

"Something you do very well." That did not help, but I couldn't think of anything better to say.

The Captain came in, a shambling bear who surveyed the wreckage with a cold eye. He came over. "How many did we get, Croaker?"

"Count's not in yet. Most of their command structure, I'd guess."

He nodded. "You hurt?"

"Worn out. Physically and emotionally. Been a while since I was so scared."

He righted a table, dragged up a chair, produced a case of maps. The Lieutenant joined him. Later, Candy brought Madle over. Somehow, the innkeeper had survived.

"Our friend has some names for you, Croaker."

I spread my paper, scratched out those Madle named.

The company commanders began drafting prisoners for grave-digging detail. Idly, I wondered if they realized they were preparing their own resting places. No Rebel soldier is paroled unless we can enlist him inescapably into the Lady's cause. Madle we enlisted. We gave him a story to explain his survival and eliminated everyone who could deny it. Candy, in a fit of generosity, had the bodies removed from his well.

Silent returned, with Goblin and One-Eye, the two smaller wizards bickering caustically. As usual. I do not recall the argument. It didn't matter. The struggle was all, and it was all decades old.

The Captain gave them a sour look, asked the Lieutenant, "Heart or Tome?" Heart and Tome are the only substantial towns in Tally. There is a king at Heart who is allied with the Lady. She crowned him two years ago, after Whisper slew his predecessor. He is not popular with the Tallylanders. My opinion, never asked, is that she should dispose of him before he does her further harm.

Goblin laid a fire. The morning hours were nippy. He knelt before it, toasting his fingers.

One-Eye poked around behind Madle's counter, found a beer jar miraculously unscathed. He drained it in a single draft, wiped his face, surveyed the room, winked at me.

"Here we go," I murmured.

The Captain glanced up. "Eh?"

"One-Eye and Goblin."

"Oh." He went back to work and did not look up again.

A face formed in the flames before frog-faced little Goblin. He did not see it. His eyes were closed. I looked at One-Eye. His eye was sealed, too, and his face was all pruned, wrinkles atop wrinkles, shadowed by the brim of his floppy hat. The face in the fire took on detail.

"Eh!" It startled me for a moment. Staring my way, it looked like the Lady. Well, like the face the Lady wore the one time I actually saw her. That was during the battle at Charm. She called me in to dredge my mind for suspicions about a conspiracy among the Ten Who Were Taken. . . . A thrill of fear. I have lived with it for years. If ever she questions me again, the Black Company will be short its senior physician and Annalist. I now have knowledge for which she would flatten kingdoms.

The face in the fire extended a tongue like that of a salamander. Goblin squealed. He jumped up clutching a blistered nose.

One-Eye was draining another beer, back to his victim. Goblin scowled, rubbed his nose, seated himself again. One-Eye turned just enough to place him at the corner of his vision. He waited till Goblin began to nod.

This has been going on forever. Both were with the Company before I joined, One-Eye for at least a century. He is *old*, but is as spry as men my age.

Maybe spryer. Lately I've felt the burden of time more and more, all too often dwelling on everything I've missed. I can laugh at peasants and townies chained all their lives to a tiny corner of the earth while I roam its face and see its wonders, but when I go down, there will be no child to carry my name, no family to mourn me save my comrades, no one to remember, no one to raise a marker over my cold bit of ground. Though I have seen great events, I will leave no enduring accomplishment save these Annals.

Such conceit. Writing my own epitaph disguised as Company history.

I am developing a morbid streak. Have to watch that.

One-Eye cupped his hands palms-down on the countertop, murmured, opened them. A nasty spider of fist size stood revealed, wearing a bushy squirrel tail. Never say One-Eye has no sense of humor. It scuttled down to the floor, skipped over to me, grinned up with a One-Eye black face wearing no eyepatch, then zipped toward Goblin.

The essence of sorcery, even for its nonfraudulent practitioners, is misdirection. So with the bushy-tailed spider.

Goblin was not snoozing. He was lying in the weeds. When the spider got close, he whirled and swung a stick of firewood. The spider dodged. Goblin hammered the floor. In vain. His target darted around, chuckling in a One-Eye voice.

The face formed in the flames. Its tongue darted out. The seat of Goblin's trousers began to smoulder.

"I'll be damned," I said.

"What?" the Captain asked, not looking up. He and the Lieutenant had taken opposite ends of an argument over whether Heart or Tome would be the better base of operations.

Somehow, word gets out. Men streamed in for the latest round of the feud. I observed, "I think One-Eye is going to win one."

"Really?" For a moment old grey bear was interested. One-Eye hadn't bested Goblin in years.

Goblin's frog mouth opened in a startled, angry howl. He slapped his bottom with both hands, dancing. "You little snake!" he screamed. "I'll strangle you! I'll cut your heart out and eat it! I'll. . . . I'll. . . ."

Amazing. Utterly amazing. Goblin never gets mad. He gets even. Then One-Eye will put his twisted mind to work again. If Goblin is even, One-Eye figures he's behind.

"Settle that down before it gets out of hand," the Captain said.

Elmo and I got between the antagonists. This thing was disturbing. Goblin's threats were serious. One-Eye had caught him in a bad temper, the first I'd ever seen. "Ease up," I told One-Eye.

He stopped. He, too, smelled trouble.

Several men growled. Some heavy bets were down. Usually, nobody will put a copper on One-Eye. Goblin coming out on top is a sure thing, but this time he looked feeble.

Goblin did not want to quit. Did not want to play the usual rules, either. He snatched a fallen sword and headed for One-Eye.

I couldn't help grinning. That sword was huge and broken, and Goblin was so small, yet so ferocious, that he seemed a caricature. A bloodthirsty caricature. Elmo couldn't handle him. I signaled for help. Some quick thinker splashed water on Goblin's back. He whirled, cussing, started a deadly spell.

Trouble for sure. A dozen men jumped in. Somebody threw another bucket of water. That cooled Goblin's temper. As we relieved him of the blade, he looked abashed. Defiant, but abashed.

I led him back to the fire and settled beside him. "What's the matter? What happened?" I glimpsed the Captain from the corner of my eye. One-Eye stood before him, drained by a heavy-duty dressing down.

"I don't know, Croaker." Goblin slumped, stared into the fire. "Suddenly everything was too much. This ambush tonight. Same old thing. There's always another province, always more Rebels. They breed like maggots in a cowpie. I'm getting older and older, and I haven't done anything to make a better world. In fact, if you backed off to look at it, we've all made it worse." He shook his head. "That isn't right. Not what I want to say. But I don't know how to say it any better."

"Must be an epidemic."

"What?"

"Nothing. Thinking out loud." Elmo. Myself. Goblin. A lot of the men, judging by their tenor lately. Something was wrong in the Black Company. I had suspicions, but wasn't ready to analyze. Too depressing.

"What we need is a challenge," I suggested. "We haven't stretched ourselves since Charm." Which was a half-truth. An operation which compelled us to become totally involved in staying alive might be a prescription for symptoms, but was no remedy for causes. As a physician, I was not fond of treating symptoms alone. They could recur indefinitely. The disease itself had to be attacked.

"What we need," Goblin said in a voice so soft it almost vanished in the crackle of the flames, "is a cause we can believe in."

"Yeah," I said. "That, too."

From outside came the startled, outraged cries of prisoners discovering that they were to fill the graves they had dug.

Juniper: Death Pays

Shed grew increasingly frightened as the days passed. He had to get some money. Krage was spreading the word. He was to be made an example.

He recognized the tactic. Krage wanted to scare him into signing the Lily over. The place wasn't much, but it was damned sure worth more than he owed.

Krage would resell it for several times his investment. Or turn it into whore cribs. And Marron Shed and his mother would be in the streets, with winter's deadly laughter howling in their faces.

Kill somebody, Krage had said. Rob somebody. Shed considered both. He would do anything to keep the Lily and protect his mother.

If he could just get real customers! He got nothing but one-night chiselers and scroungers. He needed residential regulars. But he could not get those without fixing the place up. And that he couldn't do without money.

Asa rolled through the doorway. Pale and frightened, he scuttled to the counter. "Find a wood supply yet?" Shed asked.

The little man shook his head, slid two gersh across the counter. "Give me a drink."

Shed scooped the coins into his box. One did not question money's provenance. It had no memory. He poured a full measure. Asa reached eagerly.

"Oh, no," Shed said. "Tell me about it."

"Come on, Shed. I paid you."

"Sure. And I'll deliver when you tell me why you're so rocky."

"Where's that Raven?"

"Upstairs. Sleeping." Raven had been out all night.

Asa shook a little more. "Give me that, Shed."

"Talk."

"All right. Krage and Red grabbed me. They wanted to know about Raven."

So Shed knew how Asa had come by money. He had tried to sell Raven. "Tell me more."

"They just wanted to know about him."

"What did they want to know?"

"If he ever goes out."

"Why?"

Asa stalled. Shed pulled the mug away. "All right. They had two men watching him. They disappeared. Nobody knows anything. Krage is furious." Shed let him have the wine. He drained it in a single gulp.

Shed glanced toward the stair, shuddered. Maybe he had underestimated Raven. "What did Krage say about me?"

"Sure could use another mug, Shed."

"I'll give you a mug. Over the noggin."

"I don't need you, Shed. I made a connection. I can sleep over to Krage's any time I want."

Shed grunted, made a mask of his face. "You win." He poured wine.

"He's going to put you out of business, Shed. Whatever it takes. He's decided you're in it with Raven." Wicked little smile. "Only he can't figure where you got the guts to buck him."

"I'm not. I don't have anything to do with Raven, Asa. You know that."

Asa enjoyed his moment. "I tried to tell Krage, Shed. He didn't want to hear it."

"Drink your wine and get out, Asa."

"Shed?" The old whine filled Asa's voice.

"You heard me. Out. Back to your new friends. See how long they have a use for you."

"Shed! . . ."

"They'll throw you back into the street, Asa. Right beside me and Mom. Git, you bloodsucker."

Asa downed his wine and fled, shoulders tight against his neck. He had tasted the truth of Shed's words. His association with Krage would be fragile and brief.

Shed tried to warn Raven. Raven ignored him. Shed polished mugs, watched Raven chatter with Darling in the utter silence of sign language, and tried to imagine some way of making a hit in the upper city. Usually he spent these early hours eying Darling and trying to imagine a way to gain access, but lately sheer terror of the street had abolished his customary randiness.

A cry like that of a hog with a cut throat came from upstairs. "Mother!" Shed took the stairs two steps at a time.

His mother stood in the doorway of the big bunkroom, panting. "Mom? What's wrong?"

"There's a dead man in there."

Shed's heart fluttered. He pushed into the room. An old man lay in the bottom right bunk inside the door.

There had been only four bunkroom customers last night. Six gersh a head. The room was six feet wide and twelve long, with twenty-four platforms stacked six high. When the room was full, Shed charged two gersh to sleep leaning on a rope stretched down the middle.

Shed touched the old-timer. His skin was cold. He had been gone for hours.

"Who was he?" old June asked.

"I don't know." Shed probed his ragged clothing. He found four gersh and an iron ring. "Damn!" He could not take that. The Custodians would be suspicious if they found nothing. "We're jinxed. This is our fourth stiff this year."

"It's the customers, son. They have one foot in the Catacombs already."

Shed spat. "I'd better send for the Custodians."

A voice said, "He's waited this long, let him wait a little longer."

Shed whirled. Raven and Darling stood behind his mother. "What?"

"He might be the answer to your problems," Raven said. And immediately

Darling began flashing signs so fast Shed could not catch one in twenty. Evidently she was telling Raven not to do something. Raven ignored her.

Old June snapped, "Shed!" Her voice was heavy with admonition.

"Don't worry, Mom. I'll handle it. Go ahead with your work." June was blind, but when her health permitted, she dumped the slops and handled what passed for maid service—mainly dusting beds between guests to kill fleas and lice. When her health confined her to bed, Shed brought in his cousin Wally, a ne'er-do-well like Asa, but with a wife and kids. Shed used him out of pity for the wife.

He headed downstairs. Raven followed, still arguing with Darling. Momentarily, Shed wondered if Raven was diddling her. Be a damned waste of fine womanflesh if someone wasn't.

How could a dead man with four gersh get him out from under Krage? Answer: He could not. Not legitimately.

Raven settled onto his usual stool. He scattered a handful of copper. "Wine. Buy yourself a mug, too."

Shed collected the coins, deposited them in his box. Its contents were pitiful. He wasn't making expenses. He was doomed. His debt to Krage could miraculously be discharged and still he'd be doomed.

He deposited a mug before Raven, seated himself on a stool. He felt old beyond his years, and infinitely weary. "Tell me."

"The old man. Who was he? Who were his people?"

Shed shrugged. "Just somebody who wanted to get out of the cold. The Buskin is full of them."

"So it is."

Shed shuddered at Raven's tone. "Are you proposing what I think?"

"What's that?"

"I don't know. What use is a corpse? I mean, even the Custodians only stuff them in the Catacombs."

"Suppose there was a buyer?"

"I've been supposing that."

"And?"

"What would I have to do?" His voice barely carried across the table. He could imagine no more disgusting crime. Even the least of the city's dead were honored above the living. A corpse was a holy object. The Enclosure was Juniper's epicenter.

"Very little. Late tonight, have the body at the back door. You could do that?"

Shed nodded weakly.

"Good. Finish your wine."

Shed downed it in a gulp. He drew another mug, polished his stoneware industriously. It was a bad dream. It would go away.

* * *

The corpse seemed almost weightless, but Shed had difficulty negotiating the stairs. He had drunk too much. He eased through the shadowed common, stepping with exaggerated care. The people clustered near the fireplace looked demonic in the sullen red of the last coals.

One of the old man's feet toppled a pot as Shed entered the kitchen. He froze. Nothing happened. His heartbeat gradually slowed. He kept reminding himself that he was doing this so his mother would not have to freeze on winter streets.

He thumped the door with his knee. It swung inward immediately. A shadow hissed, "Hurry up," and seized the old man's feet, helped Shed heave it into a wagon.

Panting, terrified, Shed croaked, "What now?"

"Go to bed. You get your share in the morning."

Shed's relieved sigh nearly became tears. "How much?" he gasped.

"A third."

"Only a third?"

"I'm taking all the risk. You're safe already."

"All right. How much would it be?"

"The market varies." Raven turned away. Shed closed the door, leaned against it with closed eyes. What had he done?

He built up the fire and went to bed, lay listening to his mother's snores. Had she guessed? Maybe she wouldn't. The Custodians often waited for night. He would tell her she had slept through everything.

He could not sleep. Who knew about the death? If word got out, people would wonder. They would begin to suspect the unsuspectable.

What if Raven got caught? Would the Inquisitors make him talk? Bullock could make a stone sing.

He watched his mother all next morning. She did not speak except in monosyllables, but that was her custom.

Raven appeared shortly after noon. "Tea and a bowl of porridge, Shed." When he paid, he did not shove copper across the counter.

Shed's eye widened. Ten silver leva lay before him. Ten? For one dead old man? That was a third? And Raven had done this before? He must be rich. Shed's palms grew moist. His mind howled after potential crimes.

"Shed?" Raven said softly when he delivered the tea and porridge. "Don't even think about it."

"What?"

"Don't think what you're thinking. *You* would end up in the wagon."

Darling scowled at them from the kitchen doorway. For a moment Raven seemed embarrassed.

* * *

Shed slunk into the hostel where Krage held court. From the outside the place was as crummy as the Lily. Timidly, he looked for Count, tried to ignore Asa. Count would not torment him for fun. "Count, I need to see Krage."

Count opened big brown cow eyes. "Why?"

"I brought him some money. On account."

Count heaved himself upright. "All right. Wait here." He stalked off.

Asa sidled up. "Where'd you get the money, Shed?"

"Where do you get yours, Asa?" Asa did not answer. "It isn't polite to ask. Mind your own business or stay away from me."

"Shed, I thought we were friends."

"I tried to be friends, Asa. I even let you have a place to sleep. And as soon as you hooked up with Krage. . . ."

A shadow crossed Asa's face. "I'm sorry, Shed. You know me. I don't think so fast. I do dumb things."

Shed snorted. So Asa had come to the inevitable conclusion: Krage would dump him once he settled with Raven.

Shed was tempted to betray Raven. The man had to have a fortune hidden. But he was afraid of a thousand things, and his guest stood at the top of the list.

Asa said, "I found a way to get deadwood from the Enclosure." His face brightened in pathetic appeal. "Mostly pine, but it's wood."

"The Enclosure?"

"It's not illegal, Shed. It keeps the Enclosure cleaned up."

Shed scowled righteously.

"Shed, it's less wrong than going through somebody's. . . ."

Shed controlled his anger. He needed allies inside the enemy camp. "Firewood could be like money, Asa. No provenance."

Asa smiled fawningly. "Thanks, Shed."

Count called, "Shed."

Shed shook as he crossed the room. Krage's men smirked.

This wouldn't work. Krage wouldn't listen. He was going to throw his money away.

"Count says you've got something to give me on account," Krage said.

"Uhm." Krage's den could have been ripped whole from a mansion high up the wall of the valley. Shed was stunned.

"Stop gawking and get on with it. You'd better not give me a handful of copper and beg for an extension, either. Picked a warm doorway yet? Your payments are a joke, Shed."

"No joke, Mr. Krage. Honest. I can pay over half of it."

Krage's eyebrows rose. "Interesting." Shed laid nine silver leva before him. "Very interesting." He fixed Shed with a penetrating stare.

Shed stammered, "That's over half, counting interest. I hoped maybe seeing as how that would put me ahead. . . ."

"Quiet." Shed shut up. "You think I should forget what happened?"

"That wasn't my fault, Mr. Krage. I didn't tell him to. . . . You don't know what Raven is like."

"Shut up." Krage stared at the coins. "Maybe something can be arranged. I know you didn't put him up to it. You don't have the guts."

Shed stared at the floor, unable to deny his cowardice.

"Okay, Shed. You're a regular client. Back to the regular schedule." He eyed the money. "You're ahead three weeks, looks like."

"Thank you, Mr. Krage. Really. You don't know how much this means. . . ."

"Shut up. I know exactly what it means. Get out. Start getting another payment together. This is your last reprieve."

"Yes, sir." Shed retreated. Count opened the door.

"Shed! I may want something sometime. A favor for a favor. Understand?"

"Yes, sir."

"All right. Go."

Shed left, a sinking feeling replacing relief. Krage would make him help get Raven. He almost wept as he tramped homeward. It never got any better. He was always in a trap.

Tally Turnaround

Tome was typical of towns we had garrisoned recently. Small, dirty, boring. One wondered why the Lady bothered. What use were these remote provinces? Did she insist they bend the knee merely to puff her ego? There was nothing here worth having, unless it was power over the natives.

Even they viewed their country with a certain contempt.

The presence of the Black Company strained the resources of the area.

Within a week the Captain started talking about shifting a company to Heart and billeting smaller units in the villages. Our patrols seldom encountered the Rebel, even when our wizards helped hunt. The engagement at Madle's had all but eliminated the infestation.

The Lady's spies told us the few committed Rebels left had fled into Tambor, an even bleaker kingdom to the northeast. I supposed Tambor would be our next mission.

I was scribbling away at these Annals one day, when I decided I needed an estimate of the mileage we'd covered in our progression eastward. I was appalled to learn the truth. Tome was two thousand miles east of Charm! Far beyond the bounds of the empire as it had existed six years ago. The great bloody conquests of the Taken Whisper had established a border arc just this side of the Plain of Fear. I ran down the line of city-states forming that forgotten frontier. Frost and Ade, Thud and Barns, and Rust, where the Rebel had defied the Lady successfully for years. Huge cities all, formidable, and the last such we had seen. I still shuddered, recalling the Plain of Fear.

We crossed it under the aegis of Whisper and Feather, two of the Taken, the Lady's black apprentices, both sorceresses orders of magnitude above our three puny wizards. Even so, and travelling with entire armies of the Lady's regulars, we suffered there. It is a hostile, bitter land where none of the normal rules apply. Rocks speak and whales fly. Coral grows in the desert. Trees walk. And the inhabitants are the strangest of all. . . . But that is neither here nor there. Just a nightmare from the past. A nightmare that haunts me still, when the screams of Cougar and Fleet come echoing down the corridors of time, and once again I can do nothing to save them.

"What's the trouble?" Elmo asked, slipping the map from beneath my fingers, cocking his head sideways. "Look like you saw a ghost."

"Just remembering the Plain of Fear."

"Oh. Yeah. Well, buck up. Have a beer." He slapped my back. "Hey! Kingpin! Where the hell you been?" He charged away, in pursuit of the Company's leading malingerer.

One-Eye arrived a moment later, startling me. "How's Goblin?" he asked softly. There had been no intercourse between them since Madle's. He eyed the map. "The Empty Hills? Interesting name."

"Also called the Hollow Hills. He's all right. Why don't you check him out?"

"What the hell for? He was the one who acted the ass. Can't take a little joke. . . ."

"Your jokes get a bit rough, One-Eye."

"Yeah. Maybe. Tell you what. You come with me."

"Got to prepare my reading." One night a month the Captain expects me to exhort the troops with a reading from the Annals. So we'll know where we came from, so we'll recall our ancestors in the outfit. Once that meant a lot. The Black Company. Last of the Free Companies of Khatovar. All brethren. Tight. Great esprit. Us against the world, and let the world watch out. But the something that had manifested itself in Goblin's behavior, in the low-grade depression of Elmo and others, was affecting everybody. The pieces were coming unglued.

I had to pick a good reading. From a time when the Company had its back against the wall and survived only by clinging to its traditional virtues. There have been many such moments in four hundred years. I wanted one recorded by one of the more inspired Annalists, one with the fire of a White Rose revivalist speaking to potential recruits. Maybe I needed a series, one that I could read several nights running.

"Crap," One-Eye said. "You know those books by heart. Always got your nose in them. Anyway, you could fake the whole thing and nobody would know the difference."

"Probably. And nobody would care if I did. It's going sour, old-timer. Right. Let's go see Goblin."

Maybe the Annals needed a rereading on a different level. Maybe I was treating symptoms. The Annals have a certain mystic quality, for me. Maybe I could identify the disease by immersing myself, hunting something between the lines.

Goblin and Silent were playing no-hands mumbletypeg. I'll say this for our three spook-pushers: They aren't great, but they keep their talents polished. Goblin was ahead on points. He was in a good mood. He even nodded to One-Eye.

So. It was over. The stopper could be put into the bottle. One-Eye just had to say the right thing.

To my amazement, he even apologized. By sign, Silent suggested we get out and let them conclude their peace in private. Each had an overabundance of pride.

We stepped outside. As we often did when no one could intercept our signs, we discussed old times. He, too, was privy to the secret for which the Lady would obliterate nations.

Half a dozen others suspected once, and had forgotten. We knew, and would never forget. Those others, if put to the question, would leave the Lady with serious doubts. We two, never. We *knew* the identity of the Lady's most potent enemy—and for six years we had done nothing to apprise her of the fact that that enemy even existed as more than a Rebel fantasy.

The Rebel tends to a streak of superstition. He loves prophets and prophecies and grand, dramatic foretellings of victories to come. It was pursuit of a prophecy which led him into the trap at Charm, nearly causing his extinction.

He regained his balance afterward by convincing himself that he was the victim of false prophets and prophecies, laid upon him by villains trickier than he. In that conviction he could go on, and believe more impossible things.

The funny thing was, he lied to himself with the truth. I was, perhaps, the only person outside the Lady's inner circle who knew he had been guided into the jaws of death. Only, the enemy who had done the guiding was not the Lady, as he believed. That enemy was an evil greater still, the Dominator, the Lady's one-time spouse, whom she had betrayed and left buried but alive in a grave in the Great Forest north of a far city called Oar. From that grave he had reached out, subtly, and twisted the minds of men high in Rebel circles, bending them to his will, hoping to use them to drag the Lady down and bring about his own resurrection. He failed, though he had help from several of the original Taken in his scheme.

If he knew of my existence, I must be high on his list. He lay up there still, scheming, maybe hating me, for I helped betray the Taken helping him. . . . Scary, that. The Lady was medicine bad enough. The Dominator, though, was the body of which her evil was but a shadow. Or so the legend goes. I sometimes wonder why, if that is true, she walks the earth and he lies restless in the grave.

I have done a good deal of research since discovering the power of the thing in the north, probing little-known histories. Scaring myself each time. The Domination, an era when the Dominator actually ruled, smelled like an era of hell on earth. It seemed a miracle that the White Rose had put him down. A pity she could not have destroyed him. And all his minions, including the Lady. The world would not be in the straits it is today.

I wonder when the honeymoon will end. The Lady hasn't been that terrible. When will she relax, and give the darkness within her free rein, reviving the terror of the past?

I also wonder about the villainies attributed to the Domination. History, inevitably, is recorded by self-serving victors.

A scream came from Goblin's quarters. Silent and I stared at one another a moment, then rushed inside.

I honestly expected one of them to be bleeding his life out on the floor. I did not expect to find Goblin having a fit while One-Eye desperately strove to keep him from hurting himself. "Somebody made contact," One-Eye gasped. "Help me. It's strong."

I gaped. Contact. We hadn't had a direct communication since the desperately swift campaigns when the Rebel was closing in on Charm, years ago. Since then, the Lady and Taken have been content to communicate through messengers.

The fit lasted only seconds. That was customary. Then Goblin relaxed, whimpering. It would be several minutes before he recovered enough to relay the message. We three looked at one another with card-playing faces, frightened inside. I said, "Somebody ought to tell the Captain."

"Yeah," One-Eye said. He made no move to go. Neither did Silent.

"All right. I'm elected." I went. I found the Captain doing what he does best. He had his feet up on his worktable, was snoring. I wakened him, told him.

He sighed. "Find the Lieutenant." He went to his map cases. I asked a couple questions he ignored, took the hint and got out.

He had expected something like this? There was a crisis in the area? How could Charm have heard first?

Silly, worrying before I heard what Goblin had to say.

The Lieutenant seemed no more surprised than the Captain. "Something up?" I asked.

"Maybe. A courier letter came after you and Candy left for Tally. Said we might be called west. This could be it."

"West? Really?"

"Yeah." Such dense sarcasm he put into the word!

Stupid. If we chose Charm as the customary demarcation point between east and west, Tally lay two thousand plus miles away. Three months' travel under perfect conditions. The country between was anything but perfect. In places roads just didn't exist. I thought six months sounded too optimistic.

But I was worrying before the fact again. I had to wait and see.

It turned out to be something even the Captain and Lieutenant hadn't anticipated.

We waited in trepidation while Goblin pulled himself together. The Captain had his map case open, sketching a tentative route to Frost. He grumbled because all westbound traffic had to cross the Plain of Fear. Goblin cleared his throat.

Tension mounted. He did not lift his eyes. The news had to be unpleasant. He squeaked, "We've been recalled. That was the Lady. She seemed disturbed. The first leg goes to Frost. One of the Taken will meet us there. He'll take us on to the Barrowland."

The others frowned, exchanged puzzled looks. I muttered, "Shit. Holy Shit."

"What is it, Croaker?" the Captain asked.

They didn't know. They paid no attention to historical things. "That's where the Dominator is buried. Where they all were buried, back when. It's in the forest north of Oar." We'd been to Oar seven years ago. It was not a friendly city.

"Oar!" the Captain yelled. "Oar! That's twenty-five hundred miles!"

"Add another hundred or two to the Barrowland."

He stared at the maps. "Great. Just great. That means not just the Plain of Fear but the Empty Hills and the Windy Country too. Just fandamntastic great. I suppose we've got to get there next week?"

Goblin shook his head. "She didn't seem rushed, Captain. Just upset and wanting us headed the right way."

"She give you any whys or wherefores?"

Goblin smirked. Did the Lady ever? Hell, no.

"Just like that," the Captain muttered. "Out of the blue. Orders to hike halfway around the world. I love it." He told the Lieutenant to begin preparations for movement.

It was bad news, mad news, insanity squared, but not as bad as he made out. He had been preparing since receiving the courier letter. It wasn't that hard to get rolling. The trouble was, nobody wanted to roll.

The west was far nicer than anything we'd known out here, but not so great anybody wanted to walk that far.

Surely she could have summoned a closer unit?

We are the victims of our own competence. She always wants us where the going threatens to become toughest. She knows we will do the best job.

Damn and double damn.

Juniper: Night Work

Shed had given Krage only nine of ten leva. The coin he held back bought firewood, wine, and beer to replenish his stocks. Then other creditors caught wind of his prosperity. A slight upturn in business did him no good. He met his next payment to Krage by borrowing from a moneylender named Gilbert.

He found himself wishing somebody would die. Another ten leva would put him in striking distance of getting through the winter.

It was a hard one, that winter. Nothing moved in the harbor. There was no work in the Buskin. Shed's only bit of good fortune was Asa. Asa brought wood whenever he got away from Krage, in a pathetic effort to buy a friend.

Asa arrived with a load. Privately, he said, "Better watch out, Shed. Krage heard about you borrowing from Gilbert." Shed went grey. "He's got a buyer for the Lily lined up. They're rounding up girls already."

Shed nodded. The whoremasters recruited desperate women this time of year. By the time summer brought its sailors, they were broken to their trade.

"The bastard. Made me think he'd given me a break. I should have known better. This way he gets my money *and* my place. The bastard."

"Well, I warned you."

"Yeah. Thanks, Asa."

Shed's next due date came on like a juggernaut. Gilbert refused him another loan. Smaller creditors besieged the Lily. Krage was aiming them Shed's way.

He took Raven a complimentary drink. "May I sit?"

A hint of a smile crossed Raven's lips. "It's your place." And: "You haven't been friendly lately, Shed."

"I'm nervous," Shed lied. Raven irritated his conscience. "Worried about my debts."

Raven saw through the excuse. "You thought maybe I could help?"

Shed almost groaned. "Yes."

Raven laughed softly. Shed thought he detected a note of triumph. "All right, Shed. Tonight?"

Shed pictured his mother being carted off by the Custodians. He swallowed his self-disgust. "Yeah."

"All right. But this time you're a helper, not a partner." Shed swallowed and nodded. "Put the old woman to bed, then come back downstairs. Understand?"

"Yes," Shed whispered.

"Good. Now go away. You irritate me."

"Yes, sir." Shed retreated. He couldn't look anyone in the eye the rest of that day.

A bitter wind howled down the Port valley, freckled with flakes of snow. Shed huddled miserably, the wagon seat a bar of ice beneath him. The weather was worsening. "Why tonight?" he grumbled.

"Best time." Raven's teeth chattered. "We're not likely to be seen." He turned into Chandler's Lane, off which innumerable narrow alleyways ran. "Good hunting territory here. In this weather they crawl back in the alleys and die like flies."

Shed shivered. He was too old for this. But that was why he was here. So he wouldn't have to face the weather every night.

Raven stopped the wagon. "Check that passageway."

Shed's feet started aching the instant he put weight on them. Good. At least he felt something. They weren't frozen.

There was little light in the alley. He searched more by feel than sight. He found one lump under an overhang, but it stirred and muttered. He ran.

He reached the wagon as Raven dumped something into the bed. Shed averted his eyes. The boy couldn't have been more than twelve. Raven concealed the body with straw. "That's one. Night like this, we ought to find a load."

Shed choked his protests, resumed his seat. He thought about his mother. She wouldn't last one night in this.

Next alley he found his first corpse. The old man had fallen and frozen because he couldn't get up again. Aching in his soul, Shed dragged the body to the wagon.

"Going to be a good night," Raven observed. "No competition. The Custodians won't come out in this." Softly: "I hope we can make the hill."

Later, after they had moved to the waterfront and each had found another corpse, Shed asked, "Why're *you* doing this?"

"I need money, too. Got a long way to travel. This way I get a lot, fast, without much risk."

Shed thought the risks far greater than Raven would admit. They could be torn apart. "You're not from Juniper, are you?"

"From the south. A shipwrecked sailor."

Shed did not believe it. Raven's accent was not at all right for that, mild though it was. He hadn't the nerve to call the man a liar, though, and press for the truth.

The conversation continued by fits and starts. Shed didn't uncover anything more of Raven's background or motives.

"Go that way," Raven told him. "I'll check over here. Last stop, Shed. I'm done in."

Shed nodded. He wanted to get the night over. To his disgust, he had begun seeing the street people as objects, and he hated them for dying in such damned inconvenient places.

He heard a soft call, turned back quickly. Raven had one. That was enough. He ran to the wagon.

Raven was on the seat, waiting. Shed scrambled up, huddled, tucked his face away from the wind. Raven kicked the mules into motion.

The wagon was halfway across the bridge over the Port when Shed heard a moan. "What?" One of the bodies was moving! "Oh. Oh, shit, Raven. . . ."

"He's going to die anyway."

Shed huddled back down, stared at the buildings on the north bank. He wanted to argue, wanted to fight, wanted to do anything to deny his part in this atrocity.

He looked up an hour later and recognized nothing. A few large houses flanked the road, widely spaced, their windows dark. "Where are we?"

"Almost there. Half an hour, unless the road is too icy."

Shed imagined the wagon sliding into a ditch. What then? Abandon everything and hope the rig couldn't be traced? Fear replaced loathing.

Then he realized where they were. There wasn't anything up here but that accursed black castle. "Raven. . . ."

"What's the matter?"

"You're headed for the black castle."

"Where'd you think we were going?"

"People live there?"

"Yes. What's your problem?"

Raven was a foreigner. He couldn't understand how the black castle affected Juniper. People who got too close disappeared. Juniper preferred to pretend that the place did not exist.

Shed stammered out his fears. Raven shrugged. "Shows your ignorance."

Shed saw the castle's dark shape through the snow. The fall was lighter on the ridge, but the wind was more fierce. Resigned, he muttered, "Let's get it over with."

The shape resolved into battlements, spires, towers. Not a light shown anywhere. Raven halted before a tall gate, went forward on foot. He banged a heavy knocker. Shed huddled, hoping there would be no response.

The gate opened immediately. Raven scrambled onto the wagon's seat. "Get up, mules."

"You're not going inside?"

"Why not?"

"Hey. No way. No."

"Shut up, Shed. You want your money, you help unload."

Shed stifled a whimper. He hadn't bargained for this.

Raven drove through the gate, turned right, halted beneath a broad arch. A single lantern battled the darkness clotting the passageway. Raven swung down. Shed followed, his nerves shrieking. They dragged the bodies out of the wagon and swung them onto stone slabs nearby. Then Raven said, "Get back on the wagon. Keep your mouth shut."

The one body stirred. Shed grunted. Raven pinched his leg savagely. "Shut up."

A shadowy shape appeared. It was tall, thin, clad in loose black pantaloons and a hooded shirt. It examined each body briefly, seemed pleased. It faced

Raven. Shed glimpsed a face all of sharp angles and shadows, lustrous, olive, cold, with a pair of softly luminous eyes.

"Thirty. Thirty. Forty. Thirty. Seventy," it said.

Raven countered, "Thirty. Thirty. Fifty. Thirty. One hundred."

"Forty. Eighty."

"Forty-five. Ninety."

"Forty. Ninety."

"Done."

They were dickering! Raven was not interested in quibbling over the old people. The tall being would not advance his offer for the youth. But the dying man was negotiable.

Shed watched the tall being count out coins at the feet of the corpses. That was a damned fortune! Two hundred twenty pieces of silver! With that he could tear the Lily down and build a new place. He could get out of the Buskin altogether.

Raven scooped the coins into his coat pocket. He gave Shed five.

"That's all?"

"Isn't that a good night's work?"

It was a good month's work, and then some. But to get only five of. . . .

"Last time we were partners," Raven said, swinging onto the driver's seat. "Maybe we will be again. But tonight you're a hired hand. Understand?" There was a hard edge to his voice. Shed nodded, beset by new fears.

Raven backed the wagon. Shed felt a sudden chill. That archway was hot as hell. He shuddered, feeling the hunger of the thing watching them.

Dark, glassy, jointless stone slid past. "My god!" He could see into the wall. He saw bones, fragments of bones, bodies, pieces of bodies, all suspended as if floating in the night. As Raven turned toward the gate, he saw a staring face. "What kind of place is this?"

"I don't know, Shed. I don't want to know. All I care is, they pay good money. I need it. I have a long way to go."

12

The Barrowland

The Taken called the Limper met the Company at Frost. We'd spent a hundred and forty-six days on the march. They were long days and hard, grinding, men and animals going on more by habit than desire. An outfit in good shape, like ours, is capable of covering fifty or even a hundred miles in a day, pushing hell out of it, but not day after week after month, upon incredibly miserable roads. A smart commander does not push on a long march. The days add up, each leaving its residue of fatigue, till men begin collapsing if the pace is too desperate.

Considering the territories we crossed, we made damned good time. Between Tome and Frost lie mountains where we were lucky to make five miles a day, deserts we had to wander in search of water, rivers that took days to cross using makeshift rafts. We were fortunate to reach Frost having lost only two men.

The Captain shone with a glow of accomplishment—till the military governor summoned him.

He assembled the officers and senior noncoms when he returned. "Bad news," he told us. "The Lady is sending the Limper to lead us across the Plain of Fear. Us and the caravan we'll escort."

Our response was surly. There was bad blood between the Company and the Limper. Elmo asked, "How soon will we leave, sir?" We needed rest. None had been promised, of course, and the Lady and the Taken seem unconscious of human frailties, but still. . . .

"No time specified. Don't get lazy. He's not here now, but he could turn up tomorrow."

Sure. With the flying carpets the Taken use, they can turn up anywhere within days. I muttered, "Let's hope other business keeps him away a while."

I did not want to encounter him again. We had done him wrong, frequently, way back. Before Charm we worked closely with a Taken called Soulcatcher. Catcher used us in several schemes to discredit Limper, both out of old enmity and because Catcher was secretly working on behalf of the Dominator. The Lady was taken in. She nearly destroyed the Limper, but rehabilitated him instead, and brought him back for the final battle.

Way, way back, when the Domination was aborning, centuries before the foundation of the Lady's empire, the Dominator overpowered his greatest rivals and compelled them into his service. He accumulated ten villains that way, soon known as the Ten Who Were Taken. When the White Rose raised the world against the Dominator's wickedness, the Ten were buried with him. She could destroy none of them outright.

Centuries of peace sapped the will of the world to guard itself. A curious wizard tried to contact the Lady. The Lady manipulated him, effected her release. The Ten rose with her. Within a generation she and they forged a new dark empire. Within two they were embattled with the Rebel, whose prophets agreed the White Rose would be reincarnated to lead them to a final victory.

For a while it looked like they would win. Our armies collapsed. Provinces fell. Taken feuded and destroyed one another. Nine of the Ten perished. The Lady managed to Take three Rebel chieftains to replace a portion of her losses: Feather, Journey, and Whisper—likely the best general since the White Rose. She gave us a terrible time before her Taking.

The Rebel prophets were correct in their prophecies, except about the last battle. They expected a reincarnated White Rose to lead them. She did not. They did not find her in time.

She was alive then. But she was living on our side of the battleline, unaware of what she was. I learned who she was. It is that knowledge which makes my life worthless should I be put to the question.

"Croaker!" the Captain snapped. "Wake up!" Everybody looked at me, wondering how I could daydream through whatever he'd said.

"What?"

"You didn't hear me?"

"No, sir."

He glowered his best bear glower. "Listen up, then. Be ready to travel by carpet when the Taken arrive. Fifty pounds of gear is your limit."

Carpet? Taken? What the hell? I looked around. Some of the men grinned. Some pitied me. Carpet flight? "What for?"

Patiently, the Captain explained, "The Lady wants ten men sent to help Whisper and Feather in the Barrowland. Doing what I don't know. You're one of the ones she picked."

Flutter of fear. "Why me?" It was rough, back when I was her pet.

"Maybe she still loves you. After all these years."

"Captain. . . ."

"Because she said so, Croaker."

"I guess that's good enough. Sure can't argue with it. Who else?"

"Pay attention and you'd know these things. Worry about it later. We have other fish to fry now."

Whisper came to Frost before the Limper. I found myself tossing a pack aboard her flying carpet. Fifty pounds. The rest I had left with One-Eye and Silent.

The carpet was a carpet only by courtesy, because tradition calls it that. Actually, it is a piece of heavy fabric stretched on a wooden frame a foot high when grounded. My fellow passengers were Elmo, who would command our team, and Kingpin. Kingpin is a lazy bastard, but he swings a mean blade.

Our gear, and another hundred pounds belonging to men who would follow us later, rested at the center of the carpet. Shaking, Elmo and Kingpin tied themselves in place at the carpet's two rear corners. My spot was the left front. Whisper sat at the right. We were heavily bundled, almost to immobility. We would be flying fast and high, Whisper said. The temperature upstairs would be low.

I shook as much as Elmo and Kingpin, though I had been aboard carpets before. I loved the view and dreaded the anticipation of falling that came with flight. I also dreaded the Plain of Fear, where strange, fell things cruise the upper air.

Whisper queried, "You all use the latrine? It's going to be a long flight." She did not mention us voiding ourselves in fear, which some men do up there. Her voice was cool and melodious, like those of the women who populate your last dream before waking. Her appearance belied that voice. She looked every bit the tough old campaigner she was. She eyed me, evidently recalling our previous encounter in the Forest of Cloud.

Raven and I had lain in wait where she was expected to meet the Limper and lead him over to the Rebel side. The ambush was successful. Raven took the Limper. I captured Whisper. Soulcatcher and the Lady came and finished up. Whisper became the first new Taken since the Domination.

She winked.

Taut fabric smacked my butt. We went up fast.

Crossing the Plain of Fear was faster by air, but still harrowing. Windwhales quartered across our path. We zipped around them. They were too slow to keep pace. Turquoise manta things rose from their backs, flapped clumsily, caught updrafts, rose above us, then dived past like plunging eagles, challenging our presence in their airspace. We could not outrun them, but outclimbed them easily. However, we could not climb higher than the windwhales. So high and the air becomes too rare for human beings. The whales could rise another mile, becoming diving platforms for the mantas.

There were other flying things, smaller and less dangerous, but determinedly obnoxious. Nevertheless, we got through. When a manta did attack, Whisper defeated it with her thaumaturgic craft.

To do so, she gave up control of the carpet. We fell, out of control, till she drove the manta away. I got through without losing my breakfast, but just barely. I never asked Elmo and Kingpin, figuring they might not want their dignity betrayed.

Whisper would not attack first. That is the prime rule for surviving the Plain of Fear. Don't hit first. If you do, you buy more than a duel. Every monster out there will go after you.

We crossed without harm, as carpets usually do, and raced on, all day long, into the night. We turned north. The air became cooler. Whisper dropped to lower altitudes and slower speeds. Morning found us over Forsberg, where the Company had served when new in the Lady's service. Elmo and I gawked over the side.

Once I pointed, shouted, "There's Deal." We had held that fortress briefly. Then Elmo pointed the other way. There lay Oar, where we had pulled some fine, bloody tricks on the Rebel, and earned the enmity of the Limper. Whisper flew so low we could distinguish faces in the streets. Oar looked no more friendly than it had eight years ago.

We passed on, rolled along above the treetops of the Great Forest, ancient and virgin wilderness from which the White Rose had conducted her campaigns against the Dominator. Whisper slowed around noon. We drifted down into a wide sprawl that once had been cleared land. A cluster of mounds in its middle betrayed the handiwork of man, though now the barrows are scarcely recognizable.

Whisper landed in the street of a town that was mostly ruin. I presumed it to be the town occupied by the Eternal Guard, whose task it is to prevent tampering with the Barrowland. They were effective till betrayed by apathy elsewhere.

It took the Resurrectionists three hundred seventy years to open the Barrowland, and then they did not get what they wanted. The Lady returned, with the Taken, but the Dominator remained chained.

The Lady obliterated the Resurrectionist movement root and branch. Some reward, eh?

A handful of men left a building still in good repair. I eavesdropped on their exchange with Whisper, understood a few words. "Recall your Forsberger?" I asked Elmo, while trying to shake the stiffness out of my muscles.

"It'll come back. Want to give Kingpin a look? He don't seem right."

He wasn't bad off. Just scared. Took a while to convince him we were back on the ground.

The locals, descendants of the Guards who had watched the Barrowland for centuries, showed us to our quarters. The town was being restored. We were the forerunners of a horde of new blood.

Goblin and two of our best soldiers came in on Whisper's next flight, three days later. They said the Company had left Frost. I asked if it looked like the Limper was holding a grudge.

"Not that I could see," Goblin said. "But that don't mean anything."

No, it didn't.

The last four men arrived three days later. Whisper moved into our barracks. We formed a sort of bodyguard cum police force. Besides protecting her, we were supposed to help make sure unauthorized persons did not get near the Barrowland.

The Taken called Feather appeared, bringing her own bodyguard. Specialists determined to investigate the Barrowland came up with a battalion of laborers hired in Oar. The laborers cleared the trash and brush, up to the Barrowland proper. Entry there, without appropriate protection, meant a slow, painful death. The protective spells the White Rose left hadn't faded with the Lady's resurrection. And she had added her own. I guess she is terrified he will break loose.

The Taken Journey arrived, bringing troops of his own. He established outposts in the Great Forest. The Taken took turns making airborne patrols. We minions watched one another as closely as we watched the rest of the world.

Something big was afoot. Nobody was saying so, but that much was obvious. The Lady definitely anticipated a breakout attempt.

I spent my free time reviewing the Guard's records, especially for the period when Bomanz lived here. He spent forty years in the garrison town, disguised as an antique digger, before he tried to contact the Lady and unintentionally freed her. He interested me. But there was little to dig out, and that little was colored.

Once I'd had his personal papers, having stumbled onto them shortly before Whisper's Taking. But I passed them on to our then mentor Soulcatcher for transportation to the Tower. Soulcatcher kept them for her own reasons, and they fell into my hands again, during the battle at Charm, as the Lady and I pursued the renegade Taken. I didn't mention the papers to anyone but a friend, Raven. The Raven, who deserted to protect a child he believed to be the reincarnation of the White Rose. When I got a chance to pick up the papers from where I hid them, they were gone. I guess Raven took them with him.

I often wonder what became of him. His declared intent was to flee so far no one could find him again. He did not care about politics. He just wanted to protect a child he loved. He was capable of doing anything to protect Darling. I guess he thought the papers might turn into insurance someday.

In the Guard headquarters there are a dozen landscapes painted by past members of the garrison. Most portray the Barrowland. It was magnificent in its day.

It had consisted of a central Great Barrow on a north-south axis, containing the Dominator and his Lady. Surrounding the Great Barrow was a star of earth raised above the plain, outlined by a deep, water-filled moat. At the points of that star stood lesser barrows containing five of The Ten Who Were Taken. A circle rising above the star connected its inward points, and there, at each, stood another barrow containing another Taken. Every barrow was surrounded by spells and fetishes. Within the inner ring, around the Great Barrow, were rank on rank of additional defenses. The last was a dragon curled around the Great Barrow, its tail in its mouth. A later painting by an eyewitness shows the dragon belching fire on the countryside the night of the Lady's resurrection. Bomanz is walking into the fire.

He was caught between Resurrectionists and the Lady, all of whom were manipulating him. His accident was their premeditated event.

The records say his wife survived. She said he went into the Barrowland to stop what was happening. No one believed her at the time. She claimed he carried the Lady's true name and wanted to reach her with it before she could wriggle free.

Silent, One-Eye and Goblin will tell you the direst fear of any sorcerer is that knowledge of his true name will fall to some outsider. Bomanz's wife claimed the Lady's was encoded in papers her husband possessed. Papers that vanished that night. Papers that I recovered decades later. What Raven snatched may contain the only lever capable of dumping the empire.

Back to the Barrowland in its youth. Impressive construction. Its weather faces were sheathed in limestone. The moat was broad and blue. The surrounding countryside was park-like. . . . But fear of the Dominator faded, and so did appropriations. A later painting, contemporary with Bomanz, shows the countryside gone to seed, the limestone facings in disrepair, and the moat becoming a swamp. Today you can't tell where the moat was. The limestone has disappeared beneath brush. The elevations and barrows are nothing but humps. That part of the Great Barrow where the Dominator lies remains in fair shape, though it, too, is heavily overgrown. Some of the fetishes anchoring the spells keeping his friends away still stand, but weather has devoured their features.

The edge of the Barrowland is now marked by stakes trailing red flags, put there when the Lady announced she was sending outsiders to investigate. The Guards themselves, having lived there always, need no markers to warn them off.

I enjoyed my month and a half there. I indulged my curiosities, and found Feather and Whisper remarkably accessible. That hadn't been true of the old

Taken. Too, the commander of the Guard, called the Monitor, bragged up his command's past, which stretches back as far as the Company's. We swapped lies and tales over many a gallon of beer.

During the fifth week someone discovered something. We peons were not told what. But the Taken got excited. Whisper started lifting in more of the Company. The reinforcements told harrowing fables about the Plain of Fear and the Empty Hills. The Company was at Lords now, only five hundred miles distant.

At the end of the sixth week Whisper assembled us and announced another move. "The Lady wants me to take some of you out west. A force of twenty-five. Elmo, you'll be in command. Feather and I, some experts, and several language specialists will join you. Yes, Croaker. You're on the list. She wouldn't deny her favorite amateur historian, would she?"

A thrill of fear. I didn't want her getting interested again.

"Where're we headed?" Elmo asked. Professional to the core, the son-of-a-bitch. Not a single complaint.

"A city called Juniper. Way beyond the western bounds of the empire. It's connected with the Barrowland somehow. It's a ways north, too. Expect it to be cold and prepare accordingly."

Juniper? Never heard of it. Neither had anyone else. Not even the Monitor. I scrounged through his maps till I found one showing the western coast. Juniper *was* way up north, near where the ice persists all year long. It was a big city. I wondered how it could exist there, where it should be frozen all the time. I asked Whisper. She seemed to know something about the place. She said Juniper benefits from an ocean current that brings warm water north. She said the city is very strange—according to Feather, who'd actually been there.

I approached Feather next, only hours before our departure. She couldn't tell me much more, except that Juniper is the demesne of a Duke Zimerlan, and he appealed to the Lady a year ago (just a while before the Captain's courier letter would have left Charm) for help solving a local problem. That someone had approached the Lady, when the world's desire is to keep her far away, argued that we faced interesting times. I wondered about the connection with the Barrowland.

The negative was that Juniper was so far away. I was pleased that I would be there when the Captain learned he was expected to head there after resting in Oar, though.

Could be I'd hear his howl of outrage even from that far. I knew he wouldn't be happy.

13

Juniper: The Enclosure

Shed slept badly for weeks. He dreamt of black glass walls and a man who hadn't been dead. Twice Raven asked him to join a night hunt. Twice he refused. Raven did not press, though they both knew Shed would jump if he insisted.

Shed prayed that Raven would get rich and disappear. He remained a constant irritant to the conscience.

Damnit, why didn't Krage go after him?

Shed couldn't figure why Raven remained unperturbed by Krage. The man was neither a fool nor stupid. The alternative, that he wasn't scared, made no sense. Not to a Marron Shed.

Asa remained on Krage's payroll, but visited regularly, bringing firewood. By the wagonload, sometimes. "What're you up to?" Shed demanded one day.

"Trying to build credit," Asa admitted. "Krage's guys don't like me much."

"Hardly anybody does, Asa."

"They might try something nasty. . . ."

"Want a place to hide when they turn on you, eh? What're you doing for Krage? Why is he bothering with you?"

Asa hemmed and hawed. Shed pushed. Here was a man he could bully. "I watch Raven, Shed. I report what he does."

Shed snorted. Krage was using Asa because he was expendable. He'd had two men disappear early on. Shed thought he knew where they were.

Sudden fear. Suppose Asa reported Raven's night adventures? Suppose he'd seen Shed. . . .

Impossible. Asa couldn't have kept quiet. Asa spent his life looking for leverage.

"You've been spending a lot lately, Asa. Where are you getting the money?"

Asa turned pale. He looked around, gobbled a few times. "The wood, Shed. Selling the wood."

"You're a liar, Asa. Where're you getting it?"

"Shed, you don't ask questions like that."

"Maybe not. But I need money bad. I owe Krage. I almost had him paid off. Then he started buying my little debts from everybody else. That damned Gilbert! . . . I need to get ahead enough so I don't have to borrow again."

The black castle. Two hundred twenty pieces of silver. How he had been tempted to attack Raven. And Raven just smiled into the wind, knowing exactly what he was thinking. "Where're you getting that money, Asa?"

"Where did you get the money you paid Krage? Huh? People are wondering, Shed. You don't come up with that kind of money overnight. Not you. You tell me and I'll tell you."

Shed backed down. Asa beamed in triumph.

"You little snake. Get out before I lose my temper."

Asa fled. He looked back once, face knotted thoughtfully. Damnit, Shed thought. Made him suspicious. He ground his rag into a tacky mug.

"What was that?"

Shed spun. Raven had come to the counter. His look brooked no crap. Shed gave him the gist.

"So Krage hasn't quit."

"You don't know him or you wouldn't ask. It's you or him, Raven."

"Then it has to be him, doesn't it?"

Shed gaped.

"A suggestion, Shed. Follow your friend when he goes wood-gathering." Raven returned to his seat. He spoke to Darling animatedly, in sign, which he blocked from Shed's view. The set of the girl's shoulders said she was against whatever it was he was proposing. Ten minutes later he left the Lily. Each afternoon he went out for a few hours. Shed suspected he was testing Krage's watchers.

Darling leaned against the door frame, watching the street. Shed watched her, his gaze sliding up and down her frame. Raven's, he thought. They're thick. I don't dare.

But she was such a fine looking thing, tall, lean of leg, ready for a man. . . . He was a fool. He did not need to get caught in that trap, too. He had troubles enough.

I think today would be good for it," Raven said as Shed delivered his breakfast.

"Eh? Good for what?"

"For a hike up the hill to watch friend Asa."

"Oh. No. I can't. Got nobody to watch the place." Back by the counter, Darling bent to pick something off the floor. Shed's eyes widened and his heart fluttered. He had to do something. Visit a whore, or something. Or get hurt. But he couldn't afford to pay for it. "Darling couldn't handle it alone."

"Your cousin Wally has stood in for you before."

Caught off balance, Shed could not marshall his excuses quickly. And Darling was driving him to distraction. She had to start wearing something that concealed the shape of her behind better. "Uh. . . . He couldn't deal with Darling. Doesn't know the signs."

Raven's face darkened slightly. "Give her the day off. Get that girl Lisa you used when Darling was sick."

Lisa, Shed thought. Another hot one. "I only use Lisa when I'm here to watch her." A hot one not attached. "She'll steal me blinder than my mother. . . ."

"Shed!"

"Eh?"

"Get Wally and Lisa here; then go keep an eye on Asa. I'll make sure they don't carry off the family silver."

"But. . . ."

Raven slapped a palm on the tabletop. "I said go!"

The day was clear and bright and, for winter, warm. Shed picked up Asa's trail outside Krage's establishment.

Asa rented a wagon. Shed was amazed. In winter stablekeepers demanded huge deposits. Draft animals slaughtered and eaten had no provenance. He thought it a miracle anyone trusted Asa with a team.

Asa went directly to the Enclosure. Shed stalked along behind, keeping his head down, confident Asa would not suspect him even if he looked back. The streets were crowded.

Asa left the wagon in a public grove across a lane running alongside the wall which girdled the Enclosure. It was one of many similar groves where Juniper's citizenry gathered for the Spring and Autumn Rites for the Dead. The wagon could not be seen from the lane.

Shed squatted in shadow and bush and watched Asa dash to the Enclosure wall. Somebody ought to clear that brush away, Shed thought. It made the wall look tacky. For that matter, the wall needed repairing. Shed crossed and found a gap through which a man could duck-walk. He crept through. Asa was crossing an open meadow, hurrying uphill toward a stand of pines.

The inner face of the wall was brush-masked, too. Scores of bundles of wood lay among the bushes. Asa had more industry than Shed had suspected. Hanging around Krage's gang had changed him. They had him scared for sure.

Asa entered the pines. Shed puffed after him. Ahead, Asa sounded like a cow pushing through the underbrush.

The whole Enclosure was tacky. In Shed's boyhood it had been park-like, a fit waiting place for those who had gone before. Now it had the threadbare look that characterized the rest of Juniper.

Shed crept toward hammering racket. What was Asa doing, making so much noise?

He was cutting wood from a fallen tree, stacking the pieces in neat bundles. Shed could not picture the little man orderly, either. What a difference terror made.

An hour later Shed was ready to give up. He was cold and hungry and stiff. He had wasted half a day. Asa was doing nothing remarkable. But he persevered. He had a time investment to recoup. And an irritable Raven awaiting his report.

Asa worked hard. When not chopping, he hustled bundles down to his wagon. Shed was impressed.

He stayed, watched, and told himself he was a fool. This was going nowhere.

Then Asa became furtive. He collected his tools and concealed them, looked around warily. This is it, Shed thought.

Asa took off uphill. Shed puffed after him. His stiff muscles protested every step. Asa traveled more than a mile through lengthening shadows. Shed almost lost him. A clinking brought him back to the track.

The little man was using flint and steel. He crouched over a supply of torches wrapped in an oilskin, taken from hiding. He got a brand burning, hastened into some brush. A moment later he clambered over some rocks beyond, disappeared. Shed gave it a minute, then followed. He slid round the boulder where he had seen Asa last. Beyond lay a crack in the earth just big enough to admit a man.

"My god," Shed whispered. "He's found a way into the Catacombs. He's looting the dead."

I came straight back," Shed gasped. Raven was amused by his distress. "I knew Asa was foul, but I never dreamed he'd commit sacrilege."

Raven smiled.

"Aren't you disgusted?"

"No. Why are *you*? He didn't steal any bodies."

Shed came within a hair's breadth of assaulting him. He *was* worse than Asa.

"He making out at it?"

"Not as well as you. The Custodians take all the burial gifts except passage urns." Every corpse in the Catacombs was accompanied by a small, sealed urn, usually fixed on a chain around the body's neck. The Custodians did not touch the few coins in those. When the Day of Passage came, the Boatmen would demand payment for passage to Paradise.

"All those souls stranded," Shed murmured. He explained.

Raven looked baffled. "How can anybody with an ounce of brains believe that crap? Dead is dead. Be quiet, Shed. Just answer questions. How many bodies in the Catacombs?"

"Who knows? They've been putting them away since. . . . Hell, for a thousand years. Maybe there's millions."

"Must have them stacked like cordwood."

Shed wondered about that. The Catacombs were vast, but a thousand years' worth of cadavers from a city Juniper's size would make a hell of a pile. He looked at Raven. Damn the man. "It's Asa's racket. Let's not try."

"Why not?"

"Too dangerous."

"Your friend hasn't suffered."

"He's smalltime. If he gets greedy, he'll get killed. There are Guardians down there. Monsters."

"Describe them."

"I can't."

"Can't or won't?"

"Can't. All they tell you is that they're there."

"I see." Raven rose. "This needs investigating. Don't discuss it. Especially not with Asa."

"Oh, no." Panicked, Asa would do something stupid.

Word drifted in off the street. Krage had sent his two best men after Raven. They had disappeared. Three more had vanished since. Krage himself had been injured by an unknown assailant. He had survived only because of Count's immense strength. Count wasn't expected to live.

Shed was terrified. Krage was neither reasonable nor rational. He asked Raven to move out. Raven stared at him in contempt. "Look, I don't want him killing you here," Shed said.

"Bad for business?"

"For my health, maybe. He's *got* to kill you now. People will stop being scared of him if he doesn't."

"He won't learn, eh? A damned city of fools."

Asa boiled through the doorway. "Shed, I got to talk to you." He was scared. "Krage thinks I turned him over to Raven. He's after me. You got to hide me, Shed."

"Like hell." The trap was closing. Two of them here. Krage would kill him for sure, would dump his mother into the street.

"Shed, I kept you in wood all winter. I kept Krage off your back."

"Oh, sure. So I should get killed, too?"

"You owe me, Shed. I never told nobody how you go out at night with Raven. Maybe Krage would want to know that, huh?"

Shed grabbed Asa's hands and yanked him forward, against the counter. As if cued, Raven stepped up behind the little man. Shed glimpsed a knife. Raven pricked Asa's back, whispered, "Let's go to my room."

Asa went pallid. Shed forced a smile. "Yeah." He released Asa, took a stoneware bottle from beneath the counter. "I want to talk to you, Asa." He collected three mugs.

Shed went up last, intensely aware of his mother's blind stare. How much had she heard? How much had she guessed? She had been cool lately. His shame had come between them. He no longer felt deserving of her respect.

He clouted his conscience. I did it for her!

Raven's room had the only door left on the upper floors. Raven held it for Asa and Shed. "Sit," he told Asa, indicating his cot. Asa sat. He looked scared enough to wet himself.

Raven's room was as Spartan as his dress. It betrayed no hint of wealth.

"I invest it, Shed," Raven said, wearing a mocking smile. "In shipping. Pour the wine." He began cleaning his nails with a knife.

Asa downed his wine before Shed finished pouring the rest. "Fill him up," Raven said. He sipped his own wine. "Shed, why have you been giving me that sour cat's piss when you had this?"

"Nobody gets it without asking. It costs more."

"I'll take this from now on." Raven locked gazes with Asa, tapped his own cheek with his knife blade.

No, Raven wouldn't have to live frugally. The body business would be lucrative. He invested? In shipping? Odd the way he said that. Where the money went might be as interesting as whence it came.

"You threatened my friend," Raven said. "Oh. Excuse me, Shed. A misstatement. It's partner, not friend. Partners don't have to like each other. Little man. You have something to say for yourself?"

Shed shuddered. Damn Raven. He'd said that so Asa would spread it around. Bastard was taking control of his life. Nibbling away at it like a mouse slowly destroying a head of cheese.

"Honest, Mr. Raven. I didn't mean nothing. I was scared. Krage thinks I tipped you. I got to hide, and Shed's scared to put me up. I was just trying to get him to. . . ."

"Shut up. Shed, I thought he was your friend."

"I just did him some favors. I felt sorry for him."

"You'd shelter him from weather, but not from enemies. You're a real gutless wonder, Shed. Maybe I made a mistake. I was going to make you a full partner.

Going to give you the whole business eventually. Thought I'd do you a favor. But you're a yellow-dog creep. Without the guts to deny it." He whirled. "Talk, little man. Tell me about Krage. Tell me about the Enclosure."

Asa went white. He didn't open up till Raven threatened to call the Custodians.

Shed's knees racketed off one another. The hilt of his butcher knife was sweat-moist and slippery. He could not have used the blade, but Asa was too scared to see that. He just squeaked at his team and started rolling. Raven followed them in his own wagon. Shed glanced across the valley. The black castle brooded on the northern skyline, casting its dread shadow across Juniper.

Why was it there? Where had it come from? He rejected the questions. Best to ignore it.

How had he gotten into this? He feared the worst. Raven had no sensibilities.

They left the wagons in the grove, entered the Enclosure. Raven examined Asa's wood stash. "Move these bundles to the wagons. Stack them alongside for now."

"You can't take my wood," Asa protested.

"Shut up." Raven pushed a bundle through the wall. "You first, Shed. Little man, I'll hunt you down if you run off."

They had moved a dozen bundles when Asa whispered, "Shed, one of Krage's goons is watching us." He was about to panic.

Raven was not displeased with the news. "You two go get bundles from the woods."

Asa protested. Raven glared. Asa headed uphill. "How does he know?" he whined at Shed. "He never followed me. I'm sure of that."

Shed shrugged. "Maybe he's a sorcerer. He always knows what I'm thinking."

Raven was gone when they returned. Shed looked around, nervously decided, "Let's get another load."

Raven was waiting next trip. "Take those bundles to Asa's wagon."

"An object lesson," Shed said, pointing into the wagon. Blood ran across the floorboards, seeping from under a pile of wood. "See what kind of man he is?"

"Up the hill now," Raven ordered when they returned. "Lead off, Asa. Collect your tools and torches to start."

Suspicion nagged Shed as he watched Raven build a litter. But no. Even Raven wouldn't stoop that low. Would he?

They stood looking down into the dark mouth of the underworld. "You first, Asa," Raven said. Reluctantly, Asa descended. "You're next, Shed."

"Have a heart, Raven."

"Get moving."

Shed moved. Raven came down behind him.

The Catacombs had a carnal smell, but weaker than Shed had anticipated. A draft stirred Asa's torch.

"Stop," Raven said. He took the brand, examined the gap through which they had entered, nodded, passed the torch back. "Lead on."

The cavern widened and joined a larger cave. Asa halted halfway across. Shed stopped, too. He was surrounded by bones. Bones on the cave floor, bones on racks on the walls, skeletons hanging from hooks. Loose bones in tumbles and piles, all mixed together. Skeletons sleeping amidst the clutter. Bones still within shreds of burial raiment. Skulls leering from wooden pegs on the far wall, empty eyes sinister in the torchlight. A passage urn shared each peg.

There were mummified bodies, too, though only a few. Only the rich demanded mummification. Here riches meant nothing. They were heaped with all the rest.

Asa volunteered, "This is a real old place. The Custodians don't come here anymore, unless maybe to get rid of loose bones. The whole cave is filled up up that way, like they just pushed them out of the way."

"Let's look," Raven said.

Asa was right. The cavern narrowed and its ceiling descended. The passageway was choked with bones. Shed noted the absence of skulls and urns.

Raven chuckled. "Your Custodians aren't as passionate about the dead as you thought, Shed."

"The chambers you see during Spring and Autumn Rites aren't like this," Shed admitted.

"I don't guess anybody cares about the old ones anymore," Asa said.

"Let's go back," Raven suggested. As they walked, he observed, "We all end up here. Rich or poor, weak or strong." He kicked a mummy. "But the rich stay in better shape. Asa, what's down the other way?"

"I only ever went about a hundred yards. More of the same." He was trying to open a passage urn.

Raven grunted, took an urn, opened it, dumped several coins onto his hand. He held them near the torch. "Uhm. How did you explain their age, Asa?"

"Money has no provenance," Shed said.

Asa nodded. "And I made out like I'd found a buried treasure."

"I see. Lead on."

Soon Asa said, "This is as far as I ever went."

"Keep going."

They wandered till even Raven responded to the oppression of the cavern. "Enough. Back to the surface." Once up top, he said, "Get the tools. Damn. I'd hoped for better."

Soon they were back with a spade and ropes. "Shed, dig a hole over there.

Asa, hang on to this end of the rope. When I yell, start pulling." Raven descended into the Catacombs.

Asa remained rooted, as instructed. Shed dug. After a while, Asa asked, "Shed, what's he doing?"

"You don't know? I thought you knew everything he did."

"I just told Krage that. I couldn't keep up with him all night."

Shed grimaced, turned another spadeful of earth. He could guess how Asa worked. By sleeping somewhere most of the time. Spying would have interfered with woodgathering and grave-robbing.

Shed was relieved. Asa didn't know what he and Raven had done. But he would before long.

He looked inside himself and found little self-disgust. Damn! He was accustomed to these crimes already. Raven was making him over in his own image.

Raven shouted. Asa hauled away. He called, "Shed, give me a hand. I can't get this by myself."

Resigned, Shed joined him. Their catch was exactly what he expected, a mummy sliding out of the darkness like some denizen of the deeps of yesteryear. He averted his gaze. "Get his feet, Asa."

Asa gagged. "My God, Shed. My God. What are you doing?"

"Be quiet and do what you're told. That's the best way. Get his feet."

They moved the body into the brush near Shed's pit. A passage urn rolled out of a bundle tied upon its chest. The bundle contained another two dozen urns. So. The hole was for burying empty urns. Why didn't Raven fill his pockets down there?

"Let's get out of here, Shed," Asa whined.

"Back to your rope." Urns took time to empty. And Raven had two men up top with little to do but think. So. They were busy-work. And an incentive, of course. Two dozen urns with each cadaver would build up quite a pile.

"Shed. . . ."

"Where you going to run to, Asa?" The day was clear and unseasonably warm, but it was still winter. There was no way out of Juniper. "He'd find you. Go back to your rope. You're in it now, like it or not." Shed resumed digging.

Raven sent up six mummies. Each carried its bundle of urns. Then Raven returned. He studied Asa's ashen face, Shed's resignation. "Your turn, Shed."

Shed gulped, opened his mouth, swallowed his protest, slunk toward the hole. He lingered over it, a hair's breadth from rebellion.

"Move it, Shed. We don't have forever."

Marron Shed went down among the dead.

It seemed he was in the Catacombs forever, numbly selecting cadavers, collecting urns, dragging his grisly booty to the rope. His mind had entered another reality. This was the dream, the nightmare. At first he did not understand when Raven called for him to come up.

He clambered into gathering dusk. "Is that enough? Can we go now?"

"No," Raven replied. "We've got sixteen. I figure we can get thirty on the wagons."

"Oh. Okay."

"You haul up," Raven said. "Asa and I will go down."

Shed hauled. In the silvery light of a three-quarters moon the dead faces seemed accusing. He swallowed his loathing and placed each with the others, then emptied urns.

He was tempted to take the money and run. He stayed more out of greed than fear of Raven. He was a partner this time. Thirty bodies at thirty leva meant nine hundred leva to share out. Even if he took the small cut, he would be richer than he'd ever dreamed.

What was that? Not Raven's order to haul away. It sounded like someone screaming. . . . He nearly ran. He did go to pieces momentarily. Raven's bellowing brought him together. The man's cold, calm contempt had vanished.

Shed heaved. This one was heavy. He grunted, strained. . . . Raven came scrambling up. His clothing was torn. A bloody gash marked one cheek. His knife was red. He whirled, grabbed the rope. "Pull!" he shouted. "Damn you, pull!"

Asa came out a moment later, tied to the rope. "What happened? My God, what happened?" Asa was breathing, and that was about it.

"Something jumped us. It tore him up before I could kill it."

"A Guardian. I warned you. Get another torch. Let's see how bad he is." Raven just sat there panting, flustered. Shed got the torch, lighted it.

Asa's wounds were not as bad as he had feared. There was a lot of blood, and Asa was in shock, but he wasn't dying. "We ought to get out of here, Raven. Before the Custodians come."

Raven recovered his composure. "No. There was only one. I killed it. We're in this now. Let's get it done right."

"What about Asa?"

"I don't know. Let's get to work."

"Raven, I'm exhausted."

"You're going to get a lot tireder before we're done. Come on. Let's get the mess cleaned up."

They moved the bodies to the wagons, then the tools, then carted Asa down. As they worked the litter through the wall, Shed asked, "What should we do with him?"

Raven looked at him as though he were a moron. "What do you think, Shed?"

"But. . . ."

"It doesn't much matter now, does it?"

"I guess not." But it did matter. Asa wasn't much, but Shed knew him. He was no friend, but they had helped one another out. . . . "No. Can't do it, Raven. He can make it. If I was sure he was checking out, yeah. Okay. No body, no questions. But I can't kill him."

"Well. A little spirit after all. How are you going to keep him quiet? He's the kind who gets throats cut with loose talk."

"I'll handle him."

"Whatever you say, partner. It's your neck."

The night was well along when they reached the black castle. Raven went in first. Shed followed closely. They pulled into the same passage as before. The drill was the same. After they laid out the bodies, a tall, lean creature went down the line. "Ten. Ten. Thirty. Ten. Ten." And so forth.

Raven protested vigorously. The only offers above ten were for the men who had followed them to the Enclosure and for Asa, who remained in his wagon.

The tall being faced Raven. "These have been dead too long. They have little value. Take them back if you're not satisfied."

"All right. All right. Let's have it."

The being counted out coins. Raven pocketed six of each ten. He handed the rest to Shed. As he did so, he told the tall being, "This man is my partner. He may come alone."

The tall figure inclined its head, took something from within its clothing, handed it to Shed. It was a silver pendant in the form of serpents entwined.

"Wear that if you come up alone," Raven said. "That's your safe-conduct." Under his icy stare Shed slipped the pendant into a pocket already filled with silver.

He ran the arithmetic. One hundred twelve leva as his share. It would have taken him half a decade to accumulate that much honestly. He was rich! Damn him, he was rich! He could do anything he wanted. No more debts. No more Krage killing him slowly. No more gruel every meal. Turn the Lily into something decent. Maybe find a place where his mother would have proper care. Women. All the women he could handle.

As he turned his wagon, he glimpsed a high chunk of wall that hadn't been there last visit. A face stared out. It was the face of the man he and Raven had brought in alive. Its eyes watched him.

14

Juniper: Duretile

Whisper delivered us to a broken-down castle named Duretile. It overlooks Juniper in general and the Enclosure in specific. For a week we had no contact with our hosts. We had no language in common. Then we were graced with the presence of a thug named Bullock who spoke the languages of the Jewel Cities.

Bullock was some kind of enforcer for the local religion. Which I could not figure out at all. It looks like a death cult at first. Look again and you find death or the dead not worshipped but revered, with bodies fanatically preserved against some millennial revival. The whole character of Juniper is shaped by this, except for the Buskin, where life has so many concerns more vital than the welfare of the dead.

I took an instant dislike to Bullock. He struck me as violence-prone and sadistic, a policeman who would solve his cases with a truncheon. He would survive when the Lady annexed Juniper. Her military governors have a need for his ilk.

I expected annexation to occur within days of the Captain's arrival. We'd have it scoped out before he got here. One word from Charm would do it. I saw no indication the Duke's people could stop it.

As soon as Feather and Whisper had all our people in, including translators, Bullock, the Duke himself, and a man named Hargadon, who was senior Custodian of the Dead—meaning he ran the Catacombs where bodies were stored—they led us into the bitter cold atop Duretile's north wall. The Duke extended an arm. "That fortress over there is why I asked for help."

I looked at it and shuddered. There was something creepy about the place.

"We call it the black castle," he said. "It's been there for centuries." And then he gave us a chunk almost too big to swallow. "It started out as a little black rock lying beside a dead man. The man who found them tried to pick the rock up. He died. And the rock started growing. It's been growing ever since. Our ancestors experimented on it. They attacked it. Nothing harmed it. Anybody who touched it died. For the sake of their sanity, they decided to ignore it."

I shaded my eyes, stared at the castle. Not that unusual, from Duretile, except it was black and gave me the creeps.

The Duke continued, "For centuries it hardly grew. It's only a few generations since it stopped looking like a rock." He got a haunted look. "They say there are things living inside there."

I smiled. What did he expect? A fortress exists to surround something, whether built or grown.

Hargadon assumed the narrative. He had been in his job too long. He'd developed an official's pompous style. "For the last several years it's grown damned fast. The Custodial Office became concerned when we heard rumors—out of the Buskin, so unreliable to be sure—saying the creatures inside were buying cadavers. The accuracy of those rumors remains a source of heated debate within the Office. However, no one can deny that we're not getting enough corpses out of the Buskin these days. Our street patrols collect fewer than they did ten years ago. Times are leaner now. The street poor are more numerous. More should be expiring of exposure."

A real sweetheart, this Hargadon. He sounded like a manufacturer whining because his profit margin was down.

He continued, "It's been hypothesized that the castle may soon be beyond a need to purchase bodies—if it is at all. I'm not convinced." Came down squarely on both sides of a question, too. That's my boy. "Its occupants may become numerous enough to come take what they want."

Elmo asked, "You think people are selling bodies, why don't you grab them and make them talk?"

Time for the policeman to enter his bit. Bullock said, "We can't catch them." He had a but-if-they'd-let-me-do-it-my-way tone. "It's happening down in the Buskin, you see. It's another world down there. You don't find out much if you're an outsider."

Whisper and Feather stood a bit apart, examining the black castle. Their faces were grim.

The Duke wanted something for nothing. In essence, he wanted to stop worrying about that fortress. He said we could do whatever it took to eliminate his worry. Only we'd have to do it his way. Like he wanted us to stay inside Duretile while *his* men and Hargadon's acted as our eyes, ears and hands. He was afraid of repercussions our presence could cause if known.

A few Rebel fugitives had come to Juniper after their defeat at Charm. The Lady was known here, though little considered. The Duke feared the refugees would incite trouble if he was suspected of collaborating.

In some ways he was an ideal overlord. All he wanted from his people was to be left alone. He was willing to grant the same favor.

So, for a while, we stayed tucked away—till Whisper became irritated by the quality of information we were given.

It was filtered. Sanitized, it was useless. She cornered the Duke and *told* him her men would be going out with his.

He actually stood up to her for a few minutes. The battle was bitter. She threatened to pull out, leaving him twisting in the wind. Pure bluff. She and Feather were intensely interested in the black castle. Armed force could not have levered them out of Juniper.

The Duke subdued, she turned on the Custodians. Bullock was stubbornly jealous of his prerogatives. I do not know how she brought him around. He never was gracious about it.

I became his companion on investigative jaunts, mainly because I learned the language quickly. Nobody down below paid me any mind.

Him they did. He was a walking terror. People crossed the street to avoid him. I guess he had a bad reputation.

Then came news which miraculously cleared the obstacles the Duke and Custodians had dumped in our path.

"You hear?" Elmo asked. "Somebody broke into their precious Catacombs. Bullock is smoking. His boss is having a shit hemorrhage."

I tried to digest that, could not. "More detail, if you please." Elmo tends to abbreviate.

"During the winter they let poor people get away with sneaking into the Enclosure. To collect deadwood for firewood. Somebody got in who decided to take more. Found a way into the Catacombs. Three or four men."

"I still don't get the whole picture, Elmo." He enjoys being coaxed.

"All right. All right. They got inside and stole all the passage urns they could lay hands on. Took them out, emptied them, and buried them in a pit. They also lifted a bunch of old-time mummies. I never seen such moaning and carrying on. You better back off your scheme for getting into the Catacombs."

I had mentioned a desire to see what went on down there. The whole setup was so alien I wanted a closer look. Preferably unchaperoned. "Think they'd get overwrought, eh?"

"Overwrought isn't the half. Bullock is talking bad. I'd hate to be those guys and get caught by him."

"Yeah? I'd better check this out."

Bullock was in Duretile at the time, coordinating his work with that of the Duke's incompetent secret police.

Those guys were a joke. They were practically celebrities, and not a one had the guts to go down into the Buskin, where really interesting things happened.

There is a Buskin in every city, though the name varies. It is a slum so bad the police dare go in only in force. Law there is haphazard at best, mostly enforced by self-proclaimed magistrates supported by toughs they recruit themselves. It is a very subjective justice they mete, likely to be swift, savage, unforgiving, and directed by graft.

I caught up with Bullock, told him, "Till this latest business is cleaned up, I stick like your leg." He scowled. His heavy cheeks reddened. "Orders," I lied, faking an apologetic tone.

"Yeah? All right. Come on."

"Where you headed?"

"The Buskin. Thing like this had to come out of the Buskin. I'm going to track it down." He had guts, for all his other failings. Nothing intimidated him.

I wanted to see the Buskin. He might be the best guide available. I'd heard he went there often, without interference. His reputation was that nasty. A good shadow to walk in.

"Now?" I asked.

"Now." He led me out into the cold and down the hill. He did not ride. One of his little affectations. He never rode. He set a brisk pace, as a man will who is accustomed to getting things done afoot.

"What're we going to look for?" I asked.

"Old coins. The chamber they defiled goes back several centuries. If somebody spent a lot of old money in the last couple days, we might get a line on our men."

I frowned. "I don't know spending patterns here. Places I've been, though, people can hang on to a family hoard for ages, then have one black sheep up and spend it all. A few old coins might not mean anything."

"We're looking for a flood, not a few. For a man who spent a fistful. There were three or four men involved. Odds are good one of them is a fool." Bullock had a good grasp of the stupid side of human nature. Maybe because he was close to it himself. Meow.

"We'll be real nice doing the tracing," he told me, as though he expected me to hammer people in outrage. His values were the only ones he could imagine. "The man we want will run when he hears me asking questions."

"We chase him?"

"Just enough so he keeps moving. Maybe he'll lead us somewhere. I know several bosses down there who could've engineered this. If one of them did, I want his balls on a platter."

He spoke in a fever, like a crusader. Did he have some special grievance against the crime lords of the slum? I asked.

"Yeah. I came out of the Buskin. A tough kid who got lucky and got on with the Custodians. My dad wasn't lucky. Tried to buck a protection gang. He paid, and they didn't protect him from another gang in the same racket. He said he wasn't going to put out good money for something he wasn't getting. They cut his throat. I was one of the Custodians who picked him up. They stood around laughing and cracking jokes. The ones responsible."

"Ever settle them up?" I asked, certain of the answer.

"Yeah. Brought them into the Catacombs, too." He glanced at the black castle, half obscured by mists drifting across the far slope. "If I'd heard the rumors about that place, maybe I'd have. . . . No, I wouldn't."

I didn't think so myself. Bullock was a fanatic of sorts. He'd never break the rules of the profession that had brought him out of the Buskin, unless he could advance its cause by so doing.

"Think we'll start right at the waterfront," he told me. "Work our way up the hill. Tavern to tavern, whorehouse to whorehouse. Maybe hint that there's a reward floating around." He ground one fist into another, a man restraining anger. There was a lot of that bottled up inside him. Someday he would blow up good.

We'd gotten an early start. I saw more taverns, cathouses, and reeking dives than I'd passed through in a dozen years. And in every one Bullock's advent engendered a sudden, frightened hush and a promise of dutiful cooperation.

But promises were all we got. We could find no trace of any old money, except a few coins that had been around too long to be the booty we sought.

Bullock was not discouraged. "Something will turn up," he said. "Times are tough. Just take a little patience." He looked thoughtful. "Might just put some of your boys down here. They aren't known, and they look tough enough to make it."

"They are." I smiled, mentally assembling a team including Elmo, Goblin, Pawnbroker, Kingpin, and a few others. Be great if Raven were still with the Company and could go in with them. They would be running the Buskin inside six months. Which gave me an idea to take up with Whisper.

If we wanted to know what was happening, we should take charge of the Buskin. We could bring in One-Eye. The little wizard was a gangster born. Stand out some, though. I hadn't seen another black face since we'd crossed the Sea of Torments.

"Had an idea?" Bullock asked, about to enter a place called the Iron Lily. "You look like your brain is smoking."

"Maybe. On something down the line. If it gets tougher than we expect."

The Iron Lily looked like every other place we'd been, only more so. The guy who ran it cringed. He didn't know nothing, hadn't heard nothing, and promised to scream for Bullock if anybody so much as spent a single gersh struck before the accession of the present Duke. Every word bullshit. I was glad to get out of there. I was afraid the place would collapse on me before he finished kissing Bullock's ass.

"Got an idea," Bullock said. "Moneylenders."

Took me a second to catch it and to see where the idea had come from. The guy in the tavern, whining about his debts. "Good thinking." A man in the snares of a moneylender would do anything to wriggle away.

"This is Krage's territory. He's one of the nastiest. Let's drop in."

No fear in the man. His confidence in the power of his office was so strong he dared walk into a den of cutthroats without blinking an eye. I faked it good, but I was scared. The villain had his own army, and it was jumpy.

We found out why in a moment. Our man had come up on the short end of somebody in the last couple days. He was down on his back, mummified in bandages.

Bullock chuckled. "Customers getting frisky, Krage? Or did one of your boys try to promote himself?"

Krage eyed us from a face of stone. "I help you with something, Inquisitor?"

"Probably not. You'd lie to me if the truth would save your soul, you bloodsucker."

"Flattery will get you nowhere. What do you want, you parasite?"

Tough boy, this Krage. Struck from the same mold as Bullock, but he had drifted into a socially less honored profession. Not much to choose between them, I thought. Priest and moneylender. And that was what Krage was saying.

"Cute. I'm looking for a guy."

"No shit."

"He's got a lot of old money. Cajian period coinage."

"Am I supposed to know him?"

Bullock shrugged. "Maybe he owes somebody."

"Money's got no provenance down here, Bullock."

Bullock told me: "A proverb of the Buskin." He faced Krage. "This money does. This money better, let's say. This is a big one, Krage. Not a little let's-look-around-and-make-a-show. Not some bump-and-run. We're going the route. Anybody covers on it, they go down with this boy. You remember Bullock said it."

For a second Bullock made an impression. The message got through. Then Krage blank-faced us again. "You're sniffing up the wrong tree, Inquisitor."

"Just telling you so you'd know."

"What did this guy do?"

"Hit somebody who don't take hitting."

Krage's eyebrows rose. He looked puzzled. He could think of no one who fit that description. "Who?"

"Uhn-uh. Just don't let your boys take any old money without you checking the source and getting back to me. Hear?"

"Said your piece, Inquisitor?"

"Yeah."

"Shouldn't you better be going, then?"

We went. I didn't know the rules of the game, so didn't know how the locals would score the exchange. I rated it too close to call.

Outside, I asked, "Would he have told us if he'd been paid in old coin?"

"No. Not until he looked into it, at least. But he hasn't seen any old money."

I wondered why he thought that. I didn't ask. These were his people. "He might know something. Thought I saw a glint in his eye a couple times."

"Maybe. Maybe not. Let him stew."

"Maybe if you'd told him why. . . ."

"No! That doesn't get out. Not even a rumor. If people thought we couldn't protect their dead or them after they kick off, all hell would break loose." He made a downward gesture with one hand. "Juniper like that. Crunch." We walked on. He muttered, "All hell would break loose." And after another half-block: "That's why we've got to get these guys. Not so much to punish them. To shut them up."

"I see." We strolled back the direction we had come, planning to resume tavern-hopping and to see a moneylender named Gilbert when we reached his territory. "Hey?"

Bullock stopped. "What?"

I shook my head. "Nothing. Thought I saw a ghost. Guy down the street. . . . Walked like somebody I used to know."

"Maybe it was."

"Nah. Long ago and far away. Long dead now. Just because I was thinking about him a little bit ago."

"I figure we got time for half a dozen more visits. Then we head uphill. Don't want to hang around here after dark."

I looked at him, one eyebrow raised.

"Hell, man, it gets dangerous down here when the sun goes down." He chuckled and gave me one of his rare smiles. It was the genuine article.

For one moment then, I liked him.

Juniper: Death of a Gangster

Shed had long, violent arguments with his mother. She never accused him directly, but she left little doubt she suspected him of hideous crimes.

He and Raven took turns nursing Asa.

Then it was time to face Krage. He did not want to go. He was afraid Krage might have lumped him with Raven and Asa. But if he didn't go, Krage would come to him. And Krage was looking for people to hurt. . . . Shaky, Shed trudged up the frozen street. Snow fell in lazy, fat flakes.

One of Krage's men ushered him into the presence. There was no sign of Count, but word was out that the big man was recovering. Too damned stupid to die, Shed thought.

"Ah, Shed," Krage said from the deeps of a huge chair. "How are you?"

"Cold. How're you keeping?" Krage worried him when he was affable.

"Be all right." Krage plucked at his bandages. "Close call. I was lucky. Come to make your payment?"

"How much do I owe, all told? You buying up my debts, I couldn't keep track."

"You can pay out?" Krage's eyes narrowed.

"I don't know. I have ten leva."

Krage sighed dramatically. "You got enough. Didn't think you had it in you, Shed. Well. You win some and you lose some. It's eight and some change."

Shed counted out nine coins. Krage made change. "You've had a run of luck this winter, Shed."

"Sure have."

"You seen Asa?" Krage's voice tautened.

"Not since three days ago. Why?"

"Nothing important. We're even, Shed. But it's time I collected that favor. Raven. I want him."

"Krage, I don't want to tell you your business, but that's one man you'd better leave alone. He's crazy. He's nasty and he's tough. He'd as soon kill you as say hi. I don't mean no disrespect, but he acts like you're a big joke."

"The joke will be on him, Shed." Krage dragged himself out of his chair, wincing. He grabbed his wound. "The joke will be on him."

"Maybe next time he won't let *you* get away, Krage."

Fear crossed Krage's features. "Shed, it's him or me. If I don't kill him, my business will fall apart."

"Where will it be if he kills you?"

Again that flicker of fear. "I don't have any choice. Be ready when I need you, Shed. Soon now."

Shed bobbed his head and retreated. He ought to get out of the Buskin, he thought. He could afford it. But where would he go? Krage could find him anywhere in Juniper. Running didn't appeal, anyway. The Lily was home. He had to weather this. One or the other would die, and either way he would be off the hook.

He was in the middle now. He hated Krage. Krage had humiliated him for years, keeping him in debt, stealing food from his mouth with ridiculous interest rates. On the other hand, Raven could connect him with the black castle and crimes in the Enclosure.

The Custodians were on the hunt, looking for somebody spending a lot of old money. Little had been said publicly, but Bullock being on the case told Shed just how seriously they were taking the case up the hill. He'd nearly had a stroke when Bullock walked into the Lily.

What had become of the passage money? Shed hadn't seen any of it. He supposed Raven still had it. He and Raven were partners now. . . .

"What did Krage say?" Raven asked when Shed reached the Lily.

"Wants me to help kill you."

"I thought so. Shed, it's late in the season. It's time to send Krage up the hill. Which way are you leaning, partner? Him or me?"

"I. . . . Uh. . . ."

"In the long run you're better off getting rid of Krage. He'd find a way to get the Lily eventually."

True, Shed reflected. "All right. What do we do?"

"Tomorrow, go tell him you think I've been selling bodies. That you think Asa was my partner. That you think I did Asa in. Asa was your friend and you're upset. It'll all be just near enough reality to confuse him. . . . What's the matter?"

Always a trap. Raven was right. Krage would believe the story. But Shed had hoped for a less direct role. If Raven screwed up, Marron Shed would be found in a gutter with his throat cut.

"Nothing."

"All right. Night after tomorrow night, I'll go out. You run to tell Krage. I'll let his men track me. Krage will want to be in at the kill. I'll ambush him."

"You did that before, didn't you?"

"He'll come anyway. He's stupid."

Shed swallowed. "That isn't a plan that does much for my nerves."

"Your nerves aren't my problem, Shed. They're yours. *You* lost them. Only you can find them again."

Krage bought Shed's story. He was ecstatic because Raven was such a villain. "If I didn't want him myself, I'd yell for the Custodians. You did good, Shed. I should have suspected Asa. He never brought no news worth hearing."

Shed whined, "Who would buy bodies, Krage?"

Krage grinned. "Don't worry your ugly head. Let me know next time he goes on one of his jaunts. We'll rig up a little surprise."

Next night Shed reported according to plan. And suffered all the disappointment he expected of life. Krage insisted he join the hunt.

"What good would I be, Krage? I'm not even armed. And he's one tough nut. You won't take him without a fight."

"I don't expect to. You're coming along just in case."

"In case?"

"In case there's a trap in this and I want to lay hands on you fast."

Shed shuddered, whined, "I done right by you. Don't I always do right by you?"

"You always do what a coward would. Which is why I don't trust you. Anybody can scare you. And you had all that money. It occurs to me you might be in the racket with Raven."

Shed went cold. Krage donned his coat. "Let's go, Shed. Stay right beside me. You try to wander off, I'll kill you."

Shed started shaking. He was dead. All he had gone through to get Krage off his back. . . . It wasn't fair. It just wasn't fair. Nothing ever worked for him. He stumbled into the street, wondering what he could do and knowing there was no escape. Tears froze on his cheeks.

No exit. If he fled, Krage would be warned. If he did not, Krage would kill him when Raven sprang his ambush. What was his mother going to do?

He had to *do* something. Had to find some guts, make a decision, *act*. He couldn't surrender to fate and hope for luck. That meant the Catacombs or black castle before dawn.

He had lied to Krage. He had a butcher knife up his left sleeve. He had put it there out of sheer bravado. Krage hadn't searched him. Old Shed armed? Ha! Not likely. He might get himself hurt.

Old Shed did go armed sometimes, but he never advertised the fact. The knife did wonders for his confidence. He could tell himself he would use it, and he'd believe the lie long enough to get by, but in any tight spot he would let fate run its course.

His fate was sealed. . . . Unless he whipped it heads-up, no holds barred.

How?

Krage's men were amused by his terror. There were six of them. . . . Then there were seven . . . and eight, as those tracking Raven reported in. Could he hope to beat those odds? Raven himself didn't stand a chance.

You are a dead man, a tiny voice whispered, over and over. *Dead man. Dead man.*

"He's working his way down Chandler's," a shadow reported. "Going into all the little alleyways."

Krage asked Shed, "Think he'll find anything this late in the winter? The weaklings have all died."

Shed shrugged. "I wouldn't know." He rubbed his left arm against his side. The knife's presence helped, but not much.

His terror peaked and began to recede. His mind cooled to an unemotional numbness. Fear in abeyance, he tried to find the unseen exit.

Again someone loomed out of the darkness, reported they were a hundred feet from Raven's wagon. Raven had gone into an alley ten minutes ago. He hadn't come out.

"He spot you?" Krage growled.

"I don't think so. But you never know."

Krage eyed Shed. "Shed, would he abandon his team and wagon?"

"How would I know?" Shed squeaked. "Maybe he found something."

"Let's take a look." They moved to the alley, one of countless dead-end breezeways opening off Chandler's Lane. Krage stared into the darkness, head canted slightly. "Quiet as the Catacombs. Check it out, Luke."

"Boss?"

"Take it easy, Luke. Old Shed is going to be right behind you. Won't you, Shed?"

"Krage. . . ."

"Move out!"

Shed shambled forward. Luke advanced cautiously, wicked knife probing the darkness. Shed tried to talk to him. "Shut up!" he snarled. "Don't you have a weapon?"

"No," Shed lied. He glanced back. It was just the two of them.

They reached the dead end. No Raven. "I'll be damned," Luke said. "How did he get out?"

"I don't know. Let's find out." This might be his chance.

"Here we go," Luke said. "He climbed this downspout."

Shed's guts knotted. His throat tightened. "Give it a try. Maybe we can follow him."

"Yeah." Luke started up.

Shed didn't think about it. The butcher knife materialized in his hand. His hand slammed forward. Luke arched back, dropped. Shed jumped on him, jammed a palm against his mouth, held on for the minute it took him to die. He backed away, unable to believe he'd done it.

"What's going on back there?" Krage demanded.

"Can't find anything," Shed yelled. He dragged Luke against a wall, buried him under trash and snow, ran to the downspout.

Krage's approach made a marvelous incentive. He grunted, strained, popped a muscle, reached the roof. It consisted of a skirt two feet wide set at a shallow angle, then twelve feet rising at forty-five degrees, above which the roof was flat. Shed leaned against the steep slate, panting, still unable to believe that he had killed a man. He heard voices below, began moving sideways.

Someone snarled, "They're gone, Krage. No Raven. No Luke and no Shed, either."

"That bastard. I knew he was setting me up."

"Why did Luke go with him, then?"

"Hell, I don't know. Don't stand there. Look around. They got out of here somehow."

"Hey. Over here. Somebody went up this spout. Maybe they're after Raven."

"Climb the damned thing. Find out. Luke! Shed!"

"Over here," a voice called. Shed froze. What the hell? Raven? Had to be Raven.

He inched along, trying to fake himself into believing there wasn't thirty-five feet of nothing behind his heels. He reached a ridged corner where he could clamber up to the flat top.

"Over here. I think we got him cornered."

"Get up there, you bastards!" Krage raged.

Lying motionless on the cold, icy tar, Shed watched two shadows appear on the skirt and begin easing toward the voice. A squeal of metal and vicious cursing proclaimed the fate of a third climber. "Twisted my ankle, Krage," the man complained.

"Come on," Krage growled. "We'll find another way up."

Run while you got the chance, Shed thought. *Go home and hole up till it's over*. But he could not. He slid down to the skirt and crept after Krage's men.

Someone cried out, scrabbled for a hold, plunged into the darkness between buildings. Krage shouted. Nobody answered.

Shed crossed to the roof next door. It was flat and forested with chimneys.

"Raven?" he called softly. "It's me. Shed." He touched the knife in his sleeve, still unable to believe that he'd used it.

A shape materialized. Shed settled into a sitting position, arms around his knees. "What now?" he asked.

"What're you doing here?"

"Krage dragged me along. I was supposed to be the first one dead if it was a trap." He told Raven what he had done.

"Damn! You've got guts after all."

"He backed me into a corner. What now?"

"The odds are getting better. Let me think about it."

Krage shouted out in Chandler's Lane. Raven yelled back, "Over here! We're right behind him." He told Shed: "I don't know how long I can fool him. I was going to pick them off one at a time. I didn't know he'd bring an army."

"My nerves are shot," Shed said. Heights were another of the thousand things that terrified him.

"Hang on. It's a long way from over." Raven yelled, "Cut him off, why don't you?" He took off. "Come on, Shed."

Shed could not keep up. He wasn't as nimble as Raven.

A shape loomed out of the darkness. He squeaked.

"That you, Shed?" It was one of Krage's men. Shed's heartbeat doubled.

"Yeah. You seen Raven?"

"No. Where's Luke?"

"Damnit, he was headed right at you. How could you miss him? Look here." Shed indicated disturbances in traces of snow.

"Look, man, I didn't see him. Don't come on at me like you was Krage. I'll kick your ass up around your ears."

"All right. All right. Calm down. I'm scared and I want to get it over. Luke fell off. Back there. Slipped on some ice or something. Be careful."

"I heard. Sounded like Milt, though. I'd have sworn it was Milt. This is stupid. He can pick us off up here. We ought to back off and try something else."

"Uhn-uh. I want him now. I don't want him tracking me down tomorrow." Shed was amazed. How easily the lies came! Silently, he cursed the man because he wouldn't turn his back. "You got an extra knife or something?"

"You? Use a knife? Come on. Stick with me, Shed. I'll look out for you."

"Sure. Look, the trail goes that way. Let's get it done."

The man turned to examine Raven's tracks. Shed drew his knife and hit him hard. The man let out a yell, twisted. The knife broke. Shed almost pitched off the roof. His victim did. People shouted questions. Krage and his men all seemed to be on the rooftops now.

When Shed stopped shaking, he started moving again, trying to recall the layout of the neighborhood. He wanted to get down and head home. Raven could finish this insanity.

Shed ran into Krage on the next roof. "Krage!" he whined. "God! Let me out of here! He'll kill us all!"

"I'll kill you, Shed. It was a trap, wasn't it?"

"Krage, no!" What could he do? He didn't have the butcher knife now. Fake. Whine and fake. "Krage, you got to get out of here. He already got Luke and Milt and somebody else. He would've gotten me when he got Luke, except he fell down and I got away—only he caught up again when I was talking to one of your guys right over there. They got fighting, and one of them went off the edge; I don't know which, but I bet it wasn't Raven. We got to get down from here, on account of we can't tell who we're running into so we got to be careful. I could have had him this last time, only I didn't have a weapon and we didn't know it wasn't one of our own guys coming. Raven don't have that problem. Anybody he sees he knows is an enemy, so he don't have to be so careful. . . ."

"Shut up, Shed."

Krage was buying it. Shed talked a little louder, hoping Raven would hear, come, and finish it.

There was a cry across the rooftops. "That's Teskus," Krage growled. "That's four. Right?"

Shed bobbed his head. "That we know about. Maybe there's only you and me now. Krage, we should get out of here before he finds us."

"Might be something to what you say, Shed. Might be. We shouldn't have come up here. Come on."

Shed followed, keeping up the chatter. "It was Luke's idea. He thought he'd make points with you. See, we saw him at the top of this drainspout and he didn't see us, so Luke said why don't we go after him and get him, and old Krage will. . . ."

"Shut up, Shed. For God's sake, shut up. Your voice sickens me."

"Yes, sir, Mr. Krage. Only I can't. I'm so scared. . . ."

"If you don't, I'll shut you up permanent. You won't have to worry about Raven."

Shed stopped talking. He had pushed as far as he dared.

Krage halted a short time later. "We'll set an ambush near his wagon. He'll come back for it, won't he?"

"I expect so, Mr. Krage. But what good will I be? I mean, I don't have a weapon, and wouldn't know how to use one if I did."

"Shut up. You're right. You're not much good, Shed. But I think you'll do fine as a distraction. You get his attention. Talk to him. I'll hit him from behind."

"Krage. . . ."

"Shut up." Krage rolled over the side of the building, clung to the parapet while getting a solid foothold. Shed leaned forward. Three stories to the ground.

He kicked Krage's fingers. Krage cursed, scrabbled for a fresh hold, missed, dropped, yelled, hit with a muted thump. Shed watched his vague shape twitch, become still.

"I did it again." He started shaking. "Can't stay here. His men might find me." He swung over the parapet and monkeyed down the side of the building, more afraid of being caught than of falling.

Krage was still breathing. In fact, he was conscious but paralyzed. "You were right, Krage. It was a trap. You shouldn't have pushed me. You made me hate you more than I was scared of you." He looked around. It wasn't as late as he had thought. The rooftop hunt hadn't lasted long. Where was Raven, anyway?

Somebody had to clean up. He grabbed Krage, dragged him toward Raven's wagon. Krage squealed. For a moment Shed was afraid someone would investigate. No one did. This was the Buskin.

Krage screamed when Shed hoisted him into the wagon. "Comfy, Krage?"

He retrieved Luke next, then went seeking other bodies. He found another three. None were Raven. He muttered, "If he doesn't show in a half hour, I'll take them up myself and the hell with him." Then: "What's come over you, Marron Shed? Letting this go to your head? So you found some guts. So what? That don't make you no Raven."

Someone was coming. He snatched a booty dagger, faded into a shadow.

Raven tumbled a body into the wagon. "How the hell?"

"I collected them," Shed explained.

"Who are they?"

"Krage and his men."

"I thought he ran for it. Figured I had to go through it all again. What happened?"

Shed explained. Raven shook his head in disbelief. "You? Shed?"

"I guess there's only so much they can scare you."

"True. But I never thought you'd figure it out. Shed, you amaze me. Disappoint me, too, some. I wanted Krage myself."

"That's him making the noise. He's got a broken back or something. Kill him if you want."

"He's worth more alive."

Shed nodded. Poor Krage. "Where are the rest of them?"

"There's one on the roof. Guess the other one got away."

"Damn. That means it's not over."

"We can get him later."

"Meanwhile, he goes and gets the others and we have them all after us."

"You think they'd risk their lives to avenge Krage? No way. They'll be fighting among themselves. Trying to take over. Wait here. I'll get the other one."

"Hurry up," Shed said. The reaction was catching up. He had survived. The old Shed was coming back, dragging all his hysteria with him.

Coming down from the castle, with pink and purple strands of dawn smearing the gaps between the Wolanders, Shed asked, "Why is he screaming?"

The tall being had laughed and paid a hundred twenty leva for Krage. His shrieks could still be heard.

"I don't know. Don't look back, Shed. Do what you have to and move on." And, a moment later: "I'm glad it's over."

"Over? What do you mean?"

"That was my last visit." Raven patted his pocket. "I have enough."

"Me, too. I'm out of debt. I can refurbish the Lily, set my mother up in her own place, and have plenty to make it next winter, no matter what business is like. I'm going to forget that castle exists."

"I don't think so, Shed. You want to get away from it, better come with me. It'll always be calling when you want some fast money."

"I couldn't leave. I have to look out for my mother."

"All right. I warned you." Then Raven asked, "What about Asa? He's going to be a problem. The Custodians are going to keep looking till they find the people who raided the Catacombs. He's the weak link."

"I can handle Asa."

"I hope so, Shed. I hope so."

Krage's disappearance was the talk of the Buskin. Shed played a baffled role, claiming he knew nothing, despite rumors to the contrary. His story held up. He was Shed the coward. The one man who knew differently did not contradict him.

The hard part was facing his mother. Old June said nothing, but her blind stare was accusing. She made him feel evil, an infidel, and disowned in the secret reaches of her mind. The gap had become unbridgeable.

16

Juniper: Nasty Surprise

Bullock looked me up next time he wanted to go downhill. Maybe he just wanted company. He had no local friends.

"What's up?" I asked when he barged into my tiny office cum dispensary.

"Get your coat. Buskin time again."

His eagerness excited me for no reason other than that I was bored with Duretile. I pitied my comrades. They hadn't yet had a chance to get out. The place was a drudge.

So away we went, and going down the hill, past the Enclosure, I asked, "Why all the excitement?"

He replied, "Not really excitement. Not even anything to do with us, probably. Remember that sweetheart of a moneylender?"

"In the bandages?"

"Yeah. Krage. He's vanished. Him and half of his boys. Seems he took a crack at the guy who cut him. And hasn't been seen since."

I frowned. That did not seem remarkable. Gangsters are always disappearing, then popping up again.

"Over there." Bullock pointed to some brush along the Enclosure wall. "That's where our men got inside." He indicated a stand of trees across the way. "Parked their wagons there. We've got a witness who saw those. Filled with wood, he says. Come on. I'll show you." He pushed into the brush, dropped to hands and knees. I followed, grumbling because I was getting wet. The north wind did nothing to improve matters.

The interior of the Enclosure was seedier than its exterior. Bullock showed me several dozen bundles of wood found in the brush near the breach.

"Looks like they were moving a lot."

"I figure they needed a lot to cover the bodies. Cut it up there." He indicated trees above us, back toward Duretile. The castle stood limned against streamers of cloud, a grey stone rockpile one earth tremor short of collapse.

I examined the bundles. Bullock's associates had dragged them out and stacked them, which may not have been smart detective work. Looked to me like they had been cut and bundled over a period of weeks. Some ends were more weathered than others. I mentioned that to Bullock.

"I noticed. Way I figure, somebody was getting wood regular. They found the Catacombs by accident. That's when they got greedy."

"Uhm." I considered the woodpile. "Figure they were selling it?"

"No. That we know. Nobody has been selling Enclosure wood. Probably a family or a group of neighbors using the wood themselves."

"You check on wagon rentals?"

"How stupid do you think people are? Rent a wagon for a raid on the Catacombs?"

I shrugged. "We're counting on one of them being stupid, aren't we?"

He admitted, "You're right. It should be checked. But it's hard when I'm the only one who has guts enough to do legwork in the Buskin. I'm hoping we get lucky somewhere else. If I have to, I'll cover it. When there's nothing more pressing."

"I see the place where they got in?" I asked.

He wanted to tell me no. Instead, he said, "It's a fair hike. Use up an hour. I'd rather go sniff around this Krage thing while it's hot."

I shrugged. "Some other time, then."

We got down into Krage's territory and started rambling. Bullock still had a few contacts left from his boyhood. Coaxed properly, with a few gersh, they would talk. I was not allowed to sit in. I spent the time sipping beer in a tavern where they alternately fawned over my money and acted like I had the plague. When asked, I did not deny being an Inquisitor.

Bullock joined me. "Maybe we don't have anything after all. There's all kinds of rumors. One says his own men did him in. One says it was his competition. He's a little pushy with his neighbors." He accepted a mug of wine on the house, something I hadn't seen him do before. I put it down to preoccupation.

"There's one angle we can check. He was obsessed about getting some foreigner who made a fool of him in public. There's some say the same foreigner was the man who cut him up." He took out a list and began to peruse it. "Not going to be a lot there for us, I expect. The night Krage disappeared there was a lot of whoop and holler. Not a single eyewitness, of course." He grinned. "Ear-witnesses say it was a running battle. That makes me favor the palace revolution theory."

"What have you got there?"

"A list of people who were maybe getting wood out of the Enclosure. Some might have seen each other. I was thinking I might find something interesting if I compared their stories." He waved for more wine. This time he paid, and covered the first mug, too, though the house would have forgiven him payment. I got the impression Juniper's people were used to giving Custodians anything they wanted. Bullock simply had a sense of ethics, at least where the people of the Buskin were concerned. He would not make their lives harder than they already were.

I could not help liking him on some levels.

"You're not going to pursue the Krage thing, then?"

"Oh, yeah. Of course. The bodies are missing. But that's not unusual. Probably turn up across the river in a couple days, if they're dead. Or screaming for blood if they're not." He tapped a name on his list. "This guy hangs around the same place. Maybe I'll talk to this guy Raven while I'm there."

I felt the blood drain from my face. "Who?"

He looked at me strangely. I forced myself to relax, to look casual. His eyebrows dropped. "Guy named Raven. The foreigner who was supposed to be feuding with Krage. Hangs out the same place as this one guy on my woodgatherer's list. Maybe I'll ask him a few questions."

"Raven. Unusual name. What do you know about him?"

"Just that he's a foreigner and supposed to be bad news. Been around a couple years. Typical drifter. Hangs out with the Crater crowd."

The Crater crowd were the Rebel refugees who had established themselves in Juniper.

"Do me a favor? It's a long shot, but this guy could be the ghost I was talking about the other day. Stand off a ways. Pretend you never heard the name. But get me a physical description. And find out if he's got anybody with him."

Bullock frowned. He didn't like it. "Is it important?"

"I don't know. It could be."

"All right."

"Keep the whole thing under your hat if you can."

"This guy means something to you, eh?"

"If he's the guy I knew, that I thought was dead, yeah. Him and me got business."

He smiled. "Personal?"

I nodded. I was feeling my way now. This was touchy. If this was my Raven, I had to go careful. I didn't dare let him get caught in the coils of our operation. He knew too damned much. He could get half the Company officers and noncoms put to the question. And made dead.

I decided Bullock would respond best if I kept it mysterious, with Raven an old enemy by implication. Somebody I would do most anything to jump in the dark, but not somebody important in any other way.

"I got you," he said. He looked at me somewhat differently, as though glad to discover I wasn't different after all.

Hell, I'm not. But I like to pretend I am, most of the time. I told him, "I'm going back to Duretile. Got to talk to a couple buddies."

"Can you find your way?"

"I can. Let me know what you find out."

"Will do."

We separated. I went up the hill as fast as forty-year-old legs would carry me.

I got Elmo and Goblin off where nobody could overhear us. "We maybe got a problem, friends."

"Like what?" Goblin wanted to know. He had been aching for me to talk from the minute I rounded him up. I guess I looked a little ragged around the fringes.

"There's a guy named Raven operating down in the Buskin. The other day, when I was down there with Bullock, I thought I saw a guy who looked like our Raven from a distance, but I shrugged it off then."

They quick got as nervous as me. "You sure it's him?" Elmo asked.

"No. Not yet. I got the hell out of there the minute I heard the name Raven. Let Bullock think he's an old enemy I want to stick a knife in. He's going to ask around for me while he's doing his own business. Get me a description. See if Darling is with him. I'm probably off in the wild blue yonder, but I wanted you guys to know. In case."

"What if it is him?" Elmo said. "What do we do then?"

"I don't know. It could be big trouble. If Whisper had some reason to get interested, like because he hangs around with the Rebel refugees here. . . . Well, you know."

Goblin mused, "Seems Silent said Raven was going to run so far nobody would ever find him again."

"So maybe he thought he'd run far enough. This is damned near the end of the world." Which, in part, was why I was so nervous. This was the kind of place I could picture Raven having gone to ground. As far from the Lady as you could get without learning to walk on water.

"Seems to me," Elmo said, "we ought to make sure before we panic. Then decide what to do. This might be the time to put our guys into the Buskin."

"That's what I was thinking. I already got a plan in front of Whisper, for something else. Let's tell her we're going with that, and have the guys watch for Raven."

"Who?" Elmo asked. "Raven would recognize anybody who knows him."

"Not true. Use guys who joined up at Charm. Send Pawnbroker just to make sure. He's not likely to remember the new guys. There were so many of them. If you want somebody reliable to run the thing, and back them up, use

Goblin. Park him where he can stay out of sight but keep his hands on the reins."

"What do you think, Goblin?" he asked.

Goblin smiled nervously. "Give me something to do, anyway. I'm going out of my skull up here. These people are weird."

Elmo chuckled. "Missing One-Eye?"

"Almost."

"All right," I said. "You'll need a guide. That'll have to be me. I don't want Bullock getting his nose any deeper into this. But they think I'm one of his men down there. You'll have to follow me from a distance. And try not to look like what you are. Don't make it hard on yourselves."

Elmo stretched. "I'll get Kingpin and Pawnbroker now. You take them down and show them a place. One can come back for the others. Go ahead and scope it out with Goblin." He left.

And so it went. Goblin and the six soldiers took rooms not far from the moneylender Krage's headquarters. Up on the hill I pretended it was all for the cause.

I waited.

17

Juniper: Travel Plans

Shed caught Asa trying to sneak out. "What the hell is this?"

"I need to get out, Shed. I'm going crazy up there."

"Yeah? You want to know something, Asa? The Inquisitors are looking for you. Bullock himself was in here the other day, and he asked for you by name." Shed was stretching the facts slightly. Bullock's interest had not been intense. But it had to have something to do with the Catacombs. Bullock and his sidekick were in the Buskin almost every day, asking, asking, asking questions. He didn't need Asa meeting Bullock face-to-face. Asa would either panic or crumble under questioning. Either way, Marron Shed would get into the heat damned fast. "Asa, if they catch you, we're all dead."

"Why?"

"You were spending those old coins. They're looking for somebody with a lot of old money."

"Damn that Raven!"

"What?"

"He gave me the passage money. As my share. I'm rich. And now you tell me I can't spend it without getting grabbed."

"He probably figured you'd hold off till the excitement died down. He'd be gone by then."

"Gone?"

"He's leaving as soon as the harbor opens."

"Where's he headed?"

"South somewhere. He won't talk about it."

"So what do I do? Keep scrambling for a living? Damn it, Shed, that's not fair."

"Look on the bright side, Asa. Nobody wants to kill you anymore."

"So? Now Bullock is after me. Maybe I could have made a deal with Krage. Bullock don't deal. It ain't fair! All my life. . . ."

Shed did not listen. He sang the same song all too often.

"What can I do, Shed?"

"I don't know. Stay holed up, I guess." He had a glimmer of a notion. "How about you get out of Juniper for a while?"

"Yeah. You might have something. That money would spend just fine somewhere else, wouldn't it?"

"I don't know. I've never traveled."

"Get Raven up here when he shows up."

"Asa. . . ."

"Hey, Shed, come on. It won't hurt to ask. All he can do is say no."

"Whatever you want, Asa. I hate to see you go."

"Sure you do, Shed. Sure you do." As Shed ducked out the doorway, Asa called, "Wait a second."

"Yeah?"

"Uh. . . . It's kind of hard. I never did thank you."

"Thank me for what?"

"You saved my life. You brought me back, didn't you?"

Shed shrugged, nodded. "No big thing, Asa."

"Sure it is, Shed. And I'll remember it. I owe you the big one."

Shed went downstairs before he could be embarrassed further. He discovered that Raven had returned. The man was in one of his animated discussions with Darling. Arguing again. They had to be lovers. Damn it all. He waited till Raven noticed him watching. "Asa wants to see you. I think he wants to go with you when you leave."

Raven chuckled. "That would solve your problem, wouldn't it?"

Shed did not deny that he would be more comfortable with Asa out of Juniper. "What do you think?"

"Not a bad idea, actually. Asa isn't much, but I need men. I have a hold on him. And him being gone would help cover my backtrail."

"Take him with my blessing."

Raven started upstairs. Shed said, "Wait." He didn't know how to approach this, because he didn't know if it was important. But he'd better tell Raven. "Bullock's been hanging around the Buskin a lot lately. Him and a sidekick."

"So?"

"So maybe he's closer than we think. For one thing, he was in here looking for Asa. For another, he's been asking about you."

Raven's face went empty. "About me? How so?"

"On the quiet. My cousin Wally's wife Sal? Her brother is married to one of Bullock's cousins. Anyway, Bullock still knows people down here, from before he got on the Custodians. He helps them out sometimes, so some of them tell him things he wants to know. . . ."

"I get the picture. Get to the point."

"Bullock was asking about you. Who you are, where you come from, who your friends are—things like that."

"Why?"

Shed could only shrug.

"All right. Thanks. I'll check it out."

Juniper: Blowing Smoke

Goblin stood across the street, leaning against a building, staring intently. I frowned angrily. What the hell was he doing on the street? Bullock might recognize him and realize we were playing games.

Obviously, he wanted to tell me something.

Bullock was about to enter another of countless dives. I told him, "Got to see a man about a horse in the alley."

"Yeah." He went inside. I slipped into the alley and made water. Goblin joined me there. "What is it?" I asked.

"What it is, Croaker, is it's him. Raven. Our Raven. Not only him, but Darling. She's a barmaid in a place called the Iron Lily."

"Holy shit," I murmured.

"Raven lives there. They're doing a show like they don't know each other that well. But Raven looks out for her."

"Damnit! It had to be, didn't it? What do we do now?"

"Maybe bend over and kiss our asses good-bye. The bastard could be smack in the middle of the body-selling racket. Everything we found could add up that way."

"How come you could find that when Bullock couldn't?"

"I got resources Bullock doesn't."

I nodded. He did. Sometimes it's handy, having a wizard around. Sometimes it's not, if it's one of those bitches up in Duretile. "Hurry it up," I said. "He'll wonder where I am."

"Raven has his own wagon and team. Keeps it way across town. Usually only takes it out late at night." I nodded. We'd already determined that bodyrunners worked the night shift. "But. . . ." he said, "and you're going to love this but, Croaker. He took it out in the daytime, once, a while back. Coincidentally, the day somebody hit the Catacombs."

"Oh boy."

"I looked that wagon over, Croaker. There was blood in it. Fairly fresh. I date it about when that moneylender and his pals disappeared."

"Oh boy. Shit. We're in for it now. Better get. Going to have to think of a story for Bullock now."

"Later."

"Yeah."

At that moment I was ready to give up. Despair overwhelmed me. That damned fool Raven—I knew exactly what he was doing. Getting together a fat bunch of running money by selling bodies and plundering graves. His conscience wouldn't bother him. In his part of the world, such things were of much less consequence. And he had a cause: Darling.

I couldn't get away from Bullock. I wanted desperately to run to Elmo, but I had to trudge hither and yon asking questions.

I looked up the northern slope, at the black castle, and thought of it as the fortress Raven had built.

I was going off the deep end. I told myself that. The evidence wasn't yet conclusive . . . but it was. Enough. My employers did not wait on legal niceties or absolute evidence.

Elmo was rattled, too. "We could kill him. No risk him giving anything away then."

"Really, Elmo!"

"I didn't mean it. But you know I'd do it if the choice got narrow enough."

"Yeah." We all would. Or we'd try. Raven might not let us. He was the toughest son-of-a-bitch I'd ever known. "If you ask me, we ought to find him and just tell him to get the hell out of Juniper."

Elmo gave me a disgusted look. "Haven't you been paying attention? Right now the only way in or out is the one we took. The harbor is frozen. The passes are snowed in. You think we could get Whisper to fly some civilian out for us?"

"Civilians. Goblin says Darling is still with him."

Elmo looked thoughtful. I started to say something else. He waved a hand for silence. I waited. He finally asked, "What would he do if he saw you? If he's been hanging around with the Crater bunch?"

I clicked my tongue. "Yeah. I didn't think of that. Let me go check something."

I hunted Bullock up. "You or the Duke got somebody inside the Crater bunch?"

He looked puzzled. "Maybe? Why?"

"Let's have a sit-down with them. An idea. It might help us break our thing here."

He looked at me a long moment. Maybe he was sharper than he pretended. "All right. Not that they would've learned much. The only reason they haven't run our guys off is we don't bother them. They just get together and talk about the old days. They don't have any fight left."

"Let's give it a look anyway. Maybe they're less innocent than they look."

"Give me a half-hour."

I did. And when that time was up, he and I sat down with two secret policemen. He and I took turns asking questions, each coming from his own private slant.

Neither knew Raven, at least not by that name. That was a relief. But there was something there, and Bullock sensed it immediately. He hung on till he had something to chew.

"I'm going to my boss," I told him. "She'll want to know about this." I had come up with a diversion. It seemed it would suit Bullock.

He said, "I'll take it up with Hargadon. Didn't occur to me this might be foreigners. Political. That could be why the money didn't show up. Maybe they're selling bodies, too."

"Rebellions do take money," I observed.

We moved next evening, at Whisper's insistence, over the objections of the Duke, but with the support of the chief Custodian. The Duke still did not want us seen. The Custodians didn't give a damn. They just wanted to salvage their reputation.

Elmo came slinking through the evening shadows. "Ready here?" he whispered.

I glanced at the four men with me. "Ready." Every Company man in Juniper was there, with the Duke's secret police and a dozen of Bullock's men. I'd thought his job silly, but even so had been astonished to discover how few men his office actually employed. All but one were there. The one was legitimately sick.

Elmo made a sound like a cow mooing, repeated three times.

The one-time Rebels were all together for their regular confab. I snickered, thinking of the surprise they were going to get. They thought they were safe from the Lady by fifteen hundred miles and seven years.

It took less than a minute. No one was injured. They just looked at us dumbly, arms hanging slack. Then one even recognized us, and groaned, "The Black Company. In Juniper."

Then another: "It's over. It's the end. She's really won."

They didn't seem to care much. Some, in fact, looked relieved.

We pulled it off so smoothly there was hardly any notice from the neighbors. The slickest raid I'd ever seen. We marched them up to Duretile, and Whisper and Feather went to work.

I just hoped one of them wouldn't know too much.

I'd made a long bet, hoping Raven would not have told them who Darling was. If he had, I'd pulled the roof down instead of misdirecting attention.

I did not hear from Whisper, so I guessed I'd won.

19

Juniper: Fear

Raven slammed through the door of the Lily. Shed looked up, startled. Raven leaned against the door frame, panting. He looked like he'd just stared his death in the face. Shed put his rag aside and hurried over, a stoneware bottle in hand.

"What happened?"

Raven stared over his shoulder, at Darling, who was waiting on Shed's lone paying customer. He shook his head, took several deep breaths, shuddered.

He was scared! By all that was holy, the man was terrified! Shed was aghast. What could have gotten him into this state? Even the black castle did not shake him.

"Raven. Come over here and sit." He took Raven's arm. The man followed docilely. Shed caught Darling's eye, signed for two mugs and another stoneware bottle.

Darling took one look at Raven and forgot her customer. She was there with mugs and bottle in seconds, her fingers flashing at Raven.

Raven did not see.

"Raven!" Shed said in a sharp whisper. "Snap out of it, man! What the hell happened?"

Raven's eyes focused. He looked at Shed, at Darling, at the wine. He tossed off a mug in one gulp, slapped it down. Darling poured again.

Her customer protested at being abandoned.

"Get it yourself," Shed told him.

The man became abusive.

"Go to hell, then," Shed said. "Raven, talk. Are we in trouble?"

"Uh. . . . No. Not we, Shed. Me." He shuddered like a dog coming out of water, faced Darling. His fingers started talking.

Shed caught most of it.

Raven told her to pack. They had to run again.

Darling wanted to know why.

Because they've found us, Raven told her.

Who? Darling asked.

The Company. They're here. In Juniper.

Darling did not seem distressed. She denied the possibility.

The Company? Shed thought. What the hell was this?

They are here, Raven insisted. I went to the meeting. I was late. Lucky. I got there after it started. The Duke's men. The Custodians. And the Company. I saw Croaker and Elmo and Goblin. I heard them call each other by name. I heard them mention Whisper and Feather. The Company is in Juniper, and the Taken are with them. We have to go.

Shed had no idea what in hell this was about. Who were these people? Why was Raven scared? "How you going to run anywhere, Raven? You can't get out of town. The harbor's still frozen."

Raven looked at him as if he were a heretic.

"Settle down, Raven. Use your head. I don't know what the hell is going on, but I can tell you this. Right now you're acting more like Marron Shed than like Raven. Old Shed is the guy who panics. Remember?"

Raven managed a feeble grin. "You're right. Yeah. Raven uses his brain." He snickered sourly. "Thanks, Shed."

"What happened?"

"Let's just say the past came back. A past I didn't expect to see again. Tell me about this sidekick you said Bullock's been pulling around lately. Word I've heard, Bullock is a loner."

Shed described the man, though he could not recall him well. His attention had been on Bullock. Darling positioned herself so she could read his lips. She formed a word with hers.

Raven nodded. "Croaker."

Shed shivered. The name sounded sinister when Raven translated it. "He some kind of hired killer?"

Raven laughed softly. "No. Actually, he's a physician. Halfway competent, too. But he has other talents. Like being crafty enough to come around looking for me in Bullock's shadow. Who would pay attention to him? They'd be too worried about the damned Inquisitor."

Darling flashed signs. She went too fast for Shed, but he thought she was admonishing Raven, telling him Croaker was his friend and would not be hunting him. It was coincidence that their paths had crossed.

"Not coincidence at all," Raven countered, both aloud and by sign. "If they aren't hunting me, why are they in Juniper? Why are two of the Taken here?"

Again Darling responded too fast for Shed to catch everything. She seemed to be arguing that if someone called the Lady had gotten to this Croaker or another someone called Silent, Croaker would not be here.

Raven stared at her a good fifteen seconds, still as stone. He downed another mug of wine. Then he said, "You're right. Absolutely right. If they were looking for me, they would have had me. And you. The Taken themselves would have been all over us. So. Coincidence, after all. But coincidence or not, the Lady's top thugs are in Juniper. And they're looking for something. What? Why?"

This was the old Raven. Cool and hard and thinking.

Darling flashed, Black castle.

Shed's humor vanished. Raven looked at the girl for several seconds, glanced in the general direction of the black castle. Then he looked at Darling again. "Why?"

Darling shrugged. She flashed, There is nothing else about Juniper that would bring Her here.

Raven thought a few minutes more. Then he turned to Shed. "Shed, have I made you rich? Have I gotten your ass far enough out of trouble?"

"Sure, Raven."

"Your turn to give me a hand, then. Some very powerful enemies of mine are in Juniper. They're working with the Custodians and the Duke, and are probably here because of the black castle. If they spot me, I'm in trouble."

Marron Shed had a full belly. He had a warm place to sleep. His mother was safe. He had no debts and no immediate threats hanging over his head. The man opposite him was responsible. Also responsible for saddling him with an agonized conscience, but that he could forgive. "Ask. I'll do what I can."

"You'll be helping yourself, too, if they're looking into the castle. You, me, and Asa. We made a mistake, raiding the Catacombs. Never mind. I want you to find out whatever you can about what's going on in Duretile. If you need bribe money, tell me. I'll cover it."

Puzzled, Shed said, "Sure. Can't you tell me a little more?"

"Not till I know a little more. Darling, get your stuff together. We have to disappear."

For the first time, Shed protested. "Hey! What're you doing? How am I supposed to run this place without her?"

"Get that girl Lisa in here. Get your cousin. I don't care. We have to disappear."

Shed frowned.

Raven said, "They want her more than they want me."

"She's just a kid."

"Shed."

"Yes, sir. How do I get in touch, sir?"

"You don't. I'll get in touch with you. Darling, go. Those are Taken up there."

"What're Taken?" Shed asked.

"If you have gods, Shed, pray that you never find out. Pray hard." And, when Darling returned with her meager belongings, Raven said, "I think you ought to reconsider leaving Juniper with me. Things are going to start happening around here, and you won't like them."

"I have to take care of my mother."

"Think about it anyway, Shed. I know what I'm talking about. I used to work for those people."

Juniper: Shadow Talk

Raven vanished on us. Even Goblin could find no trace. Feather and Whisper worked on our prisoners till each was drained, and got nothing on our old friend. I concluded that Raven had used an assumed name when dealing with them.

Why hadn't he used one down in the Buskin? Folly? Pride? As I recall, Raven had too much of that.

Raven was not his real name, any more than Croaker is mine. But that was the name we knew him by the year he served with us. None of us, unless maybe the Captain, knew his real one. He had been a man of substance once, in Opal. That I knew. He and the Limper became bitter enemies when the Limper used his wife and her lovers to do him out of his rights and titles. That I knew. But not who he was before he became a soldier of the Black Company.

I dreaded telling the Captain what we had found. He was fond of Raven. Like brothers, the two of them. The Captain, I think, was hurt when Raven deserted. He would be hurt more deeply when he learned what his friend had done in Juniper.

Whisper called us in to announce the results of the interrogations. She said roughly, "We did not exactly score a triumph, gentlemen. All but a couple of those men were dabblers. We knocked the fight out of them at Charm. But we did learn that the black castle *has* been buying corpses. Its denizens even buy live bodies. Two of our captives have sold to them. Raising money for the Rebel."

The idea of trading in corpses was repellent, but not especially wicked. I wondered what use the black castle people had for them.

Whisper continued, "They were not responsible for the raid on the Catacombs. In fact, they are of no interest to us. We're turning them over to the Custodians to do with as they please. You gentlemen will now go out into the city and resume digging."

"Excuse me, ma'am?" Elmo said.

"Somewhere in Juniper there is someone who is feeding the black castle. Find him. The Lady wants him."

Raven, I thought. Had to be Raven. Just had to be. We had to find that son-of-a-bitch, yes. And get him out of town or dead.

You have to understand what the Company means. For us, it is father, mother, family. We are men with nothing else. Raven getting caught would kill the family, figuratively and literally. The Lady would disband what remained of the outfit after she'd mauled us for not turning Raven in back when.

I told Whisper: "It might help if we knew what we're dealing with. It's hard to take something serious when nobody tells you anything. What's the point of the exercise? That castle is damned bizarre, I grant you. But why should we care?"

Whisper seemed to think about it. For several seconds her eyes were blank. She had taken the matter to higher authority. She was in communion with the Lady. When she returned, she said, "The black castle has its roots in the Barrowland."

That got our attention. I croaked, "What?"

"The black castle is the Dominator's escape hole. When it reaches a certain size and certain set of circumstances, the creatures who live there, who are his creatures, heart and soul, will conjure him out of the Great Barrow. Here."

Several men snorted in disbelief. It did seem far-fetched, for all the weirdness and sorceries we have seen.

Whisper said, "He foresaw his defeat by the White Rose, though not his betrayal by the Lady. Even before the Domination fell, he started preparing his return. He sent a faithful follower here with the seed of the black castle. Something went wrong. He never planned to spend so long waiting. Maybe he did not know of Juniper's preoccupation with preserving the dead. What are they waiting for? A ship that will carry them to paradise?"

"Roughly," I agreed. "I studied it, but the whole business is still monkey chatter to me. Go on. The Dominator is going to pop out on us here?"

"Not if we can stop him. But we may have gotten here too late. This man. If we don't take him soon, it *will* be too late. The portal is almost ready to open."

I looked at Elmo. He looked at me. Oh boy, I thought. If Raven knew what he was doing. . . . I still couldn't get upset. He did it for Darling. He couldn't have known he was doing the Dominator's work. He had that much conscience. He would have found another way. . . . What the hell was he going to do with so much money?

We had to find him. That was all there was to it. Whatever we did from now on, our main goal, for the sake of the Company, had to be to warn him off.

I glanced at Elmo. He agreed. From this moment forward we would be fighting for the survival of the outfit.

Somewhere, somehow, Raven must have smelled trouble. Goblin looked under every rock in the Buskin, watched every alley, practically lived in the Iron Lily, and still found a big bunch of nothing. Time ground past. Warmer weather threatened. And we became ever more panicky.

21

Juniper

Raven departed soon after the outer channel opened. Shed went down to say good-bye—and only then discovered the nature of Raven's shipping investment. He had had a ship built and crewed. A whole new ship, and as big a vessel as Shed had seen. "No wonder he needed a fortune," he mused. How many bodies to build that?

He returned to the Lily numbed. He poured himself some wine, sat staring into nothing. "That Raven was a man of vision," he mumbled. "Glad he's gone, though. Asa, too. Maybe things can get back to normal."

Shed bought a cottage near the Enclosure. He installed his mother with a staff of three. It was a relief to be rid of her evil, blind stare.

He had workmen into the Lily every day. They interfered with business, but business remained good. The harbor was busy. There was work for anyone who wanted it.

Shed could not handle prosperity. He hared after every impulse he had known during his impoverishment. He bought fine clothing he dared not wear. He went places frequented only by the wealthy. And he bought the attentions of beautiful women.

Women cost a lot when you pretended to be somebody off the high slope.

One day Shed went to his secret cash box and found it empty. All that money gone? Where? The improvements on the Lily weren't finished. He owed the workmen. He owed the people caring for his mother. Damn! Was he back where he started?

Hardly. He had his profits.

He scampered downstairs, to his business cash box, opened it, sighed in relief. He'd done all his spending out of the box upstairs.

But something was wrong. There wasn't anywhere near enough in the box. . . . "Hey, Wally."

His cousin looked at him, gulped, raced out the door. Baffled, Shed hurried outside, saw Wally vanish into an alley. Then the truth hit him. "Damn you!" he yelled. "Damn you, you damned thief!" He went back in and tried to figure where he stood.

An hour later he told the workmen to knock off. He left his new girl Lisa in charge, started the rounds of his suppliers.

Wally had screwed him good. He had bought on credit and pocketed monies payable. Shed covered his debts as he went, growing increasingly alarmed as his reserves dwindled. Down to little more than copper, he returned to the Lily and started an inventory.

At least Wally hadn't sold what he had bought on credit. The Lily was well-stocked.

Only what was he going to do about his mother?

The house was paid for. That was a plus. But the old girl needed her servants to survive. And he couldn't pay their wages. But he didn't want her back in the Lily. He could sell all those clothes. He'd spent a fortune on them and couldn't wear them. He did some figuring. Yes. Sell the clothes and he could support his mother till next summer.

No more clothes. No more women. No more improvements on the Lily. . . . Maybe Wally hadn't spent it all.

Finding Wally was not difficult. He returned to his family after two days in hiding. He thought Shed would endure the loss. He didn't know he was dealing with a new Shed.

Shed stormed to his cousin's tiny one-room apartment, kicked the door in. "Wally!"

Wally squealed. His children and wife and mother all screeched questions. Shed ignored them. "Wally, I want it back! Every damned copper!"

Wally's wife got in his way. "Calm down, Marron. What's the matter?"

"Wally!" Wally cowered in a corner. "Out of my way, Sal. He stole damned near a hundred leva." Shed grabbed his cousin and dragged him out the doorway. "I want it back."

"Shed. . . ."

Shed shoved him. He staggered backward, tripped, rolled down a flight of stairs. Shed charged after him, hurled him down another flight.

"Shed, please. . . ."

"Where's the money, Wally? I want the money."

"I don't have it, Shed. I spent it. Honest. The kids had to have clothes. We had to eat. I couldn't help it, Shed. You had so much. . . . You're family, Shed. You're supposed to help."

Shed shoved him into the street, kicked him in the groin, dragged him upright, started slapping. "Where is it, Wally? You couldn't have spent that much. Hell, your kids are wearing rags. I paid you enough to handle that. Because you were family. I want the money you stole." As he raged, Shed drove his cousin toward the Lily.

Wally whined and begged, refusing to tell the truth. Shed guessed he had stolen upward of fifty leva, enough to have completed the renovation of the Lily. This hadn't been petty pilfering. He hurled blows in an angry rain.

He herded Wally around behind the Lily, away from prying eyes. "Now I get nasty, Wally."

"Shed, please. . . ."

"You stole from me and you're lying about it. I could forgive you for doing it for your family. But you didn't. Tell me. Or give it back." He punched Wally hard.

The pain in his hands, from hitting the man, sapped his rage. But then Wally broke. "I lost it gambling. I know I was stupid. But I was so sure I was going to win. They took me. They let me think I was going to win big, then took me, and the only way out was to steal. They would have killed me. I borrowed from Gilbert after I told him how good you were doing. . . ."

"Lost it? Gambling? Borrowed from Gilbert?" Shed muttered. Gilbert had moved in on Krage's territories. He was as bad as his predecessor. "How could you be so stupid?" The rage took him again. He snatched a board off a scrap pile left for kindling. He hit Wally hard. And hit him again. His cousin went down, stopped trying to fend off the blows.

Shed froze, suddenly coldly rational. Wally wasn't moving. "Wally? Wally? Hey, Wally. Say something."

Wally did not respond.

Shed's stomach knotted. He tossed the board into the pile. "Have to get that inside before people cart it off." He gripped his cousin's shoulder. "Come on, Wally. I won't hit you anymore."

Wally did not move.

"Oh, shit," Shed muttered. "I killed him." This tore it. What now? There wasn't much justice in the Buskin, but what there was was quick and rough. They would hang him sure.

He whirled, looking for witnesses. He saw no one. His mind flew in a hundred directions. There was a way out. No body, no proof that murder had been done. But he'd never gone up that hill alone.

Hastily, he dragged Wally to the scrap pile and covered him. The amulet he needed to get into the black castle. Where was it? He dashed into the Lily, roared upstairs, found the amulet, examined it. Definitely serpents intertwined. The workmanship was amazingly detailed. Tiny jewels formed the eyes of the snakes. They sparkled menacingly in the afternoon sun.

He stuffed the amulet into his pocket. "Shed, get yourself together. Panic and you're dead."

How long before Sal yelled for the law? A few days, surely. Plenty of time.

Raven had left him his wagon and team. He hadn't thought to keep paying the stable-keeper. Had the man sold them? If so, he was in trouble.

He cleaned out his coin boxes, left the Lily in Lisa's care.

The stable-keeper hadn't sold off, but the mules were looking lean. Shed cursed him.

"I should feed them at my own expense, mister?"

Shed cursed him some more and paid what was owed. He said, "Feed them. And have them hitched and ready at the tenth hour."

Shed remained panicky all afternoon. Somebody might find Wally. But no lawman came stamping in. Soon after dark he stole away to the stable.

He spent the journey alternately being terrified and wondering how much Wally would bring. And how much he could get for his wagon and team. He hadn't factored them into his earlier calculations.

He ought to help Wally's family. He had to. It was the decent thing. . . . He was acquiring too many dependents.

Then he was facing the dark gate. The castle, with all its monstrous decoration, was terrible, but it didn't seem to have grown since last he had been there. He knocked as Raven had done, his heart in his throat. He gripped his amulet in his left hand.

What was taking them so long? He hammered again. The gate jumped open, startling him. He fled to his wagon, got the mules moving.

He entered exactly as Raven had done, ignoring everything but his driving. He halted in the same place, climbed down, dragged Wally out.

No one came for several minutes. He grew ever more nervous, wishing he'd had the sense to come armed. What guarantee did he have that they wouldn't turn on him? That silly amulet?

Something moved. He gasped.

The creature that stepped out of the shadow was short and wide and radiated an air of contempt. It never looked at him. Its examination of the cadaver was detailed. It was being difficult, like some petty official with a helpless citizen momentarily in his power. Shed knew how to handle that. Stubborn patience and refusal to become irritated. He stood motionless, waiting.

The creature finally placed twenty-five pieces of silver near Wally's feet.

Shed grimaced, but collected the cash. He returned to his seat, backed the wagon, got the team aligned with the gate. Only then did he register his protest. "That was a prime corpse. Next time you'll do better, or there won't be a time after that. Git up." Out the gate he went, amazed at his temerity.

Going down the hill he sang. He felt great. Except for a fading guilt about Wally—the bastard had earned it—he was at peace with his world. He was free and safe, out of debt, and now had money in reserve. He returned his team to its stable, wakened the stable-keeper, paid four months in advance. "Take good care of my animals," he admonished.

A representative of the precinct Magistrate showed up next day. He had questions about Wally's disappearance. Sal had reported the fight.

Shed admitted it. "I kicked the shit out of him. But I don't know what happened to him. He just took off. I would've run, too, if I had somebody that mad at me."

"What was the fight about?"

Shed played the role of a man who didn't want to get anybody in trouble. Finally, he admitted, "He worked for me. He stole money to pay back money he borrowed to pay gambling debts. Check with my suppliers. They'll tell how he bought on credit. He told me he was paying cash."

"How much was involved?"

"Can't say exactly," Shed replied. "More than fifty leva. My whole profit for the summer, and then some."

The questioner whistled. "I don't blame you for getting pissed."

"Yeah. I wouldn't have begrudged him money to help his family. He's got a whole mob to take care of. But to lose it gambling. . . . Damn, I was hot. I borrowed to fix this place up. The payments are rough. I probably won't make it through the winter now, because that bastard couldn't resist a game. I may still break his neck."

It was a good act. Shed pulled it off.

"You want to register a formal complaint?"

Shed played reluctant. "He's family. My cousin."

"I'd break my own father's back if he did that to me."

"Yeah. All right. I'll register it. But don't go hanging him right away. Maybe he can work it out or something. Hell, maybe he's still got some he can pay back. He could have lied about losing it all. He lied about a lot of things." Shed shook his head. "He worked for us on-and-off since my father ran this place. I never thought he'd do anything like that."

"You know how it is. You get too far into debt and the vultures start closing in, you'll do anything to save your ass. You don't worry about tomorrow. We see it all the time."

Shed nodded. He knew how it was.

After the Magistrate's man departed, Shed told Lisa: "I'm going out." He wanted one last fling before he settled in to the dreary business of managing the Lily.

He bought the most skilled, most beautiful woman he could find. She cost, but she was worth every copper. He returned to the Lily wishing he could live that way all the time. He dreamed about the woman that night.

Lisa wakened him early. "There's a man here who wants to see you."

"Who is he?"

"He didn't say."

Cursing, Shed rolled out. He did nothing to hide his nakedness. More than once he had hinted that Lisa should include more than barmaid's chores in her duties. She was not cooperating. He had to find a handle. . . . He'd better look out. He was getting obsessed with sex. That could give somebody a handle.

He descended to the common room. Lisa indicated a man. He was no one Shed knew. "You wanted to see me?"

"You got someplace private?"

A hard case. Now what? He did not owe anyone. He did not have any enemies. "What's your business?"

"Let's talk about your cousin. The one who didn't disappear the way people think."

Shed's stomach knotted. He concealed his distress. "I don't understand."

"Suppose somebody saw what happened?"

"Come into the kitchen."

Shed's visitor peeped back through the kitchen door. "Thought the split-tail might try to listen in." Then he gave Shed an accurate account of Wally's death.

"Where did you get that fairy tale?"

"I saw it."

"In a pipe dream, maybe."

"You're cooler than I heard. Here's the way it goes, friend. I have a trick memory. Sometimes I forget. Depends on how I'm treated."

"Ah. I begin to see the light. This is about hush money."

"There you go."

Shed's thoughts scurried like frightened mice. He couldn't *afford* hush money. He had to find another way out. But he couldn't do anything right now. He was too confused. He needed time to get himself together. "How much?"

"A leva a week would buy a first-class case of amnesia."

Shed goggled. He sputtered. He choked back his protest.

The extortionist made a what-can-I-do? gesture. "I have problems too. I got expenses. A leva a week. Or take your chances."

The black castle flickered through Shed's thoughts. Low cunning grabbed it, turned it over, looked at the possibilities. Murder did not bother him anymore.

But not now. Not here. "How do I pay you?"

The man grinned. "Just hand me a leva."

Shed brought his coin box into the kitchen. "You'll have to take copper. I don't have any silver."

The man's smile grew broader. He was pleased. Why?

The man left. Shed said, "Lisa, I have a job for you. Worth a bonus. Follow that man. Find out where he goes." He gave her five gersh. "Another five when you get back, if it's worth it."

Lisa zipped out in a whirl of skirts.

He wandered around a lot," Lisa reported. "Like he was killing time. Then he headed down by the Sailmakers'. To see that one-eyed moneylender."

"Gilbert?"

"Yeah. Gilbert."

"Thank you," Shed said thoughtfully. "Thanks a bunch. That casts light on the problem."

"Five gersh worth?"

"Sure. You're a good girl." He made a suggestive offer as he counted.

"I don't need money that bad, Mr. Shed."

He retreated to his kitchen, began preparing supper. So Gilbert was behind the extortionist. Did Gilbert want him financially pressed? Why?

The Lily. Why else? The renovations made the place that much more attractive a steal.

So. Assume Gilbert was opening a campaign to snatch the Lily. He had to fight. But this time nobody could help him. He was on his own.

Three days later Shed visited an acquaintance who operated on the nether edge of the Buskin. For a consideration he received a name. He visited the man attached, and left him with two pieces of silver.

Back at the Lily, he asked Lisa to tell her favorite customers that Gilbert was trying to force them out by spreading lies and making threats. He wanted the Magistrate suspicious of accusations leveled against him later.

The morning of the next payoff, Shed told Lisa, "I'll be gone all day. Anybody comes looking for me, tell them to come back after supper."

"The man I followed?"

"Him especially."

At first Shed just roamed, killing time. His nerve worsened with time. Something would go wrong. Gilbert would come back rough. . . . But he wouldn't dare, would he? That would tarnish his reputation. Shed's rumors had him on the defensive now. People would make their loans elsewhere if he pressed.

Shed found himself a woman. She cost too much, but she made him forget. For a while. He returned to the Lily at sunset. "He came by?" he asked Lisa.

"Be back, too. He looked put out. I don't think he's going to be nice, Mr. Shed."

"That's the way it goes. I'll be out back working on the woodpile." Shed glanced at a customer he'd never before seen. The man nodded, departed through the front door.

Shed chopped wood by lanternlight. Now and again he searched the shadows, saw nothing. He prayed nothing would go wrong.

The extortionist stormed out the kitchen doorway. "You trying to duck me, Shed? You know what happens if you mess with me?"

"Duck you? What do you mean? I'm right here."

"You weren't this afternoon. Now that girl of yours gives me a hard way to go, trying to steer me away. I like to had to pound her before she'd tell me where you were."

Very creative. Shed wondered how much Lisa suspected. "Save the dramatics. You want your money. I want your ugly face away from my place. Let's get on with it."

The extortionist looked puzzled. "You talking tough? They told me you were the biggest coward in the Buskin."

"Who told you? You working for somebody? This not a freelance play?"

The man's eyes narrowed as he realized his mistake.

Shed produced a handful of copper. He counted, counted, counted again, put a few coins away. "Hold out your hands."

The extortionist extended cupped hands.

Shed had not expected it to be this easy. He dumped the coins, grabbed the man's wrists.

"Hey! What the hell?"

A hand clamped over the man's mouth. A face appeared over his shoulder, mouth stretched in a grimace of effort. The extortionist rose to his toes, arching backward. His eyes widened in fear and pain, then rolled up. He slumped forward.

"All right. Perfect. Get out of here," Shed said.

Hastening footsteps faded quickly.

Shed dragged the body into shadow, quickly covered it with wood scraps, then dropped to hands and knees and began collecting coins. He found all but two.

"What are you doing, Mr. Shed?"

He jumped. "What're *you* doing?"

"I came to see if you were all right."

"I'm fine. We had an argument. He knocked some coins out of my hand. I can't find them all."

"Need help?"

"Mind the counter, girl. Or they'll steal us blind."

"Oh. Sure." She ducked back inside.

Shed gave it up a few minutes later. He would search again tomorrow.

He got antsy waiting for closing time. Lisa was too curious. He was afraid she would look for the missing coins and find the body. He did not want her disappearance on his conscience, too.

Two minutes after he closed, he was out his back door and heading for his wagon and team.

The tall being was back on duty. He paid Shed thirty pieces of silver. As he was maneuvering to leave, though, the thing demanded, "Why do you come so seldom?"

"I'm not as skilled as my partner."

"What has become of him? We have missed him."

"He's out of town."

Shed could have sworn he heard the thing chuckle as he went out the gate.

Juniper: Running Scared

A long time had passed and nothing had happened. The Taken were not pleased. Neither was Elmo. He dragged me into his quarters. "Where the hell did Raven go, Croaker?"

"I don't know," I told him. As if he were the only one disturbed. I was scared and getting more so by the day.

"I want to know. Soon."

"Look, man. Goblin's done everything but torture people trying to pick up his trail. He flat vanished. He got wind of us somehow."

"How? Will you tell me how? We've been here half our lives, it seems like. And nobody else down there has noticed. Why should Raven be any different?"

"Because we were around looking for him. He must have spotted one of us."

"If he did, I want to know that. You hike on down there and light a fire under Goblin's ass. Hear?"

"Right. Whatever you say, boss." Though he commanded the advance party, technically I outranked Elmo. But I was not about to press for prerogatives at the moment. There was too much tension in the air.

There was stress throughout Duretile, and I did not understand most of it. I remained on the periphery of the Taken's study of the black castle. Just another messenger boy, a foot-slogger bringing in data from the city. I hadn't the slightest notion what they had discovered by direct examination. Or even if they were studying the castle directly. They could be lying back, afraid they would alert the Dominator to their presence.

One of the men located me in Elmo's quarters. "Whisper wants you, Croaker."

I jumped a foot. Guilty conscience. "What for?" I had not seen her for weeks.

"You'll have to go see. She didn't say." He sneered, hoping he would see an officer in the soup. He figured I was in trouble.

He figured that; so did I. I dawdled as much as I dared, but eventually had to present myself. Whisper glared at me as I entered. "You people haven't found a damned thing down there. What are you doing? Dogging it? Taking a vacation? Well, say something."

"I. . . ."

"Do you know the black castle stopped growing after our raid on the Crater group? No? Why not? You're supposed to be finding out these things."

"None of the prisoners accounted for the. . . ."

"I know that. I know none of them knew who the main body supplier was. But that supplier must have known them. He packed up. There have been just two bodies delivered since. The latest just last night. Why didn't you know that? Why have you got people in the Buskin? They seem incapable of learning anything."

Oh, she was in a mood. I said, "Is the deadline close or something? The way I understood it, we wouldn't be in trouble if only a few bodies were delivered."

"True. As far as it goes. But we've reached a point where a handful might make all the difference."

I bit my lower lip, tried to look properly chastised, and waited.

She told me: "The Lady is pressing. She's *very* nervous. She wants something to happen up here."

So. As always, the shit rolls downhill. The normal course would be for me to go out and tromp on somebody below me.

"Half the problem is, we don't know what's going on. If you claim you know what the castle is, how it's growing and so forth, how come you don't go over and kick it down? Or turn it into grape preserves or something?"

"It's not that simple."

It never is. I tend to overlook political ramifications. I am not politically minded.

"Maybe once the rest of your company gets here. The city will have to be controlled. The Duke and his incompetents couldn't manage that."

I stood there looking expectant. Sometimes that will con people into telling you more than they plan.

"The city will go up in flames if it's not buttoned up tight when the truth comes out. Why do you think the Custodians are so determined to keep the Catacombs thing hushed? Several thousand citizens have relatives who went into that monstrosity. That's a lot of people who'll get very irate about the souls of loved ones being lost."

"I see." I did a little. It took a certain willing suspension of reason, though.

"We're going at this from a different angle," she told me. "I'm taking charge of your investigations. Report to me daily. I'll decide what you're going to do, and how. Understand?"

"Yes, ma'am." Only too well. It was going to get that much more difficult to keep her and Raven apart.

"The first thing you'll do is set a watch on the castle. And if that doesn't shake something loose, I'll send Feather down there. Understand?"

"Yes, ma'am." Again, only too well.

I wondered if Whisper suspected we were working at cross-purposes.

"You can leave. I'll expect you back tomorrow. With something to report."

"Yes, ma'am."

I went straight back to Elmo, fuming. He should have faced her, not me. Just because I'd sort of taken over. . . .

I was with Elmo barely long enough to tell him what had happened when a messenger came from Bullock. He wanted to see me right away.

Bullock was another problem. I'd become convinced he was smarter than he put on, and was almost as sure that he suspected we were up to more than we admitted.

I eased into his cubicle in the secret police headquarters. "What's up?"

"I've made a little headway on the Catacombs raid. Result of pure stubborn footwork."

"Well?" I felt pretty curt about then, and he raised an eyebrow. "Just had a face-to-face with my boss," I told him, which was as near an apology as I cared to come. "What have you got?"

"A name."

I waited. Like Elmo, Bullock liked to be coaxed. I was in no mood to play that game.

"I followed up your notion about rented wagons. Turned up the name Asa. A wood-gatherer named Asa was, probably, working through the hole I showed you. A man named Asa spent a number of old coins, but before the raid on the Catacombs. A man named Asa worked for Krage before he and his men disappeared. Everywhere I go, it's Asa-this or Asa-that."

"Anything to connect him with the black castle?"

"No. I don't think he's a principal in anything. But he must know something."

I thought back. Bullock had mentioned this name once before, referring to a man who hung around the same place as Raven. Maybe there was a connection. Maybe I ought to find this Asa before anybody else did.

"I'm headed down to the Buskin," I said. "Direct orders from her holiness. I'll have Goblin round the guy up."

Bullock scowled. There had been some ill will when he found out that we had put men into the Buskin without consulting him. "All right. But don't play any more fast shuffle with me, eh? Your people and mine aren't after the same things, but that's no reason to undermine each other, eh?"

"You're right. We're just used to doing things different. I'll see you when I get back."

"I'd appreciate that." He eyed me in a way that said he did not trust me anymore. If ever he had. I left thinking the Company and I were into it deep. Trouble on every hand. Juggling with too many balls in the air. Only we were juggling knives with poisoned edges.

I hustled on down and looked up Goblin, told him about our escalating troubles. He was no happier than Elmo or I.

23

Juniper: Interrogation

Shed had no more trouble with extortionists. Somebody did tell the Magistrate that he had killed Wally. The Magistrate did not believe it, or did not care.

Then Bullock's sidekick turned up. Shed nearly dropped a valuable piece of crockery. He had felt safe from that. The only people who knew anything were far away. He clamped down on his nerves and guilt, went to the man's table. "How may we serve you, Reverend Sir?"

"Bring me a meal and your best wine, landlord."

Shed lifted an eyebrow. "Sir?"

"I'll pay. Nobody in the Buskin can afford to give away meals."

"Ain't it the truth, sir. Ain't it the truth."

When Shed returned with the wine, the Inquisitor observed, "You seem to be doing well, landlord."

Shed snorted. "We live on the edge, Reverend Sir. On the ragged edge. One bad week would destroy me. I spend every winter borrowing from one moneylender to pay another. This summer was good, though. I found a partner. I was able to fix a few things. That made the place more attractive. Probably my last dying gasp before it gets away." He donned his sourest face.

The Inquisitor nodded. "Leave the bottle. Let the Brotherhood contribute to your prosperity."

"I'll ask no profit, Reverend Sir."

"Why be foolish? Charge me the same as anyone else."

Shed mentally upped the tab twenty percent over normal. He was glad to be rid of the bottle. Raven had left him stuck with several.

When Shed delivered the meal, the Inquisitor suggested, "Bring a mug and join me."

Shed's nerves twisted as tight as a bowstring. Something was wrong. They had caught on. "As you wish, Reverend Sir." He dragged over and collected his own mug. It was dusty. He had not done much drinking lately, afraid his tongue would wag.

"Sit down. And wipe the scowl off your face. You haven't done anything. Have you? I don't even know your name."

"Shed, Reverend Sir. Marron Shed. The Iron Lily has been in my family for three generations."

"Admirable. A place with tradition. Tradition is falling by the wayside nowadays."

"As you say, Reverend Sir."

"I guess our reputation has preceded me. Won't you calm down?"

"How may I help you, Reverend Sir?"

"I'm looking for a man named Asa. I hear he was a regular here."

"So he was, sir," Shed admitted. "I knew him well. A lazy wastrel. Hated honest work. Never a copper to his name, either. Yet he was a friend, after his fashion, and generous in his way. I let him sleep on the common room floor during the winter, because in the days of my hardship he never failed to bring wood for the fire."

The Inquisitor nodded. Shed decided to tell most of the truth. He could not hurt Asa. Asa was beyond the reach of the Custodians.

"Do you know where he acquired the wood?"

Shed pretended acute embarrassment. "He collected it in the Enclosure, Reverend Sir. I debated with myself about using it. It wasn't against the law. But it seemed reprehensible anyway."

The Inquisitor smiled and nodded. "No failing on your part, Marron Shed. The Brotherhood doesn't discourage gleaning. It keeps the Enclosure from becoming too seedy."

"Why are you looking for Asa, then?"

"I understand he worked for a man named Krage."

"Sort of. For a while. He thought he was king of the Buskin when Krage took him on. Strutting and bragging. But it didn't last."

"So I heard. It's the timing of their falling-out that intrigues me."

"Sir?"

"Krage and some of his friends disappeared. So did Asa, about the same time. And all of them vanished soon after somebody got into the Catacombs and looted several thousand passage urns."

Shed tried to look properly horrified. "Krage and Asa did that?"

"Possibly. This Asa started spending old money after he began gleaning in the Enclosure. Our investigations suggest he was petty at his grandest. We think he pilfered a few urns each time he gathered wood. Krage may have found out and decided to plunder in a big way. Their falling-out may have been over that. Assuming Asa had any conscience."

"Possibly, sir. I understood it to be a squabble over a guest of mine. A man named Raven. Krage wanted to kill him. He hired Asa to spy on him. Asa told me that himself. Krage decided he wasn't doing his job. He never did anything right. Anyway, he never did anything very well. But that doesn't invalidate your theory. Asa could have been lying. Probably was. He lied a lot."

"What was the relationship between Asa and Raven?"

"There wasn't any."

"Where is Raven now?"

"He left Juniper right after the ice broke up in the harbor."

The Inquisitor seemed both startled and pleased. "What became of Krage?"

"Nobody knows, Reverend Sir. It's one of the great mysteries of the Buskin. One day he was there; the next he wasn't. There were all kinds of rumors."

"Could he have left Juniper, too?"

"Maybe. Some people think so. Whatever, he didn't tell anybody. The people who worked for him don't know anything, either."

"Or so they say. Could he have looted enough from the Catacombs to make it worthwhile to leave Juniper?"

Shed puzzled that question. It sounded treacherous. "I don't. . . . I don't understand what you're asking, sir."

"Uhm. Shed, thousands of the dead were violated. Most were put away at a time when the wealthy were very generous. We suspect a sum of gold may have been involved."

Shed gaped. He hadn't seen any gold. The man was lying. Why? Laying traps?

"It was a major plundering operation. We'd very much like to ask Asa some questions."

"I can imagine." Shed bit his lip. He thought hard. "Sir, I can't tell you what became of Krage. But I think Asa took ship for the south." He went into a long song-and-dance about how Asa had come to him after falling out with Krage, begging to be hidden. One day he had gone out, returned later badly wounded, had hidden upstairs for a while, then had vanished. Shed claimed to have seen him from a distance only, on the docks, the day the first ships sailed for the south. "I never got close enough to talk, but he looked like he was going somewhere. He had a couple bundles with him."

"Do you recall what ship?"

"Sir?"

"What ship did he take?"

"I didn't actually see him board a ship, sir. I just assumed he did. He might still be around. Only I figure he would have gotten in touch if he was. He always came to me when he was in trouble. I guess he's in trouble now, eh?"

"Maybe. The evidence isn't conclusive. But I'm morally convinced he was in on the looting. You didn't see Krage on the dock, did you?"

"No, sir. It was crowded. Everybody always goes down to see the first ships off. It's like a holiday." Was the Inquisitor buying it? Damn. He had to. An Inquisitor wasn't somebody you got off your back by selling him into the black castle.

The Inquisitor shook his head wearily. "I was afraid you'd tell me a story like that. Damn it. You leave me no choice."

Shed's heart leapt into his throat. Crazy ideas swarmed through his head. Hit the Inquisitor, grab the coin box, make a run for it.

"I hate to travel, Shed. But it looks like either Bullock or I will have to go after those people. Guess who'll get stuck?"

Relief swamped Shed. "Go after them, Reverend Sir? But the law down there doesn't recognize the Brotherhood's right. . . ."

"Won't be easy, will it? The barbarians just don't understand us." He poured some wine, stared into it for a long while. Finally, he said, "Thank you, Marron Shed. You've been very helpful."

Shed hoped that was a dismissal. He rose. "Anything else, Reverend Sir?"

"Wish me luck."

"Of course, sir. A prayer for your mission this very evening."

The Inquisitor nodded. "Thank you." He resumed staring into his mug.

He left a fine tip. But Shed was uneasy when he pocketed it. The Inquisitors had a reputation for doggedness. Suppose they caught up with Asa?

24

Juniper: Shadow Dancing

"I think I was pretty slick," I told Goblin.

"You should have seen that Shed," Pawnbroker cackled. "A chicken sweating like a pig and lying like a dog. A one-man barnyard."

"Was he really lying?" I mused. "He didn't say anything that conflicted with what we know."

"What did you learn?" Goblin asked.

"I think he was lying," Pawnbroker insisted. "Maybe by not telling everything he knew, but he was lying. He was into it somehow."

"You keep hanging around the Lily, then. Keep an eye on him."

"What did you learn?" Goblin demanded.

Elmo came in. "How'd it go?"

"Great," I said. "I found out what happened to Raven."

"What?" he and Goblin both demanded.

"He left town. By ship. The first day the harbor was open."

"Darling, too?" Goblin asked.

"You see her around? What do you think?"

Pawnbroker mused, "Bet that Asa went with him. Old Shed said they both left the first day."

"Could be. I was proud of myself, catching him with that. Looks to me, now, like this Shed is our only outside loose end. He's the only one who knows what happened to them. No Shed, nobody to maybe tell Bullock or the Taken anything."

Elmo frowned. The suggestion was more in keeping with his style than mine. He thought I'd put it forward seriously. "I don't know. Sounds too simple. Anyway, we're starting to get noticed down there, aren't we?"

Goblin nodded. "We're supposed to be sailors who missed our ship, but people are comparing notes, trying to figure us out. If Shed got killed, there might be enough fuss to get Bullock wondering. If he gets wondering, sooner or later the news would get back to the Taken. I figure we ought to save heroic measures for heroic circumstances."

Pawnbroker agreed. "That Shed's got something to hide. I know that in my guts. Croaker told him about the raid on the Catacombs. He hardly blinked. Anybody else would have whooped off and spread the news like the plague."

"Kingpin still watching him?" I asked.

"Him and Sharkey and Tickle are taking turns. He ain't going to be able to poot without we know about it."

"Good. Keep it that way. But don't mess with him. We just want to keep him away from Bullock and the Taken." I faded away into my thoughts.

"What?" Elmo finally asked.

"I had an idea while I was talking to Shed. Bullock is our main risk, right? And we know he'll stick like a bulldog once he gets on a trail. And he's on the trail of this Asa character. So why don't we con him into going south after this Asa?"

"I don't know," Elmo muttered. "He might find him."

"What's he want him for? Questioning about a raid on the Catacombs. What kind of cooperation is he going to get someplace else? Not much. Way I hear it, the cities down the coast think Juniper is a bad joke. Anyway, we just want to buy a little time. And if he does catch up with Asa, I figure he catches up with Raven, too. Ain't nobody going to bring Raven back. Not if he thinks the Taken are after Darling. They tangle, I'll put my money on Raven. Cut out the only source of info. Temporarily or permanently. See what I mean? And if he does kill Raven, then Raven can't talk."

"How you going to talk Bullock into it?" Elmo asked. "It's dumb, Croaker. He's not going to go haring off after some minor suspect."

"Yes, he will. You remember, when we came here, he had to translate? How do you figure he learned the language of the Jewel Cities? I asked him. He spent three years there looking for a guy who wasn't any more important than Asa."

Goblin said, "This mess gets crazier every day. We got so many cons and lies going I can't keep track of them anymore. I don't think we better do anything except cover our asses till the Captain gets here."

I often had a feeling we were making things worse. But I could see no exit, other than to keep coping and hoping.

"Best way out," Elmo observed laconically, "would be to kill everybody who knows anything, then all of us fall on our swords."

"Sounds a little extreme," Goblin opined. "But if you want to go first, I'm right behind you."

"I've got to report in to Whisper," I said. "Anybody got any brilliant ideas what I should tell her?"

Nobody did. I went, dreading the encounter. I was sure guilt smouldered in my eyes whenever I faced her. I resented Elmo because he did not have to endure her daily fits of ire.

Bullock was almost too easy. He was packing almost before I finished handing him my line of bull. He wanted that Asa bad.

I wondered if he knew something we did not. Or if he'd just worked up an obsession with the mystery of the invaded Catacombs.

Whisper was more of a problem.

She told me: "I want you to send somebody with him." I had had to tell her something, so had told her most of the truth. I figured the chances of anybody tracking Asa and Raven were nil. But. . . . She seemed a little too interested, too. Perhaps she knew more than she pretended. She was, after all, one of the Taken.

Elmo picked three men, put Kingpin in charge, and told him to stick a knife in Bullock if he looked like needing it.

The Captain and Company were, I was told, in the Wolander Mountains a hundred miles from Juniper. They faced a slow passage through tough passes, but I began to anticipate their arrival. Once the Old Man showed, the weight would be off Elmo and me. "Hurry," I muttered, and returned to tangling our skein of deceits.

Juniper: Lovers

Marron Shed fell in love. In love in the worst possible way—with a woman far younger, who had tastes far beyond his means. He charged into the affair with all the reserve of a bull in rut, disdaining consequences, squandering his cash reserve as though it came from a bottomless box. His boxes dried up. Two weeks after he met Sue, he made a loan with Gilbert, the moneylender. Another loan followed that, then another. Within a month he had gone into debt farther than he had been during the winter.

And he did not care. The woman made him happy, and that was that. Compounding his negative attributes was a tendency toward willful stupidity and an unconscious confidence that money could be no problem ever again.

Wally's wife Sal visited the Lily one morning, grim and slightly ashamed. "Marron," she said, "can we talk?"

"What's the matter?"

"You were going to help with rent and stuff."

"Sure. So what's the problem?"

"Well, I don't want to sound ungrateful or like I have any right to expect you to support us, but our landlord is threatening to throw us out on account of the rent hasn't been paid for two weeks. We can't get work on account of nobody is putting out any sewing right now."

"The rent isn't paid? But I saw him just the other day. . . ." It hadn't been just the other day. He had forgotten. His mother, too. Her servants' salaries would be due in a few days. Not to mention Lisa's. "Oh my," he said. "I'm sorry. I forgot. I'll take care of it."

"Shed, you've been good to us. You didn't have to be. I don't like seeing you get into this kind of mess."

"What kind of mess?"

"With that woman. She's trying to destroy you."

He was too puzzled to become angry. "Sue? Why? How?"

"Give her up. It'll hurt less if you break it off. Everybody knows what she's doing."

"What's she doing?" Shed's voice was plaintive.

"Never mind. I said more than I should already. If there's ever anything we can do for you, let us know."

"I will. I will," he promised. He went upstairs, to his hidden cash box, and found it barren.

There was not a gersh in the place, upstairs or down. What was going on? "Lisa. Where's all the money?"

"I hid it."

"What?"

"I hid it. The way you're carrying on, you're going to lose this place. You have a legitimate expense, tell me. I'll cover it."

Shed goggled. He sputtered. "Who the hell do you think you are, girl?"

"The girl who's going to keep you in business in spite of yourself. The girl who's going to stop you from being a complete fool with Gilbert's woman."

"Gilbert's?"

"Yes. What did you think was going on?"

"Get out," Shed snapped. "You don't work here anymore."

Lisa shrugged. "If that's what you want."

"Where's the money?"

"Sorry. Come see me when you get your common sense back."

Shed raged around the common room. His customers clapped, egging him on. He threatened. He cajoled. Nothing worked. Lisa remained adamant. "It's my family!" he protested.

"You go prove that woman isn't Gilbert's whore. Then I'll give you the money and walk."

"I'll do that."

"What if I'm right?"

"You're not. I know her."

"You don't know shit. You're infatuated. What if I'm right?"

He was incapable of entertaining the possibility. "I don't care."

"All right. If I'm right, I want to run things here. You let me get us out of debt."

Shed bobbed his head once and stormed out. He was not risking anything. She was wrong.

What was her game? She was acting like a partner or something. Like his mother had, after his father died and before she lost her sight. Treating him like he did not have twice her experience of business and the world.

He wandered for half an hour. When he came up from his melancholy, he saw he was near Sailmakers' Hall. Hell. He was there; he'd just go see Gilbert. Make a loan so he could see Sue that night. Little bitch Lisa could hide his money, maybe, but she couldn't keep him away from Gilbert.

Half a block later he began to suffer conscience pangs. Too many people depended upon him. He shouldn't make his financial situation worse.

"Damned woman," he muttered. "Shouldn't talk to me that way. Now she's got me doubting everybody." He leaned against a wall and fought his conscience. Sometimes lust pulled ahead, sometimes the urge toward responsibility. He ached for Sue. . . . He should not need money if she really loved him. . . .

"What?" he said aloud. He looked again. His eyes had not deceived him. That was Sue stepping into Gilbert's place.

His stomach sank like a falling rock. "No. She couldn't. . . . There must be an explanation."

But his traitor mind started cataloguing little oddities about their relationship, particularly mauling her penchant for spending. A low-grade anger simmered over the fire of his hurt. He slipped across the street, hurried into the alley leading behind Gilbert's place. Gilbert's office was in the back. It had an alley window. Shed did not expect that to be open. He did hope to sneak a peek.

The window was not open, but he could hear. And the sounds of lovemaking in no way approximated what he *wanted* to hear.

He considered killing himself on the spot. Considered killing himself on Sue's doorstep. Considered a dozen other dramatic protests. And knew none would move either of these villains.

They began talking. Their chatter soon killed Shed's hold-out doubts. The name Marron Shed came up.

"He's ready," the woman said. "I've taken him as far as I can. Maybe one more loan before he starts remembering his family."

"Do it, then. I want him wrapped up. Make the hill steep, then grease it. He got away from Krage."

Shed shook with anger.

"How far down do you have him?"

"Eighteen leva, and nearly another ten in interest."

"I can work him for another five."

"Do it. I have a buyer hot to go."

Shed left. He wandered the Buskin for hours. He looked so grim people crossed the street. There is no vengeance as terrible as the vengeance a coward plots in the dark of his heart.

Late that afternoon Shed strolled into Gilbert's office, all emotion locked back in the shadows he had discovered the night he had run with Krage's hunters. "I need fifteen leva, Gilbert. In a hurry."

Gilbert was startled. His one eye opened wide. "Fifteen? What the hell for?"

"I've set up a sweet deal, but I have to close it tonight. I'll go a couple extra points if you want."

"Shed, you're into me big now. I'm worried about you covering that."

"This deal goes off and I can clear it all."

Gilbert stared. "What's up, Shed?"

"Up?"

"You're awful sure of yourself."

Shed told the lie that hurt most. "I'm going to get married, Gilbert. Going to ask the lady tonight. I want to close this deal so I can make the Lily over into a decent place for her."

"Well," Gilbert breathed. "Well, well, well. Marron Shed getting married. Interesting. All right, Shed. It's not good business, but I'll take a chance. Fifteen, you said?"

"Thank you, Mr. Gilbert. I'm really grateful. . . ."

"You sure you can meet the payments?"

"I'll have you ten leva before the end of the week. Guaranteed. And with Sue helping out at the Lily, I'll have no problem clearing enough to cover the rest."

Gilbert controlled a thin smile. "Then you won't mind putting up collateral more valuable than your word?"

"Sir?"

"I want a lien on the Iron Lily."

Shed pretended to think hard. Finally: "All right. She's worth the risk."

Gilbert smiled the smile of a hungry stoat, but managed to look worried at the same time. "Wait here. I'll have a note drawn up and get the money."

Shed smiled nastily as Gilbert departed.

26

Juniper: Lovers' Parting

Shed pulled his rig into the alleyway behind Sue's place, raced around front, pounded on the door. It was a class place for the Buskin. A man guarded the entrance from within. Eight women lived there, each in her own apartment. Each in the same business as Sue. Each commanding a substantial premium for her time.

"Hello, Mr. Shed," the door guard said. "Go on up. She's expecting you."

Shed tipped him, something he hadn't done before. The man became obsequious. Shed ignored him, mounted the stair.

Now came the difficult part. Playing cow-eyed lover when he was no longer blind. But he would fool her, just as she had fooled him.

She answered the door, radiantly beautiful. Shed's heart climbed into his throat. He shoved something into her hand. "This is for you."

"Oh, Marron, you shouldn't have." But, if he hadn't, he would not have gotten past her door. "What a strange necklace. Are these serpents?"

"Real silver," he said. "And rubies. It caught my fancy. Ugly, but the craftsmanship is superb."

"I think it's gorgeous, Marron. How much did it cost?"

"Too much," Shed replied, smiling sardonically. "I couldn't tell you. More than I should have paid for anything."

Sue did not press. "Come here, Marron." She must have had orders to play him carefully. Usually she gave him a hard time before surrendering. She began disrobing.

Shed went. He took her rough, something he had not done before. Then he took her again. When it was over, she asked, "What's gotten into you?"

"I have a big surprise for you. A big surprise. I know you'll love it. Can you sneak out without anyone knowing?"

"Of course. But why?"

"That's the surprise. Will you do it? You won't be disappointed, I promise."

"I don't understand."

"Just do it. Slip out a few minutes after I leave. Meet me in the alley. I want to take you somewhere and show you something. Be sure to wear the necklace."

"What are you up to?" She seemed amused, not suspicious.

Good, Shed thought. He finished dressing. "No answers now, darling. This will be the biggest surprise of your life. I don't want to spoil it." He headed for the door.

"Five minutes?" she called.

"Don't make me wait. I'm a bear when I have to wait. And don't forget the necklace."

"I won't, dear."

Shed waited nearly fifteen minutes. He grew impatient, but was certain greed would bring Sue out. The hook was set. She was playing with him.

"Marron?" Her voice was soft and musical. His heart twisted. How could he do this?

"Here, love." She came to him. He enfolded her in his arms.

"Now, now. Enough of that. I want my surprise. I can hardly wait."

Shed took a deep breath. Do it! he yelled inside. "I'll help you up." She turned. *Now!* But his hands were made of lead.

"Come on, Marron."

He swung. Sue slammed into the wagon, a mewl the only sound she made. He hit her again as she bounced back. She sagged. He took a gag from the wagon, forced it into her mouth before she could scream, then tied her hands quickly. She began kicking when he went for her ankles. He kicked her back, nearly let anger carry him away.

She quit fighting. He finished binding her, then propped her on the wagon seat. In the darkness they looked like man and wife about some late business.

He did not speak till they were across the Port. "You're probably wondering what's going on, darling."

Sue grunted. She was pale and frightened. He retrieved his amulet. While he was at it, he stripped her of jewelry and valuables.

"Sue, I loved you. I really did. I would have done anything for you. When you kill a love like that, you turn it into a big hatred." At least twenty leva worth of jewelry, he guessed. How many men had she destroyed? "Working for Gilbert like that. Trying to steal the Lily. Anything else I could have forgiven. Anything."

He talked all the way up the hill. It distracted her till the black castle loomed so large it could no longer be overlooked. Then her eyes got huge. She began to shake, to stink as she lost all control.

"Yes, darling," Shed said, voice pleasantly rational, conversational. "Yes. The black castle. You were going to deliver me to the mercy of *your* friends. You made a bet and lost. Now I deliver you to *mine*." He halted, climbed down, went to the gate. It opened immediately.

The tall being met him, wringing spidery hands. "Good," it said. "Very good. Your partner never brought healthy game."

Shed's guts knotted. He wanted to change his mind. He only wanted to hurt and humiliate Sue. . . . But it was too late. He could not turn back. "I'm sorry, Sue. You shouldn't have done it. You and Gilbert. His turn will come. Marron Shed isn't what everybody thinks."

A whining noise came from behind Sue's gag. Shed turned away. He had to get out. He faced the tall creature. It began counting coins directly into his hand.

As always, Shed did not barter. In fact, he did not look at the money, just kept stuffing his pockets. His attention was on the darkness behind the creature.

More of its kind were back there, hissing, jostling. Shed recognized the short one he'd dealt with once.

The tall being stopped counting. Absently, Shed put the coins into a pocket, returned to his wagon. The things in shadow swept forward, seized Sue, began ripping her clothing. One yanked the gag out of her mouth. Shed started packing his rig.

"For God's sake, Marron. Don't leave me."

"It's done, woman. It's done." He snapped his traces. "Back up, mules."

She started screaming as he turned toward the gate. He did not look. He did not want to know. "Keep moving, mules."

"Come again soon, Marron Shed," the tall creature called after him.

27

Juniper: Banished

The summons from Whisper caught me unprepared. It was too early for the daily report. I'd barely finished breakfast. I knew it meant trouble.

I was not disappointed.

The Taken prowled like a caged animal, radiating tension and anger. I went inside by the numbers, stood at a perfect attention, giving no excuse for the picking of nits—in case whatever it was was not my fault.

She ignored me for several minutes, working off energy. Then she seated herself, stared at her hands thoughtfully.

Her gaze rose. And she was in complete control. She actually smiled. Had she been as beautiful as the Lady, that smile would have melted granite. But she was what she was, a scarred old campaigner, so a smile only ameliorated the grimness of her face.

"How were the men disposed last night?" she asked.

Baffled, I responded, "Excuse me? You mean their temper?"

"Where were they stationed?"

"Oh." That was properly Elmo's province, but I knew better than to say so. The Taken do not tolerate excuses, sound though they may be. "The three men on the ship south with Bullock, looking for that man Asa." I worried about her having sent them. When I do not understand the motives of the Taken, I get paranoid. "Five down in the Buskin pretending to be foreign sailors. Three more down there watching people we've found especially interesting. I'd have to double-check with Elmo to be positive, but at least four more were in other parts of the city, trying to pick up something of interest. The rest of us were here in the castle, off duty. Wait. One man would have been down in the Duke's secret police office, and two would have been at the Enclosure, hanging around with the Custodians. I was with the Inquisitors most of the night, picking their brains. We're scattered pretty thin right now. I'll be glad when the Captain gets here. We've got too much going for the available manpower. The occupation planning is way behind."

She sighed, rose, resumed pacing. "My fault as much as anyone's, I suppose." She looked out a window for a long time. Then she beckoned. I joined her.

She indicated the black castle. "Just whiskers short. They're trying to open the way for the Dominator already. It's not yet time, but they're getting hurried. Maybe they've sensed our interest."

This Juniper business was like some giant, tentacled sea beast from a sailor's lie. No matter where we turned or what we did, we got deeper into trouble. By working at cross-purposes with the Taken, trying to cover an increasingly more obvious trail, we were complicating their efforts to deal with the peril of the black castle. If we did cover well, we just might make it possible for the Dominator to emerge into an unprepared world.

I did not want that horror upon my conscience.

Though I fear I tend not to record it that way, we were embroiled in substantial moral quandaries. We are not accustomed to such problems. The lot of the mercenary does not require much moralizing or making of moral decisions. Essentially, the mercenary sets morality aside, or at best reorders the customary structures to fit the needs of his way of life. The great issues become how well he does his job, how faithfully he carries out his commission, how well he adheres to a standard demanding unswerving loyalties to his comrades. He dehumanizes the world outside the bounds of his outfit. Then anything he does, or witnesses, becomes of minor significance as long as its brunt is borne outside the Company.

We had drifted into a trap where we might have to face the biggest choice in the Company's history. We might have to betray four centuries of Company mythos on behalf of the greater whole.

I knew I could not permit the Dominator to restore himself, if that turned out to be the only way we could keep the Lady from finding out about Darling and Raven.

Yet. . . . The Lady was not much better. We served her, and, till lately, well and faithfully, obliterating the Rebel wherever we found him, but I don't think many of us were indifferent to what she was. She was less evil than the Dominator only because she was less determined about it, more patient in her drive for total and absolute control.

That presented me with another quandary. Was I capable of sacrificing Darling to prevent the Dominator's return? If that became the price?

"You seem very thoughtful," Whisper said.

"Uhm. There're too many angles to this business. The Custodians. The Duke. Us. Bullock, who has axes of his own to grind." I had told her about Bullock's Buskin origins, feeding her seemingly irrelevant information to complicate and distract her thinking.

She pointed again. "Didn't I suggest a close watch be kept on that place?"

"Yes, ma'am. We did for a while, too. But nothing ever happened, and then we were told to do some other things. . . ." I broke off, quaking with a sudden nasty suspicion.

She read my face. "Yes. Last night. And this delivery was still alive."

"Oh boy," I murmured. "Who did it? You know?"

"We just sensed the consequent changes. They tried to open the way. They weren't strong enough yet, but they came very close."

She began to prowl. Mentally, I ticked off the roster for the Buskin last night. I was going to ask some very pointed questions.

"I consulted the Lady directly. She's very worried. Her orders are to let ancillary business slide. We're to prevent any more bodies reaching the castle. Yes, the rest of your Company will be here soon. From six to ten days. And there is much to be done to prepare for their arrival. But, as you observed, there is too much to do and too few to do it. Let your Captain cope when he arrives. The black castle must be isolated."

"Why not fly some men in?"

"The Lady has forbidden that."

I tried to look perplexed. "Buy why?" I had a sweating, fearful suspicion that I knew.

Whisper shrugged. "Because she doesn't want you wasting time making hellos and briefing newcomers. Go see what can be done about isolating the castle."

"Yes, ma'am."

I departed, thinking it had gone both better and worse than I had anticipated. Better, because she did not throw one of her screaming rages. Worse, because she had in effect announced that we who were here already were suspect, that we might have succumbed to a moral infection the Lady did not want communicated to our brethren.

Scary.

"Yeah," Elmo said when I told him. He did not need it explained. "Which means we got to make contact with the Old Man."

"Messenger?"

"What else? Who can we break loose and cover?"

"One of the men from the Buskin."

Elmo nodded. "I'll handle that. You go ahead and figure how to isolate the castle with the manpower we have."

"Why don't you go scout the castle? I want to find out what those guys were doing last night."

"That's neither here nor there now, Croaker. I'm taking over. Not saying you done a bad job, just you didn't get it done. Which is my fault, really. I'm the soldier."

"Being a soldier won't make any difference, Elmo. This isn't soldier's work. It's spy stuff. And spies need time to worm into the fabric of a society. We haven't had enough of that."

"Time is up now. Isn't that what you said?"

"I guess," I admitted. "All right. I'll scout the castle. But you find out what went on down there last night. Especially around that placed called the Iron Lily. It keeps turning up, just like that guy Asa."

All the while we talked, Elmo was changing. Now he looked like a sailor down on his luck, too old to ship, but still tough enough for dirty work. He would fit right in down in the Buskin. I told him so.

"Yeah. Let's get moving. And don't plan on getting much sleep till the Captain gets here."

We looked at one another, not saying what lay in the backs of our minds. If the Taken did not want us in touch with our brethren, what might they do when the Company hove in sight, coming out of the Wolanders?

* * *

Up close, the black castle was both intriguing and unsettling. I took a horse over, circled the place several times, even flipped a cheerful wave at the one movement I detected atop its glassy ramparts.

There was some difficult ground behind it—steep, rocky, overgrown with scraggly, thorny brush which had a sagey odor. Nobody lugging a corpse would reach the fortress from that direction. The ground was better along the ridgeline to east and west, but even there an approach was improbable. Men of the sort who sold corpses would do things the easy way. That meant using the road which ran from the Port River waterfront, through the scatter of merchant class houses on the middle slopes, and just kept on to the castle gate. Someone had followed that course often, for wheel ruts ran from the end of the road to the castle.

My problem was, there was no place a squad could lie in wait without being seen from the castle wall. It took me till dusk to finalize my plan.

I found an abandoned house a ways down the slope and a little upriver. I would conceal my squad there and post sentries down the road, in the populated area. They could run a message to the rest of us if they saw anything suspicious. We could hustle up and across the slope to intercept potential body-sellers. Wagons would be slow enough to allow us the time needed.

Old Croaker is a brilliant strategist. Yes, sir. I had my troops in place and everything set by midnight. And had two false alarms before breakfast. I learned the embarrassing way that there was legitimate night traffic past my sentry post.

I sat in the old house with my team, alternately playing Tonk and worrying, and on rare occasions napping. And wondering a lot about what was happening down in the Buskin and across the valley in Duretile.

I prayed Elmo could keep his fingers on all the strings.

28

Juniper: Lisa

Shed spent an entire day lying in his room, staring at the ceiling, hating himself. He had sunk as low as a man could. There was no deed too foul for him anymore, and nothing more he could do to blacken his soul. A million-leva passage fee could not buy him aboard on Passage Day. His name had to be written in the Black Book with those of the greatest villains.

"Mr. Shed?" Lisa said from the doorway next morning, as he was contemplating another day of ceiling study and self-pity. "Mr. Shed?"

"Yeah?"

"Bo and Lana are here."

Bo and Lana, with a daughter, were his mother's servants. "What do they want?"

"Their accounts settled for the month, I expect."

"Oh." He got up.

Lisa stopped him at the head of the stair. "I was right about Sue, wasn't I?"

"You were."

"I'm sorry. I wouldn't have said anything if we could have afforded it."

"We? What do you mean, we? Oh, hell. Never mind. Forget about it. I don't want to hear about it anymore."

"Whatever you say. But I'm going to hold you to your promise."

"What promise?"

"To let me manage the Lily."

"Oh. All right." At that moment he did not care. He collected the monthly accounting from the servants. He had chosen them well. They were not cheating him. He suggested they deserved a small bonus.

He returned upstairs for the money. Lisa watched him go, perplexed. He realized his mistake too late. Now she wondered why he had money today when he'd had none yesterday. He located his dirty clothing, emptied his pockets onto his bed. And gasped.

"Oh, damn! Damn," he muttered. "What the hell am I going to do with three gold pieces?"

There was silver, too, and even a fistful of copper, but. . . . It was a gyp! A fortune he could not spend. Juniper law made it illegal for commoners to hold minted gold. Even incoming foreigners had to exchange theirs for silver—though foreign silver was as welcome as local. Lucky, too, for the black castle mintage was a decidedly odd coinage, though in the standard weights.

How could he get rid of the gold? Sell it to some ship captain headed south? That was the usual procedure. He slipped it into his most secret hiding place, with the amulet from the black castle. A useless fortune. He assessed the remainder. Twenty-eight pieces of silver, plus several leva in copper. Enough to take care of his mother and Sal. Way short of enough to pry Gilbert off his back. "Still be in the damned money trap," he whined.

He recalled Sue's jewelry, smiled nastily, muttered, "I'll do it." He pocketed everything, returned to the ground floor, paid his mother's servants, told Lisa, "I'm going out for a while."

First he made sure Wally's family was cared for, then ambled down toward Gilbert's place. No one seemed to be around. Gilbert was not like Krage, in that he felt he needed an army on hand, but he did have his bone-breakers. They were all away. But someone was in Gilbert's office because lamplight illuminated the curtains. He smiled thoughtfully, then hustled back to the Lily.

He went to a table back in the shadows, near where Raven used to sit. A couple of foreign sailors were seated there. Tough merchandise if he'd ever seen it. They'd been around for some time. They said they and their friends, who came and went, had missed their ship. They were waiting for another. Shed could not recall having heard the name of their home port.

"You men like to pick up some easy money?" he asked.

"Who doesn't?" one responded.

And the other, "What you got in mind?"

"I have a little problem. I've got to do some business with a man. He's liable to get vicious."

"Want some back-up, eh?"

Shed nodded.

The other sailor looked at him narrowly. "Who is he?"

"Name's Gilbert. A moneylender. You heard of him?"

"Yeah."

"I was just past his place. Don't look like there's anybody there but him."

The men exchanged glances. The taller said, "Tell you what. Let me go get a friend of ours."

"I can't afford a whole army."

"Hey, no problem. You two work out what you'd pay two of us; he'll come along free. Just feel more comfortable having him with us."

"Tough?"

Both men grinned. One winked at the other. "Yeah. Like you wouldn't believe."

"Then get him."

One man left. Shed dickered with the other. Lisa watched from across the room, eyes narrow and hard. Shed decided she was getting too much into his business too fast.

The third man was a frog-faced character barely five feet tall. Shed frowned at him. His fetcher reminded, "He's tough. Remember?"

"Yeah? All right. Let's go." He felt a hundred percent better with three men accompanying him, though he had no real assurance they would help if Gilbert started something.

There were a couple of thugs in the front room when Shed arrived. He told them: "I want to see Gilbert."

"Suppose he don't want to see you?" It was standard tough-guy game-playing. Shed did not know how to respond. One of his companions saved him the worry.

"He don't got much choice, does he? Unless that fat's all muscle in disguise." He produced a knife, began cleaning his nails. The deed was so reminiscent of Raven that Shed was startled.

"He's back in the office." The fat thug exchanged a look with his companion. Shed figured one would run for help.

He started moving. His frog-faced companion said, "I'll just stay out here."

Shed pushed into Gilbert's office. The moneylender had a sack of leva on his desk, was weighing coins one at a time on a fine scale, sorting out those that had been clipped. He looked up angrily. "What the hell is this?"

"Couple of friends wanted to stop by with me and watch how you do business."

"I don't like what this says about our relationship, Shed. It says you don't trust me."

Shed shrugged. "There's some nasty rumors out there. About you and Sue working on me. To do me out of the Lily."

"Sue, eh? Where is she, Shed?"

"There is a connection, eh?" Shed let his face fall. "Damn you. That's why she turned me down. You villain. Now she won't even see me. That ape at the door keeps telling me she isn't there. You arrange that, Mister Gilbert? You know, I don't like you much."

Gilbert gave the lot of them a nasty one-eyed stare. For a moment he seemed to consider his chances. Then the small man ambled in, leaned against the wall, his wide mouth wrinkled into a sneer.

Gilbert said, "You come to talk or to do business? If it's business, get at it. I want these creeps out of here. They'll give the neighborhood a bad name."

Shed produced a leather bag. "You have the bad name, Gilbert. I hear people saying they won't do business with you anymore. They don't think it's right you should try to screw people out of their property."

"Shut up and give me some money, Shed. You just want to whine, get out."

"Sure talks tough for being down four to one," one of the men remarked. A companion admonished him in another language. Gilbert glared in a way that said he was memorizing faces. The little man grinned and beckoned with one finger. Gilbert decided it could wait.

Shed counted coins. Gilbert's eyes widened as the stack grew. Shed said, "Told you I was working on a deal." He tossed in Sue's jewelry.

One of his companions picked up a bracelet, examined it. "How much do you owe this character?"

Gilbert snapped a figure, which Shed suspected to be inflated.

The sailor observed, "You're shorting yourself, Shed."

"I just want quit of this jackal's lien on my place."

Gilbert stared at the jewelry, pallid, stiff. He licked his lips and reached for a ring. His hand shook.

Shed was both fearful and filled with malicious glee. Gilbert knew the ring. Now maybe he would be a little nervous about messing with Marron Shed. Or he might decide to cut a few throats. Gilbert had some of the same ego problems Krage had had.

"This should more than cover everything, Mr. Gilbert. The big, too. Even with the extra points. Let's have my lien back."

Dully, Gilbert retrieved that from a box on a nearby shelf. His eyes never left the ring.

Shed destroyed the lien immediately. "Don't I still owe you a little something, though, Mr. Gilbert? Yes, I think so. Well, I'll do my best to see you get everything you've got coming."

Gilbert squinted angrily. Shed thought he saw a hint of fear, too. That pleased him. Nobody was ever afraid of Marron Shed, except maybe Asa, who did not count.

Best make his exit, before he stretched his luck. "Thank you, Mr. Gilbert. See you again soon."

Passing through the outer room, he was astonished to find Gilbert's men snoring. The frog-faced man grinned. Outside, Shed paid his guardians. "He wasn't as much trouble as I expected."

"You had us with you," the little man said. "Let's go to your place and have a beer."

One of the others observed, "He looked like he was in shock."

The little man asked, "How'd you ever get that far into a moneylender, anyway?"

"A skirt. I thought I was going to marry her. She was just taking me for my money. I finally woke up."

His companions shook their heads. One said, "Women. Got to watch them, buddy. They'll pick your bones."

"I learned my lesson. Hey. Drinks on the house. I've got some wine I used to keep for a special customer. He left town, so I'm stuck with it."

"That bad, eh?"

"No. That good. Nobody can afford it."

Shed spent his entire evening sipping wine, even after the sailors decided they had business elsewhere. He broke into a grin each time he recalled Gilbert's reaction to the ring. "Got to be careful now," he muttered. "He's as crazy as Krage."

In time the good feeling departed. Fear took over. He'd face anything Gilbert did alone, and he was still very much the same old Shed under the patina left by Raven and a few deals since.

"Ought to haul the bastard up the hill," he muttered into his mug. Then: "Damn! I'm as bad as Raven. Worse. Raven never delivered them alive. Wonder what that bastard is doing now, with his fancy ship and slick young slot?"

He got himself very, very drunk and very, very filled with self-pity.

The last guest went to his bunk. The last outsider went home. Shed sat there nursing his wine and glowering at Lisa, angry with her for no reason he could define. Her body, he thought. Ripe. But she wouldn't. Too good for him. And her pushiness lately. Yeah.

She studied him as she cleaned up. Efficient little witch. Better even than Darling, who had worked hard but hadn't the economy of movement Lisa had. Maybe she *did* deserve to manage the place. He hadn't done such a great job.

He found her seated opposite him. He glowered. She did not retreat. A hard lass, too. Wouldn't bluff. Didn't scare. Tough Buskin bitch. Be trouble someday.

"What's the matter, Mr. Shed?"

"Nothing."

"I hear you paid Gilbert off. On a loan you took on this place. How could you take a loan on the Lily? It's been in your family for ages."

"Don't give me that sentimental crap. You don't believe it."

"Where did you get the money?"

"Maybe you shouldn't be so nosy. Maybe nosiness could be bad for your health." He was talking surly and tough but not meaning what he said.

"You've been acting strange lately."

"I was in love."

"That wasn't it. What happened to that, anyway? I hear Sue disappeared. Gilbert says you did her in."

"Did what? I was over to her place today."

"You see her?"

"No. The door guard said she wasn't home. Which means she didn't want to see me. Probably had somebody else up there."

"Maybe it meant she wasn't home."

Shed snorted. "I told you I don't want to talk about her anymore. Understand?"

"Sure. Tell me where you got the money."

Shed glared. "Why?"

"Because if there's more, I want a chunk. I don't want to spend my life in the Buskin. I'll do whatever it takes to get out."

Shed smirked.

She misunderstood. "This job is just to keep body and soul together till I find something."

"A million people have thought that, Lisa. And they've frozen to death in Buskin alleys."

"Some make it. I don't intend to fail. Where did you get the money, Mr. Shed?" She went for a bottle of the good wine. Vaguely, Shed thought it must be about gone.

He told her about his silent partner.

"That's a crock. I've been here long enough to know that."

"Better believe it, girl." He giggled. "You keep pushing and you're liable to meet him. You won't like him, I guarantee." He recalled the tall creature telling him to hurry back.

"What happened to Sue?"

Shed tried to rise. His limbs were limp. He fell back into his seat. "I'm drunk. Drunker than I thought. Getting out of shape." Lisa nodded gravely. "I loved her. I really loved her. She shouldn't ought to have done that. I would have treated her like a queen. Would have gone into hell for her. Almost did." He chuckled. "Went in with her. . . . Oops."

"Would you do that for me, Mr. Shed?"

"What?"

"You're always trying to get me. What's it worth?"

Shed leered. "Don't know. Can't tell till I've tried you."

"You don't have anything to give me, old man."

"Know where to get it, though."

"Where?"

Shed just sat there grinning, a bit of drool trailing from one corner of his mouth.

"I give up. You win. Come on. I'll help you get up the stairs before I go home."

The climb was an epic. Shed was one drink short of passing out. When they reached his room, he just toppled into bed. "Thanks," he mumbled. "What're you doing?"

"You have to get undressed."

"Guess so." He made no effort to help. "What're you doing now? Why're you grabbing me like that?"

"You want me, don't you?" A moment later she was in the bed with him, rubbing her nakedness against his. He was too drunk to make anything of the situation. He held her, and became maudlin, spouting his trials. She played to it.

29

Juniper: Payoff

Shed sat up so suddenly his head twisted around. Somebody started beating drums inside. He rolled to the edge of the bed and was noisily sick. And then became sick in another way. With terror.

"I told her. I told her the whole damned thing." He tried to jump up. He had to get out of Juniper before the Inquisitors came. He had gold. A foreign captain might take him south. He could catch up with Raven and Asa. . . . He settled onto the cot, too miserable to act. "I'm dying," he muttered. "If there's a hell, this is what it's going to be like."

Had he told her? He thought so. And for nothing. He had gotten nothing. "Marron Shed, you were born to lose. When will you ever learn?"

He rose once more, cautiously, and fumbled through his hiding place. The gold was there. Maybe he hadn't told her everything. He considered the amulet. Lisa could follow the trail blazed by Sue. If she hadn't told anybody yet. But she would be wary, wouldn't she? Be hard to catch her off guard. Even assuming he could find her.

"My head! Gods! I can't think." There was a sudden racket downstairs. "Damn," he muttered. "She left the place unlocked. They'll steal everything." Tears rolled down his cheeks. Such an end he had come to. Maybe that was Bullock and his thugs knocking around down there.

Best to meet his fate. Cursing, he eased into his clothing, began the long journey downstairs.

"Good morning, Mr. Shed," Lisa called brightly. "What will you have for breakfast?"

He stared, gulped, finally stumbled to a table, sat there with his head in his hands, ignoring the amused stare of one of his companions of the Gilbert adventure.

"A little hung over, Mr. Shed?" Lisa asked.

"Yes." His own voice sounded thunderous.

"I'll mix you something my father taught me to make. He's a master drunkard, you know."

Shed nodded weakly. Even that proved painful. Lisa's father was one reason he had hired her. She needed all the help she could get. Another of his charities gone sour.

She returned with something so foul even a sorcerer would not have touched it. "Drink fast. It goes down easier that way."

"I can imagine." Half praying it would poison him, he gulped the malodorous concoction. After gasping for breath, he murmured, "When are they coming? How long do I have?"

"Who, Mr. Shed?"

"The Inquisitors. The law. Whoever you called."

"Why would they come here?"

Painfully, he raised his gaze to meet hers.

She whispered, "I told you I'll do anything to get out of the Buskin. This is the chance I've been looking for. We're partners now, Mr. Shed. Fifty-fifty."

Shed buried his head in his hands and groaned. It would never end. Not till it devoured him. He cast curses on Raven and all his house.

The common room was empty. The door was closed. "First we have to take care of Gilbert," Lisa said.

Shed bobbed his head, refused to look up.

"That was stupid, giving him jewelry he would recognize. He'll kill you if we don't kill him first."

Again Shed bobbed his head. Why me? he whined to himself. What have I done to deserve this?

"And don't you think you can get rid of me the way you did Sue and that blackmailer. My father has a letter he'll take to Bullock if I disappear."

"You're too smart for your own good." And: "It won't be long till winter."

"Yes. But we won't do it Raven's way. Too risky and too much work. We'll get charitable. Let all the derelicts in. One or two can disappear every night."

"You're talking murder!"

"Who'll care? Nobody. They'll be better off themselves. Call it mercy."

"How can anybody so young be so heartless?"

"You don't prosper in the Buskin if you have a heart, Mr. Shed. We'll fix a place where the outside cold will keep them till we get a wagonload. We can take them up maybe once a week."

"Winter is. . . ."

"Is going to be my last season in the Buskin."

"I won't do it."

"Yes, you will. Or you'll hear from Bullock. You don't have a choice. You have a partner."

"God, deliver me from evil."

"Are you less evil than me? You killed five people."

"Four," he protested weakly.

"You think Sue is still alive? You're splitting hairs. Any way you look at it, you're guilty of murder. You're a murderer so dumb about money he doesn't have a gersh to his name. So stupid he keeps getting tangled with Sues and Gilberts. Mr. Shed, they only execute you once."

How to argue with sociopathic reasoning? Lisa was the heart of Lisa's universe. Other people existed only to be exploited.

"There are some others we should think about after Gilbert. That man of Krage's who got away. He knows there was something strange about the bodies not turning up. He hasn't talked or it would be all over the Buskin. But someday he might. And there's the man you hired to help you with the blackmailer."

She sounded like a general planning a campaign. Planning murder wholesale. How could anybody? . . .

"I want no more blood on my hands, Lisa."

"How much choice do you have?"

He could not deny that Gilbert's death had meaning in the equation of his survival. And after Gilbert, one more. Before she destroyed him. She would let her guard down sometime.

What about that letter? Damn. Maybe her father had to go first. . . . The trap was vast and had no apparent exits.

"This could be my only chance to get out, Mr. Shed. You'd better believe I'm going to grab it."

Shed shook his lethargy, leaned forward, stared into the fireplace. His own survival came first. Gilbert had to go. That was definite.

What about the black castle? Had he told her about the amulet? He could not recall. He had to imply the existence of a special passkey, else she might try to kill and sell *him*. He would become a danger to her once they implemented her plan. Yes. For sure. She would try to rid herself of him once she made her connection with the things in the castle. So add another to his must-kill list.

Damn. Raven had done the smart thing, the only thing possible. Had taken the only exit. Leaving Juniper was the only way out.

"Going to have to follow him," he muttered. "There isn't any choice."

"What?"

"Just muttering, girl. You win. Let's get to work on Gilbert."

"Good. Stay sober and get up early tomorrow. You'll need to watch the Lily while I check something out."

"All right."

"Time you pulled your own weight again, anyway."

"Probably so."

Lisa eyed him suspiciously. "Good night, Mr. Shed."

Lisa told Shed: "It's set up. He'll meet me at my place tonight. Alone. You bring your wagon. I'll make sure my dad isn't around."

"I hear Gilbert won't go anywhere without a bodyguard now."

"He will tonight. He's supposed to pay me ten leva to help get control of the Lily. I let him think he's going to get something else, too."

Shed's stomach growled. "What if he catches on?"

"There's two of us and one of him. How did such a chicken-shit manage everything you have?"

He had dealt with the lesser fear. But he kept that thought to himself. There was no point giving Lisa more handles than she had. It was time to find handles on her. "Aren't you scared of anything, child?"

"Poverty. Especially of being old and poor. I get the grey shakes whenever I see the Custodians haul some poor old stiff out of an alley."

"Yeah. That I can understand." Shed smiled thinly. That was a beginning.

Shed stopped the wagon, glanced at the window of a downstairs rear apartment. No candle burning there. Lisa hadn't yet arrived. He snapped the traces, rolled on. Gilbert might have scouts out. He was not stupid.

Shed pulled around a kink in the alleyway, strolled back pretending to be a drunk. Before long someone lighted a candle in the apartment. Heart hammering, Shed slunk to the rear door.

It was unlocked. As promised. Maybe Gilbert *was* stupid. Gently, he eased inside. His stomach was a mess of knots. His hands shook. A scream lay coiled in his throat.

This was not the Marron Shed who had fought Krage and his troops. That Shed had been trapped and fighting for his life. He had had no time to think himself into a panic. This Shed did. He was convinced he would foul up.

The apartment consisted of two tiny rooms. The first, behind the door, was dark and empty. Shed moved through carefully, eased to a ragged curtain. A man murmured beyond the doorway. Shed peeked.

Gilbert had disrobed and was resting a knee on a bedraggled excuse of a bed. Lisa was in it, covers pulled to her neck, pretending second thoughts. Gilbert's withered, wrinkled, blue-veined old body contrasted bizarrely with her youth.

Gilbert was angry.

Shed cursed mutely. He wished Lisa would stop playing games. Always she had to do more than go directly to her goal. She had to manipulate along the way, just to satisfy something within herself.

He wanted to get it over.

Lisa pretended surrender, made room for Gilbert beside her.

The plan was for Shed to strike once Lisa enwrapped Gilbert in arms and legs. He decided to play a game of his own. He let it wait. He stood there grinning while her face betrayed her thoughts, while Gilbert sated himself upon her.

Finally, Shed moved in.

Three quick, quiet steps. He looped a garotte around Gilbert's skinny neck, leaned back. Lisa tightened her grip. How small and mortal the moneylender appeared. How unlike a man feared by half the Buskin.

Gilbert struggled, but could not escape.

Shed thought it would never end. He hadn't realized it took so long to strangle a man. Finally, he stepped back. His shakes threatened to overcome him.

"Get him off!" Lisa squealed.

Shed rolled the corpse aside. "Get dressed. Come on. Let's get out of here. He might have some men hanging around. I'll get the wagon." He swept to the door, peeped into the alleyway. Nobody around. He recovered the wagon fast.

"Come on!" he snapped when he returned and found Lisa still undressed. "Let's get him out of here."

She could not tear herself away.

Shed shoved clothing into her arms, slapped her bare behind. "Get moving, damn it."

She dressed slowly. Shed fluttered to the door, checked the alley. Still no one around. He scooted back to the body, hustled it to the wagon and covered it with a tarp. Funny how they seemed lighter when they were dead.

Back inside: "Will you come on? I'll drag you out the way you are."

The threat had no effect. Shed grabbed her hand, dragged her out the door. "Up." He hoisted her onto the seat, jumped up himself.

He flicked the traces. The mules plodded forward. Once he crossed the Port River bridge, they knew where they were headed and needed little guidance. Idly, he wondered how many times they had made the journey.

The wagon was halfway up the hill before he calmed down enough to study Lisa. She seemed to be in shock. Suddenly, murder was not just talk. She had helped kill. Her neck was in a noose. "Not as easy as you thought, eh?"

"I didn't know it would be like that. I was holding him. I felt the life go out. It. . . . It wasn't what I expected."

"And you want to make a career of it. I'll tell you something. I'm not killing my customers. You want it done that way, you do it yourself."

She tried a feeble threat.

"You don't have any power over me anymore. Go to the Inquisitors. They'll take you to a truth-sayer. Partner."

Lisa shivered. Shed held his tongue till they neared the black castle. "Let's not play games anymore." He was considering selling her along with Gilbert, but decided he could not muster the hatred, anger or downright meanness to do it.

He stopped the mules. "You stay here. Don't get off the wagon no matter what. Understand?"

"Yes." Lisa's voice was small and distant. Terrified, he thought.

He knocked on the black gate. It swung inward. He resumed his seat and drove inside, stepped down, swung Gilbert onto a stone slab. The tall creature came forth, examined the body, looked at Lisa.

"Not this one," Shed said. "She's a new partner."

The creature nodded. "Thirty."

"Done."

"We need more bodies, Marron Shed. Many bodies. Our work is nearing completion. We grow eager to finish."

Shed shuddered at its tone. "There'll be more soon."

"Good. Very good. You shall be rewarded richly."

Shed shuddered again, looked around. The thing asked, "You seek the woman? She has not yet become one with the portal." It snapped long, yellow fingers.

Feet scuffed in the darkness. Shadows came forth. They held the arms of a naked Sue. Shed swallowed hard. She had been used badly. She had lost weight, and her skin was colorless where not marked with bruises or abrasions. One of the creatures raised her chin, made her look at Shed. Her eyes were hollow and vacant. "The walking dead," he whispered.

"Is the revenge sweet enough?" the tall creature asked.

"Take her away! I don't want to see her."

The tall being snapped its fingers. Its compatriots retreated into the shadows.

"My money!" Shed snarled.

Chuckling, the being counted coins at Gilbert's feet. Shed scooped them into his pocket. The being said, "Bring us more live ones, Marron Shed. We have many uses for live ones."

A scream echoed from the darkness. Shed thought he heard his name called.

"She recognized you, friend."

A whimper crawled out of Shed's throat. He vaulted onto the wagon seat, snarled at his mules.

The tall creature eyed Lisa with unmistakable meaning. Lisa read it. "Let's get out of here, Mr. Shed. Please?"

"Git up, mules." The wagon creaked and groaned and seemed to take forever getting through the gate. Screams continued echoing from somewhere deep inside the castle.

Outside, Lisa looked at Shed with a decidedly odd expression. Shed thought he detected relief, fear, and a little loathing. Relief seemed foremost. She sensed how vulnerable she had been. Shed smiled enigmatically, nodded, and said nothing. Like Raven, he recalled.

He grinned. Like Raven.

Let her think. Let her worry.

The mules halted. "Eh?"

Men materialized out of the darkness. They held naked weapons. Military-type weapons.

A voice said, "I'll be damned. It's the innkeeper."

30

Juniper: More Trouble

Otto rolled in out of the night. "Hey! Croaker! We got a customer."

I folded my hand but did not throw the cards in. "You sure?" I was damned tired of false alarms.

Otto looked sheepish. "Yeah. For sure."

Something was wrong here. "Where is he? Let's have all of it."

"They're going to make it inside."

"They?"

"Man and a woman. We didn't think they were anything to worry about till they were past the last house and still headed uphill. It was too late to stop them then."

I slapped my hand down. I was pissed. There would be hell to pay in the morning. Whisper had had it up to her chin with me already. This might be her excuse to park me in the Catacombs. Permanently. The Taken are not patient.

"Let's go," I said in as calm a voice as I could manage, while glaring a hole through Otto. He made sure he stayed out of reach. He knew I was not pleased. Knew I was in a tight place with the Taken. He did not want to give me any excuse to wrap my hands around his neck. "I'm going to cut some throats if this gets screwed up again." We all grabbed weapons and rushed into the night.

We had our place picked, in brush two hundred yards below the castle gate. I got the men into position just as somebody started screaming inside.

"Sounds bad," one of the men said.

"Keep it down," I snapped. Cold crept my spine. It did sound bad.

It went on and on and on. Then I heard the muted jangle of harness and the creak of wheels improperly greased. Then the voices of people talking softly.

We jumped out of the brush. One of the men opened the eye of a lantern. "I'll be damned!" I said. "It's the innkeeper."

The man sagged. The woman stared at us, eyes widening. Then she sprang off the wagon and ran.

"Get her, Otto. And heaven help you if you don't. Crake, drag this bastard down. Walleye, take the wagon around to the house. The rest of us will cut across."

The man Shed did not struggle, so I detailed another two men to help Otto. He and the woman were crashing through the brush. She was headed toward a small precipice. She should corner herself there.

We led Shed to the old house. Once in the light, he became more deflated, more resigned. He said nothing. Most captives resist detention somehow, if only by denying that there is any reason to detain them. Shed looked like a man who thought he was overdue for the worst.

"Sit," I said, and indicated a chair at the table where we had played cards. I took another, turned it, parked myself with forearms atop its back and chin upon my forearms. "We've got you dead, Shed."

He just stared at the tabletop, a man without hope.

"Anything to say?"

"There's nothing to be said, is there?"

"Oh, I think there's a whole lot. You've got your ass in a sling for sure, but you're not dead yet. You maybe could talk your way out of this."

His eyes widened slightly, then emptied again. He did not believe me.

"I'm not an Inquisitor, Shed."

His eyes flickered with momentary life.

"It's true. I followed Bullock around because he knew the Buskin. My job had very little to do with his. I couldn't care less about the Catacombs raid. I do care about the black castle, because it's a disaster in the making, but not as much as I care about you. Because of a man named Raven."

"One of your men called you Croaker. Raven was scared to death of somebody named Croaker that he saw one night when the Duke's men grabbed some of his friends."

So. He'd witnessed our raid. Damn, but I had cut it close to the wind that time.

"I'm that Croaker. And I want to know everything you know about Raven and Darling. And everything about anybody else who knows anything."

The slightest hint of defiance crossed his face.

"A lot of folks are looking for you, Shed. Bullock isn't the only one. My boss wants you, too. And she's worse trouble than he is. You wouldn't like her at all. And she'll get you if you don't do this right."

I would rather have given him to Bullock. Bullock wasn't interested in our problems with the Taken. But Bullock was out of town.

"There's Asa, too. I want to know everything you haven't told me about him." I heard the woman cursing in the distance, carrying on like Otto and the guys were trying to rape her. I knew better. They hadn't the nerve after having screwed up once already tonight. "Who's the slot?"

"My barmaid. She. . . ." And his story boiled out. Once he started, there was no stopping him.

I had a notion how to wriggle out of a potentially embarrassing situation. "Shut him up." One of the men clamped a hand over Shed's mouth. "Here's what we're going to do, Shed. Assuming you want out of this alive."

He waited.

"The people I work for will know a body was delivered tonight. They'll expect me to catch whoever did it. I'll have to give them someone. That could be you, the girl, or both of you. *You* know some things I don't want the Taken to find out. One way I can avoid handing you over is having you turn up dead. I can make that real if I have to. Or you can fake it for me. Let the slot see you looking like you've been wrecked. You follow?"

Shaking, he replied, "I think so."

"I want to know everything."

"The girl. . . ."

I held up a hand, listened. The uproar was close. "She won't come back from her meeting with the Taken. There's no reason we couldn't turn you loose once we're done doing what we have to do."

He did not believe me. He had committed crimes he believed deserved the harshest punishment, and he expected it.

"We're the Black Company, Shed. Juniper is going to get to know that real well soon. Including the fact that we keep our promises. But that's not important to you. Right now you want to stay alive long enough to get a break. That means you'd damned well better fake being dead, and do it better than any stiff you ever hauled up the hill."

"All right."

"Take him over by the fire and make him look like he's had it rough."

The men knew what to do. They sort of scattered Shed around without actually hurting him. I tossed a few things around to make it look like there had been a fight, and finished just in time.

The girl came sailing through the doorway, propelled by Otto's fist. She looked the worse for wear. So did Otto and the men I'd sent to help. "Wildcat, eh?"

Otto tried to grin. Blood leaked from the corner of his mouth. "Ain't the half of it, Croaker." He kicked the girl's feet from under her. "What happened to the guy?"

"Got a little feisty. I stuck a knife in him."

"I see."

We stared at the girl. She stared back, the fire gone. Each few seconds she glanced at Shed, looked back more subdued.

"Yep. You're in a heap of trouble, sweetheart."

She gave us the song-and-dance I'd expected from Shed. We ignored it, knowing it was bullshit. Otto cleaned up, then bound her hands and ankles. He parked her in a chair. I made sure it faced away from Shed. The poor bastard had to breathe.

I sat down opposite the girl and began to question her. Shed said he had told her almost everything. I wanted to know if she knew anything about Raven that could give him or us away.

I got no chance to find out.

There was a great rush of air around the house. A roar like a tornado passing. A crack like thunder.

Otto said it all. "Oh shit! Taken."

The door blew inward. I rose, stomach twisting, heart hammering. Feather came in looking like she'd just walked through a burning building. Wisps of smoke rose from her smouldering apparel.

"What the hell?" I asked.

"The castle. I got too close. They almost knocked me out of the sky. What have you got?"

I told my story quickly, not omitting the fact that we had allowed a corpse to get past. I indicated Shed. "One dead, trying to fight questioning. But this one is healthy." I indicated the girl.

Feather moved close to the girl. She had taken a real blast out there. I did not feel the aura of great power rigidly constrained that one usually senses in the presence of the Taken. And she did not sense the life still throbbing in Marron Shed. "So young." She lifted the girl's chin. "Oh. What eyes. Fire and steel. The Lady will love this one."

"We keep the watch?" I asked, assuming she would confiscate the prisoner.

"Of course. There may be others." She faced me. "No more will get through. The margin is too narrow. Whisper will forgive the latest. But the next is your doom."

"Yes, ma'am. Only it's hard to do and not attract the attention of the locals. We can't just go set up a roadblock."

"Why not?"

I explained. She had scouted the black castle and knew the lay of the land. "You're right. For the moment. But your Company will be here soon. There'll be no need for secrecy then."

"Yes, ma'am."

Feather took the girl's hand. "Come," she said.

I was amazed at how docilely our hellcat followed Feather. I went outside and watched Feather's battered carpet rise and hurry toward Duretile. One despairing cry floated in its wake.

I found Shed in the doorway when I turned to go inside. I wanted to smack him for that, but controlled myself.

"Who was *that*?" he asked. "*What* was that?"

"Feather. One of the Taken. One of my bosses."

"Sorceress?"

"One of the greatest. Go sit. Let's talk. I need to know exactly what that girl knows about Raven and Darling."

Intense questioning convinced me that Lisa did not know enough to arouse Whisper's suspicions. Unless Whisper connected the name Raven with the man who had helped capture her years ago.

I continued grilling Shed till first light. He practically begged to tell every filthy detail of his story. He had a big need to confess. Over coming days, when I sneaked down to the Buskin, he revealed everything recorded where he appears as the focal character. I do not think I have met many men who disgusted me more. Nastier men, yes. I have encountered scores. Greater villains come by the battalion. Shed's leavening of self-pity and cowardice reduced him from those categories to an essentially pathetic level.

Poor dolt. He was born to be used.

And yet. . . . There was one guttering spark in Marron Shed, reflected in his relationships with his mother, Raven, Asa, Lisa, Sal, and Darling, that he noted but did not recognize himself. He had a hidden streak of charity and decency. It was the gradual growth of that spark, with its eventual impact upon the Black Company, which makes me feel obligated to record all the earlier noxious details about that frightened little man.

The morning following his capture, I rode into the city in Shed's wagon and allowed him to open the Iron Lily as usual. During the morning I got Elmo and Goblin in for a conference. Shed was unsettled when he discovered that we all knew one another. Only through sheer luck had he not been taken earlier.

Poor fellow. The grilling never ceased. Poor us. He could not tell us everything we wanted to know.

"What are we going to do about the girl's father?" Elmo asked.

"If there is a letter, we've got to grab it," I replied. "We can't have anybody stirring up more problems. Goblin, you take care of the papa. He's even a little suspicious, see he has a heart attack."

Sourly, Goblin nodded. He asked Shed for the father's whereabouts, departed. And returned within half an hour. "A great tragedy. He didn't have a letter. She was bluffing. But he did know too much that would come out under questioning. This business is beginning to get to me. Hunting Rebels was cleaner. You knew who was who and where you stood."

"I'd better get back up the hill. The Taken might not be understanding about me being down here. Elmo, better keep somebody in Shed's pocket."

"Right. Pawnbroker lives there from now on. That clown takes a crap, he's holding his hand."

Goblin looked remote and thoughtful. "Raven buying a ship. Imagine that. What do you figure he was going to do?"

"I think he wanted to head straight out to sea," I said. "I hear there're islands out there, way out. Maybe another continent. A guy could hide pretty good out there."

I went back up the hill and loafed for two days, except to slip off and get everything I could out of Shed. Not a damned thing happened. Nobody else tried to make a delivery. I guess Shed was the only fool in the body business.

Sometimes I looked at those grim black battlements and wondered. They had taken a crack at Feather. Somebody in there knew the Taken meant trouble. How long before they realized they had been cut off and did something to get the meat supply moving again?

31

Juniper: The Return

Shed was still rattled two days after his capture. Each time he looked across the common room and saw one of those Black Company bastards, he started falling apart again. He was living on borrowed time. He was not sure what use they had for him, but he was sure that when he was used up, they would dump him with the garbage. Some of his babysitters clearly thought him trash. He could not refute their viewpoint in his own mind.

He was behind his counter, washing mugs, when Asa walked through the door. He dropped a mug.

Asa met his eye for only an instant, sidled around the L and headed upstairs. Shed took a deep breath and followed. The man called Pawnbroker was a step behind when he reached the head of the stair, moving as silent as death. He had a knife ready for business.

Shed stepped into what had been Raven's room. Pawnbroker remained outside. "What the hell are you doing here, Asa? The Inquisitors are after you. About that Catacombs business. Bullock himself went south looking for you."

"Easy, Shed. I know. He caught up with us. It got hairy. We left him cut up, but he'll mend. And he'll come back looking for you. I came to warn you. You've got to get out of Juniper."

"Oh, no," Shed said softly. Another tooth in the jaws of fate. "Been considering that anyway." That would not tell Pawnbroker anything he could not guess for himself. "Things have gotten rotten here. I've started looking for a buyer." Not true, but he would before day's end.

For some reason Asa's return restored his heart. Maybe just because he felt he had an ally, somebody who shared his troubles.

Most of the story poured out. Pawnbroker did not take exception. He did not make an appearance.

Asa had changed. He did not seem shocked. Shed asked why not.

"Because I spent so much time with Raven. He told me stories that would curl your hair. About the days before he came to Juniper."

"How is he?"

"Dead."

"Dead?" Shed gasped.

"What?" Pawnbroker bulled through the doorway. "Did you say Raven was dead?"

Asa looked at Pawnbroker, at Shed, at Pawnbroker again. "Shed, you bastard. . . ."

"You shut up, Asa," Shed snapped. "You haven't got the faintest what's happened while you were gone. Pawnbroker is a friend. Sort of."

"Pawnbroker, eh? Like from the Black Company?"

Pawnbroker's eyebrows rose. "Raven been talking?"

"He had some tales about the old days."

"Uh-huh. Right, buddy. That's me. Let's get back to Raven being dead."

Asa looked at Shed. Shed nodded. "Tell us."

"Okay. I don't really know what happened. We were clearing out after our mix-up with Bullock. Running. His hired thugs caught us by surprise. We're hiding in some woods outside of town when all of a sudden he starts screaming and jumping around. It don't make no sense to me." Asa shook his head. His face was pale and sweaty.

"Go on," Shed urged gently.

"Shed, I don't know."

"What?" Pawnbroker demanded.

"I don't know. I didn't hang around."

Shed grimaced. That was the Asa he knew.

"You're a real buddy, fellow," Pawnbroker said.

"Look. . . ."

Shed motioned for silence.

Asa said, "Shed, you've got to get out of Juniper. Fast. Any day a ship could bring a letter from Bullock."

"But. . . ."

"It's better down there than we thought, Shed. You got money; you're all right. They don't care about the Catacombs. Think it was a big joke on the Custodians. That's how Bullock found us. Everybody was laughing about the raid. There was even some guys talking about getting up an expedition to come clean them out."

"How did anybody find out about the Catacombs, Asa? Only you and Raven knew."

Asa looked abashed.

"Yeah. Thought so. Had to brag, didn't you?" He was confused and frightened and starting to take it out on Asa. He did not know what to do. He had to get out of Juniper, like Asa said. But how to give his watchdogs the slip? Especially when they knew he had to try?

"There's a ship at the Tulwar dock that leaves for Meadenval in the morning, Shed. I had the Captain hold passage for two. Should I tell him you'll be there, too?"

Pawnbroker stepped into position to block the doorway. "Neither one of you will be there. Some friends of mine want to talk to you."

"Shed, what is this?" Panic edged Asa's voice.

Shed looked at Pawnbroker. The mercenary nodded. Shed poured out most everything. Asa did not understand. Shed did not himself, because his chaperones had not told him everything, so there was some sense missing from the picture he had.

Pawnbroker was alone at the Lily. Shed suggested, "How about I go get Goblin?"

Pawnbroker smiled. "How about we just wait?"

"But. . . ."

"Somebody will turn up. We'll wait. Let's go downstairs. You." He indicated Asa with his blade. "Don't get any funny ideas."

Shed said, "Be careful, Asa. These are the guys Raven was scared of."

"I will. I heard enough from Raven."

"That's a pity, too," Pawnbroker said. "Croaker and Elmo aren't going to like that. Down, gents. Shed, just go on about your business."

"Somebody's liable to recognize Asa," Shed warned.

"We'll take a chance. Git." Pawnbroker stood aside and allowed both men to pass. Downstairs, he seated Asa at the shadowiest table and joined him, cleaning his nails with his knife. Asa watched in fascination. Seeing ghosts, Shed figured.

He could get away now if he wanted to sacrifice Asa. They wanted Asa more than they wanted him. If he just headed out through the kitchen, Pawnbroker would not come after him.

His sister-in-law came from the kitchen, a platter balanced on each hand. "When you get a minute, Sal." And when she got the minute: "You think you and the kids could run the place for me for a few weeks?"

"Sure. Why?" She looked puzzled. But she glanced quickly into the shadows.

"I might have to go somewhere for a while. I'd feel better if I knew somebody in the family was running the place. I don't really trust Lisa."

"You haven't heard from her yet?"

"No. You'd have thought she'd turn up when her father died, wouldn't you?"

"Maybe she's shacked up somewhere and hasn't heard yet." Sal did not sound convinced. In fact, Shed suspected, she thought he had something to do with the disappearance. Way too many people had disappeared around him. He was afraid she would do her sums and decide he had had something to do with Wally disappearing, too.

"There's one rumor I heard said she got arrested. Keep an eye out for Mom. She's got good people taking care of her, but they need supervising."

"Where are you going, Marron?"

"I don't know yet." He was afraid it might be just a way up the hill, to the Enclosure. If not that, then certainly somewhere, away from everything that had happened here. Away from these merciless men and their even less merciful employers. Have to talk to Asa about the Taken. Maybe Raven had told him something.

He wished he could get a moment with Asa to plan something. The two of them making a break. But not on the Tulwar ship. Asa had mentioned that, damn him. Some other ship, headed south.

What had become of Raven's big new vessel? And Darling?

He went over to the table. "Asa. What happened to Darling?"

Asa reddened. He stared at his folded hands. "I don't know, Shed. Honest. I panicked. I just ran for the first ship headed north."

Shed walked away, shaking his head in disgust. Leaving the girl alone like that. Asa hadn't changed much after all.

The one called Goblin came through the door. He began to beam at Asa before Pawnbroker said anything. "My, my, my, my, my," he said. "Is this who I think it is, Pawn?"

"You got it. The infamous Asa himself, home from the wars. And does he have stories to tell."

Goblin seated himself opposite Asa. He wore a big frog grin. "Such as?"

"Mainly, he claims Raven is dead."

Goblin's smile vanished. In an eye's blink he became deadly serious. He made Asa tell his story again while staring into a mug of wine. When he finally looked up, he was subdued. "Better talk this over with Elmo and Croaker. Good job, Pawnbroker. I'll take him. Keep your eye on friend Shed."

Shed winced. In the back of his head had lain the small hope that both would leave with Asa.

His mind was made up. He would flee at the first opportunity. Get south, change his name, use his gold pieces to buy into an inn, behave himself so thoroughly nobody would notice him ever again.

Asa showed a spark of rebellion. "Who the hell do you guys think you are? Suppose I don't want to go anywhere?"

Goblin smiled nastily, muttered something under his breath. Dark brown smoke drifted out of his mug, illuminated by a bloody inner glow. Goblin stared at Asa. Asa stared at the mug, unnerved.

The smoke coalesced, formed a small, headlike shape. Points began glowing where eyes might be. Goblin said, "My little friend *wants* you to argue. He feeds on pain. And he hasn't eaten for a long time. I've had to keep a low profile in Juniper."

Asa's eyes kept getting bigger. So did Shed's. Sorcery! He had sensed it in the thing called the Taken, but that had not upset him much. It had been removed, not experienced. Something that had happened to Lisa, out of sight. But this. . . .

It was a minor sorcery, to be sure. Some slight trick. But it was sorcery in a city which saw none other than that involved in the slow growth of the black castle. The dark arts hadn't gained any following in Juniper.

"All right," Asa said. "All right." His voice was high and thin and squeaky, and he was trying to push his chair back. Pawnbroker prevented him.

Goblin grinned. "I see Raven mentioned Goblin. Good. You'll behave. Come along."

Pawnbroker released Asa's chair. The little man followed Goblin docilely.

Shed sidled over and looked into Goblin's mug. Nothing. He frowned. Pawnbroker grinned. "Cute trick, eh?"

"Yeah." Shed took the mug to his sink. When Pawnbroker was not looking, he dropped it into the trash. He was more scared than ever. How did he get away from a sorcerer?

His head filled with tales he had heard from southern sailors. Bad business, wizards were.

He wanted to weep.

32

Juniper: Visitors

Goblin brought me the man Asa, and insisted we wait for Elmo before questioning him. He had sent someone to dig Elmo out of Duretile, where he was trying to placate Whisper. Whisper was getting goosed by the Lady regular and taking it out on anyone handy.

Goblin was unsettled by what he had learned. He did not play the usual game and try to make me guess what was going on. He blurted, "Asa says him and Raven had a run-in with Bullock. Raven is dead. He lit out. Darling is on her own down there."

Excitement? Better believe it. I was ready to put the little man to the question, then and there. But I controlled myself.

Elmo was a while showing up. Goblin and I got damned antsy before he did, while Asa worked himself up for a stroke.

The wait proved worthwhile. Elmo did not come alone.

The first hint was a faint but sour odor that seemed to come from the fireplace, where I'd had a small fire lighted. Just in case, you know. With a few iron rods set by, ready to be heated, so Asa could look them over and think, and maybe convince himself he ought not to leave anything out.

"What's that smell?" somebody asked. "Croaker, you let that cat in again?"

"I kicked him out after he sprayed my boots," I said. "Like halfway down the hill. Maybe he got the firewood before he left."

The odor grew stronger. It wasn't really obnoxious, just mildly irritating. We took turns examining the firewood. Nothing.

I was in the middle of a third search for the source when the fire caught my eye. For a second I saw a face in the flames.

My heart nearly stopped. For half a minute I was in a panic, nothing but the face's presence having registered. I considered every evil that could happen: Taken watching, the Lady watching, the things from the black castle, maybe the Dominator himself peeking through our fire. . . . Then something calm, back in the far marches of mind, reiterated something I hadn't noticed because I had no reason to expect it. The face in the flames had had only one eye.

"One-Eye," I said without thinking. "That little bastard is in Juniper."

Goblin spun toward me, eyes wide. He sniffed the air. His famous grin split his face. "You're right, Croaker. Absolutely right. That stink is the little skunk himself. Should have recognized it straight off."

I glanced at the fire. The face did not reappear.

Goblin mused, "What would be a suitable welcome?"

"Figure the Captain sent him?"

"Probably. Be logical to send him or Silent ahead."

"Do me a favor, Goblin."

"What?"

"Don't give him no special welcome."

Goblin looked deflated. It had been a long time. He did not want to miss an opportunity to refresh his acquaintance with One-Eye with a flash and a bang.

"Look," I said. "He's here on the sneak. We don't want the Taken to know. Why give them anything to sniff out?"

Bad choice of words. The smell was about to drive us outside.

"Yeah," Goblin grumbled. "Wish the Captain had sent Silent. I was all worked up for this. Had him the biggest surprise of his life."

"So get him later. Meantime, why not clear this smell out? Why not get his goat by just ignoring him?"

He thought about it. His eyes gleamed. "Yeah," he said, and I knew he had shaped my suggestion to his own warped sense of humor.

A fist hammered on the door. It startled me even though I was expecting it. One of the men let Elmo in.

One-Eye came in behind Elmo, grinning like a little black mongoose about to eat snake. We paid him no heed. Because the Captain came in behind him.

The Captain! The last man I expected to reach Juniper before the Company itself.

"Sir?" I blurted. "What the hell are *you* doing here?"

He lumbered to the fire, extended his hands. Summer had begun to fade, but it was not that cold. He was as bear-like as ever, though he had lost weight and aged. It had been a hard march indeed.

"Stork," he replied.

I frowned, looked at Elmo. Elmo shrugged, said, "I sent Stork with the message."

The Captain expanded, "Stork didn't make any sense. What's this about Raven?"

Raven, of course, had been his closest friend before deserting. I began to get a glimmer.

I indicated Asa. "This guy was in the thick of it from the beginning. Been Raven's sidekick. He says Raven is dead, down. . . . What's the name of that place, Asa?"

Asa stared at the Captain and One-Eye and swallowed about six times without being able to say anything. I told the Captain, "Raven told stories about us that turned his hair grey."

"Let's hear the story," the Captain said. He was looking at Asa.

So Asa told his tale for the third time, while Goblin hovered, listening for the clunk of untruth. He ignored One-Eye in the most masterful show of ignoring I've ever seen. And all for nought.

The Captain dropped Asa completely the moment he finished his tale. A matter of style, I think. He wanted the information to percolate before he trotted it out for reexamination. He had me review everything I had experienced since arriving in Juniper. I presumed he had gotten Elmo's story already.

I finished. He observed, "You're too suspicious of the Taken. The Limper has been with us all along. He doesn't act like there's anything up." If anyone had a cause for malice toward us, the Limper did.

"Nevertheless," I said, "there're wheels within wheels within wheels with the Lady and the Taken. Maybe they didn't tell him anything because they figured he couldn't keep it secret."

"Maybe," the Captain admitted. He shuffled around, occasionally gave Asa a puzzled look. "Whatever, let's not get Whisper wondering any more than she is. Play it close. Pretend you're not suspicious. Do your job. One-Eye and his boys will be around to back you up."

Sure, I thought. Against the Taken? "If the Limper is with the Company, how did you get away? If he knows you're gone, the word will be out to the Lady, won't it?"

"He shouldn't find out. We haven't spoken in months. He stays to himself. Bored, I think."

"What about the Barrowland?" I was primed to find out everything that had happened during the Company's long trek, for I had nothing in the Annals concerning the majority of my comrades. But it was not yet time to exhume details. Just to feel for high points.

"We never saw it," the Captain said. "According to the Limper, Journey and the Lady are working that end. We can expect a major move as soon as we have Juniper under control."

"We haven't done squat to prepare," I said. "The Taken kept us busy fussing about the black castle."

"Ugly place, isn't it?" He looked us over. "I think you might've gotten more done had you not been so paranoid."

"Sir?"

"Most of your trail-covering strikes me as needless and a waste of time. The problem was Raven's, not yours. And he solved it in typical fashion. Without help." He glared at Asa. "In fact, the problem seems solved for all time."

He had not been here and had not felt the pressures, but I did not mention that. Instead, I asked, "Goblin, you figure Asa is telling the truth?"

Warily, Goblin nodded.

"How about you, One-Eye? You catch any false notes?"

The little black man responded with a cautious negative.

"Asa. Raven should have had a bunch of papers with him. He ever mention them?"

Asa looked puzzled. He shook his head.

"He have a trunk or something that he wouldn't let anybody near?"

Asa seemed baffled by the direction my questions had taken. The others did too. Only Silent knew about those papers. Silent, and maybe Whisper, who had possessed them once herself.

"Asa? Anything he treated unusually?"

A light dawned in the little man's mind. "There was a crate. About the size of a coffin. I remember making a joke about it. He said something cryptic about it being somebody's ticket to the grave."

I grinned. The papers still existed. "What did he do with that crate down there?"

"I don't know."

"Asa. . . ."

"Honest. I only saw it a couple times on the ship. I never thought anything about it."

"What are you getting at, Croaker?" the Captain asked.

"I have a theory. Just based on what I know about Raven and Asa."

Everyone frowned.

"Generally, what we know about Asa suggests he's a character Raven wouldn't take up with on a bet. He's chicken. Unreliable. Too talkative. But Raven *did* take up with him. Took him south and made him part of the team. Why? Maybe that don't bother you guys, but it does me."

"I don't follow you," the Captain said.

"Suppose Raven wanted to disappear so people wouldn't even bother looking for him? He tried to vanish once, by coming to Juniper. But we turned up. Looking for him, he thought. So what next? How about he dies? In front of a witness. People don't hunt for dead men."

Elmo interrupted. "You saying he staged his death and used Asa to report it so nobody would come looking?"

"I'm saying we ought to consider the possibility."

The Captain's sole response was a thoughtful, "Uhm."

Goblin said, "But Asa did see him die."

"Maybe. And maybe he only thinks he did."

We all looked at Asa. He cowered. The Captain said, "Take him through his story again, One-Eye. Step-by-step."

For two hours One-Eye dragged the little man through again and again. And we could not spot one flaw. Asa insisted he had seen Raven die, devoured from within by something snake-like. And the more my theory sprung leaks, the more I was sure it was valid.

"My case depends on Raven's character," I insisted, when everybody ganged up on me. "There's the crate, and there's Darling. Her and a damned expensive ship that he, for godsakes, had built. He left a trail going out of here, and he knew it. Why sail a few hundred miles and tie up to a dock when somebody is going to come looking? Why leave Shed alive behind you, to tell about you being in on the raid on the Catacombs? And there's no way in hell he'd leave Darling twisting in the wind. Not for a minute. He would have had arrangements made for her. You know that." My arguments were beginning to sound a little strained to me, too. I was in the position of a priest trying to sell religion. "But Asa says they just left her hanging around some inn. I tell you, Raven had a plan. I bet, if you went down there now, you'd find Darling gone without a trace. And if the ship is still there, that crate wouldn't be aboard."

"What is this with the crate?" One-Eye demanded. I ignored him.

"I think you have too much imagination, Croaker," the Captain said. "But, on the other hand, Raven is crafty enough to pull something like that. Soon as I can spring you, figure on going down to check."

"If Raven's crafty enough, how about the Taken being villainous enough to try something against us?"

"We'll cross that bridge when we come to it." He faced One-Eye. "I want you and Goblin to save the games. Understand? Too much clowning around and the Taken will get curious. Croaker. Hang on to this Asa character. You'll want him to show you where Raven died. I'm heading back to the outfit. Elmo. Come ride with me part way."

So. A little private business. Bet it had to do with my suspicions about the Taken. After a while you get so used to some people you can almost read their minds.

Juniper: The Encounter

Things changed after the Captain's visit. The men became more alert. Elmo's influence waxed while mine waned. A less wishy-washy, more inflexible tone characterized the Company deputation. Every man became ready to move at an instant's notice.

Communications improved dramatically while time available for sleep declined painfully. None of us were ever out of touch more than two hours. And Elmo found excuses to get everyone but himself out of Duretile, into places where the Taken would have trouble finding them. Asa became my ward out on the black castle slope.

Tension mounted. I felt like one of a flock of chickens poised to scatter the moment a fox landed among us. I tried to bleed off my shakiness by updating the Annals. I had let them slide sadly, seldom having done more than keep notes.

When the tension became too much for me, I walked uphill to stare at the black castle.

It was an intentional risk-taking, like that of a child who crawls out a tree branch overhanging a deadly fall. The closer I approached the castle, the more narrow my concentration. At two hundred yards all other cares vanished. I felt the dread of that place down to my ankle bones and the shallows of my soul. At two hundred yards I felt what it meant to have the shadow of the Dominator overhanging the world. I felt what the Lady felt when she considered her husband's potential resurrection. Every emotion became edged with a hint of despair.

In a way, the black castle was more than a gateway through which the world's great old evil might reappear. It was a concretization of metaphorical concepts, and a living symbol. It did things a great cathedral does. Like a cathedral, it was far more than an edifice.

I could stare at its obsidian walls and grotesque decoration, recall Shed's stories, and never avoid dipping into the cesspool of my own soul, never avoid searching myself for the essential decency shelved through most of my adult life. That castle was, if you like, a moral landmark. If you had a brain. If you had any sensitivity at all.

There were times when One-Eye, Goblin, Elmo or another of the men accompanied me. Not one of them went away untouched. They could stand there with me, talking trivialities about its construction or, weightily, about its significance in the Company's future, and all the while something would be happening inside.

I do not believe in evil absolute. I have recounted that philosophy in specific elsewhere in the Annals, and it affects my every observation throughout my tenure as Annalist. I believe in our side and theirs, with the good and evil decided after the fact, by those who survive. Among men you seldom find the good with one standard and the shadow with another. In our war with the Rebel, eight and nine years ago, we served the side perceived as the shadow. Yet we saw far more wickedness practiced by the adherents of the White Rose than by those of the Lady. The villains of the piece were at least straightforward.

The world knows where it stands with the Lady. It is the Rebel whose ideals and morals conflict with fact, becoming as changeable as the weather and as flexible as a snake.

But I digress. The black castle has that effect. Makes you amble off into all the byways and cul-de-sacs and false trails you have laid down during your life. It makes you reassess. Makes you *want* to take a stand somewhere, even if on the black side. Leaves you impatient with your own malleable morality.

I suspect that is why Juniper decided to pretend the place did not exist. It is an absolute demanding absolutes in a world with a preference for relatives.

Darling was in my thoughts often while I stood below those black, glossy walls, for she was the castle's antipode when I was up there. The white pole, and absolute in opposition to what the black castle symbolized. I had not been much in her presence since realizing what she was, but I could recall being morally unnerved by her, too. I wondered how she would affect me now, after having had years to grow.

From what Shed said, she did not reek the way the castle did. His main interest in her had been hustling her upstairs. And Raven had not been driven into puritanical channels. If anything, he had slipped farther into the darkness—though for the highest of motives.

Possibly there was a message there. An observation upon means to ends. Here was Raven who had acted with the pragmatic amorality of a prince of Hell, all so he could save the child who represented the best hope of the world against the Lady and the Dominator.

Oh, 'twould be marvelous if the world and its moral questions were like some game board, with plain black players and white, and fixed rules, and nary a shade of grey.

Even Asa and Shed could be made to feel the aura of the castle if you took them up during the daytime and made them stand there looking at those fell walls.

Shed especially.

Shed had achieved a position where he could afford conscience and uncertainty. I mean, he had none of the financial troubles that had plagued him earlier, and no prospect of digging himself a hole with us watching him, so he could reflect upon his place in things and become disgusted with himself. More than once I took him up and watched as that deep spark of hidden decency flared, twisted him upon a rack of inner torment.

I do not know how Elmo did it. Maybe he went without sleep for a few weeks. But when the Company came down out of the Wolanders, he had an occupation plan prepared. It was crude, to be sure, but better than any of us expected.

I was in the Buskin, at Shed's Iron Lily, when the first rumors raged down the waterfront and stirred one of the most massive states of confusion I've ever seen. Shed's wood-seller neighbor swept into the Lily, announced, "There's an army coming down out of the pass! Foreigners! Thousands of them! They say. . . ."

During the following hour a dozen patrons brought the news. Each time the army was larger and its purpose more obscure. Nobody knew what the Company wanted. Various witnesses assigned motives according to their own fears. Few came anywhere near the mark.

Though the men were weary after so long a march, they spread through the city quickly, the larger units guided by Elmo's men. Candy brought a reinforced company into the Buskin. The worst slums are always the first site of rebellion, we've found. There were few violent confrontations. Juniper's citizens were taken by surprise and had no idea what to fight about anyway. Most just turned out to watch.

I got myself back up to my squad. This was the time the Taken would do their deed. If they planned anything.

Nothing happened. As I might have guessed, knowing that men from our forerunner party were guiding the new arrivals. Indeed, nobody got in touch with me, up there, for another two days. By then the city was pacified. Every key point was in our hands. Every state building, every arsenal, every strong point, even the Custodians' headquarters in the Enclosure. And life went on as usual. What little trouble there was came when Rebel refugees tried to start an uprising, accurately accusing the Duke of having brought the Lady to Juniper.

The people of Juniper didn't much care.

There were problems in the Buskin, though. Elmo wanted to straighten the slum out. Some of the slum dwellers didn't want to be straightened. He used

Candy's company forcefully, cracking the organizations of the crime bosses. I did not see the necessity, but wiser heads feared the gangs could become the focus of future resistance. Anything with that potential had to be squashed immediately. I think there was a hope the move would win popular favor, too.

Elmo brought the Lieutenant to my hillside shack the third day after the Company's arrival. "How goes it?" I asked. The Lieutenant had aged terribly since I had seen him last. The passage westward had been grim.

"City's secure," he said. "Stinking dump, isn't it?"

"Better believe. It's all snake's belly. What's up?"

Elmo said, "He needs a look at the target."

I lifted an eyebrow.

The Lieutenant said, "The Limper says we're going to take this place. I don't know how soon. Captain wants me to look it over."

"Fun times tomorrow," I muttered. "Ain't going to grab it on the sneak." I donned my coat. It was chilly up on the slopes. Elmo and One-Eye tagged along when I took the Lieutenant up. He eyeballed the castle, deep in thought. Finally, he said, "I don't like it. Not even a little bit." He felt the cold dread of the place.

"I got a man who's been inside," I said. "But don't let the Taken know. He's supposed to be dead."

"What can he tell me?"

"Not much. He's only been there at night, in a court behind the gate."

"Uhm. The Taken have a girl up at Duretile, too. I talked to her. She couldn't tell me nothing. Only in there once, and was too scared to look around."

"She's still alive?"

"Yeah. That's the one you caught? Yeah. She's alive. Lady's orders, apparently. Nasty little witch. Let's hike around it."

We got onto the far slope, where the going was rough, to the accompaniment of constant crabbing by One-Eye. The Lieutenant stated the obvious. "No getting at it from here. Not without help from the Taken."

"Going to take a big lot of help to get at it from any direction."

He looked me a question.

I told him about Feather's troubles the night we took Shed and his barmaid.

"Anything since?"

"Nope. Not before, either. My man who's been inside never saw anything extraordinary, either. But, dammit, the thing connects with the Barrowland. It's got the Dominator behind it. You *know* it's not going to be a pushover. They know there's trouble out here."

One-Eye made a squeaking sound. "What?" the Lieutenant snapped.

One-Eye pointed. We all looked up the wall, which loomed a good sixty feet above us. I did not see anything. Neither did the Lieutenant. "What?" he asked again.

"Something was watching us. Nasty-looking critter."

"I saw it too," Elmo volunteered. "Long, skinny, yellowish guy with eyes like a snake."

I considered the wall. "How could you tell from here?"

Elmo shivered and shrugged. "I could. And I didn't like it. Looked like he wanted to bite me." We dragged on through brush and over boulders, keeping one eye on the castle, the other on the down slope. Elmo muttered, "Hungry eyes. That's what they were."

We reached the ridgeline west of the castle. The Lieutenant paused. "How close can you get?"

I shrugged. "I haven't had the balls to find out."

The Lieutenant moved here, there, as if sighting on something. "Let's bring up some prisoners and find out."

I sucked spittle between my teeth, then said, "You won't get the locals anywhere near the place."

"Think not? How about in exchange for a pardon? Candy's rounded up half the villains in the Buskin. Got a regular anti-crime crusade going. He gets three complaints about somebody, he nabs them."

"Sounds a little simple," I said. We were moving around for a look at the castle gate. By simple I meant simplistic, not easy.

The Lieutenant chuckled. Months of hardship had not sapped his bizarre sense of humor. "Simple minds respond to simple answers. A few months of Candy's reforms and the Duke will be a hero."

I understood the reasoning. Juniper was a lawless city, ruled by regional strongmen. There were hordes of Sheds who lived in terror, continuously victimized. Anyone who lessened the terror would win their affection. Adequately developed, that affection would survive later excesses.

I wondered, though, if the support of weaklings was worth much. Or if, should we successfully infect them with courage, we might not be creating trouble for ourselves later. Take away daily domestic oppression and they might imagine oppression on our part.

I have seen it before. Little people have to hate, have to blame someone for their own inadequacies.

But that was not the problem of the moment. The moment demanded immediate, vigorous, violent attention.

The castle gate popped open as we came in line. A half-dozen wild beings in black rushed us. A fog of lethargy settled upon me, and I found fear fading the moment it sparked into existence. By the time they were halfway to us, all I wanted was to lie down.

Pain filled my limbs. My head ached. Cramps knotted my stomach. The lethargy vanished.

One-Eye was doing strange things, dancing, yelping like a wolf pup, throwing his hands around like wounded birds. His big, weird hat flew off and tumbled with the breeze, downhill, till it became tangled in the brush. Between yelps he snapped, "Do something, you idiots! I can't hold them forever."

Shang! Elmo's sword cleared its scabbard. The Lieutenant's did the same. I was carrying nothing but a long dagger. I whipped it out and joined the rush. The castle creatures stood frozen, surprise in their ophidian eyes. The Lieutenant reached them first, stopped, wound up, took a mighty two-handed swing.

He lugs a hanger that is damned near an executioner's sword. A blow like that would have severed the necks of three men. It did not remove the head of his victim, though it did bite deep. Blood sprayed the three of us.

Elmo went with a thrust, as did I. His sword drove a foot into his victim. My dagger felt like it had hit soft wood. It sank but three inches into my victim. Probably not deeply enough to reach anything vital.

I yanked my blade free, poked around in my medical knowledge for a better killing point. Elmo kicked his victim in the chest to get his weapon free.

The Lieutenant had the best weapon and approach. He hacked another neck while we diddled around.

Then One-Eye lost it. The eyes of the castle creatures came alive. Pure fiery venom burned there. I feared the two not yet harmed would swarm all over us. But the Lieutenant threw a wild stroke and they retreated. The one I had wounded staggered after them. He fell before he reached the gate. He kept crawling. The gate closed in his face.

"So," the Lieutenant said. "There's a few lads we don't have to face later. My commendation, One-Eye." He spoke calmly enough, but his voice was up in the squeak range. His hands shook. It had been close. We would not have survived had One-Eye not come along. "I think I've seen enough for today. Let's hike."

Ninety percent of me wanted to run as fast as I could. Ten percent stuck to business. "Let's drag one of these bastards along," it croaked out of a mouth dry with fear.

"What the hell for?" Elmo demanded.

"So I can carve it up and see what it is."

"Yeah." The Lieutenant squatted and grabbed a body under the arms. It struggled feebly. Shuddering, I took hold of booted feet and hoisted. The creature folded in the middle.

"Hell with that," the Lieutenant said. He dropped his end, joined me. "You pull that leg. I'll pull this one."

We pulled. The body slid sideways. We started bickering about who should do what.

"You guys want to stop crapping around?" One-Eye snarled. He stabbed a wrinkled black finger. I looked back. Creatures had appeared on the battlements. I felt an increase in the dread the castle inspired.

"Something's happening," I said, and headed downhill, never letting go of the body. The Lieutenant came along. Our burden took a beating going through the rock and brush.

Wham! Something hit the slope like the stamp of a giant's foot. I felt like a roach fleeing a man who hated cockroaches and had his stomping boots on. There was another stamp, more earth-shaking.

"Oh, shit," Elmo said. He came past me, arms and legs pumping. One-Eye was right behind him, flying low, gaining ground. Neither offered to help.

A third thump, and a fourth, about equally spaced in time, each closer than the last. The last sent chunks of stone and dead brush arcing overhead.

Fifty yards down-slope One-Eye halted, whirled, did one of his magic things. A chunk of pale blue fire exploded in his upraised hands, went roaring up the hill, moaning past me less than a foot away. The Lieutenant and I passed One-Eye. A fifth giant stomp spattered our backs with shards of rock and brush.

One-Eye let out a mad howl and ran again. He yelled, "That was my best shot. Better dump that clown and scatter." He pulled away, bounding like a hare fleeing hounds.

A scream filled the valley of the Port. A pair of dots came hurtling over from the southern slope, almost too fast for the eye to follow. They passed over with a hollow, deep roar, and boomed like a god's drum behind us. I was not sure, but it seemed the dots were connected.

Another pair appeared, revolving about a common center. I got a better look. Yes, they were connected. They roared. They boomed. I glanced back. The face of the black castle had vanished behind a wall of color like paint thrown against, then running down, a pane of glass to which it would not adhere.

"Taken are on the job," the Lieutenant panted. His eyes were wild, but he clung to his side of our burden.

The damned creature got hung up. Panicky, we hacked its clothing free from a thorn bush. I kept looking up, expecting something to come down and smash us all over the slope.

Another pair of balls arrived, spraying color. They did no obvious harm, but kept the castle occupied.

We freed our booty, hurried on.

A different sort of dot pair came, dropping from high above. I pointed. "Feather and Whisper." The Taken plunged toward the black castle, preceded by a high-pitched shriek. Fire enveloped the castle wall. Obsidian seemed to melt and run like candle wax, shifting the already grotesque decorations into forms even more bizarre. The Taken pulled out, gained altitude, came around for another pass. In the interim another pair of dots screamed across the Port valley and painted the planes of the air. It would have been a great show if I had not been so damned busy getting away.

The slope resounded to the stamp of an invisible giant. A circle fifteen feet across and five deep appeared above us. Sticks and stones flew. It missed by only a dozen feet. The impact knocked us down. A line of like imprints marched back up the slope.

Mighty though that blow was, it was less forceful than its predecessors.

Feather and Whisper swooped again, and again the face of the black castle melted, ran, shifted form. Then thunder racked the air. *Bam-bam!* Both Taken vanished in clouds of smoke. They wobbled out, fighting for control of their carpets. Both smouldered the way Feather had the night we captured Shed. They fought for altitude.

The castle turned its entire attention to them. The Lieutenant and I made our escape.

34

Juniper: Flight

The Lily shuddered several times.

Shed was doing mugs and wondering which of his customers were Black Company. The shaking made him nervous. Then a shriek flashed overhead, rising, then falling as it whipped away north. A moment later the earth shivered again, strong enough to rattle crockery. He rushed into the street. One small, cunning part of him kept watching his customers, trying to determine who was watching him. His chance of escape had lessened drastically with the advent of the Company. He no longer knew who was who. They all knew him.

He hit the street as a second shriek came from the direction of the Enclosure. He followed pointing hands. A pair of balls joined by a cord whipped away to the north. Seconds later all Juniper was illuminated by a particolored glare.

"The black castle!" people said. "They hit the black castle."

Shed could see it from his street. It had vanished behind a curtain of color. Terror gripped his heart. He could not understand it. He was safe down here. Wasn't he?

Wasn't he? The Company had great wizards supporting it. They would not let the castle do anything. . . . A mighty hammer blow threw stuff around the north slope. He could not see what was happening, but instantly sensed that the castle had struck at someone. Possibly that Croaker, who was up there keeping the place isolated. Maybe the castle was trying to open the road.

Crowd yammer directed his attention to two dots dropping from the blue. Fire enveloped the castle. Obsidian shifted form, writhing, then found its normal shape again. The flying attackers soared, turned. Another pair of balls hurtled in, apparently thrown from Duretile. And down came the carpet riders.

Shed knew who they were and what was happening, and he was terrified. Around him, the Buskin, taken unawares, went berserk.

He retained the presence of mind to consider his own position. Here, there, members of the Black Company were running for battle stations. Squads formed up, hurried off. Pairs of soldiers took stations apparently assigned against times when rioting and looting looked possible. Nowhere did Shed see anyone identifiable as his babysitter.

He slipped back inside the Lily, upstairs, into his room, dug into his secret place. He stuffed gold and silver into his pockets, dithered over his amulet, then hung it around his neck, under his clothing. He scanned the room once, saw nothing else he wanted to take, hurried back downstairs. There was no one in the common room but Sal, who stood at the door watching the display on the north slope. He'd never seen her more homebody and calm.

"Sal."

"Marron? Is it time?"

"Yes. I'm leaving twenty leva in the box. You'll do fine as long as the soldiers keep coming in."

"Is that up there what's been going on?"

"That's where it's been headed. It'll probably get worse. They're here to destroy the castle. If they can."

"Where are you going?"

"I don't know." He honestly did not. "Wouldn't tell you if I did. They would find out from you."

"When will you be back?"

"Maybe never. Certainly not before they pull out." He doubted the Company ever would. Or, if it did, it would be replaced. Its Lady seemed the type not to turn loose of anything.

He gave Sal a peck on the cheek. "Take care. And don't short yourself or the kids. If Lisa turns up, tell her she's fired. If Wally does, tell him I forgive him."

He headed for the back door. The flash and roar on the slope continued. At one point there was a howling which fluttered toward Duretile, but it broke up somewhere over the Enclosure. He put his head down and his collar up and followed alleyways toward the waterfront.

Only twice did he encounter patrols. Neither boasted a man who knew him. The first ignored him. The corporal commanding the second told him to get his ass off the street and went on.

From Wharf Street he could see the black castle once more, through the masts and stays of countless ships. It seemed to have gotten the worst of the exchange, which had died away. Thick, black smoke boiled out of the fortress, an oily column leaning a few degrees and rising thousands of feet, then spreading in a dark haze. On the slopes below the castle there was a twinkling and seething, an anthill-like suggestion of movement. He supposed the Company was hurrying into action.

The waterfront was in a frenzy. The channel boasted a dozen vessels heading out. Every other foreign ship was preparing to sail. The river itself seemed strangely disturbed and choppy.

Shed tried three ships before he found one where money talked loudly enough to be heard. He paid ten leva to a piratical purser and found himself a spot where he would not be seen from shore.

Nevertheless, as the crew were casting off, the man called Pawnbroker came racing along the pier with a squad of soldiers, shouting at the ship's master to hold fast.

The ship's master made an obscene gesture, told them where they could go, and began drifting with the current. There were too few tugs for the number of ships moving out.

For his defiance the skipper got an arrow through the throat. Astonished sailors and officers stood frozen, aghast. Arrows stormed aboard, killed more than a dozen men, including the mate and boatswain. Shed cowered in his hiding place, gripped by a terror deeper than any he had known before.

He had known they were hard men, men who did not play games. He had not realized just how hard they were, how savage they could be. The Duke's men would have thrown up their hands in despair and wandered away cursing. They would not have massacred anyone.

The arrows kept coming, in a light patter, till the vessel was out of range.

Only then did Shed peep out and watch the city dwindle slowly. Oh, slowly, did it drift away.

To his surprise none of the sailors were angry with him. They were angry, true, but had not made a connection between the attack and their last-minute passenger.

Safe, he thought, elated. That lasted till he began to wonder where he was bound and what he would do once he got there.

A sailor called, "Sir, they're coming after us in a launch." Shed's heart dropped to his ankles. He looked and saw a small ship pulling out, trying to put on sail. Men in Black Company uniform abused the crew, hurrying them.

He got back into hiding. After the mauling these men had taken, there was no doubt they would surrender him rather than suffer more. If they realized he was what Pawnbroker wanted.

How had the man picked up his trail?

Sorcery. Of course. Had to be.

Did that mean they could find him anywhere?

35

Juniper: Bad News

The fuss was over. It had been a dramatic display while it lasted, though not as impressive as some I've seen. The battle on the Stair of Tear. The fighting around Charm. This was all flash and show, more rattling to Juniper's people than to us or the denizens of the black castle. They did us no harm. The worst they suffered was the direct deaths outside their gate. The fire inside did no real harm. Or so the Taken reported.

Grimy, Whisper grounded her carpet outside my headquarters, trundled inside looking the worse for wear but unharmed. "What started it?" she asked.

The Lieutenant explained.

"They're getting frightened," she said. "Maybe desperate. Were they trying to scare you off or take you prisoner?"

"Definitely prisoner," I said. "They hit us with some kind of sleepy spell before they came after us." One-Eye supported me with a nod.

"Why were they unsuccessful?"

"One-Eye broke the spell. Turned it around on them. We killed three."

"Ah! No wonder they were upset. You brought one down with you?"

"I thought we could understand them better if I cut one up to see how he was made."

Whisper did one of her mental fades, communing with the mistress of us all. She returned. "A good idea. But Feather and I will do the cutting. Where is the corpse? I'll take it to Duretile now."

I indicated the body. It was in plain sight. She had two men carry it to her carpet. I muttered, "Don't damn trust us to do anything anymore." Whisper heard me. She did not comment.

Once the body was loaded, she told the Lieutenant, "Begin your preliminary siegework immediately. A circumvallation. Limper will support you. It's likely the Dominator's creatures will try to break out or take prisoners, or both. Don't permit it. A dozen captives would allow them to open the pathway. You would find yourself facing the Dominator. He would not be kind."

"No shit." The Lieutenant is a tough guy's tough guy when it suits him. In those moments not even the Lady could intimidate him. "Why don't you clear out? Tend to your job and let me tend to mine."

His remarks didn't fit the moment, but he was fed up with Taken in general. He had been on the march with the Limper for months, and the Limper fancied himself a commander. He gave the Lieutenant and Captain both a bellyful. And maybe that was the source of the friction between the Company and Taken. The Captain had his limits, too, though he was more diplomatic than the Lieutenant. He would ignore orders that did not suit him.

I went out to watch the circumvallation of the black castle. Drafts of laborers arrived from the Buskin, shovels over their shoulders and terror in their eyes. Our men put down their tools and assumed guardianship and supervisory roles. Occasionally the black castle sputtered, making a feeble attempt to interfere, like a volcano muttering to itself after its energy has been spent. The locals sometimes scattered and had to be rounded up. We lost a lot of good will won earlier.

A sheepish yet angry Pawnbroker came looking for me, gravity accentuated by the afternoon sunlight. I eased away and went to meet him. "What's the bad news?"

"That damned Shed. Made a run for it in the confusion."

"Confusion?"

"The city went crazy when the Taken started sniping at the castle. We lost track of Shed. By the time Goblin found him, he was on a ship headed for Meadenvil. I tried to keep it from pulling out, but they wouldn't stop. I shot them up, then grabbed a boat and went after them, but I couldn't catch up."

After cursing Pawnbroker, and stifling an urge to strangle him, I sat down to think. "What's the matter with him, Pawn? What's he afraid of?"

"Everything, Croaker. His own shadow. I reckon he figured we were going to kill him. Goblin says it was more than that, but you know how he loves to complicate stuff."

"Like what?"

"Goblin says he wants to make a clean break with the old Shed. Fear of us was the motivation he needed to get moving."

"Clean break?"

"You know. Like from guilt about everything he did. And from reprisals by the Inquisitors. Bullock knows he was in on the Catacombs raid. Bullock would jump on him as soon as he got back."

I stared down at the shadowed harbor. Ships were getting under way still. The waterfront looked naked. If outsiders kept running, we would become very unpopular. Juniper depended heavily on trade.

"You find Elmo. Tell him. Say I think you ought to go after Shed. Find Kingpin and those guys and bring them back. Check on Darling and Bullock while you're at it."

He looked like a man condemned, but did not protest. He had several screw-ups to his credit. Being separated from his comrades was a cheap penalty to pay. "Right," he said, and hustled off.

I returned to the task at hand.

Disorganization resolved itself as the troops formed the locals into work crews. The earth was flying. First a good deep trench so the creatures from the castle would have trouble getting out, then a palisade behind that.

One of the Taken remained airborne, circling high above, watching the castle.

Wagons began coming up from the city, carrying timber and rubble. Down there other work crews were demolishing buildings for materials. Though they were structures unfit for occupation and long overdue for replacement, they housed people who were not going to love us for destroying their homes.

One-Eye and a sergeant named Shaky took a large labor draft around the castle, down to the roughest slope, and began a mine designed to drop part of the castle wall down the steep slope. They did nothing to conceal their purpose. Wasn't much point trying. The things we faced had the power to knife through any subterfuge.

Actually managing to breach the wall would be a tough job. It might take weeks, even with One-Eye helping. The miners would have to cut through many yards of solid rock.

The project was one of several feints the Lieutenant would employ, though the way he plans a siege, one day's feint can become another's main thrust. Drawing on a manpower pool like Juniper, he could exercise every option.

I felt a certain pride, watching the siege take shape. I have been with the Company a long time. Never had we undertaken so ambitious a project. Never had we been given the wherewithal. I wandered around till I found the Lieutenant. "What's the plan here, anyway?" Nobody ever told me anything.

"Just nail them down so they can't get out. Then the Taken will jump all over them."

I grunted. Basic and simple. I expected it would get more complicated. The creatures inside would fight. I suspect the Dominator was lying restless, shaping a counterstroke.

Must be hell to be buried alive, able to do nothing but wish and hope at minions far beyond direct control. Such impotence would destroy me in a matter of hours.

I told the Lieutenant about Shed's escape. He did not get excited. Shed meant little to him. He did not know about Raven and Darling. To him, Raven was a deserter and Darling his camp follower. Nothing special. I wanted him to know about Shed so he would mention it to the Captain. The Captain might want to take action more vigorous than my recommendation to Elmo.

I stayed with the Lieutenant a while, he watching the work crews, I watching a wagon train come uphill. This one should be bringing supper. "Getting damned tired of cold meals," I muttered.

"Tell you what you ought to do, Croaker. You ought to get married and settle down."

"Sure," I replied, more sarcastically than I felt. "Right after you."

"No, really. This might be the place to do it. Set yourself up in practice, catering to the rich. That Duke's family, say. Then, when your girlfriend gets here, you pop the question and you're all set."

Daggers of ice drove into my soul, twisting. I croaked, "Girlfriend?"

He grinned. "Sure. Nobody told you? She's coming out for the big show. Going to run it personally. Be your big chance."

My big chance. But for what?

He was talking about the Lady, of course. It had been years, but still they rode me about some romantic stories I wrote before I actually met the Lady. They always ride anybody about anything they know will get their goat. All part of the game. All part of the brotherhood.

I bet the son-of-a-bitch had been boiling with the news since first he heard it, waiting to spring it on me.

The Lady. Coming to Juniper.

I considered deserting for real. While there was a ship or two left to get away.

36

Juniper: Fireworks

The castle lulled us. Let us think we could slam the door without a squawk. For two days the labor crews ripped at the north ridge, gouging out a good deep trench, getting up much of the needed stockade, hammering out a nice beginning of a mine. Then they let us in on their displeasure.

It was a little bit chaotic and a whole lot hairy, and in retrospect, it seems it may not have started as what it became.

It was a moonless night, but labor crews were working by firelight, torchlight, lanternlight. The Lieutenant had wooden towers going up each hundred feet where the trench and palisade were complete, and nearby them small ballistae for mounting atop them. A waste of time, I thought. What value mundane siege equipment against minions of the Dominator? But the Lieutenant was our siege specialist. He was determined to do things properly, by the numbers, even if the ballistae never were used. They had to be available.

Sharp-eyed Company members were in the towers nearing completion, trying to see into the castle. One detected movement at the gate. Instead of raising a fuss, he sent a message down. The Lieutenant went up. He decided that someone had left the castle and slipped around to One-Eye's side. He had drums sounded, trumpets blown, and fire arrows shot into the air.

The alarm wakened me. I rushed up to see what was happening. For a while there was nothing to see.

On the far slope One-Eye and Shaky stood to arms. Their workers panicked. Many were killed or crippled trying to flee across the brushy, rocky, steep slope. A minority had sense enough to stand fast.

The castle folks wanted to make a quick strike and catch some of One-Eye's workers, drag them inside, and complete whatever rites were necessary to bring the Dominator through. Once they were discovered, their strategy shifted. The men in the towers yelled that more were coming out. The Lieutenant ordered harassing fire. He had a couple of small trebuchets chuck balls of burning brush into the area near the gate. And he sent men to find Goblin and Silent, figuring they could do more than he to provide needed illumination.

Goblin was down in the Buskin. It would take him an hour to respond. I had no idea where Silent might be. I had not seen him, though he had been in Juniper a week.

The Lieutenant had signal fires lighted to warn watchers on Duretile's walls that we had a situation.

The Taken above finally came down to investigate. It proved to be the Limper. His first act was to take a handful of javelins, do something to them, then cast them to earth from above. They became pillars of chartreuse light between trench and castle.

On the far slope One-Eye provided his own illumination by spinning spiderwebs of violet and hanging their corners on the breeze. They quickly betrayed the approach of a half-dozen shapes in black. Arrows and javelins flew.

The creatures suffered several casualties before they took exception. Light blazed, then faded into a shimmer which surrounded each. They attacked.

Other shapes appeared atop the castle wall. They hurled objects downslope. The size of a man's head, they bounded toward the minehead. One-Eye did something to alter their course. Only one escaped him. It left a trail of unconscious soldiers and workers.

The castle creatures had, evidently, planned for every possibility but One-Eye. They were able to give the Limper hell, but did nothing about One-Eye at all.

He shielded his men and made them fight toe-to-toe when the castle creatures closed. Most of his men were killed, but they wiped out their attackers.

By then the castle creatures were mounting a sortie against the trench and wall, directly toward where I stood watching. I recall being more puzzled than fearful.

How many were there? Shed had given the impression the castle was practically untenanted. But a good twenty-five of them, attacking with wizardry backing them, made the trench and wall almost pointless.

They came out the gate. And something came over the castle wall, vast and bladder-like. It hit the ground, bounded twice, mashed down on the trench and palisade, crushing one and filling the other. The sortie streaked for the opening. Those creatures could *move.*

The Limper came down out of the night, shrieking with the fury of his descent, glowing ever more brightly as he dropped. The glow peeled off in flakes the size of maple seeds, which fluttered in his wake, spinning and twisting earthward, eating into whatever they contacted. Four or five attackers went down.

The Lieutenant launched a hasty counterattack, finished several of the injured, then had to retreat. Several of the creatures dragged fallen soldiers toward the castle. The others came on.

Without a heroic bone in my body, I picked up my heels and headed across the slope. And a wise move that proved.

The air crackled and sparked and opened like a window. Something poured through from somewhere else. The slope froze so cold and so fast the air itself turned to ice. The air around me rushed into the affected area, and it too froze. The cold took most of the castle creatures, enveloping them in frost. A random javelin struck one. The creature shattered, turning to powder and small shards. Men hurled whatever missiles were available, destroying the others.

The opening closed after only a few seconds. The relative warmth of the world sapped the bitter cold. Fogs boiled up, concealed the area for several minutes. When they cleared, no trace of the creatures could be found.

Meantime, three untouched creatures raced down the road toward Juniper. Elmo and an entire platoon raged in pursuit. Above, the Limper passed the apex of a climb and descended for a strike upon the fortress. As another band of creatures came out.

They grabbed up whatever bodies they could and hurried back. Limper adjusted his descent and hit them. Half went down. The others dragged at least a dozen dead men inside.

A pair of those flying balls came shrieking across from Duretile and impacted the castle wall, hurling up a shield of color. Another carpet dropped behind Limper. It released something which plunged into the black castle. There was a flash so brilliant it blinded people for miles around. I was facing away at the moment, but, even so, fifteen seconds passed before my vision recovered enough to show me the fortress afire.

This was not the shifting fire we had seen earlier. This was more like a conflagration actually consuming the stuff of the fortress itself. Strange screams came from inside. They set chills crawling my spine. They were screams not of pain but of rage. Creatures appeared on the battlements, flailing away with what looked like cats-o'-nine-tails, extinguishing the flames. Wherever the flames had burned, the fortress was visibly diminished.

A steady stream of ball pairs howled across the valley. I do not see that they contributed anything, yet I'm sure there was purpose behind them.

A third carpet dropped while Limper and the other were climbing. This one trailed a cloud of dust. Wherever the dust touched, it had an effect like Limper's maple seeds, only generalized. Exposed castle creatures shrieked in agony. Several seemed to melt. The others abandoned the walls.

Events proceeded in like fashion for quite a while, with the black castle appearing to get the worst of it. Yet they had gotten those bodies inside, and I suspected that meant trouble.

Sometime during all this Asa made a getaway. I was unaware of it. So was everyone else, till hours later, when Pawnbroker spotted him going into the Iron

Lily. But Pawnbroker was a good distance away, and the Lily was doing a booming business despite the hour, with everyone who could gathered for drinks while watching the fury on the north ridge. Pawnbroker lost him in the mob. I expect Asa spoke to Shed's sister-in-law and learned that he, too, had escaped. We never had time to interview her.

Meantime, the Lieutenant was getting things under control. He had the casualties cleared away from the break in the circumvallation. He moved ballistae into position to fire into any further break-out attempt. He had pit traps dug. He sent laborers around to replace those One-Eye had lost.

The Taken continued their harassment of the castle, though at a more leisurely pace. They had shot their best bolts early.

The occasional pair of balls howled over from Duretile. I later learned that Silent was throwing them, having been taught by the Taken.

The worst of it seemed over. Except for the three escapees Elmo was hunting, we had contained the thing. The Limper peeled off to join the hunt for the three. Whisper returned to Duretile to refurbish her store of nasty tricks. Feather patrolled above the castle, dipping down occasionally when its denizens came out to battle the last consuming flames. Relative peace had returned.

Nobody rested, though. Bodies had been hauled inside. We all wondered if they had gleaned enough to bring the Dominator through.

But they were up to something else in there.

A group of creatures appeared on the wall, setting up a device pointing down-slope. Feather dove.

Bam! Smoke boiled around her, illuminated from within. She came out wobbling. *Bam!* And *bam!* again. And thrice more still. And after the last she could no longer hold it. She was afire, a comet arcing up, out, away, and down into the city. A violent explosion occurred where she hit. In moments a savage conflagration raged upon the waterfront. The fire spread swiftly among the tightly packed tenements.

Whisper was out of Duretile and hitting the black castle in minutes, with the vicious dust that melted and the fire that burned the stuff of the fortress itself. There was an intensity to her flying that betrayed her anger over Feather's fall.

The Limper, meantime, broke off hunting escapees to help fight the fire in the Buskin. With his aid it was controlled within hours. Without him the entire district might have burned.

Elmo got two of the fugitives. The third vanished utterly. When the hunt resumed with the help of the Taken, no trace could be found.

Whisper maintained her attack till she exhausted her resources. That came well after sunrise. The fortress looked more like a giant hunk of slag than a castle, yet she had not overcome it. One-Eye, when he came around seeking more tools, told me there was plenty of activity inside.

37

Juniper: The Calm

I caught a two-hour nap. The Lieutenant allowed half the troops and workers the same, then the other half. When I wakened, I found few changes, except that the Captain had sent Pockets over to establish a field hospital. Pockets had been down in the Buskin, trying to win friends with free medical attention. I looked in, found only a handful of patients and the situation under control, went on to check the siegework.

The Lieutenant had repaired the gap in the palisade and trench. He had extended both, intending to take them all the way around, despite the difficulty of the nether slope. New, heavier missile weapons were under construction.

He was not content to rely upon the Taken to reduce the place. He did not trust them to do the necessary.

Sometime during my brief sleep, drafts of Candy's prisoners came up. But the Lieutenant did not permit the civilians to leave. He put them to gathering earth while he scoped out a site for building a ramp.

I suggested, "You'd better get some sleep."

"Need to ride herd," he said. He had a vision. His talent had gone unused for years. He wanted this. I suspect he found the Taken an irritation, despite the formidable nature of the black castle.

"It's your show," I said. "But you won't be much good if they hit back and you're too exhausted to think straight."

We were communicating on a level outside words. Weariness had us all fragmented and choppy, neither our thoughts nor actions nor speech moving logically or linearly. He nodded curtly. "You're right." He surveyed the slope. "Seems to be clicking. I'll go down to the hospital. Have somebody get me if something happens."

The hospital tent was the nearest place out of the sun. It was a bright, clear, intense day, promising to be unseasonably warm. I looked forward to that. I was tired of shivering. "Will do."

He was right about things running smoothly. They usually do once the men know what has to be done.

From the viewpoint of the Limper, who again had the air patrol, the slope must have looked like an overturned anthill. Six hundred Company troops were supervising the efforts of ten times as many men from the city. The road uphill carried so much traffic it was being destroyed. Despite the night's excitement and their lack of sleep, I found the men in excellent spirits.

They had been on the march so long, doing nothing else, that they had developed a big store of violent energy. It was pouring out now. They worked with an eagerness which infected the locals. Those seemed pleased to participate in a task which required the concerted efforts of thousands. Some of the more thoughtful mentioned that Juniper had mounted no major communal effort in generations. One man suggested that that was why the city had gone to seed. He believed the Black Company and its attack on the black castle would be great medicine for a moribund body politic.

That, however, was not a majority opinion. Candy's prisoners, especially, resented being used as a labor force. They represented a strong potential for trouble.

I have been told I always look at the dark underbelly of tomorrow. Possibly. You're less likely to be disappointed that way.

The excitement I expected did not materialize for days. The castle creatures seemed to have pulled their hole in after them. We eased the pace slightly, ceased working as if everything had to be done before tomorrow.

The Lieutenant completed the circumvallation, including the back slope, looping around One-Eye's excavation. He then broke the front wall and began building his ramp. He did not use many mantlets, for he designed it to provide its own shielding. It rose steeply at our end, with steps constructed of stone from demolished buildings. The work crews downtown were now pulling down structures ruined in the fire following Feather's crash. There were more materials than could be used in the siege. Candy's outfit was salvaging the best to use in new housing planned for the cleared sites.

The ramp would rise till it overtopped the castle by twenty feet, then it would descend to the wall. The work went faster than I expected. So did One-Eye's project. He found a combination of spells which turned stone soft enough to be worked easily. He soon reached a point beneath the castle.

Then he ran into the material that looked like obsidian. And could go no farther. So he started spreading out.

The Captain himself came over. I had been wondering what he was doing. I asked.

"Finding ways to keep people busy," he said. He shambled around erratically. If we did not pay attention, we found ourselves wandering off after he made some sudden turn and went to inspect something apparently trivial. "Damned Whisper is turning me into a military governor."

"Uhm?"

"What, Croaker?"

"I'm the Annalist, remember? Got to get this all down somewhere."

He frowned, eyeballed a barrel of water set aside for animals. Water was a problem. A lot had to be hauled to augment the little we caught during the occasional shower. "She has me running the city. Doing what the Duke and city fathers should." He kicked a rock and said nothing more till it stopped rolling. "Guess I'm coping. Isn't anybody in town who isn't working. Aren't getting paid anything but keep, but they're working. Even got people lined up with projects they want done as long as we're making people work. The Custodians are driving me crazy. Can't tell them all their clean-ups may be pointless."

I caught an odd note in that. It underscored a feeling I'd had already, that he was depressed about what was happening. "Why's that?"

He glanced around. No natives were within earshot. "Just a guess, mind. Nobody's put it in words. But I think the Lady plans to loot the Catacombs."

"People aren't going to like that."

"I know. You know; I know; even Whisper and Limper know. But we don't give the orders. There's talk about how the Lady is short of money."

In all the years we'd been in her service we'd never missed a payday. The Lady played that straight. The troops got paid, be they mercenaries or regulars. I suspect the various outfits could tolerate a few delays. It's almost a tradition for commanders to screw their troops occasionally.

Most of us didn't much care about money, anyway. We tended toward inexpensive and limited tastes. I suppose attitudes would shift if we had to do without, though.

"Too many men under arms on too many frontiers," the Captain mused. "Too much expansion too fast for too long. The empire can't take the strain. The effort in the Barrowland ate up her reserves. And it's still going. If she whips the Dominator, look for things to change."

"Maybe we made a mistake, eh?"

"Made a lot. Which one are you talking about?"

"Coming north, over the Sea of Torments."

"Yes. I've known that for years."

"And?"

"And we can't get out. Not yet. Someday, maybe, when our orders take us back to the Jewel Cities, or somewhere where we could leave the empire and still find ourselves in a civilized country." There was an almost bottomless yearning in his voice. "The longer I spend in the north, the less I want to end my days here, Croaker. Put that in your Annals."

I had him talking, a rare occurrence. I merely grunted, hoping he would continue filling the silence. He did.

"We're running with the darkness, Croaker. I know that don't make no never-mind, really. Logically. We're the Black Company. We're not good or evil. We're just soldiers with swords for sale. But I'm tired of having our work turned to wicked ends. If this looting thing happens, I may step aside. Raven had the right idea back at Charm. He got the hell out."

I then set forth a notion that had been in the back of my mind for years. One I'd never taken seriously, knowing it quixotic. "That doesn't contribute anything, Captain. We also have the option of going the other way."

"Eh?" He came back from whatever faraway place ruled him and really looked at me. "Don't be silly, Croaker. That's a fool's game. The Lady squashes anybody who tries." He ground a heel into the earth. "Like a bug."

"Yeah." It *was* a silly idea, on several levels, not the least of which was that the other side could not afford us. I could not picture us in the Rebel role anyway. The majority of Rebels were idiots, fools or ambitious types hoping to grab a chunk of what the Lady had. Darling was the outstanding exception, and she was more symbol than substance, and a secret symbol at that.

"Eight years since the comet was in the sky," the Captain said. "You know the legends. She won't fall till the Great Comet is up there. You want to try surviving twenty-nine years on the run from the Taken? No, Croaker. Even if our hearts were with the White Rose, we couldn't make that choice. That's suicide. Getting out of the empire is the way."

"She'd come after us."

"Why? Why shouldn't she be satisfied with what she's had of us these ten years? We're no threat to her."

But we were. We very much were, if only because we knew of the existence of the reincarnation of the White Rose. And I was sure that, once we left the empire, either Silent or I would spill that secret.

Of course, the Lady did not know that we knew.

"This chatter is an exercise in futility," the Captain said. "I'd rather not talk about it."

"As you wish. Tell me what we're going to do here."

"The Lady is coming in tonight. Whisper says we'll begin the assault as soon as the auspices are right."

I glanced at the black castle.

"No," he said. "It won't be easy. It may not be possible, even with the Lady helping."

"If she asks about me, tell her I'm dead. Or something," I said.

That won a smile. "But, Croaker, she's your. . . ."

"Raven," I snapped. "I know things about him that could get us all killed. So does Silent. Get him out of Duretile before she gets here. Neither one of us dares face the Eye."

"For that, neither do I. Because I know you know something. We're going to have to take our chances, Croaker."

"Right. So don't put notions into her head."

"I expect she's forgotten you long since, Croaker. You're just another soldier."

38

Juniper: The Storm

The Lady hadn't forgotten me. Not even a little. Shortly after midnight a grim Elmo rousted me out. "Whisper is here. Wants you, Croaker."

"Eh?" I hadn't done anything to arouse her ire. Not for weeks.

"They want you over to Duretile. *She* wants you. Whisper is here to take you back."

Ever seen a grown man faint? I haven't. But I came close. I may have come close to having a stroke, too. My blood pressure must have soared. For two minutes I was vertiginous and unable to think. My heart pounded. My guts ached with fear. I *knew* she was going to drag me in for a session with the Eye, which sees every secret buried in a man's mind. And yet I could do nothing to evade her. It was too late to run. I wished I had been aboard the ship to Meadenvil with Pawnbroker.

Like a man walking to the gallows, I went out to Whisper's carpet, settled myself behind her, and dwindled into my thoughts as we rose and rushed through the chill night toward Duretile.

As we passed over the Port, Whisper called back, "You must have made quite an impression back when, physician. You were the first person she asked about when she got here."

I found enough presence of mind to ask, "Why?"

"I suspect because she wants her story recorded again. As she did during the battle at Charm."

I looked up from my hands, startled. How had she known that? I'd always pictured the Taken and Lady as uncommunicative among themselves.

What she said was true. During the battle at Charm the Lady had dragged me around with her so the events of the day would be recorded as they happened. And she did not demand special treatment. In fact, she insisted I write stuff as I saw it. There was just the faintest whiff of a hint that she expected to be toppled sometime, and, once she was, expected maltreatment by historians. She wanted a neutral record to exist. I hadn't thought about that for years. It was one of the more curious anomalies I'd noted about her. She did not care what people thought of her, but was frightened that the record would be bastardized to suit someone else's ends.

The tiniest spark of hope rose from that. Maybe she *did* want a record kept. Maybe I *could* get through this. If I could remain nimble enough to avoid the Eye.

The Captain met us when we landed on Duretile's northern wall. A glance at the carpets there told me all the Taken were on hand. Even Journey, whom I had expected to remain in the Barrowland. But Journey would have a grudge to soothe. Feather had been his wife.

A second glance told me the Captain was silently apologetic about my situation, that there were things he wanted to say but dared not. I fed him a tiny shrug, hoped we would get a moment later. We did not. Whisper led me from the wall directly into the Lady's presence.

She hadn't changed an iota since I had seen her last. The rest of us had aged terribly, but she remained twenty forever, radiantly gorgeous with stunning black hair and eyes into which a man could fall and die. She was, as always, such a focal point of glamor that she could not be physically described. A detailed description would be pointless anyway, as what I saw was not the true Lady. The Lady who looked like that hadn't existed for four centuries, if ever.

She rose and came to greet me, a hand extended. I could not tear my eyes away. She rewarded me with the slightly mocking smile I recalled so well, as though we shared a secret. I touched her hand lightly, and was astonished to find it warm. Away from her, when she vanished from mind except as a distant object of dread, like an earthquake, I could think of her only as cold, dead, and deadly. More on the order of a lethal zombie than a living, breathing, even possibly vulnerable person.

She smiled a second time and invited me to take a seat. I did so, feeling grotesquely out of place amidst a company which included all but one of the great evils of the world. And the Dominator was there in spirit, casting his cold shadow.

I was not there to contribute, that became obvious. The Captain and Lieutenant did the talking for the Company. The Duke and Custodian Hargadon were there, too, but contributed little more than I. The Taken carried the discussion, questioning the Captain and Lieutenant. Only once was I addressed, and that by the Captain, who inquired as to my readiness to treat casualties from the fighting.

The meeting had only one point so far as I was concerned. The assault was set for dawn, day after the one coming up. It would continue till the black castle was destroyed or we lost our capacity to attack.

"The place is a hole in the bottom of the ship of empire," the Lady said. "It has to be plugged or we all drown." She entertained no protests from the Duke or Hargadon, both of whom regretted asking her for help. The Duke was now impotent within his own domain, and Hargadon little better. The Custodian suspected he would be out of work entirely, once the threat of the castle ended. Few of the Company and none of the Taken had been at any pains to conceal their disdain for Juniper's odd religion. Having spent a lot of time among the people, I could say they took it only as seriously as the Inquisitors, Custodians and a few fanatics made them.

I hoped she went slow if she intended changes, though. Like so slow the Company would be headed elsewhere before she started. You mess with people's religion and you mess with fire. Even people who don't much give a damn. Religion is something that gets hammered in early, and never really goes away. And has powers to move which go beyond anything rational.

Morning after the day coming up. Total war. All-out effort to eradicate the black castle. Every resource of the Lady, Taken, Company and Juniper to be bent to that end, for as long as it took.

Morning after the day coming up. But it did not work that way. Nobody told the Dominator he was supposed to wait.

He got in the first strike six hours before jump-off, while most of the troops and all the civilian laborers were asleep. While the only Taken patrolling was Journey, who was the least of the Lady's henchmen.

It began when one of those bladder-like things bounced over the wall and filled the gap remaining in the Lieutenant's ramp. At least a hundred creatures stormed out of the castle and crossed.

Journey was alert. He had sensed a strangeness in the castle and was watching for trouble. He came down fast and drenched those attackers with the dust that melted.

Bam! Bam-bam-bam! The castle hit him the way it had hit his one-time wife. He fishtailed through the air, evading the worst, but caught the edge of every crack, and went down smouldering, his carpet destroyed.

The banging wakened me. It wakened the entire camp, for it started the same time as the alarms and drowned them entirely.

I charged out of the hospital, saw the castle creatures boiling down the steps of the Lieutenant's ramp. Journey hadn't stopped more than a handful. They were enveloped by that protective glow One-Eye had encountered once before. They spread out, sprinting through a storm of missiles from the men who had the watch. A few more fell, but not many. They began extinguishing lights, I suppose because their eyes were more suited to darkness than ours.

Men were running everywhere, dragging their clothing on as they rushed toward or away from the enemy. The laborers panicked and greatly hampered the Company's response. Many were killed by our men, vexed at finding them in the way.

The Lieutenant charged through the chaos bellowing orders. First he got his batteries of heavy weapons manned and trained on the steps. He sent messengers everywhere, ordering every ballista, catapult, mangonel and trebuchet moved to a position where it could fire on the ramp. That baffled me only till the first castle creature headed home with a body under each arm. A storm of missiles hit him, tore the bodies to shreds, battered him to a pulp, and nearly buried him.

The Lieutenant had trebuchets throw cannisters of oil which smashed on the steps and caught fire when flaming balls were thrown after them. He kept the oil and fire flying. The castle creatures would not run through the flames.

So much for my thinking the Lieutenant was wasting time building useless engines.

The man knew his job. He was good. His preparation and quick response were more valuable than anything done by the Lady or Taken that night. He held the line in the critical minutes.

A mad battle began the moment the creatures realized they were cut off. They promptly attacked, trying to reach the engines. The Lieutenant signaled his under-officers and brought the bulk of his available manpower to bear. He had to. Those creatures were more than a match for any two soldiers, and they benefited from the protective glow as well.

Here, there, a brave citizen of Juniper grabbed a fallen weapon and jumped into the struggle. Most paid the ultimate price, but their sacrifice helped keep the enemy away from the engines.

It was obvious to everyone that if the creatures escaped with many bodies, our cause was lost. We'd soon be face-to-face with their master himself.

The ball pairs began coming over from Duretile, splashing the night with terrible color. Then Taken dropped from the night, Limper and Whisper each depositing an egg which hatched the fire that fed on the stuff of the castle. Limper dodged several attacks from the castle, swooped around, brought his carpet to ground near my hospital, where we were swamped by customers already. I had to retreat there to do the job for which I was paid. I kept the uphill tent flaps open so I could watch.

Limper left his aerial steed, marched uphill with a long, black sword that glimmered evilly in the light from the burning fortress. He radiated a glow not unlike that protecting the castle creatures. His, however, was far more puissant than theirs, as he demonstrated when he pushed through the press and attacked them. Their weapons could not reach him. His sliced through them as though they were made of lard.

The creatures, by that time, had slaughtered at least five hundred men. The majority were workers, but the Company had taken a terrible beating, too. And that beating went on even after the Limper turned the tide, for he could engage but one creature at a time. Our people strove to keep the enemy contained till the Limper could get to them.

They responded by trying to swamp the Limper, which they managed with some success, fifteen or twenty piling on and keeping him pinned by sheer body weight. The Lieutenant shifted the fire of the engines temporarily, pounded that seething pile till it broke up and the Limper regained his feet.

That ploy having failed, a band of the creatures clotted up and tried to break out to the west. I don't know whether they planned to escape entirely or meant to swing around and strike from behind. The dozen who made it through encountered Whisper, and a heavy fall of the melting dust. The dust killed a half-dozen workers for every castle creature, but it stopped the charge. Only five creatures survived it.

Those five immediately encountered the portal from elsewhere that expelled the cold breath of the infinite. They all perished.

Whisper, meantime, was scrambling for altitude. A drumroll procession of bangs pursued her up the sky. She was a better flyer than Journey, but even so could not evade injury. Down she came, eventually touching down beyond the fortress.

Within the castle itself creatures were out with the cats-o'-nine-tails, extinguishing the fires started by Whisper and the Limper. The structure had begun to look pathetic, so much of its substance had been consumed. Gone was the dark, dreadful grace of weeks before. It was one big, dark, glassy lump, and it seemed impossible that creatures could survive inside it, yet they did, and continued the fight. A handful came out on the ramp and did something which gnawed black chunks out of the Lieutenant's conflagration. All the creatures on the slope ran for home, not a one forgetting to scoop up at least one body.

The ice door opened again, its breath dumping on the steps. The fires died instantly. A score of the creatures died too, hammered to powder by the Lieutenant's missiles.

The things inside took a tack I had anticipated fearfully since I had seen Feather crash. They turned their booming spell on the slope.

If it wasn't the thing that had pursued the Lieutenant, Elmo, One-Eye and me that day, it was a close cousin. There wasn't much flash or smoke when they used it on the slope, but huge holes appeared, often with bloody pulp smashed into their bottoms.

All this happened so swiftly, so dramatically, that nobody really had time to think. I don't doubt that even the Company would have run had events been stretched out enough to allow thinking time. As it was, in their confusion, the men had a chance only to pursue roles for which they had been preparing since reaching Juniper. They stood their ground and, too often, died.

The Limper scampered around the slope like an insane chicken, cackling and hunting creatures who hadn't died on the steps. There were a score of those, most surrounded by angry soldiers. Some of the creatures were slain by their own side, for those knots made tempting targets for the booming spell.

Teams of creatures appeared on the ramparts, assembling devices like the one we'd seen them try to use before. This time there was no Taken above to drop and give them hell.

Not till fool Journey came rushing past the hospital, looking cruelly battered, and stole the Limper's carpet.

It had been my notion that one Taken could not use another's vehicle. Not so, apparently, for Journey got the thing aloft and dove upon the castle again, dumping dust and another fire egg. The castle knocked him down again, and despite the tumult, I heard the Limper howling and cursing him for it.

Ever see how a child draws a straight line? None too straight. Something as shaky as a child's hand scribbled a wobbly line from Duretile to the black castle. It hung against the night like an improbable clothesline, wriggling, of indeterminate color, irridescent. Its tip threw sparks off the obsidian material, like the meeting of flint and steel magnified ten thousand times, generating an actinic glare too intense to view directly. The entire slope was bathed in wild bluish light.

I put aside my instruments and stepped out to better observe, for down in my gut I knew the Lady anchored the nether end of that scrawl, having entered the lists for the first time. She was the big one, the most powerful, and if the castle could be reduced at all, hers was the might that would do it.

The Lieutenant must have been distracted. For a few seconds his fires dwindled. A half-dozen castle creatures went up the steps, dragging two and three corpses apiece. A rush of their compatriots came out to meet the Limper, who was in hot pursuit. My guess is they got twelve bodies inside. Some might not have lost the spark of life entirely.

Chunks flew from the castle where the Lady's line touched, each blazing with that brilliant light. Thin cracks, in crimson, appeared against the black, spreading slowly. The creatures assembling the devices retreated, were replaced by others trying to lessen the effects of the Lady's attack. They had no luck. Several were knocked down by missiles from the Lieutenant's batteries.

The Limper reached the head of the stairs and stood limned against the glow of a section of castle still afire, sword raised high. A giant runt, if you will pardon the contradiction. He is a tiny thing, yet stood huge at that moment. He bellowed, "Follow me!" and charged down the ramp.

To my everlasting amazement, men followed him. Hundreds of men. I saw Elmo and the remnants of his company go roaring up, across, and disappear. Even scores of gutsy citizens decided to take part.

Part of the story of Marron Shed had come out recently, without names or such, but with heavy emphasis on how much wealth he and Raven had garnered. Obviously, the story had been planted against this moment, when a storm of manpower would be needed to subdue the castle. In ensuing minutes the call of wealth led many a man from the Buskin up those steps.

Down on the far side of the castle Whisper reached One-Eye's camp. One-Eye and his men, of course, had stood to arms, but had taken part in nothing yet. His mine operation had stalled once he was certain there was no way to get around or to breech the substance of the castle.

Whisper brought one of those eggs of fire, planted it against the obsidian exposed by One-Eye's mine. She set it off and let it gnaw at the fortress's underbelly.

That, I learned later, had been in the plan for some time. She had done some fancy flying to bring her crippled carpet down near One-Eye so she could carry it out.

Seeing the men pour into the castle, seeing the walls abandoned and being broken up by the Lady, seeing fires burning unchecked, I decided the battle was ours and was all over but the crying. I went back into the hospital and resumed cutting and stitching, setting and just plain shaking my head over men for whom there was nothing I could do. I wished One-Eye weren't on the far side of the ridge. He'd always been my principal assistant, and I missed him. While I could not denigrate Pockets' skill, he did not have One-Eye's talent. Often there was a man beyond my help who could be saved with a little magic.

A whoop and howl told me Journey was back, home from his latest crash and rushing his enemies once more. And not far behind him came those elements of the Company which had been stationed in the Buskin. The Lieutenant met Candy and prevented him from rushing over the ramp. Instead, he manned the perimeter and began rounding up those laborers who could be found still close to the action. He started putting things back together.

The *bam!* weapon had continued pounding away all along. Now it began to falter. The Lieutenant loudly cursed the fact that there were no carpets to drop fire eggs.

There *was* one. The Lady's. And I was sure she knew the situation. But she did not abandon her rope of irridescent light. She must have felt it to be more important.

Down in the mine the fire gnawed through the bottom of the fortress. A hole slowly expanded. One-Eye says there is very little heat associated with those flames. The moment Whisper considered it opportune, she led his force into the fortress.

One-Eye says he really considered going, but had a bad feeling about it. He watched the mob charge in, workers and all, then hiked around to our side. He joined me in the hospital and updated me as he worked.

Moments after he arrived, the backside of the castle collapsed. The whole earth rumbled. A long roar rolled down the thousand feet of the back slope. Very dramatic, but to little effect. The castle creatures were not inconvenienced at all.

Parts of the forewall were falling too, broken by the Lady's incessant attack.

Company members continued to arrive, accompanied by frightened formations of the Duke's men and even some Custodians rigged out as soldiers. The Lieutenant fed them into his lines. He allowed no one else to enter the castle.

Strange lights and fires, fell howls and noises, and terrible, terrible odors came out of that place. I don't know what happened in there. Maybe I never will. I gather that hardly anyone came back.

A strange, deep-throated, almost inaudible moaning began. It had me shuddering before I noted it consciously. It climbed in pitch with extreme deliberation, in volume much more rapidly. Soon it shook the whole ridge. It came from everywhere at once. After a while it seemed to have meaning, like speech incredibly slowed. I could detect a rhythm, like words stretched over minutes.

One thought. One thought alone. The Dominator. He was coming through.

For an instant I thought I could interpret the words. "Ardath, you bitch." But that went away, chased by fear.

Goblin appeared at the hospital, looked us over, and seemed relieved to find One-Eye there. He said nothing, and I got no chance to ask what he had been up to recently. He returned to the night, parting with a wave.

Silent appeared a few minutes later, looking grim. Silent, my partner in guilty knowledge, whom I had not seen in more than a year, whom I had missed during my visit to Duretile. He looked taller, leaner and bleaker than ever. He nodded, began talking rapidly in deaf speech. "There is a ship on the waterfront flying a red banner. Go there immediately."

"What?"

"Go to the ship with the red banner immediately. Stop only to inform others of the old Company. These are orders from the Captain. They are not to be disobeyed."

"One-Eye. . . ."

"I caught it, Croaker," he said. "What the hell, hey, Silent?"

Silent signed, "There will be trouble with the Taken. This ship will sail to

Meadenvil, where loose ends must be tied off. Those who know too much must disappear. Come. We just gather the old brothers and go."

There weren't many old brothers around. One-Eye and I hurried around telling everyone we could find, and in fifteen minutes a crowd of us were headed toward the Port River bridge, one as baffled as another. I kept looking back. Elmo was inside the castle. Elmo, who was my best friend. Elmo, who might be taken by the Taken. . . .

39

On The Run

Ninety-six men reported aboard, as ordered. A dozen were men for whom the order had not been meant, but who could not be sent away. Missing were a hundred brothers from the old days, before we crossed the Sea of Torments. Some had died on the slopes. Some were inside the castle. Some we hadn't been able to find. But none of the missing were men who had dangerous knowledge, except Elmo and the Captain.

I was there. Silent, One-Eye and Goblin were there. The Lieutenant was there, more baffled than anyone else. Candy, Otto, Hagop. . . . The list goes on and on. They were all there.

But Elmo wasn't, and the old man wasn't, and there was a threat of mutiny when Silent passed the word to put out without them. "Orders," was all he would say, and that in the finger speech many of the men could not follow, though we had been using it for years. It was a legacy Darling had left the Company, a mode of communication useful on the hunt or battlefield.

The moment the ship was under way, Silent produced a sealed letter marked with the Captain's sign. Silent took the officers present into the cabin of the ship's master. He instructed me to read the letter aloud.

"You were right about the Taken, Croaker," I read. "They do suspect, and they do intend to move against the Company. I have done what I can to circumvent them by hiring a ship to take my most endangered brothers to safety. I will not be able to join you, as my absence would alert the Taken. Do not dawdle. I do not expect to last long once they discover your desertion. As you and Goblin can attest, no man hides from the Lady's Eye.

"I do not know that flight will present much hope. They will hunt you, for they will get things from me unless I am quick on my feet. I know enough to set them on the trail. . . ."

The Lieutenant interrupted. "What the hell is going on?" He knew there were secrets some of us shared, to which he was not privy. "I'd say we're past playing games and keeping things from each other."

I looked at Silent, said, "I think we should tell everybody, just so there's a chance the knowledge won't die."

Silent nodded.

"Lieutenant, Darling is the White Rose."

"What? But. . . ."

"Yes. Silent and I have known since the battle at Charm. Raven figured it out first. That's why he deserted. He wanted to get her as far from the Lady as he could. You know how much he loved her. I think a few others guessed too."

The announcement did not cause a stir. Only the Lieutenant was surprised. The others had suspected.

The Captain's letter hadn't much more to say. Farewells. A suggestion we elect the Lieutenant to replace him. And a final, private word to me.

"Circumstances seem to have dictated a shift to the option you mentioned, Croaker. Unless you can outrun the Taken back to the south." I could hear the sardonic chuckle that went with the comment.

One-Eye wanted to know what had become of the Company treasure chest. Way, way back in our service to the Lady we had grabbed off a fortune in coin and gems. It had traveled with us through the years, through good times and bad—our final, secret insurance against tomorrow.

Silent told us it was up in Duretile with the old man. There had been no chance to get it out.

One-Eye broke down and wept. That chest meant more to him than all vicissitudes past, present or promised.

Goblin got down on him. Sparks flew. The Lieutenant was about to take a hand when someone shoved through the door. "You guys better come topside and see this." He was gone before we could find out what he meant.

We hurried up to the main deck.

The ship was a good two miles down the Port, riding the current and tide. But the glow from the black castle illuminated both us and Juniper as brightly as a cloudy day.

The castle formed the base of a fountain of fire reaching miles into the sky.

A vast figure twisted in the flames. Its lips moved. Long, slow words echoed down the Port. "Ardath. You bitch."

I had been right.

The figure's hand rose slowly, lazily, pointed toward Duretile.

"They got enough bodies inside," Goblin squeaked. "The old bastard is coming through."

The men watched in rapt awe. So did I, able only to think we were lucky to escape in time. At the moment I felt nothing for the men we had left behind. I could think only of myself.

"There," somebody said softly. "Oh, look there."

A ball of light formed on Duretile's wall. It swelled rapidly, shedding many colors. It was gorgeous, like a giant moon of stained glass rotating slowly. It was at least two hundred yards in diameter when it separated from Duretile and drifted toward the black castle. The figure there reached, grabbed at the globe, was unable to affect it.

I giggled.

"What's so damned funny?" the Lieutenant demanded.

"Just thinking how the people of Juniper must feel, looking up at that. They've never seen sorcery."

The stained glass ball rolled over and over. For a moment it presented a side I hadn't noticed before. A side that was a face. The Lady's face. Those great glassy eyes stared right into me, hurting. Without thinking I said, "I didn't betray you. You betrayed me."

Swear to the gods there was some form of communication. Something in the eyes said *she* had heard, and was pained by the accusation. Then the face rolled away, and I did not see it again.

The globe drifted into the fountain of fire. It vanished there. I thought I heard the long, slow voice say, "I have you, Ardath."

"There. Look there," the same man said, and we turned to Duretile. And upon the wall where the Lady had begun moving toward her husband there was another light. For a while I could not make out what was happening. It came our way, faltering, rising, falling.

"That's the Lady's carpet," Silent signed. "I have seen it before."

"But who? . . ." There was no one left who could fly one. The Taken were all over at the black castle.

The thing began to move faster, converting rickety up-and-down into ever-increasing velocity. It came our way, faster and faster, dropping lower and lower.

"Somebody who doesn't know what they're doing," One-Eye opined. "Somebody who is going to get killed if. . . ."

It came directly toward us, now not more than fifty feet off the water. The ship had begun the long turn which would take her around the last headland to the open sea. I said, "Maybe it was sent to hit us. Like a missile. To keep us from getting away."

"No," One-Eye said. "Carpets are too precious. Too hard to create and maintain. And the Lady's is the only one left. Destroy it and even she would have to walk home."

The carpet was down to thirty feet, swelling rapidly, sending an audible murmur ahead. It must have been traveling a hundred fifty miles an hour.

Then it was on us, ripping through the rigging, brushing a mast, and spinning on to impact on the sound half a mile away. A gout of spray arose. The carpet skipped like a flat stone, hit again, bounced again, and smashed into the face of a cliff. The spell energies ruling the carpet degenerated in a violet flash.

And not a word was spoken by any member of the Company. For as that carpet had torn through the rigging, we had glimpsed the face of its rider.

The Captain.

Who knows what he was doing? Trying to join us? Probably. I suspect he went to the wall planning to disable the carpet so it could not be used to pursue us. Maybe he planned to throw himself off the wall afterward, to avoid being questioned later. And maybe he had seen the carpet in action often enough to have been tempted by the idea of using it himself.

No matter. He had succeeded. The carpet would not be used to chase us. He would not be exposed to the Eye.

But he had failed his personal goal. He had died in the north.

His flight and death distracted us while the ship moved down the channel till both Juniper and the north ridge dropped behind the headland. The fire over the black castle continued, its terrible flames extinguishing the stars, but it shrank slowly. Oncoming dawn lessened its brilliance. And when one great shriek rolled across the world, announcing someone's defeat, we were unable to determine who had won.

For us the answer did not matter. We would be hunted by either the Lady or her long-buried spouse.

We reached the sea and turned south, with sailors still cursing as they replaced lines torn by the Captain's passage. We of the Company remained very silent, scattered about the deck, alone with our thoughts. And only then did I begin to worry for comrades left behind.

We held a long service two days out. We mourned everyone left behind, but the Captain especially. Every survivor took a moment to eulogize him. He had been head of the family, patriarch, father to us all.

40

Meadenvil: Pathfinding

Fair weather and good winds carried us to Meadenvil in good time. The ship's master was pleased. He had been well-paid beforehand for his trouble, but was eager to shed a manifest of such vile temper. We had not been the best of passengers. One-Eye was terrified of the sea, a grand victim of seasickness, and insisted everyone else be as scared and sick as he. He and Goblin never let up on one another, though the Lieutenant threatened to throw the pair of them to the sharks. The Lieutenant was in such a foul temper himself that they took him half seriously.

In accordance with the Captain's wishes, we elected the Lieutenant our commander and Candy to become second. That position should have fallen to Elmo. . . . We did not call the Lieutenant Captain. That seemed silly with the outfit so diminished. There weren't enough of us left to make a good street gang.

Last of the Free Companies of Khatovar. Four centuries of brotherhood and tradition reduced to this. A band on the run. It did not make sense. Did not seem right. The great deeds of our forebrethren deserved better of their successors.

The treasure chest was lost, but the Annals themselves had, somehow, found their way aboard. I expect Silent brought them. For him they were almost as important as for me. The night before we entered Meadenvil harbor, I read to the troops, from the Book of Woeg, which chronicled the Company's history after its defeat and near destruction in the fighting along the Bake, in Norssele. Only a hundred four men survived that time, and the Company had come back.

They were not ready for it. The pain was too fresh. I gave it up halfway through.

Fresh. Meadenvil was refreshing. A real city, not a colorless berg like Juniper. We left the ship with little but our arms and what wealth we'd carried in Juniper. People watched us fearfully, and there was no little trepidation on our part, too, for we were not strong enough to make a show if the local Prince took exception to our presence. The three wizards were our greatest asset. The Lieutenant and Candy had hopes of using them to pull something that would provide the wherewithal to move on, aboard another ship, with further hopes of returning to lands we knew on the southern shore of the Sea of Torments. To do that, though, meant an eventual overland journey at least partly through lands belonging to the Lady. I thought we would be wiser to move down the coast, confuse our trail, and hook on with someone out here, at least till the Lady's armies closed in. As they would someday.

The Lady. I kept thinking of the Lady. It was all too likely that her armies now owed allegiance to the Dominator.

We located both Pawnbroker and Kingpin within hours of going ashore. Pawnbroker had arrived only two days before us, having faced unfavorable seas and winds during his journey. The Lieutenant started on Kingpin immediately.

"Where the hell you been, boy?" It was a sure thing Kingpin had turned his assignment into an extended vacation. He was that sort. "You were supposed to come back when. . . ."

"Couldn't, sir. We're witnesses in a murder case. Can't leave town till after the trial."

"Murder case?"

"Sure. Raven's dead. Pawn says you know that. Well, we fixed it so that Bullock guy took the rap. Only we've got to hang around and get him hanged."

"Where is he?" I asked.

"In jail."

The Lieutenant reamed him good, cussing and fussing while passersby nervously eyed the hard guys abusing each other in a variety of mystery tongues.

I suggested, "We ought to get off the street. Keep a low profile. We got trouble enough without attracting attention. Lieutenant, if you don't mind, I'd like a chat with Kingpin. Maybe these other guys can show you places to hole up. King, come with me. You, too." I indicated Silent, Goblin and One-Eye.

"Where we going?" Kingpin asked.

"You pick it. Someplace where we can talk. Serious like."

"Right." He led the way, setting a brisk pace, wanting to put distance between himself and the Lieutenant. "That really true? What happened up there? The Captain dead and everything?"

"Too damned true."

He shook his head, awed by the idea of the Company having been destroyed. Finally, he asked, "What do you want to know, Croaker?"

"Just everything you found out since you been here. Especially about Raven. But also about that guy Asa. And the tavern-keeper."

"Shed? I saw him the other day. At least I think I did. Didn't realize it was him till later. He was dressed different. Yeah. Pawn told me he got away. The Asa guy, too. Him I think I know where to find. The Shed guy, though. . . . Well, if you really want him, you'll have to start looking where I thought I saw him."

"He see you?"

That idea caught Kingpin by surprise. Apparently, it hadn't occurred to him to wonder. He isn't the brightest fellow sometimes. "I don't think so."

We went into a tavern favored by foreign sailors. The customers were a polyglot lot and as ragged as we were. They spoke a dozen languages. We settled in at a table, used the language of the Jewel Cities. Kingpin did not speak it well, but understood it. I doubted that anyone else there could follow our discussion.

"Raven," I said. "That's what I want to know about, Kingpin."

He told us a story which matched Asa's closely, the edges being about as uneven as you would expect from someone who hadn't been an eyewitness.

"You still think he faked it?" One-Eye asked.

"Yeah. It's half hunch, but I think he did. Maybe when we go look the place over, I'll change my mind. There a way you guys could tell if he's in town?"

They put their heads together, returned a negative opinion. "Not without we had something that belonged to him to start with," Goblin opined. "We don't got that."

"Kingpin. What about Darling? What about Raven's ship?"

"Huh?"

"What happened to Darling after Raven supposedly died? What happened to his ship?"

"I don't know about Darling. The ship is tied up down at its dock."

We exchanged glances around the table. I said, "That ship gets visited if we have to fight our way aboard. Those papers I told you about. Asa couldn't account for them. I want them to turn up. They're the only thing we got that can get the Lady off our back."

"If there is a Lady," One-Eye said. "Won't be much pumpkin if the Dominator broke through."

"Don't even think that." For no sound reason I had convinced myself that the Lady had won. Mostly, it was wishful thinking, I'm sure. "Kingpin, we're going to visit that ship tonight. What about Darling?"

"Like I said. I don't know."

"You were supposed to look out for her."

"Yeah. But she kind of vanished."

"Vanished? How?"

"Not how, Croaker," One-Eye said, in response to vigorous signing from Silent. "How is irrelevant now. When."

"All right. When, Kingpin?"

"I don't know. Nobody's seen her since the night before Raven died."

"Bingo," Goblin said in a soft, awed voice. "Damn your eyes, Croaker, your instincts were right."

"What?" Kingpin asked.

"There's no way she would have disappeared beforehand unless she knew something was going to happen."

"Kingpin," I said, "did you go look at the place they were staying? Inside, I mean."

"Yeah. Somebody got there before me."

"What?"

"The place was cleaned out. I asked the innkeeper. He said they didn't move out. They was paid up for another month. That sounded to me like somebody knew about Raven getting croaked and decided to clean his place out. I figured it was that Asa. He disappeared right after."

"What did you do then?"

"What? I figured you guys didn't want Bullock back in Juniper, so we got him charged with Raven's murder. There was plenty of witnesses besides us saw them fighting. Enough to maybe convince a court we really saw what we said."

"You do anything to trace Darling?"

Kingpin had nothing to say. He stared at his hands. The rest of us exchanged irritated glances. Goblin muttered, "I told Elmo it was dumb to send him."

I guess it was. In minutes we had come up with several loose ends overlooked by Kingpin.

"How come you're so damned worried about it, anyway, Croaker?" Kingpin demanded. "I mean, it all looks like a big so-what to me."

"Look, King. Like it or not, when the Taken turned on us, we got pushed over to the other side. We're White Rose now. Whether we want it or not. They're going to come after us. The only thing the Rebel has going is the White Rose. Right?"

"If there is a White Rose."

"There is. Darling is the White Rose."

"Come on. Croaker. She's a deaf-mute."

One-Eye observed, "She's also a magical null-point."

"Eh?"

"Magic won't work around her. We noticed that clean back at Charm. And if she follows true for her sort, the null will get stronger as she gets older."

I recalled noting oddities about Darling during the battle of Charm, but hadn't made anything of it then. "What are you talking about?"

"I told you. Some people are negatives. Instead of having a talent for sorcery, they go the other way. It won't work around them. And when you think about it, that's the only way the White Rose makes sense. How could a deaf and dumb kid grow up to challenge the Lady or Dominator on their own ground? I'll bet the original White Rose didn't."

I didn't know. There had been nothing in the histories about her powers or their noteworthy absence. "This makes it more important to find her."

One-Eye nodded.

Kingpin looked baffled. It was easy to fuddle King, I decided. I explained. "If magic won't work around her, we've got to find her and stay close. Then the Taken won't be able to hurt us."

One-Eye said, "Don't forget that they have whole armies they can send after us."

"If they want us that bad. . . . Oh my."

"What?"

"Elmo. If he didn't get killed. He knows enough to put the whole empire on our trail. Maybe not so much for us as in hopes we'll lead them to Darling."

"What're we going to do?"

"Why're you looking at me?"

"You're the one seems to know what's going on, Croaker."

"Okay. I guess. First we find out about Raven and Darling. Especially Darling. And we ought to catch Shed and Asa again, in case they know something useful. We got to move fast and get out of town before the empire closes in. Without upsetting the locals. We better have a sit-down with the Lieutenant. Get everything on the table for everybody, then decide exactly what we'll do."

41

Meadenvil: The Ship

Ours, apparently, was the last ship out of Juniper. We kept waiting for a later vessel to bring news. None came. The crew of our vessel did us no favor, either. They yammered all over town. We were buried by nosy locals, people concerned about relatives in Juniper, and the city government, concerned that a group of tough refugees might cause trouble. Candy and the Lieutenant dealt with all that. The struggle for survival devolved on the rest of us.

The three wizards, Otto, Kingpin and Pawnbroker, and I stole through the shadowed Meadenvil waterfront district after midnight. There were strong police patrols to dodge. We evaded them with help from One-Eye, Goblin and Silent. Goblin was especially useful. He possessed a spell capable of putting men to sleep.

"There she is," Kingpin whispered, indicating Raven's ship. Earlier I'd tried to find out how her docking fees were being paid. I'd had no luck.

She was a fine, big ship with a look of newness the darkness could not conceal. Only the normal lights burned aboard her: bow, stern masthead, port and starboard, and one at the head of the gangway, where a single bored sailor stood watch.

"One-Eye?"

He shook his head. "Can't tell."

I polled the others. Neither Silent nor Goblin detected anything remarkable, either.

"Okay, Goblin. Do your stuff. That'll be the acid test, won't it?"

He nodded. If Darling was aboard, his spell would not affect the watch.

Now that everyone had accepted my suspicions about Raven being alive, I'd begun to question them. I could see no sense in his not having slipped away by now, taking his very expensive ship somewhere far away. Perhaps out to the islands.

Those islands intrigued me. I thought we might grab a ship and head out there. Had to take someone who knew the way, though. The islands were a long way out and there was no regular commerce. No way to get there by guesswork.

"Okay," Goblin said. "He's out."

The sailor on the quarterdeck had slumped onto a handy stool. He had his arms folded on the rail and his forehead on his arms.

"No Darling," I said.

"No Darling."

"Anybody else around?"

"No."

"Let's go, then. Keep low, move fast, all that."

We crossed the pier and scampered up the gangway. The sailor stirred. Goblin touched him and he went out like the dead. Goblin hustled forward, then aft, to the men on the rat guards. He returned nodding. "Another eight men below, all asleep. I'll put them under. You go ahead."

We started with the biggest cabin, assuming it would be the owner's. It was. It sat in the stern, where the master's cabin usually is, and was split into sections. I found things in one indicating that it had been occupied by Darling. On

Raven's side we found soiled clothing discarded some time ago. There was enough dust to indicate that no one had visited the cabin for weeks.

We did not find the papers I sought.

We did find money. Quite a substantial amount. It was cunningly hidden, but One-Eye's sense for those things is infallible. Out came a chest brimming with silver.

"I don't reckon Raven is going to need that if he's dead," One-Eye said. "And if he ain't—well, tough. His old buddies are in need."

The coins were odd. After studying them, I recognized what that oddness was. They were the same as the coins Shed had received at the black castle. "Sniff these things," I told One-Eye. "They're black castle. See if there's anything wrong with them."

"Nope. Good as gold." He chuckled.

"Uhm." I hadn't any scruples about lifting the money. Raven had obtained it by foul means. That put it up for grabs. It had no provenance, as they say in Juniper. "Gather round here. I got an idea." I backed up to the stern lights, where I could watch the dock through the glass window.

They crowded in on me and the chest. "What?" Goblin demanded.

"Why settle for the money? Why not take the whole damned ship? If Raven's dead, or even faking he's dead, what's he going to say about it? We could make it our headquarters."

Goblin liked the idea. So One-Eye didn't. The more so because ships had to do with water. "What about the crew?" he asked. "What about the harbormaster and his people? They'd get the law down on us."

"Maybe. But I think we can handle it. We move in and lock the crew up, there's nobody to complain. Nobody complains, why should the harbormaster be interested?"

"The whole crew ain't aboard. Some's out on the town."

"We grab them when they come back. Hell, man, what better way to be ready to move out in a hurry? And what better place to wait for Raven to turn up?"

One-Eye gave up objecting. He is essentially lazy. Too, there was a gleam in his eye which said he was thinking ahead of me. "Better talk to the Lieutenant," he said. "He knows ships."

Goblin knew One-Eye well. "Don't look at me if you're thinking about going pirate. I've had all the adventure I want. I want to go home."

They got into it, and got loud about it, and had to be shut up.

"Let's worry about getting through the next few days," I growled. "What we do later we can worry about later. Look. We got clothes that belonged to Darling and Raven. Can you guys find them now?"

They put their heads together. After some discussion Goblin announced,

"Silent thinks he can. Trouble is, he has to do it like a dog. Lock on the trail and follow around everywhere Raven went. Right up till he died. Or didn't. If he didn't, right on to where he is now."

"But that. . . . Hell. You're spotting him a couple months lead."

"People spend a lot of time not moving around, Croaker. Silent would skip over that."

"Still sounds slow."

"Best you can get. Unless he comes to us. Which maybe he can't."

"All right. All right. What about the ship?"

"Ask the Lieutenant. Let's see if we can find your damned papers."

There were no papers. One-Eye was able to detect nothing hidden anywhere. If I wanted to trace the papers, I'd have to start with the crew. Someone had to help Raven take them off.

We left the ship. Goblin and Pawnbroker found a good spot from which they could watch it. Silent and Otto took off on Raven's trail. The rest of us went back and wakened the Lieutenant. He thought taking the ship was a good idea.

He'd never liked Raven much. I think he was motivated by more than practical considerations.

42

Meadenvil: The Refugee

The rumors and incredible stories swept through Meadenvil rapidly. Shed heard about the ship from Juniper within hours of her arrival. He was stunned. The Black Company run out? Crushed by their masters? That made no sense. What the hell was going on up there?

His mother. Sal. His friends. What had become of them? If half the stories were true, Juniper was a desolation. The battle with the black castle had consumed the city.

He wanted desperately to go find somebody, ask about his people. He fought the urge. He had to forget his homeland. Knowing that Croaker and his bunch, the whole thing could be a trick to smoke him out.

For a day he remained in hiding, in his rented room, debating, till he convinced himself that he should do nothing. If the Company was on the run, it would be leaving again. Soon. Its former masters would be looking for it.

Would the Taken come after him, too? No. They had no quarrel with him. They did not care about his crimes. Only the Custodians wanted him. . . . He wondered about Bullock, rotting in prison, accused of Raven's murder. He did not understand that at all, but was too nervous to investigate. The answer was not significant in the equation of Marron Shed's survival.

After his day in isolation he decided to resume his quest for a place of business. He was looking for a partnership in a tavern, having decided to stick with what he knew.

It had to be a better place. One that would not lead him into financial difficulties the way the Lily had. Each time he recalled the Lily, he suffered moments of homesickness and nostalgia, of bottomless loneliness. He had been a loner all his life, but never alone. This exile was filled with pain.

He was walking a narrow, shadowed street, slogging uphill through mud left by a nighttime rain, when something in the corner of his eye sent chills to the deeps of his soul. He stopped and whirled so swiftly he knocked another pedestrian down. As he helped the man rise, apologizing profusely, he glared into the shadows of an alley.

"Conscience playing tricks on me, I guess," he murmured, after parting with his victim. But he knew better. He had seen it. Had heard his name called softly. He went to the mouth of the gap between buildings. But it had not waited for him.

A block later he laughed nervously, trying to convince himself it had been a trick of imagination after all. What the hell would the castle creatures be doing in Meadenvil? They'd been wiped out. . . . But the Company guys who had fled here didn't know that for sure, did they? They had run off before the fight was over. They just hoped their bosses had won, because the other side was even worse than theirs.

He was being silly. How could the creature have gotten here? No ship's master would sell passage to a thing like that.

"Shed, you're worrying yourself silly about nothing." He entered a tavern called the Ruby Glass, operated by a man named Selkirk. Shed's landlord had recommended both.

Their discussions were fruitful. Shed agreed to return the following afternoon.

* * *

Shed was sharing a beer with his prospective partner. His proposition seemed beneficial, for Selkirk had satisfied himself as to his character and now was trying to sell him on the Ruby Glass. "Night business will pick up once the scare is over."

"Scare?"

"Yeah. Some people have disappeared around the neighborhood. Five or six in the last week. After dark. Not the kind usually grabbed by the press gangs. So people have been staying inside. We aren't getting the usual night traffic."

The temperature seemed to drop forty degrees. Shed sat rigid as a board, eyes vacant, the old fear sliding through him like the passage of snakes. His fingers rose to the shape of the amulet hidden beneath his shirt.

"Hey, Marron, what's the matter?"

"That's how it started in Juniper," he said, unaware that he was speaking. "Only it was just the dead. But they wanted them living. If they could get them. I have to go."

"Shed? What the hell is wrong?"

He came out of it momentarily. "Oh. Sorry, Selkirk. Yeah. We have a deal. But there's something I have to do first. Something I need to check on."

"What?"

"Nothing to do with you. With us. We're ready to go. I'll bring my stuff up tomorrow and we can get together with the people we need to close the deal legally. I just have something else to do right now."

He went out of the place practically running, not sure what he could do or where he could start, not even if he was sane in his assumption. But he was sure that what had happened in Juniper would reoccur in Meadenvil. And a lot faster if the creatures were doing their own collecting.

He touched his amulet again, wondering how much protection it afforded. Was it puissant? Or just a promise?

He hurried to his rooming house, where people were patient with his questions, knowing he was from out of town. He asked about Raven. The murder had been the talk of the town, what with a foreign policeman having been charged on the accusation of his own men. But nobody knew anything. There was no eyewitness to Raven's death except Asa. And Asa was in Juniper. Probably dead. The Black Company would not have wanted him turning witness against them.

He shed an impulse to contact the survivors. They might want him out of the way, too.

He was on his own with this.

The place where Raven had died seemed a likely place to start. Who knew where that was? Asa. Asa was not available. Who else? How about Bullock?

His guts knotted. Bullock represented everything he feared back home. In a cage here, but still very much a symbol. Could he face the man?

Would the man tell him anything?

Finding Bullock was no problem. The main prison did not move. Finding the courage to face him, even from beyond bars, was another matter. But this entire city lay under a shadow.

Torment racked Shed. Guilt cut him apart. He had done things that left him unable to endure himself. He had committed crimes for which there was no way of making restitution. Yet here was something. . . .

"You're a fool, Marron Shed," he told himself. "Don't worry about it. Meadenvil can look out for itself. Just move on to another city."

But something deeper than cowardice told him he could not run. And not just from himself. A creature from the black castle had appeared in Meadenvil. Two men who had had dealings with the castle had come here. That could not be coincidence. Suppose he moved on? What was to keep the creatures from turning up again, wherever he went?

He had made a deal with a devil. On a gut level he sensed that the net in which he had been taken had to be unwoven strand by strand.

He moved the everyday, cowardly Shed to a throne far behind his eyes and brought forward the Shed who had hunted with Krage and eventually killed his tormentor.

He did not recall the cock-and-bull story he used to get past the wards, but did bullshit his way in to see Bullock.

The Inquisitor had lost none of his spirit. He came to the bars spitting and cursing and promising Shed an excruciating death.

Shed countered, "You ain't never going to punish nobody but maybe a cockroach in there. Shut up and listen. Forget who you were and remember where you are. I'm the only hope you got of getting out." Shed was amazed. Could he have been half as firm without the intervening bars?

Bullock's face went blank. "Go ahead. Talk."

"I don't know how much you hear in here. Probably nothing. I'll run it down. After you left Juniper, the rest of the Black Company showed up. They took over. Their Lady and what-not came to town. They attacked the black castle. I don't know how that turned out. What word there is makes it sound like the city was wiped out. During the fighting some of the Company guys grabbed a ship and got out on account of their masters were going to turn on them. Why I don't know."

Bullock stared at him, considering. "That's the truth?"

"From what I've heard second-hand."

"It was those Black Company bastards got me in here. Framed me. I only had a fight with Raven. Hell, he almost killed *me*."

"He's dead now." Shed described what Asa had seen. "I have a notion what killed him and why. What I need to know is where it happened. So I can make sure. You tell me that and I'll try to get you out."

"I only know approximately. I know where I caught up with him and which way him and Asa went when they got away. That should pin it down pretty close. Why do you want to know?"

"I think the castle creatures planted something on Raven. Like a seed. I think that's why he died. Like the man who brought the original seed to Juniper."

Bullock frowned.

"Yeah. Sounds tall. But listen to this. The other day I saw one of the creatures near where I'm staying. Watching me. Wait! I know what they look like. I met them. Also, people are disappearing. Not too many yet. Not enough to cause a big stink. But enough to scare people."

Bullock moved to the back of his cell, settled on the floor, placed his back against the wall. He was quiet for more than a minute. Shed waited nervously.

"What's your interest, innkeeper?"

"Repayment of a debt. Bullock, the Black Company kept me prisoner for a while. I learned a lot about that castle. It was nastier than anybody guessed. It was a doorway of sorts. Through which a creature called the Dominator was trying to get into the world. I contributed to the growth of that thing. I helped it reach the point where it attracted the Black Company and its sorcerer friends. If Juniper has been destroyed, it's as much my fault as anybody's. Now the same fate threatens Meadenvil. I can do something to stop it. If I can find it."

Bullock sniggered. Sniggers turned into chuckles. Chuckles became laughter.

"Then rot here!" Shed shouted, and started to leave.

"Wait!"

Shed turned.

Bullock stifled his mirth. "Sorry. It's so incongruous. You, so righteous. I mean, I really believe you mean it. All right, Marron Shed. Give it a shot. And if you manage it and you get me out of here, I might not drag you back to Juniper."

"There's no Juniper to drag me to, Bullock. Rumor says the Lady planned to loot the Catacombs after she finished the black castle. You know what that means. All-out rebellion."

Bullock's humor vanished. "Straight down the Shaker Road, past the twelfth mile marker. Left on the first farm track, under a dead oak tree. You go at least six miles on that. Way past the farms. That's wild country. You better go armed."

"Armed?" Shed grinned a big, self-conscious grin. "Marron Shed never had guts enough to learn to use a weapon. Thanks."

"Don't forget me, Shed. My trial comes up first week next month."

"Right."

* * *

Shed dismounted and began leading the rented mule when he reached a point he estimated to be six miles from the Shaker Road. He went on another half-mile. The track was little more than a game trail, winding through rugged country densely covered with hardwood. He saw no evidence man ever traveled this way. Odd. What had Raven and Asa been doing out here? He could think of no reason that made sense. Asa had claimed they were running from Bullock. If so, why hadn't they kept on going down the Shaker Road?

His nerves tautened. He touched the amulet, the knife hidden up his sleeve. He had splurged and bought himself two good short weapons, one for his belt and one for his sleeve.

They did little to boost his confidence.

The trail turned downhill, toward a brook, ran beside that for several hundred yards, and debouched into a broad clearing. Shed almost walked into that. He was a city boy. Never before had he been into country more wild than the Enclosure.

Some innate sense of caution stopped him at the clearing's edge. He dropped to one knee, parted the undergrowth, cursed softly when the mule nudged him with its nose.

He had guessed right.

A great black lump stood out there. It was the size of a house already. Shed stared at faces frozen in screams of terror and agony.

A perfect place for it, out here. Growing this fast, it would become complete before anyone discovered it. Unless by accident. And the accidental discoverer would become one with it.

Shed's heart hammered. He wanted nothing more than to race back to Meadenvil and cry the city's danger in the streets. He had seen enough. He knew what he had come to learn. Time to get away.

He went forward, slowly. He dropped the mule's reins, but it followed, interested in the tall grass. Shed approached the black lump carefully, a few steps at a time. Nothing happened. He circled it.

The shape of the thing became more evident. It would be identical to the fortress overlooking Juniper, except for the way its foundations conformed to the earth. Its gate would face south. A well-beaten path led to a low hole there. Further confirmation of his suspicions.

Where had the creatures come from? Did they roam the world at will, hidden on the edge of night, seen only by those who bargained with them?

Returning to the side from which he had approached, he stumbled over something.

Bones. Human bones. A skeleton—head, arms, legs, with part of the chest missing. Still clad in tatters he'd seen Raven wear a hundred times. He knelt.

"Raven. I hated you. But I loved you, too. You were the worst villain I ever knew. And as good a friend as I ever had. You made me start thinking like a man." Tears filled his eyes.

He searched childhood memories, finally found the prayer for the passage of the dead. He began to sing in a voice that had no notion how to carry a tune.

The grass swished only once, just on the edge of audibility. A hand closed on his shoulder. A voice said, "Marron Shed."

Shed shrieked and grabbed for his belt knife.

43

Meadenvil: Warm Trail

I did not have a good night after visiting Raven's ship. It was a night of dreams. Of nightmares, if you will. Of terrors I dared not mention when I wakened, for the others had troubles and fears enough.

She came to me in my sleep, as she had not done since our grim retreats when the Rebel was closing in on Charm, so long ago. She came, a golden glow that might have been no dream at all, for it seemed to be there in the room I shared with five other men, illuminating them and the room while I lay with heart hammering, staring in disbelief. The others did not respond, and later I was not sure I had not imagined the whole thing. It had been that way with the visits in the way back when.

"Why did you abandon me, physician? Did I treat you less than well?"

Baffled, confused, I croaked out, "It was run or be killed. We would not have fled had there been a choice. We served you faithfully, through hazards and horrors greater than any in our Company's history. We marched to the ends of the earth for you, without complaint. And when we came to the city Juniper, and spent half our strength storming the black castle, we learned that we were to be rewarded by being destroyed."

That marvelous face formed in the golden cloud. That marvelous face drawn in sadness. "Whisper planned that. Whisper and Feather. For reasons of their own. But Feather is gone and Whisper has been disciplined. I would not have allowed such a crime in any case. You were my chosen instruments. I would permit no machination of the Taken to harm you. Come back."

"It's too late. Lady. The die is cast. Too many good men have been lost. Our heart is gone. We have grown old. Our only desire is to return to the South, to rest in the warm sun and forget."

"Come back. There is much to be done. You are my chosen instruments. I will reward you as no soldiers have ever been rewarded."

I could detect no hint of treachery. But what did that mean? She was ancient. She had deluded her husband, who was far harder to fuddle than I.

"It's too late, Lady."

"Come back, physician. You, if no one else. I need your pen."

I do not know why I said what I did next. It was not the wisest thing to do, if she was feeling the least benevolent toward us, the least disinclined to come howling after us. "We will do one more thing for you. Because we are old and tired and want to be done with war. We will not stand against you. If you do not stand against us."

Sadness radiated from the glow. "I am sorry. Truly sorry. You were one of my favorites. A mayfly who intrigued me. No, physician. That cannot be. You cannot remain neutral. You never could. You must stand with me or against me. There is no middle ground."

And with that the golden cloud faded, and I fell into a deep sleep—if ever I had been awake.

I woke feeling rested but worried, at first unable to recall the visit. Then it slammed back into consciousness. I dressed hurriedly, raced to the Lieutenant. "Lieutenant, we got to start moving faster. She won. She's going to come after us."

He looked startled. I told him about the night vision. He took it with a pound of salt till I told him that she had done the same before, during the long retreat and series of encounters that had brought the Rebel main forces to the gates of Charm. He did not want to believe me, but he dared not do otherwise. "Get out there and find that Asa, then," he said. "Candy, we move on that ship tonight. Croaker, you pass the word. We're pulling out in four days, whether you guys find Raven or not."

I sputtered a protest. The critical thing now was to find Darling. Darling was our hope. I asked, "Why four days?"

"It took us four days to sail here from Juniper. Good winds and seas all the way. If the Lady left when you turned her down, she couldn't get here any quicker. So I'll give you that long. Then we hit the sea. If we have to fight our way out."

"All right." I didn't like it, but he was the man who made the decisions. We had elected him to do that. "Hagop, find Kingpin. We're going looking for Asa."

Hagop hurried away like his tail was aflame. He brought Kingpin back in minutes, King crabbing because he hadn't yet eaten, hadn't yet gotten his eight hours of sleep.

"Shut up, King. Our ass is in a vise." I explained, though it wasn't necessary. "Grab something cold and eat on the run. We've got to find Asa."

Hagop, Kingpin, One-Eye and I hit the street. As always, we drew a lot of attention from morning marketers, not only because we had come from Juniper, but because One-Eye was an oddity. They'd never seen a black man in Meadenvil. Most people hadn't heard of blacks.

Kingpin led us a mile through twisting streets. "I figure he'll hole up in the same area as before. He knows it. He's not very bright, either, so it wouldn't occur to him to move because you guys came to town. Probably just plans to keep his head down till we pull out. He's got to figure we have to keep moving."

His reasoning seemed sound. And so it proved. He interviewed a few people he had met in the course of previous poking around, quickly discovered that Asa was, indeed, hiding out in the area. Nobody was sure where, though.

"We'll take care of that in a hurry," One-Eye said. He parked himself on a doorstep and performed a few cheap magic tricks that were all flash and show. That arrested the attention of the nearest urchins. Meadenvil's streets are choked with children all the time.

"Let's fade," I told the others. We had to be intimidating to small eyes. We moved up the street and let One-Eye draw his crowd.

He gave the kids their money's worth. Of course. And fifteen minutes later he rejoined us, trailed by an entourage of street mites. "Got it," he said. "My little buddies will show us where."

He amazes me sometimes. I would have bet he hated kids. I mean, when he mentions them at all, which is about once a year, it is in the context of whether they are tastier roasted or boiled.

Asa was holed up in a tenement typical of slums the world over. A real rat- and firetrap. I guess having come into money hadn't changed his habits. Unlike old Shed, who had gone crazy when he had money to spend.

There was but one way out, the way we went in. The children followed us. I did not like that, but what could I do?

We pushed into the room Asa called home. He was lying on a pallet in a corner. Another man, reeking of wine, lay nearby, in a pool of vomit. Asa was curled into a ball, snoring. "Time to get up, sweetheart." I shook him gently.

He stiffened under my hand. His eyes popped open. Terror filled them. I pressed down as he tried to jump up. "Caught you again," I said.

He gobbled air. No words came out.

"Take it easy, Asa. Nobody's going to get hurt. We just want you to show us where Raven went down." I withdrew my hand.

He rolled over slowly, watched us like a cat cornered by dogs. "You guys are always saying you just want something."

"Be nice, Asa. We don't want to play rough. But we will if we have to. We have four days before the Lady gets here. We're going to find Darling before then. You're going to help. What you do afterward is your own business."

One-Eye snorted softly. He had visions of Asa with a cut throat. He figured the little man deserved no better.

"You just go down the Shaker Road. Turn left on the first farm road past the twelfth milestone. Keep heading east till you get to the place. It's about seven miles. The road turns into a trail. Don't worry about that. Just keep going and you'll get there." He closed his eyes, rolled over, and pretended to snore.

I indicated Hagop and Kingpin. "Get him up."

"Hey!" Asa yelped. "I told you. What more do you want?"

"I want you to come along. Just in case."

"In case what?"

"In case you're lying and I want to lay hands on you fast."

One-Eye added, "We don't believe Raven died."

"I *saw* him."

"You saw something," I countered. "I don't think it was Raven. Let's go." We grabbed his arms. I told Hagop to see about rounding up horses and provisions. I sent Kingpin to tell the Lieutenant we wouldn't be back till tomorrow. Hagop I gave a fistful of silver from Raven's chest. Asa's eyes widened slightly. He recognized the mintage, if not the immediate source.

"You guys can't push me around here," he said. "You're not anything more than I am. We go out in the street, all I have to do is yell and. . . ."

"And you'll wish you hadn't," One-Eye said. He did something with his hands. A soft violet glow webbed his fingers, coalesced into something serpent-like that slithered over and under his digits. "This little fellow here can crawl into your ear and eat out your eyes from behind. You can't yell loud enough or fast enough to keep me from siccing him on you."

Asa gulped and became amenable.

"All I want is for you to show me the place," I said. "Quickly. I don't have much time."

Asa surrendered. He expected the worst of us, of course. He had spent too much time in the company of villains nastier than us.

Hagop had the horses within half an hour. It took Kingpin another half-hour to rejoin us. Being Kingpin, he dawdled, and when he appeared, One-Eye gave him such a look he blanched and half drew his sword.

"Let's get moving," I growled. I did not like the way the Company was turning upon itself, like a wounded animal snapping at its own flank. I set a stiff pace, hoping to keep everybody too tired and busy to fuss.

Asa's directions proved sound and were easily followed. I was pleased, and when he saw that, he asked permission to turn back.

"How come you're so anxious to stay away from this place? What's out there that's got you scared?"

It took a little pressure, with One-Eye conjuring his violet snake again, to loosen Asa's jaw.

"I came out here right after I got back from Juniper. Because you guys didn't believe me about Raven. I thought maybe you were right and he'd fooled me somehow. So I wanted to see how he maybe did it. And. . . ."

"And?"

He checked us over, estimating our mood. "There's another of those *places* out there. It wasn't there when he died. But it is now."

"Places?" I asked. "What kind of places?"

"Like the black castle. There's one right where he died. Out in the middle of the clearing."

"Tricky," One-Eye snarled. "Trying to send us into that. I'm going to cut this guy, Croaker."

"No, you're not. You let him be." Over the next mile I questioned Asa closely. He told me nothing more of importance.

Hagop was riding point, being a superb scout. He threw up a hand. I joined him. He indicated droppings in the trail. "We're following somebody. Not far behind." He swung down, poked the droppings with a stick, duckwalked up the trail a way. "He was riding something big. Mule or plowhorse."

"Asa!"

"Eh?" the little man squeaked.

"What's up ahead? Where is this guy headed?"

"Nothing's up there. That I know of. Maybe it's a hunter. They sell a lot of game in the markets."

"Maybe."

"Sure," One-Eye said, sarcastic, playing with his violet snake.

"How about you put a little silence on the situation, One-Eye? No! I mean so nobody can hear us coming. Asa. How far to go?"

"Couple miles, anyway. Why don't you guys let me head back now? I can still get to town before dark."

"Nope. You go where we go." I glanced at One-Eye. He was doing as I had requested. We would be able to hear one another talk. That was all. "Saddle up, Hagop. He's only one guy."

"But which guy, eh, Croaker? Suppose it's one of them creepy things? I mean, if that place in Juniper had a whole battalion that came out of nowhere, why shouldn't this place have some?"

Asa made sounds that indicated he had been having similar thoughts. Which explained why he was anxious to get back to town.

"You see anything when you were there, Asa?"

"No. But I seen where the grass was trampled like something was coming and going."

"You pay attention when we get there, One-Eye. I don't want no surprises."

Twenty minutes later Asa told me, "Almost there. Maybe two hundred yards up the creek. Can I stay here?"

"Quit asking stupid questions." I glanced at Hagop, who pointed out tracks. Somebody was ahead of us still. "Dismount. And stow the chatter. Finger talk from here on in. You, Asa, don't open your mouth for nothing. Understand?"

We dismounted, drew our weapons, went forward under cover of One-Eye's spell. Hagop and I reached the clearing first. I grinned, waved One-Eye forward, pointed. He grinned too. I waited a couple of minutes, for the right time, then strode out, stepped up behind the man, and grabbed his shoulder. "Marron Shed."

He shrieked and tried to pull a knife, tried to run at the same time. Kingpin and Hagop headed him off and herded him back. By that time I was kneeling where he had knelt, examining the scatter of bones.

44

Meadenvil: The Clearing

I looked up at Shed. He looked resigned. "Caught up faster than you expected, eh?"

He babbled. I could make little sense of what he said because he was talking about several things at once. Raven. Black castle creatures. His chance to make a new life. What-not.

"Calm down and be quiet, Shed. We're on your side." I explained the situation, telling him we had four days to find Darling. He found it difficult to believe that the girl who had worked in the Iron Lily could be the Rebel's White Rose. I did not argue, just presented the facts. "Four days, Shed. Then the Lady and Taken could be here. And I guarantee you she'll be looking for you, too. By now they know we faked your death. By now they've probably questioned enough people to have an idea what was going on. We're fighting for our lives. Shed." I looked at the big black lump and said to no one in particular, "And that thing don't help one damned bit."

I looked at the bones again. "Hagop, see what you can make of this. One-Eye, you and Asa go over exactly what he saw that day. Walk through it. Kingpin, you play Raven for them. Shed, come here with me."

I was pleased. Both Asa and Shed did as they were told. Shed, though shaken by our return to the stage of his life, did not seem likely to panic. I watched him as Hagop examined the ground inch by inch. Shed seemed to have grown, to have found something in himself that had not had a chance in the sterile soil of Juniper.

He whispered, "Look, Croaker. I don't know about that stuff about the Lady coming and how you got to find Darling. I don't much care." He indicated the black lump. "What're you going to do about that?"

"Good question." He did not have to explain what it meant. It meant the Dominator had not endured final defeat in Juniper. He had hedged his bet beforehand. He had another gateway growing here, and growing fast. Asa was right to be afraid of castle creatures. The Dominator knew he had to hurry—though I doubted he had expected to be found out so soon. "There isn't much we *can* do, when you get down to it."

"You got to do something. Look, I know. I dealt with those things. What they did to me and Raven and Juniper. . . . Hell, Croaker, you can't let that happen again here."

"I didn't say I didn't want to do something. I said I can't. You don't ask a man with a penknife to chop down a forest and build a city. He doesn't have the tools."

"Who does?"

"The Lady."

"Then. . . ."

"I have my limits, friend. I'm not going to get myself killed for Meadenvil. I'm not going to get my outfit scrubbed for people I don't know. Maybe we owe a moral debt. But I don't think it's that big."

He grunted, understanding without accepting. I was surprised. Without his having said as much, I sensed that he had launched a crusade. A grand villain trying to buy redemption. I did not begrudge him in the least. But he could do it without the Company and me.

I watched One-Eye and Asa walk Kingpin through everything Raven had done the day he died. From where I sat I could see no flaw in Asa's story. I hoped One-Eye had a better view. He, if anyone, could find the angle. He was as good at stage magic as at true wizardry.

I recalled that Raven had been pretty good with tricks. His biggie had been making knives appear out of thin air. But he had had other tricks with which he had entertained Darling.

Hagop said, "Look here, Croaker."

I looked. I did not see anything abnormal. "What?"

"Going through the grass toward the lump. It's almost gone now, but it's there. Like a trail." He held blades of grass parted.

It took me a while to see it. Just the faintest hint of a sheen, like an old snail track. A closer scrutiny showed that it should have started roughly where the corpse's heart would have lain. It took a little work to figure, because scavengers had torn the remains.

I examined a fleshless hand. Rings remained on the fingers. Various metal accoutrements and several knives also lay around.

One-Eye worked Kingpin over to the bones. "Well?" I asked.

"It's possible. With a little misdirection and stage magic. I couldn't tell you how he did it. If he did."

"We got a body," I said, indicating the bones.

"That's him," Asa insisted. "Look. He's still wearing his rings. And that's his belt buckle and sword and knives." But a shadow of doubt lingered in his voice. He was coming around to my way.

And I still wondered why the nice new ship had not been claimed.

"Hagop. Hunt around for signs somebody went off in another direction. Asa. You said you lit out as soon as you saw what was happening?"

"Yeah."

"So. Let's quit worrying about that and try to figure what happened here. Just to look at it, this dead man had something that became that." I indicated the lump. I was surprised I had so little trouble ignoring it. I guess you can get used to anything. I'd paraded around the big one in Juniper till I'd lost that cold dread that had moved me for a while. I mean, if men can get used to slaughter-houses, or my business—soldier *or* surgeon—they can get used to anything.

"Asa, you hung around with Raven. Shed, he lived at your place for a couple years, and you were his partner. What did he bring from Juniper that could have come to life and become that?"

They shook their heads and stared at the bones. I told them, "Think harder. Shed, it had to be something he had when you knew him. He stopped going up the hill a long time before he headed south."

A minute or two passed. Hagop had begun working his way along the edge of the clearing. I had little hope he would find traces this long after the fact. I was no woodsman, but I knew Raven.

Asa suddenly gasped.

"What?" I snapped.

"Everything is here. You know, all the metal. Even his buttons and stuff. But one thing."

"Well?"

"This necklace he wore. I only seen it a couple times. . . . What's the matter, Shed?"

I turned. Shed was gripping his chest over his heart. His face was marble white. He gobbled for words that would not come. He started trying to rip his shirt.

I thought he was having an attack. But as I reached him, to help, he opened his shirt and grabbed something he was wearing around his neck. Something on a chain. He tried to get it off by main force. The chain would not break.

I forced him to take it off over his head, pried it out of stiff fingers, held it out to Asa.

Asa looked a little pale. "Yeah. That's it."

"Silver," One-Eye said, and looked at Hagop meaningfully.

He would think that way. And he might be right. "Hagop! Come here."

One-Eye took the thing, held it to the light. "Some craftsmanship," he mused. . . . Then flung it down and dived like a frog off his lily pad. As he arced through the air, he barked like a jackal.

Light flashed. I whirled. Two castle creatures stood at the side of the black lump, frozen in midstep, in the act of rushing us. Shed cursed. Asa shrieked. Kingpin zipped past me and drove his blade deep into a chest. I did the same, so rattled I did not recall the difficulty I'd had during our previous encounter.

We both hit the same one. We both yanked out weapons free. "The neck," I gasped. "Go for the vein in the neck."

One-Eye was up again, ready for action. He told me later he had glimpsed motion in the corner of his eye, jumped just in time to evade something thrown. They had known who to take first. Who was most potent.

Hagop came up from behind as the things started moving, added his blade to the contest. As did Shed, to my surprise. He jumped in with a knife about a foot long, got low, went for a hamstring.

It was brief. One-Eye had given us the moment we needed. They were stubborn about it, but they died. The last to go looked up at Shed, smiled, and said, "Marron Shed. You will be remembered."

Shed started shaking.

Asa said, "He knew you, Shed."

"He's the one I delivered bodies to. Every time but one."

"Wait a minute," I countered. "Only one creature got away at Juniper. Don't seem likely it would be the one who knew you. . . ." I stopped. I had noticed something disturbing. The two creatures were identical. Even to a scar across the chest when I peeled back their dark clothing. The creature the Lieutenant and I had hauled down the hill, after having slain it before the castle gate, had had such a scar.

While everyone else was suffering post-combat shakes, One-Eye asked Hagop, "You see anything silver around Old Bones? When you were checking first?"

"Uh. . . ."

One-Eye held up Shed's necklace. "It might have looked something like this. It was what killed him."

Hagop gulped and dug into a pocket. He handed over a necklace identical to Shed's, except that the serpents had no eyes.

"Yeah," One-Eye said, and again held Shed's necklace to the light. "Yeah. The eyes it was. When the time was right. Time and place."

I was more interested in what else might come out of the black lump. I pulled Hagop around the side, found the entrance. It looked like the entrance to a mud hut. I supposed it wouldn't become a real gate till the place grew up. I indicated the tracks. "What do they tell you?"

"They tell me it's busy and we ought to get out of here. There's more of them."

"Yeah."

We rejoined the others. One-Eye was wrapping Shed's necklace in a piece of cloth. "We get back to town, I'm sealing this in something made of steel and sinking it in the harbor."

"Destroy it, One-Eye. Evil always finds its way back. The Dominator is a perfect example."

"Yeah. All right. If I can."

Elmo's rush into the black castle came to mind while I was getting everybody organized to get out of there. I had changed my mind about overnighting. We could get most of the way back before nightfall. Meadenvil, like Juniper, had neither walls nor gates. We would not be locked outside.

I let Elmo lie in the back of my mind till the thought ripened. When it did, I was aghast.

A tree ensures reproduction by shedding a million seeds. One certainly will survive, and a new tree will grow. I pictured a horde of fighters bursting into the guts of the black castle and finding silver amulets everywhere. I pictured them filling their pockets.

Had to be. That place was doomed. The Dominator would have known that even before the Lady.

My respect for the old devil rose. Crafty bastard.

It was not till we were back on the Shaker Road that I thought to ask Hagop if he had seen any evidence that anyone had left the clearing by another route.

"Nope," he said. "But that don't mean anything."

"Let's not spend so much time yakking," One-Eye said. "Shed, can't you make that damned mule go any faster?"

He was scared. And if he was, I was more so.

Meadenvil: Hot Trail

We made the city. But I swear I could sense something sniffing along our backtrail before we reached the safety of the lights. We returned to our lodgings only to find most of the men gone. Where were they? Off to take over Raven's ship, I learned.

I had forgotten about that. Yes. Raven's ship. . . . And Silent was on Raven's trail. Where was he now? Damn! Sooner or later Raven would lead him to the clearing. . . . A way to find out if Raven had left it, for sure. Also a way to lose Silent. "One-Eye. Can you get hold of Silent?"

He looked at me strangely. He was tired and wanted to sleep.

"Look, if he follows Raven's every move, he's going to head out to that clearing."

One-Eye groaned and went through several dramatic shows of disgust. Then he dug into his magic sack for something that looked like a desiccated finger. He took it to a corner and communed with it, then returned to say, "I got a line on him. I'll find him."

"Thanks."

"Yeah. You bastard. I ought to make you come with me."

I settled by the fire, with a big beer, and lost myself in thought. After a while, I told Shed: "We have to go back out there."

"Eh?"

"With Silent."

"Who's Silent?"

"Another guy from the Company. Wizard. Like One-Eye and Goblin. He's on Raven's trail, tracing every move he made from the minute he arrived. He figured he could track him down, or at least tell from his movements if he was planning to trick Asa."

Shed shrugged. "If we have to, we have to."

"Hunh. You amaze me, Shed. You've changed."

"I don't know. Maybe I could have done it all along. I just know that this thing can't happen again, to anybody else."

"Yeah." I did not mention my visions of hundreds of men looting amulets from the fortress at Juniper. He did not need that. He had a mission. I couldn't make it sound hopeless.

I went downstairs and asked the landlord for more beer. Beer makes me sleepy. I had a notion. A possibility. I did not share it with anyone. The others would not have been pleased.

After an hour I took a leak and dragged off to my room, more intimidated by the thought of returning to that clearing than by what I hoped to accomplish now.

Sleep was a time coming, beer or not. I could not relax. I kept trying to reach out and bring her to me. Which meant nothing at all.

It was a weak fool's hope that she would return so soon. I had put her off. Why should she? Why shouldn't she forget me till her minions caught up and could bring me to her in chains?

Maybe there *is* a connection on a level I do not understand. For I wakened from a drowse, thinking I needed to visit the head again, and found that golden glow hanging above me. Or maybe I did not waken, but only dreamed that I did. I can't get that straight. It always seems so dream-like in retrospect.

I did not wait for her to start. I started talking. I talked fast and told her everything she needed to know about the lump in Meadenvil and about the possibility the troops had carried hundreds of seeds out of the black castle.

"You tell me this when you are determined to be my enemy, physician?"

"I don't want to be your enemy. I'll be your enemy only if you leave me no option." I abandoned debate. "We can't handle this. And it has to be handled. All its like must be handled. There is evil enough in the world as it is." I told her we had found an amulet upon a citizen of Juniper. I named no name. I told her we would leave it where she could be sure to find it when she arrived.

"Arrive?"

"Aren't you on your way here?"

Thin smile, secretive, perfectly aware that I was fishing. No answer. Just a question. "Where will you be?"

"Gone. Long gone, and headed far away."

"Perhaps. We shall see." The golden glow faded.

There were things I wanted to say yet, but they had nothing to do with the problem at hand. Questions I wanted to ask. I did not.

The last golden mote left me with a whispered, "I owe you one, physician."

One-Eye rambled into the place shortly after sunrise, looking a lot worse for wear. Silent came along behind him, looking pretty beaten himself. He had been on Raven's trail without let-up. One-Eye said, "I caught him just in time. Another hour and he would have headed out. I conned him into waiting till daylight."

"Yeah. You want to wake the troops? We get an earlier start today, we ought to be able to get back before dark."

"What?"

"I thought I was pretty clear. We've got to go back out there. Now. We've used one of our days."

"Hey, man, I'm ripped. I'll die if you make me. . . ."

"Sleep in the saddle. That's always been one of your big talents. Sleep anywhere, any time."

"Oh, my aching butt."

An hour later I was headed down the Shaker Road again, with Silent and Otto added to the crew. Shed insisted on coming along, though I was willing to excuse him. Asa decided he wanted in, too. Maybe because he thought Shed would extend an umbrella of protection. He had started talking mission like Shed, but a deaf man could hear its false ring.

We moved faster this time, pressed harder, and had Shed on a real horse. We got down to the clearing by noon. While Silent sniffed around, I worked myself up and took a closer look at the lump.

No change. Except the two dead creatures were gone. I did not need Hagop's eye to see that they had been dragged through the entry hole.

Silent worked his way around the clearing to a point almost identical with that where the creature trail entered the forest. Then he threw up an arm, beckoned. I hurried over, and did not have to read the dance of his fingers to know what he had found. His face revealed the answer.

"Found it, eh?" I asked more brightly than I felt. I had started to count on Raven being dead. I did not like what the skeleton implied.

Silent nodded.

"Yo!" I called. "We found it. Let's go. Bring the horses."

The others gathered. Asa looked a little peaked. He asked, "How did he do it?"

Nobody had an answer. Several of us wondered whose skeleton lay in the clearing and how it had come to wear Raven's necklace. I wondered how Raven's plot for vanishing had dovetailed so neatly with the Dominator's for seeding a new black castle.

Only One-Eye seemed in a mood to talk, and that all complaint. "We follow this and we're not going to get back to town before dark," he said. He said a lot more, mostly about how tired he was. Nobody paid attention. Even those of us who had rested were tired.

"Lead off, Silent," I said. "Otto, you want to take care of his horse? One-Eye, bring up the rear. So we don't get any surprises from behind."

The track was no track at all for a while, just a straight shot through the brush. We were winded by the time it intercepted a game trail. Raven, too, must have been exhausted, for he had turned onto that trail and followed it over a hill, along a creek, up another hill. Then he had turned onto a less traveled path which ran along a ridge, toward the Shaker Road. Over the next two hours we encountered several such forkings. Each time Raven had taken the one which tended more directly westward.

"Bastard was headed back to the high road," One-Eye said. "Could have figured that, gone the other way, and saved all this tramping through the brush."

Men growled at him. His complaints were grating. Even Asa tossed a nasty look over one shoulder.

Raven had taken the long way, no doubt about it. I would guess we walked at least ten miles before coming across a ridgeline and viewing cleared land which descended to the high road. A number of farms lay on our right. In the distance ahead lay the blue haze of the sea. The countryside was mostly brown, for autumn had come to Meadenvil. The leaves were turning. Asa indicated a stand of maples and said they would look real pretty in another week. Odd. You don't think of guys like him as having a sense of beauty.

"Down there." Otto indicated a cluster of buildings three-quarters of a mile south. It did not look like a farm. "Bet that's a roadside inn," he said. "What do you want to bet that was where he was headed?"

"Silent?"

He nodded, but hedged. He wanted to stick to the track to make sure. We mounted up, let him do what walking remained to be done. I, for one, had had enough tramping around.

"How about we stay over?" One-Eye asked.

I checked the sun. "I'm considering it. How safe you figure we'd be?"

He shrugged. "There's smoke coming up down there. Don't look like they had any trouble yet."

Mind-reader. I had been examining farmsteads as we passed, seeking indications that the lump creatures were raiding the neighborhood. The farms had seemed peaceful and active. I suppose the creatures confined their predations to the city, where they would cause less excitement.

Raven's track hit the Shaker Road a half-mile above the buildings Otto thought an inn. I checked landmarks, could not guess how far south of the twelfth mile we were. Silent beckoned, pointed. Raven had indeed turned south. We followed and soon passed milestone sixteen.

"How far are you going to follow him, Croaker?" One-Eye asked. "Bet you he met Darling out here and just kept hiking."

"I suspect he did. How far to Shaker? Anybody know?"

"Two hundred forty-seven miles," Kingpin replied.

"Rough country? Likely to have trouble along the way. Bandits and such?"

King said, "Not that I ever heard of. There's mountains, though. Pretty rough ones. Take a while to get through them."

I did some calculating. Say three weeks to cover that distance, not pushing. Raven wouldn't push, what with Darling along, and the papers. "A wagon. He'd have to have a wagon."

Silent, too, was mounted now. We reached the buildings quickly. Otto proved right. Definitely an inn. A girl came outside as we dismounted, looked at us with wide eyes, raced inside. I guess we were a rough-looking lot. Those who did not show tough looked nasty.

A worried fat man came out strangling an apron. His face could not decide if it wanted to remain ruddy or to go pallid. "Afternoon," I said. "We get a meal and some fodder for the animals?"

"Wine," One-Eye called out as he loosened his cinch. "I need to dive into a gallon of wine. And a feather bed."

"I reckon," the man said. His speech proved difficult to follow. The language of Meadenvil is a dialect of that spoken in Juniper. In the city it wasn't hard to get along, what with the constant intercourse between Meadenvil and Juniper. But this fellow spoke a country dialect with an altered rhythm. "And you can afford it."

I produced two of Raven's silver pieces, handed them over. "Let me know when we're over that limit." I dropped my reins over the hitching rail, climbed the steps, patted his arm as I passed. "Not to worry. We're not bandits. Soldiers. Following somebody who passed this way a while back."

He rewarded me with a frown of disbelief. It was obvious we did not serve the Prince of Meadenvil.

The inn was pleasant, and though the fat man had several daughters, everyone stayed in line. After we had eaten and most had gone off to rest, the innkeeper began to relax. "You answer me some questions?" I asked. I placed a silver piece upon my table. "Might be worth something."

He settled opposite me, regarded me narrowly over a gigantic beer mug. He had drained the thing at least six times since our arrival, which explained his girth. "What do you want to know?"

"The tall man who can't talk. He's looking for his daughter."

"Eh?"

I indicated Silent, who had made himself at home near the fire, seated on the floor, folded forward in sleep. "A deaf and dumb girl who passed this way a while back. Probably driving a wagon. Met a guy here, maybe." I described Raven.

His face went blank. He remembered Raven. And did not want to talk about it.

"Silent!"

He snapped out of sleep as if stung. I sent a message with finger signs. He smiled nastily. I told the innkeeper, "He don't look like much, but he's a sorcerer. Here's how it stands. The man who was here maybe told you he'd come back and cut your throat if you said anything. That's a remote risk. On the other hand, Silent there can cast a few spells and make your cows go dry, your fields barren, and all your beer and wine go sour."

Silent did one of those nasty little tricks which amuse him, One-Eye and Goblin. A ball of light drifted around the common room like a curious puppy, poking into things.

The innkeeper believed me enough not to want to call my bluff. "All right. They was here. Like you said. I get a lot of people through in the summer, so I wouldn't have noticed except like you say, the girl was deaf and the guy was a hard case. She come in in the morning, like she traveled all night. On a wagon. He come in the evening, walking. They stayed off in the corner. They left next morning." He looked at my coin. "Paid in that same funny coin, come to think."

"Yeah."

"Come from a long way off, eh?"

"Yeah. Where'd they go?"

"South. Down the road. Questions I heard the guy ask, I figure they was headed for Chimney."

I raised an eyebrow. I'd never heard of any place called Chimney.

"Down the coast. Past Shaker. Take the Needle Road out of Shaker. The Tagline Road from Needle. Somewhere south of Tagline there's a crossroad where you head west. Chimney is on the Salada Peninsula. I don't know where for sure. Only what I heared from travelers."

"Uhm. Long hike. How far, you think?"

"See. Two hundred twenty-four miles to Shaker. Round two hundred more to Needle. Tagline is about one eighty on from Needle, I think. Or maybe it's two eighty. I don't rightly recollect. That crossroad must be another hundred down from Tagline, then out to Chimney. Don't know how far that would be. Least another hundred. Maybe two, three. Seen a map oncet, that a fellow showed me. Peninsula sticks way out like a thumb."

Silent joined us. He produced a scrap of paper and a tiny, steel-tipped pen. He had the innkeeper run through it again. He drew a crude map that he adjusted as the fat man said it did or did not resemble the map he had seen. Silent kept juggling a column of figures. He came up with an estimate in excess of nine hundred miles from Meadenvil. He knocked off the last digit, then wrote the word *days* and a plus sign. I nodded.

"Probably a four-month trip at least," I said. "Longer if they spend much time resting up in any of those cities."

Silent drew a straight line from Meadenvil to the tip of the Salada Peninsula, wrote, *est. 600 mi. a. 6 knots = 100 hrs.*

"Yeah," I said. "Yeah. That's why the ship never left. Had to give him a head start. Think we'll have a talk with the crew tomorrow. Thanks, innkeeper." I pushed the coin over. "Anything odd happened around here lately?"

A weak smiled stretched his lips. "Not till today."

"Right. No. I mean like neighbors disappearing, or what-not."

He shook his head. "Nope. Less you count Moleskin. Hain't seen him in a while. But that don't make no never-mind."

"Moleskin?"

"Hunter. Works the forest over east. Mainly for furs and hides, but brings me game when he needs salt or something. He don't come around regular, but I reckon he's overdue. Usually comes in come fall, to get staples for the winter. Thought it was him when your friend come through the door."

"Eh? Which friend?"

"The one you're hunting. That carried off this feller's daughter."

Silent and I exchanged glances. I said, "Better not count on seeing Moleskin again. I think he's dead."

"What brings you to say that?"

I told him a little about Raven faking his own death and leaving a body that had been confused for his.

"Bad thing, that. Yep. Bad thing, doing like that. Hope you catch him up." His eyes narrowed slightly, cunning. "You fellers wouldn't be part of that bunch come down from Juniper, would you? Everybody headed south talks about how. . . ." Silent's glower shut him up.

"I'm going to get some sleep," I said. "If none of my men are up yet, roust me out at first light."

"Yes, sir," the innkeeper said. "And a fine breakfast we'll fix you, sir."

46

Meadenvil: Trouble

And a fine breakfast we had. I tipped the innkeeper another piece of silver. He must have thought me mad.

Half a mile up the road One-Eye called a halt. "You just going to leave them?" he asked.

"What?"

"Those people. First Taken comes down this way is going to find out everything we did."

My heart flip-flopped. I knew what he was getting at. I had thought about it earlier. But I could not order it. "No point," I said. "Everybody in Meadenvil is going to see us put out."

"Everybody in Meadenvil don't know where we're headed. I don't like the idea any better than you do, Croaker. But we have to cut the trail somewhere. Raven didn't. And we're on to him."

"Yeah. I know." I glanced at Asa and Shed. They were not taking it well. Asa, at least, figured he was next.

"Can't take them with us, Croaker."

"I know."

He swung around, started back. Alone. Not even Otto joined him, and Otto has very little conscience.

"What's he going to do?" Asa asked.

"Use his magic to make them forget," I lied. "Let's move along. He can catch up."

Shed kept giving me looks. Looks like he must have given Raven when he first found out Raven was in the body business. He did not say anything.

One-Eye caught up an hour later. He busted out laughing. "They were gone," he said. "Every blessed one, with all their dogs and cattle. Into the woods. Damned peasants." He laughed again, almost hysterically. I suspect he was relieved.

"We got two days and some gone," I said. "Let's push it. The bigger head start we have, the better."

We reached the outskirts of Meadenvil five hours later, not having pressed as hard as I wanted. As we penetrated the city, our pace lagged. I think we all sensed it. Finally, I stopped. "King, you and Asa wander around and see what you hear. We'll wait at yonder fountain." There were no children in the streets. The adults I saw seemed dazed. Those who passed us moved by as widely as they could navigate.

King was back in two minutes. No lollygagging. "Big trouble, Croaker. The Taken got here this morning. Big blowout down at the waterfront."

I glanced in that direction. A ghost of smoke rose there, as if marking the aftermath of a major fire. The sky to the west, in the direction the wind was blowing, had a dirty look.

Asa returned a minute later with the same news and more. "They got in a big fight with the Prince. Not over yet, some say."

"Wouldn't be much of a fight," One-Eye said.

"I don't know," I countered. "Even the Lady can't be everywhere at once. How the hell did they get here so fast? They didn't have any carpets."

"Overland," Shed said.

"Overland? But. . . ."

"It's shorter than the sea trip. Road cuts across. If you ride hard, day and night, you can make it in two days. When I was a kid, they used to have races. They stopped that when the new Duke took over."

"Guess it doesn't matter. So. What now?"

"Got to find out what happened," One-Eye said. He muttered, "If that bastard Goblin got himself killed, I'll wring his neck."

"Right. But how do we do that? The Taken know us."

"I'll go," Shed volunteered.

Harder looks you cannot imagine than those we bent upon Marron Shed. He quailed for a moment. Then: "I won't let them catch me. Anyway, why should they bother me? They don't know me."

"Okay," I said. "Get moving."

"Croaker. . . ."

"Got to trust him, One-Eye. Unless you want to go yourself."

"Nope. Shed, you screw us over and I'll get you if I have to come back from the grave."

Shed smiled weakly, left us. On foot. Not many people rode through Meadenvil's streets. We found a tavern and made ourselves at home, two men staying in the street to watch. It was sundown before Shed returned.

"Well?" I said, signaling for another pitcher of beer.

"It's not good news. You guys are stuck. Your Lieutenant took the ship out. Twenty, twenty-five of your guys were killed. The rest went out on the ship. The Prince lost. . . ."

"Not all of them," One-Eye said, and tipped a pointing finger over the top of his mug. "Somebody followed you, Shed."

Shed whirled, terrified.

Goblin and Pawnbroker stood in the doorway. Pawn had been carved up some. He limped over and collapsed into a chair. I checked his wounds. Goblin and One-Eye exchanged looks that might have meant anything, but probably meant they were glad to see one another.

The tavern's other customers began to fade. Word who we were had gotten out. They knew some bad people were hunting us.

"Sit, Goblin," I said. "King, you and Otto go get some fresh horses." I gave them most of the money I had. "All the staples that will buy, too. I think we got a long ride ahead. Right, Goblin?"

He nodded.

"Let's hear it."

"Whisper and Limper turned up this morning. Came with fifty men. Company men. Looking for us. Made enough fuss we heard them coming. The Lieutenant sent word to everybody ashore. Some didn't get aboard in time. Whisper headed for the ship. The Lieutenant had to cut loose. We left nineteen men behind."

"What're you doing here?"

"I volunteered. Went over the side off the point, swam to shore, came back to wait for you guys. Supposed to tell you where to meet the ship. Ran into Pawn by accident. I was patching him up when I seen Shed poking around. We followed him back here."

I sighed. "They're headed for Chimney, right?"

He was surprised. "Yeah. How'd you know that?"

I explained briefly.

He said, "Pawn, better tell them what you know. Pawn was caught ashore. Only survivor I could find."

"This is a private adventure with the Taken," Pawn said. "They snuck down here. Supposed to be somewhere else. Figured it was a chance to get even, I guess, now we're not on the list of the Lady's favorites."

"She doesn't know they're here?"

"No."

I chuckled. Despite the gravity of the situation, I could not help that. "They're in for a surprise, then. The old bitch herself is going to turn up. We got another black castle growing here."

Several of them looked at me askance, wondering how I would know what the Lady was doing. I had not explained my dream to anyone but the Lieutenant. I finished patching Pawnbroker. "You'll be able to travel, but take it easy. How'd you find that out?"

"Shaky. We talked some before he tried to kill me."

"Shaky!" One-Eye snarled. "What the hell?"

"I don't know what the Taken told those guys. But they were cranked up. Wanted our asses bad. Suckers. Most of them got killed for their trouble."

"Killed?"

"Prince what's-it got righteous about the Taken walking in like they owned the place. There was a big fight with the Limper and our boys. Our guys practically got wiped out. Maybe they'd have done better if they could've rested first."

Funny. We talked it over like those men and we had not somehow become mortal enemies, sympathizing. And, in my case, feeling bitter toward the Taken for having turned and squandered them.

"Shaky say anything about Juniper?"

"Yeah. They had a real old-fashioned blood bath up there. Not much left of anything. Counting us, the Company was down six hundred guys when the Lady finished with the castle. Lot more guys was killed in the riots that came after, when she cleaned out the Catacombs. The whole damned city went crazy, with that Hargadon leading the rebellion. Had our guys trapped in Duretile. Then the Lady lost her temper. She wrecked what was left of the town."

I shook my head. "The Captain guessed right about the Catacombs."

"Journey took over what was left of the Company," Goblin said. "They was supposed to pull out with the plunder as soon as they got it all together. City is so wrecked there isn't no reason to stay around."

I looked at Shed. A bleaker face could not be imagined. Pain and questions twisted inside him. He wanted to know about his people. Did not want to speak for fear someone would accuse him. "Not your fault, man," I told him. "The Duke asked the Lady in before you got involved. It would have happened no matter what you did."

"How can people do stuff like that?"

Asa gave him the odd look. "Shed, that's dumb. How could you do all the stuff you did? Desperate, that's what. Everybody's desperate. They do crazy things."

One-Eye gave me a how-about-that? look. Even Asa could think sometimes.

"Pawn. Shaky say anything about Elmo?" Elmo remained my main regret.

"No. I didn't ask. We didn't have much time."

"What's the plan?" Goblin said.

"We'll head south when King and Otto get here with the horses and supplies." A sigh. "Going to be hard times. I got maybe two leva. How about you guys?"

We catalogued our resources. I said, "We're in trouble."

"The Lieutenant sent this." Goblin deposited a small sack on the table. It contained fifty silver castle coins from Raven's horde.

"That'll help. Still going to make it on prayer, though."

"I have some money," Shed volunteered. "Quite a bit. It's back where I was staying."

I eyeballed him. "You don't have to go. You're not part of this."

"Yes, I am."

"For as long as I've known you, you've been trying to run away. . . ."

"Got something to fight for now, Croaker. What they did to Juniper. I can't let that go."

"Me, too," Asa said. "I still got most of the money Raven gave me after we raided the Catacombs."

I polled the others silently. They did not respond. It was up to me. "All right. Get it. But don't dawdle. I want to pull out as soon as I can."

"I can catch you on the road," Shed said. "I don't see why Asa can't too." He rose. Shyly, he extended a hand. I hesitated only a moment.

"Welcome to the Black Company, Shed."

Asa did not make the same offer.

"Think they'll come back?" One-Eye asked after they left.

"What do you think?"

"Nope. I hope you know what you're doing, Croaker. They could get the Taken after us if they get caught."

"Yeah. They could." I was counting on it, in fact. A vicious notion had come to me. "Let's have another round here. Be our last for a long time."

47

The Inn: On The Run

Very much to my amazement, Shed overtook us ten miles south of Meadenvil. And he was not alone.

"Holy shit!" I heard One-Eye yell from the rear, and: "Croaker, come and look at this."

I turned back. And there was Shed. With a bedraggled Bullock. Shed said,

"I promised to get him out if I could. Had to bribe some people, but it wasn't that hard. It's every man for himself up there right now."

I looked at Bullock. He looked at me. "Well?" I said.

"Shed gave me the word, Croaker. I guess I'm in with you guys. If you'll take me. I don't have anywhere else to go."

"Damn. Asa shows up, I'll lose my faith in human nature. Also blow an idea I have. Okay, Bullock. What the hell. Just remember we're not in Juniper. None of us. We're on the run from the Taken. And we don't have time to fuss over who did what to whom. You want a fight, save it for them."

"You're the boss. Just give me a shot at evening things up." He followed me back to the head of the column. "Not much difference between your Lady and somebody like Krage, is there?"

"Matter of proportion," I said. "Maybe you'll get your shot sooner than you think."

Silent and Otto came trotting out of the darkness. "You did good," I said. "Dogs never barked." I had sent Silent because he handled animals well.

"They're all back out of the woods and tucked in their beds," Otto reported.

"Good. Let's move in. Quietly. And I don't want anybody hurt. Understand? One-Eye?"

"I hear you."

"Goblin. Pawnbroker. Shed. You watch the horses. I'll signal with a lantern."

Occupying the inn was easier than planning it. We caught everyone asleep because Silent had fuddled their dogs. The innkeeper wakened puffing and blowing and terrified. I took him downstairs while One-Eye watched everybody else, including some northbound travelers who represented a complication, but who caused no trouble.

"Sit," I told the fat man. "You have tea or beer in the morning?"

"Tea," he croaked.

"It's making. So. We're back. We didn't expect to be, but circumstances dictated an overland trip. I want to use your place a couple days. You and me need to make an accommodation."

Hagop brought out tea so strong it reeked. The fat man drained a mug the size of that from which he drank his beer.

"I don't want to hurt anybody," I continued, after taking a sip myself. "And I'll pay my way. But if you want it that way, you'll have to cooperate."

He grunted.

"I don't want anybody to know we're here. That means no customers leave. People who come through have to see things looking normal. You get my drift?"

He was smarter than he looked. "You're waiting for somebody." None of the men had figured that out, I don't think.

"Yes. Somebody who will do unto you as you expect me to, just for being here. Unless my ambush works." I had a crazy idea. It would die if Asa turned up.

I think he believed me when I claimed no wicked plans for his family. Now. He asked, "That the same somebody who kicked up the ruckus in the city yesterday?"

"News travels fast."

"Bad news does."

"Yes. The same somebody. They killed about twenty of my people. Busted the city up pretty good, too."

"I heard. Like I said, bad news travels fast. My brother was one of the people they killed. He was in the Prince's guard. A sergeant. Only one of us ever amounted to anything. He was killed by something that ate him, I heared. Sorcerer sicced it on him."

"Yeah. He's a bad one. Nastier than my friend who can't talk." I did not know who would come after us. I was counting on someone doing so, with Asa to point the way. I also figured the pursuit would develop quickly. Asa would tell them the Lady was on her way to Meadenvil.

The fat man eyed me cautiously. Hatred smouldered behind his eyes. I tried to direct it. "I'm going to kill him."

"All right. Slow? Like my brother?"

"I don't think so. If it isn't fast and sneaky, he wins. Or she. There's two of them, actually. I don't know which one will come." I figured we could buy a lot of time if we could take out one of the Taken. The Lady would be damned busy with black castles for a while with only two pairs of hands to help her. Also, I had an emotional debt to pay, and a message to make clear.

"Let me send the wife and kids away," he said. "I'll stand in with you."

I let my gaze flick to Silent. He nodded slightly. "All right. What about your guests?"

"I know them. They'll sit tight."

"Good. Go take care of your part."

He left. Then I had it out with Silent and the others. I had not been elected to command. I was running on momentum as senior officer present. It got angry for a while. But I won my point.

Fear is a wonderful motivator. It moved Goblin and One-Eye like nothing I've ever seen. Moved the men, too. They set up every gimmick they could imagine. Booby traps. Hiding places prepared from which an attack could be carried out, each glossed with a concealing spell. Weapons prepared with fanatical attention.

The Taken are not invulnerable. They're just hard to reach, and more so when they're ready for trouble. Whoever came would be.

Silent went into the woods with the fat man's family. He returned with a hawk that he tamed in record time, and cast it aloft to patrol the road between Meadenvil and the inn. We would be forewarned.

The landlord prepared dishes tainted with poison, though I advised him that the Taken seldom eat. He petitioned Silent for advice concerning his dogs. He had a whole pack of savage mastiffs and wanted them in on the action. Silent found them a spot in the plan. We did everything we could, and then settled in to wait. When my shift came, I took my turn getting some rest.

She came. Almost the moment my eyes closed, it seemed. I was in a panic for a moment, trying to banish my location and plan from my mind. But what was the point? She had found me already. The thing to conceal was the ambush.

"Have you reconsidered?" she asked. "You cannot outrun me. I want you, physician."

"That why you sent Whisper and the Limper? To return us to the fold? They killed half our men, lost most of theirs, wrecked the city, and didn't make a single friend. Is that how you win us back?"

She had not been party to that, of course. Pawnbroker had said the Taken were acting on their own. I wanted her angry and distracted. I wanted to know her reaction.

She said, "They're supposed to be headed back to the Barrowland."

"Sure they are. They just go off on their own any time they feel like it, to settle grudges ten years old."

"Do they know where you are?"

"Not yet." I now had the feeling she could not locate me precisely. "I'm outside the city, lying low."

"Where?"

I let an image seep through. "Near the place where the new castle is growing. It was the nearest place we could put up." I figured a strong thread of truth was in order. Anyway, I wanted her to find the gift I meant to leave.

"Stay where you are. Do not attract attention. I will be there soon."

"Thought so."

"Do not test my patience, physician. You amuse me, but you are not invulnerable. I am short of temper these days. Whisper and Limper have pressed their luck one time too many."

The door of the room opened. One-Eye said, "Who you talking to, Croaker?"

I shuddered. He stood on the far side of the glow without seeing it. I was awake. I replied, "My girlfriend," and giggled.

An instant later I endured a moment of intense vertigo. Something parted from me, leaving a flavor both of amusement and irritation. I recovered, found One-Eye kneeling, frowning. "What's the matter?" he demanded.

I shook my head. "Head feels like it's on backwards. Shouldn't have had that beer. What's up?"

He scowled suspiciously. "Silent's hawk came in. They're coming. Come on downstairs. We need to redo the plan."

"They?"

"The Limper and nine men. That's what I mean, we need to redo. Right now the odds look too good for the other side."

"Yeah." Those would be Company men. The inn wouldn't fool them. Inns are the axes of life in the hinterlands. The Captain used them frequently to draw the Rebel.

Silent did not have much to add, except that we had only as long as it would take our pursuers to cover six miles.

"Hey!" The old comes-the-dawn. Suddenly I *knew* why the Taken had come to Meadenvil. "You got a wagon and team?" I asked the innkeeper. I still did not know his name.

"Yeah. Use it to haul supplies down from Meadenvil, from the miller's, from the brewer's. Why?"

"Because the Taken are looking for those papers I've been on about." I had to reveal their provenance.

"The same ones we dug up in the Forest of Cloud?" One-Eye asked.

"Yes. Look. Soulcatcher told me they have the Limper's true name in them. They also include the wizard Bomanz's secret papers, where the Lady's true name is supposedly encoded."

"Wow!" Goblin said.

"Right."

One-Eye demanded, "What's that got to do with us?"

"The Limper wants his name back. Suppose he sees a bunch of guys and a wagon light out of here? What's he going to figure? Asa gave him bum dope about them being with Raven. Asa doesn't know everything we've been up to."

Silent interjected, in sign, "Asa is with the Limper."

"Fine. He did what I wanted. Okay. The Limper figures that's us making a run for it with the papers. 'Specially if we let a few pieces go fluttering around."

"I get it," One-Eye said. "Only we don't have enough men to work it. Only Bullock and the landlord that Asa don't know about."

Goblin said, "I think you better stop talking and start doing. They're getting closer."

I called the fat man. "Your friends from the south have to do us a favor. Tell them it's their only chance of getting out of this alive."

48

The Inn: Ambush

The four southerners were shaking and sweating. They did not know what was going on, did not like what they saw. But they had become convinced that cooperation was their only hope. "Goblin!" I shouted upstairs. "Can you see them yet?"

"Almost time. Count to fifty, then turn it loose."

I counted. Slowly, forcing myself to keep the pace down. I was as scared as the southerners.

"Now!"

Goblin came boiling downstairs. We all roared out to the barn, where the animals and wagon were waiting, whooped out of there, stormed into the road, and went howling off south like eight men very nearly taken by surprise. Behind us the Limper's party halted momentarily, talked it over, then came after us. I noted that the Limper was setting the pace. Good. His men were not eager to tangle with their old buddies.

I brought up the rear, behind Goblin and One-Eye and the wagon. One-Eye was driving. Goblin kept his mount right beside the wagon.

We roared into a rising curve where the road began climbing a wooded hill south of the inn. The innkeeper said the forest went on for miles. He had gone ahead with Silent and Bullock and the men the southerners were pretending to be.

"Yo!" someone shouted back. A scrap of red cloth whipped past. One-Eye stood up on the wagon, clinging to the traces as he edged over. Goblin swung in close. One-Eye jumped.

For a moment I did not think he would make it. Goblin almost missed. One-Eye's feet trailed in the dust. Then he scrambled up, lay on his stomach behind his friend. He glared back at me, daring me to grin.

I grinned anyway.

The wagon hit the timber prepared, flung up, twisted. Horses screamed, fought, could not hold it. Wagon and team went thrashing off the road, crashed against trees, the animals screaming in pain and terror while the vehicle disintegrated. The men who had upset the wagon vanished immediately.

I spurred my mount forward, past Goblin and One-Eye and Pawnbroker, yelled at the southerners, gave them the sign to go on, keep riding, get the hell away.

A quarter mile farther on I swung onto the track the fat man had told me about, got down into the woods far enough not to be seen, halted long enough for One-Eye to get himself seated. Then we moved on hurriedly, headed for the inn.

Above us, Limper and his bunch came pounding up to where the wrecked wagon lay, the animals still crying their distress.

It started.

Cries. Shrieks. Men dying. Hiss and howl of spells. I didn't think Silent stood a chance, but he had volunteered. The wagon was supposed to distract the Limper long enough for the massed attack to reach him.

The clangor was still going on, muted by distance, when we reached open country. "Can't be going all wrong," I shouted. "Been going on a while."

I did not feel as optimistic as I pretended. I did not want it to go on. I'd wanted them to hit quick, hurt the Limper, and fade away, doing enough damage to make him retreat to the inn to lick his wounds.

We hustled the animals into the barn and headed for our hiding places. I muttered, "You know, we wouldn't be in this spot if Raven had killed him when he had a chance." Way back, when I had helped capture Whisper, when she was trying to bring Limper over to her side, Raven had had a fantastic opportunity to finish him off. He had not been able, though he had had grievances against the Taken. His mercy had come back to haunt us all.

Pawnbroker went into the pig shed, where we had installed a crude, light ballista built as part of our earlier plan. Goblin cast a weak spell that made him seem like just another hog. I wanted him to stay out of it if possible. I doubted the ballista would get used.

Goblin and I raced upstairs to watch the road and the ridgeline to the east. Once he broke off, which he had not done when he was supposed to, Silent would fake in the direction taken by the southerners, retreat through the wood to that ridge, watch what happened at the inn. It was my hope that some of the Limper's men would keep after the southerners. I hadn't told those guys that. I hoped they had sense enough to keep running.

"Ho!" Goblin said. "There's Silent. He made it."

The men appeared briefly. I could not tell who was who. "Only three of them," I muttered. That meant four had not made it. "Damn!"

"It had to work," Goblin said. "Else they wouldn't be up there."

I did not feel reassured. I hadn't had many shots at field command. I hadn't learned to deal with the feelings that come when you know men have been killed trying to carry out your orders.

"Here they come."

Riders left the woods, coming up the Shaker Road amidst lengthening shadows. "I make it six men," I said. "No. Seven. They must not have gone after those guys."

"Looks like they're all hurt."

"Element of surprise. The Limper with them? Can you tell?"

"No. That one. . . . That's Asa. Hell, that's old Shed on the third horse, and the innkeeper next to last."

A slight positive, then. They were half as strong as they had been. I'd lost only two of seven committed.

"What do we do if the Limper ain't with them?" Goblin asked.

"Take what comes to us." Silent had vanished off the far ridge.

"There he is, Croaker. In front of the innkeeper. Looks like he's unconscious."

That was too much to hope. Yet it did indeed look like the Taken was out. "Let's get downstairs."

I watched through a cracked shutter as they turned into the yard. The only member of the group uninjured was Asa. His hands were bound to his saddle, his feet to his stirrups. One of the injured men dismounted, released Asa, held a knife on him while he helped the others. A variety of injuries were evident. Shed looked like he shouldn't be alive at all. The innkeeper was in better shape. Just seemed to have been knocked around a lot.

They made Asa and the fat man get the Limper off his animal. I nearly gave myself away then. The Taken was missing most of his right arm. He had several additional wounds. But, of course, he would recover if he remained protected by his allies. The Taken are tough.

Asa and the fat man started toward the door. Limper sagged like a wet rope. The man who had covered Asa pushed the door open.

The Limper wakened. "No!" he squeaked. "Trap!"

Asa and the innkeeper dropped him. Asa began heeling and toeing it, eyes closed. The innkeeper whistled shrilly. His dogs came raging out of the barn.

Goblin and One-Eye cut loose. I jumped out and went for the Limper as he tried to gain his feet.

My blade bit into the Limper's shoulder above the stump of his right arm. His remaining fist came up and brushed me across the belly.

The air exploded out of me. I nearly passed out. I settled to the ground, heaving my guts out, only vaguely aware of my surroundings.

The dogs boiled over the Limper's men, mauling them savagely. Several hit the Taken. He hammered them with his fist, each blow leaving an animal dead.

Goblin and One-Eye charged out, hit him with everything they had. He shed their spells like rainwater, punched One-Eye, turned on Goblin.

Goblin ran. The Limper trundled after him, weaving, the surviving mastiffs snapping at his back.

Goblin raced toward the pig shed. He went sprawling before he reached it, twitched feebly in the mire. Limper rolled up behind him, fist raised for the kill.

Pawnbroker's shaft split his breastbone, stood three feet out of his back. He stood there swaying, a ragged little man in brown picking at the shaft. His whole will seemed to focus upon that. Goblin wriggled away. Inside the shed Pawn cranked the ballista back and dropped another javelin into its trough.

Whomp! This one ripped all the way through the Limper. It knocked him off his feet. The dogs went for his throat.

I regained my breath. I looked for my sword. Vaguely, I was aware of screeching from a patch of blackberries along a ditch two hundred feet north. A lone dog trotted back and forth, snarling. Asa. He had ducked into the only cover available.

I got my feet under me. The fat man helped One-Eye get up, then snagged a fallen weapon. We three closed in on the Limper. He lay in the mire, twisted slightly sideways, his mask slipped so we could see the ruined face it had concealed. He could not believe what was happening. Feebly, he waved at the dogs.

"All for nothing," I told him. "The papers haven't been here for months."

And the fat man: "This is for my brother." He swung his weapon. He was so badly bruised, and getting so stiff, that he did not get much into it.

The Limper tried to strike back. He did not have anything left. He realized that he was going to die. After all those centuries. After having survived the White Roses, and the anger of the Lady after he had betrayed her in the battle at Roses and in the Forest of Cloud.

His eyes rolled up and he went away, and I knew he was yelling for Mama's help.

"Kill him quick," I said. "He's calling the Lady."

We hacked and slashed and chopped. The dogs snarled and bit. He would not die. Even when we ran out of energy, a spark of life remained.

"Let's drag him around front."

We did. And I saw Shed, lying on the ground with men who used to be brothers in the Black Company. I looked up at the waning light, saw Silent approaching, followed by Hagop and Otto. I felt a numb pleasure because those two had survived. They had been best friends for as long as I could recall. I could not picture one surviving without the other.

"Bullock's gone, eh?"

The fat man said, "Yeah. Him and this Shed. You should have seen them.

They jumped into the road and pulled the sorcerer off his horse. Bullock chopped his arm off. Between them they killed four men."

"Bullock?"

"Somebody split his head open. Like hitting a melon with a cleaver."

"Kingpin?"

"Got trampled to death. But he got his licks in."

I levered myself down beside Shed. One-Eye did the same. "How'd they catch you?" I asked the innkeeper.

"Too fat to run fast." He managed a feeble smile. "Never was meant to be a soldier."

I smiled. "What do you think, One-Eye?" A glance told me there was nothing I could do for Shed.

One-Eye shook his head.

Goblin said, "Two of these guys are still alive, Croaker. What you want we should do?"

"Take them inside. I'll patch them up." They were brothers. That the Taken had twisted them and made them enemies did not make them less deserving of my help.

Silent came up, looming tall in the twilight. He signed, "A maneuver worthy of the Captain, Croaker."

"Right." I stared at Shed, moved more than I thought I should be.

A man lay before me. He had sunk as low as any I'd ever known. Then he had fought his way back, and back, and had become worthy. A man far better than I, for he had located his moral polestar and set his course by it, though it had cost his life. Maybe, just a little, he had repaid his debt.

He did another thing by getting himself killed in a fight I did not consider his. He became a sort of patron saint of mine, an example for days to come. He set a high standard in his last few days.

He opened his eyes before the end. He smiled. "Did we do it?" he asked.

"We did it, Shed. Thanks to you and Bullock."

"Good." Still smiling, he closed his eyes.

Hagop hollered, "Hey, Croaker. What you want to do about this Asa creep?"

Asa was still in the blackberries, yelling for help. The dogs had the patch surrounded.

"Put a couple javelins in him," One-Eye muttered.

"No," Shed said in a tiny whisper. "Let him be. He was my friend. He tried to get back, but they caught him. Let him go."

"All right, Shed. Hagop! Dig him out and turn him loose."

"What?"

"You heard me." I looked back at Shed. "Okay, Shed?"

He didn't say anything. He couldn't. But he was smiling.

I got up and said, "At least somebody died the way he wanted. Otto. Get a damned shovel."

"Aw, Croaker. . . ."

"Get a goddamned shovel and get to work. Silent, One-Eye, Goblin, inside. We got plans to make."

The light was nearly gone. By the Lieutenant's estimate it would be but hours before the Lady reached Meadenvil.

49

On The Move

We need rest," One-Eye protested.

"There won't be any rest till we're dead," I countered. "We're on the other side now, One-Eye. We did what the Rebel couldn't. We've done in the Limper, the last of the original Taken. She'll be after us hard as soon as she's cleaned up these black castle leavings. She has to. If she doesn't get us fast, every Rebel in five thousand miles will get worked up to try something. There are only two Taken left, and only Whisper worth much."

"Yeah. I know. Wishful thinking. Can't stop a man wishing, Croaker."

I stared at the necklace Shed had worn. I had to leave it for the Lady, yet the silver in it might become a lifesaver down the long road we had to travel. I screwed up my courage and began digging out the eyes.

"What the hell you doing?"

"Going to leave these with the Limper. Going to feed them to him. I figure they'll hatch."

"Ha!" Goblin said. "Ironic. Fitting."

"I thought it an interesting turn of justice. Give him back to the Dominator."

"And the Lady will have to destroy him. I like it."

Grudgingly, One-Eye agreed.

"Thought you guys would. Go see if they've got everybody buried."

"Only been ten minutes since they got back with the bodies."

"All right. Go help." I levered myself up and went to check on the men I had patched up. I don't know if everyone Hagop and Otto brought back from the ambush site was dead when they got there. They certainly were now. Kingpin had been dead for a long time, though they had brought him to me to examine.

My patients were doing fine. One was aware enough to be frightened. I patted his arm and limped outside.

They had King in the ground now, beside Shed and Bullock and the Limper's boy they had buried earlier. Only two corpses remained unburied. Asa was making the dirt fly. Everyone else stood and watched. Till they saw me glowering.

"What's the take?" I asked the fat man. I'd had him strip the dead of valuables.

"Not a lot." He showed me a hat filled with odds and ends.

"Take what you need to cover the damages."

"You guys will need it more than me."

"You're out a wagon and a team, not to mention the dogs. Take what you need. I can always rob somebody I don't like." No one knew that I had filched Shed's purse. Its weight had surprised me. It would be my secret reserve. "Take a couple horses, too."

He shook his head. "I'm not getting caught with somebody else's animals after the dust settles and the Prince starts looking for scapegoats." He selected a few silver coins. "I got what I wanted."

"Okay. You'd better hide in the woods for a while. The Lady will come here. She's nastier than the Limper."

"Will do."

"Hagop. If you're not going to dig, go get the horses ready. Move!" I beckoned Silent. He and I dragged the Limper to a shade tree out front. Silent tossed a rope over a limb. I forced the eyes of the serpents down the Taken's throat. We hoisted him up. He turned slowly in the chill moonlight. I rubbed my hands together and considered him. "Took a while, guy, but somebody finally got you." For ten years I had wanted to see him go down. He had been the most inhuman of the Taken.

Asa came to me. "All buried, Croaker."

"Good. Thanks for the help." I started toward the barn.

"Can I go with you guys?"

I laughed.

"Please, Croaker? Don't leave me here where. . . ."

"I don't give a damn, Asa. But don't expect me to look out for you. And don't try any slick tricks. I'd as soon kill you as look at you."

"Thanks, Croaker." He raced ahead, hastily saddled another horse. One-Eye looked at me and shook his head.

"Mount up, men. Let's go find Raven."

Though we pushed hard, we were not twenty miles south of the inn when something hit my mind like a fighter's fist. A golden cloud materialized, radiating anger. "You have exhausted my patience, physician."

"You exhausted mine a long time ago."

"You'll rue this murder."

"I'll exult in it. It's the first decent thing I've done this side of the Sea of Torments. Go find your castle eggs. Leave me alone. We're even."

"Oh, no. You will hear from me again. As soon as I close the last door on my husband."

"Don't press your luck, old witch. I'm ready to get out of the game. Push and I'll learn TelleKurre."

That caught her from the blind side.

"Ask Whisper what she lost in the Forest of Cloud and hoped to recover in Meadenvil. Then reflect upon what an angry Croaker could do with it if he knew where to find it."

There was a vertiginous moment as she withdrew.

I found my companions looking at me weirdly. "Just saying good-bye to my girl," I told them.

We lost Asa in Shaker. We took a day off there, to prepare for the next leg, and when it came time to leave, Asa was not to be seen. Nobody bothered looking for him. On Shed's behalf I left him with a wish for luck. Judging from his past, he probably had it, and all bad.

My farewell to the Lady did not take. Three months to the day after the Limper's fall, as we were resting prior to hazarding the last range of hills between us and Chimney, the golden cloud visited me again. This time the Lady was less belligerent. In fact, she seemed mildly amused.

"Greetings, physician. I thought you might want to know, for the sake of your Annals, that the threat of the black castle no longer exists. Every seed has been located and destroyed." More amusement. "There is no way my husband can rise short of exhumation. He is cut off, totally incapable of communicating with his sympathizers. A permanent army occupies the Barrowland."

I could think of nothing to say. It was no less than I had expected, and had hoped she would accomplish, for she was the lesser evil, and, I suspect, remained possessed of a spark that had not committed itself to the darkness. She had shown restraint on several occasions when she could have indulged her cruelty. Maybe if she felt unchallenged, she would drift toward the light rather than farther toward the shadow.

"I interviewed Whisper. With the Eye. Stand clear, Croaker."

Never before had she called me by name. I sat up and took notice. There was no amusement in her now.

"Stand clear?"

"Of those papers. Of the girl."

"Girl? What girl?"

"Don't come the innocent. I know. You left a wider trail than you thought. And even dead men answer questions for one who knows how they must be asked. Such of your Company as remained when I returned to Juniper told most of the story. If you wish to live out your days in peace, kill her. If you don't, I will. Along with anyone near her."

"I don't know what you're talking about."

Amusement again, but a hard sort. A malignant sort. "Keep your Annals, physician. I will be in touch. I will keep you apprised of the advance of the empire."

Puzzled, I asked, "Why?"

"Because it amuses me. Behave yourself." She faded away.

We went down into Chimney, tired men three-quarters dead. We found the Lieutenant and the ship and—Lo!—Darling, who was living aboard with the Company. The Lieutenant had taken employment with the private constabulary of a mercantile factor. He added our names to the roll as soon as we recuperated.

We did not find Raven. Raven had evaded reconciliation or confrontation with his old comrades by cheating his way out.

Fate is a fickle bitch who dotes on irony. After all he had been through, all he had done, all he had survived, the very morning the Lieutenant arrived he slipped on a wet marble diving platform in a public bath, split his head open, fell into the pool, and drowned.

I refused to believe it. It could not be true, after what he had pulled up north. I dug around. I poked. I pried. But there were scores of people who had seen the body. The most reliable witness of all, Darling, was absolutely convinced. In the end, I had to give in. This time no one would hear my doubts.

The Lieutenant himself claimed to have seen and recognized the corpse as the flames of a pyre had risen about it the morning of his arrival. It was there he had encountered Darling and had brought her back into the keeping of the Black Company.

What could I say? If Darling believed, it must be true. Raven could never lie to her.

Nineteen days after our arrival in Chimney, there was another arrival, which explained the Lady's nebulous remark about interviewing only those she could find when she returned to Juniper.

Elmo rode into town with seventy men, many brethren from the old days, whom he had spirited out of Juniper while all the Taken were absent but Journey, and Journey was in such a state of confusion due to conflicting orders from the Lady that he let slip the true state of affairs in Meadenvil. He followed me down the coast.

So, in two years, the Black Company had crossed the breadth of the world, from the nethermost east to the farthest west, close to four thousand miles, and in the process had come near destruction, and had found a new purpose, a new life. We were now the champions of the White Rose, a bedraggled joke of a nucleus for the force legend destined to bring the Lady down.

I did not believe a word of that. But Raven had told Darling what she was, and she, at least, was ready to play her part.

We could but try.

I hoisted a glass of wine in the master's cabin. Elmo, Silent, One-Eye, Goblin, the Lieutenant and Darling raised theirs. Above, men prepared to cast off. Elmo had brought the Company treasure chest. We had no need to work. I proposed my toast. "To the twenty-nine years."

Twenty-nine years. According to legend it would be that long before the Great Comet returned and fortune would smile upon the White Rose.

They responded, "The twenty-nine years."

I thought I detected the faintest hint of gold in the corner of my eye, felt the faintest hint of amusement.

The White Rose

For Nancy Edwards, just because

The Plain of Fear

The still desert air had a lenselike quality. The riders seemed frozen in time, moving without drawing closer. We took turns counting. I could not get the same number twice running.

A breath of a breeze whined in the coral, stirred the leaves of Old Father Tree. They tinkled off one another with the song of wind chimes. To the north, the glimmer of change lightning limned the horizon like the far clash of warring gods.

A foot crunched sand. I turned. Silent gawked at a talking menhir. It had appeared in the past few seconds, startling him. Sneaky rocks. Like to play games.

"There are strangers on the Plain," it said.

I jumped. It chuckled. Menhirs have the most malevolent laughs this side of fairy stories. Snarling, I ducked into its shadow. "Hot out here already." And: "That's One-Eye and Goblin, back from Tanner."

It was right and I was wrong. I was too narrowly focused. The patrol had been away a month longer than planned. We were worried. Lately the Lady's troops have been more active along the bounds of the Plain of Fear.

Another chuckle from the block of stone.

It towered over me, thirteen feet tall. A middle-sized one. Those over fifteen feet seldom move.

The riders were closer, yet seemed no nearer. Blame nerves. Times are desperate for the Black Company. We cannot afford casualties. Any man lost would be a friend of many years. I counted again. Seemed right this time. But there was a riderless mount. . . . I shivered despite the heat.

They were on the downtrail leading to a creek three hundred yards from where we watched, concealed within a great reef. The walking trees beside the ford stirred, though the breeze had failed.

The riders urged their mounts to hurry. The animals were tired. They were reluctant, though they knew they were almost home. Into the creek. Water splashing. I grinned, pounded Silent's back. They were all there. Every man, and another.

Silent shed his customary cool, returned a smile. Elmo slipped out of the coral and went to meet our brethren. Otto, Silent, and I hurried after him.

Behind us, the morning sun was a great seething ball of blood.

Men piled off horses, grinning. But they looked bad. Goblin and One-Eye worst of all. But they had come back to territory where their wizards' powers were useless. This near Darling they are no greater than the rest of us.

I glanced back. Darling had come to the head of the tunnel, stood like a phantom in its shadow, all in white.

Men hugged men; then old habit took charge. Everybody pretended it was just another day. "Rough out there?" I asked One-Eye. I considered the man accompanying them. He was not familiar.

"Yes." The dried-up little black man was more diminished than first I had thought.

"You all right?"

"Took an arrow." He rubbed his side. "Flesh wound."

From behind One-Eye, Goblin squeaked, "They almost got us. Been chasing us a month. We couldn't shake them."

"Let's get you down in the Hole," I told One-Eye.

"Not infected. I cleared it."

"I still want a look." He has been my assistant since I enlisted as Company physician. His judgment is sound. Yet health is my responsibility, ultimately.

"They were waiting for us, Croaker." Darling was gone from the mouth of the tunnel, back to the stomach of our subterranean fastness. The sun remained bloody in the east, legacy of the change storm's passing. Something big drifted across its face. Windwhale?

"Ambush?" I glanced back at the patrol.

"Not us specifically. For trouble. They were on the ball." The patrol had had a double mission: to contact our sympathizers in Tanner to find out if the Lady's people were coming alive after a long hiatus, and to raid the garrison there in order to prove we could hurt an empire that bestrides half a world.

As we passed it the menhir said, "There are strangers on the Plain, Croaker."

Why do these things happen to me? The big stones talk to me more than to anyone else.

Twice a charm? I paid attention. For a menhir to repeat itself meant it considered its message critical. "The men hunting you?" I asked One-Eye.

He shrugged. "They wouldn't give up."

"What's happening out there?" Hiding on the Plain, I might as well be buried alive.

One-Eye's face remained unreadable. "Corder will tell it."

"Corder? That the guy you brought in?" I knew the name though not the man. One of our best informants.

"Yeah."

"No good news, eh?"

"No."

We slipped into the tunnel which leads down to our warren, our stinking, moldering, damp, tight little rabbit-hole fortress. It is disgusting, but it is the heart and soul of the New White Rose Rebellion. The New Hope, as it is whispered among the captive nations. The Joke Hope to those of us who live here. It is as bad as any rat-infested dungeon—though a man *can* leave. If he does not mind a venture into a world where all the might of an empire is turned upon him.

The Plain of Fear

Corder was our eyes and ears in Tanner. He had contacts everywhere. His work against the Lady goes back decades. He is one of the few who escaped her wrath at Charm, where she obliterated the Rebel of old. In great part, the Company was responsible. In those days we were her strong right arm. We piloted her enemies into the trap.

A quarter million men died at Charm. Never was there a battle so vast or grim, nor an outcome so definitive. Even the Dominator's bloody failure in the Old Forest consumed but half as many lives.

Fate compelled us to switch sides—once there was no one left to help us in our fight.

One-Eye's wound was as clean as he claimed. I cut him loose, ambled off to my quarters. Word was, Darling wanted the patrol rested before she accepted its report. I shivered with premonition, afraid to hear their tidings.

An old, tired man. That is what I am. What became of the old fire, drive, ambition? There were dreams once upon a time, dreams now all but forgotten. On sad days I dust them off and fondle them nostalgically, with a patronizing wonder at the naivete of the youth who dreamed them.

Old infests my quarters. My great project. Eighty pounds of ancient documents, captured from the general Whisper when we served the Lady and Whisper the Rebel. They are supposed to contain the key to breaking the Lady and the Taken. I have had them six years. And in six years I have found nothing. So much failure. Depressing. Nowadays, more often than not I merely shuffle them, then turn to these Annals.

Since our escape from Juniper they have been little more than a personal journal. The remnant of the Company generates little excitement. What outside news we get is so slim and unreliable I seldom bother recording it. Moreover, since her victory over her husband in Juniper, the Lady seems to be in stasis even more than we, running on inertia.

Appearances deceive, of course. And the Lady's essence is illusion.

"Croaker."

I looked up from a page of Old TelleKurre already studied a hundred times. Goblin stood in the doorway. He looked like an old toad. "Yeah?"

"Something happening up top. Grab a sword."

I grabbed my bow and a leather cuirass. I am too ancient for hand-to-hand. I'd rather stand off and plink if I have to fight at all. I considered the bow as I followed Goblin. It had been given me by the Lady herself, during the battle at Charm. Oh, the memories. With it I helped slay Soulcatcher, the Taken who brought the Company into the Lady's service. Those days now seemed almost prehistoric.

We galloped into sunlight. Others came out with us, dispersed amidst cactus and coral. The rider coming down the trail—the only path in here—would not see us.

He rode alone, on a moth-eaten mule. He was not armed. "All this for an old man on a mule?" I asked. Men scooted through coral and between cacti, making one hell of a racket. The old-timer had to know we were there. "We'd better work on getting out here more quietly."

"Yeah."

Startled, I whirled. Elmo was behind me, one hand shading his eyes. He looked as old and tired as I felt. Each day something reminds me that none of us are young anymore. Hell, none of us were young when we came north, over the Sea of Torments. "We need new blood, Elmo."

He sneered.

Yes. We will be a lot older before this is done. If we last. For we are buying time. Decades, hopefully.

The rider crossed the creek, stopped. He raised his hands. Men materialized, weapons held negligently. One old man alone, at the heart of Darling's null, presented no danger.

Elmo, Goblin, and I strolled down. As we went I asked Goblin, "You and One-Eye have fun while you were gone?" They have been feuding for ages. But here, where Darling's presence forbids it, they cannot play sorcerous tricks.

Goblin grinned. When he grins, his mouth spreads from ear to ear. "I loosened him up."

We reached the rider. "Tell me later."

Goblin giggled, a squeaking noise like water bubbling in a teakettle. "Yeah."

"Who are you?" Elmo asked the mule rider.

"Tokens."

That was not a name. It was a password for a courier from the far west. We had not heard it for a long time. Western messengers had to reach the Plain through the Lady's most tamed provinces.

"Yeah?" Elmo said. "How about that? Want to step down?"

The old man eased off his mount, presented his bona fides. Elmo found them acceptable. Then he announced, "I've got twenty pounds of stuff here." He tapped a case behind his saddle. "Every damn town added to the load."

"Make the whole trip yourself?" I asked.

"Every foot from Oar."

"Oar? That's. . . ."

More than a thousand miles. I hadn't known we had anyone up there. But there is a lot I do not know about the organization Darling has assembled. I spend my time trying to get those damned papers to tell me something that may not be there.

The old man looked at me as though subjecting my soul to an accounting. "You the physician? Croaker?"

"Yeah. So?"

"Got something for you. Personal." He opened his courier case. For a moment everyone was alert. You never know. But he brought out an oilskin packet wrapped to protect something against the end of the world. "Rains all the time up there," he explained. He gave me the packet.

I weighed it. Not that heavy, oilskin aside. "Who's it from?"

The old man shrugged.

"Where'd you get it?"

"From my cell captain."

Of course. Darling has built with care, structuring her organization so that it is almost impossible for the Lady to break more than a fraction. The child is a genius.

Elmo accepted the rest, told Otto, "Take him down and find him a bunk. Get some rest, old-timer. The White Rose will question you later."

An interesting afternoon upcoming, maybe, what with this guy and Corder both to report. I hefted the mystery packet, told Elmo, "I'll go give this a look." Who could have sent it? I knew no one outside the Plain. Well . . . but the Lady would not inject a letter into the underground. Would she?

Twinge of fear. It had been a while, but she *had* promised to keep in touch.

The talking menhir that had forewarned us about the messenger remained rooted beside the path. As I passed, it said, "There are strangers on the Plain, Croaker."

I halted. "What? More of them?"

It reverted to character, would say no more.

Never will I comprehend those old stones. Hell, I still don't understand why they are on our side. They hate all outsiders separately but equally. They and every one of the weird sentiences out here.

I slipped into my quarters, unstrung my bow, left it leaning against the earth wall. I settled at my worktable and opened the packet.

I did not recognize the hand. I found the ending was not signed. I began to read.

3 Story From Yesteryear

Croaker:

The woman was bitching again. Bomanz massaged his temples. The throbbing did not slacken. He covered his eyes. "Saita, sayta, suta," he murmured, his sibilants angry and ophidian.

He bit his tongue. One did not make a sending upon one's wife. One endured with humbled dignity the consequences of youthful folly. Ah, but what temptation! What provocation!

Enough, fool! Study the damned chart.

Neither Jasmine nor the headache relented.

"Bloody hell!" He slapped the weights off the corners of the chart, rolled the thin silk around a wisp of glass rod. He slipped the rod inside the shaft of a fake antique spear. That shaft was shiny with handling. "Besand would spot it in a minute," he grumbled.

He ground his teeth as his ulcer took a bite of gut. The closer the end drew, the greater was the danger. His nerves were shot. He was afraid he might crack at the last barrier, that cowardice would devour him and he would have lived in vain.

Thirty-seven years was a long time to live in the shadow of the headsman's axe.

"Jasmine," he muttered. "And call a sow Beauty." He flung the door-hanging aside, shouted downstairs, "What is it now?"

It was what it always was. Nagging unconnected with the root of her dissatisfaction. An interruption of his studies as a payback for what she fancied was his having misspent their lives.

He could have become a man of consequence in Oar. He could have given her a great house overstuffed with fawning servants. He could have draped her in cloth-of-gold. He could have fed her tumble-down fat with meat at every meal. Instead, he had chosen a scholar's life, disguising his name and profession, dragging her to this bleak, haunted break in the Old Forest. He had given her nothing but squalor, icy winters, and indignities perpetrated by the Eternal Guard.

Bomanz stamped down the narrow, squeaky, treacherous stairway. He cursed the woman, spat on the floor, thrust silver into her desiccated paw, drove her away with a plea that supper, for once, be a decent meal. Indignity? he thought. I'll tell you about indignity, you old crow. I'll tell you what it's like to live with a perpetual whiner, a hideous old bag of vapid, juvenile dreams. . . .

"Stop it, Bomanz," he muttered. "She's the mother of your son. Give her her due. She hasn't betrayed you." If nothing else, they still shared the hope represented by the map on silk. It was hard for her, waiting, unaware of his progress, knowing only that nearly four decades had yielded no tangible result.

The bell on the shop door tinkled. Bomanz clutched at his shopkeeper persona. He scuttled forward, a fat, bald little man with blue-veined hands folded before his chest. "Tokar." He bowed slightly. "I didn't expect you so soon."

Tokar was a trader from Oar, a friend of Bomanz's son Stancil. He had a bluff, honest, irreverent manner Bomanz deluded himself into seeing as the ghost of his own at a younger age.

"Didn't plan to be back so soon, Bo. But antiques are the rage. It surpasses comprehension."

"You want another lot? Already? You'll clean me out." Unsaid, the silent complaint: Bomanz, this means replenishment work. Time lost from research.

"The Domination is hot this year. Stop pottering around, Bo. Make hay, and all that. Next year the market could be as dead as the Taken."

"They're not. . . . Maybe I'm getting too old, Tokar. I don't enjoy the rows with Besand anymore. Hell. Ten years ago I went looking for him. A good squabble killed boredom. The digging grinds me down, too. I'm used up. I just want to sit on the stoop and watch life go by." While he chattered, Bomanz set out his best antique swords, pieces of armor, soldiers' amulets, and an almost perfectly preserved shield. A box of arrowheads with roses engraved. A pair of broad-bladed thrusting spears, ancient heads mounted on replica shafts.

"I can send you some men. Show them where to dig. I'll pay you commission. You won't have to do anything. That's a damned fine axe, Bo. TelleKurre? I could sell a bargeload of TelleKurre weaponry."

"UchiTelle, actually." A twinge from his ulcer. "No. No helpers." That was all he needed. A bunch of young hotshots hanging over his shoulder while he made his field calculations.

"Just a suggestion."

"Sorry. Don't mind me. Jasmine was on me this morning."

Softly, Tokar asked, "Found anything connected with the Taken?"

With the ease of decades, Bomanz dissembled, feigning horror. "The Taken? Am I a fool? I wouldn't touch it if I *could* get it past the Monitor."

Tokar smiled conspiratorily. "Sure. We don't want to offend the Eternal Guard. Nevertheless . . . there's one man in Oar who would pay well for something that could be ascribed to one of the Taken. He'd sell his soul for something that belonged to the Lady. He's in love with her."

"She was known for that." Bomanz avoided the younger man's gaze. How much had Stance revealed? Was this one of Besand's fishing expeditions? The older Bomanz became, the less he enjoyed the game. His nerves could not take this double life. He was tempted to confess just for the relief.

No, damnit! He had too much invested. Thirty-seven years. Digging and scratching every minute. Sneaking and pretending. The most abject poverty. No. He would not give up. Not now. Not when he was this close.

"In my way, I love her, too," he admitted. "But I haven't abandoned good sense. I'd scream for Besand if I found anything. So loud you'd hear me in Oar."

"All right. Whatever you say." Tokar grinned. "Enough suspense." He produced a leather wallet. "Letters from Stancil."

Bomanz seized the wallet. "Haven't heard from him since last time you were here."

"Can I start loading, Bo?"

"Sure. Go ahead." Absently, Bomanz took his current inventory list from a pigeonhole. "Mark off whatever you take."

Tokar laughed gently. "All of it this time, Bo. Just quote me a price."

"Everything? Half is junk."

"I told you, the Domination is hot."

"You saw Stance? How is he?" He was halfway through the first letter. His son had nothing substantial to relate. His missives were filled with daily trivia. Duty letters. Letters from a son to his parents, unable to span the timeless chasm.

"Sickeningly healthy. Bored with the university. Read on. There's a surprise."

Tokar was here," Bomanz said. He grinned, danced from foot to foot.

"That thief?" Jasmine scowled. "Did you remember to get paid?" Her fat, sagging face was set in perpetual disapproval. Generally her mouth was open in the same vein.

"He brought letters from Stance. Here." He offered the packet. He could not contain himself. "Stance is coming home."

"Home? He can't. He has his position at the university."

"He's taking a sabbatical. He's coming for the summer."

"Why?"

"To see us. To help with the shop. To get away so he can finish a thesis."

Jasmine grumbled. She did not read the letters. She had not forgiven her son for sharing his father's interest in the Domination. "What he's doing is coming here to help you poke around where you're not supposed to poke, isn't he?"

Bomanz darted furtive glances at the shop's windows. His was an existence of justifiable paranoia. "It's the Year of the Comet. The ghosts of the Taken will rise to mourn the passing of the Domination."

This summer would mark the tenth return of the comet which had appeared at the hour of the Dominator's fall. The Ten Who Were Taken would manifest strongly.

Bomanz had witnessed one passage the summer he had come to the Old Forest, long before Stancil's birth. The Barrowland had been impressive with ghosts walking.

Excitement tightened his belly. Jasmine would not appreciate it, but this was the summer. End of the long quest. He lacked only one key. Find it and he could make contact, could begin drawing out instead of putting in.

Jasmine sneered. "Why did I get into this? My mother warned me."

"It's Stancil we're talking about, woman. Our only."

"Ah, Bo, don't call me a cruel old lady. Of course I'll welcome him. Don't I cherish him, too?"

"Wouldn't hurt to show it." Bomanz examined the remnants of his inventory. "Nothing left but the worst junk. These old bones ache just thinking of the digging I'll have to do."

His bones ached, but his spirit was eager. Restocking was a plausible excuse for wandering the edges of the Barrowland.

"No time like now to start."

"You trying to get me out of the house?"

"That wouldn't hurt my feelings."

Sighing, Bomanz surveyed his shop. A few pieces of time-rotted gear, broken weapons, a skull that could not be attributed because it lacked the triangular inset characteristic of Domination officers. Collectors were not interested in the bones of kerns or in those of followers of the White Rose.

Curious, he thought. Why are we so intrigued by evil? The White Rose was more heroic than the Dominator or Taken. She has been forgotten by everybody but the Monitor's men. Any peasant can name half the Taken. The Barrowland, where evil lies restless, is guarded, and the grave of the White Rose is lost.

"Neither here nor there," Bomanz grumbled. "Time to hit the field. Here. Here. Spade. Divining wand. Bags. . . . Maybe Tokar was right. Maybe I should get a helper. Brushes. Help carry that stuff around. Transit. Maps. Can't forget those. What else? Claim ribbons. Of course. That wretched Men fu."

He stuffed things into a pack and hung equipment all about himself. He gathered spade and rake and transit. "Jasmine. Jasmine! Open the damned door."

She peeped through the curtains masking their living quarters. "Should've opened it first, dimwit." She stalked across the shop. "One of these days, Bo, you're going to get organized. Probably the day after my funeral."

He stumbled down the street grumbling, "I'll get organized the day you die. Damned well better believe. I want you in the ground before you change your mind."

4

The Near Past: Corbie

The Barrowland lies far north of Charm, in the Old Forest so storied in the legends of the White Rose. Corbie came to the town there the summer after the Dominator failed to escape his grave through Juniper. He found the Lady's minions in high morale. The grand evil in the Great Barrow was no longer to be feared. The dregs of the Rebel had been routed. The empire had no more enemies of consequence. The Great Comet, harbinger of all catastrophes, would not return for decades.

One lone focus of resistance remained, a child claimed to be the reincarnation of the White Rose. But she was a fugitive, running with the remnants of the traitorous Black Company. Nothing to fear there. The Lady's overwhelming resources would swamp them.

Corbie came limping up the road from Oar, alone, a pack on his back, a staff gripped tightly. He claimed to be a disabled veteran of the Limper's Forsberg campaigns. He wanted work. There was work aplenty for a man not too proud. The Eternal Guard were well-paid. Many hired drudgework taken off their duties.

At that time a regiment garrisoned the Barrowland. Countless civilians orbited its compound. Corbie vanished among those. When companies and battalions transferred out, he was an established part of the landscape.

He washed dishes, curried horses, cleaned stables, carried messages, mopped floors, peeled vegetables, assumed any burden for which he might earn a few coppers. He was a quiet, tall, dusky, brooding sort who made no special friends, but made no enemies either. Seldom did he socialize.

After a few months he asked for and received permission to occupy a ramshackle house long shunned because once it belonged to a sorcerer from Oar. As time and resources permitted, he restored the place. And like the sorcerer before him, he pursued the mission that had brought him north.

Ten, twelve, fourteen hours a day Corbie worked around town, then went home and worked some more. People wondered when he rested.

If there was anything that detracted from Corbie, it was that he refused to assume his role completely. Most scutboys had to endure a lot of personal abuse. Corbie would not accept it. Victimize him and his eyes went cold as winter steel. Only one man ever pressed Corbie once he got that look. Corbie beat him with ruthless, relentless efficiency.

No one suspected him of leading a double life. Outside his home he was Corbie the swamper, nothing more. He lived the role to his heart. When he was home, in the more public hours, he was Corbie the renovator, creating a new home from an old. Only in the wee hours, while all but the night patrol slept, did he become Corbie the man with a mission.

Corbie the renovator found a treasure in a wall of the wizard's kitchen. He took it upstairs, where Corbie the driven came up from the deeps.

The scrap of paper bore a dozen words scribbled in a shaky hand. A cipher key.

That lean, dusky, long-unsmiling face shed its ice. Dark eyes sparkled, Fingers turned up a lamp. Corbie sat, and for an hour stared at nothing. Then, still smiling, he went downstairs and out into the night. He raised a hand in gentle greeting whenever he encountered the night patrol.

He was known now. No one challenged his right to limp about and watch the constellations wheel.

He went home when his nerves settled. There would be no sleep for him. He scattered papers, began to study, to decipher, to translate, to write a story-letter that would not reach its destination for years.

5

The Plain of Fear

One-Eye stopped by to tell me Darling was about to interview Corder and the messenger. "She's looking peaked, Croaker. You been watching her?"

"I watch. I advise. She ignores. What can I do?"

"We got twenty-some years till the comet shows. No point her working herself to death, is there?"

"Tell *her* that. She just tells me this mess will be settled long before the comet comes around again. That it's a race against time."

She believes that. But the rest of us cannot catch her fire. Isolated in the Plain of Fear, cut off from the world, we find the struggle with the Lady sometimes slips in importance. The Plain itself too often preoccupies us.

I caught myself outdistancing One-Eye. This premature burial has not been good for him. Without his skills he has weakened physically. He is beginning to show his age. I let him catch up.

"You and Goblin enjoy your adventure?"

He could not choose between a smirk or a scowl.

"Got you again, eh?" Their battle has been on since the dawn. One-Eye starts each skirmish. Goblin usually finishes.

He grumbled something.

"What?"

"Yo!" someone shouted. "Everybody up top! Alert! Alert!"

One-Eye spat. "Twice in one day? What the hell?"

I knew what he meant. We have not had twenty alerts our whole two years out here. Now two in one day? Improbable.

I dashed back for my bow.

This time we went out with less clatter. Elmo had made his displeasure painfully apparent in a few private conversations.

Sunlight again. Like a blow. The entrance to the Hole faces westward. The sun was in our eyes when we emerged.

"You damned fool!" Elmo was yelling. "What the hell you doing?" A young soldier stood in the open, pointing. I let my gaze follow.

"Oh, damn," I whispered. "Oh, double bloody damn."

One-Eye saw it too. "Taken."

The airborne dot drifted higher, circling our hideout, spiraling inward. It wobbled suddenly.

"Yeah. Taken. Whisper or Journey?"

"Good to see old friends," Goblin said as he joined us.

We had not seen the Taken since reaching the Plain. Before that they had been in our hair constantly, having pursued us all the four years it had taken us to get here from Juniper.

They are the Lady's satraps, her understudies in terror. Once there were ten. In the time of the Domination, the Lady and her husband enslaved the greatest of their contemporaries, making them their instruments: the Ten Who Were Taken. The Taken went into the ground with their masters when the White Rose defeated the Dominator four centuries ago. And they arose with the Lady, two turns of the comet back. And in fighting among themselves—for some remained loyal to the Dominator—most perished.

But the Lady obtained new slaves. Feather. Whisper. Journey. Feather and the last of the old ones, the Limper, went down at Juniper, when we overcame the Dominator's bid for his own resurrection. Two are left. Whisper. Journey.

The flying carpet wobbled because it had reached the boundary where Darling's null was enough to overpower its buoyancy. The Taken turned away, falling outward, got far enough to recover complete control. "Pity it didn't come straight in," I said. "And come down like a rock."

"They're not stupid," Goblin said. "They're just scouting us now." He shook his head, shuddered. He knew something I did not. Probably something learned during his venture outside the Plain.

"Campaign heating up?" I asked.

"Yep. What're you doing, bat-breath?" he snapped at One-Eye. "Pay attention."

The little black man was ignoring the Taken. He stared at the wild wind-carved bluffs south of us.

"Our job is to stay alive," One-Eye said, so smug you knew he had something to get Goblin's goat. "That means don't get distracted by the first flashy show you see."

"What the hell does that mean?"

"Means while the rest of you are eyeballing that clown up there another one sneaked up behind the bluffs and put somebody down."

Goblin and I glared at the red cliffs. We saw nothing.

"Too late," One-Eye said. "It's gone. But I reckon somebody should go collect the spy."

I believed One-Eye. "Elmo! Get over here." I explained.

"Beginning to move," he murmured. "Just when I was hoping they'd forgotten us."

"Oh, they haven't," Goblin said. "They most certainly haven't." Again I felt he had something on his mind.

Elmo scanned the ground between us and the bluffs. He knew it well. We all do. One day our lives may depend on our knowing it better than someone hunting us. "Okay," he told himself. "I see it. I'll take four men. After I see the Lieutenant."

The Lieutenant does not come up for alerts. He and two other men camp in the doorway to Darling's quarters. If ever the enemy reaches Darling, it will be over their bodies.

The flying carpet went away westward. I wondered why it had gone unchallenged by the creatures of the Plain. I went to the menhir that had spoken to me earlier. I asked. Instead of answering, it said, "It begins, Croaker. Mark this day."

"Yeah. Right." And I do call that day the beginning, though parts of it started years before. That was the day of the first letter, the day of the Taken, and the day of Tracker and Toadkiller Dog.

The menhir had a final remark. "There are strangers on the Plain." It would not defend the various flyers for not resisting the Taken.

Elmo returned. I said, "The menhir says we might have more visitors."

Elmo raised an eyebrow. "You and Silent have the next two watches?"

"Yep."

"Be careful. Goblin. One-Eye. Come here." They put their heads together. Then Elmo picked four youngsters and went hunting.

The Plain of Fear

I went up top for my watch. There was no sign of Elmo and his men. The sun was low. The menhir was gone. There was no sound but the voice of the wind.

Silent sat in shadow inside a reef of thousand-coral, dappled by sunlight come through twisted branches. Coral makes good cover. Few of the Plain's denizens dare its poisons. The watch is always in more danger from native exotica than from our enemies.

I twisted and ducked between deadly spines, joined Silent. He is a long, lean, aging man. His dark eyes seemed focused on dreams that had died. I deposited my weapons. "Anything?"

He shook his head, a single minuscule negative. I arranged the pads I had brought. The coral twisted around us, branches and fans climbing twenty feet high. We could see little but the creek crossing and a few dead menhirs, and the walking trees on the far slope. One tree stood beside the brook, taproot in the water. As though sensing my attention, it began a slow retreat.

The visible Plain is barren. The usual desert life—lichens and scrub brush, snakes and lizards, scorpions and spiders, wild dogs and ground squirrels—is present but scarce. You encounter it mainly when that is inconvenient. Which sums up Plain life generally. You encounter the real strangeness only when that is most inopportune. The Lieutenant claims a man trying to commit suicide here could spend years without becoming uncomfortable.

The predominant colors are reds and browns, rust, ochre, blood- and wine-shaded sandstones like the bluffs, with here and there the random stratum of orange. The corals lay down scattered white and pink reefs. True verdance is absent. Both walking trees and scrub plants have leaves a dusty grey-green, in which green exists mainly by acclamation. The menhirs, living and dead, are a stark grey-brown unlike any stone native to the Plain.

A bloated shadow drifted across the wild scree skirting the cliffs. It covered many acres, was too dark to be the shadow of a cloud. "Windwhale?"

Silent nodded.

It cruised the upper air between us and the sun, but I could not spot it. I had not seen one in years. Last time Elmo and I were crossing the Plain with Whisper, on the Lady's behalf. . . . That long ago? Time does flee, and with little fun in it. "Strange waters under the bridge, my friend. Strange waters under."

He nodded, but he did not speak. He is Silent.

He has not spoken in all the years I have known him. Nor in the years he has been with the Company. Yet both One-Eye and my predecessor as Annalist say he is quite capable of speech. From hints accumulated over the years, it has become my firm conviction that in his youth, before he signed on, he swore a great oath never to speak. It being the iron law of the Company not to pry into a man's life before he enlisted, I have been unable to learn anything about the circumstances.

I have seen him come close to speaking, when he was angry enough, or amused enough, but always he caught himself at the last instant. For a long time men made a game of baiting him, trying to get him to break his vow, but most abandoned the effort quickly. Silent had a hundred little ways of discouraging a man, like filling his bedroll with ticks.

Shadows lengthened. Stains of darkness spread. At last Silent rose, stepped over me, returned to the Hole, a darkly clad shadow moving through darkness. A strange man, Silent. Not only does he not talk; he does not gossip. How can you get a handle on a guy like that?

Yet he is one of my oldest and closest friends. Go explain that.

"Well, Croaker." The voice was as hollow as a ghost's. I started. Malicious laughter rattled through the coral reef. A menhir had slipped up on me. I turned slightly. It stood square on the path Silent had taken, twelve feet tall and ugly. A runt of its kind.

"Hello, rock."

Having amused itself at my expense, it now ignored me. Stayed as silent as a stone. Ha-ha.

The menhirs are our principal allies upon the Plain. They interlocute for the other sentient species. They let us know what is happening only when it suits them, however.

"What's happening with Elmo?" I asked.

Nothing.

Are they magic? I guess not. Otherwise they would not survive inside the nullity Darling radiates. But what are they? Mysteries. Like most of the bizarre creatures out here.

"There are strangers on the Plain."

"I know. I know."

Night creatures came out. Dots of luminescence fluttered and swooped above. The windwhale whose shadow I saw came far enough eastward to show me its glimmering underbelly. It would descend soon, trailing tendrils to trap whatever came its way. A breeze rose.

Sagey scents trickled across my nostrils. Air chuckled and whispered and murmured and whistled in the coral. From farther away came the wind-chimes tinkle of Old Father Tree.

He is unique. First or last of his kind, I do not know. There he stands, twenty feet tall and ten thick, brooding beside the creek, radiating something akin to dread, his roots planted on the geographical center of the Plain. Silent, Goblin, and One-Eye have all tried to unravel his significance. They have gotten nowhere. The scarce wild human tribesmen of the Plain worship him. They say he has been here since the dawn. He does have that timeless feel.

The moon rose. While it lay torpid and pregnant on the horizon I thought I saw something cross it. Taken? Or one of the Plain creatures?

A racket rose around the mouth of the Hole. I groaned. I did not need this. Goblin and One-Eye. For half a minute, uncharitably, I wished they had not come back. "Knock it off. I don't want to hear that crap."

Goblin scooted up outside the coral, grinned, dared me to do something. He looked rested, recuperated. One-Eye asked, "Feeling cranky, Croaker?"

"Damned straight. What're you doing out here?"

"Needed some fresh air." He cocked his head, stared at the line of cliffs. So. Worried about Elmo.

"He'll be all right," I said.

"I know." One-Eye added, "I lied. Darling sent us. She felt something stir at the west edge of the null."

"Ah?"

"I don't know what it was, Croaker." Suddenly he was defensive. Pained. He would have known but for Darling. He stands where I would were I stripped of my medical gear. Helpless to do what he has trained at all his life.

"What're you going to do?"

"Build a fire."

"What?"

That fire roared. One-Eye got so ambitious he dragged in enough deadwood to serve half a legion. The flames beat back the darkness till I could see fifty yards beyond the creek. The last walking trees had departed. Probably smelled One-Eye coming.

He and Goblin dragged in a fallen tree of the ordinary sort. We leave the walkers alone, except to right clumsies that trip on their own roots. Not that that happens often. They do not travel much.

They were bickering about who was dogging his share of work. They dropped the tree. "Fade," Goblin said, and in a moment there was no sign of them. Baffled, I surveyed the darkness. I saw nothing, heard nothing.

I found myself having trouble remaining awake. I broke up the dead tree for something to do. Then I felt the oddness.

I stopped in midbreak. How long had the menhirs been gathering? I counted fourteen on the verges of the light. They cast long, deep shadows. "What's up?" I asked, my nerves a bit frayed.

"There are strangers on the Plain."

Hell of a tune they played. I settled near the fire, back to it, tossed wood over my shoulder, building the flames. The light spread. I counted another ten menhirs. After a time I said, "That's not exactly news."

"One comes."

That *was* new. And spoken with passion, something I had not witnessed before. Once, twice, I thought I caught a flicker of motion, but I could not be sure. Firelight is tricky. I piled on more wood.

Movement for sure. Beyond the creek. Manshape coming toward me, slowly. Wearily. I settled in pretended boredom. He came nearer. Across his right shoulder he carried a saddle and blanket held with his left hand. In his right he carried a long wooden case, its polish gleaming in the firelight. It was seven feet long and four inches by eight. Curious.

I noticed the dog as they crossed the creek. A mongrel, ragged, mangy, mostly a dirty white but with a black circle around one eye and a few daubs of black on its flanks. It limped, carrying one forepaw off the ground. The fire caught its eyes. They burned bright red.

The man was over six feet, maybe thirty. He moved lithely even in his weariness. He had muscles on muscles. His tattered shirt revealed arms and chest crisscrossed with scars. His face was empty of emotion. He met my gaze as he approached the fire, neither smiling nor betraying unfriendly intent.

Chill touched me, lightly. He looked tough, but not tough enough to negotiate the Plain of Fear alone.

First order of business would be to stall. Otto was due out to relieve me soon. The fire would alert him. He would see the stranger, then duck down and rouse the Hole.

"Hello," I said.

He halted, exchanged glances with his mongrel. The dog came forward slowly, sniffing the air, searching the surrounding night. It stopped a few feet away, shook as though wet, settled on its belly.

The stranger came forward just that far. "Take a load off," I invited.

He swung his saddle down, lowered his case, sat. He was stiff. He had trouble crossing his legs.

"Lose your horse?"

He nodded. "Broke a leg. West of here, five, six miles. I lost the trail."

There *are* trails through the Plain. Some of them the Plain honors as safe. Sometimes. According to a formula known only to its denizens. Only someone desperate or stupid hazards them alone, though. This fellow did not look like an idiot.

The dog made a whuffling sound. The man scratched its ears.

"Where you headed?"

"Place called the Fastness."

That is the legend-name, the propaganda name, for the Hole. A calculated bit of glamor for the troops in faraway places.

"Name?"

"Tracker. This is Toadkiller Dog."

"Pleased to meet you, Tracker. Toadkiller."

The dog grumbled. Tracker said, "You have to use his whole name. Toadkiller Dog."

I kept a straight face only because he was such a big, grim, tough-looking man. "What's this Fastness?" I asked. "I never heard of it."

He lifted hard, dark eyes from the mutt, smiled. "I've heard it lies near Tokens."

Twice in one day? Was it the day of twos? No. Not bloody likely. I did not like the look of the man, either. Reminded me too much of our one-time brother Raven. Ice and iron. I donned my baffled face. It is a good one. "Tokens? That's a new one on me. Must be somewhere way the hell out east. What are you headed there for, anyway?"

He smiled again. His dog opened one eye, gave me a baleful look. They did not believe me.

"Carrying messages."

"I see."

"Mainly a packet. Addressed to somebody named Croaker."

I sucked spittle between teeth, slowly scanned the surrounding darkness. The circle of light had shrunk, but the number of menhirs remained undiminished.

I wondered about One-Eye and Goblin. "Now there's a name I've heard," I said. "Some kind of sawbones." Again the dog gave me that look. This time, I decided, it was sarcastic.

One-Eye stepped out of the darkness behind Tracker, sword ready to do the dirty deed. Damn, but he came quiet. Witchery or no.

I gave him away with a flicker of surprise. Tracker and his dog looked back. Both were startled to see someone there. The dog rose. Its hackles lifted. Then it sank to the ground again, having twisted till it could keep us both in sight.

But then Goblin appeared, just as quietly. I smiled. Tracker glanced over. His eyes narrowed. He looked thoughtful, like a man discovering he was in a card game with rogues sharper than he had expected. Goblin chuckled. "He wants in, Croaker. I say we take him down."

Tracker's hand twitched toward the case he had carried. His animal growled. Tracker closed his eyes. When they opened, he was in control. His smile returned. "Croaker, eh? Then I've found the Fastness."

"You've found it, friend."

Slowly, so as not to alarm anyone, Tracker took an oilskin packet from his saddlebag. It was the twin of that I had received only half a day before. He offered it to me. I tucked it inside my shirt. "Where'd you get it?"

"Oar." He told the same story as the other messenger.

I nodded. "You've come that far, then?"

"Yes."

"We *should* take him in, then," I told One-Eye. He caught my meaning. We would let this messenger come face to face with the other. See if sparks flew. One-Eye grinned.

I glanced at Goblin. He approved.

None of us felt quite right about Tracker. I am not sure why.

"Let's go," I said. I hoisted myself off the ground with my bow.

Tracker eyed the stave. He started to say something, shut up. As though he recognized it. I smiled as I turned away. Maybe he thought he had fallen foul of the Lady. "Follow me."

He did. And Goblin and One-Eye followed him, neither helping with his gear. His dog limped beside him, nose to the ground. Before we went inside, I glanced southward, concerned. When would Elmo come home?

We put Tracker and mutt into a guarded cell. They did not protest. I went to my quarters after wakening Otto, who was overdue. I tried to sleep, but that damned packet lay on the table screaming.

I was not sure I wanted to read its contents.

It won the battle.

The Second Letter

Croaker:

Bomanz peered through his transit, sighting on the prow of the Great Barrow. He stepped back, noted the angle, opened one of his crude field maps. This was where he had unearthed the TelleKurre axe. "Wish Occules' descriptions weren't so vague. This must have been the flank of their formation. The axis of their line should have paralleled the others, so. Shifter and the knights would have bunched up over there. I'll be damned."

The ground there humped slightly. Good. Less ground water to damage buried artifacts. But the overgrowth was dense. Scrub oak. Wild roses. Poison ivy. Especially poison ivy. Bomanz hated that pestilential weed. He started scratching just thinking about it.

"Bomanz."

"What?" He whirled, raising his rake.

"Whoa! Take it easy, Bo."

"What's the matter with you? Sneaking up like that. Ain't funny, Besand. Want me to rake that idiot grin off your face?"

"Ooh! Nasty today, aren't we?" Besand was a lean old man approximately Bomanz's age. His shoulders slumped, following his head, which thrust forward as though he was sniffing a trail. Great blue veins humped the backs of his hands. Liver spots dotted his skin.

"What the hell do you expect? Come jumping out of the bushes at a man."

"Bushes? What bushes? Your conscience bothering you, Bo?"

"Besand, you've been trying to trap me since the moon was green. Why don't you give up? First Jasmine gives me a hard way to go, then Tokar buys me out so I have to go digging fresh stock, and now I have to dance with you? Go away. I'm not in the mood."

Besand grinned a big, lopsided grin, revealing pickets of rotten teeth. "I haven't caught you, Bo, but that don't mean you're innocent. It just means I never caught you."

"If I'm not innocent, you must be damned stupid not to catch me in forty years. Damn, man, why the hell can't you make life easy for both of us?"

Besand laughed. "Real soon now I'll be out of your hair for good. They're putting me out to pasture."

Bomanz leaned on his rake, considered the Guardsman. Besand exuded a sour odor of pain. "Really? I'm sorry."

"Bet you are. My replacement might be smart enough to catch you."

"Give it a rest. You want to know what I'm doing? Figuring where the TelleKurre knights went down. Tokar wants spectacular stuff. That's the best I can do. Short of going over there and giving you an excuse to hang me. Hand me that dowser."

Besand passed the divining rod. "Mound robbing, eh? Tokar suggest that?"

Icy needles burrowed into Bomanz's spine. This was more than a casual question. "We have to do this constantly? Haven't we known each other long enough to do without the cat-and-mouse?"

"I enjoy it, Bo." Besand trailed him to the overgrown hummock. "Going to have to clear this out. Just can't keep up anymore. Not enough men, not enough money."

"Could you get it right away? That's where I want to dig, I think. Poison ivy."

"Oh, 'ware poison ivy, Bo." Besand snickered. Each summer Bomanz cursed his way through numerous botanical afflictions. "About Tokar. . . ."

"I don't deal with people who want to break the law. That's been my rule forever. Nobody bothers me anymore."

"Oblique but acceptable."

Bomanz's wand twitched. "I'll be dipped in sheep shit. Right in the middle."

"Sure?"

"Look at it jump. Must've buried them in one big hole."

"About Tokar. . . ."

"What about him, dammit? You want to hang him, go ahead. Just give me time to hook up with somebody else who can handle my business as good."

"I don't want to hang anybody, Bo. I just want to warn you. There's a rumor out of Oar that says he's a Resurrectionist."

Bomanz dropped his rod. He gobbled air. "Really? A Resurrectionist?"

The Monitor scrutinized him intently. "Just a rumor. I hear all kinds. Thought you might want to know. We're as close as two men get around here."

Bomanz accepted the olive branch. "Yeah. Honestly, he's never dropped a hint. Whew! That's a load to drop on a man." A load which deserved some heavy thinking. "Don't tell anybody what I found. That thief Men fu. . . ."

Besand laughed yet again. His mirth had a sephulchral quality.

"You enjoy your work, don't you? I mean, harassing people who don't dare fight back."

"Careful, Bo. I could drag you in for questioning." Besand spun, stalked away.

Bomanz sneered at his back. Of course Besand enjoyed his job. It let him play dictator. He could do anything to anyone without having to answer for it.

Once the Dominator and his minions fell and were buried in their mounds behind barriers wrought of the finest magicks of their day, the White Rose decreed that an eternal guard be posted. A guard beholden to none, charged with preventing the resurrection of the undead evil beneath the mounds. The White Rose understood human nature. Always there would be those who would see profit in using or following the Dominator. Always there would be worshippers of evil who wished their champion freed.

The Resurrectionists appeared almost before the grass sprouted on the barrows.

Tokar a Resurrectionist? Bomanz thought. Don't I have enough trouble? Besand will pitch his tent in my pocket now.

Bomanz had no interest in reviving the old evils. He merely wanted to make contact with one of them so as to illuminate several ancient mysteries.

Besand was out of sight. He should stomp all the way back to his quarters. There would be time for a few forbidden observations. Bomanz realigned his transit.

The Barrowland did not have the look of great evil, only of neglect. Four hundred years of vegetation and weather had restructured that once marvelous work. The barrows and mystical landscaping were all but lost amidst the brush covering them. The Eternal Guard no longer had the wherewithal to perform adequate upkeep. Monitor Besand was fighting a desperate rearguard action against time itself.

Nothing grew well on the Barrowland. The vegetation was twisted and stunted. Still, the shapes of the mounds, and the menhirs and fetishes which bound the Taken, were often concealed.

Bomanz had spent a lifetime sorting out which mound was which, who lay where, and where each menhir and fetish stood. His master chart, his silken treasure, was nearly complete. He could, almost, thread the maze. He was so close he was tempted to try before he was truly ready. But he was no fool. He meant to try nursing sweet milk from the blackest of cows. He dared make no mistake. He had Besand on the one hand, the poisonous old wickedness on the other.

But if he succeeded. . . . Ah, if he succeeded. If he made contact and nursed away the secrets. . . . Man's knowledge would be extended dramatically. He would become the mightiest of living mages. His fame would course with the wind. Jasmine would have everything she quarreled about sacrificing. *If* he made contact.

He would, by damn! Neither fear nor the infirmity of age would stay him now. A few months and he would have the last key.

Bomanz had lived his lies so long he often lied to himself. Even in his honest moments he never confessed his most powerful motive, his intellectual affair with the Lady. It was she who had intrigued him from the beginning, she whom he was trying to contact, she who made the literature endlessly fascinating. Of all the lords of the Domination she was the most shadowed, the most surrounded by myth, the least encumbered by historical fact. Some scholars called her the greatest beauty ever to have lived, claiming that simply to have seen her was to have fallen into her thrall. Some called her the true motive force of the Domination. A few admitted that their documentaries were really little more than romantic fantasies. Others admitted nothing while demonstrably embellishing. Bomanz had become perpetually bemused while still a student.

Back in his attic, he spread his silken chart. His day had not been a complete waste. He had located a previously unknown menhir and had identified the spells it anchored. And he had found the TelleKurre site. That would buy the mutton and beans.

He glared at the chart, as if pure will might conjure the information he needed.

There were two diagrams. The upper was a five-pointed star within a slightly larger circle. Such had been the shape of the Barrowland when newly constructed. The star had stood a fathom above the surrounding terrain, retained by limestone walls. The circle represented the outer bank of a moat, the earth from which had been used to build the barrows, the star, and a pentagon within the star. Today the moat was little more than boggy ground. Besand's predecessors had been unable to keep up with Nature.

Within the star, drawn off the points where the arms met, was a pentagon another fathom high. It, too, had been retained, but the walls had fallen and become overgrown. Central to the pentagon, on a north-south axis, lay the Great Barrow where the Dominator slept.

At the points of his chart star, clockwise from the top, Bomanz had penned the odd numbers from one to nine. Accompanying each was a name: Soulcatcher, Shapeshifter, Nightcrawler, Stormbringer, Bonegnasher. The occupants of the five outer barrows had been identified. The five inner points were numbered evenly, beginning at the right foot of the arm of the star pointing northward. At four was the Howler, at eight the Limper. The graves of three of the Ten Who Were Taken remained unidentified.

"Who's in that damned six spot?" Bomanz muttered. He slammed a fist against the table. "Dammit!" Four years and he was no closer to that name. The mask concealing that identity was the one remaining substantial barrier. Everything else was plain technical application, a matter of negating wardspells, then of contacting the great one in the central mound.

The wizards of the White Rose had left volumes bragging about their performances of their art, but not one word of where their victims lay. Such was human nature. Besand bragged about the fish he caught, the bait he used, and seldom produced the veritable piscine trophy.

Below his star chart Bomanz had drawn a second portraying the central mound. It was a rectangle on a north-south axis surrounded by and filled with ranks of symbols. Outside each corner was a representation of a menhir which, on the Barrowland, was a twelve-foot pillar topped by a two-faced owl's head. One face glared inward, the other out. The menhirs formed the corner posts anchoring the first line of spells warding the Great Barrow.

Along the sides were the line posts, little circles representing wooden fetish poles. Most had rotted and fallen, their spells drooping with them. The Eternal Guard had no staff wizard capable of restoring or replacing them.

Within the mound proper there were symbols ranked in three rectangles of declining size. The outermost resembled pawns, the next knights, and the inner, elephants. The crypt of the Dominator was surrounded by men who had given their lives to bring him down. Ghosts were the middle line between old evil and a world capable of recalling it. Bomanz anticipated no difficulty getting past them. The ghosts were there, in his opinion, to discourage common grave robbers.

Within the three rectangles Bomanz had drawn a dragon with its tail in its mouth. Legend said a great dragon lay curled round the crypt, more alive than the Lady or Dominator, catnapping the centuries away while awaiting an attempt to recall the trapped evil.

Bomanz had no way of coping with the dragon, but he had no need, either. He meant to communicate with the crypt, not to open it.

Damn! If he could only lay hands on an old Guardsman's amulet. . . . The early Guards had worn amulets which had allowed them to go into the Barrowland to keep it up. The amulets still existed, though they were no longer used. Besand wore one. The others he kept squirreled away.

Besand. That madman. That sadist.

Bomanz considered the Monitor his closest acquaintance—but a friend, never. No, never a friend. Sad commentary on his life, that the man nearest him would be one who would jump at a chance to torture or hang him.

What was that about retirement? Someone outside this forsaken forest had recalled the Barrowland?

"Bomanz! Are you going to eat?"

Bomanz muttered imprecations and rolled his chart.

* * *

The Dream came that night. Something sirenic called him. He was young again, single, strolling the lane that passed his house. A woman waved. Who was she? He didn't know. He didn't care. He loved her. Laughing, he ran toward her. . . . Floating steps. Effort took him no nearer. Her face saddened. She faded. . . . "Don't go!" he called. "Please!" But she disappeared, and took with her his sun.

A vast starless night devoured his dream. He floated in a clearing within a forest unseen. Slowly, slowly, a diffuse silver something limned the trees. A big star with a long silver mane. He watched it grow till its tail spanned the sky.

Twinge of uncertainty. Shadow of fear. "It's coming right at me!" He cringed, threw his arm across his face. The silver ball filled the sky. It had a face. The woman's face. . . .

"Bo! Stop it!" Jasmine punched him again.

He sat up. "Uhn? What?"

"You were yelling. That nightmare again?"

He listened to his heart hammer, sighed. Could it take much more? He was an old man. "The same one." It recurred at unpredictable intervals. "It was stronger this time."

"Maybe you ought to see a dream doctor."

"Out here?" He snorted disgustedly. "I don't need a dream doctor anyway."

"No. Probably just your conscience. Nagging you for luring Stancil back from Oar."

"I didn't lure. . . . Go to sleep." To his amazement, she rolled over, for once unwilling to pursue their squabble.

He stared into the darkness. It had been so much clearer. Almost too crisp and obvious. Was there a meaning hidden behind the dream's warning against tampering?

Slowly, slowly, the mood of the beginning of the dream returned. That sense of being summoned, of being but one intuitive step from heart's desire. It felt good. His tension drained away. He fell asleep smiling.

Besand and Bomanz stood watching Guardsmen clear the brush from Bomanz's site. Bomanz suddenly spat, "Don't burn it, you idiot! Stop him, Besand."

Besand shook his head. A Guard with a torch backed away from the brush pile. "Son, you don't burn poison ivy. The smoke spreads the poison."

Bomanz was scratching. And wondering why his companion was being so reasonable. Besand smirked. "Get itchy just thinking about it, don't you?"

"Yes."

"There's your other itch." He pointed. Bomanz saw his competitor Men fu observing from a safe distance. He growled, "I never hated anybody, but he tempts me. He has no ethics, no scruples, and no conscience. He's a thief and a liar."

"I know him, Bo. And lucky for you I do."

"Let me ask you something, Besand. *Monitor* Besand. How come you don't aggravate him the way you do me? What do you mean, lucky?"

"He accused you of Resurrectionist tendencies. I don't shadow him because his many virtues include cowardice. He doesn't have the hair to recover proscribed artifacts."

"And I do? That little wart libeled me? With capital crimes? If I weren't an old man. . . ."

"He'll get his, Bo. And you do have the guts. I've just never caught you with the inclination."

Bomanz rolled his eyes. "Here we go. The veiled accusations. . . ."

"Not so veiled, my friend. There's a moral laxness in you, an unwillingness to accept the existence of evil, that stinks like an old corpse. Give it its head and I'll catch you, Bo. The wicked are cunning, but they always betray themselves."

For an instant Bomanz thought his world was falling apart. Then he realized Besand was fishing. A dedicated fisherman, the Monitor. Shaken, he countered, "I'm sick of your sadism. If you really suspected anything, you'd be on me like a snake on shit. Legalities never meant anything to you Guards. You're probably lying about Men fu. You'd haul your own mother in on the word of a sorrier villain than him. You're sick, Besand. You know that? Diseased. Right here." He tapped his temple. "You can't relate without cruelty."

"You're pushing your luck again, Bo."

Bomanz backed down. Fright and temper had been talking. In his own odd way Besand had shown him special tolerance. It was as though he were necessary to the Monitor's emotional health. Besand needed one person, outside the Guard, whom he did not victimize. Someone whose immunity repaid him in a sort of validation. . . . I'm symbolic of the people he defends? Bomanz snorted. That was rich.

That business about being retired. Did he say more than I heard? Is he calling off all bets because he's leaving? Maybe he does have a sense for scofflaws. Maybe he wants to go out with a flash.

What about the new man? Another monster, unblinkered by the gossamer I've spun across Besand's eyes? Maybe someone who will come in like the bull into the corrida? And Tokar, the possible Resurrectionist. . . . How does he fit?

"What's the matter?" Besand asked. Concern colored his words.

"Ulcer's bothering me." Bomanz massaged his temples, hoping the headache would not come too.

"Plant your markers. Men fu might jump you right here."

"Yeah." Bomanz took a half dozen stakes from his pack. Each trailed a strip of yellow cloth. He planted them. Custom dictated that the ground so circumscribed was his to exploit.

Men fu could make night raids, or whatever, and Bomanz would have no legal recourse. Claims had no standing in law, only in private treaty. The antique miners exercised their own sanctions.

Men fu was under every sanction but violence. Nothing altered his thieving ways.

"Wish Stancil was here," Bomanz said. "He could watch at night."

"I'll growl at him. That's always good for a few days. I heard Stance was coming home."

"Yeah. For the summer. We're excited. We haven't seen him in four years."

"Friend of Tokar, isn't he?"

Bomanz whirled. "Damn you! You never let up, do you?" He spoke softly, in genuine rage, without the shouts and curses and dramatic gestures of his habitual semi-rage.

"All right, Bo. I'll drop it."

"You'd better. You'd damned well better. I won't have you crawling all over him all summer. Won't have it, you hear?"

"I said I'd drop it."

8

The Barrowland

Corbie came and went at will around the Guard compound. The walls inside the headquarters building boasted several dozen old paintings of the Barrowland. He studied those often while he cleaned, shivering. His reaction was not unique. The Dominator's attempt to escape through Juniper had rocked the Lady's empire. Stories of his cruelties had fed upon themselves and grown fat in the centuries since the White Rose laid him down.

The Barrowland remained quiet. Those who watched saw nothing untoward. Morale rose. The old evil had shot its bolt.

But it waited.

It would wait throughout eternity if need be. It could not die. Its apparent last hope was no hope. The Lady was immortal, too. She would allow nothing to open her husband's grave.

The paintings recorded progressive decay. The latest dated from shortly after the Lady's resurrection. Even then the Barrowland had been much more whole.

Sometimes Corbie went to the edge of town, stared at the Great Barrow, shook his head.

Once there had been amulets which permitted Guards safely within the spells making the Barrowland lethal, to allow for upkeep. But those had disappeared. The Guard could but watch and wait now.

Time ambled. Slow and grey and limping, Corbie became a town fixture. He spoke seldom, but occasionally enlivened the lie sessions at Blue Willy with a wooly anecdote from the Forsberg campaigns. The fire blazed in his eyes then. No one doubted he had been there, even if he saw those days a little walleyed.

He made no true friends. Rumor said he did share the occasional private chess game with the Monitor, Colonel Sweet, for whom he had done some special small services. And of course, there was the recruit Case, who devoured his tales and accompanied him on his hobbling walks. Rumor said Corbie could read. Case hoped to learn.

No one ever visited the second floor of Corbie's home. There, in the heart of the night, he slowly unravelled the treacherous mare's nest of a tale that time and dishonesty had distorted out of any parallel with truth.

Only parts were encrypted. Most was hastily scribbled in TelleKurre, the principal language of the Domination era. But scattered passages were in UchiTelle, a TelleKurre regional vulgate. Times were, when battling those passages, Corbie smiled grimly. He might be the only man alive able to puzzle through those sometimes fragmentary sentences. "Benefit of a classical education," he would murmur with a certain sarcasm. Then he would become reflective, introspective. He would take one of his late night walks to shake revenant memory. One's own yesterday is a ghost that will not be laid. Death is the only exorcism.

He saw himself as a craftsman, did Corbie. A smith. An armorer cautiously forging a lethal sword. Like his predecessor in that house, he had dedicated his life to the search for a fragment of knowledge.

The winter was astonishing. The first snows came early, after an early and unusually damp autumn. It snowed often and heavily. Spring came late.

In the forests north of the Barrowland, where only scattered clans dwelt, life was harsh. Tribesmen appeared bearing furs to trade for food. Factors for the furriers of Oar were ecstatic.

Old folks called the winter a harbinger of worse to come. But old folks always see today's weather as more harsh than that of yore. Or milder. Never, never the same.

Spring sprung. A swift thaw set the creeks and rivers raging. The Great Tragic, which looped within three miles of the Barrowland, spread miles beyond its banks. It abducted tens and hundreds of thousands of trees. The flood was so spectacular that scores from town wandered out to watch it from a hilltop.

For most, the novelty faded. But Corbie limped out any day Case could accompany him. Case was yet possessed of dreams. Corbie indulged him.

"Why so interested in the river, Corbie?"

"I don't know. Maybe because of its grand statement."

"What?"

Corbie swung an encompassing hand. "The vastness. The ongoing rage. See how significant we are?" Brown water gnawed at the hill, furious, fumbling forests of driftwood. Less turbulent arms hugged the hill, probed the woods behind.

Case nodded. "Like the feeling I get when I look at the stars."

"Yes. Yes. But this is more personal. Closer to home. Not so?"

"I guess." Case sounded baffled. Corbie smiled. Legacy of a farm youth.

"Let's go back. It's peaked. But I don't trust it with those clouds rolling in."

Rain did threaten. Were the river to rise much more, the hill would become an island.

Case helped Corbie cross the boggy parts and up to the crest of the low rise which kept the flood from reaching cleared land. Much of that was a lake now, shallow enough to be waded if some fool dared. Under grey skies the Great Barrow stood out poorly, reflecting off the water as a dark lump. Corbie shuddered. "Case. He's still there."

The youth leaned on his spear, interested only because Corbie was interested. He wanted to get out of the drizzle.

"The Dominator, lad. Whatever else did not escape. Waiting. Filling with ever more hatred for the living."

Case looked at Corbie. The older man was taut with tension. He seemed frightened.

"If he gets loose, pity the world."

"But didn't the Lady finish him in Juniper?"

"She stopped him. She didn't destroy him. That may not be possible.... Well, it must be. He has to be vulnerable somehow. But if the White Rose couldn't harm him...."

"The Rose wasn't so strong, Corbie. She couldn't even hurt the Taken. Or even *their* minions. All she could do was bind and bury them. It took the Lady and the Rebel. . . ."

"The Rebel? I doubt that. *She* did it." Corbie lunged forward, forcing his leg. He marched along the edge of the lake. His gaze remained fixed on the Great Barrow.

Case feared Corbie was obsessed with the Barrowland. As a Guard, he had to be concerned. Though the Lady had exterminated the Resurrectionists in his grandfather's time, still that mound exerted its dark attraction. Monitor Sweet remained frightened someone would revive that idiocy. He wanted to caution Corbie, could think of no polite way to phrase himself.

Wind stirred the lake. Ripples ran from the Barrow toward them. Both shivered. "Wish this weather would break," Corbie muttered. "Time for tea?"

"Yes."

The weather continued chill and wet. Summer came late. Autumn arrived early. When the Great Tragic did at last recede, it left a mud plain strewn with the wrecks of grand trees. Its channel had shifted a half mile westward.

The woodland tribes continued selling furs.

Serendipity. Corbie was near done renovating. He was restoring a closet. In removing a wooden clothes rod he fumbled. The rod separated into parts when it hit the floor.

He knelt. He stared. His heart hammered. A slim spindle of white silk lay exposed. . . . Gently, gently, he put the rod back together, carried it upstairs.

Carefully, carefully, he removed the silk, unrolled it. His stomach knotted.

It was Bomanz's chart of the Barrowland, complete with notes about which Taken lay where, where fetishes were located and why, the puissance of protective spells, and a scatter of known resting places of minions of the Taken who had gone into the ground with their captains. A cluttered chart indeed. Mostly annotated in TelleKurre.

Also noted were burial sites outside the Barrowland proper. Most of the ordinary fallen had gone into mass graves.

The battle fired Corbie's imagination. For a moment he saw the Dominator's forces standing firm, dying to the last man. He saw wave after wave of the White Rose horde give themselves up to contain the shadow within the trap. Overhead, the Great Comet seared the sky, a vast flaming scimitar.

He could only imagine, though. There were no reliable histories.

He commiserated with Bomanz. Poor foolish little man, dreaming, seeking the truth. He had not earned his dark legend.

Corbie remained fixed over the chart all night, letting it seep into bone and soul. It did little to help him translate, but it did illuminate the Barrowland some. And even more, it illuminated a wizard so dedicated he had spent his entire adult life studying the Barrowland.

Dawn's light stirred Corbie. For a moment he doubted himself. Could he become prey to the same fatal passion?

The Plain of Fear

The Lieutenant himself stirred me out. "Elmo's back, Croaker. Eat some breakfast, then report to the conference room." He was a sour man getting sourer every day. Sometimes I regret having voted for him after the Captain died in Juniper. But the Captain wished it. It was his dying request.

"Be there soonest," I said, piling out without my customary growl. I grabbed clothing, stirred papers, silently mocked myself. How often did I doubt voting for the Captain himself? Yet when he wanted to resign, we did not let him.

My quarters look nothing like a physician's den. The walls are floor to ceiling with old books. I have read most, after having studied the languages in which they are written. Some are as old as the Company itself, recounting ancient histories. Some are noble genealogies, stolen from widely dispersed old temples and civil offices. The rarest, and most interesting, chronicle the rise and growth of the Domination.

The rarest of all are those in TelleKurre. The followers of the White Rose were not gentle victors. They burned books and cities, transported women and children, profaned ancient works of art and famous shrines. The customary afterglow of a great conflagration.

So there is little left to key one into the languages and thinking and history of the losers. Some of the most plainly written documents I possess remain totally inaccessible.

How I wish Raven were with us still, instead of dwelling among the dead men. He had a passing familiarity with written TelleKurre. Few outside the Lady's intimate circle do.

Goblin stuck his head in. "You coming or not?"

I cried on his shoulder. It was the old lament. No progress. He laughed. "Go blow in your girlfriend's ear. She might help."

"When will you guys let up?" It had been fifteen years since I wrote my last simpleminded romance about the Lady. That was before the long retreat which led the Rebel to his doom before the Tower at Charm. They do not let you forget.

"Never, Croaker. Never. Who else has spent the night with her? Who else goes carpet-flying with her?"

I would rather forget. Those were times of terror, not romance.

She became aware of my annalistic endeavors and asked me to show her side. More or less. She did not censor or dictate, but did insist I remain factual and impartial. I recall thinking she expected defeat, wanted an unbiased history set down somewhere.

Goblin glanced at the mound of documents. "You can't get any handle on it?"

"I don't think there is a handle. Everything I do translate turns out a big nothing. Somebody's expense record. An appointment calendar. A promotions list. A letter from some officer to a friend at court. Everything way older than what I'm looking for."

Goblin raised an eyebrow.

"I'll keep on trying." There was *something* there. We took them from Whisper, when she was a Rebel. They meant a lot to her. And our mentor then, Soulcatcher, thought them of empire-toppling significance.

Thoughtfully, Goblin remarked, "Sometimes the whole is greater than the sum of its parts. Maybe you should look for what ties it all together."

The thought had occurred to me. A name here, there, elsewhere, revealing the wake of someone through his or her earlier days. Maybe I would find it. The comet would not return for a long time.

But I had my doubts.

Darling is a young thing yet, just into her middle twenties. But the bloom of youth has abandoned her. Hard years have piled on hard years. There is little feminine about her. She had no chance to develop in that direction. Even after two years on the Plain none of us think of her as Woman.

She is tall, maybe two inches under six feet. Her eyes are a washed-out blue that often seems vacant, but they become swords of ice when she is thwarted. Her hair is blond, as from much exposure to the sun. Without continuous attention it hangs in straggles and strings. Not vain, she keeps it shorter than is stylish. In dress, too, she leans toward the utilitarian. Some first-time visitors are offended because she dresses so masculine. But she leaves them with no doubts that she can handle business.

Her role came to her unwanted, but she has made peace with it, has assumed it with stubborn determination. She shows a wisdom remarkable for her age, and for one handicapped as she is. Raven taught her well during those few years he was her guardian.

She was pacing when I arrived. The conference room is earth-sided, smoky, crowded even when empty. It smells of long occupation by too many unclean men. The old messenger from Oar was there. So were Tracker and Corder and several other outsiders. Most of the Company were present. I finger-signed a greeting. Darling gave me a sisterly hug, asked if I had any progress to report.

I spoke for the group and signed for her. "I am sure we don't have all the documents we found in the Forest of Cloud. Not just because I can't identify what I'm looking for, either. Everything I do have is too old."

Darling's features are regular. Nothing stands out. Yet you sense character, will, that this woman cannot be broken. She has been to Hell already. It did not touch her as a child. She will not be touched now.

She was not pleased. She signed, "We will not have the time we thought."

My attention was half elsewhere. I had hoped for sparks between Tracker and the other westerner. On a gut level I had responded negatively to Tracker. I found myself with an irrational hope for evidence to sustain that reaction.

Nothing.

Not surprising. The cell structure of the movement keeps our sympathizers insulated from one another.

Darling wanted to hear from Goblin and One-Eye next.

Goblin used his squeakiest voice. "Everything we heard is true. They are reinforcing their garrisons. But Corder can tell you better. For us, the mission was a bust. They were ready. They chased us all over the Plain. We were lucky to get away. We didn't get no help, either."

The menhirs and their weird pals are on our side, supposedly. Sometimes I wonder. They are unpredictable. They help or don't according to a formula only they understand.

Darling was little interested in details of the failed raid. She moved on to Corder. He said, "Armies are gathering on both sides of the Plain. Under command of the Taken."

"Taken?" I asked. I knew of only the two. He sounded like he meant many.

A chill then. There is a longtime rumor that the Lady has been quiet so long because she is raising a new crop of Taken. I had not believed it. The age is sorrowfully short of characters of the magnificently villainous vitality of those the

Dominator took in olden times: Soulcatcher, the Hanged Man, Nightcrawler, Shapeshifter, the Limper, and such. Those were nastymen of the grand scope, nearly as wild and hairy in their wickedness as the Lady and Dominator themselves. This is the era of the weak sister, excepting only Darling and Whisper.

Corder responded shyly. "The rumors are true, Lord."

Lord. Me. Because I stand near the heart of the dream. I hate it, yet eat it up. "Yes?"

"They may not be Stormbringers or Howlers, these new Taken." He smiled feebly. "Sir Tucker observed that the old Taken were wild devils as unpredictable as the lightning, and the new ones are the predictable tame thunder of bureaucracy. If you follow my meaning."

"I do. Go on."

"It is believed that there are six new ones, Lord. Sir Tucker believes they are about to be unleashed. Thus the great buildup around the Plain. Sir Tucker believes the Lady has made a competition of our destruction."

Tucker. Our most dedicated agent. One of the few survivors of the long siege of Rust. His hatred knows no bounds.

Corder had a strange look. A green-around-the-edges look. A look that said there was more, and all bad. "Well?" I said. "Spit it out."

"The names of the Taken have been enscribed on stelae raised in their respective demesnes. At Rust the army commander is named Benefice. His stela appeared after a carpet arrived by night. He has not actually been seen."

That bore investigation. Only the Taken can manage a carpet. But no carpet can reach Rust without crossing the Plain of Fear. The menhirs have reported no such passage. "Benefice? Interesting name. The others?"

"In Thud the stela bears the name Blister."

Chuckles. I said, "I liked it better when the names were descriptive. Like the Limper, Moonbiter, the Faceless Man."

"At Frost we have one called the Creeper."

"That's better." Darling gave me a cautionary look.

"At Rue there is one called Learned. And at Hull, one called Scorn."

"Scorn. I like that, too."

"The western bounds of the Plain are held by Whisper and Journey, both operating from a village called Spit."

Being a natural mathematical phenom, I summed and said, "That's five new ones and two old. Where is the other new one?"

"I don't know. The only other is the commander over all. His stela stands in the military compound outside Rust."

The way he said that abraded my nerves. He was pale. He started shaking. A premonition gripped me. I knew I would not like what he said next. But, "Well?"

"That stela bears the sigil of the Limper."

Right. So right. I did not like it at all.

The feeling was universal.

"Oh!" Goblin shrieked.

One-Eye said, "Holy shit," in a soft awed tone that was all the more meaningful for its reserve.

I sat down. Right there. Right in the middle of the floor. I folded my head in my hands. I wanted to cry. "Impossible," I said. "I killed him. With my own hands." And saying it, I did not believe it anymore, though I had had faith in that fact for years. "But how?"

"Can't keep a good man down," Elmo chided. That he was shaken was evidenced by the smart remark. Elmo says nothing gratuitously.

The feud between the Limper and the Company dates to our arrival north of the Sea of Torments, for it was then that we enlisted Raven, a mysterious native of Opal, a man of former high estate who had been done out of his titles and livings by minions of the Limper. Raven was as tough as they come, and utterly fearless. The robbery sanctioned by Taken or not, he struck back. He slew the villains, among them the Limper's most competent people. Then our path kept crossing the Limper's. Each time something worsened the weather between us. . . .

In the confusion after Juniper, Limper thought to settle with us. I engineered an ambush. He charged in. "I would have bet anything I killed him." I tell you, at that moment I was as rattled as ever I have been. I was on the precipice of panic.

One-Eye noticed. "Don't get hysterical, Croaker. We survived him before."

"He's one of the old ones, idiot! One of the real Taken. From times when they had real wizards. And he's never really been allowed to go full speed at us before. And with all that help." Eight Taken and five armies to assault the Plain of Fear. Seldom were there more than seventy of us here in the Hole.

My head filled with terrible visions. Those Taken might be second-rate, but they were so many. Their fury would fire the Plain. Whisper and the Limper have campaigned here before. They are not ignorant of the Plain's perils. In fact, Whisper battled here both as a Rebel and as Taken. She won most of the most famous battles of the eastern war.

Reason reasserted itself but did little to brighten tomorrow. Once I thought, I reached the inescapeable conclusion that Whisper knows the Plain too well. Might even have allies out here.

Darling touched my shoulder. That was more calming than any words from friends. Her confidence is contagious. She signed, "Now we know," and smiled.

Still, time has become a hanging hammer about to fall. The long wait for the comet has been rendered irrelevant. We have to survive right now. Trying for a bright side, I said, "The Limper's true name is somewhere in my document collection."

But that recalled my problem. "Darling, the specific document I want is not there."

She raised an eyebrow. Unable to speak, she has developed one of the most expressive faces I've ever seen.

"We have to have a sit-down. When you have time. To go over exactly what happened to those papers while Raven had them. Some are missing. They were there when I turned them over to Soulcatcher. They were there when I got them back from her. I am sure they were there when Raven took them. What happened to them later?"

"Tonight," she signed. "I will make time." She seemed distracted suddenly. Because I mentioned Raven? He meant a lot to her, but you'd think the edge would be off by now. Unless there was more to the story than I knew. And that was plenty possible. I really have no idea what their relationship became in the years after Raven left the Company. His death certainly bothers her still. Because it was so pointless. I mean, after surviving everything the shadow threw his way, he drowned in a public bath.

The Lieutenant says there are nights she cries herself to sleep. He does not know why, but he suspects Raven is at the root.

I have asked her about those years when they were on their own, but she will not tell the tale. The emotional impression I get is one of sorrow and grave disappointment.

She pushed her troubles away now, turned to Tracker and his mutt. Behind them, the men Elmo caught on the bluff squirmed. Their turn was coming. They knew the reputation of the Black Company.

But we did not get to them. Nor even to Tracker and Toadkiller Dog. For the watch above shrieked another alert.

This was getting tiresome.

The rider crossed the stream as I entered the coral. Water splashed. His mount staggered. It was covered with foam. Never again would it run well. It hurt me to see an animal so broken. But its rider had cause.

Two Taken darted about just beyond the bound of the null. One flung a violet bolt. It perished long before it reached us. One-Eye cackled and raised a middle finger. "Always wanted to do that."

"Oh, wonder of wonders," Goblin squeaked, looking the other way. A number of mantas, big blue-blacks, soared off the rosy bluffs, caught updrafts. Must have been a dozen, though they were hard to count, maneuvering as they did to avoid stealing one another's wind. These were giants of their kind. Their wings spanned almost a hundred feet. When they were high enough, they dove at the Taken in pairs.

The rider halted, fell. He had an arrow in his back. He remained conscious just long enough to gasp, "Tokens!"

The first manta pair, seeming to move with slow stately grace, though actually they streaked ten times faster than a man can run, ripped past the nearer Taken just inside Darling's null. Each loosed a brilliant lightning bolt. Lightning could speed where Taken witchery would not survive.

One bolt hit. Taken and carpet reeled, glowed briefly. Smoke appeared. The carpet twisted and spun earthward. We sent up a ragged cheer.

The Taken regained control, rose clumsily, drifted away.

I knelt by the messenger. He was little more than a boy. He was alive. He had a chance if I got to work. "A little help here, One-Eye."

Manta pairs ripped along the boundary of the null, blasting away at the second Taken. This one evaded effortlessly, did nothing to fight back. "That's Whisper," Elmo said.

"Yeah," I said. She knows her way around.

One-Eye grumbled, "You going to help this kid or not, Croaker?"

"All right. All right." I hated to miss the show. It was the first I had seen so many mantas, the first I had seen them support us. I wanted to see more.

"Well," said Elmo, while calming the boy's horse and going through his saddlebags, "another missive for our esteemed annalist." He proffered another oilskin packet. Baffled, I tucked it under my arm, then helped One-Eye carry the messenger down into the Hole.

10

Bomanz's Story

Croaker:

Jasmine's squeal rattled the windows and doors. "Bomanz! You come down here! Come down right now, you hear me?"

Bomanz sighed. A man couldn't get five minutes alone. What the hell did he get married for? Why did any man? You spent the rest of your life doing hard time, doing what other people wanted, not what you wanted.

"Bomanz!"

"I'm coming, dammit! Damned woman can't blow her nose without me there to hold her hand," he added sotto voce. He did a lot of talking under his breath. He had feelings to vent, and peace to maintain. He compromised. Always, he compromised.

He stamped downstairs, each footfall a declaration of irritation. He mocked himself as he went: You know you're getting old when everything aggravates you.

"What do you want? Where are you?"

"In the shop." There was an odd note in her voice. Suppressed excitement, he decided. He entered the shop warily.

"Surprise!"

His world came alive. Grouchiness deserted him. "Stance!" He flung himself at his son. Powerful arms crushed him. "Here already? We didn't expect you till next week."

"I got away early. You're getting pudgy, Pop." Stancil opened his arms to include Jasmine in a three-way hug.

"That's your mother's cooking. Times are good. We're eating regular. Tokar's been. . . ." He glimpsed a faded, ugly shadow. "So how are you? Back up. Let me look at you. You were still a boy when you left."

And Jasmine: "Doesn't he look great? So tall and healthy. And such nice clothes." Mock concern. "You haven't been up to any funny business, have you?"

"Mother! What could a junior instructor get up to?" He met his father's eye, smiled a smile that said "Same old Mom."

Stancil was four inches taller than his father, in his middle twenties, and looked athletic despite his profession. More like an adventurer than a would-be don, Bomanz thought. Of course, times changed. It had been eons since his own university days. Maybe standards had changed.

He recalled the laughter and pranks and all-night, dreadfully serious debates on the meaning of it all, and was bitten by an imp of nostalgia. What had become of that mentally quick, foxy young Bomanz? Some silent, unseen Guardsman of the mind had interred him in a barrow in the back of his brain, and there he lay dreaming, while a bald, jowly, potbellied gnome gradually usurped him. . . . They steal our yesterdays and leave us no youth but that of our children. . . .

"Well, come on. Tell us about your studies." Get out of that self-pitying mindset, Bomanz, you old fool. "Four years and nothing but letters about doing laundry and debates at the Stranded Dolphin. Stranded he would be in Oar. Before I die I want to see the sea. I never have." Old fool. Dream out loud and that's the best you can do? Would they really laugh if you told them the youth is still alive in there somewhere?

"His mind wanders," Jasmine explained.

"Who are you calling senile?" Bomanz snapped.

"Pop. Mom. Give me a break. I just got here."

Bomanz gobbled air. "He's right. Peace. Truce. Armistice. You referee, Stance. Two old warhorses like us are set in their ways."

Jasmine said, "Stance promised me a surprise before you came down."

"Well?" Bomanz asked.

"I'm engaged. To be married."

How can this be? This is my son. My baby. I was changing his diapers last week. . . . Time, thou unspeakable assassin, I feel thy cold breath. I hear thine iron-shod hooves. . . .

"Hmph. Young fool. Sorry. Tell us about her, since you won't tell us about anything else."

"I would if I could get a word in."

"Bomanz, be quiet. Tell us about her, Stance."

"You probably know something already. She's Tokar's sister, Glory."

Bomanz's stomach plunged to the level of his heels. Tokar's sister. Tokar, who might be a Resurrectionist.

"What's the matter now, Pop?"

"Tokar's sister, eh? What do you know about that family?"

"What's wrong with them?"

"I didn't say anything was. I asked you what you know about them."

"Enough to know I want to marry Glory. Enough to know Tokar is my best friend."

"Enough to know if they're Resurrectionists?"

Silence slammed into the shop. Bomanz stared at his son. Stancil stared back. Twice he started to respond, changed his mind. Tension rasped the air. "Pop. . . ."

"That's what Besand thinks. The Guard is watching Tokar. And me, now. It's the time of the comet, Stance. The tenth passage. Besand smells some big Resurrectionist plot. He's making life hard. This thing about Tokar will make it worse."

Stancil sucked spittle between his teeth. He sighed. "Maybe it was a mistake, coming home. I won't get anything done wasting time ducking Besand and fighting with you."

"No, Stance," Jasmine said. "Your father won't start anything. Bo, you weren't starting a fight. You're not going to start one."

"Uhm." My son engaged to a Resurrectionist? He turned away, took a deep breath, quietly berated himself. Jumping to conclusions. On word no better than Besand's. "Son, I'm sorry. He's been riding me." He glanced at Jasmine. Besand wasn't his only persecutor.

"Thanks, Pop. How's the research coming?"

Jasmine grumbled and muttered. Bomanz said, "This conversation is crazy. We're all asking questions and nobody is answering."

"Give me some money, Bo," Jasmine said.

"What for?"

"You two won't say hello before you start your plotting. I might as well go marketing."

Bomanz waited. She eschewed her arsenal of pointed remarks about Woman's lot. He shrugged, dribbled coins into her palm. "Let's go upstairs, Stance."

"She's mellowed," Stancil said as they entered the attic room.

"I hadn't noticed."

"So have you. But the house hasn't changed."

Bomanz lighted the lamp. "Cluttered as ever," he admitted. He grabbed his hiding spear. "Got to make a new one of these. It's getting worn." He spread his chart on the little table.

"Not much improvement, Pop."

"Get rid of Besand." He tapped the sixth barrow. "Right there. The only thing standing in my way."

"That route the only option, Pop? Could you get the top two? Or even one. That would leave you a fifty-fifty chance of guessing the other two."

"I don't guess. This isn't a card game. You can't deal a new hand if you play your first one wrong."

Stancil took the one chair, stared at the chart. He drummed the tabletop with his fingers. Bomanz fidgeted.

A week passed. The family settled into new rhythms, including living with the Monitor's intensified surveillance.

Bomanz was cleaning a weapon from the TelleKurre site. A trove, that was. A veritable trove. A mass burial, with weapons and armor almost perfectly preserved. Stancil entered the shop. Bomanz looked up. "Rough night?"

"Not bad. He's ready to give up. Only came round once."

"Men fu or Besand?"

"Men fu. Besand was there a half dozen times."

They were working shifts. Men fu was the public excuse. In reality, Bomanz hoped to wear Besand down before the comet's return. It was not working.

"Your mother has breakfast ready." Bomanz began assembling his pack.

"Wait up, Pop. I'll go too."

"You need to rest."

"That's all right. I feel like digging."

"Okay." Something was bothering the boy. Maybe he was ready to talk.

They'd never done much of that. Their pre-university relationship had been one of confrontation, with Stance always on the defensive. . . . He had grown, these four years, but the boy was still there inside. He was not yet ready to face his father man-to-man. And Bomanz had not grown enough to forget that Stancil was his little boy. Those growths sometimes never come. One day the son is looking back at his own son, wondering what happened.

Bomanz resumed rubbing flakes off a mace. He sneered at himself. Thinking about relationships. This isn't like you, you old coot.

"Hey, Pop," Stance called from the kitchen. "Almost forgot. I spotted the comet last night."

A claw reached in and grabbed a handful of Bomanz's guts. The comet! Couldn't be. Not already. He was not ready for it.

Nervy little bastard," Bomanz spat. He and Stancil knelt in the brush, watching Men fu toss artifacts from their diggings. "I ought to break his leg."

"Wait here a minute. I'll circle around and cut him off when he runs."

Bomanz snorted. "Not worth the trouble."

"It's worth it to me, Pop. Just to keep the balance."

"All right." Bomanz watched Men fu pop up to look around, ugly little head jerking like that of a nervous pigeon. He dropped back into the excavation. Bomanz stalked forward.

He drew close enough to hear the thief talking to himself. "Oh. Lovely.

Lovely. A stone fortune. Stone fortune. That fat little ape don't deserve it. All the time sucking up to Besand. That creep."

"Fat little ape? You asked for it." Bomanz shed his pack and tools, got a firm grip on his spade.

Men fu came up out of the pit, his arms filled. His eyes grew huge. His mouth worked soundlessly.

Bomanz wound up.

"Now Bo, don't be. . . ."

Bomanz swung. Men fu danced, took the blow on his hip, squawked, dropped his burden, flailed the air, and toppled into the pit. He scrambled out the far side, squealing like a wounded hog. Bomanz wobbled after him, landed a mighty stroke across his behind. Men fu ran. Bomanz charged after him, spade high, yelling, "Stand still, you thieving son-of-a-bitch! Take it like a man."

He took a last mighty swing. It missed. It flung him around. He fell, bounced back up, continued the chase sans avenging spade.

Stancil threw himself into Men fu's way. The thief put his head down and bulled through. Bomanz ploughed into Stancil. Father and son rolled in a tangle of limbs.

Bomanz gasped, "What the hell? He's gone now." He sprawled on his back, panted. Stancil started laughing. "What's so damned funny?"

"The look on his face."

Bomanz sniggered. "You weren't much help." They guffawed. Finally, Bomanz gasped, "I'd better find my spade."

Stancil helped his father stand. "Pop, I wish you could have seen yourself."

"Glad I didn't. Lucky I didn't have a stroke." He lapsed into a fit of giggles.

"You all right, Pop?"

"Sure. Just can't laugh and catch my breath at the same time. Oh. Oh, my. I won't be able to move again if I sit down."

"Let's go dig. That'll keep you loose. You dropped the spade around here, didn't you?"

"There it is."

The giggles haunted Bomanz all morning. He would recall Men fu's flailing retreat and his self-control would go.

"Pop?" Stancil was working the far side of the pit. "Look here. This may be why he didn't notice you coming."

Bomanz limped over, watched Stancil brush loose soil off a perfectly preserved breastplate. It was as black and shiny as rubbed ebony. An ornate ornament in silver bossed its center. "Uhm." Bomanz popped out of the pit. "Nobody around. That half-man, half-beast design. That's Shapeshifter."

"He led the TelleKurre."

"He wouldn't be buried here, though."

"It's his armor, Pop."

"I can see that, dammit." He popped up like a curious groundhog. No one in sight. "Sit up here and keep watch. I'll dig it out."

"You sit, Pop."

"You were up all night."

"I'm a lot younger than you are."

"I'm feeling just fine, thank you."

"What color is the sky, Pop?"

"Blue. What kind of question. . . ."

"Hallelujah. We agree on something. You're the most contrary old goat. . . ."

"Stancil!"

"Sorry, Pop. We'll take turns. Flip a coin to see who goes first."

Bomanz lost. He settled down with his pack as a backrest. "Going to have to spread the dig out. Going straight down like this, it'll cave in first heavy rain."

"Yeah. Be a lot of mud. Ought to think about a drainage trench. Hey, Pop, there's nobody in this thing. Looks like the rest of his armor, too." Stancil had recovered a gauntlet and uncovered part of a greave.

"Yeah? I hate to turn it in."

"Turn it in? Why? Tokar could get a fortune for it."

"Maybe so. But what if friend Men fu did spot it? He'll tell Besand out of spite. We've got to stay on his good side. We don't *need* this stuff."

"Not to mention he might have planted it."

"What?"

"It shouldn't be here, right? And no body inside the armor. And the soil is loose."

Bomanz grunted. Besand was capable of a frame. "Leave everything the way it is. I'll go get him."

Sour-faced old fart," Stancil muttered as the Monitor departed. "I bet he did plant it."

"No sense cussing. We can't do anything." Bomanz settled against his pack.

"What're you doing?"

"Loafing. I don't feel like digging anymore." He ached all over. It had been a busy morning.

"We should get what we can while the weather is good."

"Go ahead."

"Pop. . . ." Stancil thought better of it. "How come you and Mom fight all the time?"

Bomanz let his thoughts drift. The truth was elusive. Stance would not remember the good years. "I guess because people change and we don't want them to." He could find no better words. "You start out with a woman; she's magical and mysterious and marvelous, the way they sing it. Then you get to know each other. The excitement goes away. It gets comfortable. Then even that fades. She starts to sag and turn grey and get lined and you feel cheated. You remember the fey, shy one you met and talked with till her father threatened to plant a boot in your ass. You resent this stranger. So you take a poke. I guess it's the same for your mother. Inside, I'm still twenty, Stance. Only if I pass a mirror, or if my body won't do what I want, do I realize that I'm an old man. I don't see the potbelly and the varicose veins and the grey hair where I've got any left. She has to live with it.

"Every time I see a mirror I'm amazed. I end up wondering who's taken over the outside of me. A disgusting old goat, from the look of him. The kind I used to snicker at when I was twenty. He scares me, Stance. He looks like a dying man. I'm trapped inside him, and I'm not ready to go."

Stancil sat down. His father never talked about his feelings. "Does it have to be that way?"

Maybe not, but it always is. . . . "Thinking about Glory, Stance? I don't know. You can't get out of getting old. You can't get out of having a relationship change."

"Maybe none of it has to be. If we manage this. . . ."

"Don't tell me about maybes, Stance. I've been living on maybes for thirty years." His ulcer took a sample nibble from his gut. "Maybe Besand is right. For the wrong reasons."

"Pop! What are you talking about? You've given your whole life to this."

"What I'm saying, Stance, is that I'm scared. It's one thing to chase a dream. It's another to catch it. You never get what you expect. I have a premonition of disaster. The dream might be stillborn."

Stancil's expression ran through a series of changes. "But you've got to. . . ."

"I don't have to do anything but be Bomanz the antiquary. Your mother and I don't have much longer. This dig should yield enough to keep us."

"If you went ahead, you'd have a lot more years and a lot more. . . ."

"I'm scared, Stance. Of going either way. That happens when you get older. Change is threatening."

"Pop. . . ."

"I'm talking about the death of dreams, son. About losing the big, wild make-believes that keep you going. The impossible dreams. That kind of jolly pretend is dead. For me. All I can see is rotten teeth in a killer's smile."

Stancil hoisted himself out of the pit. He plucked a strand of sweetgrass, sucked it while gazing into the sky. "Pop, how did you feel right before you married Mom?"

"Numb."

Stancil laughed. "Okay, how about when you went to ask her father? On the way there?"

"I thought I was going to dribble down my leg. You never met your grandfather. He's the one who got them started telling troll stories."

"Something like you feel now?"

"Something. Yes. But it's not the same. I was younger, and I had a reward to look forward to."

"And you don't now? Aren't the stakes bigger?"

"Both ways. Win or lose."

"Know what? You're having what they call a crisis of self-confidence. That's all. Couple of days and you'll be raring to go again."

That evening, after Stancil had gone out, Bomanz told Jasmine, "That's a wise boy we've got. We talked today. Really talked, for the first time. He surprised me."

"Why? He's your son, isn't he?"

The dream came stronger than ever before, more quickly than ever. It wakened Bomanz twice in one night. He gave up trying to sleep. He went and sat on the front stoop, taking in the moonlight. The night was bright. He could make out rude buildings along the dirty street.

Some town, he thought, remembering the glories of Oar. The Guard, us antiquaries, and a few people who scratch a living serving us and the pilgrims. Hardly any of those anymore, even with the Domination fashionable. The Barrowland is so disreputable nobody wants to look at it.

He heard footsteps. A shadow approached. "Bo?"

"Besand?"

"Uhm." The Monitor settled on the next step down. "What're you doing?"

"Couldn't sleep. Been thinking about how the Barrowland has gotten so blighted even self-respecting Resurrectionists don't come here anymore. You? You're not taking the night patrol yourself, are you?"

"Couldn't sleep either. That damned comet."

Bomanz searched the sky.

"Can't see it from here. Have to go around back. You're right. Nobody knows we're here anymore. Us or those things in the ground over there. I don't know what's worse. Neglect or plain stupidity."

"Uhm?" Something was gnawing at the Monitor.

"Bo, they're not replacing me because I'm old or incompetent, though I guess I'm enough of both. They're moving me out so somebody's nephew can have a post. An exile for a black sheep. That hurts, Bo. That really hurts. They've forgotten what this place is. They're telling me I wasted my whole life doing a job any idiot can sleep his way through."

"The world is full of fools."

"Fools die."

"Eh?"

"They laugh when I talk about the comet or about Resurrectionists striking this summer. They can't believe that I believe. They don't believe there's anything under those mounds. Not anything still alive."

"Bring them out here. Walk them through the Barrowland after dark."

"I tried. They told me to quit whining if I wanted a pension."

"You've done all you can, then. It's on their heads."

"I took an oath, Bo. I was serious about it then, and I'm serious now. This job is all I have. You've got Jasmine and Stance. I might as well have been a monk. Now they're discarding me for some young . . ." He began making strange noises.

Sobs? Bomanz thought. From the Monitor? From this man with a heart of flint and all the mercy of a shark? He took Besand's elbow. "Let's go look at the comet. I haven't seen it yet."

Besand got hold of himself. "You haven't? That's hard to believe."

"Why? I haven't been up late. Stancil has done the night work."

"Never mind. Slipping into my antagonistic character again. We should've been lawyers, you and I. We've got the argumentative turn of mind."

"You could be right. Spent a lot of time lately wondering what I'm doing out here."

"What *are* you doing here, Bo?"

"I was going to get rich. I was going to study the old books, open a few rich graves, go back to Oar and buy into my uncle's drayage business." Idly, Bomanz wondered how much of his faked past Besand accepted. He had lived it so long that he now remembered some fraudulent anecdotes as factual unless he thought hard.

"What happened?"

"Laziness. Plain old-fashioned laziness. I found out there's a big difference between dreaming and getting in there and doing. It was easier to dig just enough to get by and spend the rest of the time loafing." Bomanz made a sour face. He was striking near the truth. His researches were, in fact, partly an excuse for not competing. He simply did not have the drive of a Tokar.

"You haven't had too bad a life. One or two hard winters when Stancil was a pup. But we all went through those. A helping hand here or there and we all survived. There she is." Besand indicated the sky over the Barrowland.

Bomanz gasped. It was exactly what he had seen in his dreams. "Showy, isn't it?"

"Wait till it gets close. It'll fill half the sky."

"Pretty, too."

"Stunning, I'd say. But also a harbinger. An ill omen. The old writers say it'll keep returning till the Dominator is freed."

"I've lived with that stuff most of my life, Besand, and even I find it hard to believe there's anything to it. Wait! I get that spooky feeling around the Barrowland, too. But I just can't believe those creatures could rise again after four hundred years in the ground."

"Bo, maybe you are honest. If you are, take a hint. When I leave, you leave. Take the TelleKurre stuff and head for Oar."

"You're starting to sound like Stance."

"I mean it. Some idiot unbeliever kid takes over here, all Hell is going to break loose. Literally. Get out while you can."

"You could be right. I'm thinking about going back. But what would I do? I don't know Oar anymore. The way Stance tells it, I'd get lost. Hell, this is home now. I never really realized that. This dump is home."

"I know what you mean."

Bomanz looked at that great silver blade in the sky. Soon now. . . .

"What's going on out there? Who is that?" came from Bomanz's back door. "You clear off, hear? I'll have the Guard after you."

"It's me, Jasmine."

Besand laughed. "And the Monitor, mistress. The Guard is here already."

"Bo, what're you doing?"

"Talking. Looking at the stars."

"I'll be getting along," Besand said. "See you tomorrow." From his tone Bomanz knew tomorrow would be a day of normal harassments.

"Take care." He settled on the dewy back step, let the cool night wash over him. Birds called in the Old Forest, their voices lonely. A cricket chirruped optimistically. Humid air barely stirred the remnants of his hair. Jasmine came out and sat beside him. "Couldn't sleep," he told her.

"Me either."

"Must be going around." He glanced at the comet, was startled by an instant of déjà vu. "Remember the summer we came here? When we stayed up to see the comet? It was a night like this."

She took his hand, entwined her fingers with his. "You're reading my mind. Our first month anniversary. Those were fool kids, those two."

"They still are, inside."

11

The Barrowland

For Corbie the unravelling came quickly now. When he kept his mind on business. But more and more he became distracted by that old silk map. Those strange old names. In TelleKurre they had a ring absent in modern tongues. Soulcatcher. Stormbringer. Moonbiter. The Hanged Man. They seemed so much more potent in the old tongue.

But they were dead. The only great ones left were the Lady and the monster who started it all, out there under the earth.

Often he went to a small window and stared toward the Barrowland. The devil in the earth. Calling, perhaps. Surrounded by lesser champions, few of them recalled in the legends and few the old wizard identified. Bomanz had been interested only in the Lady.

So many fetishes. And a dragon. And fallen champions of the White Rose, their shades set to eternal guard duty. It seemed so much more dramatic than the struggle today.

Corbie laughed. The past was always more interesting than the present. For those who lived through the first great struggle it must have seemed deadly slow, too. Only in the final battle were the legends and legacies created. A few days out of decades.

He worked less now, now that he had a sound place to live and a little saved. He spent more time wandering, especially by night.

Case came calling one morning, before Corbie was fully wakened. He allowed the youth inside. "Tea?"

"All right."

"You're nervous. What is it?"

"Colonel Sweet wants you."

"Chess again? Or work?"

"Neither. He's worried about your wandering around at night. I told him I go with you and all you do is look at the stars and stuff. Guess he's getting paranoid."

Corbie smiled a smile he did not feel. "Just doing his job. Guess my life looks odd. Getting past it. Lost in my own mind. Do I act senile sometimes? Here. Sugar?"

"Please." Sugar was a treat. The Guard could not provide it.

"Any rush? I haven't eaten."

"He didn't put it that way."

"Good." More time to prepare. Fool. He should have guessed his walks would attract attention. The Guard was paranoid by design.

Corbie prepared oats and bacon, which he shared with Case. For all they were well paid, the Guard ate poorly. Because of ongoing foul weather the Oar road was all but impassable. The army quartermasters strove valiantly but often could not get through.

"Well, let's see the man," Corbie said. And: "That's the last bacon. The Colonel better think about farming here, just in case."

"They talked about it." Corbie had befriended Case partly because he served at headquarters. Colonel Sweet would play chess and talk old times, but he never revealed any plans.

"And?"

"Not enough land. Not enough fodder."

"Pigs. They get fat on acorns."

"Need herdsmen. Else the tribemen would get them."

"I guess so."

The Colonel ushered Corbie into his private quarters. Corbie joked, "Don't you ever work? Sir?"

"The operation runs itself. Been rolling four centuries, that's the way it goes. I have a problem, Corbie."

Corbie grimaced. "Sir?"

"Appearances, Corbie. This is a world that lives by perceptions. You aren't presenting a proper appearance."

"Sir?"

"We had a visitor last month. From Charm."

"I didn't know that."

"Neither did anyone else. Except me. What you might call a prolonged surprise inspection. They happen occasionally." Sweet settled behind his worktable, pushed aside the chess set over which they had contested so often. He drew a long sheet of southern paper from a cubby at his right knee. Corbie glimpsed printing in a crabbed hand.

"Taken? Sir?"

Corbie never sirred anyone except as an afterthought. The habit disturbed Sweet. "Yes. With the Lady's carte blanche. He did not abuse it. But he did make recommendations. And he did mention people whose behavior he found unacceptable. Your name was first on the list. What the hell are you doing, wandering around all night?"

"Thinking. I can't sleep. The war did something. The things I saw. . . . The guerrillas. You don't want to go to sleep because *they* might attack. If you do sleep, you dream about the blood. Homes and fields burning. Animals and children screaming. That was the worst. The babies crying. I still hear the babies crying." He exaggerated very little. Each time he went to bed he had to get past the crying of babes.

He told most of the truth and wound it into an imaginative lie. Babies crying. The babies who haunted him were his own, innocents abandoned in a moment of fear of commitment.

"I know," Sweet replied. "I know. At Rust they killed their children rather than let us capture them. The hardest men in the regiment wept when they saw the mothers hurling their infants down from the walls, then jumping after them. I never married. I have no children. But I know what you mean. Did you have any?"

"A son," Corbie said, in a voice both soft and strained, from a body almost shaking with pain. "And a daughter. Twins, they were. Long ago and far away."

"And what became of them?"

"I don't know. I would hope they're living still. They would be about Case's age."

Sweet raised an eyebrow but let the remark slide past. "And their mother?"

Corbie's eyes became iron. Hot iron, like a brand. "Dead."

"I'm sorry."

Corbie did not respond. His expression suggested he was not sorry himself.

"You understand what I'm saying, Corbie?" Sweet asked. "You were noticed by one of the Taken. That's never healthy."

"I get the message. Which was it?"

"I can't say. Which of the Taken are where when could be of interest to the Rebel."

Corbie snorted. "What Rebel? We wiped them out at Charm."

"Perhaps. But there is that White Rose."

"I thought they were going to get her?"

"Yeah. The stories you hear. Going to have her in chains before the month is out. Been saying that since first we heard of her. She's light on her feet. Maybe light enough." Sweet's smile faded. "At least I won't be around next time the comet comes. Brandy?"

"Yes."

"Chess? Or do you have a job?"

"Not right away. I'll go you one game."

Halfway through, Sweet said, "Remember what I said. Eh? The Taken claimed he was leaving. But there's no guarantee. Could be behind a bush someplace watching."

"I'll pay more attention to what I'm doing."

He would. The last thing he wanted was a Taken interested in *him.* He had come too far to waste himself now.

12

The Plain of Fear

I had the watch. My belly gnawed, weighted by lead. All day dots had traversed the sky, high up. A pair were there now, patroling. The continuous presence of Taken was not a good omen.

Closer, two manta pairs planed the afternoon air. They would ride the updrafts up, then circle down, taunting the Taken, trying to lure them across the boundary. They resented outsiders. The more so these, because these would crush them but for Darling—another intruder.

Walking trees were on the move beyond the creek. The dead menhirs glistened, somehow changed from their usual dullness. Things were happening on the Plain. No outsider could comprehend their import fully.

One great shadow clung to the desert. Way up there, daring the Taken, a lone windwhale hovered. An occasional, barely perceptible bass roar tumbled down. I'd never heard one talk before. They do so only when enraged.

A breeze muttered and whimpered in the coral. Old Father Tree sang counterpoint to the windwhale.

A menhir spoke behind me. "Your enemies come soon." I shivered. It recalled the flavor of a nightmare I have been having lately. I can recall no specifics afterward, only that it is filled with terror.

I refused to be unsettled by the sneaky stone. Much.

What are they? Where did they come from? Why are they different from normal stones? For that matter, why is the Plain ridiculously different? Why so bellicose? We are here on sufferance only, allied against a greater enemy. Shatter the Lady and see how our friendship prospers.

"How soon?"

"When they are ready."

"Brilliant, old stone. Positively illuminating."

My sarcasm did not go unnoticed, just unremarked. The menhirs have their own flare for sarcasm and the sharp-edged tongue.

"Five armies," said the voice. "They will not wait long."

I indicated the sky. "The Taken cruise at will. Unchallenged."

"They have not challenged." True. But a weak excuse. Allies should be allies. More, windwhales and mantas usually consider appearance on the Plain sufficient challenge. It occurred to me the Taken might have bought them off.

"Not so." The menhir had moved. Its shadow now fell across my toes. I finally looked. This one was just ten feet tall. A real runt.

It had guessed my thought. Damn.

It continued telling me what I already knew. "It is not possible to deal from a position of strength always. Take care. There has been a call to the Peoples to reassess your acceptance on the Plain."

So. This overtalkative hunk was an emissary. The natives were scared. Some thought they could save themselves trouble by booting us out.

"Yes."

"The Peoples" doesn't properly describe the parliament of species that makes decisions here, but I know no better title.

If the menhirs are to be believed—and they lie only by omission or indirection—over forty intelligent species inhabit the Plain of Fear. Those I know include menhirs, walking trees, windwhales and mantas, a handful of humans (both primitives and hermits), two kinds of lizard, a bird like a buzzard, a giant white bat, and an extremely scarce critter that looks like a camel-centaur put together backward. I mean, the humanoid half is behind. The creature runs toward what most would take as its fanny.

No doubt I have encountered others without recognizing them.

Goblin says there is a tiny rock monkey that lives in the hearts of the great coral reefs. He claims it looks like a miniature One-Eye. But Goblin is not to be trusted where One-Eye is concerned.

"I am charged with delivering a warning," the menhir said. "There are strangers on the Plain."

I asked questions. When it did not answer I turned irritably. It was gone. "Damned stone. . . ."

Tracker and his mutt stood in the mouth of the Hole, watching the Taken.

Darling interviewed Tracker thoroughly, I'm told. I missed that. She was satisfied.

I had an argument with Elmo. Elmo liked Tracker. "Reminds me of Raven," he said. "We could use a few hundred Ravens."

"Reminds *me* of Raven, too. And that's what I don't like." But what good arguing? We cannot always like everyone. Darling thinks he is all right. Elmo thinks so. The Lieutenant accepts him. Why should I be different? Hell, if he is from the same mold as Raven, the Lady is in trouble.

He will be tested soon enough. Darling has something in mind. Something preemptive, I suspect. Possibly toward Rust.

Rust. Where the Limper had raised his stella.

The Limper. Back from the dead. I did everything but burn the body. Should have done that, I guess. Bloody hell.

The scary part is wondering if he is the only one. Did others survive apparent certain death? Are they hidden away now, waiting to astound the world?

A shadow fell across my feet. I returned to the living. Tracker stood beside me. "You look distressed," he said. He did show one every courtesy, I must admit.

I looked toward those patroling reminders of the struggle. I said, "I am a soldier, grown old and tired and confused. I have been fighting since before you were born. And I have yet to see anything gained."

He smiled a thin, almost secretive smile. It made me uncomfortable. Everything he did made me uncomfortable. Even his damned dog made me uncomfortable, and it did nothing but sleep. Much as it loafed, how had it managed the journey from Oar? Too much like work. I swear, that dog won't even get in a hurry to eat.

"Be of good faith, Croaker," Tracker said. "She *will* fall." He spoke with absolute conviction. "She hasn't the strength to tame the world."

There was that scariness again. True or not, the way he expressed the sentiment was disturbing.

"We'll bring them all down." He indicated the Taken. "They aren't real, like those of old."

Toadkiller Dog sneezed on Tracker's boot. He looked down. I thought he would kick the mutt. But instead he bent to scratch the dog's ear.

"Toadkiller Dog. What kind of name is that?"

"Oh, it's an old joke. From when we were both a lot younger. He took a shine to it. Insists on it now."

Tracker seemed only half there. His eyes were vacant, his gaze far away, though he continued to watch the Taken. Weird.

At least he admitted to having been young. There was a hint of human vulnerability in that. It is the apparent invulnerability of characters like Tracker and Raven that rattles me.

13

The Plain of Fear

"Yo! Croaker!" The Lieutenant had come outside.

"What?"

"Let Tracker cover you." I had only minutes left in my watch. "Darling wants you."

I glanced at Tracker. He shrugged. "Go ahead." He assumed a stance facing westward. I swear, it was like he turned the vigilance on. As though on the instant he became the ultimate sentinel.

Even Toadkiller Dog opened an eye and went to watching.

I brushed the dog's scalp with my fingers as I left, what I thought a friendly gesture. He growled. "Be like that," I said, and joined the Lieutenant.

He seemed disturbed. Generally, he is a cold customer. "What is it?"

"She's got one of her wild hairs."

Oh, boy. "What?"

"Rust."

"Oh yeah! Brilliant! Get it all over with fast! I thought that was just talk. I trust you tried to argue her out of it?"

You would think a man would grow accustomed to stench after having lived with it for years. But as we descended into the Hole my nose wrinkled and tightened. You just can't keep a bunch of people stuffed in a pit without ventilation. We have precious little.

"I tried. She says, 'Load the wagon. Let me worry about the mule being blind.' "

"She's right most of the time."

"She's a damned military genius. But that don't mean she can pull off any cockamamie scheme she dreams up. Some dreams are nightmares. Hell, Croaker. The Limper is out there."

Which is where we started when we reached the conference room. Silent and I bore the brunt because we are Darling's favorites. Seldom do I see such unanimity among my brethren. Even Goblin and One-Eye spoke with a single voice, and those two will fight over whether it is night or day with the sun at high noon.

Darling prowled like a caged beast. She had doubts. They nagged her.

"Two Taken in Rust," I argued. "That's what Corder said. One of them our oldest and nastiest enemy."

"Break them and we will shatter their entire plan of campaign," she countered.

"Break them? Girl, you're talking about the Limper. I proved he is invincible before."

"No. You proved that he will survive unless you are thorough. You might have burned him."

Yeah. Or cut him into pieces and fed him to the fish, or given him a swim in a vat of acid or a dust bath in quicklime. But those things take time. We had the Lady herself coming down on us. We barely got away as it was.

"Assuming we can get there undetected—which I do not believe for a moment—and manage total surprise, how long before all the Taken get on us?" I signed vigorously, more angry than frightened. I never refuse Darling, ever. But this time I was ready.

Her eyes flashed. For the first time ever I saw her battle her temper. She signed, "If you will not accept orders you should not be here. I am not the Lady. I do not sacrifice pawns for small gain. I agree, there is great risk in this operation. But far less than you argue. With potential impact far greater than you suppose."

"Convince me."

"That I cannot do. If you are captured, you must not know."

I was primed. "You just telling me that is enough for the Taken to get on a trail." Maybe I was more scared than I could admit. Or maybe it was just an all-time case of the contraries.

"No," she signed. There was something more, but she held it back.

Silent dropped a hand on my shoulder. He had given up. The Lieutenant joined him. "You're overstepping yourself, Croaker."

Darling repeated, "If you will not accept orders, Croaker, leave."

She meant it. Really! I stood with mouth open, stunned.

"All right!" I stamped out. I went to my quarters, shuffled those obstinate old papers and, of course, found not a damned thing new.

They left me alone for a while. Then Elmo came. He did not announce himself. I just glanced up and found him leaning against the door frame. By then I was half ashamed of my performance. "Yeah?"

"Mail call," he said, and tossed me another of those oilskin packets.

I snapped it out of the air. He departed without explaining its appearance. I placed it on my worktable, wondered. Who? I knew no one in Oar.

Was it some sort of trick?

The Lady is patient and clever. I would not put past her some grand maneuver using me.

I guess I must have thought about it an hour before, reluctantly, I opened the packet.

14

The Story of Bomanz

Croaker:

Bomanz and Tokar stood in one corner of the shop. "What do you think?" Bomanz asked. "Bring a good price?"

Tokar stared at the *pièce de résistance* of Bomanz's new TelleKurre collection, a skeleton in perfectly restored armor. "It's marvelous, Bo. How did you do it?"

"Wired the joints together. See the forehead jewel? I'm not up on Domination heraldry, but wouldn't a ruby mean somebody important?"

"A king. That would be the skull of King Broke."

"His bones, too. And armor."

"You're rich, Bo. I'll just take a commission on this one. A wedding present to the family. You took me serious when I said come up with something good."

"The Monitor confiscated the best. We had Shapeshifter's armor."

Tokar had brought helpers this trip, a pair of hulking gorilla teamsters. They were carrying antiques to wagons outside. Their back-and-forth made Bomanz nervous.

"Really? Damn! I'd give my left arm for that."

Bomanz spread his hands apologetically. "What could I do? Besand keeps me on a short leash. Anyway, you know my policy. I'm stretching it to deal with a future daughter-in-law's brother."

"How's that?"

Stuck my foot in it now, Bomanz thought. He ploughed ahead. "Besand has heard you're a Resurrectionist. Stance and I are getting a hard time."

"Now that's sick. I'm sorry, Bo. Resurrectionist! I shot my mouth off once, years ago, and said even the Dominator would be better for Oar than our clown Mayor. One stupid remark! They never let you forget. It's not enough that they hounded my father into an early grave. Now they have to torment me and my friends."

Bomanz had no idea what Tokar was talking about. He would have to ask Stance. But it reassured him; which was all he really wanted.

"Tokar, keep the profits from this lot. For Stance and Glory. As my wedding present. Have they set a date?"

"Nothing definite. After his sabbatical and thesis. Come winter, I guess. Thinking about coming down?"

"Thinking about moving back to Oar. I don't have enough fight left to break in a new Monitor."

Tokar chuckled. "Probably won't be much call for Domination artifacts after this summer anyway. I'll see if I can find you a place. You do work like the king here, you won't have trouble making a living."

"You really like it? I was thinking about doing his horse, too." Bomanz felt a surge of pride in his craftsmanship.

"Horse? Really? They buried his horse with him?"

"Armor and all. I don't know who put the TelleKurre in the ground, but they didn't loot. We've got a whole box of coins and jewelry and badges."

"Domination coinage? That's hotter than hot. Most of it was melted down. A Domination coin in good shape can bring fifty times its metal value."

"Leave King Whosis here. I'll put his horse together for him. Pick him up next trip."

"I won't be long, either. I'll unload and zip right back. Where's Stance, anyway? I wanted to say hello." Tokar waved one of those leather wallets.

"Glory?"

"Glory. She ought to write romances. Going to break me, buying paper."

"He's out to the dig. Let's go. Jasmine! I'm taking Tokar out to the dig."

During the walk Bomanz kept glancing over his shoulder. The comet was now so bright it could be seen, barely, by day. "Going to be one hell of a sight when it peaks out," he predicted.

"I expect so." Tokar's smile made Bomanz nervous. I'm imagining, he told himself.

Stancil used his back to open the shop door. He dumped a load of weapons. "We're getting mined out, Pop. Pretty much all common junk last night."

Bomanz twisted a strand of copper wire, wriggled out of the framework supporting the horse skeleton. "Then let Men fu take over. Not much more room here anyway."

The shop was almost impassable. Bomanz would not have to dig for years, were that his inclination.

"Looking good," Stance said of the horse, tarrying before going for another armful from a borrowed cart. "You'll have to show me how to get the king on top so I can put them together when I go back."

"I may do it myself."

"Thought you'd decided to stay."

"Maybe. I don't know. When are we going to start that thesis?"

"I'm working on it. Making notes. Once I get organized I can write it up like that." He snapped his fingers. "Don't worry. I've got plenty of time." He went outside again.

Jasmine brought tea. "I thought I heard Stance."

Bomanz jerked his head. "Outside."

She looked for a place to set teapot and cups. "You're going to have to get this mess organized."

"I keep telling myself that."

Stancil returned. "Enough odds and ends here to make a suit of armor. Long as nobody tries to wear it."

"Tea?" his mother asked.

"Sure. Pop, I came past headquarters. That new Monitor is here."

"Already?"

"You're going to love him. He brought a coach and three wagons filled with clothing for his mistress. And a platoon of servants."

"What? Ha! He'll die when Besand shows him his quarters." The Monitor lived in a cell more fit for a monk than for the most powerful man in the province.

"He deserves it."

"You know him?"

"By reputation. Polite people call him the Jackal. If I'd known it was him . . . What could I have done? Nothing. He's lucky his family got him sent here. Somebody would have killed him if he'd stayed around the city."

"Not popular, eh?"

"You'll find out if you stay. Come back, Pop."

"I've got a job to do, Stance."

"How much longer?"

"A couple of days. Or forever. You know. I've got to get that name."

"Pop, we could try now. While things are confused."

"No experiments, Stance. I want it cold. I won't take chances with the Ten."

Stancil wanted to argue but sipped tea instead. He went out to the cart again. When he returned, he said, "Tokar should be turned around by now. Maybe he'll bring more than two wagons."

Bomanz chuckled. "Maybe he'll bring more than wagons, you mean? Like maybe a sister?"

"I was thinking that, yes."

"How are you going to get a thesis written?"

"There's always a spare moment."

Bomanz ran a dust cloth over the jewel in the brow of his dead king's horse. "Enough for now, Dobbin. Going out to the dig."

"Swing by and check the excitement," Stancil suggested.

"I wouldn't miss it."

Besand came to the dig that afternoon. He caught Bomanz napping. "What is this?" he demanded. "Sleeping on the job?"

Bomanz sat up. "You know me. Just getting out of the house. I hear the new man showed up."

Besand spat. "Don't mention him."

"Bad?"

"Worse than I expected. Mark me, Bo. Today writes the end of an era. Those fools will rue it."

"You decide what you're going to do?"

"Go fishing. Bloody go fishing. As far from here as I can get. Take a day to break him in, then head south."

"I always wanted to retire to one of the Jewel Cities. I've never seen the sea. So you're headed out right away, eh?"

"You don't have to sound so damned cheerful about it. You and your Resurrectionist friends have won, but I'll go knowing you didn't beat me on my own ground."

"We haven't fought much lately. That's no reason to make up for lost time."

"Yeah. Yeah. That was uncalled for. Sorry. It's frustration. I'm helpless, and everything is going under."

"It can't be that bad."

"It can. I have my sources, Bo. I'm not some lone crazy. There are knowledgeable men in Oar who fear the same things I do. They say the Resurrectionists are going to try something. You'll see, too. Unless you get out."

"I probably will. Stancil knows this guy. But I can't go before we finish the dig."

Besand gave him a narrow-eyed look. "Bo, I ought to make you clean up before I go. Looks like Hell puked here."

Bomanz was not a fastidious worker. For a hundred feet around his pit the earth was littered with bones, useless scraps of old gear, and miscellaneous trash. A gruesome sight. Bomanz did not notice.

"Why bother? It'll be overgrown in a year. Besides, I don't want to make Men fu work any harder than he has to."

"You're all heart, Bo."

"I work at it."

"See you around."

"All right." And Bomanz tried to puzzle out what he had done wrong, what Besand had come for and not found. He shrugged, snuggled into the grass, closed his eyes.

The woman beckoned. Never had the dream been so clear. And never so successful. He went to her and took her hand, and she led him along a cool green tree-lined path. Thin shafts of sunlight stabbed through the foliage. Golden dust danced in the beams. She spoke, but he could not decipher her words. He did not mind. He was content.

Gold became silver. Silver became a great blunt blade stabbing a nighttime sky, obscuring the weaker stars. The comet came down, came down . . . and a great female face opened upon him. It was shouting. Shouting angrily. And he could not hear. . . .

The comet vanished. A full moon rode the diamond-studded sky. A great shadow crossed the stars, obscuring the Milky Way. A head, Bomanz realized. A head of darkness. A wolf's head, snapping at the moon. . . . Then it was gone. He was with the woman again, walking that forest path, tripping over sunbeams. She was promising him something. . . .

He wakened. Jasmine was shaking him. "Bo! You're dreaming again. Wake up."

"I'm all right," he mumbled. "It wasn't that bad."

"You've got to stop eating so many onions. A man your age, and with an ulcer."

Bomanz sat up, patted his paunch. The ulcer had not bothered him lately. Maybe he had too much else on his mind. He swung his feet to the floor and stared into the darkness.

"What are you doing?"

"Thinking about going out to see Stance."

"You need your rest."

"Bull. Old as I am? Old people don't need to rest. Can't afford to. Don't have the time left to waste." He felt for his boots.

Jasmine muttered something typical. He ignored her. He had that down to a fine art. She added, "Take care out there."

"Eh?"

"Be careful. I don't feel comfortable now that Besand is gone."

"He only left this morning."

"Yes, but. . . ."

Bomanz left the house muttering about superstitious old women who could not stand change.

He took a random roundabout route, occasionally pausing to watch the comet. It was spectacular. A great mane of glory. He wondered if his dream had been trying to tell him something. A shadow devouring the moon. Not solid enough, he decided.

Nearing the edge of town, he heard voices. He softened his step. People were not usually out at this time of night.

They were inside an abandoned shack. A candle flickered inside. Pilgrims, he supposed. He found a peephole, but he could see nothing save a man's back. Something about those slumped shoulders. . . . Besand? Of course not. Too wide. More like that one ape of Tokar's. . . .

He could not identify the voices, which were mostly whispers. One did sound a lot like Men fu's habitual whine. The words were distinct enough, though.

"Look, we did everything we could to get him out of here. You take a man's job and home, he ought to realize he's not wanted. But he won't go."

A second voice: "Then it's time for heroic measures."

Whiny voice: "That's going too far."

Short of disgust. "Yellow. I'll do it. Where is he?"

"Holed up in the old stable. The loft. Fixed himself a pallet, like an old dog in a corner."

A grunt as someone rose. Feet moving. Bomanz grabbed his belly, mouse-stepped away and hid in a shadow. A hulking figure crossed the road. Comet light glittered upon a naked blade.

Bomanz scuttled to a more distant shadow and stopped to think.

What did it mean? Murder, surely. But who? Why? Who had moved into the abandoned stable? Pilgrims and transients used the empty places all the time. . . . Who were those men?

Possibilities occurred. He banished them. They were too grim. When his nerves returned, he hurried to the dig.

Stancil's lantern was there, but he was nowhere in sight. "Stance?" No answer. "Stancil? Where are you?" Still no answer. Almost in panic, he shouted, "Stancil!"

"That you, Pop?"

"Where are you?"

"Taking a crap."

Bomanz sighed, sat down. His son appeared a moment later, brushing sweat off his forehead. Why? It was a cool night.

"Stance, did Besand change his mind? I saw him leave this morning. A while ago I heard men plotting to kill somebody. Sounded like they meant him."

"Kill? Who?"

"I don't know. One of them might have been Men fu. There were three or four of them. Did he come back?"

"I don't think so. You didn't dream something, did you? What are you doing out in the middle of the night, anyway?"

"That nightmare again. I couldn't sleep. I didn't imagine it. Those men were going to kill somebody because he wouldn't leave."

"That doesn't make sense, Pop."

"I don't care. . . ." Bomanz whirled. He heard the strange noise again. A figure staggered into the light. It took three steps and fell.

"Besand! It is Besand. What did I tell you?"

The former Monitor had a bloody wound across his chest. "I'm okay," he said. "I'll be okay. Just shock. It's not as bad as it looks."

"What happened?"

"Tried to kill me. Told you all hell would break loose. Told you they'd make a play. Beat them this round, though. Got their assassin instead."

"I thought you left. I saw you leave."

"I changed my mind. Couldn't go. I took an oath, Bo. They took away my job but not my conscience. I've got to stop them."

Bomanz met his son's gaze. Stancil shook his head. "Pop, look at his wrist."

Bomanz looked. "I don't see anything."

"That's the point. His amulet is gone."

"He turned it in when he left. Didn't you?"

"No," Besand said. "Lost it in the fight. Couldn't find it in the dark." He made that funny sound.

"Pop, he's bad hurt. I better go to the barracks."

"Stance," Besand gasped. "Don't tell *him*. Get Corporal Husky."

"Right." Stancil hurried off.

The light of the comet filled the night with ghosts. The Barrowland seemed to twist and crawl. Momentary shapes drifted amongst the brush. Bomanz shuddered and tried to convince himself that his imagination was acting up now.

Dawn was approaching. Besand was over his shock, sipping broth Jasmine had sent. Corporal Husky came to report the result of his investigation. "Couldn't find anything, sir. Not no body, not no amulet. Not even no sign of no fight. It's like it never happened."

"I sure as hell didn't try to kill myself."

Bomanz became thoughtful. Had he not overheard the conspirators, he would have doubted Besand. The man was capable of staging an assault for sympathy.

"I believe you, sir. I was just saying what I found."

"They blew their best chance. We're warned now. Keep alert."

"Better not forget who's in charge now," Bomanz interjected. "Don't get anybody in trouble with our new leader."

"That rockbrain. Do what you can, Husky. Don't crawl out on a limb."

"Yes, sir." The corporal departed.

Stancil said, "Pop, you ought to get back to the house. You're looking grey."

Bomanz rose. "You all right now?" he asked.

Besand replied, "I'll be fine. Don't worry about me. The sun is up. That kind don't try anything in broad daylight."

Don't bet on it, Bomanz thought. Not if they're devotees of the Domination. They'll bring the darkness to high noon.

Out of earshot, Stancil said, "I was thinking last night, Pop. Before this got started. About our name problem. And suddenly it hit me. There's an old stone in Oar. A big one with runic carvings and pictographs. Been around forever. Nobody knows what it is or where it came from. Nobody really cares."

"So?"

"Let me show you what's carved on it." Stancil picked up a twig, brushed a dusty area clear of debris. He started drawing. "There's a crude star in a circle at the top. Then some lines of runes nobody can read. I can't remember those. Then some pictures." He sketched rapidly.

"That's pretty rough."

"So is the original. But look. This one. Stick figure with a broken leg. Here. A worm? Here, a man superimposed over an animal. Here, a man with a lightning bolt. You see? The Limper. Nightcrawler. Shifter. Stormbringer."

"Maybe. And maybe you're reaching."

Stancil kept drawing. "Okay. That's the way they are on the rock. The four I named. In the same order as on your chart. Look here. At your empty spots. They could be the Taken whose graves we haven't identified." He tapped what looked like a simple circle, a stick figure with its head cocked, and a beast head with a circle in its mouth.

"The positions match," Bomanz admitted.

"So?"

"So what?"

"You're being intentionally thick, Pop. A circle is a zero, maybe. Maybe a sign for the one called the Faceless Man or Nameless man. And here the Hanged Man. And here Moondog or Moonbiter?"

"I see it, Stance. I'm just not sure I want to." He told Stance about having dreamed of a great wolf's head snapping at the moon.

"You see? Your own mind is trying to tell you. Go check the evidence. See if it don't fit this way."

"I don't have to."

"Why not?"

"I know it by heart. It fits."

"Then what's the matter?"

"I'm not sure I want to do it anymore."

"Pop. . . . Pop, if you won't, I will. I mean it. I'm not going to let you throw away thirty-seven years. What's changed, anyway? You gave up a hell of a future to come out here. Can you just write that off?"

"I'm used to this life. I don't mind it."

"Pop. . . . I've met people who knew you back when. They all say you could have been a great wizard. They wonder what happened to you. They know that you had some great secret plan and went off to chase it. They figure you're dead now, 'cause anybody with your talent would've been heard from. Right now I'm wondering if they're not right."

Bomanz sighed. Stancil would never understand. Not without getting old under the threat of the noose.

"I mean it, Pop. I'll do it myself."

"No, you won't. You have neither the knowledge nor the skill. I'll do it. I guess it's fated."

"Let's go!"

"Not so eager. This isn't a tea party. It'll be dangerous. I need rest and time to get into the right frame of mind. I have to assemble my equipment and prepare the stage."

"Pop. . . ."

"Stancil, who is the expert? Who is going to do this?"

"I guess you are."

"Then shut your mouth and keep it shut. The quickest I could try is tomorrow night. Assuming I stay comfortable with those names."

Stancil looked pained and impatient.

"What's the hurry? What's your stake in it?"

"I just. . . . I think Tokar is bringing Glory. I wanted everything out of the way when she got here."

Bomanz raised a despairing eyebrow. "Let's go to the house. I'm exhausted." He glanced back at Besand, who was staring into the Barrowland. The man was stiff with defiance. "Keep him out of my hair."

"He won't be getting around too good for a while."

Later Bomanz muttered, "I wonder what it was all about, anyway? Really Resurrectionists?"

Stancil said, "The Resurrectionists are a myth Besand's bunch use to keep themselves employed."

Bomanz recalled some university acquaintances. "Don't be too sure."

When they reached the house, Stance trudged upstairs to study the chart. Bomanz ate a small meal. Before lying down, he told Jasmine, "Keep an eye on Stance. He's acting funny."

"Funny? How?"

"I don't know. Just funny. Pushy about the Barrowland. Don't let him find my gear. He might try to open the path himself."

"He wouldn't."

"I hope not. But watch him."

15

The Barrowland

Case heard Corbie was back at last. He ran to the old man's home. Corbie greeted him with a hug. "How you been, lad?"

"We thought you were gone for good." Corbie had been away eight months.

"I tried to get back. There's damned near no roads anymore."

"I know. The Colonel asked the Taken to fly supplies in."

"I heard. The military government in Oar got off their butts when that hit. Sent a whole regiment to start a new road. It's about a third of the way built. I came up on part of it."

Case donned his serious face. "Was it really your daughter?"

"No," Corbie said. On departing he had announced that he was off to meet a woman who might be his daughter. He claimed to have given over his savings to a man who would find his children and bring them to Oar.

"You sound disappointed."

He was. His researches had not worked out well. Too many records were missing.

"What sort of winter was it, Case?"

"Bad."

"It was bad down there, too. I worried for you all."

"We had trouble with the tribes. That was the worst part. You can always stay inside and throw another log on. But you can't eat if thieves steal your stores."

"I thought it might come to that."

"We watched your house. They broke in some of the empty places."

"Thank you." Corbie's eyes narrowed. His home had been violated? How thoroughly? A careful searcher might have found enough to hang him. He glanced out a window. "Looks like rain."

"It always looks like rain. When it don't look like snow. It got twelve feet deep last winter. People are worried. What's happened to the weather?"

"Old folks say it goes this way, after the Great Comet. The winters turn bad for a few years. Down in Oar it never got that cold. Plenty of snow, though."

"Wasn't that cold here. Just snowed so much you couldn't get out. I like to went crazy. The whole Barrowland looked like a frozen lake. You could hardly tell where the Great Barrow was."

"Uhm? I have to unpack yet. If you don't mind? Let everyone know I'm back. I'm near broke. I'll need work."

"Will do, Corbie."

Corbie watched from a window as Case ambled back to the Guard compound, taking an elevated walkway built since his departure. The mud below explained it. That and Colonel Sweet's penchant for keeping his men occupied. Once Case vanished he went to the second floor.

Nothing had been disturbed. Good. He peeped out a window, toward the Barrowland.

How it had changed in just a few years. A few more and you would not be able to find it.

He grunted, stared the harder. Then he retrieved the silken map from its hiding place, studied it, then the Barrowland again. After a time he fished sweat-stained papers from inside his shirt, where he had carried them since stealing them from the university in Oar. He spread them over the map.

Late that afternoon he rose, donned a cloak, gathered the cane he now carried, and went out. He limped through the water and mud and drizzle till he reached a point overlooking the Great Tragic River.

It was in flood, as always. Its bed had continued to shift. After a time he cursed, smote an old oak with his cane, and turned back.

The day had gone grey with the hour. It would be dark before he got home.

"Damned complications," he muttered. "I never counted on this. What the hell am I going to do?"

Take the high risk. The one chance he wished most to avoid, though its possible necessity was his real reason for having wintered in Oar.

For the first time in years he wondered if the game were worth the candle.

Whatever his course, it would be dark before he got home.

16

The Plain of Fear

You get mad and walk out on Darling, you can miss a lot. Elmo, One-Eye, Goblin, Otto, those guys like to bait me. They were not about to clue me in. They got everybody else to go along. Even Tracker, who seemed to be taking a shine to me and chattered at me more than everybody else combined, would not drop a hint. So when the day came, I went topside in total ignorance.

I'd packed the usual field gear. Our traditions are heavy infantry, though mostly we ride these days. All of us are too old to lug eighty pounds of gear. I dragged mine to the cavern that serves as a stable and smells like the grandfather of them all—and found that not one animal was saddled. Well, one. Darling's.

The stable boy just grinned when I asked what was going on. "Go on up," he said. "Sir."

"Yeah? Rotten bastards. They play games with me? I'll get them. They damned well better start remembering who keeps the Annals around here." I bitched and moaned all the way into the pre-moonset shadows that lurked around the tunnel mouth. There I found the rest of the outfit, all already up, with light gear. Each man carried his weapons and a sack of dried food.

"What you doing, Croaker?" One-Eye asked with suppressed laughter. "Look like you're taking everything you own. You a turtle? Carry your house on your back?"

And Elmo: "We ain't moving, boy. Just going on a raid."

"You're a bunch of sadists, you know that?" I stepped into the wan light. The moon was half an hour from setting. Far, Taken drifted on the night. Those son-of-a-bitches were determined to keep a close watch. Nearer, a whole horde of menhirs had gathered. They looked like a graveyard out on the desert, there were so many of them. There were a lot of walking trees, too.

More, though there was no breeze, I could hear Old Father Tree tinkling. No doubt that meant something. A menhir might have explained. But the stones remain closemouthed about themselves and their fellow species. Especially about Father Tree. Most of them won't admit he exists.

"Better lighten your load, Croaker," the Lieutenant said. He would not explain either.

"You going too?" I asked, surprised.

"Yep. Move it. We don't have long. Weapons and field medical kit should do it. Scoot."

I met Darling going down. She smiled. Grouchy as I was, I smiled back. I can't stay mad at her. I have known her since she was so high. Since Raven rescued her from the Limper's thugs long ago, in the Forsberg campaigns. I cannot see the woman that is without recalling the child that was. I get all sentimental and soft.

They tell me I suffer from a crippling romantic streak. Looking back, I'm almost inclined to agree. All those silly stories I wrote about the Lady. . . .

The moon was on the rim of the world when I returned topside. A whisper of excitement coursed among the men. Darling was up there with them, astride her flashy white mare, moving around, gesturing at those who understood sign. Above, the spots of luminescence that are characteristic of windwhale tentacles drifted lower than I'd ever heard tell of. Except in horror stories about starved whales dropping down to drag their tentacles on the ground, ripping up every plant and animal in their path.

"Hey!" I said. "We'd better look out. That sucker is coming down." A vast shadow blotted out thousands of stars. And it was expanding. Mantas swarmed around it. Big ones, little ones, in-between ones—more than I'd ever seen.

My expostulation drew laughter. I turned surly again. I moved among the men, harassing them about the medical kits I expect them to carry on a mission. I was in a better mood when I finished. They all had them.

The windwhale kept coming down.

The moon disappeared. The instant it did the menhirs began to move. Moments later they began to glow on the side toward us. The side away from the Taken.

Darling rode along the pathway they marked. When she passed a menhir its light went out. I suspect it moved to the far end of the line.

I had no time to check. Elmo and the Lieutenant herded us into a line of our own. Above, the night filled with the squeaks and flutter of mantas squabbling for flying room.

The windwhale settled astride the creek.

My god, it was big. Big! I had no idea. . . . It stretched from the coral over the creek another two hundred yards. Four, five hundred yards long, altogether. And seventy to a hundred wide.

A menhir spoke. I could not make out its words. But the men began moving forward.

In a minute my worst suspicions were confirmed. They were climbing the creature's flank, onto its back, where mantas normally nested.

It smelled. Smelled unlike anything I've ever smelled before, and strongly. Richly, you might say. Not necessarily a bad smell, but overpowering. And it felt strange to the touch. Not hairy, scaly, horny. Not exactly slimy, but still spongy and slick, like a full, exposed intestine. There were plenty of handholds. Our fingers and boots did not bother it.

The menhir mumbled and grumbled like an old first sergeant, both issuing orders and relaying complaints from the windwhale. I got the impression the windwhale was a naturally grouchy sort. He did not like this any more than did I. Can't say I blame him.

Up top there were more menhirs, each balanced precariously. As I arrived, one menhir told me to go to another of its kind. That one told me to sit about twenty feet away. The last men climbed aboard only moments later.

The menhirs vanished.

I began to feel odd. At first blush I thought that was because the whale was lifting off. When I flew with the Lady or Whisper or Soulcatcher, my stomach was in continual rebellion. But this was a different malaise. It took a while to understand it as an absence.

Darling's null was fading. It had been with me so long it had become part of my life. . . .

What was happening?

We were going up. I felt the breeze shift. The stars turned ponderously. Then, suddenly, the whole north lighted up.

Mantas were attacking the Taken. A whole mess of them. The stroke was a complete surprise, for all the Taken must have sensed their presence. But the mantas were not doing that sort of thing. . . .

Oh, hell, I thought. They're pushing them our way. . . .

I grinned. Not our way at all. Toward Darling and her null, in a place unexpected.

As the thought occurred I saw the flash of vain sorceries, saw a carpet stagger, flutter earthward. A score of mantas swarmed it.

Maybe Darling was not as dumb as I thought. Maybe these Taken could be taken out. A profit, for sure, if nothing else went right.

But what were we doing? The lightning illuminated my companions. Nearest me were Tracker and Toadkiller Dog. Tracker seemed bored. But Toadkiller Dog was as alert as I had seen him. He was sitting up, watching the display. The only time I ever saw him not on his belly was at mealtime.

His tongue was out. He panted. Had he been human, I would have said he was grinning.

The second Taken tried to impress the mantas with his power. He was too immensely outnumbered. And below, Darling was moving. That second Taken suddenly entered her null. Down he went. The manta swarm pursued.

Both would survive landing. But then they would be afoot at the heart of the Plain, which tonight had taken a stand. Their chances of walking out looked grim.

The windwhale was up a couple thousand feet now, moving northeast, gaining speed. How far to the edge of the Plain nearest Rust? Two hundred miles? Fine. We might make it before dawn. But what about the last thirty miles, beyond the Plain?

Tracker started singing. His voice was soft at first. His song was old. Soldiers of the north countries had sung it for generations. It was a dirge, a song-before-death sung in memory of those about to die. I heard it in Forsberg, sung on both sides. Another voice took it up. Then another and another. Perhaps fifteen men knew it, of forty or so.

The windwhale glided northward. Far, far below, the Plain of Fear slid away, utterly invisible.

I began to sweat, though the upper air was cold.

Rust

My first false assumption was that the Limper would be home when we called. Darling's maneuver against the Taken obviated that. I should have recalled that the Taken touch one another over long distances, mind to mind. Limper and Benefice passed nearby as we moved north.

"Down!" Goblin squealed when we were fifty miles short of the edge of the Plain. "Taken. Nobody move."

As always, old Croaker considered himself the exception to the rule. For the Annals, of course. I crept nearer the side of our monster mount, peered out into the night. Way below, two shadows raced down our backtrack. Once they were past I took a cussing from Elmo, the Lieutenant, Goblin, One-Eye, and anybody else who wanted a piece. I settled back beside Tracker. He just grinned and shrugged.

He came ever more to life as action approached.

My second false assumption was that the windwhale would drop us at the edge of the Plain. I was up again as that drew near, ignoring naughty remarks directed my way. But the windwhale did not go down. It did not descend for many minutes yet. I began to babble sillinesses when I resumed my place by Tracker.

He had his till-now mysterious case open. It contained a small arsenal. He checked his weapons. One long-bladed knife did not please him. He began applying a whetstone.

How many times had Raven done the same in the brief year he spent with the Company?

The whale's descent was sudden. Elmo and the Lieutenant passed among us, telling us to get off in a hurry. Elmo told me, "Stick close to me, Croaker. You too, Tracker. One-Eye. You feel anything down there?"

"Nothing. Goblin has his sleeping spell ready. Their sentries will be snoring when we touch down."

"Unless they aren't and raise the alarm," I muttered. Damn, but didn't I have it for the dark side?

No problems. We grounded. Men poured over the side. They spread out as if this part had been rehearsed. Parts may have been while I was sulking.

I could do nothing but what Elmo told me.

The early going reminded me of another barracks raid, long ago, south of the Sea of Torments, ere we enlisted with the Lady. We had slaughtered the Urban Cohorts of the Jewel City Beryl, our wizards keeping them snoozing while we murdered them.

Not work I enjoy, I'll tell you. Most of them were just kids who enlisted for want of something better to do. But they were the enemy, and we were making a grand gesture. A grander gesture than I had supposed Darling could order, or had in mind.

The sky began to lighten. Not one man of an entire regiment, save perhaps a few AWOL for the night, survived. Out on the main parade of the compound, which stood well outside Rust proper, Elmo and the Lieutenant began to yell. Hurry, hurry. More to do. This squad to wreck the stellae of the Taken. That squad to plunder regimental headquarters. Another to set out stuff to fire the barracks buildings. Still another to search the Limper's quarters for documents. Hurry, hurry. Got to get gone before the Taken return. Darling cannot distract them forever.

Somebody screwed up. Naturally. It always happens. Somebody fired one barracks early. Smoke rose.

Over in Rust, we soon learned, there was another regiment. In minutes a squadron of horse were galloping our way. And again, someone had screwed up. The gates were not secured. Almost without warning the horsemen were among us.

Men shouted. Weapons clanged. Arrows flew. Horses shrieked. The Lady's men got out, leaving half their number behind.

Now Elmo and the Lieutenant were in a hurry for sure. Those boys were going for help.

While we were scattering the imperials the windwhale lifted off. Maybe half a dozen men managed to scramble aboard. It rose just enough to clear the rooftops, then headed south. There was not yet enough light to betray it.

You can imagine the cussing and shouting. Even Toadkiller Dog found the energy to snarl. I slumped in defeat, dropped my butt onto a hitching rail, sat there shaking my head. A few men sped arrows after the monster. It did not notice.

Tracker leaned on the rail beside me. I grumped, "You wouldn't think something that big would be chicken." I mean, a windwhale can destroy a city.

"Do not impart motives to a creature you do not understand. You have to see its reasoning."

"What?"

"Not reasoning. I don't know the right word." He reminded me of a four-year-old struggling with a difficult concept. "It's outside the lands it knows. Beyond bounds its enemies believe it can breech. It runs for fear it will be seen and a secret betrayed. It has never worked with men. How can it remember them in a desperate moment?"

He was right, probably. But at the moment I was more interested in him than in his theory. That I would have stumbled across after I settled down. He made it seem one huge and incredibly difficult piece of thinking.

I wondered about his mind. Was he just slightly more than a half-wit? Was his Ravenlike act not a product of personality but of simpleness?

The Lieutenant stood on the parade ground, hands on hips, watching the windwhale leave us in the enemy's palm. After a minute he shouted, "Officers! Assemble!" After we gathered, he said, "We're in for it. As I see it, we have one hope. That that big bastard gets in touch with the menhirs when it gets back. And that *they* decide we're worth saving. So what we do is hold out till nightfall. And hope."

One-Eye made an obscene noise. "I think we better run for it."

"Yeah? And let the imperials track us? We're how far from home? You think we can make it with the Limper and his pals after us?"

"They'll be after us here."

"Maybe. And maybe they'll keep them busy out there. At least, if we're here, they'll know where to find us. Elmo, survey the walls. See if we can hold them. Goblin, Silent, get those fires put out. The rest of you, clean out the Taken's documents. Elmo! Post sentries. One-Eye. Your job is to figure out how we can get help from Rust. Croaker, give him a hand. You know who we have where. Come on. Move."

A good man, the Lieutenant. He kept his cool when, like all of us, what he wanted to do was run in circles and scream.

We didn't have a chance, really. This was the end of it. Even if we held off the troops from the city, there was Benefice and the Limper. Goblin, One-Eye, and Silent would be of no value against them. The Lieutenant knew that, too. He did not have them put their heads together to plot a surprise.

We could not get the fire controlled. The barracks had to burn itself out. While I tended two wounded men the others made the compound as defensible as thirty men could. Finished doctoring, I went poking through the Limper's documents. I found nothing immediately interesting.

"About a hundred men coming out of Rust!" someone shouted.

The Lieutenant snapped, "Make this place look abandoned!" Men scurried.

I popped up to the wall top for a quick peek at the scrub woods north of us. One-Eye was out there, creeping toward the city, hoping to get to Corder's friends.

Even after having been triply decimated in the great sieges and occupied for years, Rust remained adamant in its hatred for the Lady.

The imperials were careful. They sent scouts around the wall. They sent a few men up close to draw fire. Only after an hour of cautious maneuver did they rush the half-open gate.

The Lieutenant let fifteen get inside before tripping the portcullis. Those went down in a storm of arrows. Then we hustled to the wall and let fly at those milling around outside. Another dozen fell. The others retreated beyond bowshot. There they milled and grumbled and tried to decide what next.

Tracker remained nearby all that time. I saw him loose only four arrows. Each ripped right through an imperial. He might not be bright, but he could use a bow.

"If they're smart," I told him, "they'll set a picket line and wait for the Limper. No point them getting hurt when he can handle us."

Tracker grunted. Toadkiller Dog opened one eye, grumbled deep in his throat. Down the way, Goblin and Silent crouched with heads together, alternately popping up to look outside. I figured they were plotting.

Tracker stood up, grunted again. I looked myself. More imperials were leaving Rust. Hundreds more.

Nothing happened for an hour, except that more and more troops appeared. They surrounded us.

Goblin and Silent unleashed their wizardry. It took the form of a cloud of moths. I could not discern their provenance. They just gathered around the two. When they were maybe a thousand strong, they fluttered away.

For a while there was a lot of screaming outside. When that died I ambled over and asked a grim-faced Goblin, "What happened?"

"Somebody with a touch of talent," he squeaked. "Almost as good as us."

"We in trouble?"

"In trouble? Us? We got it whipped, Croaker. We got them on the run. They just don't know it yet."

"I meant. . . ."

"He won't hit back. He don't want to give himself away. There's two of us and only one of him."

The imperials began assembling artillery pieces. The compound had not been built to withstand bombardment.

Time passed. The sun climbed. We watched the sky. When would doom come riding in on a carpet?

Certain the imperials would not immediately attack, the Lieutenant had some of us gather our plunder on the parade ground, ready to board a windwhale. Whether he believed it or not, he insisted we would be evacuated after sunset. He would not entertain the possibility that the Taken might arrive first.

He did keep morale up.

The first missile fell an hour after noon. A ball of fire smacked down a dozen feet short of the wall. Another arced after it. It fell on the parade ground, sputtered, fizzled.

"Going to burn us out," I muttered to Tracker. A third missile came. It burned cheerfully, but also upon the parade.

Tracker and Toadkiller Dog stood and stared over the ramparts, the dog stretching on his hind legs. After a while Tracker sat down, opened his wooden case, withdrew a half dozen overly long arrows. He stood again, stared toward the artillery engines, arrow across his bow.

It was a long flight, but reachable even with my weapon. But I could have plinked all day and not come close.

Tracker fell into a state of concentration almost trancelike. He lifted and bent his bow, pulled it to the head of his arrow, let fly.

A cry rolled up the slope. The artillerymen gathered around one of their number.

Tracker loosed shafts smoothly and quickly. I'd guess he put four in the air at one time. Each found a target. Then he sat down. "That's that."

"Say what?"

"No more good arrows."

"Maybe that's enough to discourage them."

It was. For a while. About long enough for them to move back and put up some protective mantlets. Then the missiles came again. One found a building. The heat was vicious.

The Lieutenant prowled the wall restlessly. I joined his silent prayer that the imperials would not get worked up and rush us. There would be no way to stop them.

18

Siege

The sun was settling. We were alive still. No Taken carpet had come swooping out of the Plain. We had begun to believe there was a chance.

Something hammered on the gate, a great loud pounding, like the hammer of doom. One-Eye roared up, "Let me in, damnit!"

Somebody scooted down and opened up. He came to the ramparts. "Well?" Goblin demanded.

"I don't know. Too many imperials. Not enough Rebels. They wanted to argue it out."

"How did you get through?" I asked.

"Walked," he snapped. Then, less belligerently, "Trade secret, Croaker."

Sorcery. Of course.

The Lieutenant paused to hear One-Eye's report, resumed his ceaseless prowl. I watched the imperials. There were indications they were out of patience.

One-Eye evidently supported my suspicion with direct evidence. He, Goblin, and Silent started plotting.

I am not certain what they did. Not moths, but the results were similar. A big outcry, soon stifled. But now we had three spook doctors to work the mine. The extra man sought the imperial who negated the spell.

A man ran toward the city, aflame. Goblin and One-Eye howled victoriously. Not two minutes later an artillery engine burst into flames. Then another. I watched our wizards closely.

Silent remained all business. But Goblin and One-Eye were getting carried away, having a good time. I feared they would go too far, that the imperials would attack in hope of overwhelming them.

They came, but later than I expected. They waited till nightfall. And then they were more cautious than the situation demanded.

Meantime, smoke began to waft up over the ruined walls of Rust. One-Eye's mission had succeeded. Somebody was doing something. Some of the imperials pulled out and hurried back to deal with it.

As the stars came out I told Tracker, "Guess we'll soon know if the Lieutenant was right."

He just looked puzzled.

Imperial horns sounded signals. Companies moved toward the wall. He and I stood to our bows, seeking targets that were difficult in the darkness, though there was a bit of moon. Out of the nowhere, he asked, "What's she like, Croaker?"

"What? Who?" I let fly.

"The Lady. They say you met her."

"Yeah. A long time ago."

"Well? What's she like?" He loosed. A cry answered the twang of his bowstring. He seemed perfectly calm. Seemed unaware that he might die in minutes. That disturbed me.

"About what you'd expect," I replied. What could I say? My contacts with her were but sketchy memories now. "Hard and beautiful."

The answer did not satisfy him. It never satisfies anyone. But it is the best I can give.

"What did she look like?"

"I don't know, Tracker. I was scared shitless. And she did things to my mind. I saw a young, beautiful woman. But you can see those anywhere."

His bow twanged, was answered by another cry. He shrugged. "I sort of wondered." He began loosing more quickly. The imperials were close now.

I swear, he never missed. I loosed when I saw something, but. . . . He has eyes like an owl. All I saw was shadows among shadows.

Goblin, One-Eye, and Silent did what they could. Their witcheries painted the field with short-lived little flares and screams. What they could do was not enough. Ladders slapped against the wall. Most went right back over again. But men came up a few. Then there were a dozen more. I scattered arrows into the darkness, almost randomly, as quickly as I could, then drew my sword.

The rest of the men did likewise.

The Lieutenant shouted, "It's here!"

I flicked a glance at the stars. Yes. A vast shape had appeared overhead. It was settling. The Lieutenant had guessed right.

Now all we had to do was get aboard.

Some of the young men broke for the parade ground. The Lieutenant's curses did not slow them. Neither did Elmo's snarls and threats. The Lieutenant yelled for the rest of us to follow.

Goblin and One-Eye loosed something nasty. For a moment I thought it was some cruel conjured demon. It looked vile enough. And it did stall the imperials. But like much of their magic, it was illusion, not substance. The enemy soon caught on.

But we had us a head start. The men reached the parade before the imperials recollected themselves. They roared, certain they had us.

I reached the windwhale as it touched down. Silent snagged my arm as I started to scramble aboard. He indicated the documents we had scrounged. "Oh, damn! There isn't time."

Men scrambled past me during my moment of indecision. Then I tossed sword and bow topside and began pitching bundles up to Silent, who got somebody to relay them to the top.

A gang of imperials charged toward us. I started for an abandoned sword, saw I could not reach it in time, thought: Oh, shit—not now; not here.

Tracker stepped between me and them. His blade was like something out of legend. He killed three men in the blink of an eye, wounded another two before the imperials decided they faced someone preternatural. He took the offensive, though still outnumbered. Never have I seen a sword used with such skill, style, economy, and grace. It was a part of him, an extension of his will. Nothing could stand before it. For that moment I could believe old tales about magic swords.

Silent kicked me in the back, signed at me, "Quit gawking and get moving." I tossed up the last two bundles, began scaling the monster.

The men Tracker faced received reinforcements. He retreated. From up top someone sped arrows down. But I did not think he would make it. I kicked at a man who had gotten behind him. Another took his place, leapt at me. . . .

Toadkiller Dog came out of nowhere. He locked his jaws in my assailant's throat. The man gurgled, responded as he might have if bitten by a krite. He lasted only a second.

Toadkiller Dog dropped away. I climbed a few feet, still trying to guard Tracker's back. He reached up. I caught his hand and heaved.

There were awful shouts and screams among the imperials. It was too dark to see why. I figured One-Eye, Goblin, and Silent were earning their keep.

Tracker flung up past me, took a firm hold, helped me. I climbed a few feet, looked down.

The ground was fifteen feet below. The windwhale was going up fast. The imperials stood around gawking. I fought my way to the top.

I looked down again as someone dragged me to safety. The fires in Rust were beneath us. Several hundred feet below. We were going up fast. No wonder my hands were cold.

Chills were not the reason I lay down shaking, though.

After it passed, I asked, "Anybody hurt? Where's my medical kit?"

Where, I wondered, were the Taken? How had we gotten through the day without a visit from our beloved enemy the Limper?

Going home I noticed more than I did coming north. I felt the life beneath me, the grumble and hum within the monster. I noted pre-adolescent mantas peeping from nesting places among the appendages which forested parts of the whale's back. And I saw the Plain in a different light, with the moon up to illuminate it.

It was another world, spare and crystalline at times, luminescent at others, sparkling and glowing in spots. What looked like lava pools lay to the west. Beyond, the flash and curl of a change storm illuminated the horizon. I suppose we were crossing its backtrail. Later, deeper into the Plain, the desert became more mundane.

Our steed was not the cowardly windwhale. This one was smaller and smelled less strongly. It was more spritely, too, and less tentative in its movements.

About twenty miles from home Goblin squealed, "Taken!" and everyone went flat. The whale climbed. I peeked over its side.

Taken for sure, but not interested in us. There was a lot of flash and roar way down there. Patches of desert were aflame. I saw the long, creepy shadows of walking trees on the move, the shapes of mantas rushing across the light. The Taken themselves were afoot, except one desperado aloft battling the mantas. The one aloft was not the Limper. I would have recognized his tattered brown even at that distance.

Whisper, surely. Trying to escort the others out of enemy territory. Great. They would be busy for a few days.

The windwhale began to descend. (For the sake of these Annals, I wish part of a passage had taken place by day so I could record more details.) It touched down shortly. From the ground a menhir called, "Get down. Hurry."

Getting off was more trouble than boarding. The wounded now realized they were hurt. Everyone was tired and stiff. And Tracker would not move.

He was catatonic. Nothing reached him. He just sat there, staring at infinity.

"What the hell?" Elmo demanded. "What's wrong with him?"

"I don't know. Maybe he got hit." I was baffled. And the more so once we got him into some light so I could examine him. There was nothing physically wrong. He had come through without a bruise.

Darling came outside. She signed, "You were right, Croaker. I am sorry. I thought it would be a stroke so bold it would fire the whole world." Of Elmo, she asked, "How many lost?"

"Four men. I don't know if they were killed or just got left." He seemed ashamed. The Black Company does not leave its brethren behind.

"Toadkiller Dog," Tracker said. "We left Toadkiller Dog."

One-Eye disparaged the mutt. Tracker rose angrily. He had salvaged nothing but his sword. His magnificent case and arsenal remained in Rust with his mongrel.

"Here now," the Lieutenant snapped. "None of that. One-Eye, go below. Croaker, keep an eye on this man. Ask Darling if the guys who ran out yesterday made it back."

Elmo and I both did.

Her answer was not reassuring. The great cowardly windwhale dumped them a hundred miles north, according to the menhirs. At least it descended before forcing them off.

They were walking home. The menhirs promised to shield them from the natural wickedness of the Plain.

We all went down into the Hole bickering. There is nothing like failure to set the sparks flying.

Failure, of course, can be relative. The damage we did was considerable. The repercussions would echo a long time. The Taken had to be badly rattled. Our capture of so many documents would force a restructuring of their plan of campaign. But still the mission was unsatisfactory. Now the Taken knew windwhales were capable of ranging beyond traditional bounds. Now the Taken knew we had resources beyond those they had suspected.

When you gamble, you do not show all your cards till after the final bet.

I scrounged around and found the captured papers, took them to my quarters. I did not feel like participating in the conference room postmortem. It was sure to get nasty—even with everyone agreeing.

I shed my weapons, lighted a lamp, picked one of the document bundles, turned to my worktable. And there lay another of those packets from the west.

19

Bomanz's Tale

Croaker:

Bomanz walked his dreams with a woman who could not make him understand her words. The green path of promise led past moon-eating dogs, hanged men, and sentries without faces. Through breaks in the foliage he glimpsed a sky-spanning comet.

He did not sleep well. The dream invariably awaited him when he dozed off. He did not know why he could not slide down into deep sleep. As nightmares went, this was mild.

Most of the symbolism was obvious, and most of it he refused to heed.

Night had fallen when Jasmine brought tea and asked, "Are you going to lie here all week?"

"I might."

"How are you going to sleep tonight?"

"I probably won't till late. I'll work in the shop. What's Stance been up to?"

"He slept a while, went and brought a load from the site, pottered around the shop, ate, and went back out when somebody came to say Men fu was out there again."

"What about Besand?"

"It's all over town. The new Monitor is furious because he didn't leave. Says he won't do anything about it. The Guards are calling him a horse's ass. They won't take his orders. He's getting madder and madder."

"Maybe he'll learn something. Thanks for the tea. Is there anything to eat?"

"Leftover chicken. Get it yourself. I'm going to bed."

Grumbling, Bomanz ate cold, greasy chicken wings, washing them down with tepid beer. He thought about his dream. His ulcer gave him a nip. His head started aching. "Here we go," he muttered, and dragged himself upstairs.

He spent several hours reviewing the rituals he would use to leave his body and slide through the hazards of the Barrowland. . . . Would the dragon be a problem? Indications were, it was meant for physical intruders. Finally: "It'll work. As long as that sixth barrow is Moondog's." He sighed, leaned back, closed his eyes.

The dream began. And midway through he found himself staring into green ophidian eyes. Wise, cruel, mocking eyes. He started awake.

"Pop? You up there?"

"Yeah. Come on up."

Stancil pushed into the room. He looked awful.

"What happened?"

"The Barrowland. . . . The ghosts are walking."

"They do that when the comet gets close. I didn't expect them so soon. Must be going to get frisky this time. That's no call to get shook up."

"Wasn't that. I expected that. That I could handle. No. It's Besand and Men fu."

"What?"

"Men fu tried to get into the Barrowland with Besand's amulet."

"I was right! That little. . . . Go on."

"He was at the dig. He had the amulet. He was scared to death. He saw me coming and headed downhill. When he got near where the moat used to be, Besand came out of nowhere, screaming and waving a sword. Men fu started running. Besand kept after him. It's pretty bright out there, but I lost track when they got up around the Howler's barrow. Besand must have caught him. I heard them yelling and rolling around in the brush. Then they started screaming."

Stancil stopped. Bomanz waited.

"I don't know how to describe it, Pop. I never heard sounds like that. All the ghosts piled onto the Howler's barrow. It went on a long time. Then the screaming started getting closer."

Stancil, Bomanz concluded, had been shaken deeply. Shaken the way a man is when his basic beliefs are uprooted. Odd. "Go on."

"It was Besand. He had the amulet, but it didn't help. He didn't make it across the moat. He dropped it. The ghosts jumped him. He's dead, Pop. The Guards were all out there. . . . They couldn't do anything but look. The Monitor wouldn't give them amulets so they could get him."

Bomanz folded his hands on the tabletop, stared at them. "So now we have two men dead. Three counting the one last night. How many will we have tomorrow night? Will I have to face a platoon of new ghosts?"

"You're going to do it tomorrow night?"

"That's right. With Besand gone there's no reason to delay it. Is there?"

"Pop. . . . Maybe you shouldn't. Maybe the knowledge out there should stay buried."

"What's this? My son parroting *my* misgivings?"

"Pop, let's don't fight. Maybe I pushed too hard. Maybe I was wrong. You know more about the Barrowland than me."

Bomanz stared at his son. More boldly than he felt, he said, "I'm going in. It's time to put doubts aside and get on with it. There's the list. See if there's an area of inquiry that I've forgotten."

"Pop. . . ."

"Don't argue with me, boy." It had taken him all evening to shed the ingrained Bomanz persona and surface the wizard so long and artfully hidden. But he was out now.

Bomanz went to a corner where a few seemingly innocuous objects were piled. He stood taller than usual. He moved more precisely, more quickly. He began piling things on the table. "When you go back to Oar, you can tell my old classmates what became of me." He smiled thinly. He could recall a few who would shudder even now, knowing he had studied at the Lady's knee. He'd never forgotten, never forgiven. And they knew him that well.

Stancil's pallor had disappeared. Now he was uncertain. This side of the father had not been seen since before the son's birth. It was outside his experience. "Do you want to go out there, Pop?"

"You brought back the essential details. Besand is dead. Men fu is dead. The Guards aren't going to get excited."

"I thought he was your friend."

"Besand? Besand had no friends. He had a mission. . . . What're you looking at?"

"A man with a mission?"

"Could be. Something kept me here. Take this stuff downstairs. We'll do it in the shop."

"Where do you want it?"

"Doesn't matter. Besand was the only one who could have separated it from the junk."

Stancil went out. Later, Bomanz finished a series of mental exercises and wondered what had become of the boy. Stance hadn't returned. He shrugged, went on.

He smiled. He was ready. It was going to be simple.

The town was in an uproar. A Guard had tried to assassinate the new Monitor. The Monitor was so bewildered and frightened he had locked himself in his quarters. Crazy rumors abounded.

Bomanz walked through it with such calm dignity that he startled people who had known him for years. He went to the edge of the Barrowland, considered his long-time antagonist. Besand lay where he had fallen. The flies were thick. Bomanz threw a handful of dirt. The insects scattered. He nodded thoughtfully. Besand's amulet had disappeared again.

Bomanz located Corporal Husky. "If you can't do anything to get Besand out, then toss dirt in on him. There's a mountain around my pit."

"Yes, sir," Husky said, and only later seemed startled by his easy acquiescence.

Bomanz walked the perimeter of the Barrowland. The sun shone a little oddly through the comet's tail. Colors were a trifle strange. But there were no ghosts aprowl now. He saw no reason not to make his communication attempt. He returned to the village.

Wagons stood before the shop. Teamsters were busy loading them. Jasmine shrilled inside, cursing someone who had taken something he shouldn't. "Damn you, Tokar," Bomanz muttered. "Why today? You could have waited till it was over." He felt a fleeting concern. He could not rely on Stance if the boy were distracted. He shoved into the shop.

"It's grand!" Tokar said of the horse. "Absolutely magnificent. You're a genius, Bo."

"You're a pain in the butt. What's going on here? Who the hell are all these people?"

"My drivers. My brother Clete. My sister Glory. Stance's Glory. And our baby sister Snoopy. We called her that because she was always spying on us."

"Pleased to meet you all. Where's Stance?"

Jasmine said, "I sent him to get something for supper. With this crowd I'll have to start cooking early."

Bomanz sighed. Just what he needed, this night of nights. A house full of guests. "You. Put that back where you got it. You. Snoopy? Keep your hands off of stuff."

Tokar asked, "What's with you, Bo?"

Bomanz raised one eyebrow, met the man's gaze, did not answer. "Where's the driver with the big shoulders?"

"Not with me anymore." Tokar frowned.

"Thought not. I'll be upstairs if something critical comes up." He stamped through the shop, went up, settled in his chair, willed himself to sleep. His dreams were subtle. It seemed he could hear at last, but could not recall what he heard. . . .

Stancil entered the upstairs room. Bomanz asked, "What are we going to do? That crowd is gumming up the works."

"How long do you need, Pop?"

"This could go all night every night for weeks if it works out." He was pleased. Stancil had recovered his courage.

"Can't hardly run them off."

"And can't go anywhere else, either." The Guards were in a hard, bitter mood.

"How noisy will you be, Pop? Could we do it here, on the quiet?"

"Guess we'll have to try. Going to be crowded. Get the stuff from the shop. I'll make room."

Bomanz's shoulders slumped when Stancil left. He was getting nervous. Not about the thing he would challenge, but about his own foresight. He kept thinking he had forgotten something. But he had reviewed four decades of notes without detecting a flaw in his chosen approach. Any reasonably educated apprentice should be able to follow his formulation. He spat into a corner. "Antiquarian's cowardice," he muttered. "Old-fashioned fear of the unknown."

Stancil returned. "Mom's got them into a game of Throws."

"I wondered what Snoopy was yelling about. Got everything?"

"Yes."

"Okay. Go down and kibbitz. I'll be there after I set up. We'll do it after they're in bed."

"Okay."

"Stance? Are you ready?"

"I'm okay, Pop. I just had the jitters last night. It's not every day I see a man killed by ghosts."

"Better get a feel for that kind of thing. It happens."

Stancil looked blank.

"You're sneaking studies on Black Campus, aren't you?" Black Campus was that hidden side of the university on which wizards learned their trade. Officially, it did not exist. Legally, it was prohibited. But it was there. Bomanz was a laureate graduate.

Stancil gave one sharp nod and left.

"I thought so," Bomanz whispered, and wondered: How black are you, son?

He pottered around till he had triple-checked everything, till he realized that caution had become an excuse for not socializing. "You're something," he mumbled to himself.

One last look. Chart laid out. Candles. Bowl of quicksilver. Silver dagger. Herbs. Censers. . . . He still had that feeling. "What the hell could I have missed?"

Throws was essentially four-player checkers. The board was four times the usual size. Players played from each side. An element of chance was added by throwing a die before each move. If a player's throw came up six, he could move any combination of pieces six moves. Checkers rules generally applied, except that a jump could be declined.

Snoopy appealed to Bomanz the moment he appeared. "They're ganging up on me!" She was playing opposite Jasmine. Glory and Tokar were on her flanks.

Bomanz watched a few moves. Tokar and the older sister were in cahoots. Conventional elimination tactics.

On impulse Bomanz controlled the fall of the die when it came to Snoopy. She threw a six, squealed, sent men charging all over. Bomanz wondered if he had been that rich in adolescent enthusiasm and optimism. He eyed the girl. How old? Fourteen?

He made Tokar throw a one, let Jasmine and Glory have what fate decreed, then gave Snoopy another six and Tokar another one. After a third time around Tokar grumbled, "This is getting ridiculous." The balance of the game had shifted. Glory was about to abandon him and side with her sister against Jasmine.

Jasmine gave Bomanz the fish-eye when Snoopy threw yet another six. He winked, let Tokar throw free. A two. Tokar grumbled, "I'm on the comeback trail now."

Bomanz wandered into the kitchen, poured himself a mug of beer. He returned to find Snoopy on the edge of disaster again. Her play was so frenetic she had to throw fours or better to survive.

Tokar, on the other hand, played a tediously conservative game, advancing in echelon, trying to occupy his flankers' king rows. A man much like himself, Bomanz reflected. First he plays to make sure he doesn't lose; then he worries about the win.

He watched Tokar roll a six and send a piece on an extravagant tour in which he took three men from his nominal ally, Glory.

Treacherous, too, Bomanz thought. That's worth keeping in mind. He asked Stancil, "Where's Clete?"

Tokar said, "He decided to stay with the teamsters. Thought we were crowding you too much."

"I see."

Jasmine won that game, and Tokar the next, whereupon the antique merchant said, "That's all for me. Take my seat, Bo. See you all in the morning."

Glory said. "I'm done, too. Can we go for a walk, Stance?"

Stancil glanced at his father. Bomanz nodded. "Don't go far. The Guards are in a bad mood."

"We won't," Stance said. His father smiled at his eager departure. It had been that way for him and Jasmine, long ago.

Jasmine observed, "A lovely girl. Stance is lucky."

"Thank you," Tokar said. "We think she's lucky, too."

Snoopy made a sour face. Bomanz allowed himself a wry smile. Somebody had a crush on Stancil. "Three-handed game?" he suggested. "Take turns playing the dummy till somebody is out?"

He let chance have its way with the players' throws but turned five and sixes for the dummy. Snoopy went out and took the dummy. Jasmine seemed amused. Snoopy squealed delightedly when she won. "Glory, I won!" she enthused when her sister and Stancil returned. "I beat them."

Stancil looked at the board, at his father. "Pop. . . ."

"I fought all the way. She got the lucky throws."

Stancil smiled a disbelieving smile.

Glory said, "That's enough, Snoopy. Bedtime. This isn't the city. People go to bed early here."

"Aw. . . ." The girl complained but went. Bomanz sighed. Being sociable was a strain.

His heartbeat quickened as he anticipated the night's work.

Stancil completed a third reading of his written instructions. "Got it?" Bomanz asked.

"I guess."

"Timing isn't important—as long as you're late, not early. If we were going to conjure some damnfool demon, you'd study your lines for a week."

"Lines?" Stancil would do nothing but tend candles and observe. He was there to help if his father got into trouble.

Bomanz had spent the past two hours neutralizing spells along the path he intended to follow. The Moondog name had been a gold strike.

"Is it open?" Stancil asked.

"Wide. It almost pulls you. I'll let you go yourself later in the week."

Bomanz took a deep breath, exhaled. He surveyed the room. He still had that nagging feeling of having forgotten something. He hadn't a hint what it might be. "Okay."

He settled into the chair, closed his eyes. "Dumni," he murmured. "Um muji dumni. Haikon. Dumni. Um muji dumni."

Stancil pinched herbs into a diminutive charcoal brazier. Pungent smoke filled the room. Bomanz relaxed, let the lethargy steal over him. He achieved a quick separation, drifted up, hovered beneath the rafters, watched Stancil. The boy showed promise.

Bo checked his ties with his body. Good. Excellent! He could hear with both his spiritual and physical ears. He tested the duality further as he drifted downstairs. Each sound Stance made came through clearly.

He paused in the shop, stared at Glory and Snoopy. He envied them their youth and innocence.

Outside, the comet's glow filled the night. Bomanz felt its power showering the earth. How much more spectacular would it become by the time the world entered its mane?

Suddenly, *she* was there, beckoning urgently. He reexamined his ties to his flesh. Yes. Still in trance. Not dreaming. He felt vaguely ill at ease.

She led him to the Barrowland, following the path he had opened. He reeled under the awesome power buried there, away from the might radiating from the menhirs and fetishes. Seen from his spiritual viewpoint, they took the form of cruel, hideous monsters leashed on short chains.

Ghosts stalked the Barrowland. They howled beside Bomanz, trying to breach his spells. The power of the comet and the might of the warding spells joined in a thunder which permeated Bomanz's being. How mighty were the ancients, he thought, that all this should remain after so long.

They approached the dead soldiers represented by pawns on Bomanz's chart. He thought he heard footsteps behind him. . . . He looked back, saw nothing, realized he was hearing Stancil back at the house.

A knight's ghost challenged him. Its hatred was as timeless and relentless as the pounding surf along a cold, bleak shore. He sidled around.

Great green eyes stared into his own. Ancient, wise, merciless eyes, arrogant, mocking, and contemptuous. The dragon exposed its teeth in a sneer.

This is it, Bomanz thought. What I overlooked. . . . But no. The dragon could not touch him. He sensed its irritation, its conviction that he would make a tasty morsel in the flesh. He hurried after the woman.

No doubt about it. She was the Lady. She had been trying to reach him, too. Best be wary. She wanted more than a grateful chela.

They entered the crypt. It was massive, spacious, filled with all the clutter that had been the Dominator's in life. Clearly, that life had not been spartan.

He pursued the woman around a furniture pile—and found her vanished. "Where . . .?"

He saw them. Side by side, on separate stone slabs. Shackled. Enveloped by crackling, humming forces. Neither breathed, yet neither betrayed the grey of death. They seemed suspended, marking time.

Legend exaggerated only slightly. The Lady's impact, even in this state, was immense. "Bo, you have a grown son." Part of him wanted to stand on its hind legs and howl like an adolescent in rut.

He heard steps again. Damn that Stancil. Couldn't he stand still? He was making racket enough for three people.

The woman's eyes opened. Her lips formed a glorious smile. Bomanz forgot Stancil.

Welcome, said a voice within his mind. *We have waited a long time, haven't we?*

Dumbstruck, he simply nodded.

I have watched you. Yes, I see everything in this forsaken wilderness. I tried to help. The barriers were too many and too great. That cursed White Rose. She was no fool.

Bomanz glanced at the Dominator. That huge, handsome warrior-emperor slept on. Bomanz envied him his physical perfection.

He sleeps a deeper sleep.

Did he hear mockery? He could not read her face. The glamor was too much for him. He suspected that had been true for many men, and that it was true that she had been the driving force of the Domination.

I was. And next time. . . .

"Next time?"

Mirth surrounded him like the tinkle of wind chimes in a gentle breeze. *You came to learn, O wizard. How will you repay your teacher?*

Here was the moment for which he had lived. His triumph lay before him. One part to go. . . .

You were crafty. You were so careful, took so long, even that Monitor discounted you. I applaud you, wizard.

The hard part. Binding this creature to his will.

Wind-chimes laughter. *You don't plan to bargain? You mean to compel?*

"If I have to."

You won't give me anything?

"I can't give you what you want."

Mirth again. Silver-bells mirth. *You can't compel me.*

Bomanz shrugged imaginary shoulders. She was wrong. He had a lever. He had stumbled onto it as a youth, had recognized its significance immediately, and had set his feet on the long path leading to this moment.

He had found a cipher. He had broken it and it had given him the Lady's patronym, a name common in pre-Domination histories. Circumstances implicated one of that family's several daughters as the Lady. A little historical detective work had completed the task.

So he had solved a mystery that had baffled thousands for hundreds of years.

Knowing her true name gave him the power to compel the Lady. In wizardry, the true name is identical with the thing. . . .

I could have shrieked. It seemed my correspondent ended on the brink of the very revelation for which I had been searching these many years. Damn his black heart.

This time there was a postscript, a little something more than story. The letter-writer had added what looked like chicken scratches. That they were meant to communicate I had no doubt. But I could make nothing of them.

As always, there was neither signature nor seal.

20

The Barrowland

The rain never ceased. Mostly it was little more than a drizzle. When the day went especially well, it slackened to a falling mist. But always there was precipitation. Corbie went out anyway, though he complained often about aches in his leg.

"If the weather bothers you so, why stay here?" Case asked. "You said you think your kids live in Opal. Why not go down there and look for them yourself? At least the weather would be decent."

It was a tough question. Corbie had yet to create a convincing answer. He had not yet found one that would do himself, let alone enemies who might ask.

There was nothing Corbie was afraid to do. In another life, as another man, he had challenged the hellmakers themselves, unafraid. Swords and sorcery and death could not intimidate him. Only people, and love, could terrify him.

"Habit, I guess," he said. Weakly. "Maybe I could live in Oar. Maybe. I don't deal well with people, Case. I don't like them that much. I couldn't stand the Jewel Cities. Did I tell you I was down there once?"

Case had heard the story several times. He suspected Corbie had been more than down there. He thought one of the Jewel Cities was Corbie's original home. "Yeah. When the big Rebel push in Forsberg started. You told me about seeing the Tower on the way up."

"That's right. I did. Memory's slipping. Cities. I don't like them, lad. Don't like them. Too many people. Sometimes there's too many of them *here.* Was when I first came. Nowadays it's about right. About right. Maybe too much fuss and bother because of the undead over there." He poked his chin toward the Great Barrow. "But otherwise about right. One or two of you guys I can talk to. Nobody else to get in my way."

Case nodded. He thought he understood while not understanding. He had known other old veterans. Most had had their peculiarities. "Hey! Corbie. You ever run into the Black Company when you was up here?"

Corbie froze, stared with such intensity the young soldier blushed. "Uh. . . . What's the matter, Corbie? I say something wrong?"

Corbie resumed walking, his limp not slowing a furiously increased pace. "It was odd. Like you were reading my mind. Yes. I ran into those guys. Bad people. *Very* bad people."

"My dad told us stories about them. He was with them during the long retreat to Charm. Lords, the Windy Country, the Stair of Tear, all those battles. When he got leave time after the battle at Charm, he came home. Told awful stories about those guys."

"I missed that part. I got left behind at Roses, when Shifter and the Limper lost the battle. Who was your dad with? You've never talked about him much."

"Nightcrawler. I don't talk about him because we never got along."

Corbie smiled. "Sons seldom get on with their fathers. And that's the voice of experience speaking."

"What did your father do?"

Corbie laughed. "He was a farmer. Of sorts. But I'd rather not talk about him."

"What are we doing out here, Corbie?"

Double-checking Bomanz's surveys. But Corbie could not tell the lad that. Nor could he think of an adequate lie. "Walking in the rain."

"Corbie. . . ."

"Can we keep it quiet for a while, Case? Please?"

"Sure."

Corbie limped all the way around the Barrowland, maintaining a respectful distance, never being too obvious. He did not use equipment. That would bring Colonel Sweet on the run. Instead, he consulted the wizard's chart in his mind. The thing blazed with its own life there, those arcane TelleKurre symbols glowing with a wild and dangerous life. Studying the remains of the Barrowland, he could find but a third of the map's referents. The rest had been undone by time and weather.

Corbie was no man to have trouble with his nerve. But he was afraid now. Near the end of their stroll he said, "Case, I want a favor. Perhaps a double favor."

"Sir?"

"Sir? Call me Corbie."

"You sounded so serious."

"It is serious."

"Say on, then."

"Can you be trusted to keep your mouth shut?"

"If necessary."

"I want to extract a conditional vow of silence."

"I don't understand."

"Case, I want to tell you something. In case something happens to me."

"Corbie!"

"I'm not a young man, Case. And I have a lot wrong with me. I've been through a lot. I feel it catching up. I don't *expect* to go soon. But things happen. If something should, there's something I don't want to die with me."

"Okay, Corbie."

"If I suggested something, can you keep it to yourself? Even if you think you maybe shouldn't? Can you do something for me?"

"You're making it hard, not telling me."

"I know. It's not fair. The only other man I trust is Colonel Sweet. And his position wouldn't let him make such a promise."

"It's not illegal?"

"Not strictly speaking."

"I guess."

"Don't guess, Case."

"All right. You have my word."

"Good. Thank you. It *is* appreciated, never doubt that. Two things. First. If something happens to me, go to the room on the second floor of my home. If I have left an oilskin packet on the table there, see that it gets to a blacksmith named Sand, in Oar."

Case looked suitably dubious and baffled.

"Second, after you do that—and only after—tell the Colonel the undead are stirring."

Case stopped walking.

"Case." There was a note of command in Corbie's voice the youth had not heard before.

"Yes. All right."

"That's it."

"Corbie. . . ."

"No questions now. In a few weeks, maybe I can explain everything. All right?"

"Okay."

"Not a word now. And remember. Packet to Sand the blacksmith. Then word to the Colonel. Tell you what. If I can, I'll leave the Colonel a letter, too."

Case merely nodded.

Corbie took a deep breath. It had been twenty years since he had attempted the simplest divining spell. Never had he tried anything on the order of what he now faced. Back in those ancient times, when he was another man, or boy, sorcery was a diversion for wealthy youths who would rather play wizard than pursue legitimate studies.

All was ready. The tools of the sorcerer appropriate to the task lay on the table on the second floor of the house that Bomanz built. It was fitting that he follow the old one.

He touched the oilskin packet left for Case, the opaque letter to Sweet, and prayed neither would touch the young man's hands. But if what he suspected were true, it was better the enemy knew than the world be surprised.

There was nothing left to do but do it. He gulped half a cup of cold tea, took his seat. He closed his eyes, began a chant taught him when he was younger than Case. His was not the method Bomanz had used, but it was as effective.

His body would not relax, would not cease distracting him. But at last the full lethargy closed in. His ka loosed its ten thousand anchors to his flesh.

Part of him insisted he was a fool for attempting this without the skills of a master. But he hadn't the time for the training a Bomanz required. He had learned what he could during his absence from the Old Forest.

Free of the flesh, yet connected by invisible bonds that would draw him back. If his luck held. He moved away carefully. He conformed to the rule of bodies exactly. He used the stairway, the doorway, and the sidewalks built by the Guard. Maintain the pretense of flesh and the flesh would be harder to forget.

The world looked different. Each object had its unique aura. He found it difficult to concentrate on the grand task.

He moved to the bounds of the Barrowland. He shuddered under the impact of thrumming old spells that kept the Dominator and several lesser minions bound. The power there! Carefully, he walked the boundary till he found the way that Bomanz had opened, still not fully healed.

He stepped over the line.

He drew the instant attention of every spirit, benign and malign, chained within the Barrowland. There were far more than he expected. Far more than the wizard's map indicated. Those soldier symbols that surrounded the Great Barrow. . . . They were not statues. They were men, soldiers of the White Rose, who had been set as spirit guards perpetually standing between the world and the monster that would devour it. How driven must they have been. How dedicated to their cause.

The path wound past the former resting places of old Taken, outer circle, inner circle, twisting. Within the inner circle he saw the true forms of several lesser monsters that had served the Domination. The path stretched like a trail of pale silver mist. Behind him that mist became more dense, his passage strengthening the way.

Ahead, stronger spells. And all those men who had gone into the earth to surround the Dominator. And beyond them, the greater fear. The dragon thing that, on Bomanz's map, lay coiled around the crypt in the heart of the Great Barrow.

Spirits shrieked at him in TelleKurre, in UchiTelle, in languages he did not know and tongues vaguely like some still current. One and all, they cursed him. One and all, he ignored them. There was a thing in a chamber beneath the greatest mound. He had to see if it lay as restless as he suspected.

The dragon. Oh, by all the gods that never were, that dragon was real. Real, alive, of flesh, yet it sensed and saw him. The silver trail curved past its jaws, through the gap between teeth and tail. It beat at him with a palpable will. But he would not be stayed.

No more guardians. Just the crypt. And the monster man inside was constrained. He had survived the worst. . . .

The old devil should be sleeping. Hadn't the Lady defeated him in his attempt to escape through Juniper? Hadn't she put him back down?

It was a tomb like many around the world. Perhaps a bit richer. The White Rose had laid her opponents down in style. There were no sarcophagi, though. There. That empty table was where the Lady would have lain.

The other boasted a sleeping man. A big man, and handsome, but with the mark of the beast upon him, even in repose. A face full of hot hatred, of the anger of defeat.

Ah, then. His suspicions were groundless. The monster slept indeed. . . .

The Dominator sat up. And smiled. His smile was the most wicked Corbie had ever seen. Then the undead extended a hand in welcome. Corbie ran.

Mocking laughter pursued him.

Panic was an emotion entirely unfamiliar. Seldom had he experienced it. He could not control it. He was only vaguely aware of passing the dragon and the hate-filled spirits of White Rose soldiers. He barely sensed the Dominator's creatures beyond, all howling in delight.

Even in his panic he clung to the misty trail. He made only one misstep. . . .

But that was sufficient.

The storm broke over the Barrowland. It was the most furious in living memory. The lightning clashed with the ferocity of heavenly armies, hammers and spears and swords of fire smiting earth and sky. The downpour was incessant and impenetrable.

One mighty bolt struck the Barrowland. Earth and shrubbery flew a hundred yards into the air. The earth staggered. The Eternal Guard scrambled to arms terrified, sure the old evil had broken its chains.

On the Barrowland two large shapes, one four-footed, one bipedal, formed in the afterglow of the lightning strike. In a moment both raced along a twisting path, leaving no mark upon water or mud. They passed the bounds of the Barrowland, fled toward the forest.

No one saw them. When the Guard reached the Barrowland, carrying weapons and lanterns and fear like vast loads of lead, the storm had waned. The lightning had ceased its boisterous brawl. The rain had fallen off to normal.

Colonel Sweet and his men spent hours roaming the bounds of the Barrowland. No one found a thing.

The Eternal Guard returned to its compound cursing the gods and weather.

On the second floor of Corbie's house Corbie's body continued to breathe one breath each five minutes. His heart barely turned over. He would be a long time dying without his spirit.

The Plain of Fear

I asked to see Darling and got an immediate audience. She expected me to come in raising hell about ill-advised military actions by outfits that could not afford losses. She expected lessons in the importance of maintaining cadres and forces-in-being. I surprised her by coming with neither. Here she was, primed to weather the worst, to get it over so she could get back to business, and I disappointed her.

Instead, I took her the letters from Oar, which I had shared with no one yet. She expressed curiosity. I signed: "Read them."

It took a while. The Lieutenant ducked in and out, growing more impatient each time. She finished, looked at me. "Well?" she signed.

"That comes from the core of the documents I am missing. Along with a few other things, that story is what I have been hunting. Soulcatcher gave me to believe that the weapon we want is hidden inside this story."

"It is not complete."

"No. But does it not give you pause?"

"You have no idea who the writer is?"

"No. And no way to find out, short of looking him up. Or her." Actually, I had a couple of suspicions, but each seemed more unlikely than the other.

"These have come with swift regularity," Darling observed. "After all this time." That made me suspect she shared one of my suspicions. That "all this time."

"The couriers believe they were forwarded over a more spread period."

"It is interesting, but not yet useful. We must await more."

"It will not hurt to consider what it means. The end part of the last, there. That is beyond me. I have to work on that. It may be critical. Unless it is meant to baffle someone who intercepts the fragment."

She shuffled out the last sheet, stared at it. A sudden light illuminated her face. "It is the finger speech, Croaker," she signed. "The letters. See? The speaking hand, as it forms the alphabet."

I circled behind her. I saw it now, and felt abysmally stupid for having missed it. Once you saw that, it was easy to read. If you knew your sign. It said:

This may be the last communication, Croaker. There is something I must do. The risks are grave. The chances hang against me, but I must go ahead. If you do not receive the final installment, about Bomanz's last days, you will have to come collect it. I will conceal one copy within the home of the wizard, as the story describes. You may find another in Oar. Ask for the blacksmith named Sand.

Wish me luck. By now you must have found a place of safety. I would not bring you forth unless the fate of the world hinged upon it.

There was no signature here, either.

Darling and I stared at one another. I asked, "What do you think? What should I do?"

"Wait."

"And if no further episodes are forthcoming?"

"Then you must go looking."

"Yes." Fear. The world was marshaled against us. The Rust raid would have the Taken in a vengeful frenzy.

"It may be the great hope, Croaker."

"The Barrowland, Darling. Only the Tower itself could be more dangerous."

"Perhaps I should accompany you."

"No! You will not be risked. Not under any circumstances. The movement can survive the loss of one beat-up, worn-out old physician. It cannot without the White Rose."

She hugged me hard, backed off, signed, "I am not the White Rose, Croaker. She is dead four centuries. I am Darling."

"Our enemies call you the White Rose. Our friends do. There is power in a name." I waved the letters. "That is what this is about. One name. What you have been named you must be."

"I am Darling," she insisted.

"To me, maybe. To Silent. To a few others. But to the world you are the White Rose, the hope and the salvation." It occurred to me that a name was missing. The name Darling wore before she became a ward of the Company. Always she had been Darling, because that was what Raven called her. Had he known her birthname? If so, it no longer mattered. She was safe. She was the last alive to know it, if even she remembered. The village where we found her, mauled by the Limper's troops, was not the sort that kept written records.

"Go," she signed. "Study. Think. Be of good faith. Somewhere, soon, you will find the thread."

The Plain of Fear

The men who fled Rust with the cowardly windwhale eventually arrived. We learned that the Taken had escaped the Plain, all in a rage because but one carpet survived. Their offensive would be delayed till the carpets were replaced. And carpets are among the greatest and most costly magicks. I suspect the Limper had to do a lot of explaining to the Lady.

I drafted One-Eye, Goblin, and Silent into an expanded project. I translated. They extracted proper names, assembled them in charts. My quarters became all but impenetrable. And barely livable while they were there, for Goblin and One-Eye had had a couple of tastes of life outside Darling's null. They were at one another constantly.

And I began having nightmares.

One evening I posed a challenge, half as a result of no further courier arriving, half as busywork meant to stop Goblin and One-Eye from driving me mad. I said, "I may have to leave the Plain. Can you do something so I don't attract any special attention?"

They had their questions. I answered most honestly. They wanted to go too, as if a journey west was established fact. I said, "No way are you going. A thousand miles of this crap? I'd commit suicide before we got off the Plain. Or murder one of you. Which I'm considering anyway."

Goblin squeaked. He pretended mortal terror. One-Eye said, "Get within ten feet of me and I'll turn you into a lizard."

I made a rude noise. "You can barely turn food into shit."

Goblin cackled. "Chickens and cows do better. You can fertilize with theirs."

"You got no room to talk, runt," I snapped.

"Getting touchy in his old age," One-Eye observed. "Must be rheumatiz. Got the rheumatiz, Croaker?"

"He'll wish his problem was rheumatism if he keeps on," Goblin promised. "It's bad enough I have to put up with you. But you're at least predictable."

"Predictable?"

"Like the seasons."

They were off. I sped Silent a look of appeal. The son-of-a-bitch ignored me.

Next day Goblin ambled in wearing a smug smile. "We figured something out, Croaker. In case you do go wandering."

"Like what?"

"We'll need your amulets."

I had two that they had given me long ago. One was supposed to warn me of the proximity of the Taken. It worked quite well. The other, ostensibly, was protective, but it also let them locate me from a distance. Silent tracked it the time Catcher sent Raven and me to ambush Limper and Whisper in the Forest of Cloud, when Limper tried to go over to the Rebel.

Long ago and far away. Memories of a younger Croaker.

"We'll work up some modifications. So you can't be located magically. Let me have them. Later we'll have to go outside to test them."

I eyed him narrowly.

He said, "You'll have to come so we can test them by trying to find you."

"Yeah? Sounds like a drummed-up excuse to get outside the null."

"Maybe." He grinned.

Whatever, Darling liked the notion. Next evening we headed up the creek, skirting Old Father Tree. "He looks a little peaked," I said.

"Caught the side wash of a Taken spell during the brouhaha," One-Eye explained. "I don't think he was pleased."

The old tree tinkled. I stopped, considered it. It had to be thousands of years old. Trees grow very slow on the Plain. What stories it would tell!

"Come on, Croaker," Goblin called. "Old Father ain't talking." He grinned his frog grin.

They know me too well. Know when I see anything old I wonder what it has seen. Damn them, anyhow.

We left the watercourse five miles from the Hole, quartered westward into desert where the coral was especially dense and dangerous. I guess there were five hundred species, in reefs so close they were almost impenetrable. The colors were riotous. Fingers, fronds, branches of coral soared thirty feet into the air. I remain eternally amazed that the wind does not topple them.

In a small sandy place surrounded by coral, One-Eye called a halt. "This is far enough. We'll be safe here."

I wondered. Our progress had been followed by mantas and the creatures that resemble buzzards. Never will I trust such beasts completely.

Long, long ago, after the Battle at Charm, the Company crossed the Plain en route to assignments in the east. I saw horrible things happen. I could not shake the memories.

Goblin and One-Eye played games but also tended to business. They remind me of active children. Always into something, just to be doing. I lay back and watched the clouds. Soon I fell asleep.

Goblin wakened me. He returned my amulets. "We're going to play hide-and-seek," he said. "We'll give you a head start. If we've done everything right, we won't be able to find you."

"Now that's wonderful," I replied. "Me alone out here, wandering around lost." I was just carping. I could find the Hole. As a nasty practical joke I was tempted to head straight there.

This was business, though.

I set off to the southwest, toward the buttes. I crossed the westward trail and went into hiding among quiescent walking trees. Only after darkness fell did I give up waiting. I walked back to the Hole, wondering what had become of my companions. I startled the sentry when I arrived.

"Goblin and One-Eye come in?"

"No. I thought they were with you."

"They were." Concerned, I went below, asked the Lieutenant's advice.

"Go find them," he told me.

"How?"

He looked at me like I was a half-wit. "Leave your silly amulets, go outside the null, and wait."

"Oh. Okay."

So I went back outside, walked up the creek, grumbling. My feet ached. I was not used to so much hiking. Good for me, I told myself. Had to be in shape if there was a trip to Oar in the cards.

I reached the edge of the coral reefs. "One-Eye! Goblin! You guys around?"

No answer. I was not going on looking, though. The coral would kill me. I circled north, assuming they had moved away from the Hole. Each few minutes I dropped to my knees, hoping to spot a menhir's silhouette. The menhirs would know what had become of them.

Once I saw some flash and fury from the corner of my eye and, without thinking, ran that way, thinking it was Goblin and One-Eye squabbling. But a direct look revealed the distant rage of a change storm.

I stopped immediately, belatedly remembering that only death hurries on the Plain by night.

I was lucky. Just steps onward the sand became spongy, loose. I squatted, sniffed a handful. It held the smell of old death. I backed away carefully. Who knows what lay in waiting beneath that sand?

"Better plant somewhere and wait for the sun," I muttered. I was no longer certain of my position.

I found some rocks that would break the wind, some brush for firewood, and pitched camp. The fire was more to declare myself to beasts than to keep warm. The night was not cold.

Firemaking was a symbolic statement out there.

Once the flames rose I found that the place had been used before. Smoke had blackened the rocks. Native humans, probably. They wander in small bands. We have little intercourse with them. They have no interest in the world struggle.

Will failed me sometime after the second hour. I fell asleep.

The nightmare found me. And found me unshielded by amulets or null.

She came.

It had been years. Last time it was to report the final defeat of her husband in the affair at Juniper.

A golden cloud, like dust motes dancing in a sunbeam. An all-over feeling of being awake while sleeping. Calmness and fear together. An inability to move. All the old symptoms.

A beautiful woman formed in the cloud, a woman out of daydream. The sort you hope to meet someday, knowing there is no chance. I cannot say what she wore, if she wore anything. My universe consisted of her face and the terror its presence inspired.

Her smile was not at all cold. Long ago, for some reason, she took an interest in me. I supposed she retained some residue of the old affection, as one does for a pet long dead.

"Physician." Breeze in the reeds beside the waters of eternity. The whisper of angels. But never could she make me forget the reality whence the voice sprang.

Nor was she ever so gauche as to tempt me, either with promises or herself. That, perhaps, is one reason I think she felt a certain fondness. When she used me, she gave it to me straight going in.

I could not respond.

"You are safe. Long ago, by your standard of time, I said I would remain in touch. I have been unable. You cut me off. I have been trying for weeks."

The nightmares explained.

"What?" I squeaked like Goblin.

"Join me at Charm. Be my historian."

As always when she touched me, I was baffled. She seemed to consider me outside the struggle while yet a part of it. On the Stair of Tear, on the eve of the most savage sorcerous struggle ever I witnessed, she came to promise me I would come to no harm. She seemed intrigued with my lesser role as Company historian. Back when, she insisted I record events as they happened. Without regard to pleasing anyone. I had done so within the limits of my prejudices.

"The heat in the crucible is rising, physician. Your White Rose is crafty. Her attack behind the Limper was a grand stroke. But insignificant on the broader canvas. Don't you agree?"

How could I argue? I did agree.

"As your spies have no doubt reported, five armies stand poised to cleanse the Plain of Fear. It is a strange and unpredictable land. But it will not withstand what is being marshaled."

Again I could not argue, for I believed her. I could but do what Darling so often spoke of: Buy time. "You may be surprised."

"Perhaps. Surprises have been calculated into my plans. Come out of that cold waste, Croaker. Come to the Tower. Become my historian."

This was as near temptation as ever she had come. She spoke to a part of me I do not understand, a part almost willing to betray comrades of decades. If I went, there was so much I would *know*. So many answers illuminated. So many curiosities satisfied.

"You escaped us at Queen's Bridge."

Heat climbed my neck. During our years on the run the Lady's forces had overtaken us several times. Queen's Bridge was the worst. A hundred brothers had fallen there. And to my shame, I left the Annals behind, buried in the river bank. Four hundred years worth of Company history, abandoned.

There was just so much that could be carried away. The papers down in the Hole were critical to our future. I took them instead of the Annals. But I suffer frequent bouts of guilt. I must answer the shades of brethren who have gone before. Those Annals *are* the Black Company. While they exist, the Company lives.

"We escaped and escaped, and will continue to escape. It is fated."

She smiled, amused. "I have read your Annals, Croaker. New and old."

I began throwing wood onto the embers of my fire. I was not dreaming. "You have them?" Till that moment I had silenced guilt with promises to recover them.

"They were found after the battle. They came to me. I was pleased. You are honest, as historians go."

"Thank you. I try."

"Come to Charm. There is a place for you in the Tower. You can see the grand canvas from here."

"I can't."

"I cannot shield you there. If you stay, you must face what befalls your Rebel friends. The Limper commands that campaign. I will not interfere. He is not what he was. You hurt him. And he had to be hurt more to be saved. He has not forgiven you that, Croaker."

"I know." How many times had she used my name? In all our contacts previously, over years, she had used it but once.

"Don't let him take you."

A slight, twisted bit of humor rose from somewhere inside me. "You are a failure, Lady."

She was taken aback.

"Fool that I am, I recorded my romances in the Annals. You read them. You know I never characterized you as black. Not, I think, as I would characterize your husband. I suspect an unconsciously sensed truth lies beneath the silliness of those romances."

"Indeed?"

"I don't think you *are* black. I think you're just trying. I think that, for all the wickedness you've done, part of the child that was remains untainted. A spark remains, and you can't extinguish it."

Unchallenged, I became more daring. "I think you've selected me as a symbolic sop to that spark. I am a reclamation project meant to satisfy a hidden streak of decency, the way my friend Raven reclaimed a child who became the White Rose. You read the Annals. You know to what depths Raven sank once he concentrated all decency in one cup. Better, perhaps, that he had had none at all. Juniper might still exist. So might he."

"Juniper was a boil overdue for lancing. I am not come to be mocked, physician. I will not be made to look weak even before an audience of one."

I started to protest.

"For I know that this, too, will end up in your Annals."

She knew me. But then, she had had me before the Eye.

"Come to the Tower, Croaker. I demand no oath."

"Lady. . . ."

"Even the Taken bind themselves with deadly oaths. You may remain free. Just do what you do. Heal, and record the truth. What you would do anywhere. You have value not to be wasted out there."

Now there was a sentiment with which I could agree wholeheartedly. I would take it back and rub some people's noses in it. "Say what?"

She started to speak. I raised a warning hand. I had spoken to myself, not to her. Was that a footfall? Yes. Something big coming. Something moving slowly, wearily.

She sensed it, too. An eye blink and she was gone, her departure sucking something from my mind, so that once more I was not certain I had not dreamed everything, for all that every word remained immutably inscribed on the stone of my mind.

I shuffled brush onto my fire, backed into a crack behind the dagger that was the only weapon I'd had sense enough to bring.

It came closer. Then paused. Then came on. My heartbeat increased. Something thrust into the firelight.

"Toadkiller Dog! What the hell, hey? What're you doing? Come on in out of the cold, boy." The words tumbled out, bearing fear away. "Boy, will Tracker be glad to see you. What happened to you?"

He came forward cautiously, looking twice as mangy as ever. He dropped onto his belly, rested his chin on forepaws, closed one eye.

"I don't have any food. I'm sort of lost myself. You're damned lucky, know that? Making it this far. The Plain is a bad place to be on your own."

Right then that old mongrel looked like he agreed. Body language, if you will. He had survived, but it had not been easy.

I told him, "Sun comes up, we'll head back. Goblin and One-Eye got lost; it's their own tough luck."

After Toadkiller Dog's arrival I rested better. I guess the old alliance is imprinted on people, too. I was confident he would warn me if trouble beckoned.

Come morning we found the creek and headed for the Hole. I stopped, as I often do, to approach Old Father Tree for a little one-sided conversation about what he had seen during his long sentinelship. The dog would not come anywhere near. Weird. But so what? Weird is the order of the day on the Plain.

I found One-Eye and Goblin snoring, sleeping in. They had returned to the Hole only minutes after my departure in search of them. Bastards. I would redress the balance when the chance came.

I drove them crazy by not mentioning my night out.

"Did it work?" I demanded. Down the tunnel Tracker was having a noisy reunion with his mutt.

"Sort of," Goblin said. He was not enthusiastic.

"Sort of? What's *sort of*? Does it work or doesn't it?"

"Well, what we got is a problem. Mainly, we can keep the Taken from locating you. From getting a fix on you, so to speak."

Obfuscation is a sure sign of trouble with this guy. "But? But me the *but*, Goblin."

"If you go outside the null, there's no hiding the fact that you are out."

"Great. Real great. What good are you guys, anyway?"

"It's not that bad," One-Eye said. "You wouldn't attract any attention unless they find out you're out from some other source. I mean, they wouldn't be watching for you, would they? No reason to. So it's just as good as if we got it to do everything we wanted."

"Crap! You better start praying that next letter comes through. Because if I go out and get my ass killed, guess who's going to haunt whom forever?"

"Darling wouldn't send you out."

"Bet? She'll go through three or four days of soul-searching. But she'll send me. Because that last letter will give us the key."

Sudden fear. Had the Lady probed my mind?

"What's the matter, Croaker?"

I was saved a lie by Tracker's advent. He bounced in and pumped my hand like a mad fool. "Thank you, Croaker. Thanks for bringing him home." Out he went.

"What the hell was that?" Goblin asked.

"I brought his dog home."

"Weird."

One-Eye chortled. "The pot calling the kettle black."

"Yeah? Lizard snot. Want me to tell you about weird?"

"Stow it," I said. "If I get sent out of here I want this stuff in perfect order. I just wish we had people who could read this junk."

"Maybe I can help." Tracker was back. The big dumb lout. A devil with a sword, but probably unable to write his own name.

"How?"

"I could read some of that stuff. I know some old language. My father taught me." He grinned as if at a huge joke. He selected a piece written in TelleKurre. He read it aloud. The ancient language rolled off his tongue naturally, as I had heard it spoken among the old Taken. Then he translated. It was a memo to a castle kitchen about a meal to be prepared for visiting notables. I went over it painstakingly. His translation was faultless. Better than I could do. A third of the words evaded me.

"Well. Welcome to the team. I'll tell Darling." I slipped out, exchanging a puzzled glance with One-Eye behind Tracker's back.

Stranger and stranger. What was this man? Besides weird. At first encounter he reminded me of Raven, and fit the role. When I came to think of him as big, slow, and clumsy, he fit that role. Was he a reflection of the image in his beholder?

A good fighter, though, bless him. Worth ten of anyone else we have.

23

The Plain of Fear

It was the time of the Monthly Meeting. The big confab during which nothing gets done. During which all heads yammer of pet projects on which action cannot be taken. After six or eight hours of which Darling closes debate by telling us what to do.

The usual charts were up. One showed where our agents believed the Taken to be. Another showed incursions reported by the menhirs. Both showed a lot of white, areas of Plain unknown to us. A third chart showed the month's change storms, a pet project of the Lieutenant's. He was looking for something. As always, most were along the periphery. But there was an unusually large number, and higher than normal percentage, in this chart's interior. Seasonal? A genuine shift? Who knew? We had not been watching long enough. The menhirs will not bother explaining such trivia.

Darling took charge immediately. She signed, "The operation in Rust had the effect I hoped. Our agents have reported anti-imperial outbreaks almost everywhere. They have diverted some attention from us. But the armies of the Taken keep building. Whisper has become especially aggressive in her incursions."

Imperial troops entered the Plain almost every day, probing for a response and preparing their men for the Plain's perils. Whisper's operations, as always, were very professional. Militarily, she is to be feared far more than the Limper.

Limper is a loser. That is not his fault, entirely, but the stigma has attached itself. Winner or loser, though, he is running the other side.

"Word came this morning that Whisper has established a garrison a day's march inside the boundary. She is erecting fortifications, daring our response."

Her strategy was apparent. Establish a network of mutually supporting fortresses; build it slowly until it is spread out over the Plain. She was dangerous, that woman. Especially if she sold the idea to the Limper and got all the armies into the act.

As a strategy it goes back to the dawn of time, having been used again and again where regular armies face partisans in wild country. It is a patient strategy that depends on the will of the conqueror to persevere. It works where that will exists and fails where it does not.

Here it will work. The enemy has twenty-some years to root us out. And feels no need to hold the Plain once done with us.

Us? Let us say, instead, Darling. The rest of us are nothing in the equation. If Darling falls, there is no Rebellion.

"They are taking away time," Darling signed. "We need decades. We have to do something."

Here it comes, I thought. She had on that look. She was going to announce the result of much soul-searching. So I was not struck down with astonishment when she signed, "I am sending Croaker to recover the rest of his correspondent's story." News of the letters had spread. Darling will gossip. "Goblin and One-Eye will accompany and support him."

"What? There ain't no way. . . ."

"Croaker."

"I won't do it. Look at me. I'm a nothing guy. Who's going to notice me? One old guy wandering around. The world is full of them. But three guys? One of them black? One of them a runt with. . . ."

Goblin and One-Eye sped me milk-curdling looks.

I snickered. My outburst put them in a tight place. Though they wanted to go no more than I wanted them along, they now dared not agree with me publicly. Worse, they had to agree with each other. Ego!

But my point remained. Goblin and One-Eye are known characters. For that matter, so am I, but as I pointed out, I'm not physically remarkable.

Darling signed, "Danger will encourage their cooperation."

I fled to my last citadel. "The Lady touched me on the desert that night I was out, Darling. *She* is watching for me."

Darling thought a moment, signed back, "That changes nothing. We must have that last piece of story before the Taken close in."

She was right about that. But. . . .

She signed, "You three will go. Be careful."

Tracker followed the debate with Otto's help. He offered, "I'll go. I know the north. Especially the Great Forest. That's where I got my name." Behind him, Toadkiller Dog yawned.

"Croaker?" Darling asked.

I was not yet resigned to going. So I passed it back to her. "Up to you."

"You could use a fighter," she signed. "Tell him you accept."

I mumbled and muttered, faced Tracker. "She says you go."

He looked pleased.

As far as Darling was concerned, that was that. The thing was settled. They hastened down the agenda to a report from Corder suggesting Tanner was ripe for a raid like that on Rust.

I fussed and fumed and no one paid me any mind, except Goblin and One-Eye, who sent me looks saying I would rue my insults.

No fooling around. We left fourteen hours later. With everything arranged for us. Dragged out of bed soon after midnight, I quickly found myself topside, beside the coral, watching a small windwhale descend. A menhir yammered behind me, instructing me in the care and stroking of the windwhale ego. I ignored him. This had come on too swiftly. I was being shoved into the saddle before I'd made up my mind to go. I was living behind events.

I had my weapons, my amulets, money, food. Everything I should need. Likewise Goblin and One-Eye, who had provided themselves with a supplementary arsenal of thaumaturgic gewgaws. The plan was to purchase a wagon and team after the windwhale dropped us behind enemy lines. All the junk they were bringing, I grumbled, we might need two.

Tracker traveled light, though. Food, an array of weapons selected from what we had on hand, and his mutt.

The windwhale rose. Night enveloped us. I felt lost. I hadn't gotten so much as a good-bye hug.

The windwhale went up where the air was chill and thin. To the east, the south, and northwest I spied the glimmer of change storms. They *were* becoming more common.

I guess I was getting blasé about windwhale-riding. Shivering, huddling into myself, ignoring Tracker, who was a positive chatterbox yammering about trivia, I fell asleep. I wakened to a shaking hand and Tracker's face inches from mine.

"Wake up, Croaker," he kept saying. "Wake up. One-Eye says we got trouble."

I rose, expecting to find Taken circling us.

We were surrounded, but by four windwhales and a score of mantas. "Where did they come from?"

"Showed up while you were sleeping."

"What's the trouble?"

Tracker pointed, off what I guess you would call our starboard bow.

Change storm. Shaping.

"Just popped out of nowhere," Goblin said, joining us, too nervous to remember he was mad at me. "Looks like a bad one, too, the rate it's growing."

The change storm was no more than four hundred yards in diameter now, but the pastel-lightninged fury in its heart said it would grow swiftly and terribly. Its touch would be more than normally dramatic. Varicolored light painted faces and windwhales bizarrely. Our convoy shifted course. The windwhales are not as much affected as humans, but they prefer to dodge trouble where possible. It was clear, though, that fringes of the monster would brush us.

Even as I recognized and thought about it, the storm's size increased. Six hundred yards in diameter. Eight hundred. Roiling, boiling color within what looked like black smoke. Serpents of silent lightning snapped and snarled soundlessly around one another.

The bottom of the change storm touched ground.

All those lightnings found their voices. And the storm expanded even more rapidly, hurling in another direction that growth which should have gone earthward. It was terrible with energy, this one.

Change storms seldom came nearer than eight miles to the Hole. They are impressive enough from that distance, when you catch only a whiff that crackles in your hair and makes your nerves go frazzled. In olden times, when we still served the Lady, I talked to veterans of Whisper's campaigns who told me of suffering through the storms. I never wholly credited their tales.

I did so as the boundary of the storm gained on us.

One of the mantas was caught. You could see through it, its bones white against sudden darkness. Then it *changed.*

Everything changed. Rocks and trees became protean. Small things that followed and pestered us shifted form. . . .

There is a hypothesis which states that the strange species of the Plain have appeared as a result of change storms. It has been proposed, too, that the change storms are responsible for the Plain itself. That each gnaws a bit more off our normal world.

The whales gave up trying to outrun the storm and plunged earthward, below the curve of expanding storm, getting down where the fall would be shorter if they changed into something unable to fly. Standard procedure for anyone caught in a change storm. Stay low and don't move.

Whisper's veterans spoke of lizards growing to elephant size, of spiders becoming monstrous, of poisonous serpents sprouting wings, of intelligent creatures going mad and trying to murder everything about them.

I was scared.

Not too scared to observe, though. After the manta showed us its bones it resumed its normal form, but grew. As did a second when the boundary overtook it. Did that mean a common tendency toward growth on a storm's outward pulse?

The storm caught our windwhale, which was the slowest getting down. Young it was, but conscientious about its burden. The crackle in my hair peaked. I thought my nerves would betray me completely. A glance at Tracker convinced me we were going to have a major case of panic.

Goblin or One-Eye, one, decided to be a hero and stay the storm. Might as well have ordered the sea to turn. The crash and roar of a major sorcery vanished in the rage of the storm.

There was an instant of utter stillness when the boundary reached me. Then a roar out of hell. The winds inside were ferocious. I thought of nothing but getting down and hanging on. Around me gear was flying about, changing shape as it flew. Then I spied Goblin. And nearly threw up.

Goblin indeed. His head had swelled ten times normal size. The rest of him looked inside out. Around him swarmed a horde of the parasites that live on a windwhale's back, some as big as pigeons.

Tracker and Toadkiller Dog were worse. The mutt had become something half as big as an elephant, fanged, possessed of the most evil eyes I've ever seen. He looked at me with a starved lust that chilled my soul. And Tracker had become something demonic, vaguely apelike yet certainly much more. Both looked like creatures from an artist's or sorcerer's nightmares.

One-Eye was the least changed. He swelled, but remained One-Eye. Perhaps he is well-rooted in the world, being so damned old. Near as I can tell, he is pushing a hundred fifty.

The thing that was Toadkiller Dog crept toward me with teeth bared. . . . The windwhale touched down. Impact sent everyone tumbling. The wind screamed around us. The strange lightning hammered earth and air. The landing area itself was in a protean mood. Rocks crawled. Trees changed shape. The animals of that part of the Plain were out and gamboling in revised forms, onetime prey turning upon predator. The horror show was illuminated by a shifting, sometimes ghastly light.

Then the vacuum at the heart of the storm enveloped us. Everything froze in the form it had at the last instant. Nothing moved. Tracker and Toadkiller Dog were down on the ground, thrown there after impact. One-Eye and Goblin faced one another, in the first phase of letting their feud go beyond its customary gamesmanship. The other windwhales lay nearby, not visibly affected. A manta plunged out of the color above, crashed.

That stasis lasted maybe three minutes. In the stillness sanity returned. Then the change storm began to collapse.

The devolution of the storm was slower than its growth. But saner, too. We suffered it for several hours. And then it was done. And our sole casualty was the one manta that had crashed. But damn, was it ever a shaking experience.

"Damn lucky," I told the others, as we inventoried our possessions. "Lucky we weren't all killed."

"No luck to it, Croaker," One-Eye replied. "The moment these monsters saw a storm coming they headed for safe ground. A place where there would be nothing that could kill us. Or them."

Goblin nodded. They were doing a lot of agreeing lately. But we all recalled how close they had come to murder.

I asked, "What did I look like? I didn't feel any change, except a sort of nervous turmoil. Like being drunk, drugged, and half-crazy all at the same time."

"Looked like Croaker to me," One-Eye said. "Only twice as ugly."

"And dull," Goblin added. "You made the most inspiring speech about the glories the Black Company won during the campaign against Chew."

I laughed. "Come on."

"Really. You were just Croaker. Maybe those amulets are good for something."

Tracker was going over his weaponry. Toadkiller Dog was napping near his feet. I pointed. One-Eye signed, "Didn't see."

Goblin signed, "He grew up and got claws."

They did not seem concerned. I decided I should not be. After all, the whale lice were the nastiest thing after the mutt.

The windwhales remained grounded, for the sun was rising. Their backs assumed the dun color of the earth, complete with sage-colored patches, and we waited for the night. The mantas nested down on the other four whales. None came near us. You get the feeling humans make them uncomfortable.

The Wide World

They never tell me anything. But I should complain? Secrecy is our armor. Need to know. All that crap. In our outfit it is the iron rule of survival.

Our escort was not along just to help us break out of the Plain of Fear. They had their own mission. What I had not been told was that Whisper's headquarters was to be attacked.

Whisper had no warning. Our companion windwhales dropped away slowly as the edge of the Plain approached. Their mantas dropped with them.

They caught favorable winds and pulled ahead. We climbed higher, into the pure shivers and gasp for breaths.

The mantas struck first. In twos and threes they crossed the town at treetop level, loosing their bolts into Whisper's quarters. Rock and timbers flew like the dust around stamping hooves. Fires broke out.

The monsters of the upper air rolled in behind as soldiers and civilians hit the streets. They unleashed bolts of their own. But the real horror was their tentacles.

The windwhales gorged upon men and animals. They ripped houses and fortifications apart. They yanked trees out by their roots. And they pounded away at Whisper with their bolts.

The mantas, meantime, rose a thousand feet and plunged again, in their pairs and threes, this time to strike at Whisper as she responded.

Her response, though it did set a broad patch of one windwhale's flank gruesomely aglow, pinpointed her for the mantas. They slapped her around good, though she did bring one down.

We passed over, the flash and fires illuminating our monster's belly. If anyone in the crucible spotted us, I doubt they guessed we were going on. Goblin and One-Eye detected no interest in anything but survival.

It continued as we lost sight of the town. Goblin said they had Whisper on the run, too busy saving her own ass to help her men.

"Glad they never pulled any of this crap on us," I said.

"It's a one-shot," Goblin countered. "Next time they'll be ready."

"I'd have thought they'd be now, because of Rust."

"Maybe Whisper has an ego problem."

No maybe about it. I had dealt with her. It was her weak spot. She would have made no preparations because she believed we feared her too much. She was, after all, the most brilliant of the Taken.

Our mighty steed ploughed the night, back brushing the stars, body gurgling, chugging, humming. I began to feel optimistic.

At dawn we dropped into a canyon in the Windy Country, another big desert. Unlike the Plain, though, it is normal. A big emptiness where the wind blows all the time. We ate and slept. When night fell we resumed our journey.

We left the desert south of Lords, turned north over the Forest of Cloud, avoiding settlements. Beyond the Forest of Cloud, though, the windwhale descended. And we were on our own.

I wish we could have gone the whole way airborne. But that was as far as Darling and the windwhales were willing to risk. Beyond lay heavily inhabited country. We could not hope to come down and pass the daylight hours unseen. So from there on we would travel the old-fashioned way.

The free city of Roses was about fifteen miles away.

Roses has been free throughout history, a republican plutocracy. Even the

Lady did not see fit to buck tradition. One huge battle took place nearby, during the northern campaigns, but the site was of Rebel choosing, not ours. We lost. For several months Roses lost its independence. Then the Lady's victory at Charm ended Rebel dominion. All in all, though unaligned, Roses is a friend of the Lady.

Crafty bitch.

We hiked. Our journey was an all-day affair. Neither I nor Goblin nor One-Eye was in good shape. Too much loafing. Getting too old.

"This isn't smart," I said as we approached a gate in Roses' pale red walls, toward sunset. "We've all been here before. You two should be well-remembered, what with having robbed half the citizens."

"Robbed?" One-Eye protested. "Who robbed . . .?"

"Both of you clowns. Selling those damned guaranteed-to-work amulets when we were after Raker."

Raker was a one-time Rebel general. He had beaten the crap out of the Limper farther north; then the Company, with a little help from Soulcatcher, had sucked him into a trap in Roses. Both Goblin and One-Eye had preyed on the populace. One-Eye was an old hand at that. Back when we were in the south, beyond the Sea of Torments, he had been involved in every shady scheme he could find. Most of his ill-gotten gains he soon lost at cards. He is the world's worst cardplayer.

You'd think by one-fifty he would learn to count them.

The plan was for us to lay up at some sleazy no-questions-asked inn. Tracker and I would go out next day and buy a wagon and team. Then we would head out the way we had come, pick up what gear we had been unable to carry, and circle the city by heading north.

That was the plan. Goblin and One-Eye did not stick to it.

Rule Number One for a soldier: Stick to the mission. The mission is paramount.

For Goblin and One-Eye all rules are made to be broken. When Tracker and I returned, with Toadkiller Dog loping along behind, it was late afternoon. We parked. Tracker stood by while I went upstairs.

No Goblin. No One-Eye.

The proprietor told me they had left soon after I had, chattering about finding some women.

My fault. I was in charge. I should have foreseen it. It had been a long, long, long time. I paid for another two nights, just in case. Then I turned animals and wagon over to the hostler's boy, had supper with a silent Tracker, and retreated to our room with several quarts of beer. We shared it, Tracker, me, and Toadkiller Dog.

"You going looking for them?" Tracker asked.

"No. If they haven't come back in two days or pulled the roof in on us, we'll go ahead without them. I don't want to be seen around them. There'll be people here who remember them."

We got pleasantly buzzed. Toadkiller Dog seemed capable of drinking people under the table. Loved his beer, that dog. Actually got up and moved around when he didn't have to.

Next morning, no Goblin. No One-Eye. But plenty of rumors. We entered the common room late, after the morning crowd and before the noontime rush. The hostler had no other ears to bend.

"You guys hear about the ruckus over in the east end last night?"

I groaned before he got to the meat of it. I knew.

"Yeah. Regular wahoo war party. Fires. Sorcery. Lynch mob. Excitement like this old town hain't seen since that time they were after that General What's-it the Lady wanted."

After he went to pester another customer, I told Tracker, "We'd better get out now."

"What about Goblin and One-Eye?"

"They can take care of themselves. If they got themselves lynched, tough. I'm not going poking around and getting myself a stretched neck, too. If they got away, they know the plan. They can catch up."

"I thought the Black Company didn't leave its dead behind."

"We don't." I said it, but maintained my determination to let the wizards stew in what juice they had concocted. I did not doubt that they had survived. They had been in trouble before, a thousand times. A good hike might have a salutary effect on their feel for mission discipline.

Meal finished, I informed the proprietor that Tracker and I were departing, but that our companions would keep the room. Then I led a protesting Tracker to the wagon, put him aboard, and when the boy had the hitch ready, headed for the western gate.

It was the long way, through tortuous streets, over a dozen arched bridges spanning canals, but it led away from yesterday's silliness. As we went I told Tracker how we had tricked Raker into a noose. He appreciated it.

"That was the Company's trademark," I concluded. "Get the enemy to do something stupid. We were the best when it came to fighting, but we only fought when nothing else worked."

"But you were paid to fight." Things were black-and-white to Tracker. Sometimes I thought he had spent too much time in the woods.

"We were paid for results. If we could do the job without fighting, all the better. What you do is, you study your enemy. Find a weakness, then work on it. Darling is good at that. Though working on the Taken is easier than you would think. They're all vulnerable through their egos."

"What about the Lady?"

"I couldn't say. She doesn't seem to have a handle. A touch of vanity, but I don't see how to get hold of it. Maybe through her drive to dominate. By getting her to overextend herself. I don't know. She's cautious. And smart. Like when she sucked the Rebel in at Charm. Killed three birds with one stone. Not only did she eliminate the Rebel; she exposed the unreliable among the Taken and squashed the Dominator's attempt to use them to get free."

"What about him?"

"He isn't a problem. He's probably more vulnerable than the Lady, though. He don't seem to think. He's like a bull. So damned strong that's all he needs. Oh, a little guile, like at Juniper, but mostly just the hammer-strokes type."

Tracker nodded thoughtfully. "Could be something to what you say."

25

The Barrowland

Corbie miscalculated. He forgot that others beside Case were interested in his fate.

When he failed to show for work various places, people came looking for him. They pounded on doors, tapped on windows, and got no response. One tried the door. It was locked. Now there was genuine concern.

Some argued for kicking a break-in up the chain of command, others for moving now. The latter view prevailed. They broke the lock and spread out inside.

They found a place obsessive in its neatness, spartan in its furnishings. The first man upstairs yelped, "Here he is. He's had a stroke or something."

The pack crowded into the little upstairs room. Corbie sat at a table on which lay an oilskin packet and a book. "A book!" someone said. "He was weirder than we thought."

A man touched Corbie's throat, felt a feeble pulse, noted that Corbie was taking shallow breaths spaced far more widely than those of a man sleeping. "Guess he did have a stroke. Like he was sitting here reading and it hit him."

"Had an uncle went like that," someone said. "When I was a kid. Telling us a story and just went white and keeled over."

"He's still alive. We better do something. Maybe he'll be all right."

A big rush downstairs, men tumbling over men.

Case heard when the group rushed into headquarters. He was on duty. The news put him in a quandary. He had promised Corbie. . . . But he could not run off.

Sweet's personal interest got the news bucked up the ladder fast. The Colonel came out of his office. He noted Case looking stricken. "You heard. Come along. Let's have a look. You men. Find the barber. Find the vet."

Made you reflect on the value of men when the army provided a vet but not a physician.

The day had begun auspiciously, with a clear sky. That was rare. Now it was cloudy. A few raindrops fell, spotting the wooden walks. As Case followed Sweet, and a dozen men followed him, he barely noted the Colonel's remarks about necessary improvements.

A crowd surrounded Corbie's place. "Bad news travels fast," Case said. "Sir."

"Doesn't it? Make a hole here, men. Coming through." He paused inside. "He always this tidy?"

"Yes, sir. He was obsessive about order and doing things by the numbers."

"I wondered. He stretched the rules a bit with his night walks."

Case gnawed his lip and wondered if he ought to give the Colonel Corbie's message. He decided it was not yet time.

"Upstairs?" the Colonel asked one of the men who had found Corbie.

"Yes, sir."

Case was up the stairs already. He spied Corbie's oilskin packet, without thinking started to slide it inside his jacket.

"Son."

Case turned. Sweet stood in the doorway, frowning.

"What are you doing?"

The Colonel was the most intimidating figure Case could imagine. More so than his father, who had been a harsh and exacting man. He did not know how to respond. He stood there shaking.

The Colonel extended a hand. Case handed the packet over. "What were you doing, son?"

"Uh . . . Sir . . . One day. . . ."

"Well?" Sweet examined Corbie without touching him. "Well? Out with it."

"He asked me to deliver a letter for him if anything happened to him. Like he thought his time was running out. He said it would be in an oilskin packet. On account of the rain and everything. Sir."

"I see." The Colonel slipped fingers under Corbie's chin, lifted. He returned the packet to the table, peeled back one of Corbie's eyelids. The pupil revealed was a pinprick. "Hmm." He felt Corbie's forehead. "Hmm." He flicked several reflex points with his finger or fist. Corbie did not respond. "Curious. Doesn't look like a stroke."

"What else could it be, sir?"

Colonel Sweet straightened. "Maybe you'd know better than I."

"Sir?"

"You say Corbie expected something."

"Not exactly. He was afraid something would happen. Talked like he was getting old and his time was running out. Maybe he had something wrong he never told nobody about."

"Maybe. Ah. Holts." The horse doctor had arrived. He followed the course the Colonel had, straightened, shrugged.

"Beyond me, Colonel."

"We'd better move him where we can keep an eye on him. Your job, son," he told Case. "If he doesn't come out of it soon, we'll have to force-feed him." He poked around the room, checked the titles of the dozen or so books. "A learned man, Corbie. I thought so. A study in contrasts. I've often wondered what he really was."

Case was nervous for Corbie now. "Sir, I think that way back he was somebody in one of the Jewel Cities, but his luck turned and he joined the army."

"We'll talk about it after we move him. Come along."

Case followed. The Colonel seemed very thoughtful. Maybe he *should* give him Corbie's message.

On the Road

After three days during which Tracker and I returned to our landing place, loaded the wagon, then headed north on the Salient Road, I began to wonder if I had not erred. Still no Goblin or One-Eye.

I need not have been concerned. They caught up near Meystrikt, a fortress in the Salient the Company once held on behalf of the Lady. We were off the road, in some woods, getting ready for supper. We heard a ruckus on the road.

A voice undeniably Goblin's shouted, "And I *insist* it's your fault, you maggot-lipped excuse for fish bait. I'd turn your brain into pudding for getting me into it if you had one."

"My fault. My fault. Gods! He even lies to himself. I had to talk him into his own idea? Look there, guano breath. Meystrikt is around that hill. They'll remember us even better than they did in Roses. Now I'm going to ask you once. How do we get through without getting our throats cut?"

After an initial relief I halted my rush toward the road. I told Tracker, "They're riding. Where do you suppose they got horses?" I tried finding a bright side. "Maybe they got into a game and got away with cheating. If One-Eye let Goblin do it." One-Eye is as inept at cheating as at games of chance themselves. There are times I think he has a positive death wish.

"You and your damned amulet," Goblin squeaked. "The Lady can't find him. That's great. But neither can we."

"*My* amulet? *My* amulet? Who the hell gave it to him in the first place?"

"Who designed the spell that's on it now?"

"Who cast it? Tell me that, toad face. Tell me that."

I moved to the edge of the woods. They had passed already. Tracker joined me. Even Toadkiller Dog came to watch.

"Freeze, Rebel!" I shouted. "First one moves is dead meat."

Stupid, Croaker. Real stupid. Their response was swift and gaudy. It damn near killed me.

They vanished in shining clouds. Around Tracker and me insects erupted.

More kinds of bugs than I imagined existed, every one interested only in having me for supper.

Toadkiller Dog snarled and snapped.

"Knock it off, you clowns," I yelled. "It's me. Croaker."

"Who's Croaker?" One-Eye asked Goblin. "You know anybody named Croaker?"

"Yeah. But I don't think we ought to stop," Goblin replied, after sticking his head out of the shining to check. "He deserves it."

"Sure," One-Eye agreed. "But Tracker is innocent. I can't fine-tune it enough to get just Croaker."

The bugs returned to routine bug business. Eating each other, I guess. I constrained my anger and greeted One-Eye and Goblin, both of whom had donned expressions of innocence and contrition. "What you got to say for yourselves, guys? Nice horses. Think the people they belong to will come looking for them?"

"Wait up," Goblin squawked. "Don't go accusing us of. . . ."

"I know you guys. Get down off those animals and come eat. We'll decide what to do with them tomorrow."

I turned my back on them. Tracker had returned to our cook fire already. He dished up supper. I went to work on it, my temper still frayed. Stupid move, stealing horses. What with the uproar they had caused already. . . . The Lady has agents everywhere. We may not be enemies of the grand sort, but we are what she has. Someone was bound to conclude that the Black Company was back in the north.

I fell asleep contemplating turning back. The least likely direction for hunters to look would be on the route to the Plain of Fear. But I could not give the order. Too much depended on us. Though now my earlier optimism stood in serious jeopardy.

Damned irresponsible clowns.

Way back down the line the Captain, who perished at Juniper, must have felt the same. We all gave him cause.

I braced for a golden dream. I slept restlessly. No dream came. Next morning I packed Goblin and One-Eye into the wagon, beneath all the clutter we deemed necessary for our expedition, abandoned the horses, and took the wagon past Meystrikt. Toadkiller Dog ran point. Tracker strolled along beside. I drove. Under the tucker, Goblin and One-Eye sputtered and grumbled. The garrison at the fort merely asked where we were bound, in such a bored manner I knew they did not care.

These lands had been tamed since last I passed through. This garrison could not conceive of trouble lifting its naughty head.

Relieved, I turned up the road that led to Elm and Oar. And to the Great Forest beyond.

27

Oar

Don't this weather ever let up?" One-Eye whined. For a week we had slogged northward, had been victimized by daily showers. The roads were bad and promised to get worse. Practicing my Forsberger on wayside farmers, I learned that this weather had been common for years. It made getting crops to town difficult and, worse, left the grains at risk from disease. There had been an outbreak of the firedance in Oar already, a malady traceable to infected rye. There were a lot of insects, too. Especially mosquitos.

The winters, though abnormal in snow and rainfall, were milder than when we had been stationed here. Mild winters do not augur well for pest control. On the other hand, game species were diminished because they could not forage in the deep snows.

Cycles. Just cycles, the old-timers assured me. The bad winters come around after the Great Comet passes. But even they thought this a cycle among cycles.

Today's weather is already the most impressive of all time.

Deal," Goblin said, and he did not mean cards. That fortress, which the Company took from the Rebel years ago, loomed ahead. The road meanders beneath its scowling walls. I was troubled, as always I was when our path neared an imperial bastion. But there was no need this time. The Lady was so confident of Forsberg that the great fortress stood abandoned. In fact, close up, it looked ragged. Its neighbors were stealing it piece by piece, after the custom of peasants the world over. I expect that is the only return they get on taxes, though they may have to wait generations for the worm to turn.

"Oar tomorrow," I said as we left the wagon outside an inn a few miles past Deal. "And this time there will be no screwups. Hear?"

One-Eye had the grace to look abashed. But Goblin was ready to argue.

"Keep it up," I said. "I'll have Tracker thrash you and tie you up. We aren't playing games."

"Life is a game, Croaker," One-Eye said. "You take it too damned serious."

But he behaved himself, both that night and the next day when we entered Oar.

I found a place well outside areas we frequented before. It catered to small-time traders and travelers. We drew no especial attention. Tracker and I kept a watch on Goblin and One-Eye. They did not seem inclined to play the fool again, though.

Next day I went looking for a smith named Sand. Tracker accompanied me. Goblin and One-Eye stayed behind, constrained by the most terrible threats I could invent.

Sand's place was easily found. He was a longtime member of his trade, well-known among his peers. We followed directions. They led me through familiar streets. Here the Company had had some adventures.

I discussed them with Tracker as we walked. I noted, "Been a lot of rebuilding since then. We tore the place up good."

Toadkiller Dog was on point, as often he was of late. He stopped suddenly, looked around suspiciously, took a few tentative steps, sank onto his belly. "Trouble," Tracker said.

"What kind?" There was nothing obvious to the eye.

"I don't know. He can't talk. He's just doing his watch-out-for-trouble act."

"Okay. Don't cost anything to be careful." We turned into a place that sold and repaired harness and tack. Tracker yakked about needing a saddle for a hunter of large beasts. I stood in the doorway watching the street.

I saw nothing unusual. The normal run of people went about their normal business. But after a while I noted that Sand's smithy had no custom. That no smithery sounds came forth. He was supposed to supervise a platoon of apprentices and journeymen.

"Hey. Proprietor. Whatever happened to the smith over there? Last time we were here he did us some work. Place looks empty."

"Grey boys is what happened." He looked uncomfortable. Grey boys are imperials. The troops in the north wear grey. "Fool didn't learn back when. Was into the Rebellion."

"Too bad. He was a good smith. What leads regular folks to get into politics, anyway? People like us, we got trouble enough just trying to make a living."

"I heard that, brother." The tackmaker shook his head. "Tell you this. You got smithery needs doing, take your custom elsewhere. The grey boys been hanging around, taking anybody who comes around."

About then an imperial strolled around the side of the smithy and crossed to a pasty stall. "Damned clumsy," I said. "And crude."

The tackmaker looked at me askance. Tracker covered well, drawing him back to business. Not as dumb as he appeared, I noted. Maybe just not socially adept.

Later, after Tracker expressed a desire to think on the deal the tackmaker offered and we departed, Tracker asked, "What now?"

"We could bring up Goblin and One-Eye after dark, use their sleeping spell, go in and see what's to see. But it don't seem likely the imperials would leave anything interesting. We could find out what they did with Sand and try to reach him. Or we could go on to the Barrowland."

"Sounds the safest."

"On the other hand, we wouldn't know what we were headed into. Sand's being taken could mean anything. We better talk it over with the others. Catalog our resources."

Tracker grunted. "How long before that sutler gets suspicious? The more he thinks about it, the more he's going to realize we were interested in the smith."

"Maybe. I'm not going to sweat it."

Oar is a city like most of substantial size. Crowded. Filled with distractions. I understood how Goblin and One-Eye had been seduced by Roses. The last major city the Company dared visit was Chimney. Six years ago. Since then it has been all the hard times and small towns you can imagine. I battled temptations of my own. I knew places of interest in Oar.

Tracker kept me on the straight line. I've never met a man less interested in the traps which tempt men.

Goblin thought we should put the imperials to sleep, give them the question. One-Eye wanted to get out of town. Their solidarity had perished like frost in the sun.

"Logically," I said, "they would get a stronger guard after dark. But if we drag you down there now, somebody is sure to recognize you."

"Then find that old boy who brought the first letter," Goblin said.

"Good idea. But. Think about it. Assuming he had perfect luck, he'd still be a long way from here. He didn't catch a ride like we did. No go. We get out. Oar is making me nervous." Too many temptations, too many chances to be recognized. And just too many people. Isolation had grown on me out there on the Plain.

Goblin wanted to argue. He had heard the north roads were terrible.

"I know," I countered. "I also know the army is building a new route to the Barrowland. And they've pushed its north end far enough so traders are using it."

No more argument. They wanted out as much as I. Only Tracker now seemed reluctant. He who first thought it best to go.

28

To the Barrowland

Oar's weather was less than exciting. Farther north it became misery curdled, though the imperial engineers had done their best to make the forest road usable. Much of it was corduroy, of logs trimmed and tarred and laid side by side. In areas where snow became obnoxious, there were frameworks to support canvas coverings.

"Amazing scope," One-Eye said.

"Uhm." There was supposed to be zero concern about the Dominator since the Lady's triumph at Juniper. This seemed a lot of effort to keep a road open.

The new road swung many miles west of the old because the Great Tragic River had shifted its bed and continued doing so. The trip from Oar to the Barrowland was fifteen miles longer. The last forty-five were not wholly finished. We endured some rough going.

We encountered the occasional trader headed south. They all shook their heads and told us we were wasting our time. The fortunes to be had had evaporated. The tribes had hunted the furbearers to extinction.

Tracker had been preoccupied since we left Oar. I could not draw out why. Maybe superstition. The Barrowland remains a great dread to Forsberg's lower classes. The Dominator is the bogeyman mothers conjure to frighten children. Though he has been gone four hundred years, his stamp remains indelible.

It took a week to cover the final forty-five miles. I was growing time-concerned. We might not get done and home before winter.

We were scarcely out of the forest, into the clearing at the Barrowland. I stopped. "It's changed."

Goblin and One-Eye crept up behind me. "Yuck," Goblin squeaked. "It sure has."

It seemed almost abandoned. A swamp now, with only the highest points of the Barrowland proper still identifiable. When last we visited, a horde of imperials was clearing, repairing, studying with a relentless clatter and bustle.

Near silence reigned. That bothered me more than the decayed state of the Barrowland. Slow, steady drizzle under deep grey skies. Cold. And no sound.

The corduroy was completed here. We rolled forward. Not till we entered the town, buildings now for the most part paintless and dilapidated, did we see a soul. A voice called, "Halt and state your business."

I stopped. "Where are you?"

Toadkiller Dog, more than normally ambitious, loped to a derelict structure and sniffed. A grumbling Guard stepped into the drizzle. "Here."

"Oh. You startled me. Name is Candle. Of Candle, Smith, Smith, Tailor, and Sons. Traders."

"Yeah? These others?"

"Smith and Tailor inside here. That's Tracker. He works for us. We're from Roses. We heard the road north was open again."

"Now you know better." He chuckled. I learned that he was in a good humor because of the weather. It was a nice day for the Barrowland.

"What's the procedure?" I asked. "Where do we put up?"

"Blue Willy is the only place. They'll be glad for the custom. Get yourself settled. Report to headquarters by tomorrow."

"Right. Where is the Blue Willy?"

He told me. I snapped the traces. The wagon rolled. "Seem pretty lax," I said.

"Where are you going to run?" One-Eye countered. "They know we're here. There's only one way out. We don't play by their book, they stick the stopper in the bottle."

The place did have that feel.

It also had a feel that went with its weather. Down. Depressing. Smiles were scarce, and those mostly commercial.

The hostler at Blue Willy didn't ask names, just payment up front. Other traders ignored us, though the fur trade, traditionally, is an Oar monopoly.

Next day a few locals came around to examine our goods. I had loaded up with what I had heard would sell well, but we got few nibbles. Only the liquor drew any offers. I asked how to get in touch with the tribes.

"You wait. They come when they come."

That done, I went to Guard headquarters. It was unchanged, though the surrounding compound seemed seedier.

The first man I encountered was one I remembered. He was the one with whom I had to do business. "Candle's the name," I said. "Of Candle, Smith, Smith, Tailor, and Sons, out of Roses. Traders. I was told to report here."

He looked at me oddly, like something way back was nagging him. He remembered something. I did not want him worrying it like a cavity in a tooth. He might come up with an answer. "Been some changes since I was here in the army."

"Going to the dogs," he grumbled. "The dogs. Worse every day. You think anybody cares? We're going to rot out here. How many in your party?"

"Four. And one dog."

Wrong move. He scowled. No sense of humor. "Names?"

"Candle. One Smith. Tailor. Tracker. He works for us. And Toadkiller Dog. Got to call him by his whole name or he gets upset."

"Funny man, eh?"

"Hey. No offense. But this place needs some sunshine."

"Yeah. Can you read?"

I nodded.

"Rules are posted over there. You got two choices. Obey them. Or be dead. Case!"

A soldier came from a back office. "Yeah, Sarge?"

"New trader. Go check him out. You at Blue Willy, Candle?"

"Yes." The list of rules had not changed. It was the same paper, almost too faded to read. Basically, it said don't mess with the Barrowland. Try it and if *it* don't kill you, we will.

"Sir?" the trooper said. "When you're ready?"

"I'm ready."

We returned to Blue Willy. The soldier looked our gear over. The only things that intrigued him were my bow and the fact that we were well armed. "Why so many weapons?"

"Been talk about trouble with the tribesmen."

"Must have gotten exaggerated. Just stealing." Goblin and One-Eye attracted no special attention. I was pleased. "You read the rules. Stick to them."

"I know them of old," I said. "I was stationed here when I was in the army."

He looked at me a bit narrowly, nodded, departed.

We all sighed. Goblin took the spell of concealment off the gear he and One-Eye had brought. The empty corner behind Tracker filled with clutter.

"He might come right back," I protested.

"We don't want to hold any spell any longer than we have to," One-Eye said. "There might be somebody around who could detect it."

"Right." I cracked the shutters to our one window. The hinges shrieked. "Grease," I suggested. I looked across the town. We were on the third floor of the tallest building outside the Guard compound. I could see the Bomanz house. "Guys. Look at this."

They looked.

"In damned fine shape, eh?" When last seen it was a candidate for demolition. Superstitious fear had kept it unused. I recalled pottering around in there several times. "Feel like a stroll, Tracker?"

"No."

"Whatever makes you comfortable"—I wondered if he had enemies here—"I'd feel better if you were along."

He strapped on his sword. Out we went, down, into the street—if that expanse of mud could be so called. The corduroy ran only to the compound, with a branch as far as Blue Willy. Beyond, there were walkways only.

We pretended to sightsee. I told Tracker stories about my last visit, most cast near the truth. I was trying to assume a foreign persona, voluble and jolly. I wondered if I was wasting my time. I saw no one interested in what I might say.

The Bomanz house had been lovingly restored. It did not appear to be occupied, though. Or guarded. Or set up as a monument. Curious. Come supper I asked our host. He had me pegged as a nostalgic fool already. He told us, "Some old boy moved in there about five years ago. Cripple. Did scut work for the Guard. Fixed the place up in his spare time."

"What happened to him?"

"While back, couple four months I guess, he had a stroke or something. They found him still alive but like a vegetable. They took him over to the compound. Far as I know, he's still there. Feeding him like a baby. That kid that was here to inspect you is the one to ask. Him and Corbie was friends."

"Corbie, eh? Thanks. Another pitcher."

"Come on, Croaker," One-Eye said in a low voice. "Lay off the beer. The guy makes it himself. It's terrible."

He was right. But I was getting adjusted for some heavy thinking.

We had to get into that house. That meant night moves and wizards' skills. It also meant our greatest risks since Goblin and One-Eye went silly in Roses.

One-Eye asked Goblin, "Think we're up against a haunt?"

Goblin sucked his lip. "Have to look."

"What's this?" I asked.

"I'd have to see the man to know for sure, Croaker, but what happened to that Corbie don't sound like a stroke."

Goblin nodded. "Sounds like somebody pulled out of body and caught."

"Maybe we can arrange to see him. What about the house?"

"First thing is to make sure there isn't a big-time haunt. Like maybe Bomanz's ghost."

That kind of talk makes me nervous. I do not believe in ghosts. Or do not want to.

"If he was caught out, or pulled out, you have to wonder how and why. The fact that that's where Bomanz lived has to be considered. Something left over from his time could have gotten this Corbie. Could be what gets us if we're not careful."

"Complications," I grumbled. "Always the complications."

Goblin snickered.

"You watch yourself," I said. "Or I just might sell you to the highest bidder."

An hour later a savage storm arrived. It howled and hammered at the inn. The roof leaked under the downpour. When I reported that, our host blew up, though not at me. Evidently making repairs was not easy under current conditions, yet repairs had to be made lest a place deteriorate entirely.

"The damned winter firewood is the worst," he complained. "Can't leave it set out. Either gets buried under snow or so damned waterlogged you can't dry it out. In a month this place will be loaded ceiling to floor. At least filling the place up makes it less hard to heat."

Along about midnight, after the Guard had changed watches and the oncoming had had time to grow bored and sleepy, we slipped out. Goblin made sure everyone inside the inn was asleep.

Toadkiller Dog trotted ahead, seeking witnesses. He found only one. Goblin took care of him, too. On a night like that nobody was out. I wished I was not.

"Make sure nobody can see any light," I said after we slipped inside. "At a guess, I'd say we start upstairs."

"At a guess," One-Eye countered, "I'd say we find out if there are any haunts or booby traps first."

I glanced at the door. I hadn't thought about that before pushing through.

29

The Barrowland, Back When

The Colonel summoned Case. He shook as he stood before Sweet's desk. "There are questions to be answered, lad," Sweet said. "Start by telling me what you know about Corbie."

Case swallowed. "Yes, sir." He told. And told much more when Sweet insisted on rehashing every word that had passed between them. He told everything but the part about the message and the oilskin.

"Curious," Sweet said. "Very. Is that all?"

Case shifted nervously. "What's this about, sir?"

"Let's say what we found in the oilskin was interesting."

"Sir?"

"It appeared to be a long letter, though no one could read it. It was in a language nobody knows. It could be the language of the Jewel Cities. What I want to know is, who was supposed to get it? Was it unique or part of a series? Our friend is in trouble, lad. If he recovers, he's in hot water. Deep. Real bums don't write long letters to anybody."

"Well, sir, like I said, he was trying to track down his kids. And he may have come from Opal. . . ."

"I know. There is circumstantial evidence on his side. Maybe he can satisfy me when he comes around. On the other hand, this being the Barrowland, anything remarkable becomes suspicious. Question, son. And you must answer satisfactorily or you're in hot water, too. Why did you try to hide the packet?"

The crux. The moment from which there was no escape. He had prayed it would not arrive. Now, facing it, Case knew his loyalty to Corbie was unequal to the test.

"He asked me if, if anything happened to him, I would get a letter delivered to Oar. A letter in oilskin."

"He did expect trouble, then?"

"I don't know. I don't know what was in the letter or why he wanted it delivered. He just gave me a name. And then he said to tell you something after the letter was delivered."

"Ah?"

"I don't remember his exact words. He said to tell you the thing in the Great Barrow isn't asleep anymore."

Sweet came out of his seat as though stung. "He did? And how did he know? Never mind. The name. Now! Who was the packet to go to?"

"A smith in Oar. Named Sand. That's all I know, sir. I swear."

"Right." Sweet seemed distracted. "Back to your duties, lad. Tell Major Klief I want him."

"Yes, sir."

Next morning Case watched Major Klief and a detail ride out, under orders to arrest Sand Smith. He felt terribly guilty. And yet, just how had he betrayed anyone? He might have been betrayed himself if Corbie was a spy.

He assuaged his guilt by tending Corbie with religious devotion, keeping him clean and fed.

30

A Barrowland Night

It took Goblin and One-Eye only minutes to examine the house. "No traps," One-Eye announced. "No ghost, either. Some old resonances of sorcery overlaid by more recent ones. Upstairs."

I produced a scrap of paper. Upon it were my notes from the Bomanz letters. We went upstairs. Confident though they were, Goblin and One-Eye let me go first. Some friends.

I checked to make certain the window was shuttered before permitting a light. Then: "Do your stuff. I'll poke around." Tracker and Toadkiller Dog remained in the doorway. It was not a big room.

I examined book titles before starting a serious search. The man had had eclectic tastes. Or had collected what was cheapest, perhaps.

I found no papers.

The place did not look ransacked. "One-Eye. Can you tell if this place was searched?"

"Probably not. Why?"

"The papers aren't here."

"You looked where he hid stuff? Like he said?"

"All but one." A spear stood in a corner. Sure enough, when I twisted it, its head came off and revealed a hollow shaft. Out came the map mentioned in the story. We spread it on the table.

Chills crept up my back.

This was real history. This chart had shaped today's world. Despite my limited grasp of TelleKurre and my even more feeble knowledge of wizardly symbols, I felt the power mapped there. For me, at least, it radiated something that left me teetering on the boundary between discomfort and true dread.

Goblin and One-Eye did not feel it. Or were too intrigued. They put their heads together and examined the route Bomanz used to reach the Lady.

"Thirty-seven years of work," I said.

"What?"

"It took him thirty-seven years to accumulate that information." I noticed something. "What's this?" It was something that should not have been there, as I recalled the story. "I see. Our correspondent added notes of his own."

One-Eye looked at me. Then he looked at the chart. Then he looked at me again. Then he bent to examine the route on the map. "That has to be it. No other answer."

"What?"

"I know what happened."

Tracker stirred uncomfortably.

"Well?"

"He tried to go in there. The only way you can. And couldn't get out."

He had written me saying there was something he had to do, that the risks were great. Was One-Eye right?

Brave man.

No papers. Unless they were hidden better than I thought. I would have Goblin and One-Eye search. I made them reroll the chart and return it to the spear shaft, then said, "I'm open to suggestions."

"About what?" Goblin squeaked.

"About how to get this guy away from the Eternal Guard. And how we get his soul back inside him so we can ask him questions. Like that."

They did not look enthused. One-Eye said, "Somebody will have to go in there to see what's wrong. Then spring him and guide him out."

"I see." Too well. We had to lay hands on the living body before doing that. "Look this place over. See what you can find that's hidden."

It took them half an hour. I became a nervous wreck. "Too much time, too much time," I kept saying. They ignored me.

The search produced one scrap of paper, very old, which contained a cipher key. It was folded into one of the books, not really hidden. I tucked it away. It might be used on the papers back at the Hole.

We got out. We got back to Blue Willy without being detected. We all heaved sighs of relief once we reached our room.

"What now?" Goblin asked.

"Sleep on it. Tomorrow is soon enough to start worrying." I was wrong, of course. I was worrying already.

With each step forward it became more complicated.

Night in the Barrowland

The thunder and lightning continued to strut about. The sound and flash penetrated the walls as though they were paper. I slept restlessly, my nerves frazzled more than they should be. The others were dead to the world. Why couldn't I be?

It started as a pinprick in a corner, a mote of golden light. The mote multiplied. I wanted to lunge across and hammer on Goblin or One-Eye, calling them liars. The amulet was supposed to keep me invisible. . . .

Faintest, most ghostly of whispers, like the cry of a ghost down a long, cold cavern. "Physician. Where are you?"

I did not respond. I wanted to pull my blanket over my head, but could not move.

She remained diffuse, wavering, uncertain. Maybe she did have trouble spotting me. When her face did assume substance momentarily, she did not look my way. Her eyes seemed blind.

"You have gone from the Plain of Fear," she called in that faraway voice. "You are in the north somewhere. You left a broad trail. You are foolish, my friend. I will find you. Don't you know that? You cannot hide. Even an emptiness can be seen."

She had no idea where I was. I did the right thing by not responding. She wanted me to betray myself.

"My patience is not unlimited, Croaker. But you may come to the Tower still. Make it soon, though. Your White Rose does not have long."

I finally managed to pull my blanket to my chin. What a sight I must have made. Amusing, in retrospect. Like a little boy afraid of ghosts.

The glow slowly faded. With it went the nervousness that had plagued me since returning from the Bomanz house.

As I settled down I glanced at Toadkiller Dog. I caught lightning glinting off a single open eye.

So. For the first time there was a witness to one of the visitations. But a mutt. I don't think anybody believed me about them, ever, except that what I reported always panned out true.

I slept.

Goblin wakened me. "Breakfast."

We ate. We made a show of looking for markets for our goods, of seeking a longer term connection for future loads. Business was not good, except our host offered to purchase distilled spirits regularly. There was a demand among the Eternal Guard. The soldiers had little to do but drink.

Lunch. And while we ate and prepared our thoughts for the head-butting session to follow, soldiers entered the inn. They asked the landlord if any of his guests had been out last night. Good old landlord denied the possibility. He claimed he was the lightest of sleepers. He knew if anyone came or went.

That was good enough for the soldiers. They left.

"What was that?" I asked when next the proprietor passed our way.

"Somebody broke into Corbie's house last night," he said. Then his eyes narrowed. He remembered other questions. My mistake.

"Curious," I said. "Why would anyone do that?"

"Yes. Why?" He went about his business, but remained thoughtful.

I, too, was thoughtful. How had they detected our visit? We were careful to leave no traces.

Goblin and One-Eye were disturbed, too. Only Tracker did not seem bothered. His lone discomfort was being there, near the Barrowland.

"What can we do?" I asked. "We're surrounded and outnumbered, and maybe now we're suspect. How do we lay hands on this Corbie?"

"That's no problem," One-Eye said. "The real trouble is getting away after we do. If we could call in a windwhale just in time. . . ."

"Tell me how it's not so hard."

"The middle of the night we go over to the Guard compound, use the sleep spell, get our man and his papers, call his spirit back, and get him out. But then what? Eh, Croaker? Then what?"

"Where do we run?" I mused. "And how?"

"There is one answer," Tracker said. "The forest. The Guard couldn't find us in the forest. If we could cross the Great Tragic, we'd be safe. They don't have the manpower for a hunt."

I nibbled the edge of a fingernail. Something to what Tracker said. I assumed he knew the woodlands and tribes well enough for us to survive with the burden of an injured man. But jumping past that only led to other problems.

There were still a thousand miles to cross to reach the Plain of Fear. With the empire alert. "Wait here," I told everybody, and left.

I hurried to the imperial compound, entered the office I had visited before, shook myself dry, examined a map on the wall. The kid who had checked us for contraband came over. "Help you somehow?"

"I don't think so. Just wanted to check the map. It pretty accurate?"

"Not anymore. The river has shifted more than a mile this way. And most of the flood plain isn't covered with woods anymore. All washed away."

"Hmm." I laid fingers on, making estimates.

"What do you want to know that for?"

"Business," I lied. "Heard we might be able to contact one of the bigger tribes around a place called Eagle Rocks."

"That's forty-five miles. You wouldn't make it. They'd kill you and take what you had. The only reason they don't bother the Guard and the road is that those have the Lady's protection. If this coming winter is as bad as the last few, that won't stop them, either."

"Uhm. Well, it was an idea. You the one called Case?"

"Yes." His eyes narrowed suspiciously.

"Heard you been taking care of some guy. . . ." I let it drop. His reaction was not what I expected. "Well, that's what they're saying around town. Thanks for the advice." I got out. But I feared I had goofed.

I soon *knew* I had goofed.

A squad commanded by a major showed up at the inn only minutes after my return. They had the bunch of us under arrest before we knew what was happening. Goblin and One-Eye barely had time to cast spells of concealment on their gear.

We played ignorant. We cursed and grumbled and whined. It did us no good. Our captors knew less about why we were being grabbed than we did. Just following orders.

The landlord had a look which made me certain he had reported us as suspicious. I expect Case said something about my visit that tipped a balance somewhere. Whatever, we were on our way to cells.

Ten minutes after the door clanged shut, the very commander of the Eternal Guard turned up. I sighed in relief. He hadn't been here before. At least he was no one we knew. He shouldn't know us.

We had had time to rehearse using the deaf speech. All but Tracker. But Tracker seemed lost within himself. They had not allowed his mutt to accompany him. He had been angry about that. Scared the crap out of the guys who arrested us. For a minute they thought they would have to fight him.

The commander studied us, then introduced himself. "I'm Colonel Sweet. I command the Eternal Guard." Case hovered behind him, anxious. "I asked you men here because aspects of your behavior have been unusual."

"Have we unwittingly broken a rule not publicly posted?" I asked.

"Not at all. Not at all. The matter is entirely circumstantial. What you might call a question of undeclared intent."

"You've lost me, sir."

He began pacing up and down the passageway outside our cell. Up and down. "There is the old saw about actions speaking louder than words. I've had reports on you from several sources. About your excessive curiosity about matters not connected with your business."

I did my best to appear baffled. "What's unusual about asking questions in new country? My associates haven't been here before. It's been years since I was. Things have changed. Anyway, this is one of the most interesting places in the empire."

"Also one of the most dangerous, trader. Candle, is it? Mr. Candle, you were stationed here in service. What unit?"

That I could answer without hesitation. "Drake Crest. Colonel Lot. Second Battalion." I *was* here, after all.

"Yes. The Roses mercenary brigade. What was the Colonel's favorite drink?"

Oh, boy. "I was a pikeman, Colonel. I didn't drink with the brigadier."

"Right." He paced. I could not tell if that answer worked or not. Drake Crest hadn't been a flashy, storied outfit like the Black Company. Who the hell would remember anything about them? After a time. "You must understand my position. With that thing buried out there paranoia becomes an occupational hazard." He pointed in the direction the Great Barrow must lie. Then he stalked off.

"What the hell was all that?" Goblin asked.

"I don't know. And I'm not sure I want to find out. Somehow, we got ourselves into big trouble." That for the benefit of eavesdroppers.

Goblin accepted his cue. "Damnit, Candle, I told you we shouldn't come up here. I told you the Oar people would have an arrangement with the Guard."

One-Eye jumped in then. They really ragged me. Meantime, we talked it over with the finger speech, decided to wait the Colonel out.

Not much choice anyway, without tipping our hands.

Imprisoned in the Barrowland

It was bad. Far worse than we suspected. Those Guard guys were paranoid plus. I mean, they didn't have an inkling who we were. But they did not let that slow them.

Half a platoon showed up suddenly. Rattle and clang at the door. No talk. Grim faces. We had trouble.

"I don't think they're going to turn us loose," Goblin said.

"Out," a sergeant told us.

We went out. All but Tracker. Tracker just sat there. I tried a funny. "He misses his dog."

Nobody laughed.

One of the Guards punched Tracker's arm. Tracker took a long time turning, looking at the man, his face an emotional blank.

"You shouldn't ought to have done that," I said.

"Shut up," the sergeant snapped. "Get him moving."

The man who had punched Tracker went to hit him again.

It might have been a love tap in slowed motion. Tracker reached around the moving fist, caught the advancing wrist, broke it. The Guardsman shrieked. Tracker tossed him aside. His face remained a blank. His gaze followed the man belatedly. He seemed to begin wondering what was happening.

The other Guards gaped. Then a couple jumped in with bared weapons.

"Hey! Take it easy!" I yelled. "Tracker. . . ."

Still in that sort of mental nowhere, Tracker took their weapons away, tossed them into a corner, and beat the crap out of both men. The sergeant was torn between awe and outrage.

I tried to mollify him. "He's not very bright. You can't come at him like that. You have to explain things slow like, two or three times."

"I'll explain!" He started to send the rest of his men into the cell.

"You get him mad, you're going to get somebody killed." I talked fast, and wondered what the hell it was with Tracker and his damned pooch. That mutt went away, Tracker became a moron. With homicidal tendencies.

The sergeant let sense override anger. "You get him under control."

I worked on it. I knew the immediate future boded no good from the attitude of the soldiers, but was not overly worried. Goblin and One-Eye could handle whatever trouble developed. The thing to do now was keep our heads and lives.

I wanted to tend the three injured soldiers, but dared not. Just looking at One-Eye and Goblin would give clues enough for the other side to figure out, eventually, who we were. No sense giving them more. I concentrated on Tracker. Once I got him to focus on me it was no great task to get through, to calm him down, to explain that we were going somewhere with the soldiers.

He said, "They shouldn't ought to do me like that, Croaker." He sounded like a child whose feelings had been hurt. I grimaced. But the Guards did not react to the name.

They surrounded us, all with hands upon weapons, except those trying to get their injured companions to the horse doctor who served as the Guard's physician. Some of them were itching to get even. I worked hard to keep Tracker calm.

The place they took us did not encourage me. It was a sodden cellar beneath the headquarters. It looked like a caricature of a torture chamber. I suspect it was meant to intimidate. Having seen real torture and real torture implements, I recognized half the equipment as prop or unusually antiquated. But there were some serviceable implements, too. I exchanged glances with Goblin and One-Eye.

Tracker said, "I don't like it here. I want to go outside. I want to see Toadkiller Dog."

"Stand easy. We'll be out in a little while."

Goblin grinned his famous grin, though it was a little lopsided. Yes. We would be out soon. Maybe feet first, but out.

Colonel Sweet was there. He did not seem pleased by our reaction to his stage. He said, "I want to talk to you men. You didn't seem eager to chat earlier. Are these surroundings more amenable?"

"Not exactly. They make one wonder, though. Is this the penalty for stepping on the heels of the gentlemen traders of Oar? I didn't realize they had the blessing of the Guard in their monopoly."

"Games. No games, Mr. Candle. Straight answers. Now. Or my men will make your next few hours extremely unpleasant."

"Ask. But I have a bad feeling I don't have the answers you want to hear."

"Then that will be your misfortune."

I glanced at Goblin. He had gone into a sort of trance.

The Colonel said, "I do not believe you when you say you're just traders. The pattern of your questions indicate an inordinate interest in a man named Corbie and his house. Corbie, let it be noted, is suspected of being either a Rebel agent or Resurrectionist. Tell me about him."

I did, almost completely, and truthfully: "I never heard of him before we got here."

I think he believed me. But he shook his head slowly.

"You see. You won't believe me even when you know I'm telling the truth."

"But how much are you telling? That is the question. The White Rose compartments its organization. You could have had no idea who Corbie was and still have come looking for him. Has he been out of touch for a while?"

This sucker was sharp.

My face must have been too studiedly blank. He nodded to himself, scanned the four of us, zeroed in on One-Eye. "The black man. Pretty old, isn't he?"

I was surprised he did not make more of One-Eye's skin color. Black men are extremely rare north of the Sea of Torments. Chances are the Colonel had not seen one before. That a black man, very old, is one of the cornerstones of the Black Company is not exactly a secret.

I did not answer.

"We'll start with him. He looks least likely to stand up."

Tracker asked, "You want me to kill them, Croaker?"

"I want you to keep your mouth shut and stand still, that's what I want." Damn. But Sweet missed the name. Either that or I was less famous than I thought and overdue for ego deflation.

Sweet did seem amazed that Tracker was so confident.

"Take him to the rack." He indicated One-Eye.

One-Eye chuckled and extended his hands to the men who approached him. Goblin snickered. Their amusement disturbed everyone. Me not least, for I knew their senses of humor.

Sweet looked me in the eye. "They find this amusing? Why?"

"If you don't indulge a sudden whim of civilized behavior, you're going to find out."

He was tempted to back down, but decided we were running some colossal bluff.

They took One-Eye to the rack. He grinned and climbed up himself. Goblin squeaked, "I been waiting to see you on one of those things for thirty years. Damn my luck if somebody else doesn't get to turn the crank when the chance finally comes."

"We'll see who turns that crank on who, horse apple," One-Eye replied.

They bantered back and forth. Tracker and I stood like posts. The imperials became ever more disturbed. Sweet, obviously, wondered if he shouldn't take One-Eye down and work on me.

They strapped One-Eye down. Goblin cackled, danced a little jig. "Stretch him till he's ten feet tall, guys," he said. "You'll still have a mental midget."

Somebody swung a backhand Goblin's way. He leaned only slightly. When the man pulled his hand back, having missed entirely and been only lightly brushed by a warding hand, he looked at his own paw in astonishment.

Ten thousand pinpricks of blood had appeared. They formed a pattern. Almost a tattoo. And that tattoo showed two serpents intertwined, each with its fangs buried in the other's neck. If necks are what snakes have behind their heads.

A distraction. I recognized it, of course. After the first moment, I concentrated on One-Eye. He just grinned.

The men who were to stretch him turned back after a moment, whipped by their Colonel's snarl. Sweet was damned uncomfortable now. He had a suspicion he faced something extraordinary, but he refused to be intimidated.

As the torturers stepped up to One-Eye his naked belly heaved. And a big, nasty spider crawled out of his navel. It came out in a ball, dragging itself with two legs, then unwrapped the others from around a body half the size of my thumb. It stepped aside and another crawled forth. The first ambled down One-Eye's leg, toward the man who held the crank to which One-Eye's ankles were strapped. The fellow's eyes just kept getting bigger. He turned to his commanding officer.

Absolute silence filled the cellar. I don't think the imperials even remembered to breathe.

Another spider crawled out of One-Eye's heaving belly. And another. And he seemed diminished just a bit more each time. His faced changed, slowly shifting toward what a spider's face looks like if you look real close. Most people do not have the nerve.

Goblin giggled.

"Turn the crank!" Sweet roared.

The man at One-Eye's feet tried. The first spider scuttled up the lever onto his hand. He shrieked, flung his hand around, hurled the arachnid into the shadows.

"Colonel," I said in as businesslike a voice as I could muster, "this has gone far enough. Let's not get someone hurt."

There was a whole mob of them and four of us and Sweet wanted badly to rely on that. But already several men were edging toward the exit. Most were edging away from us. Everyone stared at Sweet.

Damned Goblin. Had to let his enthusiasm get away. He squeaked, "Hold on, Croaker. This is a once-in-a-lifetime chance. Let them stretch One-Eye a little."

I saw the light dawn behind Sweet's eyes, though he tried to conceal it.

"Damn you, Goblin. Now you've done it. We're going to have a talk after this is over. Colonel. What will it be? I have the edge here. As you now know."

He elected for the better part of valor. "Release him," he told the man nearest One-Eye.

There were spiders all over One-Eye. He had them popping out of his mouth and ears now. Getting enthusiastic, he had them turning up as gaudy as you can imagine, hunters, web-spinners, jumpers. All big and revolting. Sweet's men refused to go near him.

I told Tracker, "Go stand in the doorway. Don't let anybody out." He had no trouble understanding that. I released One-Eye. I had to keep reminding myself the arachnids were illusions.

Some illusions. I *felt* the little creepies. . . . Belatedly, I realized One-Eye's legions were marching on Goblin. "Damn it, One-Eye! Grow up!" The son-of-a-bitch wasn't satisfied to bluff the imperials. He had to play games with Goblin, too. I wheeled on Goblin. "If you do one damned thing to get involved in this, I'll see you never leave the Hole again. Colonel Sweet. I can't say I've enjoyed your hospitality. If you and your men will come over here? We'll just be on our way."

Reluctantly, Sweet gestured. Half of his men refused to move toward the spiders. "One-Eye. Game time is over. It's get-out-alive time. Would you mind?"

One-Eye gestured. His eight-legged troops rushed into the shadows behind the rack, where they vanished into that mad oblivion from which such things spring. One-Eye strutted over to stand by Tracker. He was cocky now. For weeks we would hear about how he had saved us. If we lived to get away tonight.

I shooed Goblin over, then joined them myself. I told Goblin and One-Eye, "I want no sound to escape this room. And I want that door sealed like it was part of the wall. Then I want to know where we find this character Corbie."

"You got it," One-Eye said. Eye twinkling, he added, "So long, Colonel. It was fun."

Sweet forebore making threats. Sensible man.

Fixing the room took the wizards ten minutes, which I found inordinately long. I became mildly suspicious, but forgot that notion when they said they were done and that the man we wanted was in another building nearby.

I should have harkened to my suspicions.

Five minutes later we stood in the doorway of the building where Corbie was supposed to be. We had encountered no difficulty getting there. "One second, Croaker," One-Eye said. He faced the building we had vacated, snapped his fingers.

The whole damned place fell in.

"You bastard," I whispered. "What did you do that for?"

"Now there's nobody who knows who we are."

"Whose fault was it they did know?"

"Chopped off the head of the snake, too. Be so much confusion we could walk off with the Lady's jewelry if we wanted."

"Yeah?" There would be those who knew we were brought in. They would wonder some if they saw us wandering around. "Tell me, O genius. Did you locate the documents I want before you tumbled the place down? If they're in there, you're the gent who's going to dig them out."

His face dropped.

Yes. I expected that. Because that is my kind of luck. And that is the way One-Eye is. He never thinks things through.

"We'll worry about Corbie first," I said. "Inside."

As we pushed through the door we encountered Case coming to investigate the uproar.

33

Missing Man

"Hi, fellow," One-Eye said, punching a finger into the soldier's chest, pushing him back. "Yeah. It's your old pals."

Behind me, Tracker stared across the compound. The collapse of the headquarters building was complete. Fire snapped and crackled inside. Toadkiller Dog loped around the end of the ruin.

"Look at that." I punched Goblin's arm. "He's running." I faced Case. "Show us your friend Corbie."

He did not want to do that.

"You don't want to argue. We're not in the mood. Move it or we walk over you."

The compound had begun to fill with yammering soldiers. None noticed us. Toadkiller Dog loped up, sniffed Tracker's calves, made a sound deep in his throat. Tracker's face gleamed.

We pushed in behind Case. "To Corbie," I reminded him.

He led us to a room where a single oil lamp illuminated a man on a bed, neatly blanketed. Case turned the lamp up.

"Oh, holy shit," I murmured. I plopped my butt on the edge of the bed. "It ain't possible. One-Eye?" But One-Eye was in another universe. He just stood there with his mouth open. Like Goblin.

Finally, Goblin squeaked, "But he's dead. He died six years ago."

Corbie was the Raven who played such a grand part in the Company past. The Raven who had set Darling on her present course.

Even I had been convinced he was dead, and I was by nature suspicious of Raven. He had tried the same stunt before.

"Nine lives," One-Eye remarked.

"Should have suspected when we heard the name Corbie," I said.

"What?"

"It's a joke. His kind. Corbie. Crow. Rook. Raven. All pretty much the same thing. Right? He waved it under our noses."

Seeing him there illuminated mysteries that had plagued me for years. Now I knew why papers I had salvaged would not come together. He had removed the key pieces before faking his last death.

"Even Darling didn't know this time," I mused. The shock had begun to wear off. I found myself reflecting that on several occasions after the letters began arriving I had skirted the suspicion that he was alive.

A raft of questions rose. Darling not knowing. Why not? That did not seem like Raven. But more, why abandon her to our mercy, as he had, when for so long he had tried to keep her away?

There was more here than met the eye. More than Raven just running off so he could poke into doings at the Barrowland. Unfortunately, I could question neither of my witnesses.

"How long has he been this way?" One-Eye asked Case. The soldier's eyes were wide. He knew who we were now. Maybe my ego did not need deflating after all.

"Months."

"There was a letter," I said. "There were papers. What became of them?"

"The Colonel."

"And what did the Colonel do? Did he inform the Taken? Did he contact the Lady?"

The trooper was about to get stubborn. "You're in trouble here, kid. We don't want to hurt you. You did right by our friend. Speak up."

"He didn't. That I know of. He couldn't read any of that stuff. He was waiting for Corbie to wake up."

"He would have waited a long time," One-Eye said. "Give us some room, Croaker. First order of business is going to be finding Raven."

"There anyone else in this building this time of night?" I asked Case.

"Not unless the bakers come in for flour. But it's stored in the cellars down to the other end. They wouldn't come around here."

"Right." I wondered how much his information could be trusted. "Tracker. You and Toadkiller Dog go stand lookout."

"One problem," One-Eye said. "Before we do anything, we need Bomanz's map."

"Oh, boy." I slipped into the hallway, to the exit, peeped out. The headquarters building was afire, sputtering halfheartedly in the rain. Most of the Guard were fighting the fire. I shuddered. Our documents were in there. If the Lady's luck held, they would burn. I returned to the room. "One-Eye, you have a more immediate problem. My documents. You better get after them. I'll try for the chart.

"Tracker, you watch the door here. Keep the kid in and everybody else out. All right?" He nodded. He needed no special coaching while Toadkiller Dog was around.

I slipped out, into the confusion. No one paid me any heed. I wondered if this was not the time to take Raven out. I exited the compound unchallenged, dashed through the drizzle to Blue Willy. The proprietor seemed astounded to see me. I did not pause to tell him what I thought of his hospitality, just went upstairs, groped around inside the concealment spell till I found the spear with the hollow shaft. Back down. One vituperous look for the landlord, then into the rain again.

By the time I returned, the fire was under control. Soldiers had begun to pull the rubble apart. Still no one challenged me. I slipped into the building where Raven lay, handed One-Eye the spear. "You do anything about those papers?"

"Not yet."

"Damn it. . . ."

"They're in a box in the Colonel's office, Croaker. What the hell do you want?"

"Ah. Tracker. Take the kid into the hallway. You guys. I want a spell where he has to do what he's told whether he wants to or not."

"What?" One-Eye asked.

"I want to send him after those papers. Can you fix it so he's got to do it and come back?"

Case was in the doorway, listening bleakly.

"Sure. No problem."

"Do it. Son, you understand? One-Eye will put a spell on you. You go help clean up that mess till you can get the box. Bring it back and we'll take the spell off."

He looked like getting stubborn again.

"You have a choice, of course. You can die an unpleasant death instead."

"I don't think he believes you, Croaker. I'd better give him a taste."

Case's expression told me he did believe. The more he thought about who we were, the more terrified he became.

How had we developed such a fierce reputation? I guess stories grow in the retelling. "I think he'll cooperate. Right, son?"

He nodded, stubbornness dead.

He looked like a good kid. Too bad he had given his loyalty to the other side.

"Do it, One-Eye. Let's get on with this."

While One-Eye worked, Goblin asked, "What do we do after we finish here, Croaker?"

"Hell, I don't know. Play it by ear. Right now don't worry about the mules, just load the wagon. Step at a time. Step at a time."

"Ready," One-Eye said.

I beckoned the youth, opened the outside door. "Get out there and do it, kid." I patted his behind. He went, but with a look that could have curdled milk.

"He's not happy with you, Croaker."

"Screw it. Get in there with Raven. Do what you have to do. Time is wasting. Come daylight this place will see some life."

I watched Case. Tracker guarded the door to the room. No one interrupted us. Case eventually found what I wanted, slipped away from the work detail. "Good job, son," I told him, taking the box. "In the room with your friend."

We entered moments before One-Eye came out of a trance. "Well?" I asked.

He took a moment to orient himself. "Going to be harder than I thought. But I think we can bring him out." He indicated the chart Goblin had spread atop Raven's stomach. "He's about here, caught, just inside the inner circle." He shook his head. "You ever hear him tell about having any background in the trade?"

"No. But there were times I wondered. Like in Roses, when he tracked Raker through a snowstorm."

"He learned something somewhere. Weren't no parlor trick, what he did. But it was too big for his skills." For a moment he was thoughtful. "It's weird in there, Croaker. Really weird. He isn't alone by a long shot. Won't be able to give you any details till we go in ourselves but. . . ."

"What? Wait. Go in yourselves? What're you talking about?"

"Figured you understood Goblin and I would have to follow him in. In order to bring him out."

"Why both of you?"

"One to cover in case the point man gets in trouble."

Goblin nodded. They were all business now. Meaning they were scared crapless.

"How long is all this going to take?"

"No telling. Quite a while. We ought to get out of here first. Out in the woods."

I wanted to argue but did not. Instead, I went and checked the compound.

They had begun bringing the bodies out of the rubble. I watched a while, got an idea. Five minutes later Case and I stepped out carrying a litter. A blanket covered what appeared to be a large broken body. Goblin's face lay exposed. He did a great corpse. One-Eye's feet stuck out the other end. Tracker carried Raven.

The documents were under the blanket with Goblin and One-Eye.

I did not expect to pull it off. But the grim business around the collapsed building preoccupied the Guard. They had reached the cellars.

I did get challenged at the compound gate. Goblin used his sleep spell. I doubted we would be remembered. Civilians were all over, helping and hindering the rescue effort.

That was the bad news. A few down in that cellar were still alive.

"Goblin, you and One-Eye get our gear. Take the kid. Tracker and I will get the wagon."

All went well. Too well, I thought, being naturally pessimistic after the way things had been going. We put Raven in the wagon and headed south.

The moment we entered the forest One-Eye said, "So we've made our getaway. Now. About Raven?"

I was without a single idea. "You call it. How close do you have to be?"

"Very." He saw I was thinking about getting out of the country first. "Darling?"

The reminder was unnecessary.

I won't say Raven was the center of her life. She will not discuss him except in the most general way. But there are nights she cries herself to sleep, remembering something. If it is for loss of Raven, we could not bring him home like this. It would break her heart all the way.

Anyway, we needed him now. He knew better than we what the hell was going on.

I appealed to Tracker for suggestions. He had none. He did not, in fact, appear pleased with what we planned. Like he expected Raven to become competition, or something.

"We've got him," One-Eye said, indicating Case, whom we had dragged along rather than leave dead. "Let's use him."

Good idea.

Twenty minutes later we had the wagon well off the road, up on rocks so it would not sink into the soggy earth. One-Eye and Goblin wound spells of concealment around it and camouflaged it with brush. We piled gear into packs, placed Raven on the litter. Case and I carried him. Tracker and Toadkiller Dog led us through the woods.

It could not have been more than three miles, yet I ached everywhere before we finished. Too old. Too out of shape. And the weather was one-hundred-ninety-proof misery. I had had enough rain to last me the rest of my life. Tracker led us to a place just east of the Barrowland. I could walk downhill a hundred yards and see its remnants. I could walk a hundred yards the other way and see the Great Tragic. Only the one narrow stretch of high ground barred it from reaching the Barrowland.

We got tents up and boughs inside so we did not have to sit on wet earth. Goblin and One-Eye took the smaller tent. The rest of us crowded into the other. Once reasonably free of the rain, I settled down to probe the rescued documents. First to catch my eye was an oilskin packet. "Case. This the letter Raven wanted you to deliver?"

He nodded sullenly. He was not talking.

Poor boy. He believed he was guilty of treason. I hoped he wouldn't get a case of the heroics.

Well, might as well keep busy while Goblin and One-Eye did their job. Start with the easy part first.

Bomanz's Story

Croaker:

Bomanz faced the Lady from another angle. He saw a ghost of fear touch her matchless features. "Ardath," he said, and saw her fear become resignation.

Ardath was my sister.

"You had a twin. You murdered her and took her name. Your true name is Ardath."

You will regret this. I will find your name. . . .

"Why do you threaten me? I mean you no harm."

You harm me by thwarting me. Free me.

"Come, come. Don't be childish. Why force my hand? That will cost us both agony and energy. I only want to rediscover the knowledge interred with you. Teaching me will cost you nothing. It won't harm you. It might even prepare the world for your return."

The world prepares already. Bomanz!

He chuckled. "That's a mask, like the antiquarian. That's not my name. Ardath. Must we fight?"

Wise men say to accept the inevitable with grace. If I must, I must. I will try to be gracious.

When pigs fly, Bomanz thought.

The Lady's smile was mocking. She sent something. He did not catch it. Other voices filled his mind. For an instant he thought the Dominator was awakening. But the voices were in his physical ears, back at the house. "Oh, damn!"

Wind-chimes mirth.

"Clete is in position." The voice was Tokar's. Its presence in the attic enraged Bomanz. He started running.

"Help me get him out of the chair." Stancil.

"Won't you wake him up?" Glory.

"His spirit is out in the Barrowland. He won't know anything unless we run into each other out there."

Wrong, Bomanz thought. Wrong, you insidious, ungrateful wart. Your old man isn't stupid. He responds to the signs even when he doesn't want to see them.

The dragon's head swung as he hurtled past. Mockery pursued him. The hatred of dead knights pounded him as he hurried on.

"Get him into the corner. Toker, the amulet is under the hearthstone in the shack. That damned Men fu! He almost blew it. I want to get my hands on the fool who sent him up here. That greedy idiot wasn't interested in anything but himself."

"At least he took the Monitor with him." Glory.

"Pure accident. Pure luck."

"The time. The time," Tokar said. "Clete's men are hitting the barracks."

"Get out of here, then. Glory, will you do something besides stare at the old man? I've got to get in there before Tokar reaches the Barrowland. The Great Ones have to be told what we're doing."

Bomanz passed the barrow of Moondog. He felt the restlessness within. He raced on.

A ghost danced beside him. A slump-shouldered, evil-faced ghost who damned him a thousand times. "I don't have time for it, Besand. But you were right." He crossed the old moat, passed his dig. Strangers dotted the landscape. Resurrectionist strangers. Where had they come from? Out of hiding in the Old Forest?

Faster. Got to go faster, he thought. That fool Stance is going to try to follow me in.

He ran like nightmare, floating through subjectively eternal steps. The comet glared down. It felt strong enough to cast shadows.

"Read the instructions again to make sure," Stancil said. "Timing isn't critical as long as you don't do anything early."

"Shouldn't we tie him up or something? Just in case?"

"We don't have time. Don't worry about him. He won't come out till way too late."

"He makes me nervous."

"Then throw a rug over him and come on. And try to keep your voice down. You don't want to waken Mother."

Bomanz charged the lights of the town. . . . It occurred to him that in this state he did not have to be a stubby-legged fat man short on breath. He changed his perception and his velocity increased. Soon he encountered Tokar, who was trotting toward the Barrowland with Besand's amulet. Bomanz judged his own startling swiftness by Tokar's apparent sluggishness. He was moving fast.

Headquarters was afire. There was heavy fighting around the barracks. Tokar's teamsters were leading the attackers. A few Guardsmen had broken out of the trap. Trouble was seeping into the town.

Bomanz reached his shop. Upstairs, Stancil told Glory, "Begin now." As Bo started up the stair, Stancil said, "Dumni. Um muji dumni." Bomanz smashed into his own body. He seized command of his muscles, surged off the floor.

Glory shrieked.

Bomanz hurled her toward a wall. Her career shattered priceless antiques.

Bomanz squealed in agony as all the pains of an old body hit his consciousness. Damn! His ulcer was tearing his gut apart!

He seized his son's throat as he turned, silencing him before he finished the cantrip.

Stancil was younger, stronger. He rose. And Glory threw herself at Bomanz. Bomanz darted backward. "Don't anybody move," he snapped.

Stancil rubbed his throat and croaked something.

"You don't think I would? Try me. I don't care who you are. You're not going to free that thing out there."

"How did you know?" Stancil croaked.

"You've been acting strange. You have strange friends. I hoped I was wrong, but I don't take chances. You should have remembered that."

Stancil drew a knife. His eyes hardened. "I'm sorry, Pop. Some things are more important than people."

Bomanz's temples throbbed. "Behave yourself. I don't have time for this. I have to stop Tokar."

Glory drew a knife of her own. She sidled a step closer.

"You're trying my patience, son."

The girl jumped. Bomanz uttered a word of power. She plunged headlong into the table, slid to the floor, almost inhumanly limp. In seconds she was limper still. She mewled like an injured kitten.

Stancil dropped to one knee. "I'm sorry, Glory. I'm sorry."

Bomanz ignored his own emotional agony. He salvaged the quicksilver spilled from the bowl that had been atop the table, mouthed words which transformed its surface into a mirror of events afar.

Tokar was two thirds of the way to the Barrowland.

"You killed her," Stancil said. "You killed her."

"I warned you, this is a cruel business." And: "You made a bet and lost. Sit your butt in the corner and behave."

"You killed her."

Remorse smashed in even before his son forced him to act. He tried to soften the impact, but the melting of bones was all or nothing.

Stancil fell across his lover.

His father fell to his knees beside him. "Why did you make me do it? You fools. You bloody damned fools! You were using me. You didn't have sense enough to make sure of me, and you want to deal with something like the Lady? I don't know. I don't know. What am I going to tell Jasmine? How can I explain?" He looked around wildly, an animal tormented. "Kill myself. That's all I can do. Save her the pain of learning what her son was. . . . Can't. Got to stop Tokar."

There was fighting in the street outside. Bomanz ignored it. He scrabbled after quicksilver.

Tokar was at the edge of the moat, staring into the Barrowland. Bomanz saw the fear and uncertainty in him.

Tokar found his courage. He gripped the amulet and crossed the line.

Bomanz began building a killing sending.

His glance crossed the doorway, spied a frightened Snoopy watching from the dark landing. "Oh, child. Child, get out of here."

"I'm scared. They're killing each other outside."

We're killing each other in here, too, he thought. Please go away. "Go find Jasmine."

A horrendous crash came from the shop. Men cursed. Steel met steel. Bomanz heard the voice of one of Tokar's teamsters. The man was deploying a defense of the house.

The Guard had made a comeback.

Snoopy whimpered.

"Stay out of here, child. Stay out. Go down with Jasmine."

"I'm scared."

"So am I. And I won't be able to help if you get in my way. Please go downstairs."

She ground her teeth and rattled away. Bomanz sighed. That was close. If she had seen Stance and Glory. . . .

The uproar redoubled. Men screamed. Bomanz heard Corporal Husky bellowing orders. He turned to the bowl. Tokar had disappeared. He could not relocate the man. In passing he surveyed the land between the town and the Barrowland. A few Resurrectionists were rushing toward the fighting, apparently to help. Others were in headlong flight. Remnants of the Guard were in pursuit.

Boots pounded upstairs. Again Bomanz interrupted the preparation of his sending. Husky appeared in the doorway. Bomanz started to order him out. He was in no mood to argue. He swung a great bloody sword. . . .

Bomanz used the word of power. Again a man's bones turned to jelly. Then again and again as Husky's troopers tried to avenge him. Bomanz dropped four before the rush ended.

He tried to get back to his sending. . . .

This time the interruption was nothing physical. It was a reverberation along the pathway he had opened into the Lady's crypt. Tokar was on the Great Barrow and in contact with the creature it contained.

"Too late," he murmured. "Too damned late." But he made the sending anyway. Maybe Tokar would die before he could release those monsters.

Jasmine cursed. Snoopy screamed. Bomanz piled over the fallen Guardsmen and charged downstairs. Snoopy screamed again.

Bo entered his bedroom. One of Tokar's men held a knife across Jasmine's throat. A pair of Guardsmen sought an opening.

Bomanz had no patience left. He killed all three.

The house rattled. Teacups clinked in the kitchen. It was a gentle tremor, but a harbinger strong enough to warn Bomanz.

His sending had not arrived in time.

Resigned, he said, "Get out of the house. There's going to be a quake."

Jasmine looked at him askance. She held the hysterical girl.

"I'll explain later. If we survive. Just get out of the house." He whirled and dashed into the street, charged toward the Barrowland.

Imagining himself tall and lean and fleet did no good now. He was Bomanz in the flesh, a short, fat old man easily winded. He fell twice as tremors shook the town. Each was stronger than the last.

The fires still burned, but the fighting had died away. The survivors on both sides knew it was too late for a decision of the sword. They stared toward the Barrowland, awaiting the unfolding of events.

Bomanz joined the watchers.

The comet burned so brightly the Barrowland was clearly illuminated.

A tremendous shock rattled the earth. Bomanz staggered. Out on the Barrowland the mound containing Soulcatcher exploded. A painful glow burned from within. A figure rose from the rubble, stood limned against the glow.

People prayed or cursed according to predilection.

The tremors continued. Barrow after barrow opened. One by one, the Ten Who Were Taken appeared against the night. "Tokar," Bomanz murmured, "I hope you rot in Hell."

There was only one chance left. One impossible chance. It rode on the time-bowed shoulders of a pudgy little man whose powers were not at their sharpest.

He marshaled his most potent spells, his greatest magicks, all the mystical tricks he had worked out during thirty-seven years worth of lonely nights. And he started walking toward the Barrowland.

Hands reached out to detain him. They found no purchase. From the crowd an old woman called, "Bo, no! Please!"

He kept walking.

The Barrowland seethed. Ghosts howled among the ruins. The Great Barrow shook its hump. Earth exploded upward, flaming. A great winged serpent rose against the night. A great scream poured from its mouth. Torrents of dragonfire inundated the Barrowland.

Wise green eyes watched Bomanz's progress.

The fat little man walked into the holocaust, unleashing his arsenal of spells. Fire enveloped him.

35

The Barrowland, from Bad to Worse

Returning Raven's letter to the oilskin, I lay back on my bough bed, let my mind go blank. So dramatic, the way Raven told it. I wondered about his sources, though. The wife? Someone had to note the tale's ending and had to hide what was found later. What *had* become of the wife, anyway? She has no place in legend. Neither does the son, for that matter. The popular stories mention only Bomanz himself.

Something there, though. Something I missed? Ah. Yes. A congruence with personal experience. The name Bomanz had relied upon. The one that, evidently, proved insufficiently powerful.

I'd heard it before. In equally furious circumstances.

In Juniper, as the contest between the Lady and the Dominator neared its climax, with her ensconced in a castle on one side of the city and the Dominator trying to escape through another on the far side, we discovered the Taken meant to do the Company evil once the crisis subsided. Under orders from the Captain we deserted. We seized a ship. As we sailed away, with husband and wife contesting above the burning city, the struggle peaked. The Lady proved the stronger.

The voice of the Dominator shook the world as he vented a last spate of frustration. He had called her by the name Bomanz had thought puissant. Apparently, even the Dominator could be mistaken.

One sister killed another and, maybe or maybe not, took her place. Soulcatcher, our one-time mentor and plotter to usurp the Lady, it proved during the great struggle at Charm, was another sister. Three sisters, then. At least. One named Ardath, but evidently not the one who became the Lady.

Maybe the beginnings of something here. All those lists, back in the Hole. And the genealogies. Find a woman named Ardath. Then discover who her sisters were.

"It's a beginning," I murmured. "Feeble, but a beginning."

"What?"

I had forgotten Case. He had not taken advantage. I suppose he was too frightened.

"Nothing." It had grown dark outside. The drizzle persisted. Out on the Barrowland ghostly lights drifted about. I shuddered. That did not seem right. I wondered how Goblin and One-Eye were getting on. I did not dare go ask. Over in a corner Tracker snored softly. Toadkiller Dog lay against his belly, making sleeping dog noises, but I caught a glint of eye which said he was not unalert.

I invested a little more attention in Case. He was shaking, and not just with the chill. He was sure we would kill him. I reached over, rested a hand on his shoulder. "It's all right, son. You won't be harmed. We owe you for looking out for Raven."

"He's really Raven? The Raven that was the White Rose's father?"

The lad knew the legends. "Yeah. Foster-father, though."

"Then he didn't lie about everything. He *was* in the Forsberg campaigns."

That struck me as humorous. I chuckled, then said, "Knowing Raven, he didn't lie about much. Just edited the truth."

"You'll really let me go?"

"When we're safe."

"Oh." He did not sound reassured.

"Let's say when we get to the edge of the Plain of Fear. You'll find plenty of friends out there."

He wanted to get into a quasi-political discussion about why we insisted on resisting the Lady. I refused. I am no evangelist. I can't make converts. I have too much trouble understanding myself and unravelling my own motives. Maybe Raven could explain after Goblin and One-Eye brought him out.

The night seemed endless, but after three eternities which took me up to midnight I heard unsteady footsteps. "Croaker?"

"In," I said. It was Goblin. Without a light I could not read him well, but got the impression that his news was not good. "Trouble?"

"Yes. We can't get him out."

"What the hell are you talking about? What do you mean?"

"I mean we don't have the skills. We don't have the talent. This's going to take someone bigger than we are. We aren't much, Croaker. Showmen. With a few handy spells. Maybe Silent could do something. His is a different sort of magic."

"Maybe you'd better back up. Where's One-Eye?"

"Resting. It was rough on him. Really rocked him, what he saw in there."

"What was that?"

"I don't know. I was just his lifeline. And I had to pull him out before he got trapped, too. All I know is, we can't get Raven without help."

"Shit," I said. "Double damned floating sheep shit. Goblin, we can't win this one unless we have Raven to help. I don't have what it takes either. I'll never translate half those papers."

"Not even with Tracker's help?"

"He reads TelleKurre. That's it. I can do that, only I take longer. Raven must know the dialects. Some of the stuff he was translating was in them. Also, there's the question of what he was doing *here.* Why he faked his death again and took off. On Darling."

Maybe I was jumping to conclusions. I do that. Or maybe I was indulging in the human penchant for oversimplification, figuring that if we just had Raven back our troubles were solved. "What are we going to do?" I wondered aloud.

Goblin rose. "I don't know, Croaker. Let's let One-Eye get his feet under him again and find out what we're up against. We can go from there."

"Right."

He slipped out. I lay down and tried to sleep.

Whenever I dropped off I had nightmares about the thing lying in the mud and slime the Barrowland had become.

Hard Times

One-Eye looked gruesome. "It was grim," he said. "Get the chart out, Croaker." I did. He indicated a point. "He's here. And stuck. Looks like he went all the way to the center along Bomanz's trail, then got in trouble on his way out."

"How? I don't understand what's going on here."

"I wish you could go in there. A realm of terrible shadows. . . . Guess I should be glad you can't. You'd try it."

"What's that crack mean?"

"Mean's you're too curious for your own good. Like old Bomanz. No. Be still." He paused a moment.

"Croaker, something that was trapped there, one of the minions of the Taken, was situated near Bomanz's path. *He* was too strong for it. But Raven was an amateur. I think Goblin, Silent, and I together would have trouble with this thing, and we're more skilled than Raven could be. He underestimated the dangers and overestimated himself. As he was leaving, this thing usurped his position and left him in its place."

I frowned, not quite understanding.

One-Eye explained, "Something used him to keep the balance of the old spells. So he's stuck in a net of old-time sorcery. And it's out here."

A sinking feeling. A feeling edging despair. "Out? And you don't know . . .?"

"Nothing. The chart indicates nothing. Bomanz must have been contemptuous of the lesser evils. He hasn't marked a dozen. There should have been scores."

The literature supported that. "What did he tell you? Were you able to communicate?"

"No. He was aware of a presence. But he's in a sinkhole of spells. I couldn't contact him without getting caught myself. There's a small imbalance there, like what went out might have been a hair more than what stayed in. I did try to get close to him. That was why Goblin had to yank me out. I did sense a great fear, not due to his situation. Only anger there. I think he got caught only because he was in so big a hurry he didn't pay attention to his surroundings."

I got the message. Been to the center, and in flight. What lay at the center? "You think whatever got away might try to open the Great Barrow?"

"It might try engineering it."

I had a brainstorm. "Why not sneak Darling out here? She could. . . ."

One-Eye gave me a don't-be-stupid look. Right. Raven was the least of the things a null would loose.

"The big guy would love that," Goblin chided. "Purely love it."

"There's nothing we can do for Raven here," One-Eye said. "Someday we might find a wizard who can. Till then?" He shrugged. "Better make a pact of silence. Darling might forget her mission if she finds out."

"Agreed," I said. Then: "But. . . ."

"But what?"

"I've been thinking about that. Darling and Raven. There's something there we don't see, I think. I mean, considering the way he always was, why did he cut out and come here? On the face of it, to sneak around the Lady and her gang. But why would he leave Darling in the dark? You see what I'm saying? Maybe she wouldn't be as upset as we think. Or maybe for different reasons."

One-Eye looked dubious. Goblin nodded. Tracker looked baffled, as usual.

"What about his body?" I asked.

"A definite encumbrance," One-Eye replied. "And I can't say but what taking him to the Plain might not snap the connection between flesh and spirit."

"Stop." I looked at Case. He looked at me. Here we had another double bind.

I knew one sure way of solving Raven's body problem. And of getting him brought out. Betray him to the Lady. That might solve several other problems, too. Like the escaped whatever, and the threat of another escape attempt by her husband. It might buy Darling time, too, for the Lady's attention would shift dramatically.

But what would become of Raven then?

He could be the key to our success or failure. Give him up to save him? Play the very long odds that we could somehow get him in hand again before his knowledge could hurt us? Ever a quandary. Ever a quandary.

Goblin suggested, "Let's give it another look. This time I'll take the point. One-Eye will cover."

One-Eye's sour look said they had had a knock-down-drag-out about this before. I kept my mouth shut. It was their area of expertise.

"Well?" Goblin demanded.

"If you think it's worthwhile."

"I do. Anyway, there's nothing to lose. Different viewpoint might help, too. I might catch something he missed."

"Having only one eye don't blind me," One-Eye snarled. Goblin glowered. This had arisen before, too.

"Don't waste time," I said. "We can't stay put forever."

Sometimes decisions get made for you.

Deep in the night. Wind in the trees. Chill fingering into the shelter, waking me to shiver till I fell asleep again. Rain pattering steadily, but not restfully. Gods, was I sick of rain. How could the Eternal Guard maintain any semblance of sanity?

A hand shook me. Tracker whispered, "Company coming. Trouble." Toadkiller Dog was at the tent flap, hackles up.

I listened. Nothing. But no point not taking his word. Better safe than dead. "What about Goblin and One-Eye?"

"Not finished yet."

"Oh-oh." I scrambled for clothing, for weapons. Tracker said, "I'll go scout them and try to scare or lead them off. You warn the others. Get ready to run." He slipped out of the tent behind Toadkiller Dog. Damned beast showed some life now!

Our whispering wakened Case. Neither of us spoke. I wondered what he would risk. I covered my head with my blanket and left. Sufficient unto the day the evil thereof.

Into the other tent, where I found both men in trances. "Shit. Now what?" Did I dare try waking One-Eye? Softly: "One-Eye. This is Croaker. We've got trouble."

Ah. His good eye opened. For a moment he seemed disoriented. Then: "What're you doing here?"

"Trouble. Tracker says there's somebody in the woods."

A cry came through the rain. One-Eye bolted upright. "The power!" he spat. "What the hell?"

"What is it?"

"Somebody just ripped off a spell almost like one of the Taken."

"Can you get Goblin out? Fast?"

"I can. . . ." Another cry ripped through the woods. This one stretched out and out, and seemed as much of despair as of agony. "I'll get him."

He sounded like all hope had gone.

Taken. Had to be. Sniffed out our tracks. Closing in. But the cries. . . . First one somebody Tracker ambushed? Second one Tracker gotten? Didn't sound like him.

One-Eye lay down and closed his eye. In moments he was back in trance, though his face betrayed the fear on his surface mind. He was good, to go under such tension.

There was a third cry from the woods. Baffled, I moved to where I could look into the rain. I saw nothing. Moments later Goblin stirred.

He looked awful. But his determination showed he had gotten the word. He forced himself upright though it was obvious he was not ready. His mouth kept opening and closing. I had a feeling he wanted to tell me something.

One-Eye came out after him but recovered more quickly. "What's happened?" he asked.

"Another yell."

"Drop everything? Run for it?"

"We can't. We have to get some of this stuff back to the Plain. Otherwise we might as well surrender right here."

"Right. Get it together. I'll take care here."

Getting things together was not much of a job. I had unpacked very little. . . . Something roared out in the woods. I froze. "What the hell?" Sounded like something bigger than four lions. A moment later there were screams.

No sense. No sense at all. I could see Tracker raising nine kinds of hell with the Guard, but not if they had one of the Taken with them.

Goblin and One-Eye showed up as I began knocking the tent down. Goblin still looked like hell. One-Eye carried half his stuff. "Where's the kid?" he asked.

I had paid no attention to his absence. It hadn't surprised me. "Gone. How are we going to carry Raven?"

My answer stepped out of the woods. Tracker. Looking a little the worse for wear, but still healthy. Toadkiller Dog was covered with blood. He seemed more animated than I had seen before. "Let's get him out of here," Tracker said, and moved to take one end of the litter.

"Your stuff."

"No time."

"What about the wagon?" I lifted the other end.

"Forget it. I'm sure they found it. March."

We marched, letting him lead the way. I asked, "What was all that uproar?"

"Caught them by surprise."

"But . . ."

"Even the Taken can be surprised. Save your breath. He isn't dead."

For a few hours it was put one foot in front of the other and don't look back. Tracker set a tough pace. In a corner of my mind where the observer still dwelt, I noted that Toadkiller Dog kept the pace with ease.

Goblin collapsed first. Once or twice he had tried to catch me and pass something along, but he just did not have the energy. When he went down, Tracker stopped, looked back irritably. Toadkiller Dog lay down in the wet leaves, rumbling. Tracker shrugged, set his end of the litter down.

That was *my* cue to drop. Like a stone. And damn the rain and mud. I couldn't get any wetter.

Gods, my arms and shoulders ached. Needles of fire drove into me where the muscles start swooping up to the neck. "This isn't going to work," I said after I caught some breath. "We're too old and weak."

Tracker considered the forest. Toadkiller Dog rose, sniffed the wet wind. I struggled up long enough to look back the way we had come, trying to guess which direction we had run.

South, of course. North made no sense and east or west would have put us in the Barrowland or river. But if we kept heading south we would encounter the old Oar road where it curved in beside the Great Tragic. That stretch was sure to be patrolled.

With my breath partially restored and my breathing no longer roaring in my ears, I could hear the river. It was no more than a hundred yards away, churning and grumbling as always.

Tracker came out of a reflective mood. "Guile, then. Guile."

"I'm hungry," One-Eye said, and I realized I was too. "Reckon we'll get a lot hungrier, though." He smiled feebly. He now had enough strength to look Goblin over. "Croaker. Want to come check him out?"

Funny that they aren't enemies when the pinch comes.

37

The Forest and Beyond

Two days passed before we ate, courtesy of Tracker's skill as a hunter. Two days we spent dodging patrols. Tracker knew those woods well. We disappeared into their deeps and drifted southward at a more relaxed pace. After the two days Tracker felt confident enough to let us have a fire. It was not much, though, because finding burnable wood was a pain. Its value was more psychological than physical.

Misery balanced by rising hope. That was the story of our two weeks in the Old Forest. Hell, trekking overland, off the road, was as fast or faster than using the road itself. We felt halfway optimistic when we neared the southern verge.

I am tempted to dwell on the misery and the arguments about Raven. One-Eye and Goblin were convinced we were doing him no good. Yet they could come up with no alternative to dragging him along.

I carried another weight in my belly, like a big stone.

Goblin got to me that second night while Tracker and Toadkiller Dog were hunting. He whispered, "I got farther in than One-Eye did. Almost to the center. I know why Raven didn't get out."

"Yeah?"

"He saw too much. What he went to see, probably. The Dominator is not asleep. I . . ." He shuddered. It took him a moment to get hold of himself. "I saw him, Croaker. Looking back at me. And laughing. If it hadn't been for One-Eye . . . I'd have been caught just like Raven."

"Oh, my," I said softly, mind abuzz with the implications. "Awake? And working?"

"Yes. Don't talk about it. Not to anybody till you can tell Darling."

There was a hint of fatalism in him then. He doubted he would be around long. Scary. "One-Eye know?"

"I'll tell him. Got to make sure word gets back."

"Why not just tell us all?"

"Not Tracker. There's something wrong with Tracker. . . . Croaker. Another thing. The old-time wizard. He's in there, too."

"Bomanz?"

"Yes. Alive. Like he's frozen or something. Not dead, but not able to do anything. . . . The dragon. . . ." He shut up.

Tracker arrived, carrying a brace of squirrels. We barely let them warm before we attacked them.

We rested a day before tackling the tamed lands. Henceforth it would be scurry from one smidgen of cover to the next, mouselike, by night. I wondered what the hell the point might be. The Plain of Fear might as well be in another world.

That night I had a golden dream.

I do not recall anything except that *she* touched me, and somehow tried to warn me. I think exhaustion more than my amulet blocked the message. Nothing stuck. I wakened retaining only a vague sense of having missed something critical.

End of the line. End of the game. Two hours out of the Great Forest I knew our time was approaching. Darkness was inadequate insulation. Nor were my amulets sufficient.

The Taken were in the air. I felt them on the prowl once it was too late to turn back. And they knew their quarry was afoot. We could hear the distant clamor of battalions moving to bar retreat into the forest.

My amulet warned me of the near passage of Taken repeatedly. When it did not, as it seemed not always to do—perhaps because the new Taken did not affect it—Toadkiller Dog gave warning. He could smell the bastards coming a league away.

The other amulet did help. That and Tracker's genius for laying a crooked trail.

But the circle closed. And closed. And we knew that it would not be long before there were no gaps through which we could slide.

"What do we do, Croaker?" One-Eye asked. His voice was shaky. He knew. But he wanted to be told. And I could neither give the order nor do it myself.

These men were my friends. We had been together all my adult life. I could not tell them to kill themselves. I could not cut them down.

But I could not allow them to be captured, either.

A vague notion formed. A foolish one, really. At first I thought it simple desperation silliness. What good?

Then something touched me. I gasped. The others felt it, too. Even Tracker and his mutt. They jumped as if stung. I gasped again. "It's her. She's here. Oh, damn." But that made up my mind. *I* might be able to buy time.

Before I could reflect and thus chicken out, I shucked my amulets, shoved them into Goblin's hands, pushed our precious documents at One-Eye. "Thanks, guys. Take care. Maybe I'll see you."

"What the hell you doing?"

Bow in hand—the bow she had given me so long ago—I leaped into darkness. Soft protests pursued me. I caught the edge of Tracker asking what the hell was going on. Then I was away.

There was a road not far off, and a little sliver of moon up top. I got onto the one and trotted by the light of the other, pushing my tired old body to its limit, trying to build as big a margin as possible before the inevitable befell me.

She would protect me for a time. I hoped. And once caught, I might stall on behalf of the others.

I felt sorry for them, though. Neither Goblin nor One-Eye was strong enough to help carry Raven. Tracker could not manage alone. If they made it to the Plain of Fear, they would not be able to evade the unenviable duty of explaining everything to Darling.

I wondered if any of them would have what it took to finish Raven. . . . Bile rose. My legs were going watery. I tried to fill my mind with nothingness, stared at the road three steps ahead of my feet, puffed hard, kept on. Count steps. By hundreds, over and over.

A horse. I could steal a horse. I kept telling myself that, concentrated on that, damning the stitch in my side, till shadows loomed before me and imperials began to shout, and I hared off into a wheat field with the Lady's hounds abay behind me.

I nearly gave them the slip. Nearly. But then the shadow descended from the heavens. Air whistled past a carpet. And a moment later darkness devoured me.

I welcomed it as the end of my miseries, hoping it was permanent.

It was light when I regained consciousness. I was in a cold place, but all places are cold in the north countries. I was dry. For the first time in weeks, I was dry. I harkened back to my run and recalled the sliver of moon. A sky clear enough for a moon. Amazing.

I cracked one eye. I was in a room with walls of stone. It had the look of a cell. Beneath me, a surface neither hard nor wet. How long since I had lain on a dry bed? Blue Willy.

I became aware of an odor. Food! Hot food, on a platter just inches from my head, atop a small stand. Some mess that looked like overcooked stew. Gods, did it smell good!

I rose so swiftly my head spun. I almost passed out. Food! The hell with anything else. I ate like the starved animal I was.

I had not quite finished when the door slammed inward. Exploded inward, ringing off the wall. A huge dark form stamped through. For a moment I sat with spoon halfway between bowl and mouth. This thing was human? It stepped to one side, weapon ready.

Four imperials followed, but I hardly noticed, so taken was I with the giant. Man, all right, but bigger than any I'd ever seen. And looking lithe and spritely as an elf for all his size.

The imperials paired to either side of the doorway, presented arms.

"What?" I demanded, determined to go down with a defiant grin. "No drumrolls? No trumpets?" I presumed I was about to meet my captor.

I can call them when I call them. Whisper came through the doorway.

I was more startled by seeing her than by the dramatic advent of her giant thug. She was supposed to be holding the western boundary of the Plain. . . . Unless. . . . I could not think it. But the worm of doubt gnawed anyway. I had been out of touch a long time.

"Where are the documents?" she demanded, without preamble.

A grin smeared my face. I had succeeded. They had not caught the others. . . . But elation faded swiftly. There were more imperials behind Whisper, and they bore a litter. Raven. They dumped him roughly onto a cot opposite mine.

Their hospitality was not niggardly. It was a grand cell. Plenty of room for the prisoner to stretch his legs.

I found my grin. "Now, you shouldn't ask questions like that. Mama wouldn't like it. Remember how angry she became last time?"

Whisper was always a cool one. Even when she led the Rebel, she never let emotion get in the way. She did remind me, "Your death can be an unpleasant one, physician."

"Dead is dead."

A slow smile spread upon her colorless lips. She was not a lovely woman. That nasty smile did not improve her looks.

I got the message. Down in the dark inside me something howled and gibbered like a monkey getting roasted. I resisted its call to terror. Now, if ever there was one, was a time to act as a brother of the Black Company. I had to buy time. Had to give the others the longest head start possible.

She might have read my mind as she stood there staring, smiling. "They won't get far. They can hide from witchery, but they cannot hide from the hounds."

My heart sank.

As if cued, a messenger arrived. He whispered to Whisper. She nodded. Then she turned to me. "I go to collect them now. Think on the Limper in my absence. For once I have drained you of knowledge, I may deliver you to him." Smile again.

"You never were a nice lady," I said, but it came feebly and got said to her departing back. Her menagerie went with her.

I checked Raven. He seemed unchanged.

I lay on my cot, closed my eyes, tried to push everything out of my mind. It had worked once before when I needed contact with the Lady.

Where was she? I knew she was near enough to sense last night. But now? Was she playing some game?

But she had said no special consideration. . . . Still. There is consideration and consideration.

38

The Fortress at Deal

Bam! The old door trick. This time I had heard the man-mountain stomping down the hall, so I did not react except to ask, "Don't you ever knock, Bruno?"

No response. Till Whisper stepped inside. "Get up, physician."

I would have made a crude remark, but something in her voice chilled me beyond the chill due my straits. I rose.

She looked terrible. Not that she was much different physically. But something inside had gone dead and cold and frightened. "What was that thing?" she demanded.

I was baffled. "What thing?"

"The thing you were traveling with. Speak."

I could not, for I hadn't the slightest notion what she was blathering about.

"We caught up. Or my men did. I arrived only in time to count the bodies. What shreds twenty hounds and a hundred men in armor, in minutes, then disappears from mortal ken?"

Gods, One-Eye and Goblin must have outdone themselves.

Still I did not speak.

"You came from the Barrowland. Where you were tampering. Did you call something forth?" She sounded as though she were musing. "It's time we found out. It's time we found out how tough you really are, soldier."

She faced the giant. "Bring him."

I gave it my best shot by playing my dirtiest. I pretended meek for just long enough to let him relax. Then I stomped his foot, running the side of my boot down his shin. Then I spun away and kicked at his crotch.

Guess I'm getting old and slow. Course, he was a lot faster than a man his size should be. He leaned back, caught my foot, and threw me across the room. Two imperials got me up and started dragging me. I went with the satisfaction of seeing the big man limp.

I tried a few more tricks, just to slow things up. They did little more than get me knocked around. The imperials strapped me down in a high-backed wooden chair in a room where Whisper had set up to practice her magicks. I saw nothing especially villainous. That only made the anticipation worse.

They got two or three good screams out of me and were working themselves up to get unpleasant when the tableau suddenly broke up. The imperials ripped me out of the chair, hustled me toward my cell. I was too foggy to wonder.

Till, in the hallway a few yards short of that cell, we encountered the Lady.

Yes. So. My message had gotten through. I'd thought the brief touch I'd received was wishful thinking at the time. But here she was.

The imperials ran. Is she that terrible to her own people?

Whisper stood her ground.

Whatever passed between them did so unspoken. Whisper helped me to my feet, pushed me into the cell. Her face was stone but her eyes were asmoulder.

"Curses. Foiled again," I croaked, and fell onto my cot.

It was plain daylight when the door closed. It was night when I wakened and she was standing over me, wearing her guise of beauty. She said, "I warned you."

"Yes." I tried to sit up. I had aches everywhere, both from maltreatment and from pushing an old body beyond its limits before my capture.

"Stay. I would not have come had my own interests not demanded it."

"I would not have called otherwise."

"Again you do me a favor."

"Only in the interest of self-preservation."

"You may, as they say, have jumped from the frying pan into the fire. Whisper lost many men today. To what?"

"I don't know. Goblin and One-Eye. . . ." I shut up. Damn groggy head. Damn sympathetic voice. Said too much already.

"It wasn't them. They haven't the skill to raise anything like that. I saw the bodies."

"I don't know, then."

"I believe you. Even so. . . . I've seen wounds like those before. I'll show you before we leave for the Tower." Was there ever any doubt about that? "When you make your examination, reflect on the fact that the last time men died in such fashion my husband ruled the world."

None of this added up. But I was not worried about it. I was worried about my own future.

"*He* has begun to move already. Long before I expected. Will he never lie quietly and let me get on with my work?"

Some sums started toting. One-Eye saying something had gotten out. Raven having been caught because of it. . . . "Dumb shit Raven, you did it again." On his own, trying to care for Darling, he had damned near let the Dominator break through at Juniper. "What did you do this time?"

Why would it follow and protect One-Eye and them?

"This is Raven, then?"

Screwup Number Two for Croaker. Why can't I keep my big damned mouth shut?

She bent over him, rested a hand on his forehead. I watched from beneath my brows, unfocused. I could not look at her direct. She did have the power to sway stone.

"I will return soon," she said, heading for the door. "Fear not. You will be safe in my absence."

The door closed.

"Sure," I murmured. "Safe from Whisper, maybe. But how safe from you?" I looked around the room, wondering if I might end my life.

Whisper took me out to look at the carnage where hounds and imperials had overhauled One-Eye and Goblin. Not pleasant, I'll tell you. The last I saw the like was when we went up against the forvalaka in Beryl, ere we joined the Lady. I wondered if that monster was back and tracking One-Eye again. But he had slain it during the Battle at Charm. Hadn't he?

But the Limper survived. . . .

Hell, yes, he did. And two days after the Lady took off—I was imprisoned in the old fortress at Deal, I'd learned—he made an appearance. A little friendly visit, just for old time's sake.

I sensed his presence before I actually saw him. And terror nearly unmanned me.

How had he known? . . . Whisper. Almost certainly Whisper.

He came to my cell, buoyed on a miniature carpet. His name no longer really described him. He could not get around without that carpet. He was but the shadow of a being, human wreckage animated by sorcery and a mad, burning will.

He floated into my cell, hovered there considering me. I did my best to appear unintimidated, failed.

A ghost of a voice stirred the air. "Your time has come. It will be a prolonged and painful ending to your tale. And I will enjoy every moment."

"I doubt it." Had to keep up the show. "Mama won't like you messing with her prisoner."

"She is not here, physician." He began to drift backward. "We will begin soon. After time for reflection." A snatch of insane chuckle drifted in behind him. I am not sure if he or Whisper was the source. She was in the hallway, watching.

A voice said, "But she *is* here."

They froze. Whisper went pallid. Limper sort of folded in upon himself.

The Lady materialized out of nowhere, appearing first as golden sparkles. She said nothing more. The Taken did not speak either, for there was nothing they could say.

I wanted to interject one of my remarks, but the better part of valor prevailed. Instead, I tried to make myself small. A roach. Beneath notice.

But roaches get squished beneath the uncaring foot. . . .

The Lady finally spoke." Limper, you were given an assignment. Nowhere in your brief is there an allowance for you to leave your command. Yet you have done so. Again. And the results are the same as when you slipped off to Roses to sabotage Soulcatcher."

Limper wilted even more.

That was one damned long time ago. One of our sneaky tricks on the Rebel of the day. What happened was, the Rebel attacked Limper's headquarters while he was away from his demesne trying to undermine Soulcatcher.

So Darling was whooping it up on the Plain.

My spirits rose. It was the confirmation I'd had that the movement had not collapsed.

"Go," the Lady said. "And know this. There will be no more understanding. Henceforth we live by the iron rules as my husband made them. Next time will be the last time. For you or anyone else who serves me. Do you understand? Whisper? Limper?"

They understood. They were careful to say so in so many words.

There was communication there beneath the level of mere words, not accessible to me, for they went away absolutely convinced their continued existence depended upon unquestioning and unswerving obedience not only to the letter but the spirit of their orders. They went with a crushed air.

The Lady faded the moment my cell door closed.

She appeared in the flesh shortly before nightfall. Her anger still simmered. I gathered, from hearing guards gossip, that Whisper had been ordered back to the Plain, too. Things had turned bad out there. The Taken on the scene could not cope.

"Give them hell, Darling," I murmured. "Give them hell." I was working hard on resigning myself to whatever fate's horror shop stocked for me.

Guards brought me out of the cell soon after nightfall. They brought Raven, too. I asked no questions. They would not have answered.

The Lady's carpet rested in the fortress' main court. The soldiers placed Raven upon it, tied him down. A glum sergeant gestured for me to board. I did so, surprising him by knowing what to do. My heart was in my heels. I knew my destination.

The Tower.

I waited half an hour. Finally she came. She looked thoughtful. Even a little disturbed and uncertain. She took her place at the leading edge of the carpet. We rose.

Riding a windwhale is more comfortable and much less trying to the nerves. A windwhale has substance, has scale.

We rose perhaps a thousand feet and began running south. I doubt we were making more than thirty miles per hour. It would be a long flight, then, unless she chose to break it.

After an hour she faced me. I could barely discern her features. She said, "I visited the Barrowland, Croaker."

I did not respond, not knowing what was expected.

"What have you done? What have you people set free?"

"Nothing."

She looked at Raven. "Perhaps there is a way." After a time: "I know the thing that is loose. . . . Sleep, physician. We'll talk another time." And I went to sleep. And when I wakened I was in another cell. And knew, by the uniforms, that my new prison was the Tower at Charm.

39

A Guest at Charm

A colonel of the Lady's household force came for me. He was almost polite. Even back when, her troops never were sure of my status. Poor babies. I had no niche in their ordered and hierarchical universe.

The Colonel said, "She wants you now." He had a dozen men with him. They did not look like an honor guard. Neither did they act like executioners.

Not that it mattered. I would go if they had to carry me.

I left with a backward glance. Raven was holding his own.

The Colonel left me at a doorway into the inner Tower, the Tower inside the Tower, into which few men pass, and from which fewer return. "March," he said. "I hear you've done this before. You know the drill."

I stepped through the doorway. When I looked back I saw only stone wall. For a moment I became disoriented. That passed and I was in another place. And she was there, framed by what appeared to be a window, though her parts of the Tower are completely ensheathed within the rest.

"Come here."

I went. She pointed. I looked out that non-window on a burning city. Taken soared above it, hurling magicks that died. Their target was a phalanx of windwhales that were devastating the city.

Darling was riding one of the whales. They were staying within her null, where they were invulnerable.

"They are not, though," the Lady said, reading my thoughts. "Mortal weapons will reach them. And your bandit girl. But it does not matter. I've decided to suspend operations."

I laughed. "Then we've won."

I do believe that was the first time I ever saw her piqued with me. A mistake, mocking her. It could make her reassess emotionally a decision made strategically.

"You have won nothing. If that is the perception a shift of focus will generate, then I will not break off. I will adjust the campaign's focus instead."

Damn you, Croaker. Learn to keep your big goddamn mouth shut around people like this. You will jack-jaw your way right into a meat grinder.

After regaining her self-control, she faced me. The Lady, from just two feet away. "Be sarcastic in your writing if you like. But when you speak, be prepared to pay a price."

"I understand."

"I thought you would." She faced the scene again. In that far city—it looked like Frost—a flaming windwhale fell after being caught in a storm of shafts hurled by ballistae bigger than any I'd ever seen. Two could play the suck-in game. "How well did your translations go?"

"What?"

"The documents you found in the Forest of Cloud, gave to my late sister Soulcatcher, took from her again, gave to your friend Raven, and took from him in turn. The papers you thought would give you the tool of victory."

"*Those* documents. Ha. Not well at all."

"You couldn't have. What you sought isn't there."

"But. . . ."

"You were misled. Yes. I know. Bomanz put them together, so they must hold my true name. Yes? But that has been eradicated—except, perhaps, in the mind of my husband." She became remote suddenly. "The victory at Juniper cost."

"He learned the lesson Bomanz did too late."

"So. You noticed. *He* has information enough to pry an answer from what happened. . . . No. My name isn't there. *His* is. *That* was why they so excited my sister. She saw an opportunity to supplant us both. She knew me. We were children together, after all. And protected from one another only by the most tangled web that could be woven. When she enlisted you in Beryl she had no greater ambition than to undermine me. But when you delivered those documents . . ."

She was thinking aloud as much as explaining.

I was stricken by a sudden insight. "*You* don't know his name!"

"It was never a love match, physician. It was the shakiest of alliances. Tell me. How do I get those papers?"

"You don't."

"Then we all lose. This is true, Croaker. While we argue and while our respective allies strive to slash one another's throats, the enemy of us all is shedding his chains. All this dying will be for naught if the Dominator wins free."

"Destroy him."

"That's impossible."

"In the town where I was born there is a folk tale about a man so mighty he dared mock the gods. In the end his might proved sheer hubris, for there is one against whom even the gods are powerless."

"What's the point?"

"To twist an old saw, death conquers all. Not even the Dominator can wrestle death and win every time."

"There are ways," she admitted. "But not without those papers. You will return to your quarters now, and reflect. I will speak to you again."

I was dismissed that suddenly. She faced the dying city. Suddenly, I knew my way out. A powerful impulse drove me toward the door. A moment of dizziness and I was outside. The Colonel came puffing along the corridor. He returned me to my cell.

I planted myself on my bunk and reflected, as ordered.

There was evidence enough that the Dominator was stirring, but . . . the business about the documents not holding the lever we had counted on—that was the shocker. That I had to swallow or reject, and my choice might have critical repercussions.

She was leading me for her own ends. Of course. I conceived numerous possibilities, none pleasant, but all making a sort of sense. . . .

She'd said it. If the Dominator broke out, we were all in the soup, good guys and bad.

I fell asleep. There were dreams, but I do not recall them. I awakened to find a hot meal freshly delivered, sitting atop a desk that had not been there before. On that desk was a generous supply of writing materials.

She expected me to resume my Annals.

I devoured half the food before noting Raven's absence. The old nerves began to rattle. Why was he gone? Where to? What use did she have for him? Leverage?

Time is funny inside the Tower.

The usual Colonel arrived as I finished eating. The usual soldiers accompanied him. He announced, "She wants you again."

"Already? I just came back from there."

"Four days ago."

I touched my cheek. I have been affecting only a partial beard of late. My face was brushy. So. One long sleep. "Any chance I could get a razor?"

The Colonel smiled thinly. "What do you think? A barber can come in. Will you come along?"

I got a vote? Of course not. I followed rather than be dragged.

The drill was the same. I found her at a window again. The scene showed some corner of the Plain where one of Whisper's fortifications was besieged. It had no heavy ballistae. A windwhale hovered overhead, keeping the garrison in hiding. Walking trees were dismantling the outer wall by the simple mechanism of growing it to death. The way a jungle destroys an abandoned city, though ten thousand times faster than the unthinking forest.

"The entire desert has risen against me," she said. "Whisper's outposts have suffered an annoying variety of attacks."

"I suspect your intrusions are resented. I thought you were going to disengage."

"I tried. Your deaf peasant isn't cooperating. Have you been thinking?"

"I've been sleeping is what I've been doing. As you know."

"Yes. So. There were matters which demanded attention. Now I can devote myself to the problem at hand." The look in her eye made me want to run. . . . She gestured. I froze. She told me to back up, to sit in a nearby chair. I sat, unable to shake the spell, though I knew what was coming.

She stood before me, one eye closed. The open eye grew bigger and bigger, reached out, devoured me. . . .

I think I screamed.

The moment had been inevitable since my capture, though I had held a foolish hope otherwise. Now she would drain my mind like a spider drains a fly. . . .

I recovered in my cell, feeling as though I had been to hell and back. My head throbbed. It was a major undertaking to rise and stagger to my medical kit, which had been returned after my captors removed the lethals. I prepared an infusion of willow inner bark, which took forever because I had no fire over which to heat the water.

Someone came in as I nursed and cursed the first weak, bitter cup. I did not recognize him. He seemed surprised to see me up. "Hello," he said. "Quick recovery."

"Who the hell are you?"

"Physician. Supposed to check you once an hour. You weren't expected to recover for a long time. Headache?"

"Goddamn well right."

"Cranky. Good." He placed his bag next to my kit, which he glanced through as he opened his. "What did you take?"

I told him, asked, "What do you mean, good?"

"Sometimes they come out listless. Never recover."

"Yeah?" I thought about whipping him just for the hell of it. Just to vent my spleen. But what was the point? Some guard would come bouncing in and make my pains the worse. Too much like work, anyway.

"Are you something special?"

"*I* think so."

A flicker of a smile. "Drink this. Better than the bark tea." I downed the drink he offered. "*She* is most concerned. Never before have I seen her care what became of one subjected to the deep probe."

"How about that?" I was having trouble keeping my foul mood. The drink he'd given me was good stuff, and fast. "What was that concoction? I could use it by the barrel."

"It's addictive. Rendered from the juice of the top four leaves of the parsifal plant."

"Never heard of it."

"Rather scarce." He was examining me at the time. "Grows in some place called the Hollow Hills. The natives use it as a narcotic."

The Company had been through those terrible hills once upon a time. "Didn't know there *were* natives."

"They're as scarce as the plant. There's been talk in council of growing it commercially after the fighting ends. As a medicinal." He clucked his tongue, which reminded me of the toothless ancient who had taught me medicine. Funny. I hadn't thought of him in ages.

Funnier still, all sorts of old odd memories were streaking to the surface, like bottom fish scared toward the light. The Lady had stirred my mind good.

I did not pursue his remark about raising the weed commercially, though that was at odds with my notion of the Lady. The black hearts don't worry about relieving pain.

"How do you feel about her?"

"The Lady? Right now? Not very charitable. How about you?"

He ignored that. "She expects to see you as soon as you recover."

"Does a bear shit in the woods?" I countered. "I get the idea I'm not exactly a prisoner. How about I get some air on the roof? Can't hardly run away from there."

"I'll see if it's permitted. Meantime, take some exercise here."

Hah. The only exercise I get is jumping to conclusions. I just wanted to get somewhere outside four walls. "Am I still among the living?" I asked when he finished examining me.

"For the time being. Though with your attitude I am amazed you survived in an outfit like yours."

"They love me. Worship me. Wouldn't harm a hair on my head." His mention of the outfit put my mood on the downswing. I asked, "You know how long it's been since I was captured?"

"No. I think you've been here more than a week. Could be longer."

So. Guess at least ten days since my capture. Give the boys the benefit of the doubt, have them moving light and hard, and they had maybe covered four hundred miles. Just one giant step out of many. Crap.

Stalling was pointless now. The Lady knew everything I did. I wondered if any of it had been of any use. Or much of a surprise.

"How is my friend?" I asked, suffering a sudden guilt.

"I don't know. He was moved north because his connection with his spirit was becoming attenuated. I'm sure the subject will arise when next you visit the Lady. I'm finished. Have a nice stay."

"Sarky bastard."

He grinned as he left.

Must run in the profession.

The Colonel stepped in a few minutes later. "I hear you want to go to the roof."

"Yeah."

"Inform the sentry when you would like to go." He had something else on his mind. After a pause he asked, "Isn't there any military discipline in your outfit?"

He was irked because I had not been sirring him. Various smart remarks occurred. I stifled them. My status might not remain enigmatic. "Yes. Though not so much as in earlier days. Not enough of us left since Juniper to make that stuff worth the trouble."

Sly shot, Croaker. Put them on the defensive. Tell them the Company fell to its current pitiful state laboring for the Lady. Remind them that it was the empire's satraps who turned first. That must be common knowledge by now, among the officer corps. Something they should think about occasionally.

"Pity, that," the Colonel said.

"You my personal watchdog?"

"Yes. She sets great store by you for some reason."

"I wrote her a poem once," I lied. "I also got the goods on her."

He frowned, decided I was bullshitting.

"Thanks," I said, by way of extending an olive branch. "I'll write for a while before I go." I was way behind. Except for a bit at Blue Willy I had done nothing but jot an occasional note since leaving the Plain.

I wrote till cramps compelled me to stop. Then I ate, for a guard brought a meal as I sanded my last sheet. Done gobbling, I went to the door, told the lad there I was ready to go topside. When he opened up I discovered I was not locked in.

But where the hell could I go if I got out? Silly even thinking of escape.

I had a feeling I was about to take on the official historian job. Like it or no, it would be the least of many evils.

Some tough decisions stared me in the eye. I wanted time to think them over. The Lady understood. Certainly she had the power and talent to be more foresighted than a physician who had spent six years out of touch.

Sunset. Fire in the west, clouds in raging flame. The sky a wealth of unusual colors. A chill breeze from the north, just enough to shiver and refresh. My guardian stayed well away, permitting the illusion of freedom. I walked to the northern parapet.

There was little evidence of the great battle fought below. Where once trenches, palisades, earthworks, and siege engines had stood, and burned, and tens of thousands had died, there was parkland. A single black stone stella marked the site, five hundred yards from the Tower.

The crash and roar returned. I remembered the Rebel horde, relentless, like the sea, wave after wave; smashing upon unyielding cliffs of defenders. I recalled the feuding Taken, their fey and fell deaths, the wild and terrible sorceries. . . .

"It was a battle of battles, was it not?"

I did not turn as she joined me. "It was. I never did it justice."

"They will sing of it." She glanced up. Stars had begun to appear. In the twilight her face seemed pale and strained. Never before had I seen her in any but the most self-possessed mood.

"What is it?" Now I did turn, and saw a group of soldiers some distance away, watching, either awed or aghast.

"I have performed a divination. Several, in fact, for I did not get satisfactory results."

"And?"

"Perhaps I got no results at all."

I waited. You do not press the most powerful being in the world. That she was on the verge of confiding in a mortal was stunning enough.

"All is flux. I divined three possible futures. We are headed for a crisis, a history-shaping hour."

I turned slightly toward her. Violet light shaded her face. Dark hair tumbled down over one cheek. It was not artifice, for once, and the impulse to touch, to hold, perhaps to comfort, was powerful. "Three futures?"

"Three. I could not find my place in any."

What do you say at a moment like that? That maybe there was an error? *You* accuse the Lady of making a mistake.

"In one, your deaf child triumphs. But it is the least likely chance, and she and all hers perish gaining the victory. In another, my husband breaks the grasp of the grave and reestablishes his Domination. That darkness lasts ten thousand years. In the third vision, he is destroyed forever and all. It is the strongest vision, the demanding vision. But the price is great. . . . Are there gods, Croaker? I never believed in gods."

"I don't know, Lady. No religion I ever encountered made any sense. None are consistent. Most gods are megalomaniacs and paranoid psychotics by their worshipers' description. I don't see how they could survive their own insanity. But it's not impossible that human beings are incapable of interpreting a power so much greater than themselves. Maybe religions are twisted and perverted shadows of truth. Maybe there *are* forces which shape the world. I myself have never understood why, in a universe so vast, a god would *care* about something so trivial as worship or human destiny."

"When I was a child . . . my sisters and I had a teacher."

Did I pay attention? You bet your sweet ass I did. I was ears from my toenails to the top of my pointy head. "A teacher?"

"Yes. He argued that *we* are the gods, that we create our own destiny. That what we are determines what will become of us. In a peasantlike vernacular, we all paint ourselves into corners from which there is no escape simply by being ourselves and interacting with other selves."

"Interesting."

"Well. Yes. There is a god of sorts, Croaker. Do you know? Not a mover and shaker, though. Simply a negator. An ender of tales. He has a hunger that cannot be sated. The universe itself will slide down his maw."

"Death?"

"I do not want to die, Croaker. All that I am shrieks against the unrighteousness of death. All that I am, was, and probably will be, is shaped by my passion to evade the end of me." She laughed quietly, but there was a thread of hysteria there. She gestured, indicating the shadowed killing ground below. "I would have built a world in which I was safe. And the cornerstone of my citadel would have been death."

The end of the dream was drawing close. I could not imagine a world without me in it, either. And the inner me was outraged. Is outraged. I have no trouble imagining someone becoming obsessed with escaping death. "I understand."

"Maybe. We're all equals at the dark gate, no? The sands run for us all. Life is but a flicker shouting into the jaws of eternity. But it seems so damned unfair!"

Old Father Tree entered my thoughts. *He* would perish in time. Yes. Death is insatiable and cruel.

"Have you reflected?" she asked.

"I think so. I'm no necromancer. But I've seen roads I don't want to walk."

"Yes. You're free to go, Croaker."

Shock. Even my heels tingled with disbelief. "Say what?"

"You're free. The Tower gate is open. You need but walk out it. But you're also free to remain, to reenter the lists in the struggle that envelops us all."

There was almost no light left except for some sun hitting very high clouds. Against the deep indigo in the east a squadron of bright pinpricks moved westward. They seemed headed toward the Tower.

I gabbled something that made no sense.

"Will she, nill she, the Lady of Charm is at war with her husband once more," she said. "And till that struggle is lost or won, there is no other. You see the Taken returning. The armies of the east are marching toward the Barrowland. Those beyond the Plain have been ordered to withdraw to garrisons farther east. Your deaf child is in no danger unless she comes looking for it. There is an armistice. Perhaps eternally." Weak smile. "If there is no Lady, there is no one for the White Rose to battle."

She left me then, in total confusion, and went to greet her champions. The carpets came down out of the darkness, settling like autumn leaves. I moved a little nearer till my personal guardian indicated that my relationship with the Lady was insufficiently close to permit eavesdropping.

The wind grew more chill, blowing out of the north. And I wondered if it might not be autumn for us all.

40

Making Up My Mind

She never once demanded anything. Even her hints were so oblique they left everything to me to work out. Two days after our evening on the ramparts I asked the Colonel if I might see her. He said he would ask. I suspect he was under instructions. Otherwise there would have been arguments.

Another day passed before he came to say the Lady had time for me.

I closed my inkwell, cleaned my quill, and rose. "Thank you." He looked at me oddly. "Is something wrong?"

"No. Just. . . ."

I understood. "I don't know either. I'm sure she has some special use for me."

That brightened the Colonel's day. That he could comprehend.

The usual routine. This time I entered her demesne as she stood at a window opening on a world of wet gloom. Grey rain, choppy brown water, and hulking to the left, shapes barely discernible, trees clinging precariously to a high river bank. Cold and misery leaked out of that portraiture. It had a too familiar smell.

"The Great Tragic River," she said. "In full flood. But it's always in flood, isn't it?" She beckoned. I followed. Since my last visit a large table had been added. Atop it was a miniature of the Barrowland, a representation so good it was spooky. You almost expected to see little Guards scurrying around the compound.

"You see?" she asked.

"No. Though I've been there twice, I'm not familiar with much but the town and the compound. What am I supposed to see?"

"The river. Your friend Raven evidently recognized its import." With one delicate finger she sketched a loop well to the east of the river's course, which curved into the ridge where we had camped.

"At the time of my triumph in Juniper the river's bed lay here. A year later the weather turned. The river flooded continuously. And crept this way. Today it's devouring this ridge. I examined it myself. The ridge is entirely earthen, without bones of stone. It won't last. Once it goes, the river will cut into the Barrowland. All the spells of the White Rose won't keep it from opening the Great Barrow. Each fetish swept away will make it that much easier for my husband to rise."

I grunted. "Against Nature there is no defense."

"There is. If one foresees. The White Rose did not. I did not when I attempted to bind him more securely. Now it's too late. So. You wanted to speak to me?"

"Yes. I have to leave the Tower."

"So. You didn't have to come to me about that. You're free to stay or go."

"I'm going because there're things I have to do. As you well know. If I walk, I'll probably get them done too late. It's a long hike to the Plain. Not to mention risky. I want to beg transportation."

She smiled, and this smile was genuine, radiant, subtly different from previous smiles. "Good. I thought you would see where the future lies. How soon can you be ready?"

"Five minutes. There is one question. Raven."

"Raven has been hospitalized at the compound at the Barrowland. Nothing can be done for him right now. Every effort will be made when an opportunity arises. Sufficient?"

I could not argue, of course.

"Good. Transport will be available. You will have a unique chauffeur. The Lady herself."

"I. . . ."

"I, too, have been thinking. My best next step is to meet your White Rose. I'm going with you."

After gulping quarts of air, I managed, "They'd jump all over you."

"Not if they don't know me. They wouldn't, unless they were told."

Well, no one was likely to recognize her. I am unique in having met her and lived to brag on it. But . . . Gods, the heaps and bales of *buts.* "If you entered the null, all your spells would fall apart."

"No. New spells wouldn't work. Spells in place would be safe."

I did not understand and said so.

"A simple glamor will fade on entering the null. It is being actively maintained. A spell which changes and leaves changed, but which isn't active on entering the null, won't be affected."

Something off in the badlands of my mind tickled me. I could not run it down. "If you turned into a frog and hopped in there, you'd stay a frog?"

"If the transformation was actual and not just an illusion."

"I see." I hung a red flag on that, told me to worry it later.

"I will become a companion acquired along the way. Say, someone who can help with your documents."

There had to be levels of deceit. Or something. I could not imagine her putting her life into my hands. I do believe I gawked.

She nodded. "You begin to understand."

"You trust me too much."

"I know you better than you know yourself. You're an honorable man, by your own lights, with enough cynicism to believe there can be a lesser of two evils. You *have* been under the Eye."

I shuddered.

She did not apologize. We both knew an apology would be false.

"Well?" she asked.

"I'm not sure why you want to do this. It makes no sense."

"There is a new situation in the world. Once there were only two poles, your peasant girl and I, with a line of conflict drawn between. But that which stirs in the north adds another point. It can be seen as a lengthening of the line, with my point near the middle, or as a triangle. The point that is my husband intends destroying both your White Rose and myself. I submit that she and I ought to eliminate the greater danger before. . . ."

"Enough. I see. But I don't see Darling being that pragmatic. There's a lot of hatred in her."

"Perhaps. But it's worth a try. Will you help?"

Having been within a stone's throw of the old darkness and seen the ghosts astalk on the Barrowland, yes, I would do most anything to keep that dread spook from shedding his grave. But how, how, how trust *her*?

She did that trick they all have, of seeming to read my mind. "You will have me within the null."

"Right. I'll need to think some more."

"Take your time. I can't leave for some time." I suspect she wanted to establish safeguards against a palace revolution.

A Town Called Horse

Fourteen days passed before we took air for Horse, a modest town lying between the Windy Country and the Plain of Fear, about a hundred miles west of the latter. Horse is a caravan stage for those traders mad enough to traipse through those two wildernesses. Of late, the city has been the logistical headquarters for Whisper's operations. What skeleton forces were not on the road to the Barrowland were in garrison there.

Damned northbound fools were going to get wet.

We drifted in after an eventless passage, me with eyes agog. Despite the removal of vast armies, Whisper's base was an anthive swirling around newly created carpets.

They came in a dozen varieties. In one field I saw a W formation of five monsters, each a hundred yards long and forty wide. A wood and metal jungle topped each. Elsewhere, other carpets in unusual shapes sat upon ground that looked to have been graded. Most were far longer than they were wide and bigger than the traditional. All had a variety of appurtenances, and all were enveloped in a light copper cage.

"What is all that?" I asked.

"Adaptation to enemy tactics. Your peasant girl isn't the only one who can change methods." She stepped down, stretched. I did the same. Those hours in the air leave you stiff. "We may get the chance to test them, despite my having backed off the Plain."

"What?"

"A large Rebel force is headed for Horse. Several thousand men and everything the desert has to offer."

Several thousand men? Where did they come from? Had things changed that much?

"They have." That damned mind-reading trick again. "The cities I abandoned poured men into her forces."

"What did you mean, test?"

"I'm willing to stop fighting. But I won't run away from a fight. If she persists in heading west, I'll show her that, null or no null, she can be crushed."

We were near one of the new carpets. I ambled over. In shape it was like a boat, about fifty feet long. It had real seats. Two faced forward, one aft. In front there was a small ballista. Aft there was a much heavier engine. Clamped to the carpet's sides and underbelly were eight spears thirty feet long. Each had a bulge the size of a nail keg five feet behind its head. Everything was painted blacker than the Dominator's heart. This boat-carpet had fins like a fish. Some humorist had painted eyes and teeth up front.

Others nearby followed similar designs, though different artisans had followed different muses in crafting the flying boats. One, instead of fish fins, had what looked like round, translucent, whisper thin dried seed pods fifteen feet across.

The Lady had no time to let me inspect her equipment and no inclination to let me wander around unchaperoned. Not as a matter of trust, but of protection. I might suffer a fatal accident if I did not stay in her shadow.

All the Taken were in Horse. Even my oldest friends.

Bold, bold Darling. Audacity. Becoming her signature, that. She had the entire strength of the Plain just twenty miles from Horse, and she was closing in. Her advance was ponderous, though, limited to the speed of the walking trees.

We went out onto the field where the carpets waited, arranged in formal array around the monsters I had spotted first. The Lady said, "I planned a small demonstration raid on your headquarters. But this will be more convincing, I think."

Men were busy around the carpets. The big ones they were loading with huge pieces of pottery which looked like those big urn-planters with the little cup-holes in the upper half for small plants. They were fifteen feet tall; the planter sites were sealed with paraffin, and the bottom boasted a twenty foot pole with a crossbar on its end. Scores were being mounted in racks.

I did a fast count. More carpets than Taken. "All these are going up? How?"

"Benefice will handle the big ones. Like the Howler before him, he has an outstanding capacity for managing a large carpet. The other four bigs will be slaved to his. Come. This one is ours."

I said something intelligent like, "Urk?!"

"I want you to see it."

"We might be recognized."

Taken circled the long, skinny boat-carpets. Soldiers were aboard them, in the second and third seats. The men facing aft checked their ballistae, munitions, cranked a spring-powered device apparently meant to help restretch bowstrings after missiles were discharged. I could see no apparent task assigned the men in the middle seats. "What's the cagework for?"

"You'll learn soon enough."

"But. . . ."

"Come to it fresh, Croaker. Without preconceptions."

I followed her around our carpet. I do not know what she checked, but she seemed satisfied. The men who had prepared it were pleased by her nod.

"Up, Croaker. Into the second seat. Fasten yourself securely. It'll get exciting before it's over."

Oh yeah.

"We're the pathfinders," she said as she buckled into the front seat. A grizzled old sergeant took the rear position. He looked at me doubtfully, but said nothing. The Taken assumed the front seat aboard every carpet. The bigs, as the Lady called them, had crews of four. Benefice rode the carpet at the center point of the W.

"Ready?" the Lady shouted.

"Right."

"Aye," the sergeant said.

Our carpet began to move.

Lumbering is the only word to describe the first few seconds. The carpet was heavy and, till it managed some forward motion, did not want to lift.

The Lady looked back and grinned as the earth dropped away. She was enjoying herself. She began shouting instructions which explained the bewildering bunch of pedals and levers surrounding me.

Push and pull on these two in combination and the carpet began to roll around its long axis. Twist those and it turned right or left. The idea was to use combinations somehow to guide the craft.

"What for?" I shouted into the wind. The words ripped away. We had donned goggles which protected our eyes but did nothing for the rest of our faces. I expected a case of windburn before the game was played out.

We were two thousand feet up, five miles from Horse, well ahead of the Taken. I could see traces of dust raised by Darling's army. Again I shouted, "What for?"

The bottom fell out.

The Lady had extinguished the spells which made the carpet go. "That's why. You'll fly the boat when we hit the null."

What the hell?

She gave me a half dozen shots at getting the hang of it, and I did see the theory, before she whipped toward the Rebel army.

We circled once, at screaming speed, well outside the null. I was astounded at what Darling had put together. About fifty windwhales, including some monsters over a thousand feet long. Mantas by the hundred. A vast wedge of walking trees. Battalions of human soldiers. Menhirs by the hundred, flickering around the walking trees, shielding them. Thousands of things that leaped and hopped and glided and flopped and flew. So gruesome and wondrous a sight.

On the westward leg of our circle I spied the imperial force, two thousand men in a phalanx on the foreslope of a ridge a mile ahead of the Rebel. A joke, them standing against Darling.

A few bold mantas cruised the edge of the null, sniping with bolts that fell short or just missed. I judged Darling herself to be aboard a windwhale about a thousand feet up. She had grown stronger, for her null's diameter had expanded since my departure from the Plain. All that bewildering Rebel array marched within its protection.

The Lady had called us pathfinders. Our carpet was not equipped like the others, but I did not know what she meant. Till she did it.

We climbed straight up. Little black balls trailing streamers of red or blue smoke scattered behind us, shoveled overboard hastily by the old sergeant. Must have been three hundred. The smoke balls scattered, hovered just feet short of the null. So. Markers by which the Taken could navigate.

And here they came. Way up, the smaller surrounding the W formation of bigs.

The men on the bigs began releasing the giant pots. Down, down, down went a score. We followed, sliding along outside the smudge pots. As they plummeted, the flowerpots turned pole-downward. Mantas and whales slid out of their way.

When the pole hit ground it drove a plunger. The paraffin seals burst. Liquid squirted. The plunger hit a striker. The fluid ignited. Gouts of fire. And when that fire reached something inside the pots, they exploded. Shards cut down men and monsters.

I watched the blooming of those flowers of fire, aghast. Above, the Taken wheeled for a second pass. There was no magic in this. The null was useless.

The second fall drew lightning from whales and mantas. Their first few successes cured them, though, for the pots they hit exploded in the air. Mantas went down. One whale was in grave trouble till others maneuvered overhead and sprayed it with ballast water.

The Taken made a third pass, again dropping pots. They would hammer Darling's troops into slime unless she did something.

She went up after the Taken.

The smoke pots slid around the flanks of the null, outlining it completely.

The Lady climbed at shrieking speed.

The W of bigs went away. The smaller carpets took on more altitude. The Lady brought us into position behind Whisper and the Limper. Clearly, she had anticipated Darling's response.

My emotions were mixed, to say the least.

Whisper's carpet tipped its nose downward. Limper followed. Then the Lady. Others of the Taken followed us.

Whisper dove toward one especially monstrous windwhale. Faster and faster she flew. Three hundred yards from the null two thirty-foot spears ripped away from her carpet, impelled by sorcery. When they hit the null they continued on in a normal ballistic trajectory.

Whisper made no effort to avoid the null. Into it she plunged, the man in her second seat guiding the carpet's fall with those fish fins.

Whisper's spears struck near the windwhale's head. Both burst into flames.

Fire is anathema to those monsters, for the gas that lifts them is violently explosive.

The Limper trailed Whisper with élan. He loosed two spears outside the null and another two inside, just dropped as his second-seat man took the carpet within inches of the windwhale.

Only one lance failed to strike home.

The whale had five fires burning upon its back.

Storms of lightning crackled round Whisper and Limper.

Then *we* hit the null. Our buoying spells failed. Panic snatched at me. Up to me? . . .

We were headed for the burning whale. I jerked and banged and kicked levers.

"Not so violently!" the Lady yelled. "Smoothly. Gently."

I got it in hand as the whale roared upward past us.

Lightning crackled. We passed between two smaller whales. They missed us. The Lady discharged her little ballista. Its bolt struck one of those monsters. What the hell was the point? I wondered. That was not a bee sting to one of them.

But that quarrel had a wire attached, running off a reel. . . .

Wham!

I was blinded momentarily. My hair crackled. Direct hit from a manta bolt. . . . We're dead, I thought.

The metal cage surrounding us absorbed the lightning's energy and passed it along the unwinding wire.

A manta was on our tail, only yards behind. The sergeant ripped off a shaft. It took our pursuer under the wing. The beast began to slide and flutter like a one-winged butterfly.

"Watch where we're going!" the Lady yelled. I turned around. A windwhale back rushed toward us. Fledgling mantas scurried in panic. Rebel bowmen threw up a barrage of arrows.

I hit and yanked every damned lever and pedal, and pissed my pants. Maybe that did it. We scraped the thing's flank, but did not crash.

Now the damned carpet began spinning and tumbling. Earth, sky, windwhales swirled around us. In one glimpse, way up, I saw a windwhale's side explode, saw the monster fold in the middle, raining gobbets of fire. Two more whales trailed smoke . . . but it was a picture there and gone in a moment. I could find none of it when the carpet again rolled to where I could see the sky.

We began our plunge from high enough that I had time to calm down. I fiddled with levers and pedals, got some of the wild spin off. . . .

Then it did not matter. We were out of the null and it was the Lady's craft again.

I looked back to see how the sergeant was. He gave me a dirty look, shook his head pityingly.

The look the Lady gave me was not encouraging either.

We climbed and moved westward. The Taken assembled, observed the results of their attack.

Only the one windwhale was destroyed. The other two managed to get under friends who doused them with ballast water. Even so, the survivors were demoralized. They had done the Taken no injury at all.

Still, they came on.

This time the Taken dropped to the surface and attacked from below, building speed from several miles away, then curving up through the null. I maneuvered between whales with a more delicate hand but still fell dangerously near the ground.

"What are we doing this for?" I yelled. We were not attacking; we were just following Whisper and Limper.

"For the hell of it. For the sheer hell of it. And so you can write about it."

"I'll fake it."

She laughed.

We went high and circled.

Darling took the whales back down. That second pass slew two more.

Down low the Taken could not throw themselves all the way through the null. None but Limper, that is. He played the daredevil. He backed off five miles and built a tremendous velocity before hitting the null.

He made that pass while the bigs were dropping the last of their pots.

I've never heard Darling called stupid. She did not do the stupid thing this time.

Despite all the flash and excitement, it was clear that she could, if she wanted, press on to Horse. The Taken had expended most of their munitions. Limper and the bigs were headed back to rearm. The others circled. . . . Horse was Darling's if she was willing to pay the price.

She decided it was too dear.

Wise choice. My guess is, it would have cost her half her force. And windwhales are too rare to give up for a prize so insignificant.

She turned back.

The Lady broke away and let her go, though she could have maintained the attacks almost indefinitely.

We touched down. I scrambled over the side even before the Lady and in a calculated, melodramatic gesture, kissed the ground. She laughed.

She had had a great time.

"You let them go."

"I made my point."

"She'll shift tactics."

"Of course she will. But for the moment the hammer is in my hand. By not using it I've told her something. She'll have thought it over by the time we get there."

"I suppose."

"You didn't do badly for a novice. Go get drunk or something. And stay out of Limper's way."

"Yeah."

What I did was go to the quarters assigned me and try to stop shaking.

Homecoming

The Lady and I entered the Plain of Fear twelve days after the aerial skirmish near Horse. We traveled on horseback, on second-grade nags, along the old trade trail the denizens of the Plain respect with free passage most of the time. Clad in castoffs, for the trail, the Lady was no longer a beauty. No kick-out-of-bed dog, but no eye-catcher.

We entered the Plain aware that by a pessimistic estimate, we had about three months before the Great Tragic River opened the Great Barrow.

The menhirs noted our presence immediately. I sensed them out there, observing. I had to point it out. For this venture the Lady had schooled herself to eschew anything but the most direct and raw sensory input. She would train herself to mortal ways during our ride so she would make no mistake once we reached the Hole.

The woman has guts.

I guess anyone willing to play heads-up power games with the Dominator has to have them.

I ignored the lurking menhirs and concentrated on explaining the ways of the Plain, revealing the thousand little traps that, at the least, might betray the Lady. It was what a man would do on bringing a newcomer to the land. It would not seem unusual.

Three days into the Plain we narrowly missed being caught in a change storm. She was awed. "What was that?" she asked.

I explained the best I could. Along with all the speculations. She, of course, had heard it all before. But seeing is believing, as they say.

Not long after that we came on the first of the coral reefs, which meant we were in the deep Plain, among the great strangenesses. "What name will you use?" I asked. "I better get used to it."

"I think Ardath." She grinned.

"You have a cruel sense of humor."

"Perhaps."

I do believe she was having fun at pretending to be ordinary. Like some great lord's lady slumming. She even took her turns at the cook fire. To my stomach's despair.

I wondered what the menhirs made of our relationship. No matter the pretense, there was a brittleness, a formality, that was hard to overcome. And the best we could fake was a partnership, which I am certain they found strange. When did man and woman travel together thus, without sharing bedroll and such?

The question of pursuing verisimilitude that far never arose. And just as well. My panic, my terror, at the suggestion would have been such that nothing else would have arisen.

Ten miles from the Hole we breasted a hill and encountered a menhir. It stood beside the way, twenty feet of weird stone, doing nothing. The Lady asked in touristy fashion, "Is that one of the talking stones?"

"Yep. Hi, rock. I'm home."

Old rock didn't have anything to say. We passed on. When I looked back it was gone.

Little had changed. As we crested the last ridge, though, we saw a forest of walking trees crowding the creek. A stand of menhirs both living and dead guarded the crossing. The backwards camel-centaurs gamboled among them. Old Father Tree stood by himself, tinkling, though there was not a breath of wind. Up high, a single buzzardlike avian soared against shattered clouds, watching. One or another of its kind had followed us for days. Of a human presence there was no sign. What did Darling do with her army? She could not pack those men into the Hole.

For a moment I was frightened that I had returned to an untenanted keep. Then, as we splashed across the creek, Elmo and Silent stepped out of the coral.

I dove off my animal and gathered them into a monster hug. They returned it, and in best Black Company tradition did not ask a single question.

"Goddamn," I said. "Goddamn, it's good to see you. I heard you guys was wiped out out west somewhere."

Elmo looked at the Lady with just the slightest hint of curiosity.

"Oh. Elmo. Silent. This is Ardath."

She smiled. "So pleased to meet you. Croaker has said so much about you."

I had not said a word. But she had read the Annals. She dismounted and offered her hand. Each took it, baffled, for only Darling, in their experience, expected treatment as an equal.

"Well, let's go down," I said. "Let's go down. I've got a thousand things to report."

"Yeah?" Elmo said. And that said a lot, for he looked up our backtrail as he said it.

Some people who had gone away with me had not come back.

"I don't know. We had half the Taken after us. We got separated. I couldn't find them again. But I never heard anything about them being captured. Let's go down. See Darling. I've got incredible news. And get me something to eat. We've been eating each other's cooking forever, and she's a worse cook than I am."

"Guck," Elmo said, and slapped me across the back. "And you lived?"

"I'm one tough old buzzard, Elmo. You ought to know. Shit, man, I. . . ." I realized I was chattering like a wacko. I grinned.

Silent signed, "Welcome home, Croaker. Welcome home."

"Come," I told the Lady as we reached the entrance to the Hole, and took her hand. "It'll seem like the pit till your eyes get used to it. And brace yourself for the smell."

Gods, the stench! Gag a maggot.

All kinds of excitement down below. It faded into studied indifference as we passed, then resumed behind us. Silent led straight to the conference room. Elmo split off to order us up something to eat.

As we entered I realized that I still held the Lady's hand. She gave me half a smile, in which there was a hell of a lot of nervousness. Talk about strutting into the dragon's lair. Bold old Croaker gave her hand a squeeze.

Darling looked ragged. So did the Lieutenant. A dozen others were there, few of whom I knew. They must have come aboard after the imperials evacuated the perimeter of the Plain.

Darling hugged me for a long time. So long I became flustered. We are not touchy people, she and I. She finally backed off and gave the Lady a look in which there was a hint of jealousy.

I signed, "This is Ardath. She will help me translate. She knows the old languages well."

Darling nodded. She asked no questions. So much was I trusted.

The food arrived. Elmo dragged in a table and chairs and shooed out everyone but myself, the Lieutenant, himself, Silent, and the Lady. He might have sent her away, too, but remained unsure of her standing with me.

We ate, and as we did I related my tale in snatches, when my hands and mouth were not full. There were some rough moments, especially when I told Darling that Raven was alive.

In retrospect I think it was harder on me than on her. I was afraid she would get all excited and hysterical. She did nothing of the sort.

First, she flat refused to believe me. And I could understand that, for till he disappeared Raven had been the cornerstone of her universe emotionally. She could not see him not including her in his biggest lie ever just so he could slip away to go poke around the Barrowland. That made no sense to her. Raven never lied to her before.

Made no sense to me, either. But then, as I have noted before, I suspected there was more in the shadows than anyone was admitting. I sniffed the faintest whiff that maybe Raven was running *from* instead of *to*.

Darling's denials did not last long. She is not one to disdain truth indefinitely only because it is unpleasant. She handled the pain far better than I anticipated, and that suggested maybe she had had a chance to bleed off some of the worst in the past.

Still, Raven's present circumstances did nothing for Darling's emotional health, already doing poorly after her defeat at Horse. That harbinger of grander defeats to come. Already she suspected she might have to face the imperials without benefit of the information I had been sent to acquire.

I conjured universal despair when I announced my failure and added, "I have it on high authority that what we sought isn't in those papers anyway. Though I can't be sure till Ardath and I finish what we have here." I did sketch what I learned from Raven's documents before losing them.

I did not lie outright. That would not be forgiven later, when the truth came out. As inevitably it must. I just overlooked a few details. I even admitted having been captured, questioned, and imprisoned.

"What the hell are you doing here, then?" Elmo demanded. "How come you're even alive?"

"They turned us loose, Ardath and me. After that business you had near Horse. That was a message. I'm supposed to deliver another."

"Such as?"

"Unless you're blind and stupid, you'll have noticed that you're not under attack. The Lady has ordered all operations against the Rebellion ceased."

"Why?"

"You haven't been paying attention. Because the Dominator is stirring."

"Come on, Croaker. We finished that business in Juniper."

"I went to the Barrowland. I saw for myself, Lieutenant. That thing is going to break loose. One of its creatures is out already, maybe dogging One-Eye and them. I'm convinced. The Dominator is a step from breaking out, and not half-assed like in Juniper." I turned to the Lady. "Ardath. What was that I figured? I lost track of how long we've been in the Plain. It was about ninety days when we came in."

"It took you eight days to get here," Elmo said.

I lifted an eyebrow.

"The menhirs."

"Of course. Eight days, then. Away from ninety for a worst-case scenario. Eighty-two days till the Great Barrow opens." I went into more detail about the Great Tragic River floods.

The Lieutenant was not convinced. Neither was Elmo. And you cannot blame them. The Lady weaves crafty, intricate plots. And they were sneaky guys who judged others by themselves. I did not proselytize. I was not wholeheartedly born-again myself.

It was of little consequence whether or not those two believed, anyway. Darling makes the decisions.

She signed for everyone to leave but me. I asked Elmo to show Ardath around and find her a place to bunk. He looked at me oddly. Like everyone else, he figured I'd brought me home a girlfriend.

I had trouble keeping a straight face. All those years they have ridden me because of a few romances written when first we entered the Lady's service. And now I'd brought her home.

I figured Darling wanted to talk about Raven. I was not wrong, but she surprised me by signing, "She has sent you to propose an alliance, has she not?"

Quick little devil. "Not exactly. Though in practice it would amount to that." I went into the details, known and reasoned, of the situation. Signing is not quick work. But Darling remained attentive and patient, not at all distracted by whatever was going on inside her. She took me over the value, or lack thereof, of my document cache. Not once did she ask about Raven. Nor about Ardath, though my friend was on her mind, too.

She signed, "She is correct in saying that our feud becomes inconsequential if the Dominator rises. My question must be, is the threat genuine or a ploy? We know just how convoluted a scheme she can manage."

"I am sure," I signed in reply. "Because Raven was sure. He had made up his mind before the Lady's people began to suspect. In fact, as far as I can tell, he developed the evidence that convinced them."

"Goblin and One-Eye. Are they safe?"

"As far as I know. I never heard of them being captured."

"They should be getting close. Those documents. They are the crux still."

"Even if they do not contain the secret of her name, but only that of her husband?"

"She wants access?"

"I would assume so. I was released for some reason, though I cannot say what the reason behind the reason was."

Darling nodded. "So I thought."

"Yet I am convinced that she is honest in this. That we must consider the Dominator the more dangerous and immediate peril. It should not be too difficult to anticipate most of the ways she could become treacherous."

"And there is Raven."

Here it comes, I thought. "Yes."

"I will reflect, Croaker."

"There is not much time."

"There is all the time in the world, in a way. I will reflect. You and your lady friend translate."

I felt I had been dismissed before we got to why she wanted to see me privately. The woman has a face like stone. You can't tell much about what is going on inside. I moved toward the door slowly.

"Croaker," she signed. "Wait."

I stopped. This was it.

"What is she, Croaker?"

Damn! Ducked around it again. Chills on my part. Guilt. I did not want to lie outright. "Just a woman."

"Not a special woman? A special friend?"

"I guess she is special. In her way."

"I see. Ask Silent to come in."

Again I went slowly, nodding. But it was not till I actually started to open the door that she beckoned me back.

In accordance with instructions, I sat. She did not. She paced. She signed, "You think I am cold toward great news. You think ill of me because I am not excited that Raven is alive."

"No. I thought it would shock you. That it would cause you great distress."

"Shock, no. I am not entirely surprised. Distressed, yes. It opens old wounds and makes them more painful."

Puzzled, I watched as she continued to prowl.

"Our Raven. He never grew up. Fearless as a stone. Utterly without the handicap of a conscience. Tough. Smart. Hard. Fierce. All those things. Yes? Yes. And a coward."

"What? How can you? . . ."

"He runs away. There were machinations around the Limper which pulled his wife in, years ago. Did he try to discover the truth and work it out? He killed people and ran away with the Black Company to kill more people. He abandoned two babies without a word of good-bye."

She was hot now. She was opening the doors on secrets and spilling stuff of which I had seen only the vaguest glimmering reflections. "Do not defend him. I have had the power to investigate, and I did," she signed.

"He fled the Black Company. For my sake? As much excuse to avoid entanglement as reason. Why did he salvage me in that village? Because of guilt over children he had abandoned. I was a safe child. And while a child I remained a safe emotional investment. But I did not remain a child, Croaker. And I knew no other man in all those years in hiding.

"I should have known better. I saw how he pushed people away if they tried to get close in any way that was not completely one-sided and under his control. But after the horrible things he did in Juniper I thought I could be the one to redeem him. On the road south, when we were running from the dark danger of the Lady and light danger of the Company, I betrayed my true feelings. I opened the lid on a chest of dreams nurtured from a time before I was old enough to think about men.

"He became a changed man. A frightened animal caught in a cage. He was relieved when news came that the Lieutenant had appeared with some of the Company. It was not but a matter of hours before he was 'dead.'

"I suspected then. I think a part of me always knew. And that is why I am not so devastated now as you want. Yes. I know you know I cry myself to sleep sometimes. I cry for a little girl's dreams. I cry because the dreams will not die, though I am powerless to make them come true. I cry because the one thing I truly want I cannot have. Do you understand?"

I thought about Lady, and Lady's situation, and nodded. I signed nothing back.

"I am going to cry again. Go out. Please. Tell Silent to come."

I did not have to look for him. He was waiting in the conference room. I watched him go inside, wondering if I was seeing things or seeing things.

She'd certainly given me something to think about.

Picnic

Put on any deadline and time accelerates. The clockwork of the universe runs off an overwound mainspring. Four days went down the jakes, *zip*! And I did not waste much time sleeping.

Ardath and I translated. And translated. And translated. She read, translating aloud. I wrote till my hands cramped. Occasionally Silent took over for me.

I spot-checked by slipping in documents already done, especially those both Tracker and I had worked. Not once did I catch a misinterpretation.

That fourth morning I did catch something. We were doing one of those lists. This soiree must have been so big that if held today, we'd call it a war. Or at least a riot. On and on. So-and-so of such-and-such, with Lady Who's-is, sixteen titles, four of which made sense. By the time the heralds finished proclaiming everyone, the party must have died of encroaching senility.

Anyway, along about the middle of the list I heard a little catch in her breath. Aha! I said to myself. A bolt strikes close. My ears pricked up.

She went on smoothly. Moments later I was not sure I had not imagined it. Reason told me the name that startled her would not be the one she was speaking. She was toddling along at my writing pace. Her eyes would be well ahead of my hand.

Not one of the names that followed clanged any bell.

I would go over the list later, just in case, hoping she had deleted something.

No such luck.

Come afternoon she said, "Break, Croaker. I'm going for tea. You want some?"

"Sure. Maybe a hunk of bread, too." I scribbled another half minute before realizing what had happened.

What? The Lady herself offering to fetch? Me putting in an order without thinking? I got a case of the nerves. How much was she role-playing? How much pretending for fun? It must be centuries since she got her own tea. If ever.

I rose, started to follow, halted outside my cell door.

Fifteen steps down the tunnel, in the grungy, feeble lamplight, Otto had cornered her against the wall. He was talking some shit. Why I had not foreseen the problem I do not know. I doubted that she had. Surely it was not one she faced normally.

Otto got pushy. I started to go break it up then vacillated. She might be angered by my interference.

A light step from the other direction. Elmo. He paused. Otto was too single-minded to notice us.

"Better do something," Elmo said. "We don't need that kind of trouble."

She did not appear frightened or upset. "I think maybe she can handle it."

Otto got a "no" that could not be misinterpreted. But he did not accept it. He tried to lay hands on.

He got a ladylike slap for his trouble. Which angered him. He decided to take what he wanted. As Elmo and I moved forward, he disappeared in a flurry of kicks and punches that set him down in the muck on the floor, holding his belly with one arm and that arm with the other. Ardath went on as though nothing had happened.

I said, "I told you she could handle it."

"Remind me not to overstep myself," Elmo said. Then he grinned and tapped my arm. "Bet she's mean on the horizontal. Eh?"

Damned if I did not blush. I gave him a foolish grin. It only confirmed his suspicions. What the hell. Anything would have. That is the way those things go.

We lugged Otto to my room. I thought he would puke up his guts. But he controlled himself. I checked for broken bones. He was just bruised. "All yours, Elmo," I said, for I knew the old sergeant was rehearsing a few choice words.

He took Otto by the elbow and said, "Step down to my office, soldier." He started dirt tumbling from the tunnel overhead when he explained the facts of life.

When Ardath returned she behaved as if nothing had happened. Perhaps she missed us watching. But after half an hour she asked, "Can we take a break? Go outside? Walk?"

"You want me to come?"

She nodded. "We need to talk. Privately."

"All right."

To tell the truth, whenever I lifted my nose from my work I got a little claustrophobic myself. My venture westward reminded me how good it is to stretch one's legs. "Hungry?" I asked. "Too serious to make a picnic?"

She looked startled, then charmed, by the idea. "Good. Let's do that."

So we went to the cook and baker and filled a bucket and went topside. Though she did not notice everyone smirking, I did.

There is but one door in the Hole. To the conference room, behind which Darling's personal quarters lie. Neither my quarters nor Ardath's had so much as a curtain closure. Folks figured we were off for the privacy of the wide open spaces.

Dream on. Up there there would be more spectators than down below. They just would not be human.

The sun was maybe three hours short of setting when we stepped outside, and it smacked us right in the eyes. Rough. But I expected it. Should have warned her.

We strolled up the creek, breathing slightly sagey air and saying nothing. The desert was silent. Not even Father Tree stirred. The breeze was insufficient to sigh in the coral. After a while I said, "Well?"

"I needed to get out. The walls were closing in. The null made it worse. I feel helpless down there. It preys on the mind."

"Oh."

We rounded a coral head and encountered a menhir. One of my old buddies, I guess, for he reported, "There are strangers on the Plain, Croaker."

"No lie?" Then: "Which strangers, rock?" But it had nothing more to say.

"They're always like that?"

"Or worse. Well. The null begins to fade. Feel better?"

"I felt better the moment I stepped outside. That's the gate to Hell. How can you people live like that?"

"It isn't much, but it's home."

We came to bare earth. She halted. "What's this?"

"Old Father Tree. You know what they think we're up to, down there?"

"I know. Let them think it. Call it protective coloration. *That* is your Father Tree?" She indicated Himself.

"That's him." I walked on. "How you doing today, old-timer?"

Must be fifty times I have asked that. I mean, the old guy is remarkable, but just a tree. Right? I did not expect a response. But Father Tree's leaves started tinkling the moment I spoke.

"Come back here, Croaker." The Lady's voice was commanding, hard, a little shaken. I turned and marched. "Back to your old self?" From the corner of my eye I caught a shadow in motion, off toward the Hole. I concentrated on a bit of coral and nearby brush. "Keep your voice down. We have an eavesdropper."

"That's no surprise." She spread the ragged blanket she had brought, sat down with her toes right at the edge of the barren. She removed the rag covering the bucket. I settled beside her, positioned so I could watch that shadow. "Do you know what that is?" she asked, nodding at the tree.

"Nobody does. It's just Old Father Tree. The desert clans call him a god. We've seen no evidence of that. One-Eye and Goblin were impressed with the fact that he stands almost exactly on the geographical center of the Plain, though."

"Yes. I suppose. . . . So much was lost in the fall. I should have suspected. . . . My husband was not the first of his kind, Croaker. Nor the White Rose the first of hers. It is a grand cycle, I believe."

"You've lost me."

"A very long time ago, even as I measure time, there was another war like that between the Dominator and the White Rose. The light overcame the shadow. But as always, the shadow left its taint on the victors. In order to end the struggle, they summoned a thing from another world, plane, dimension, what-have-you, the way Goblin might conjure a demon, only this thing was an adolescent god. Of sorts. In a sapling avatar. These events were legendary only in my youth, when much more of the past survived, so details are open to question. But it was a summoning of such scope, and such price, that thousands perished and countries were devastated. But they planted their captive god over the grave of their great enemy, where it would keep him enchained. This tree-god would live a million years."

"You mean? . . . Old Father is sitting on something like the Great Barrow?"

"I did not connect the legends and the Plain till I saw that tree. Yes. This earth constrains something as virulent as my husband. So much suddenly makes sense. It all fits. The beasts. The impossible talking rocks. Coral reefs a thousand miles from the sea. It all leaked through from that other world. The change storms are the tree's dreams."

She rattled on, not so much explaining as putting things together for herself. I gaped and remembered the change storm that caught me on the way west. Was I accursed, to be caught in a god's nightmare?

"This is crazy," I said, and at the same instant decrypted the shape I had been trying to pry from the shadows, bushes, and coral.

Silent. Squatting on his hams, motionless as a snake awaiting prey. Silent, who had been everywhere I went the last three days, like an extra shadow, seldom noticed because he *was* Silent. Well. So much for my confidence that my return with a companion had tickled no suspicions.

"This is a bad place to be, Croaker. Very bad. Tell that deaf peasant wench to move."

"If I did that, I would have to explain why and reveal who gave *me* the advice. I doubt she would be impressed."

"I suppose you're right. Well, it won't matter much longer. Let's eat."

She opened a packet and set out what looked like fried rabbit. But there are no rabbits on the Plain. "For all they got kicked around, their adventure toward Horse improved the larder." I dug in.

Silent remained motionless in the corner of my eye. You bastard, I thought. I hope you're drooling.

Three pieces of rabbit later I slowed enough to ask, "That about the old-timer is interesting, but does it have any relevance?"

Father Tree was raising a ruckus. I wondered why. "Are you afraid of him?"

She did not answer. I chucked bones down the creek bank, rose. "Back in a minute." I stomped over to Father Tree. "Old-Timer, you got any seeds? Any sprouts? A little something we could take to the Barrowland to plant on top of our own villain?"

Talking to that tree, all those times heading past, was a game. I was possessed of an almost religious awe of its age, but of no conscious belief in it as anything like either the nomads or the Lady claimed. Just a gnarly old tree with weird leaves and a bad temper.

Temper?

When I touched it, to lean against it while looking up among its bizarre leaves for nuts or seeds, it bit me. Well, not with teeth. But sparks flew. The tips of my fingers stung. When I took them out of my mouth they looked burned. "Damn," I muttered, and backed off a few steps. "Nothing personal, tree. Thought you might want to help out."

Vaguely, I was aware that a menhir now stood near Silent's lurking place. More appeared around the barren area.

Something hit me with the force of windwhale ballast dumped from a hundred feet up. I went down. Waves of power, of thought, beat upon me. I whimpered, tried to crawl toward the Lady. She extended a hand, but would not cross that boundary. . . .

Some of that power began to hint at comprehensibility. But it was like being inside fifty minds at once, with them scattered across the world. No. The Plain. And more than fifty minds. As it became more melded, more meshed . . . I was touching the menhir minds.

That all faded. The sledge of power ceased hammering the anvil that was me. I scrambled for the edge of the barren, though I knew that line demarked no true safety. I reached the blanket, caught my breath, finally turned to face the tree. Its leaves tinkled in exasperation.

"What happened?"

"Basically, he told me he's doing what he can, not for our sake but for that of his creatures. That I should go to Hell, leave him alone, quit aggravating him or find my ass in deep shit. Oh, my."

I had looked back to see how Silent had taken my encounter.

"I warned. . . ." She glanced back, too.

"I think we maybe got trouble. Maybe they recognized you."

Almost everyone from the Hole had appeared. They were lining up across the trail. The menhirs were more numerous. Walking trees were forming a circle with us at its center.

And we were unarmed, for Darling was there. We were inside the null again.

She had on her white linen. She stepped past Elmo and the Lieutenant and came toward me. Silent joined her. Behind her came One-Eye, Goblin, Tracker, and Toadkiller Dog. Those four still had the dust of the trail upon them.

They had been on the Plain for days. And I had been given no word. . . .

You talk about your trapdoor on your gallows dropping unexpectedly. For fifteen seconds I stood there with my mouth open. Then I asked, "What do we do?" in a soft squeak.

She startled me by taking my hand. "I bet and lost. I don't know. They're your people. Bluff. Oh!" Her eyes narrowed. Her stare fixed, became intense. Then a thin smile stretched her lips. "I see."

"What?"

"Some answers. The shadow of what my husband is about. You have been manipulated more than you know. He anticipated being found out with his weather. Once he had your Raven, he decided to bring your peasant girl to him. . . . Yes. I think. . . . Come."

My old comrades did not appear hostile, only puzzled.

The circle continued to close.

The Lady caught my hand again, led me to the base of Old Father Tree. She whispered, "Let there be peace between us while you observe, Ancient One. One comes whom you will remember of old." And to me: "There are many old shadows in the world. Some reach back to the dawn. Not big enough, they seldom draw attention like my husband or the Taken. Soulcatcher had minions who antedated the tree. They were interred with her. I told you I recognized the way those bodies were torn."

I stood there in the bloody light of the fading sun, baffled all to hell. She might as well have been speaking UchiTelle.

Darling, Silent, One-Eye, and Goblin came right to us. Elmo and the Lieutenant halted within a rock's throw. But Tracker and Toadkiller Dog sort of melted into the crowd.

"What is going on?" I signed at Darling, obviously frightened.

"That is what we want to find out. We have been getting disjointed, nonsensical reports from the menhirs since Goblin, One-Eye, and Tracker reached the Plain. On one hand, Goblin and One-Eye confirm everything you told me—till you parted ways."

I glanced at my two friends—and saw no friendship there. Their eyes were cold and glassy. Like somebody else had moved in behind them.

"Company," Elmo called, without shouting.

A pair of Taken, aboard boat-carpets, cruised some distance away. They came no closer. The Lady's hand twitched. She controlled herself otherwise. They remained far enough out not to be recognizable.

"More than one pair of hands is stirring this stew," I said. "Silent, get to the point. Right now you're scaring the crap out of me."

He signed, "The rumor is strong in the empire that you have sold out. That you have brought someone high-up here, to assassinate Darling. Maybe even one of the new Taken."

I could not help grinning. The planters of rumors had not dared tell the whole tale.

The grin convinced Silent. He knew me well. Which, I guess, was why *he* was watching me.

Darling, too, relaxed. But neither One-Eye nor Goblin softened.

"What's wrong with these guys, Silent? They look like zombies."

"They say you sold them out. That Tracker saw you. That if . . ."

"Bullshit! Where the hell is Tracker? Get that big stupid son-of-a-bitch out here and let him say that to my face!"

The light was weakening. The fat tomato of a sun had slipped behind the hills. Soon it would be dark. I felt a creepy tingle against my back. Was the damned tree going to act up?

Once I thought of him, I sensed an intense interest upon Old Father Tree's part. Also a sort of dreamy rage coalescing. . . .

Suddenly, menhirs flickered around all over the place, even across the creek where the brush was dense. A dog yelped. Silent signed something to Elmo. I did not catch it because his back was turned. Elmo trotted toward the turmoil.

The menhirs worked our way, forming a wall, herding something. . . . Well! Tracker and Toadkiller Dog. Tracker looked vacuously puzzled. The mutt kept trying to scoot between the menhirs. They would not let him. Our people had to stay light on their feet to keep from getting their toes squashed.

The menhirs pushed Toadkiller Dog and Tracker into the barren circle. The mongrel let out one long, despairing howl, tucked his tail between his legs, and slunk into Tracker's shadow. They stood about ten feet from Darling.

"Oh, Gods," the Lady murmured, and squeezed my hand so hard I almost yelled.

The kernel of a change storm exploded in Old Father Tree's tinkly hair.

It was huge; it was horrible; it was violent. It devoured us all, with such ferocity we could do nothing but endure it. Shapes shifted, ran, changed; yet those nearest Darling stayed exactly the same.

Tracker screamed. Toadkiller Dog unleashed a howl that spread terror like a cancer. And they changed the most, into the identical vile and violent monsters I saw while westward bound.

The Lady shouted something lost in the rage of the storm. But I caught its triumphal note. She *did* know those shapes.

I stared at her.

She had not changed.

That seemed impossible. This creature about whom I had been silly for fifteen years could not be the real woman.

Toadkiller Dog flung himself into the jaws of the storm, hideous fangs bared, trying to reach the Lady. He knew her, too. He meant to finish her while she was helpless inside the null. Tracker shambled after, just as puzzled as the Tracker that looked human had been.

One of Father Tree's great branches whipped down. It batted Toadkiller Dog the way a man might bat an attack bunny. Three times Toadkiller Dog gave it the valiant try. Three times he failed. The fourth time, what might have been the grandfather of all lightning bolts met him squarely and hurled him all the way to the creek, where he smouldered and twitched for a minute before rising and howling away into the enemy desert.

At the same time Tracker-beast went for Darling. He gathered her up and headed west. When Toadkiller Dog-beast went out of the game, Tracker got all the attention.

Old Father Tree may not be a god, but when he talks he has the voice. Coral reefs crumbled when he spoke. Everyone outside the barren grabbed their ears and screamed. For us who were closer it was less tormenting.

I do not know what he said. The language was none I knew, and it sounded like none I had ever heard. But it got through to Tracker. He put Darling down and came back, into the teeth of the storm, to stand before the god while that great voice hammered him and violent violet echoed round his misshapen bones. He bowed and did homage to the tree, and then he *did* change.

The storm died as swiftly as it had began. Everyone collapsed. Even the Lady. But unconsciousness did not come with collapse. By the wan light remaining I saw the circling Taken decide their hour had come. They fell back, gathered velocity, cut a ballistic chord through the null, each loosing four of those thirty-foot spears meant for shattering windwhales. And I sat on the hard ground drooling, hand in hand with their target.

Through sheer will, I guess, the Lady managed to murmur, "They can read the future as well as I." Which made no sense at the time. "I overlooked that."

Eight shafts arced down.

Father Tree responded.

Two carpets disintegrated beneath their riders.

The shafts exploded so high that none of their fiery charge reached the ground.

The Taken did, though. They plunged in neat arcs into a dense coral reef east of us. Then the sleepiness came. The last thing I recall wás that the glaze had left the three eyes of Goblin and One-Eye.

44

The Quickening

There were dreams. Endless, horrible dreams. Someday, if I live so long, if I survive what is yet to come, I may record them, for they were the story of a god that is a tree, and of the thing his roots bind. . . .

No. I think not. One life of struggle and horror is enough to report. And this one goes on.

The Lady stirred first. She reached over, pinched me. The pain wakened my nerves. She gasped, in a voice so soft I barely heard it, "Get up. Help me. We have to move your White Rose."

Made no sense.

"The null."

I was shivering. I thought it was reaction to whatever struck me down.

"The thing below is of this world. The tree is not."

Wasn't me shivering. It was the ground. Ever so gently and rapidly. And now I became aware of a sound. Something far away, deep down.

I began to get the idea.

Fear is one hell of a motivator. I got my feet under me. Above, the Tinkle of Old Father Tree beat maddeningly. There was panic in his wind-chimes song.

The Lady rose too. We staggered toward Darling, supporting one another. Each groggy step spiced more life into my sluggish blood. I looked into Darling's eyes. She was aware, yet paralyzed. Her face was frozen halfway between fear and disbelief. We hoisted her up, each slipping an arm around her. The Lady began counting steps. I remember no other labor so damnably great. I do not recall another time when I ran so much on will alone.

The shaking of the earth waxed rapidly into the shudder of passing horsemen, then to a landslide's uproar, then to an earthquake. The ground around Father Tree began to writhe and buckle. A gout of flame and dust blasted upward. The tree tinkled a shriek. Blue lightning rioted in his hair. We pressed even harder in our flight down and across the creek.

Something behind us began to scream.

Images in mind. That which was rising was in agony. Father Tree subjected it to the torments of Hell. But it came on, determined to be free.

I no longer looked back. My terror was too great. I did not want to see what an ancient Dominator looked like.

We made it. Gods. Somehow the Lady and I got Darling sufficiently far away for Father Tree to regain his full otherworldly power.

The shriek rose rapidly in pitch and fury; I fell down grasping my ears. And then it went away.

After a time the Lady said, "Croaker, go see if you can help the others. It's safe. The tree won."

That quickly? Out of that much fury?

Getting my feet under me seemed an all-night job.

A blue nimbus still shimmered among Father Tree's branches. You could feel his aggravation from two hundred yards. Its weight grew as I moved nearer.

The ground around the tree's feet hardly seemed disturbed, considering the violence of moments ago. It looked freshly plowed and harrowed, was all. Some of my friends were partially buried, but no one appeared injured. Everyone was moving at least a little. Faces looked wholly stunned. Except Tracker's. That ugly character had not resumed his fake human form.

He was up early, placidly helping the others, dusting their clothing with hearty, friendly slaps. You would not have known that a short time before he had been a deadly enemy. Weird.

Nobody needed any help. Except the walking trees and menhirs. The trees had been overturned. The menhirs. . . . Many of them were down, too. And unable to right themselves.

That gave me a chill.

I got me another shudder when I neared the old tree.

Reaching out of the ground, fumbling at the bark of a root, was a human hand and forearm, long, leathery, greenish, with nails grown to claws then broken and bleeding upon Father Tree. It did not belong to anyone from the Hole.

It twitched feebly, now.

Blue sparks continued to crackle above.

Something about that hand stirred the old beast within me. I wanted to run away shrieking. Or seize an axe and mutilate it. I took neither course, for I got the distinct feeling that Father Tree was watching me and glowering more than a little, and maybe blaming me personal-like for wakening the thing to which the hand belonged.

"I'm going," I said. "Know how you feel. Got my own old monster to keep down." And I backed away, bowing some each three or four steps.

"What the hell was that?"

I whirled. One-Eye was staring at me. He had a Croaker-is-up-to-another-of-his-crazies look.

"Just chatting with the tree." I looked around. People seemed to be finding their sea legs. Some of the less flustered were starting to right the walking trees. For the fallen menhirs, though, there seemed no hope. Those had gone to whatever reward a sentient stone may expect. Later they would be discovered righted, standing among the other dead menhirs near the creek ford.

I returned to Darling and the Lady. Darling was slow to come around, too groggy to communicate yet. The Lady asked, "Everyone all right?"

"Except the guy in the ground. And he came close to making himself well." I described the hand.

She nodded. "That's a mistake not likely to be made again soon."

Silent and several others had gathered around, so we could say little that would not sound suspect. I did murmur, "What now?" In the background I heard the Lieutenant and Elmo hollering about getting some torches out to shed a little light.

She shrugged.

"What about the Taken?"

"You want to go after them?"

"Hell, no! But we can't have them running around loose in our backyard, either. No telling. . . ."

"The menhirs will watch them. Won't they?"

"That depends on how pissed the old tree is. Maybe he's ready to let us go to hell in a bucket after this."

"You might find out."

"I'll go," Goblin squeaked. He wanted an excuse to put a lot of yards between him and the tree.

"Don't take all night," I said. "Why don't the rest of you help Elmo and the Lieutenant?"

That got rid of some folks, but not Silent.

There was no way I was going to get Silent out of sight of Darling. He had some reservations still.

I chaffed Darling's wrists and did other silly things when time was the only cure. After some minutes I mumbled, "Seventy-eight days."

And the Lady, "Before long it will be too late."

I lifted an eyebrow.

"He can't be beaten without her. It won't be long before the hardest ride won't get her there in time."

I do not know what Silent made of that exchange. I do know that the Lady looked up at him and smiled thinly, with that look she gets when she knows your thoughts. "We need the tree." And: "We didn't get to finish our picnic."

"Huh?"

She went away for a few minutes. When she returned she had the blanket, dirtier than ever, and the bucket. She snagged my hand and headed for the dark. "You watch for the traps," she told me.

What the hell was this game?

Bargain Struck

Later a broken boat of a moon arose. We did not go far before it did, for there was not enough starlight to risk much movement. Once the moon did rise, the Lady guided me in a slow circle toward where the Taken had come down. We halted in a clear area, sandy but not dangerous. She spread the blanket. We were outside the null. "Sit."

I sat. She sat. I asked, "What? . . ."

"Be quiet." She closed her eyes and went inside herself.

I wondered if Silent had torn himself away from Darling to stalk us. Wondered if my comrades were making crude jokes about us as they labored over the walking trees. Wondered what the hell kind of game had me caught in its toils.

You learned something out of it, anyway, Croaker.

After a while I realized she was back from wherever she had gone. "I *am* amazed," she whispered. "Who would have thought they had the guts?"

"Eh?"

"Our sky-borne friends. I expected Limper and Whisper, up to their old crimes. But I got Scorn and Blister. Though I might have suspected her, had I thought. Necromancy is her great talent."

Another round of her thinking aloud. I wondered if she did that often. I am sure she was unaccustomed to having witnesses around if she did. "What do you mean?"

She ignored me. "I wonder if they told the others?"

I harkened back, put a few things together. The Lady's divinations about three possible futures and no place in any of them. Maybe that meant there was no place in them for Taken, either. And maybe they figured they could take their futures into their own hands by ridding themselves of their mistress.

A light step startled me. But I did not get excited. I just figured Silent had chosen to follow. So I was very surprised when Darling sat down with us, unchaperoned.

How had I overlooked the return of the null? Distracted, of course.

The Lady said, as though Darling had not appeared, "They haven't yet gotten out of the coral. It's very slow going, and they're both injured. And though the coral can't kill them, it can cause a lot of pain. Right now they're lying up, waiting for first light."

"So?"

"So maybe they won't get out at all."

"Darling can read lips."

"She knows already."

Well, I have said a thousand times that the girl is not stupid.

I think Darling's knowledge was implicit in the position she took. She placed me squarely in the gap between them.

Oh yeah.

I found myself playing interpreter.

Trouble is, I cannot record what went back and forth. Because someone tampered with my memories later. I got only one chance to make notes, and those now make no sense.

Some sort of negotiation took place. I can still conjure a sense of profound astonishment at Darling's willingness to deal. Also an amazement at the Lady for the same reason.

They reached an accommodation. An uneasy one, to be sure, for the Lady henceforth stuck very close and kept me between her and anyone else while she was within the null. Great feeling, knowing you're a human shield. . . . And Darling kept near the Lady to prevent her calling on her power.

But she did turn her loose once.

That is getting ahead, slightly. First we all sneaked back, not letting anyone know there had been summit. The Lady and I returned after Darling, trying to look like we had had an energetic and thorough encounter. I could not help chuckling at some envious looks.

The Lady and I went outside the null again next morning, after Darling distracted Silent, One-Eye, and Goblin by sending them to dicker with the menhirs. Father Tree could not make up his mind. We went the other direction. And tracked Taken.

Actually, there was little tracking to do. They were not yet free of the coral. The Lady called upon that power she held over them and they ceased to be Taken.

Her patience was exhausted. Maybe she wanted them to serve as an object lesson. . . . In any event, buzzards—real buzzards—were circling before we returned to the Hole.

That easy, I thought. For her. And for me, when I tried to kill the Limper, with every damned thing going my way, impossible.

She and I went back to translating. So busy did we stay that I did not remain abreast of the news from outside. I was a little vacant, anyway, because she had expunged my memories of the meeting with Darling.

Anyhow, somehow, the White Rose got right with Father Tree. The shaky alliance survived.

One thing I did notice. The menhirs stopped ragging me about strangers on the Plain.

They meant Tracker and Toadkiller Dog all the time. And the Lady. Two of three were no longer strangers. No one knew what had become of Toadkiller Dog. Even the menhirs could not trace him.

I tried to get Tracker to explain the name. He could not remember. Not even Toadkiller Dog himself. Weird.

He was the tree's creature now.

46

Son of the Tree

I was nervous. I had trouble sleeping. Days were slipping away. Out west, the Great Tragic was gnawing its banks. A four-legged monster was running to its overlord with news that it had been found out. Darling and the Lady were doing nothing.

Raven remained trapped. Bomanz remained trapped in the long fires he had called down on his own head. The end of the world tramped ever closer. And nobody was doing anything.

I completed my translations. And was no wiser than before. It seemed. Though Silent, Goblin, and One-Eye kept fooling with charts of names, cross-indexing, seeking patterns. The Lady watched over their shoulders more than did I. I fiddled with these Annals. I bothered myself with how to phrase a request for the return of those I had lost at Queen's Bridge. I fussed. I grew ever more antsy. People became irritated with me. I began taking moonlight walks to work off my nervous energy.

One night the moon was full, a fat orange bladder just scaling the hills to the east. A grand sight, especially with patrolling mantas crossing its face. For some reason the desert had a lilac luminescence upon all its edges. The air was chill. There was a dust of powder swirling on the breeze, fallen that afternoon. A change storm flickered far away to the north. . . .

A menhir appeared beside me. I jumped three feet. “Strangers on the Plain, rock?” I asked.

“None stranger than you, Croaker.”

“I get a comedian. You want something?”

“No. The Father of Trees wants *you*.”

“Yeah? See you.” Heart pounding, I headed toward the Hole.

Another menhir blocked the path.

“Well. Since you put it that way.” Faking bravery, I headed upstream.

They would have herded me. Best accept the inevitable. Less humiliation.

The wind was bitter around the barren, but when I crossed the boundary it was like stepping into summer. No wind at all, though the old tree was tinkling. And heat like a furnace.

The moon had risen enough to flood the barren with light now argent. I approached the tree. My gaze fixed on that hand and forearm, still protruding, still gripping a root, still, it seemed, betraying the occasional feeble twitch. The root had grown, though, and seemed to be enveloping the hand, as a tree used for a line post will envelop a wire tacked to it. I stopped five feet from the tree.

“Come closer,” it said. In plain voice. In conversational tone and volume.

I said, “Yipe!” and looked for the exits.

About two skillion menhirs surrounded the barren. So much for running away.

“Stand still, ephemeral.”

My feet froze to the ground. Ephemeral, eh?

“You asked help. You demanded help. You whined and pleaded and begged for help. Stand still and accept it. Come closer.”

“Make up your mind.” I took two steps. Another would have me climbing him.

“I have considered. This thing you ephemera fear, in the ground so far from here, would be a peril to my creatures if it rose. I sense no significant strength in those who resist it. Therefore . . .”

I hated to interrupt, but I just had to scream. You see, something had me by the ankle. It was squeezing so hard I felt the bones grinding. Crushing. Sorry about that, old-timer.

The universe turned blue. I rolled in a hurricane of anger. Lightning roared in Father Tree's branches. Thunder rolled across the desert. I yelled some more.

Bolts of blue hammered around me, crisping me almost as much as my tormentor. But, at last, the hand turned me loose.

I tried to run away.

One step and down I went. I kept on, crawling, while Father Tree apologized and tried to call me back.

Like Hell. I would crawl through the menhirs if I had to. . . .

My mind filled with a waking dream, Father Tree delivering a message direct. Then the earth got quiet, except for the *wish* as menhirs vanished.

Big hoopla from the direction of the Hole. A whole gang charged out to find the cause of the uproar. Silent reached me first. "One-Eye," I said. "I need One-Eye." He is the only one beside me with medical training. And contrary though he is, I could count on him to take medical instructions.

One-Eye showed up in a moment, along with twenty others. The watch had reacted quickly. "Ankle," I told him. "Maybe crushed. Somebody get some light up here. And a damned shovel."

"A shovel? Are you off your gourd?" One-Eye demanded.

"Just get it. And do something for the pain."

Elmo materialized, still buckling buckles. "What happened, Croaker?"

"Old Tree wanted to talk. Had the rocks bring me over. Says he wants to help us. Only while I was listening, that hand got ahold of me. Like to ripped my foot off. The racket was the tree saying, 'Now stop that. That's not polite.' "

"Cut his tongue out after you fix his leg," Elmo told One-Eye. "What did it want, Croaker?"

"Your ears gone? To help with the Dominator. Said he thought it over. Decided it was in his own best interest to keep the Dominator down. Give me a hand up." One-Eye's efforts were paying dividends. He had sponged one of his wild jungle glops onto my ankle—it had swollen three times normal size already—and the pain was fading.

Elmo shook his head.

I said, "I'll break *your* damned leg if you don't get me up." So he and Silent hoisted me, but supported me.

"Bring them shovels," I said. A half dozen had appeared. They were entrenching tools, not real ditchdiggers. "You guys insist on helping, get me back over to the tree."

Elmo growled. For a moment I thought Silent might say something. I eyed him expectantly, smiling. I had been waiting twenty-some years.

No luck.

Whatever vow he had taken, whatever it was that had driven him to abstain from speech, it had put a steel lock on Silent's jaw. I have seen him so pissed he could chew nails, so excited he lost sphincter control, but nothing has shaken his resolution against talking.

Blue still sparkled in the tree's branches. Leaves tinkled. Moonlight and torchlight mixed into weird shadows the sparks sent dancing. . . . "Around him," I told my body slaves. I had not seen it myself, so it must be beyond that trunk.

Yep. There it was, out twenty feet from the base of the tree. A sapling. It stood about eight feet tall.

One-Eye, Silent, Goblin, those guys gobbled and gaped like startled apes. But not old Elmo. "Get a few buckets of water and soak the ground good," he said. "And find an old blanket we can wrap around the roots and the dirt that comes up with them."

He caught right on. Damned farmer. "Get me back downstairs," I said. "I want to see this ankle myself, in better light."

Going back, with Elmo and Silent carrying me, we encountered the Lady. She put on a suitably solicitous act, fussing all over me. I had to endure a lot of knowing grins.

Only Darling knew the truth even then. With maybe a little suspicion on Silent's part.

Shadows In Shadowland

There was no time inside the Barrowland, only shadow and fire, light without source, and endless fear and frustration. From where he stood, snared in the web of his own device, Raven could discern a score of Domination monsters. He could see men and beasts put down in the time of the White Rose to prevent those evils from escaping. He could see the silhouette of the sorcerer Bomanz limned against frozen dragon fire. The old wizard still struggled to take one more step toward the heart of the Great Barrow. Didn't he know that he had failed generations ago?

Raven wondered how long he had been caught. Had his messages gotten through? Would help come? Was he just marking time till the darkness exploded?

If there was a clock to count the time, it was the growing distress of those set to guard against the darkness. The river gnawed ever closer. There was nothing they could do. No way for them to summon the wrath of the world.

Raven thought he would have done things differently had he been in charge back when.

Vaguely, Raven recalled some things passing nearby, shades like himself. But he knew not how long ago, or even what they were. Things moved at times, and one could tell nothing certain. The world had a whole different look from this perspective.

Never had he been so helpless, so frightened. He did not like the feeling. Always he had been master of his destiny, dependent upon no one. . . .

There was, in that world, nothing to do but think. Too much, too often, his thoughts came back to what it meant to be Raven, to things Raven had done and not done and should have done differently. There was time to identify and at least confront all the fears and pains and weaknesses of the inside man, all of which had created the ice and iron and fearless mask he had presented to the world. All those things which had cost him everything he had valued and which had driven him into the fangs of death again and again, in self-punishment. . . .

Too late. Far too late.

When his thoughts cleared and coagulated and he reached this point, he sent shrieks of anger echoing through the spirit world. And those who surrounded him and hated him for what he might have triggered, laughed and reveled in his torment.

48

Flight West

Despite my exoneration by the tree, I never quite regained my former status with my comrades. Always there was a certain reserve, perhaps as much from envy of my apparent sudden female wealth as from trust slow to heal. I cannot deny the pain it caused me. I had been with those guys since I was a boy. They were my family.

I did take some ribbing about getting onto crutches in order to get out of work. But my work would have gone on had I had no legs at all.

Those damned papers. I had them committed to memory, set to music. And still I did not have the key we sought, nor what the Lady hoped to find. The cross-referencing was taking forever. The spelling of names, in pre-Domination and Domination times, had been free-form. TelleKurre is one of those languages where various letter combinations can represent identical sounds.

Pain in the damned fundament.

I do not know how much Darling told the others. I was not at the Big Meeting. Neither was the Lady. But word came out: The Company was moving out.

One day to get ready.

Topside, near nightfall, on my crutches, I watched the windwhales arrive. There were eighteen of them, all summoned by Father Tree. They came with their mantas and a whole panoply of Plain sentient forms. Three dropped to the ground. The Hole puked up its contents.

We began boarding. I got a ration because I had to be lifted, along with my papers, gear, and crutches. The whale was a small one. I would share it with just a few people. The Lady. Of course. We could not be separated now. And Goblin. And One-Eye. And Silent, after a bloody sign battle, for he did not want to be separated from Darling. And Tracker. And the child of the tree, for whom Tracker was guardian and I was *in loco parentis*. I think the wizards were supposed to keep an eye on the rest of us, though little they could have done had a situation presented itself.

Darling, the Lieutenant, Elmo, and the other old hands boarded a second windwhale. The third carried a handful of troops and a lot of gear.

We lifted off, joined the formation above.

A sunset from five thousand feet is unlike anything you will see from the ground. Unless you are atop a very lonely mountain. Magnificent.

With darkness came sleep. One-Eye spelled me under. I still had a good deal of swelling and pain.

Yes. We were outside the null. Our whale flew the far flank from Darling. Specifically for the Lady's benefit.

Even then she did not give herself away.

The winds were favorable and we had the blessing of Father Tree. Dawn found us passing over Horse. It was there the truth finally surfaced.

Taken came up, all in their fish-carpets, armed to the gills. Panic noises wakened me. I got Tracker to help me stand. After one glance at the fire of the rising sun, I spied the Taken drifting into guardian positions around our whale. Goblin and them expected an attack. They howled their hearts out. Somehow One-Eye found a way for it all to be Goblin's fault. They went at it.

But nothing happened. Almost to *my* surprise, too. The Taken merely maintained station. I glanced at the Lady. She startled me with a wink. Then: "We *all* have to cooperate, whatever our differences."

Goblin heard that. He ignored One-Eye's ranting for a moment, stared at the Taken. After a bit he looked at the Lady. Really looked.

I saw the light dawn. In a more than normally squeaky voice, and with a truly goofy look, he said, "I remember you." He remembered the one time he had had a sort of direct contact with her. Many years ago, when he tried to contact Soulcatcher, he had caught her in the Tower, in the Lady's presence. . . .

She smiled her most charming smile. The one that melts statues.

Goblin threw a hand in front of his eyes, turned away from her. He looked at me with the most awful expression. I could not help laughing. "You always accused me. . . ."

"You didn't have to go and *do* it, Croaker!" His voice climbed the scale till it became inaudible. He sat down abruptly.

No lightning bolt splattered him across the sky. After a time he looked up and said, "Elmo is going to crap!" He giggled.

Elmo was the most unremitting of them all when it came to reminding me of my romances about the Lady.

After the humor went out of it, after One-Eye had been through it, too, and Silent had had his worst fears confirmed, I began to wonder about my friends.

One and all, they were westward bound on Darling's say-so. They had not been informed, in so many words, that we were allied with our former enemies.

Fools. Or was Darling? What happened once the Dominator was down and we were ready to go after each other again? . . .

Whoa, Croaker. Darling learned to play cards from Raven. Raven was a cut-throat player.

It was the Forest of Cloud by nightfall. I wonder what they made of us in Lords. We passed right over. The streets filled with gawkers.

Roses passed in the night. Then the other old cities of our early years in the north. There was little talk. The Lady and I kept our heads together, growing more tense as our strange fleet neared its destination and we drew no nearer unearthing the nuggets we sought.

"How long?" I asked. I had lost track of time.

"Forty-two days," she said.

"We were in the desert that long?"

"Time flies when you're having fun."

I gave her a startled look. A joke? Even an old cliché? From her?

I hate it when they go human on you. Enemies are not supposed to do that. She had been crawling all over me with it for a couple months.

How can you hate?

The weather stayed halfway decent till we got to Forsberg. Then it became clabbered misery.

It was solid winter up there. Good, briskly refreshing winds loaded up with pellets of powder snow. A nice abrasive for a tender face like mine. A bombardment to clear out the lice on the backs of the whales, too. Everybody cussed and fussed and grumbled and huddled for warmth that dared not be provided by man's traditional ally, fire. Only Tracker seemed untouched. "Don't anything bother that thing?" I asked.

In the oddest voice I ever heard her use, the Lady replied, "Loneliness. If you want to kill Tracker the easy way, lock him up alone and go away."

I felt a chill that had nothing to do with the weather. Whom did I know who had been alone a long time? Who, maybe, just maybe, had begun to wonder if absolute power were worth the absolute price?

I knew beyond the glimmer of doubt that she had enjoyed every second of pretend on the Plain. Even the moments of danger. I knew that had I had the hair on my ass, there in the last days, I could have become more than a pretend boyfriend. There was a growing and quiet desperation to her in that time as going back to being the Lady approached.

Some of that I might have appropriated out of ego, for a very critical time faced her. She was under a lot of stress. She knew the enemy we faced. But not all was ego. I think she actually did like me as a person.

"I got a request," I said softly, in the middle of the huddle, banishing thoughts caused by a woman pressed against me.

"What?"

"The Annals. They're all that's left of the Black Company." Depression had set in fast. "There was an obligation undertaken ages ago, when the Free Companies of Khatovar were formed. If any of us get through this alive, someone should take them back."

I do not know if she understood. But: "They're yours," she said.

I wanted to explain, but could not. *Why* take them back? I am not sure where they are supposed to go. Four hundred years the Company drifted slowly north, waxing, waning, turning over its constituents. I have no idea if Khatovar still exists or if it is a city, country, a person, or a god. The Annals from the earliest years either did not survive or went home already. I have seen nothing but digests and excerpts from the earliest century. . . . No matter. Part of the Annalist's undertaking has always been to return the Annals to Khatovar should the Company disband.

The weather worsened. By Oar it seemed actively inimical, and may have been. That thing in the earth would know we were coming.

Just north of Oar all the Taken suddenly dropped away like rocks. "What the hell?"

"Toadkiller Dog," the Lady said. "We've caught up with him. He hasn't reached his master yet."

"Can they stop him?"

"Yes."

I crutched over to the side of the whale. I do not know what I expected to see. We were up in the snow clouds.

There were a few flashes below. Then the Taken came back. The Lady looked displeased. "What happened?" I asked.

"The monster got crafty. Ran into the null where it brushes the ground. The visibility is too poor to go after him."

"Will it make much difference?"

"No." But she did not sound entirely confident.

The weather worsened. But the whales remained undaunted. We reached the Barrowland. My group went to the Guards compound. Darling's put up at Blue Willy. The boundary of the null fell just outside the compound wall.

Colonel Sweet himself greeted us. Good old Sweet who I thought was dead for sure. He had a gimp leg now. I cannot say he was convivial. But then, it was a time when nobody was.

The orderly assigned us was our old friend Case.

49

The Invisible Maze

The first time Case appeared he rode the edge of panic. Me doing a kindly uncle act did not soothe him. The Lady doing her bit almost kicked him over the edge into hysteria. Having Tracker lurking around in natural form was no help either.

One-Eye, of all people, calmed him down. Got him onto the subject of Raven and how Raven was doing, and that did the job.

I had my own near case of hysteria. Hours after we put down, before I even got set up for it, the Lady brought Whisper and Limper to double-check our translations.

Whisper was supposed to see if any papers were missing. Limper was supposed to plumb his memory of olden times for connections we may have missed. He, it seems, was much into the social whirl of the early Domination.

Amazing. I could not imagine that hunk of hatred and human wreckage ever having been anything but nastiness personified.

I got Goblin to keep an eyeball on those two while I broke away to look in on Raven. Everyone else had given him a look-see already.

She was there, leaning against a wall, gnawing a fingernail, not looking anything like the great bitch who had tormented the world for lo! so many years. Like I said before, I hate it when they go human. And she was human and then some. Flat-assed scared.

"How is he?" I asked, and when I saw her mood: "What's the matter?"

"He's unchanged. They've taken good care of him. Nothing is the matter that a few miracles won't cure."

I dared raise a questioning eyebrow.

"All the exits are closed, Croaker. I'm headed down a tunnel. My choices grow ever more narrow, and each is worse than the other."

I settled on the chair Case used while watching over Raven, began playing doctor. Needlessly, but I liked to see for myself. Half-distracted, I said, "I expect it's lonely, being queen of the world."

Slight gasp. "You grow too bold."

Didn't I? "I'm sorry. Thinking out loud. An unhealthy habit known to be the cause of bruises and major hemorrhaging. He does look sound. You think Limper or Whisper will help?"

"No. But every angle has to be tried."

"What about Bomanz?"

"Bomanz?"

I looked at her. She seemed honestly puzzled. "The wizard who sprung you."

"Oh. What about him? What could a dead man contribute? I disposed of my necromancer. . . . You know something I don't?"

Not bloody likely. She had me under the Eye. Nevertheless. . . .

I debated for half a minute, not wanting to give up what might be a whisker of advantage. Then: "I had it from Goblin and One-Eye that he's perfectly healthy. That he's caught in the Barrowland. Like Raven, only body and all."

"How could that be?"

Was it possible she had overlooked this while interrogating me? I guess if you do not ask the right questions, you will not get the right answers.

I reflected on all we had done together. I had sketched Raven's reports for her, but she had not read those letters. In fact . . . The originals, from which Raven drew his story, were in my quarters. Goblin and One-Eye lugged them all the way to the Plain only to see them hauled right back. Nobody had plumbed them because they repeated a story already told. . . .

"Sit," I said, rising. "Back in two shakes."

Goblin fish-eyed me when I breezed in. "Be a few minutes more. Something came up." I scrounged up the case in which Raven's documents had traveled. Only the original Bomanz manuscript resided there now. I fluttered back out, ignored by the Taken.

Nice feeling, I'll tell you, being beneath their notice. Too bad it was just because they were fighting for their existence. Like the rest of us.

"Here. This is the original manuscript. I went over it once, lightly, to check Raven's translation. It looked good to me, though he did dramatize and invent dialog. But the facts and characterizations are pure Bomanz."

She read with incredible swiftness. "Get Raven's version."

Out and back, under Goblin's scowl and growl at my departing back: "How long is a few minutes these days, Croaker?"

She went through those swiftly, too. And looked thoughtful when she finished.

"Well?" I asked.

"There may be something here. Actually, something that's not here. Two questions. Who wrote this in the first place? And where is the stone in Oar that the son mentioned?"

"I assume Bomanz did most of the original and his wife finished it."

"Wouldn't he have used first person?"

"Not necessarily. It's possible the literary conventions of the time forbade it. Raven often chided me for interjecting too much of myself into the Annals. He came of a different tradition."

"We'll accept that as a hypothesis. Next question. What became of the wife?"

"She came of a family from Oar. I would expect her to go back."

"When she was known as the wife of the man responsible for loosing me?"

"Was she? Bomanz was an assumed name."

She brushed my objection aside. "Whisper acquired those documents in Lords. As a lot. Nothing connects Bomanz with them except his story. My feeling is that they were accumulated at a later date. But his papers. What were they doing between the time they left here and the time Whisper found them? Have some ancillary items been lost? It's time we consulted Whisper."

We, however, included me out.

Whatever, a fire was ignited. Before long, Taken were roaring off to faraway places. Within two days Benefice delivered the stone mentioned by Bomanz's son. It proved useless. Some Guards appropriated it and used it for a doorstep to their barracks.

I caught occasional hints of a search progressing from Oar south along the route Jasmine had taken after fleeing from the Barrowland, widowed and shamed. Hard to find tracks that old, but the Taken have remarkable skills.

Another search progressed from Lords.

I had the dubious pleasure of hanging around with the Limper while he pointed out all the mistakes we made transliterating UchiTelle and TelleKurre names. Seems not only were spellings not uniform in those days, but neither were alphabets. And some of the folks mentioned were not of UchiTelle or TelleKurre stock, but outsiders who had adapted their names to local usage. Limper busied himself doing things backwards.

One afternoon Silent gave me the high sign. He had been spying over the Limper's shoulder, off and on, with more devotion than I.

He had found a pattern.

50

Gnomen?

Darling has a self-discipline that amazes me. All that time she was over there at Blue Willy and not once did she surrender to her desire to see Raven. You could see the ache in her whenever his name came up, but she held off for a month.

But she came, as inevitably we knew she must, with the Lady's permission. I tried to ignore her visit entirely. And I made Silent, Goblin, and One-Eye stay away too, though with Silent it was a tight thing. Eventually he did agree; it was a private thing, for her alone, and his interests would not be served by sticking his nose in.

If I would not go to her, she would come to me. For a while, while everyone else was busy elsewhere. For a hug, to remind her there were those of us who cared. To have some moral support there while she worked out something in her mind.

She signed, "I cannot deny it now, can I?" And a few minutes later: "I still have the soft place for him. But he will have to earn his way back in." Which was her equivalent of our thinking aloud.

I felt more for Silent at that moment than for Raven. Raven I'd always respected for his toughness and fearlessness, but I'd never really grown to like him. Silent I did like, and did wish well.

I signed, "Do not be brokenhearted if you find he is too old to change."

Wan smile. "My heart was broken a long time ago. No. I have no expectations. This is not a fairy-tale world."

That was all she had to say. I did not take it to heart till it began to illuminate later events.

She came and she went, in sorrow for the death of dreams, and she came no more.

In moments when his needs called him away, we copied everything the Limper left behind and compared it with our own charts. "Oh, hey," I breathed once. "Oh, hey."

Here was a lord from a far western kingdom. A Baron Senjak who had four daughters said to vie with one another in their loveliness. One wore the name Ardath.

"She lied," Goblin whispered.

"Maybe," I admitted. "More likely, she didn't know. In fact, she couldn't have known. Nor could anyone else have, really. I still don't see how Soulcatcher could have been convinced that the Dominator's true name was in here."

"Wishful thinking, maybe," One-Eye guessed.

"No," I said. "You could tell she *knew* what she had. She just didn't know how to dig it out."

"Just like us."

"Ardath is dead," I said. "That leaves three possibilities. But if push comes to shove, we only get one shot."

"Catalog what else we know."

"Soulcatcher was one sister. Name not yet known. Ardath may have been the Lady's twin. I think she was older than Catcher, though they were children together and not separated by many years. Of the fourth sister we know nothing."

Silent signed, "You have four names, given and family. Consult the genealogies. Find who married whom."

I groaned. The genealogies were over at Blue Willy. Darling had had them loaded onto the cargo whale with everything else.

Time was short. The work daunted me. You do not go into those genealogies with a woman's name and find anything easily. You have to look for a man who married the woman you are seeking and hope the recorder thought enough of her to mention her name.

"How are we going to manage all this?" I wondered. "With me the only one who can decipher these chicken tracks?" Then a brilliant idea. If I say so myself. "Tracker. We'll put Tracker on it. He don't have nothing to do but watch that sapling. He can do that over at Blue Willy and read old books at the same time."

Easier said than done. Tracker was far from his new master. Getting the message into his pea brain was a major undertaking. But once that had been accomplished there was no stopping him.

One night, as I snuggled down under the covers, *she* appeared in my quarters. "Up, Croaker."

"Huh?"

"We're going flying."

"Uh? No disrespect, but it's the middle of the night. I had a hard day."

"Up."

So you don't argue when the Lady commands.

51

The Sign

A freezing rain was falling. Everything was glazed with crystal ice. "Looks like a warm snap," I said.

She was without a sense of humor that night. It took an effort to overlook my remark. She led me to a carpet. It had a crystal dome covering the forward seats. That was a feature recently added to Limper's craft.

The Lady used some small magic to melt the ice off. "Make sure it's sealed tightly," she told me.

"Looks good to me."

We lifted off.

Suddenly I was on my back. The nose of the fish pointed at unseen stars. We climbed at a dreadful rate. I expected momentarily to be so high I could not breathe.

We got that high. And higher. We broke through the clouds. And I understood the significance of the dome.

It kept in breathable air. Meaning the windwhales could no longer climb higher than the Taken. Always chipping away, the Lady and her gang.

But what the hell was *this* all about?

"There." A sigh of disappointment. A confirmation that a shadow darkened hope. She pointed.

I saw it. I knew it, for I had seen it before, in the days of the long retreat that ended in the battle before the Tower. The Great Comet. Small, but no denying its unique silver scimitar shape. "It can't be. It isn't due for twenty years. Celestial bodies don't change their cycles."

"They don't. That's axiomatic. So maybe the axiom makers are wrong."

She tilted the carpet down. "Note it in your writings, but don't mention it otherwise. Our peoples are troubled enough."

"Right." That comet has a hold on men's minds.

Back down into the yuck of a Barrowland night. We came in over the Great

Barrow itself, only forty feet up. The damned river was close. The ghosts were dancing in the rain.

I sloshed into the barracks in a numb state, checked the calendar.

Twelve days to go.

The old bastard was probably out there laughing it up with his favorite hound, Toadkiller Dog.

52

No Surprise

Something that lies down in that mind below the mind would not let me be. I tossed and turned, wakened, fell asleep, and finally, in the wee hours, it surfaced. I got up and shuffled through papers.

I found that piece that made the Lady gasp once, ploughed through that interminable guest list till I found a Lord Senjak and his daughters Ardath, Credence, and Sylith. The youngest, one Dorotea, the scribbler noted, could not attend.

"Ha!" I crowed. "The search narrows."

There was no more information, but that was a triumph. Assuming the Lady was indeed a twin and Dorotea was the youngest and Ardath dead, the odds were now fifty-fifty. A woman named Sylith or a woman named Credence. Credence? That is how it translated.

I was so excited I got no more sleep. Even that damned off-schedule comet fled my thoughts.

But excitement perished between the grinding stones of time. Nothing came from those Taken tracing Bomanz's wife and papers. I suggested the Lady go to the source himself. She was not prepared for the risk. Not yet.

Our old and stupid friend Tracker produced another gem four days after I eliminated sister Dorotea. The big goof had been reading genealogies day and night.

Silent came back from Blue Willy wearing such a look I knew something good had happened. He dragged me outside, toward town, into the null. He gave me a slip of damp paper. In Tracker's simple style, it said:

Three sisters were married. Ardath married twice, first a Baron Kaden of Dartstone, who died in battle. Six years later she married Erin NoFather, an unlanded priest of the god Vancer, from a town called Slinger, in the kingdom of Vye. Credence married Barthelme of Jaunt, a renowned sorcerer. It is in my memory that Barthelme of Jaunt became one of the Taken, but my memory is not trustworthy.

No lie.

Dorotea married Raft, Prince-in-Waiting, of Start. Sylith never married.

Tracker then proved that, slow though he might be, an occasional idea did perk through his murk of a mind.

The death rolls reveal that Ardath and her husband, Erin NoFather, an unlanded priest of the god Vancer, from a town called Slinger, in the kingdom of Vye, were slain by bandits while traveling between Lathe and Ova. My untrustworthy memory recalls that this took place just months before the Dominator proclaimed himself.

Sylith drowned in a flood of the River Dream some years earlier, swept away before countless witnesses. But no body was found.

We had an eyewitness. It never occurred to me to think of Tracker that way, though the knowledge had been there for the recognition. Maybe we could figure some way to get at his memories.

Credence perished in the fighting when the Dominator and Lady took Jaunt in the early days of their conquests. There is no record of Dorotea's death.

"Damn," I said. "Old Tracker is worth something after all."

Silent signed, "It sounds confused, but reason should provide something."

More than something. Without drawing charts, connecting all those women, I felt confident enough to say, "We knew Dorotea as Soulcatcher. We know Ardath wasn't the Lady. Odds are, the sister who engineered the ambush that killed her. . . ." There was something missing still. If I just knew which were twins. . . .

In response to my question, Silent signed, "Tracker is looking for birth records." But he was unlikely to score again. Lord Senjak was not TelleKurre.

"One of the purported dead didn't die. I'd put my money on Sylith. Assuming Credence was killed because she recognized a sister who was supposed to be dead when the Dominator and Lady took Jaunt."

"Bomanz mentions a legend about the Lady killing her twin. Is that this ambush? Or something more public?"

"Who knows?" I said. It really did get confusing. For a moment I wondered if it mattered.

* * *

The Lady called an assembly. Our original estimate of time available now appeared overly optimistic. She told us, "We appear to have been misled. There is nothing in Catcher's documents to betray my husband's name. How she reached that assumption is beyond us now. If documents are missing, we cannot be sure. Unless news comes from Lords or Oar soon, we can forget that avenue. It's time to consider alternatives."

I scribbled a note, asked Whisper to pass it to the Lady. The Lady read it, then looked at me with narrowed, thoughtful eyes. "Erin NoFather," she read aloud. "An unlanded priest of the god Vancer, from Slinger, in the kingdom of Vye. This, from our amateur historian. What you found is less interesting than the fact that you found it, Croaker. That news is five hundred years old. It was worthless then. Whoever Erin NoFather was before he left Vye, he did an absolute job of eliminating traces. By the time he became interesting enough to have his antecedents investigated, he had obliterated not only Slinger but every person to have lived in that village during his lifetime. In later years he went even farther, wasting all Vye. Which is why the notion that those papers might contain his true name constituted such a surprise."

I felt about half-size, and stupid. I should have known they would have tried to unmask the Dominator before. I had surrendered some small advantage for nothing. So much for the spirit of cooperation.

One of the new Taken—I cannot keep them straight, for they all dress the same—arrived soon afterward. He or she gave the Lady a small carved chest. The Lady smiled when she opened it. "There were no papers that survived. But there were these." She dumped some odd bracelets. "Tomorrow we go after Bomanz."

Everyone else knew. I had to ask. "What are they?"

"The amulets made for the Eternal Guard in the time of the White Rose. So they could enter the Barrowland without hazard."

The resulting excitement surpassed my understanding.

"The wife must have carried them away. Though how she laid hands on them is a mystery. Break this up now. I need time to think." She shooed us like a farm wife shooes chickens.

I returned to my room. The Limper floated in behind me. He said nary a word, but ducked into the documents again. Puzzled, I looked over his shoulder. He had lists of all the names we had unearthed, written in the alphabets of the languages whence they sprang. He seemed to be playing with both substitution codes and numerology. Baffled, I went to my bed, turned my back on him, faked sleep.

As long as he was there, I knew, sleep would evade me.

53

The Recovery

It resumed snowing that night. Real snow, half a foot an hour and no letup. The racket raised by the Guards as they strove to clear it from doorways and the carpets wakened me.

I had slept despite the Limper.

An instant of terror. I sat bolt upright. He remained at his task.

The barracks was overly warm, holding the heat because it was all but buried.

There was a bustle despite the weather. Taken had arrived while I slept. Guards not only dug but hurried about other tasks.

One-Eye joined me for a rude breakfast. I said, "So she's going ahead. Despite the weather."

"It won't get any better, Croaker. That guy out there knows what's going on." He looked grim.

"What's the matter?"

"I can count, Croaker. What do you expect from a guy with a week to live?"

My stomach tightened. Yes. I had been able to avoid thoughts of the sort so far, but. . . . "We've been in tight places before. Stair of Tear. Juniper. Beryl. We made it."

"I keep telling myself."

"How's Darling?"

"Worried. What do you think? She's a bug between hammer and anvil."

"The Lady has forgotten her."

He snorted. "Don't let your special dispensation erode your common sense, Croaker."

"Sound advice," I admitted. "But unnecessary. A hawk couldn't watch her more closely."

"You going out?"

"I wouldn't miss it. Know where I can get some snowshoes?"

He grinned. For an instant the devil of years past peeped forth. "Some guys

I know—mentioning no names, you know how it is—swiped a half dozen pairs from the Guard Armory last night. Duty man fell asleep on post."

I grinned and winked. So. I was not seeing enough of them to keep up, but they were not just sitting around and waiting.

"Couple pairs went off to Darling, just in case. Got four pair left. And just a smidgen of a plan."

"Yeah?"

"Yeah. You'll see. Brilliant, if I do say so myself."

"Where are the shoes? When are you going?"

"Meet us in the smokehouse after the Taken get off the ground."

Several guards came in to eat, looking exhausted, grumbling. One-Eye departed, leaving me in deep thought. What were they plotting?

The most carefully laid plans. . . . Like that.

The Lady marched into the mess hall. "Get your gloves and coats, Croaker. It's time."

I gaped.

"Are you coming?"

"But. . . ." I flailed around for an excuse. "If we go, somebody will have to do without a carpet."

She gave me an odd look. "Limper is staying here. Come. Get your clothing."

I did so, in a daze, passing Goblin as we went outside. I gave him a baffled little headshake.

A moment before we lifted off the Lady reached back, offering me something. "What's this?"

"Better wear it. Unless you want to go in without an amulet."

"Oh."

It did not look like much. Some cheap jaspar and jade on brittle leather. Yet when I secured the buckle around my wrist, I felt the power in it.

We passed over the rooftops very low. They were the only visual guides available. Out on the cleared land there was nothing. But being the Lady, she had other resources.

We took a turn around the bounds of the Barrowland. On the river side we descended till the water lay but a yard beneath us. "Lot of ice," I said.

She did not reply. She was studying the shoreline, now within the Barrowland itself. A sodden section of bank collapsed, revealing a dozen skeletons. I grimaced. In moments they were covered with snow or swept away.

"Just about on schedule, I'd guess," I said.

"Uhm." She moved on around the perimeter. A couple times I glimpsed other carpets circling. Something below caught my eye. "Down there!"

"What?"

"Thought I saw tracks."

"Maybe. Toadkiller Dog is nearby."

Oh, my.

"Time," she said, and turned toward the Great Barrow.

We put down at the mound's base. She piled out. I joined her. Other carpets descended. Soon there were four Taken, the Lady, and one scared old physician standing just yards from the despair of the world.

One of the Taken brought shovels. Snow began to fly. We took turns, nobody exempt. It was a bitch of a job, and became more so when we reached the buried scrub growth. It got worse when we reached frozen earth. We had to go slow. The Lady said Bomanz was barely covered.

It went on, it seemed, forever. Dig and dig and dig. We uncovered a withered humanoid thing the Lady assured us was Bomanz.

My shovel clicked against something my last turn. I bent to examine it, thinking it a rock. I brushed frosty earth away. . . .

And dived out of that hole, whirled, pointed. The Lady went down. Laughter drifted upward. "Croaker found the dragon. His jaw, anyway."

I kept on retreating, toward our carpet. . . .

Something huge vaulted it, trailing a basso snarl. I flung myself to one side, into snow that swallowed me. There were cries, growls. . . . When I emerged it was over. I glimpsed Toadkiller Dog clearing the carpet in retreat, more than a little scarred.

The Lady and Taken had been ready for him.

"Why didn't somebody warn me?" I whined.

"He could have read you. I'm just sorry we didn't cripple him."

Two Taken, probably of the male vice, lifted Bomanz. He was stiff as a statue, yet there was that about him which even I could sense. A spark, or something. No one could have mistaken him for dead.

Into a carpet he went.

The anger in the mound had been a trickle, barely sensed, like the buzzing of a fly across a room. It smacked us now, one hard hammer stroke reeking madness. Not an iota of fear informed it. That thing had an absolute confidence in its ultimate victory. We were but delays and irritants.

The carpet carrying Bomanz departed. Then another. I settled into my place and willed the Lady to hurry me away.

A spate of snarling and yelling broke out toward town. Brilliant light slashed through the snowfall. "I knew it," I growled, one fear realized. Toadkiller Dog had found One-Eye and Goblin.

Another carpet lifted. The Lady boarded ours, closed the dome. "Fools," she said. "What were they doing?"

I said nothing.

She did not see. Her attention was on the carpet, which was not behaving as it should. Something seemed to pull it toward the Great Barrow. But I saw. Tracker's ugly face passed at eye level. He carried the son of the tree.

Then Toadkiller Dog reappeared, stalking Tracker. Half the monster's face was gone. He ran on three legs. But he was plenty enough to take Tracker apart.

The Lady saw Toadkiller Dog. She spun the carpet. Systematically she loosed its eight thirty-foot shafts. She did not miss. And yet. . . .

Dragging the missiles, engulfed in flame, Toadkiller Dog crawled into the Great Tragic River. He went under and did not come up.

"That'll keep *him* out of the way for a while."

Not ten yards away, oblivious, Tracker was clearing the peak of the Great Barrow so he could plant his sapling. "Idiots," the Lady murmured. "I'm surrounded by idiots. Even the Tree is a dolt."

She would not explain. Neither did she interfere.

I sought traces of One-Eye and Goblin as we flew homeward. I saw nothing. They were not in the compound. Of course. There had not yet been time for them to snowshoe back. But when they had not appeared an hour later, I began having trouble concentrating on the reanimation of Bomanz.

That started with repeated hot baths, both to warm his flesh and to cleanse him. I did not get to see the preliminaries. The Lady kept me with her. She did not look in till the Taken were ready for the final quickening. And that was unimpressive. The Lady made a few gestures around Bomanz—who looked pretty moth-eaten—and said a few words in a language I did not understand.

Why do sorcerers always use languages nobody understands? Even Goblin and One-Eye do it. Each has confided that he cannot follow the tongue the other uses. Maybe they make it up?

Her words worked. That old wreck came to life grittily determined to push forward against a savage wind. He marched three steps before registering his altered circumstances.

He froze. He turned slowly, face collapsing into despair. His gaze locked on the Lady. Maybe two minutes passed. Then he looked the rest of us over and considered his surroundings.

"You explain, Croaker."

"Does he speak. . . ."

"Forsberger hasn't changed."

I faced Bomanz, a legend come to life. "I am Croaker. A military physician by profession. You are Bomanz. . . ."

"His name is Seth Chalk, Croaker. Let us establish that immediately."

"You are Bomanz, whose true name may be Seth Chalk, a sorcerer of Oar. Nearly a century has passed since you attempted to contact the Lady."

"Give him the whole story." The Lady used a Jewel Cities dialect likely to be outside Bomanz's capacity.

I talked till I was hoarse. The rise of the Lady's empire. The threat defeated at the battle at Charm. The threat defeated at Juniper. The present threat. He said not a word in all that time. Not once did I see in him the fat, almost obsequious shopkeeper of the story.

His first words were: "So. I did not entirely fail." He faced the Lady. "And you remain tainted by the light, Not-Ardath." He faced me again. "You will take me to the White Rose. As soon as I have eaten."

Nary a protest from the Lady.

He *ate* like a fat little shopkeeper.

The Lady herself helped me back into my wet winter coat. "Don't dawdle," she cautioned.

Hardly had we departed when Bomanz seemed to diminish. He said, "I'm too old. Don't let that back there fool you. An act. Going to play with the big boys, you have to act. What'll I do? A hundred years. Less than a week to redeem myself. How will I get a handle on things that quickly? The only principal I know is the Lady."

"Why did you think she was Ardath? Why not one of the other sisters?"

"There was more than one?"

"Four." I named them. "From your papers I've established that Soulcatcher was the one named Dorotea. . . ."

"*My* papers?"

"So called. Because the story of you wakening the Lady was prominent among them. It's always been assumed, till a few days ago, that you assembled them and your wife carried them away when she thought you had died."

"Bears investigation. I collected nothing. I risked nothing but a map of the Barrowland."

"I know the map well."

"I must see those papers. But first, your White Rose. Meanwhile, tell me about the Lady."

I had trouble staying with him. He zigged and zagged, spraying ideas. "What about her?"

"There is a detectable tension between you. Of enemies who are friends, perhaps. Lovers who are enemies? Opponents who know one another well and respect one another. If you respect her, it's with reason. It's impossible to respect total evil. It cannot respect itself."

Wow. He was right. I did respect her. So I talked a bit. And my theme was, when I noticed it, that she did remain tainted by the light. "She tried hard to be a villain. But when faced by real darkness—the thing under the mound—her weakness started to show."

"It is only slightly less difficult for us to extinguish the light within us than it is for us to conquer the darkness. A Dominator occurs once in a hundred generations. The others, like the Taken, are but imitations."

"Can you stand against the Lady?"

"Hardly. I suspect my fate is to become one of the Taken when she finds time." He'd landed on his feet, this old boy. He halted. "Lords! She's strong!"

"Who?"

"Your Darling. An incredible absorption. I feel helpless as a child."

We stamped into Blue Willy, entering through a second-floor window. The snow was banked that high.

One-Eye, Goblin, and Silent were down in the common room with Darling. The first two looked a bit shopworn. "So," I said. "You guys made it. I thought Toadkiller Dog had you for lunch."

"No problem at all," One-Eye said. "We. . . ."

"What do you mean, we?" Goblin demanded. "You were worthless as tits on a boar hog. Silent . . ."

"Shut up. This is Bomanz. He wants to meet Darling."

"*The* Bomanz?" Goblin squeaked.

"The very one."

Their meeting was about a three-question interview. Darling took charge immediately. When he realized Darling was leading him, Bomanz broke it off. He told me, "Next step. I read my alleged autobiography."

"It's not yours?"

"Unlikely. Unless my memory serves me worse than I suppose."

We returned to the compound in silence. He seemed reflective. Darling has that impact on those who meet her for the first time. She is just Darling to those of us who have known her all along.

Bomanz worked his way through the original manuscript, occasionally asking about specific passages. He was unfamiliar with the UchiTelle dialect.

"You had nothing to do with that, then?"

"No. But my wife was the primary source. Question. Was the girl Snoopy traced?"

"No."

"She is the one to follow up. She is the only survivor of significance."

"I'll tell the Lady. But there isn't time for it. In a few days Hell is going to break loose out there." I wondered if Tracker had gotten the sapling planted. Much good it would do when the Great Tragic reached the mound. Brave move but dumb, Tracker.

The effects of his effort were apparent soon, though. When I got around to relaying Bomanz's suggestion about Snoopy, the Lady asked, "Have you noted the weather?"

"No."

"It's getting better. The sapling stilled my husband's ability to shape it. Too late, of course. It will be months before the river falls."

She was depressed. She merely nodded when I told her what Bomanz had to say.

"Is it that bad? Are we defeated before we enter the lists?"

"No. But the price of victory escalates. I do not want to pay that price. I don't know if I can."

I stood there perplexed, awaiting an expansion upon the subject. None was forthcoming.

After a time she said, "Sit, Croaker." I sat in the chair she indicated, next to a roaring fire diligently tended by the soldier Case. After a time she sent Case away. But still nothing was forthcoming.

"Time tightens the noose," she murmured at one point, and at another, "I'm afraid to unravel the knot."

54

An Evening At Home

Days passed. No one of any especial allegiance gained any apparent ground. The Lady canceled all investigations. She and the Taken conferred often. I was excluded. So was Bomanz. The Limper participated only when ordered out of my quarters.

I gave up trying to sleep there. I moved in with Goblin and One-Eye. Which shows how much the Taken distressed me. Sharing a room with those two is like living amidst an ongoing riot.

Raven, as ever, changed not the least and remained mostly forgotten by all but his loyal Case. Silent did look in occasionally, on Darling's behalf, but without enthusiasm.

Only then did I realize that Silent felt more toward Darling than loyalty and protectiveness, and he was without means of expressing those feelings. Silence was enforced upon him by more than a vow.

I could not learn which sisters were twins. As I anticipated, Tracker found nothing in the genealogies. A miracle he found what he did, the way sorcerers cover their backtrails.

Goblin and One-Eye tried hypnotizing him, hoping to plumb his ancient memories. It was like stalking ghosts in a heavy fog.

The Taken moved to stall the Great Tragic. Ice collected along the western bank, turning the force of the current. But they overtinkered and a gorge developed. It threatened to raise the river level. A two-day effort won us maybe ten hours.

Occasionally large tracks appeared around the Barrowland, soon vanished beneath drifting snow. Though the skies cleared, the air grew colder. The snow neither melted nor crusted. The Taken engineered that. A wind from the east stirred the snow continuously.

Case stopped by to tell me, "The Lady wants you, sir. Right away."

I broke off playing three-handed Tonk with Goblin and One-Eye. So far had things slowed—except the flow of time. There was nothing more we could do.

"Sir," said Case as we stepped out of hearing of the others, "be careful."

"Uhm?"

"She's in a dark mood."

"Thanks." I dallied. My own mood was dark enough. It did not need to feed on hers.

Her quarters had been refurnished. Carpets had been brought in. Hangings covered the walls. A settee of sorts stood before the fireplace, where a fire burned with a comforting crackle. The atmosphere seemed calculated. Home as we dream it to be rather than as it is.

She was seated on the couch. "Come sit with me," she said, without glancing back to see who had come in. I started to take one of the chairs. "No. Here, by me." So I settled on the couch.

"What is it?"

Her eyes were fixed on something far away. Her face said she was in pain. "I have decided."

"Yes?" I waited nervously, not sure what she meant, less sure I belonged there.

"The choices have narrowed down. I can surrender and become another of the Taken."

That was a less dire penalty than I had expected. "Or?"

"Or I can fight. A battle that can't be won. Or won only in its losing."

"If you can't win, why fight?" I would not have asked that of one of the Company. With my own I would have known the answer.

Hers was not ours. "Because the outcome can be shaped. I can't win. But I can decide who does."

"Or at least make sure it isn't him?"

A slow nod.

Her bleak mood began to make sense. I have seen it on the battlefield, with men about to undertake a task likely to be fatal but which must be hazarded so others will not perish.

To cover my reaction, I slipped off the couch and added three small logs to the fire. But for our moods it would have been nice there in the crispy heat, watching the dancing flames.

We did that for a while. I sensed that I was not expected to talk.

"It begins at sunup," she said at last.

"What?"

"The final conflict. Laugh at me, Croaker. I'm going to try to kill a shadow. With no hope of surviving myself."

Laugh? Never. Admire. Respect. My enemy still, in the end unable to extinguish that last spark of light and so die in yet another way.

All this while she sat there primly, hands folded in her lap. She stared into the fire as if certain that eventually it would reveal the answer to some mystery. She began to shiver.

This woman for whom death held such devouring terror had chosen death over surrender.

What did that do for my confidence? Nothing good. Nothing good at all. I might have felt better had I seen the picture she did. But she did not talk about it.

In a very, very soft, tentative voice, she asked, "Croaker? Will you hold me?"

What? I didn't say it, but I sure as hell thought it.

I didn't say anything. Clumsily, uncertainly, I did as she asked.

She began crying on my shoulder, softly, quietly, shaking like a captive baby rabbit.

It was a long time before she said anything. I did not presume.

"No one has done this since I was a baby. My nurse. . . ."

Another long silence.

"I've never had a friend."

Another long gap.

"I'm scared, Croaker. And alone."

"No. We'll all be with you."

"Not for the same reasons." She fell silent for good then. I held her a long time. The fire burned down and its light faded from the room. Outside, the wind began to howl.

When I finally thought she had fallen asleep, and started to disengage myself, she clung more tightly, so I stilled and continued to hold her, though half the muscles in my body ached.

Eventually she peeled herself away, rose, built up the fire. I sat. She stood behind me a while, staring at the flames. Then she rested a hand on my shoulder a moment. In a faraway voice she said, "Good night."

She went into another room. I sat for ten or fifteen minutes before putting on a last log and shuffling back into the real world.

I must have worn an odd look. Neither Goblin nor One-Eye aggravated me. I rolled into my bedroll, back to them, but did not fall asleep for a long time.

55

Opening Rounds

I wakened startled. The null! I had been out of it so much it disturbed me by its presence. I rolled out hurriedly, discovered I was alone in the room. Not only there, but in the barracks, practically. There were a few Guards in the mess hall.

The sun was not yet up.

The wind still howled around the building. There was a marked chill in the air, though the fires were burning high. I shoveled boiled oats in and wondered what I was missing.

The Lady entered as I finished. "There you are. I thought I'd have to leave without you."

Whatever her problems the night before, she was brisk and confident and ready for business now.

The null faded while I got my coat. I dropped by my own room momentarily. The Limper was there still. I left frowning thoughtfully.

Into the carpet. Full crew today. Every carpet was fully crewed and armed. But I was more interested in the absence of snow between town and the Barrowland.

That howling wind had blown it away.

We went up as it became light enough to see. The Lady took the carpet up till the Barrowland resembled a map taking shape as shadows vaporized. She set us to cruising in a tight circle. The wind, I noted, had faded.

The Great Barrow looked ready to collapse into the river.

"One hundred hours," she said, as though divining my thoughts. So we were reduced to counting hours.

I looked around the horizon. There. "The comet."

"They can't see it from the ground. But tonight . . . it'll have to cloud up."

Below, tiny figures scurried around one quarter of the cleared area. The Lady unrolled a map similar to Bomanz's.

"Raven," I said.

"Today. If we're lucky."

"What're they doing down there?"

"Surveying."

More than that was happening. The Guards were out in full battle regalia, forming an arc around the Barrowland. Light siege machines were being assembled. But some men were, indeed, surveying and setting up rows of lances flying colored pennons. I did not ask why. She would not explain.

A dozen windwhales hovered to the east, beyond the river. I had thought them long departed.

The sky there burned with dawn's conflagration.

"First test," the Lady said. "A feeble monster." She frowned in concentration. Our carpet began to glow.

A white horse and white rider came from the town. Darling. Accompanied by Silent and the Lieutenant. Darling rode into an aisle marked by pennons. She halted beside the last.

The earth erupted. Something that might have been first cousin to Toadkiller Dog, and even more closely related to an octopus, burst into the light. It raced over the Barrowland, toward the river, away from the null.

Darling galloped toward town.

Wizards' fury rained from the carpets. The monster was a cinder in seconds. "One," the Lady said. Below, men began another aisle of pennons.

And so it went, slowly and deliberately, all the day long. Most of the Dominator's creatures broke for the river. The few that charged the other way encountered a barricade of missile fire before succumbing to the Taken.

"Is there time to eliminate them all?" I asked as the sun was setting. I had been itchy for hours, sitting in one place.

"More than enough. But it won't stay this easy."

I probed, but she would not expand upon what she had said.

It looked slick to me. Just pick them off and keep picking them off, and go for the big guy when they were all gone. Tough he might be, but what could he do enveloped in the null?

When I staggered into the barracks, to my room, I found the Limper still at work. The Taken need less rest than we mortals, but he had to be on the edge of collapse. What the hell was he doing?

Then there was Bomanz. He had not appeared today. What was he trying to slip up his sleeve?

I was eating a supper very much like breakfast when Silent materialized. He settled opposite me, clutching a bowl of mush as if it were an alms bowl. He looked pale.

"How was it for Darling?" I asked.

He signed, "She almost enjoyed it. She took chances she should not have. One of those things almost got to her. Otto was hurt fending it off."

"He need me?"

"One-Eye managed."

"What're you doing here?"

"It is the night to bring Raven out."

"Oh." Again I had forgotten Raven. How could I number myself among his friends when I seemed so indifferent to his fate?

Silent followed me to where I was staying with One-Eye and Goblin. Those two joined us shortly. They were subdued. They had been assigned major roles in the recovery of our old friend.

I worried more about Silent. The shadow had passed over him. He was fighting it. Would he be strong enough to win?

Part of him did not want Raven rescued.

Part of me did not, either.

A very tired Lady came to ask, "Will you participate in this?"

I shook my head. "I'd just get in the way. Let me know when it's done."

She gave me a hard look, then shrugged and went away.

Very late a feeble One-Eye wakened me. I bolted up. "Well?"

"We managed. I don't know how well. But he's back."

"How was it?"

"Rough." He crawled into his bedroll. Goblin was in his already, snoring. Silent had come with them. He was against the wall, wrapped in a borrowed blanket, cutting logs. By the time I wakened fully One-Eye was sawing with the rest.

In Raven's room there was nothing to see but Raven snoring and Case looking worried. The crowd had cleared out, leaving a ripe stench behind.

"He seem all right?" I asked.

Case shrugged. "I'm no doctor."

"I am. Let me look him over."

Pulse strong enough. Breathing a little fast for a sleeper, but not disturbingly so. Pupils dilated. Muscles tense. Sweaty. "Don't look like much to worry about. Keep feeding him broth. And get hold of me as soon as he's talking. Don't let him get up. His muscles will be clay. He might hurt himself."

Case nodded and nodded.

I returned to my bedroll, lay there a long time alternately wondering about Raven and about the Limper. A lamp still burned in my former quarters. The last of the old Taken still pursued his monomaniacal quest.

Raven became the greater worry. He was going to demand an accounting of our care for Darling. And I was in a mood to challenge his right.

56

Time Fading

Dawn comes early when you wish it would not. The hours flash when you want them to drag. The following day was another of executions. The only thing unusual was that the Limper came out to watch. He seemed satisfied we were doing things right. He returned to my quarters—where he sacked out in my bed.

My evening check on Raven showed little change. Case reported that he had come near wakening several times and was mumbling in his sleep.

"Keep pouring soup down him. And don't be afraid to yell if you need me."

I could not sleep. I tried roaming the barracks, but near silence reigned. A few sleepless Guards haunted the mess hall. They fell silent at my arrival. I thought about going over to Blue Willy. But I would find no better reception there. I was on everybody's list.

It could do nothing but get worse.

I knew what the Lady meant about lonely.

I wished I had the nerve to visit her now that *I* needed a hug.

I returned to my bedroll.

I did fall asleep this time; they had to threaten mayhem to get me up.

We polished off the last of the Dominator's pets before noon. The Lady ordered a holiday for the remainder of the day. Come next morning we were to rehearse for the big show. She guessed we had about forty-eight hours before the river opened the tomb. Time to rest, time to practice, and ample time to get in the first whack.

That afternoon Limper went out and flew around a while. He was in high spirits. I seized the opportunity to visit my quarters and poke around, but all I could find were a few black wood shavings and a hint of silver dust, and barely enough of either to leave traces. He had cleaned up hastily. I did not touch. No telling what curiosities might occur if I did. Otherwise, I learned nothing.

The practice for the Event was tense. Everyone turned out, including Limper and Bomanz, who had kept so low most everyone had forgotten him. The windwhales ranged above the river. Their mantas soared and swooped. Darling charged the Great Barrow down a prepared aisle, stopping just short of far enough. The Taken and Guards stood to their respective weapons.

It looked good. Looked like it would work. So why was I convinced we were in for big trouble?

The moment our carpet touched down Case was beside it. "I need your help," he told me, ignoring the Lady. "He won't listen to me. He keeps trying to get up. He fell on his face already twice."

I glanced at the Lady. She gave me a go-ahead nod.

Raven was seated on the edge of his bed when I arrived. "I hear you're being a pain in the ass. What's the point of pulling your butt out of the Barrowland if you're going to commit suicide?"

His gaze rose slowly. He did not appear to recognize me. Oh, damn, I thought. His mind is gone.

"He talked any, Case?"

"Some. He don't always make sense. He don't realize how long it's been, I think."

"Maybe we should restrain him."

"No."

Startled, we looked at Raven. He knew me now. "No restraints, Croaker. I'll behave." He flopped onto his back, smiling. "How long, Case?"

"Tell him the story," I said. "I'm going to go whip up some medicine."

I just wanted away from Raven. He looked worse with his soul restored. Cadaverous. Too much a reminder of my mortality. And that was one thing I did not need on my mind more than it was.

I whipped up a couple potions. One would settle Raven's shakes. The other would knock him out if he gave Case too much trouble.

Raven gave me a dark look when I returned. I do not know how far Case had gotten. "Stay off your high horse," I told him. "You got no idea what's happened since Juniper. In fact, not a whole lot since the Battle at Charm. You being the brave and rugged loner hasn't helped. Drink this. It's for the shakes." I gave Case the other mixture with whispered instructions.

In a voice little above a whisper, Raven asked, "Is it true? Darling and the Lady are going after the Dominator tomorrow? Together?"

"Yes. Do-or-die time. For everybody."

"I want to. . . ."

"You'll stay put. You, too, Case. We don't want Darling distracted."

I had managed to abolish worries about the tangled ramifications inherent in tomorrow's confrontations. Now they rushed in on me again. The Dominator would not be the end of it. Unless we lost. If he fell, the war with the Lady would resume instantly.

I wanted to see Darling badly, wanted in on her plans. I dared not go. The Lady was keeping me on the leash. She might interrogate me any time.

Lonely work. Lonely work.

Case went on tale-telling. Then Goblin and One-Eye dropped in to tell stories from their perspectives. The Lady even looked in. She beckoned me.

"Yes?" I asked.

"Come."

I followed her to her quarters.

Outside, night had fallen. In about eighteen hours the Great Barrow would open of its own accord. Sooner if we followed plan.

"Sit."

I sat. I said, "I'm getting fixated on it. Butterflies the size of horses. Can't think about anything else."

"I know. I considered you as a distraction, but I cared too much."

Well, that distracted *me.*

"Perhaps one of your potions?"

I shook my head. "There is no specific for fear in my arsenal. I've heard of wizards. . . ."

"Those antidotes cost too dearly. We'll need our wits about us. It won't go like it did in rehearsal."

I raised an eyebrow. She did not expand. I suppose she expected a lot of improvisational behavior from her allies.

The mess sergeant appeared. His crew rolled in a grand meal they set out on a table brought in special. A last feast for the condemned? After the crowd dispersed, the Lady said, "I ordered the best for everyone. Your friends in town included. Breakfast likewise." She seemed calm enough. But she was more accustomed to high-risk confrontations. . . .

I snorted at myself. I recalled being asked for a hug. She was as scared as anybody.

She saw but did not ask—tip enough that she was focused inward.

The meal was a miracle considering what the cooks had to work with. But it was nothing grand. We exchanged no words during its course. I finished first, rested my elbows on the table, retreated into thought. She followed suit. She had eaten very little. After a few minutes she went to her bedroom. She returned with three black arrows. Each had silver inlays in TelleKurre script. I had seen their like before. Soulcatcher gave Raven one the time we ambushed Limper and Whisper.

She said, "Use the bow I gave you. And stay close."

The arrows appeared identical. "Who?"

"My husband. They can't kill him. They lack his true name. But they'll slow him down."

"You don't think the rest of the plan will work?"

"Anything is possible. But all eventualities should be considered." Her eyes met mine. There was something there. . . . We looked away. She said, "You'd better go. Sleep well. I want you alert tomorrow."

I laughed. "How?"

"It's been arranged. For all but the duty section."

"Oh." Sorcery. One of the Taken would put everyone to sleep. I rose. I dithered for a few seconds, putting logs on the fire. I thanked her for the meal. Finally I managed to say what was on my mind. "I want to wish you luck. But I can't put my whole heart into it."

Her smile was wan. "I know." She followed me to the door.

Before I went out I yielded to the final impulse, turned—found her right there, hoping. I hugged her for half a minute.

Damn her for being human. But I needed that, too.

57

The Last Day

We were permitted to sleep in, then given an hour to breakfast, make peace with our gods, or whatever we had to do before entering battle. The Great Barrow was supposed to hold till noon. There was no rush.

I wondered what the thing in the earth was doing.

Battle muster came about eight. There were no absences. The Limper drifted around on his little carpet, his path seeming to intersect that of Whisper more often than was necessary. They had their heads together about something. Bomanz skulked around the edges of things, trying to remain invisible. I did not blame him. In his shoes I might have made a run for Oar. . . . In his shoes? Were mine more comfortable?

The man was a victim of his sense of honor. He believed he had a debt to repay.

A drumbeat announced time to take positions. I followed the Lady, noting that the remaining civilians were headed down the road to Oar with what possessions they could carry. It was going to be a crazy road. The troops the Lady had summoned were reported our side of Oar, coming in their thousands. They would arrive too late. Nobody thought to tell them to hold up.

Attentions had narrowed. The outside world no longer existed. I watched the civilians and for a moment wondered what difficulties faced us if we had to flee. But my concern did not persist. I could not worry past the Dominator.

Windwhales took station over the river. Mantas searched for updrafts. Taken carpets rose. But today my feet remained on the ground. The Lady intended meeting her husband toe to toe.

Thanks a bunch, friend. There was Croaker in her shadow with his puny bow and arrows.

Guards all in position, entrenched, behind low palisades, ditches, and artillery. Pennons all in place, to guide Darling's carefully surveyed ride. Tension mounting.

What more was there to do?

"Stay behind me," the Lady reminded. "Keep your arrows ready."

"Yeah. Good luck. If we win, I'll buy you dinner at the Gardens in Opal." I don't know what possessed me to say that. Frenzied attempt at self-distraction? It was a chilly morning, but I was sweating.

She seemed startled. Then she smiled. "If we win, I'll hold you to that." The smile was feeble. She had no cause to believe she would survive another hour.

She started walking toward the Great Barrow. Faithful pup, I dogged her.

The last spark of light would not die. She would not save herself through surrender.

Bomanz gave us a head start, then followed. Likewise, the Limper.

Neither's action was in the master plan.

The Lady did not react. Perforce, I let it go, too.

Taken carpets began to spiral down. The windwhales seemed a little bouncy, the mantas a little frenetic in their search for favorable air.

Edge of the Barrowland. My amulet did not tingle. All the old fetishes outside the Barrowland's heart had been removed. The dead now lay in peace.

Moist earth sucked at my boots. I had trouble maintaining my balance, keeping an arrow across my bow. I had one black shaft set to string, the other two gripped in the hand that held the bow.

The Lady halted a few feet from the pit whence we had dragged Bomanz. She became oblivious to the world, almost as if she were communing with the thing underground. I glanced back. Bomanz had halted a little to the north, about fifty feet from me. He had his hands in his pockets and wore a look that dared me to protest his presence. The Limper had set down about where the moat was when a moat surrounded the Barrowland. He did not want to fall when the null swept over him.

I glanced at the sun. About nine. Three hours margin if we wanted to use it.

My heart was setting records for carrying on. My hands shook so much it seemed the bones ought to rattle. I doubted I could put an arrow into an elephant from five feet.

How come I got lucky and got picked to be her buttboy?

I reviewed my life. What had I done to deserve this? So many choices I might have made differently. . . . "What?"

"Ready?" she asked.

"Never." I pasted on a sickly grin.

She tried to smile back, but she was more scared than I was. She knew what she faced. She believed she had only moments to live.

She had guts, that woman, going on when there was nothing she could win but, perhaps, some small redemption in the eyes of the world.

Names flashed through my mind. Sylith. Credence. Which? In a moment a choice might be critical.

I am not a religious man. But I sped a silent prayer to the gods of my youth asking that it not be me required to complete the ritual of her naming.

She faced the town and raised an arm. Trumpets winded. As though anyone were not paying attention.

Her arm dropped.

Hoofbeats. Darling in her white, with Elmo, Silent, and the Lieutenant all three dogging her, galloped the lane defined by the pennons. The null was to come sudden, then freeze. The Dominator was to be allowed to break out, but not with his power intact.

I felt the null. It hit me hard, so unaccustomed to it was I. The Lady staggered too. A mewl of fear fled her lips. She did not want to be disarmed. Not now. But it was the only way.

The ground shuddered once, gently, then geysered upward. I retreated a step. Shivering, I watched the fountain of muck disperse . . . and was amazed to see not a man but the dragon. . . .

The damned dragon! I hadn't thought about that.

It reared fifty feet high, flames boiling around its head. It roared. What now? In the null the Lady could not shield us.

The Dominator fled my mind entirely.

I drew a shaft to its head, aimed for the beast's open mouth.

A shout restrained me. I turned. Bomanz pranced and shrieked, calling insults in TelleKurre. The dragon eyeballed him. And recalled that they had unfinished business.

It struck like a snake. Flames surged ahead of it.

Fire masked Bomanz but did not harm him. He had taken his stand beyond the null.

The Lady moved a few steps to her right, to look past the dragon, whose forelegs were now free and scrabbling to drag the rest of its immense body loose. I could see nothing of our quarry. But the flying Taken were into their attack runs. Heavy fire-carrying spears were in flight already. They roared down, burst.

A thunderous voice announced, "Headed for the river."

The Lady hurried forward. Darling resumed moving, carrying the null toward the water. Ghosts cursed and pranced around me. I was too distracted to respond.

Mantas dropped in swift, dark pairs, dancing between bolts of lightning loosed by windwhales. The air went crackly, smelled dry and strange.

Suddenly Tracker was with us, muttering about having to save the tree.

I heard a rising bray of horns. I dodged a flailing dragon leg, ducked a hammering wing, looked back.

Scores of ill-clad human skeletons poured from the forest in the wake of a limping Toadkiller Dog. "I knew we hadn't seen the last of that bastard." I tried to get the Lady's attention. "The forest tribes. They're attacking the Guard." The Dominator had had at least one ace in the hole.

The Lady paid me no heed.

What the tribesmen and Guard did were of no consequence to us at the moment. We had prey on the run and dared concern ourselves with nothing else.

"In the water!" that voice thundered from above. Darling moved some more. The Lady and I scrambled over earth still rippling with the dragon's efforts to break free. It ignored us. Bomanz had its entire attention.

A windwhale dropped. Its tentacles probed the river. It caught something, dropped ballast water.

A human figure writhed in the whale's grasp, screaming. My spirits rose. We had done it. . . .

The whale lifted too high. For a moment it raised the Dominator out of the null.

Deadly mistake.

Thunder. Lightning. Terror on hot hooves. Half the town and a swath to the edge of the null shattered, scattered, burned, and blackened.

The whale exploded.

The Dominator fell. As he plunged toward both water and null, he bellowed, "Sylith! I name your name!"

I loosed an arrow.

Deadeye. One of the best wing shots I have ever made. It got him in the side. He shrieked and clawed at the shaft. Then he hit water. Manta lightning made the river boil. Another whale dropped and shoved tentacles beneath the surface. For a long moment I was terrified the Dominator would stay under and escape.

But up he came, again in a monster's grasp. This whale, too, went too high. And paid the price, though the Dominator's magic was much enfeebled, probably by my arrow. He got off one wild spell which went astray and started fires in the Guards compound. The Guards and tribesmen were closely engaged nearby. The spell slew scores from both forces.

I did not get another arrow off. I was frozen. I had been assured that the naming of a name, once suitable rituals had been observed, could not be stilled by the null. But the Lady had not faltered. She stood a step short of the edge of land, staring at the thing that had been her husband. The naming of the name Sylith had not disturbed her at all.

Not Sylith! Twice the Dominator had named her wrong. . . . Only one left to try. But my grin was hollow. *I* would have named her Sylith.

A third windwhale caught the Dominator. This one made no mistake. It carried him to shore, toward Darling and her escort. He struggled furiously. Gods! The vitality of that man!

Behind us, men screamed. Arms clashed. The Guards had not been as surprised as I. They were holding their ground. The airborne Taken hastened to support them, flinging a storm of deadly sorceries. Toadkiller Dog was the center of their attention.

Elmo, the Lieutenant, and Silent jumped the Dominator the moment the windwhale dropped him. That was like jumping a tiger. He threw Elmo thirty feet. I heard the crack as he broke the Lieutenant's spine. Silent danced away. I put another arrow into him. He staggered, but did not go down. Dazed, he started toward the Lady and me.

Tracker met him halfway. He set the son of the tree aside, grabbed hold of his man, started a wrestling match of epic scale. He and the Dominator shrieked like souls in torment.

I wanted to rush down and tend to Elmo and the Lieutenant, but the Lady gestured for me to stay. Her gaze roved everywhere. She expected something more.

A great shriek shook the earth. A ball of oily fire rolled skyward. The dragon flopped like an injured worm, screaming. Bomanz had disappeared.

To be seen was the Limper. Somehow he had dragged himself to within a dozen feet of me without my noticing. My fear was so great I nearly voided my bowels. His mask was gone. The devasted wasteland of his bare face glowered with malice. In a moment, he was thinking, he would even all scores with me. My legs turned to jelly.

He pointed a small crossbow, grinned. Then his aim drifted aside. I saw that his quarrel was close cousin to the arrow across my bow.

That electrified me, finally. I drew to the head.

He squealed, "Credence, the rite is complete. I name your name!" And then he let fly.

I loosed at the same instant. I could get the shaft off no faster, damn me. My arrow slammed into his black heart, knocked him over. But too late. Too late.

The Lady cried out.

Terror turned into unreasoning rage. I flung myself at the Limper, abandoning my bow for my sword. He did not turn to face my assault. He just held himself up on one elbow and gaped at the Lady.

I really went crazy. I guess we all can, in the right circumstances. But I had been a soldier for ages. I'd long ago learned you don't do that sort of thing and stay alive long.

The Limper was inside the null. Which meant he was barely clinging to life, barely able to sustain himself, wholly unable to defend himself. I made him pay for all the years of fear.

My first stroke half severed his neck. I kept hacking till I finished the job. Then I scattered a few limbs about, blunting my steel and madness on ancient bone. Sanity began to return. I whirled to see what had become of the Lady.

She was down on one knee, the weight of her body resting upon the other. She was trying to draw Limper's bolt. I charged over, pulled her hand away. "No. Let me. Later." This time I was less startled that the naming had not worked. This time convinced me that nothing could disarm her.

She should have been gone, damn it!

I gave myself up to a long fit of the shakes.

The Taken pounding on the forest people were having an effect. Some of the savages had begun fleeing. Toadkiller Dog was enveloped by painful sorceries. "Hang on," I told the Lady. "We're over the hump. We're going to do it." I don't know that I believed that, but it was what she needed to hear.

Tracker and the Dominator continued to roll around, grunting and cursing. Silent pranced around them with a broadbladed spear. When chance presented itself, he cut our great enemy. Nothing could survive that forever. Darling watched, stayed close, stayed out of the Dominator's way.

I scooted back to the wreck of the Limper and dug out the shaft I'd put into his chest. He glared at me. There was life in his brain still. I booted his head into the trench left by the dragon's rising.

That beast had ceased thrashing. Still no sign of Bomanz. Never any sign of Bomanz. He found the fate he feared, second try. He slew the monster from within.

Do not think Bomanz peripheral because he kept his head down. I believe the Dominator expected the dragon to preoccupy Darling and the Lady those few moments he needed to get shut of the null. Bomanz took that away. With the same determination and distinction as the Lady facing *her* inescapable fate.

I returned to the Lady. My hands had attained their battlefield steadiness. I wished for my kit. My knife would have to do. I laid her back, started digging. That quarrel would chew on her till I got it out. For all the pain, she managed a grateful smile.

A dozen men surrounded Tracker and the Dominator now, every one stabbing. Some did not seem particular as to whom they hit.

The sands were about gone for the old evil.

I packed and bound the Lady's wound with material from her own clothing. "We'll change this as soon as we can."

The tribesmen were whipped. Toadkiller Dog was dragging himself toward the high country. That old mutt had as much staying power as his boss. Guards freed of the fighting hurried our way. They carried wood for the old doom's funeral pyre.

58

End of the Game

Then I spotted Raven.

"The damned fool."

He was leaning on Case, hobbling. He carried a bare sword. His face was set. Trouble for sure. His step was not quite as feeble as he pretended.

It took no genius to guess what he had in mind. In his simple way of seeing things, he was going to make everything right with Darling by finishing off her big enemy.

The shakes came back, but this time not from fear. If somebody did not do something, I was going to be right in the middle. Right where I would have to make a choice, to act, and nothing I did would make anyone happy.

I tried distracting myself by testing the Lady's dressing.

Shadows fell upon us. I looked up into Silent's cold eyes, into Darling's more compassionate face. Silent cast a subtle glance Raven's way. He was in the middle, too.

The Lady clawed at my arm. "Lift me," she said.

I did. She was as weak as water. I had to support her.

"Not yet," she told Darling, as though Darling could hear. "He is not yet finished."

They had gotten a leg and an arm off the Dominator. Those they threw into the woodpile. Tracker hung on so they could carve on the Dominator's neck. Goblin and One-Eye stood by, waiting for the head, ready to run like hell. Some Guards planted the son of the tree. Windwhales and mantas hovered overhead. Others, with the Taken, were harassing Toadkiller Dog and the savages through the forest.

Raven was getting closer. And I was no closer to knowing where I stood.

That son-of-a-bitching Dominator was tough. He killed a dozen men before they finished carving him up. Even then he was not dead. Like Limper's, his head lived on.

Time for Goblin and One-Eye. Goblin grabbed the still-living head, sat down, held it tightly between his knees. One-Eye hammered a six-inch silver spike through its forehead, into its brain. The Dominator's lips kept forming curses.

The nail would capture his blighted soul. The head would go into the fire. When that burned out, the spike would be recovered and driven into the trunk of the son of the tree. Meaning one dark spirit would be bound for a million years.

Guards brought Limper parts to the fire, too. They did not find his head, though. The sodden walls of the trench whence the dragon had risen had collapsed upon it.

Goblin and One-Eye torched the woodpile.

The fire leapt up as if eager to fulfill its mission.

The Limper's bolt had struck the Lady four inches from the heart, midway between her left breast and collarbone. I confess to a certain pride in having drawn it under such terrible circumstances without killing her. I should have incapacitated her left arm, though.

She now lifted that arm, reached out to Darling. Silent and I were puzzled. But only for a moment.

The Lady pulled Darling to her. She had no strength, so it must be that, in a way, Darling allowed herself to be pulled. Then she whispered, "The rite is complete. I name your true name, Tonie Fisk."

Darling screamed soundlessly.

The null began to fray.

Silent's face blackened. For what seemed an eternity he stood there in obvious torment, torn between a vow, a love, a hatred, perhaps the concept of an obligation to a higher duty. Tears began coursing down his cheeks. I got an old wish, and was ready to cry myself when I did.

He spoke. "The ritual is closed." He had trouble shaping his words. "I name your true name, Dorotea Senjak. I name your true name, Dorotea Senjak."

I thought he would collapse in a faint then. But he did not.

The women did.

Raven was getting closer. So I had a pain atop all the other pains.

Silent and I stared at one another. I suspect my face was as tormented as his. Then he nodded through his tears. There was peace between us. We knelt, untangled the women. He looked worried while I felt Darling's neck. "She'll be all right," I told him. The Lady, too, but he did not care about that.

I wonder still how much each of the women expected in that moment. How much each yielded to destiny. It marked their end as powers of the world. Darling had no null. The Lady had no magic. They had canceled one another out.

I heard screaming. Carpets were raining. All those Taken had been Taken by the Lady herself, and after what had happened on the Plain, she had made certain her fate would be their fate. So now they were undone, and soon dead.

Not much magic left on that field. Tracker, too, was a goner, mauled to death by the Dominator. I believe he died happy.

But there was no end yet. No. There was Raven.

Fifty feet away, he let go of Case and bore down like nemesis itself. His gaze was fixed on the Lady, though you could tell by his very step that he was on stage, that he was going to do a deed to win back Darling.

Well, Croaker? Can you let it happen?

The Lady's hand shivered in mine. Her pulse was feeble, but it was there. Maybe. . . .

Maybe he would bluff.

I picked up my bow and the arrow recovered from Limper. "Stop, Raven."

He did not. I do not think he heard me. Oh, damn. If he didn't . . . It was going to get out of hand.

"Raven!" I bent the bow.

He stopped. He stared at me as if trying to recall who I was.

That whole battleground fell into silence. Every eye fixed upon us. Silent stopped moving Darling away, took up a sword, made certain he was between her and potential danger. It was almost amusing, the two of us there, like twins, standing guard over women whose hearts we could never have.

One-Eye and Goblin began drifting our way. I had no idea where they stood. Wherever, I did not want them involved. This had to be made into Raven against Croaker.

Damn. Damn. Damn. Why couldn't he just go away?

"It's over, Raven. There ain't going to be no more killing." I think my voice began to rise in pitch. "You hear? It's lost and won."

He looked at Silent and Darling, not at me. And took a step.

"You *want* to be the next guy dead?" Damn it, nobody could ever bluff him. Could I do it? I might have to.

One-Eye stopped a careful ten feet to one side. "What are you doing, Croaker?"

I was shaking. Everything but my hands and arms, though my shoulders had begun to ache with the strain of keeping my arrow drawn. "What about Elmo?" I asked, my throat tight with emotion. "What about the Lieutenant?"

"No good," he replied, telling me what I already knew in my heart. "Gone. Why don't you put the bow down?"

"When he drops the sword." Elmo had been my best friend for more years than I cared to count. Tears began to blur my vision. "They're gone. That leaves me in charge, right? Senior officer surviving? Right? My first order is, peace breaks out. Right now. *She* made this possible. *She* gave herself up for this. Nobody touches her now. Not while I'm alive."

"Then we'll change that," Raven said. He started moving.

"Damned stubborn fool!" One-Eye shrieked. He flung himself toward Raven. I heard Goblin pattering up behind me. Too late. Both too late. Raven had a lot more fire in him than anyone suspected. And he was more than a little crazy.

I yelled, "No!" and let fly.

The arrow took Raven in the hip. In the very side he had been pretending was crippled. He wore a look of amazement as he stumbled. Lying there on the ground, his sword eight feet away, he looked up at me, still unable to believe that, in the end, I was not bluffing.

I had trouble believing it myself.

Case yelled and tried to jump me. Hardly looking at him, I whacked him upside the head with my bow. He went away and fussed over Raven.

Silence, and stillness, again. Everyone looking at me. I slung my bow. "Fix him up, One-Eye." I limped over to the Lady, knelt, lifted her. She seemed awfully light and fragile for one who had been so terrible. I followed Silent toward what was left of the town. The barracks were still burning. We made an odd parade, the two of us lugging women. "Company meeting tonight," I threw out at the Company survivors. "You all be there."

I would not have believed myself capable before I did it. I carried her all the way to Blue Willy. And my ankle never hurt till I put her down.

Last Vote

I limped into the common room at what was left of Blue Willy, the Lady supported under one arm, bow used as a crutch. The ankle was killing me. I had thought it almost healed.

I deposited the Lady in a chair. She was weak and pale and only about half conscious despite the best One-Eye and I could do. I was determined not to let her out of my sight. Our situation was still fraught with peril. Her people no longer had any reason to be nice. And she was at risk herself—probably more from herself than from Raven or my comrades. She had fallen into a state of complete despair.

"Is this all?" I asked. Silent, Goblin, and One-Eye were there. And Otto the immortal, wounded as always after a Company action, with his eternal sidekick, Hagop. A youngster named Murgen, our standard-bearer. Three others from the Company. And Darling, of course, seated beside Silent. She ignored the Lady completely.

Raven and Case were back by the bar, present without having been invited. Raven wore a dark look but seemed to have himself under control. His gaze was fixed on Darling.

She looked grim. She had rebounded better than the Lady. But she had won. She ignored Raven more assiduously than she did the Lady.

There had been a showdown between them, and I had overheard his half. Darling had made very clear her displeasure with his inability to handle emotional commitment. She had not cut him off. She had not banished him from her heart. But he was not redeemed in her eyes.

He then had said some very unkind things about Silent, whom, it was obvious, she held in affection but nothing deeper.

And that had gotten her really angry. I had peeped then. And she had gone on in great length and fury about not being a prize in some men's game, like a princess in some dopey fairy tale where a gang of suitors ride around doing stupid and dangerous things vying for her hand.

Like the Lady, she had been in charge too long to accept a standard female role now. She was still the White Rose inside.

So Raven was not so happy. He had not been shut out, but he *had* been told he had a long way to go if he wanted to lay any claims.

The first task she had given him was righting himself with his children.

I halfway felt sorry for the guy. He knew only one role. Hard guy. And it had been stripped away.

One-Eye interrupted my thoughts. "This is it, Croaker. This is all. Going to be a big funeral."

It would. "Shall I preside as senior officer surviving? Or do you want to exercise your prerogative as oldest brother?"

"You do it." He was in no mood to do anything but brood.

Neither was I. But there were ten of us still alive, surrounded by potential enemies. We had decisions to make.

"All right. This is an official convocation of the Black Company, last of the Free Companies of Khatovar. We've lost our captain. First business is to elect a new commander. Then we have to decide how we're going to get out of here. Any nominations?"

"You," Otto said.

"I'm a physician."

"You're the only real officer left."

Raven started to rise.

I told him, "You sit down and keep quiet. You don't even belong here. You walked out on us fifteen years ago, remember? Come on, you guys. Who else?"

Nobody spoke. Nobody volunteered. Nobody met my eye, either. They all knew I did not want it.

Goblin squeaked, "Is anybody against Croaker?"

Nobody blackballed me. It's wonderful to be loved. Grand to be the least of evils.

I wanted to turn it down. The option was not there. "All right. Next order of business. Getting the hell out of here. We're surrounded, guys. And the Guard will get its balance pretty soon. We've got to get gone before they start looking around for somebody to whip on. But once we get clear, then what?"

Nobody offered an opinion. These men were as much in shock as the Guards.

"All right. I know what *I* want to do. Since time immemorial one of the jobs of the Annalist has been to return the Annals to Khatovar should the Company disband or be demolished. We've been demolished. I propose a vote to disband. Some of us have assumed obligations that are going to put us at odds as soon as we don't have anybody more dangerous to fuss at." I looked at Silent. He met my gaze. He'd just moved his seat so he was more into the gap between Darling and Raven, a gesture understood by everyone but Raven himself.

I had nominated myself guardian for the Lady, for the time being. There was no way we could keep those two women in one another's company for long. I hoped we could hold the group together as far as Oar. I would be satisfied with getting to the edge of the forest. We needed every hand. Our tactical situation could not have been worse.

"Shall we disband?" I asked.

That caused a stir. Everyone but Silent argued the negative.

I interjected, "This is a formal proposition. I want those with special interests to go their own ways without the stigma of desertion. That don't mean we *have* to split. What I'm saying is, we formally shed the name the Black Company. I'll head south with the Annals, looking for Khatovar. Anyone who wants can come. Under the usual rules."

Nobody wanted to give up the name. That would be like renouncing a patronym thirty generations old.

"So we don't give it up. Who would rather not go look for Khatovar?"

Three hands rose. All belonged to troopers who had enlisted north of the Sea of Torments. Silent abstained, though he wanted to go his own way, in pursuit of his own impossible dream.

Then another hand shot up. Belatedly, Goblin had noted that One-Eye was not opposed. They started one of their arguments. I cut it short.

"I won't insist on the majority dragging everybody along. As commander, I can discharge anyone who wants to follow another path. Silent?"

He had been a brother of the Black Company longer than I. We were his friends, his family. His heart was torn.

Finally, he nodded. He would go his own road, even without promises from Darling. The three who had opposed heading for Khatovar nodded too. I entered their discharges in the Annals. "You're out," I told them. "I'll deal out your shares of money and equipment when we clear the south edge of the forest. Till then we stick together." I did not pursue it further, or in a moment I would have been hanging all over Silent, bawling my eyes out. We had been through a lot, he and I.

I wheeled on Goblin, pen poised. "Well? Do I strike your name?"

"Go on," One-Eye said. "Hurry. Do it. Get rid of him. We don't need his kind. He's never been anything but trouble."

Goblin scowled at him. "Just for that I'm not leaving. I'm going to stay and outlive you and make your remaining days examples of misery. And I hope you live another hundred years."

I had not thought they would split. "Fine," I said, stifling a grin. "Hagop, take a couple men and round up some animals. The rest of you collect whatever might be useful. Like money, if you see any lying around."

They looked at me with eyes still dull with the impact of what had happened.

"We're getting out, guys. As soon as we can ride. Before any more trouble finds us. Hagop. Don't stint on pack animals. I want to carry off everything that isn't nailed down."

There was talk, argument, whatnot, but I closed the official debate at that point.

Cunning devil that I am, I got the Guards to do our burying. I stood over the Company graves with Silent and shed more than a few tears. "I never thought Elmo . . . He was my best friend." It had hit me. At last. Hard. Now I had done all the duties, there was nothing to hold it at bay. "He was my sponsor when I came in."

Silent lifted a hand, gently squeezed my arm. It was as much of a gesture as I could expect.

The Guards were paying their last respects to their own. Their daze was fading. Soon they would begin thinking about getting on with business. About asking the Lady what they should do. In a sense, they had been rendered unemployed.

They did not know their mistress had been disarmed. I prayed they did not learn, for I meant to use her as our ticket out.

I dreaded what might happen should her loss become general knowledge. On the broad canvas, civil wars to torment the world. On the fine, attempts at revenge upon her person.

Someday someone would begin to suspect. I just wanted the secret kept till we had a good run at getting out of the empire.

Silent took my arm again. He wanted to go. "One second," I said. I drew my sword, saluted our graves, repeated the ancient formula of parting. Then I followed him to where the others waited.

Silent's party would ride with us a while, as I'd wished. Our ways would part when we felt safe from the Guards. I did not look forward to that moment, inevitable though it was. How keep two such as Darling and the Lady in company when there was no survival imperative?

I swung into the saddle cursing my wretched aching ankle. The Lady gave me a dirty look. "Well," I said. "You're showing some spirit."

"Are you kidnapping me?"

"You want to be alone with all your folks? With maybe nothing better than a knife to keep order?" Then I forced a grin. "We've got a date. Remember? Dinner at the Gardens in Opal?"

For just a moment there was a spark of mischief behind her despair. And a look from a moment by a fire when we had come close. Then the shadow returned.

I leaned closer, trembling with the thought. I whispered, "And I need your help to get the Annals out of the Tower." I had not told anyone that I did not have them in my possession yet.

The shadow went. "Dinner? That's a promise?"

The witch could promise a lot, just with a look and her tone. I croaked, "In the Gardens. Yes."

I gave the time-honored signal. Hagop started off on point. Goblin and One-Eye followed, bickering as usual. Then Murgen, with the standard, then the Lady and I. Then most of the others, with the pack animals. Silent and Darling brought up the rear, well separated from the Lady and me.

As I urged my mount forward, I glanced back. Raven stood leaning on his cane, looking more forlorn and abandoned than he should. Case was still trying to explain it to him. The kid had no trouble understanding. I figured Raven would, once he got over the shock of not having everyone jump to do things his way, the shock of discovering that old Croaker could fill his bluff if he had to. "I'm sorry," I murmured his way, not quite sure why. Then I faced the forest and did not look back again.

I had a feeling he would be on the road himself soon enough. If Darling really meant as much to him as he wanted us to think.

That night, for the first time in who knows how long, the northern skies were completely clear. The Great Comet illuminated our way. Now the north knew what the rest of the empire had known for weeks.

It was on the wane already. The hour of decision had passed. The empire awaited in fear the news that it portended.

Away north. Three days later. In the dark of a moonless night. A beast with three legs limped from the Great Forest. It settled on its haunches on the remains of the Barrowland, scratched the earth with its one forepaw. The son of the tree flung a tiny change storm.

The monster fled.

But it would return another night, and another, and another after that. . . .